# Waggoners Gap

## Tony Peluso

WARRIORS PUBLISHING GROUP
NORTH HILLS, CALIFORNIA

WAGGONERS GAP

A Warriors Publishing Group book/published by arrangement with the author

PRINTING HISTORY
Warriors Publishing Group /February 2013

ISBN 978-0-9853388-6-2

10 9 8 7 6 5 4 3 2 1

To Colonel PEB, II and his magnificent Bride of 70 years, Ms. ADB, Ph.D. May you both rest in peace in the knowledge that you have richly earned your eternal happiness. Thank you for your immense courage on many battlefields, countless sacrifices for our country, unbounded generosity to friends and strangers alike, unfeigned altruism, genuine kindness to all, friendship to many, and for providing the inspiration for Waggoners Gap.

# Acknowledgments

Since it took more than a decade from the inception of Waggoners Gap until its publication by Warriors Publishing Group, scores of my relatives, friends, colleagues, associates, and neighbors have helped me with telling this story. It would take another 100 pages to pay proper tribute to their collective contribution. To those who do not see their name on these pages, please forgive me. Know that I understand that each of you has materially assisted this effort, and I am grateful.

First and foremost, I must thank Lieutenant Colonel Don Hansen for his friendship and collaboration. If it weren't for Don's suggestions and encouragement, I would never have begun this project in the first place.

My immediate family: Kathy, Tony, Andy, Kristle, and Lyn deserve enormous credit for their support and patience over many years. Their ideas, observations, contributions, and constructive criticism mean more than I could ever describe. Special thanks go to my dear friends Tamara Marks, Dave Fleet, Pete Sartis, Chuck DeVlaming, Tom Gonzalez, Chris Bentley, Sabrina Page and Jennifer Reynolds.

I am sincerely grateful to Gerard M. Devlin, author of *Paratrooper*, *Silent Wings*, and other Airborne non-fictions. I especially appreciate his personal effort, comments, and suggestions when he reviewed an early draft of this book.

I would also like to thank authors like Clay Blair (*Ridgway's Paratroopers*) and Grover Hall (*1000 Destroyed, The Life and Times of the 4th Fighter Group*) for their superb historical works, which made the job of researching this story so much easier.

Finally, Julia, I don't know how you mustered the patience to deal with me for all of those months. Were it not for you and your immense talent, this project would still be languishing in the dream stage. Thank you from the bottom of my heart for helping me begin to tell the tale of these amazing patriots.

# Prologue

2200 Hours
October 21, 1943
Jackson [Air] Strip
Regimental Headquarters
503d Parachute Infantry Regiment (PIR)
Port Moresby, Papua New Guinea (PNG)

> *In Papua New Guinea, it rains every day for nine months. Then, the monsoons begin.*
> —Local adage.

On a damp night in late October, Anne Calvert-Smith hung on for dear life as her lover raced his weather-beaten Jeep up the unimproved track above her hospital.

Anne's lover was Colonel Kevin Kincaid, the controversial commander of the elite American paratroopers who'd come up from Queensland to fight the Japs. In September, his regiment had made its first combat jump on a small airport in the Markham Valley, far to the north on the other side of the rugged Owen Stanley Mountains.

Weeks later, the paratroopers had returned to their lager at Jackson Strip, seven miles from Port Moresby. After refitting, they established their headquarters near the Australian hospital where Anne had been working for several months.

Anne was off-duty. Away from the hospital and the oppressing atmosphere of the orthopedics ward, she wore her beautiful auburn hair loose and undone. As she and Kevin tore up the hill, her long and elegant tresses fluttered behind her like an unruly dark red pennant. The wind rushing across her body and through her hair felt refreshing and a bit erotic.

Anne Calvert-Smith, a nurse with the Royal Australian Army Nursing Service (RAANS), was fifth-generation Aussie. The Calverts first came to Australia on a British penal ship after the Yorkshire West Riding Revolt of 1820. Convicted of treason and being lower-class radicals, the Crown sentenced them to the penal colony on Van Diemen's Land, which became Tasmania. They earned their freedom after seven years, moving to the new free colony of Victoria.

Nurse Calvert-Smith grew up in Sydney, the second oldest of five children in a working-class family. After her father lost his job in the Great Depression that lasted throughout the 1930s, the family faced the humiliation of poverty and hunger. When the Nazis invaded Poland in October of 1939, the Commonwealth interrupted the economic downturn and ramped up their military readiness to rally to Britain's call.

In early 1940, Anne married her childhood sweetheart, the handsome and charming David Smith. They tied the knot at a small chapel in Bondi Beach, where they honeymooned before he shipped out to fight the Germans in North Africa.

Australian Army Command posted David as a sapper to the 20th Infantry Brigade of the Australian Imperial Force on the Egyptian border with Libya. In short order, David and his mates squared off with the Italians and Germans.

After less than a week in combat, David died defending the Libyan town of Tobruk from the armored forces of the *Afrika Korps*, commanded by General Erwin Rommel—the infamous Desert Fox.

In September of 1941, grief stricken—but not wanting to remain idle with a war in progress—the young widow used David's death benefit to finish the nursing program that she'd begun two years earlier at a hospital in Sydney. After graduation, Anne joined the RAANS.

In January 1943, the Service transferred Anne to their field hospital at Jackson Strip, which they had named after a gallant Australian fighter pilot, "Old John" Jackson, who'd been shot down dog fighting with Jap Zeros over Port Moresby in April 1942.

Over the last ten months, Nurse Calvert-Smith had seen the worst that the Aussie Diggers had endured in the wretched battles with the Japanese on the northern slopes of the Owen Stanley Mountains.

During her tour, Anne had survived several Japanese air raids, 14-hour days, seven-day weeks, every communicable disease imaginable, flying and biting insects the size of birds, venomous snakes, hairy spiders, monsoonal storms, moldy rations, cheeky patients, randy soldiers, and the ravages of drinking American hooch—which the Yanks called jungle juice. By the southern hemispheric spring of 1943, Anne was an old hand in PNG. She lived one day at a time.

Like all nurses, Anne could not resist the opportunity to cure some illness, mend a fractured limb, bolster low morale, or fix whatever was broken in the scarred bodies or wounded psyches of the allied soldiers around her. She had a weakness for stray cats, cute puppies, good scotch whiskey—and lately—this arrogant and flawed American colonel. *Tonight, with his crazy drivin' and heavy drinkin', he's doing his best to put us both in the intensive care ward of my hospital,* Anne thought as the couple sped up the trail.

At the end of the track, Col. Kevin Kincaid pulled the Jeep into the tree-lined alcove on the edge of the gravel pit. The narrow road had become Lover's Lane. It was the one place on the Strip where they could find privacy.

Anne thought Kincaid was handsome. Due to his rank and position, he could pinch a Jeep for his personal use any time he wanted. Kincaid used—some said misused—his authority to obtain this privacy with Anne on a dozen occasions since the American combat jump into Markham Valley.

Not that anyone blamed him. Anne was a beautiful woman. She had always been a good girl and a proper wife back in Australia. After David's death, she'd remained chaste. Lately, her life had taken a new direction. *During some air raid, my luck might run out. I might never have another chance at love. Since I'm stuck in this god-forsaken mess, I might as well take up with this crazy Yank,* Anne thought

Anne had loved sharing herself with David, and now that he was gone and she could die any minute, she saw no reason to deny herself physical pleasure. Here in the rain forest, in the leeward shadow of the Owen Stanley Mountains in the midst of a worldwide conflict, she'd become that rare woman of every man's fantasy: the classy lady in the parlor and the lusty wench in the bedroom.

Anne didn't like everything about Kevin, but she was drawn to his bad-boy attitude. This evening, Anne was randy. Kevin had never failed to take her over the edge. *The trips in his Jeep aren't the only wild rides that we've shared,* Anne thought. *And—if the gossip at the hospital is true—there's another wild ride coming.*

She'd heard the rumors of the American Inspector General's inquiry into the allegations of command dereliction and abuse in the airborne regiment. *I don't care what the Americans think of Kevin. He's my man.* She was loyal. That was the end of the debate. Nothing brought out her claws like a threat to something dear to her.

After Kevin turned off the Jeep's engine, he turned to his right and fished around for the bottle of Jack Daniels. *It's a damn site better than jungle juice, but this whiskey from Tennessee is a bit rough for my taste,* Anne concluded as she watched Kevin take a hefty swig from the bottle. *But it's real whiskey, isn't it? I might as well help Kevin finish what's left.*

The crazy jaunt along the ridgeline had left Anne disheveled. Her hair was wind blown. The hem of her white smock had ridden high on her thighs, exposing the tops of her stockings. Kevin delighted in her appearance.

In a perfect world, the two lovers would be sipping a dram of single-malt scotch while reclining on an eiderdown mattress in a cool mountain retreat. In the real world of Jackson Strip, Anne sat in the Jeep and drank directly from Kevin's bottle.

Passing the bottle back and forth, the two lovers cuddled on the small single seat on the rider's side in the front of the battered Jeep. Anne stroked and caressed Kevin's arms and legs with increasing urgency. "C'mon, Kevin, I've been waitin' all week, haven't I?" Anne pleaded, impatient for the lovemaking.

Looking at Anne, Kevin thought, *No doubt about it. Anne's remarkable. She's the best piece of ass I've ever had. It's really too bad that we've come to the end.* A deeply tortured soul, Kincaid had never made an emotional connection with a lover—or any other human being.

Kevin had grown up in southern Illinois, the only child of a successful grain merchant in Cairo. He'd graduated from the Military Academy at West Point in 1926 in the bottom third of his class. Until just before the war, he'd risen no higher in rank than first lieutenant.

Kevin had struggled for more than 15 years to make ends meet in an army that paid him little and offered him no advancement prospects. He had languished until the Second World War provided him with the miraculous opportunity to become a paratrooper and the regimental commander of some of the finest soldiers in the world.

Over the last 14 months, Kincaid had squandered his good fortune in a most disturbing manner. He'd grown—for reasons that he could not articulate—to despise the men of his regiment. In response to their commander's excesses, his lack of judgment, and his disdain for them, the paratroopers of the 503d detested their colonel right back.

Earlier in the day, Kincaid had received notice that the Sixth Army Inspector General would recommend that he be relieved of his command. If General Krueger followed the IG's advice, Kevin's military career would be ruined.

After the IG departed Jackson Strip, Kincaid called a conference of the 503d's most senior officers. He intended to break the news of his imminent relief. Once the three lieutenant colonels arrived at his tent, Kevin couldn't bear to tell them about the IG's recommendation.

Instead, in a moment that the attendees later recalled as surrealistic, Kincaid broke out a bottle of Jack Daniels and poured drinks for his subordinates. Over the next hour, the four men drank whiskey and chatted amicably in the manner of professional soldiers.

After dismissing his staff, Kincaid continued to drink. He'd been working on his third bottle when he drove up to Anne's tent to pick her up for their date. By the time that the couple reached the top of the ridgeline, Colonel Kincaid was as drunk as Nurse Calvert-Smith had ever seen him.

Kevin initiated the sexual dance between them almost immediately after he finished the whiskey. Anne liked more foreplay, but tonight she was ready to get down to business. Besides, Anne couldn't be sure how the alcohol would impact on Kevin's performance. *We can make love another time. Tonight, I just want to screw his bleedin' brains out,* she thought as she pulled the hem of skirt up to her narrow waist.

A half an hour later, satisfied from some very good sex, Anne sat on Kevin's lap, facing him with the Yank's softening manhood still imbedded in her. As she tried to regain her composure, she wrapped her long arms around his broad shoulders. She rested her forehead against his sweaty chest. *The sex wasn't pretty, but it was damn good,* Anne decided.

"Well, love, next time we'll go a wee bit slower. But I have to admit that this was pretty decent," Anne said, enjoying the moment while nuzzling against Kevin's shoulder and trying to regulate her still ragged breathing.

"There's not going to be a next time," Kevin said, his voice cold as ice.

The brutal message startled Anne. She pulled her face from Kincaid's chest. She turned her head and looked into his eyes. What she saw caused her to shiver. "What do mean, love?"

"Anne, there's not going to be a next time. I mean it. To-night will be our last little rendezvous."

"Well, don't I have a say in this? Do you think that I'm going to let you toy with me?"

"Neither you nor anybody else in this godforsaken place has any say in this decision. It's my choice and I'll answer to the devil for it!" Kevin screamed, showing emotion for the first time.

As Kevin stared into Anne's eyes, his right hand swept up in a wide arch, brushing aside her left arm. It continued until his right hand came to rest in the small space between their two laps. For the first time that night Anne saw the Colt .45 caliber pistol. Kevin had cocked the hammer and his finger rested on the trigger.

"Kevin, what're you doing? Be careful love! You could hurt yourself or shoot me!"

"Don't worry, love," Kincaid said, trying to mimic Anne's accent. "I'm a trained soldier. I hit what I aim at."

Kincaid turned the pistol so that the muzzle faced his chest. With a look of utter hatred on his face, he stared into Anne's terrified eyes and pulled the trigger.

The pistol's report was loud and shocking. In the next instant, a .45 caliber bullet entered Kincaid's chest at 900 feet per second. As the big metal slug pierced his torso, a stream of blood pumped from his wound spraying Anne's face, neck, and breasts.

The crushing impact of the round picked Kincaid out of the Jeep's seat and threw him back hard. He bounced violently, dropping the pistol and bucking Anne off his lap. In less than a half-second, the slug obliterated Kevin's heart.

In June and July of 1942, during the darkest days of World War II, allied armed forces began arriving in Papua New Guinea. Their presence in PNG reflected a frantic attempt to bolster the defense of Northern Australia and to stem the onslaught of the Japanese military juggernaut.

Most of the American fleet lay smoldering at the bottom of Pearl Harbor. The island fortress of Corregidor had fallen. The Japanese had conquered the Philippines, Malaysia, Singapore, and Hong Kong. Every allied soldier knew that he and his comrades were in the Emperor's crosshairs.

The fate of Australia and the future of the South Pacific depended on the ability of the Australians to maintain their tenuous perimeter around Port Moresby. To counter the Australian tactical move, the Japanese invaded northern New Guinea in force. They threw large numbers of ships, planes, and fighting men into the battle. The three New Guinea territories were controlled by Australia and the Netherlands, and its size supported air, land, and naval bases. Responding to the threat, the Australians rushed reinforcements to southern New Guinea. Later in the year, American soldiers and airmen began to arrive in small numbers.

By the end of 1942, Australian infantrymen supported by the Papuan Infantry Battalion had ended the Japanese threat to Port Moresby along the primitive Kokoda Trail in the Owen Stanley Mountains. By force of will, undeniable courage, and thousands of separate acts of sacrifice, the allies defeated the Japanese land and naval forces in three major engagements. As a consequence, the allies maintained a fragile perimeter around Port Moresby.

In September 1943, in a decisive strategic move, General Douglas MacArthur struck north across the Owen Stanleys. His target was the small port of Lae on the northeastern coast. Operation *Postern* used combined arms on a scale never before seen in the Pacific.

The Australian 9th Division landed east of Lae in an attempt to encircle the Japanese forces there. Simultaneously, American paratroopers seized Nadzab Airfield to the west to protect the Australian flank.

The Markham Valley operation went off without a serious mishap in the first successful combat jump in the short history of the American use of vertical envelopment. The 503d, suffering very few casualties, seized Nadzab Airfield in a classic *coup de main*. The paratroopers of the 503d showed that they were equal to any elite military formation on the planet.

Basking in the glow of their unprecedented success, the airborne troopers and their officers should have been elated. Instead, the regiment suffered from a series of ill-considered command decisions.

In early October 1943, the Commanding General of the American Sixth Army ordered his inspector general to investigate the persistent allegations involving the 503d's commander. After interviewing 100 witnesses, the IG concluded that not one single officer or non-com had any faith in their commander. The IG decided to advise General Krueger that Col. Kincaid should be relieved of command.

At 2300 hours, Major Phillip E. Genero, II, stood in the tent billet of the 503d's executive officer. Major Reynolds, the obsessive-compulsive motor officer, claimed that Genero had stolen a Jeep, and Lieutenant Colonel Jones—the XO—was mediating the inane dispute.

Earlier in the month, Col. Kincaid had issued an edict precluding majors and light colonels from taking vehicles from the motor pool for their own use, as had been the habit during the months when the unit had been billeted in Gordonvale, Australia. Of course, the order could not apply to the commander himself—evidenced by the fact that another Jeep was missing.

*Colonel Kincaid is probably up on the ridgeline again. He must be screwing one of the nurses,* Jones reasoned.

LtCol. Jones was a fine officer. He was West Point grad—like Col. Kincaid—but their leadership styles were worlds apart. Jones valued the tight bond he held with the 503d paratroopers. And although he was too professional to show his anger to his men, he quietly bristled at Kincaid's personal excesses, inconsistencies, and derelictions. *It's hard to do my job when my CO is incoherent, uncommunicative, and doesn't give a rat's ass about his unit's morale,* Jones thought.

Now, the IG was interrogating everyone above the rank of corporal. Jones hoped that the ordeal would soon be over. *There is a war, after all. The regiment has battles to fight, jumps to make, and Japanese to kill.*

If the scuttlebutt was to be trusted, Gen. Krueger would soon relieve Kincaid. *I don't care who commands the regiment, as long as he is competent and takes care of the men,* Jones reflected. *I just want to get back to something resembling normal duty, which—in an airborne unit in a combat zone—is tough enough.*

Jones had cemented his relationship with his men on the troopship during the long, difficult sea voyage from California to Australia. Jones had caught several company grade officers drinking contraband booze and breaking restrictions on the ship. As a disciplinary measure, he confined them to their quarters for an entire week. The enlisted men and non-commissioned officers loved Jones for holding the officers to an equitable standard. From that time forward, they affectionately referred to Jones as *the Warden*.

Maj. Genero—who was new to the regiment—had also developed a deep respect for the XO's competence during the airborne assault in Markham Valley. In turn, Jones valued Phil's soldierly bearing and demonstrated expertise.

As a senior officer, Jones had made it a point to learn as much as he could about the new man. Genero's assignment to the Pacific presented an intriguing enigma. *Why would they send a man with his qualifications here?* Jones puzzled.

Although he was 25 years old, Genero had accomplished a great deal in his career. He had been a pioneer in the first American airborne battalion, the 501$^{st}$ at Fort Benning. He'd served with distinction with the fledgling 509$^{th}$ Parachute Infantry Battalion in several difficult battles in North Africa, for which he had received a Silver Star, a Bronze Star and a Purple Heart. Genero had more actual combat experience than any of the regiment's senior leaders.

Markham Valley had been Genero's fourth combat jump. He'd been the only paratrooper in the 509$^{th}$ to make all three of their combat jumps in Africa and live to tell about it. Despite the recent operations by the 82$^{nd}$ Airborne Division in Sicily and Italy, at this point in the war, few American paratroopers had Genero's depth of airborne warfare experience.

Analysis of the North Africa campaign had guided the 503d's planners in their flawless airborne operation in September. The planners, motivated by MacArthur's egomaniacal desire to outshine his rivals, had looked for any edge to out-do the campaigns in Europe. In that theater, operational difficulties and high casualty rates put the very concept of employing large formations of paratroopers in jeopardy. The 503d was determined to demonstrate what motivated airborne troops could accomplish.

As LtCol. Jones listened to Maj. Reynolds drone on about the overblown Jeep theft, he analyzed the other side of Genero's coin. Genero was a linguistic phenomenon. He could speak German, Italian, and French. *Why would the Army send a brave, resourceful, and experienced officer with superb language skills away from his unit in Europe to New Guinea?* Jones thought. Neither Genero's record nor any admission shed any light on this mystery.

Then there was the business of a letter of reprimand to Genero from the Commanding General of the 82$^{nd}$ Airborne Division. Jones had seen it.

*The letter is caustic, but short of essential details,* Jones concluded. *Genero must have had gotten into a brawl of some sort in General Ridgway's mess. If that's the problem, it's a pretty silly reason to exile a good officer to an assignment halfway around the world. Yet Genero seems glad to be in the Pacific Theater.*

Genero was tight-lipped about his reasons for wanting to be in the 503d. Colonel Kincaid had speculated that Genero must have lost a brother in one of the battles with the Japanese, but Phil's record showed no sign of a brother in the service.

The motor officer was about to finish his diatribe. He had to stop and take a breath. This gave LtCol. Jones an opportunity to get a word in.

"Major Reynolds, thank you!" Jones said. "Major Genero, what's your side? Didn't you read the C.O.'s directive about field grade officers and the regimental motor pool?"

"Yes, sir. I did. I fully understood it. I've done everything possible to comply with it," Phil responded, shifting his six-foot-three-inch frame.

"OK. Where did you take the Jeep, and why didn't you get Major Reynolds' permission first?" Jones asked, hoping to finish up and go back to sleep.

"Sir, I received an order to meet with General Moses. The meeting was urgent. I had to be at his quarters in Port Moresby early this evening. I looked around for Major Reynolds, you, or one of the other light colonels. I couldn't find anyone. Before I left camp, I informed the sergeant major that I was taking the Jeep, where I was going, and on whose authority. Sorry, Colonel, but I did everything that I was supposed to do," Genero responded.

"You met with General Moses?" Jones asked, surprised at the breach of protocol.

*Majors don't just meet with the special advisor to the theater commander without informing the regimental commanding officer,* Jones thought. *General Moses should have sent the request for Genero through the adjutant. This would have given Colonel Kincaid the opportunity to get his political house in order, especially during this investigation. Something is up.*

"What was the purpose of the meeting?" Jones asked.

"I'm sorry, sir, but I'm ordered not to discuss the details with anyone in the 503d," Genero said.

"Are you telling me that General Moses called you to a meeting this afternoon in Port Moresby, without notifying anyone here, and then directed you not to discuss the matter with either Colonel Kincaid or me? You can't be serious!"

"I know it's unusual, sir. By 0900 hours tomorrow, you'll receive orders detaching me from duty with the regiment for six months. I'll leave in 48 hours. That's all I can reveal at this time."

Colonel Jones was thunderstruck. *In all of my years in the Army no senior commander has ever treated the chain of command with such disrespect.*

Instantly, the misappropriation of the Jeep was a non-issue. Genero would be gone before anyone would be able to reprimand him. Jones tended to believe Genero's version of events. It was probable that no violation had occurred in the first place.

Jones was about to dismiss the majors when he heard a ruckus out in the camp. The duty officer, a brand new second lieutenant—just assigned from OCS in Brisbane—came running to the tent.

"Sir...sir! You ain't gonna believe this! There's a half-naked Aussie dame out here. She's covered in blood. She claims the C.O. shot hisself up at the gravel pit! Colonel Kincaid is dead, sir!"

As the sky lightened from an inky blue-black to a dull grey-green, most of the bowerbirds and cannibal frogs in the rainforest had begun their cacophony to greet the new sun. For their part, the harpy eagles watched silently from the tall trees, as the faint morning light provided a ghastly setting to the scene at the gravel pit.

Col. Kincaid's body was still seated on the passenger side of the Jeep. In the last few hours, the top of his torso had slumped to the left and his head now lay supported by the back of the driver's seat.

A small, greasy hole festered in his chest. A sticky pool of blood covered the front panel, windscreen, and foot well of the Jeep. A horde of screw-worm flies swarmed the pool of blood and buzzed around the colonel.

When Maj. Genero first saw the regimental commander that morning, Kincaid's eyes had been open but eerily sightless in the way of dead men. A considerate military policeman had closed them, out of respect for the deceased and to keep the flies from laying their eggs in the soft tissue around Kincaid's eyes.

Genero's blood boiled until his temple throbbed. He'd seen men killed in combat. If it were possible, you handled the remains quickly to give the insects, scavengers, and grave robbers the smallest window of opportunity.

Maj. Genero walked over to the captain in charge of gathering the evidence. Noting Genero's demeanor, the captain snapped to attention, and saluted smartly.

"Captain Adams, Colonel Jones asked me to look after things here, until he can get back this morning. I've been watching your M.P.s playing grab-ass and fuckin' around for over an hour. The sun's almost up. It's going to get hot around here. I want your investigation concluded. Get the colonel out of that Jeep and inside before one of those eagles swoops down from those trees and tries to carry him off!"

"Yes, sir!"

As Genero walked away from the captain, he turned his back on the Jeep. He glanced up in the eucalyptus trees and watched the raptors staring at the dead American commander. A powerful feeling of déjà vu swept over him, causing him to shiver.

For just a moment, he was not standing on a ridgeline near a gravel pit in a little known corner of the world, where a tortured soul had taken his own life because of dark secrets that only he could possibly know.

In his mind's eye, Phil traveled back to a wooded glade on Waggoners Gap, the bucolic sanctuary tucked into the green hills above his family's farm in Carlisle, Pennsylvania. He was a boy again.

When he stood on the rocky promontory at the edge of his special place in the Gap, Phil could see the other verdant fingers in the Appalachian Mountains, the picturesque multicolored patchwork quilt of farmland in the Cumberland Valley below, and the quaint working-class town of Carlisle. He could make out the smokestack of the clothing factory where his mom and dad had worked.

For uncounted millennia, Waggoners Gap had served as the way station for transient hawks, falcons, and golden eagles. These graceful raptors—so similar to the harpy eagles in the trees above Col. Kincaid—had used Waggoners Gap as a rest stop in their yearly intercontinental migrations.

Phil had spent many fall afternoons lying on top of his favorite boulder, watching the great birds conduct their reconnaissance. Mesmerized, Phil would close his eyes and dream about the adventures that he'd have in the future.

As a young man, he'd hike up to the Gap for solitude. When he got older, he'd take Linda with him. *Just like Col. Kincaid on the ridgeline, I guess*, thought Phil.

Waggoners Gap had been Phil's personal refuge. His secrets had been safe there. It was different now.

The cold reality of this morning struck him. Dark, unfathomable issues had caused the regimental commander to go to his New Guinea refuge, have one last drunken tryst, and then end his life. In Phil's case, his family's inscrutable secrets were now coincident with Waggoners Gap.

Phil thought of his family. *There'd once been happiness. Now there was desolation. C'est le vie et c'est la guerre!* Phil decided.

Maj. Genero turned in time to watch the soldiers begin to remove Colonel Kincaid's remains. Staring right through the men and machines, Genero thought again of his youth at Waggoners Gap.

# Chapter 1

8:25 AM
October 8, 1918
Maternity Ward, Room 12
Saint Mary's Hospital
Carlisle, Pennsylvania

A magnificent fall morning, the soft, southern breeze pushed bulbous clouds in a promenade through the cobalt blue sky. The wind was dry, guaranteeing a warm afternoon and the prospect of a cool, pleasant evening.

The leaves on the maples, oaks, hickories, and other hardwoods had begun to change from dark green into the splendid canvas of fall hues: white, gold, crimson, vermillion, and burnt orange.

Resting in her bed at the small Catholic hospital on Hanover Street, Marta Brumbach Genero gazed through her window toward the ridgeline northwest of town. Propped up in her bed, she could make out the trees that rose like a towering, multicolored fortress. The panorama stretched to infinity.

Mrs. Genero's eyes were bright with exhilaration as she tried to rest from her labor. Though her baby was healthy, fat, and gorgeous, she was not at peace.

As she cradled her nursing son, Marta stared out the window, interpreting the beauty of the fall leaves as a sign from God. Just before she'd entered the hospital, she'd gone to that special place at Waggoners Gap and prayed hard. She had assumed that all would be well with the baby but she had worried about her husband.

Phillip couldn't be with her at the birth of their first child. He was in France with the American Expeditionary Force, fighting the Kaiser's army. She hadn't seen her husband since the winter, when he'd spent his leave with her before shipping out to France as a rifleman in the 82nd Division's 328th Infantry Regiment.

That winter interlude had been bittersweet, passionate, and romantic. Their baby boy was the miraculous creation from that brief time together.

The first moment that she saw Phillip leaving old Alfie McDuff's Tavern, she fell in love. She loved him still, with a fierce loyalty she held only for those deepest in her heart. On that cold winter's night, he was walking down High Street laughing with his boisterous friends. *The young men were all a little drunk,* Marta recalled. *They were showing off, as young men will. They made snowballs and playfully tossed them at each other.*

*I remember the way Phillip looked with white snowflakes melting in his jet-black hair,* she thought. *I tingled when he looked at me with that beautiful white smile. When he gazed into my heart with those deep, penetrating blue eyes, I knew I was a goner.*

Marta's husband, Phillip Genero, was the second youngest of six sons of Italian immigrants from Milan. Over the last 20 years, the family had run a prosperous bakery in Hagerstown. Phillip was the first son of the family to be born in the United States. He finished his education at 16, left home, and traveled north to Carlisle. He found a job at the Monarch Clothing Company.

The locals found Phillip's friendly manner and infectious sense of humor irresistible. The young ladies liked his good looks. He was industrious and worked hard as a factory hand before the local board drafted him at the onset of the Great War.

Marta wanted him to come home. He wrote letters, but the words on the cold paper were small consolation. In the last two weeks, she'd received only one short and somber letter from her husband. Phillip told her very little of the war and almost nothing of the battles in which he'd been engaged. Lately, Marta had been having premonitions.

Marta's family was Pennsylvania Dutch. In contrast to her husband, she was very fair and petite. She had long blonde hair that flowed in graceful waves down her back, and soft brown eyes. The young men in Carlisle thought she was the most beautiful woman in town.

Marta had been raised in an Amish family on a working farm near Lancaster. As a child, she led a normal Amish life, filled with hard work, strict religious duties, and unending family responsibilities.

When she was 15, her mother died, leaving her the eldest girl in family with eight brothers and sisters. She tried to keep the family together, but working on the farm, caring for her siblings and dealing with her distant and unaffectionate father proved to be too much. After she left Lancaster to participate in the traditional Rumspringa Year—when Amish youths leave their culture and live among the *English* to examine and test their religious commitment—Marta realized that if she returned home, she could not survive. After much soul searching, racked with guilt, but trusting in her instincts, she sent her father an emotional letter asking for guidance. Receiving no response, she traveled west, seeking domestic employment in Harrisburg, Camp Hill, or Carlisle.

Marta found a position in the home of Daniel Monarch, the younger brother of the Monarch Company patriarch. She became his nanny and cared for his two young children.

Though relatively uneducated, Marta—who was very bright—had taught herself to read and write. After two years, she persuaded Daniel's older brother to allow her to work in the clothing factory as a clerk, where she could gain clerical skills and expand her horizons. She found a small apartment to share with an older, widowed woman in Carlisle, near the main office of the clothing company.

After she'd failed to return to the Brumbach farm, the Amish congregation in Lancaster expelled her. The Amish commonly shunned their members who wouldn't conform to their lifestyle. Since her relocation to Carlisle, her family and friends in Lancaster had refused to acknowledge her existence.

Marta had understood that her family would abandon her. She thought she could endure the isolation. As time passed in Carlisle, the reality of their rejection grew far worse than she'd imagined.

At 18, Marta was still a teenager in an era nearly Victorian in its approach to sex. Amish society hadn't prepared her for the physical desire that blossomed within her. One man, who was grateful, considerate, and discrete, inflamed her passion. She succumbed without considering the consequences. There was only one drawback—her lover was married.

Their illicit relationship continued for many months. Several times Marta tried to stop it, but her intense sexual needs always overpowered her guilty conscience. Her lover understood her weaknesses and how to exploit them. Marta realized that the break with her Amish past was complete.

Marta's rented room was a block from the local Catholic Church. When walking to work or to the market, she passed the church and watched the faithful gather. After a few months, she noticed that on Sunday, her one day off, the Genero boy attended the 9:00 a.m. mass.

Ever since the first time she saw him with his friends on High Street, she'd kept track of Phillip. The glint in his eye showed a sense of humor and fun, yet he'd also been protective of his friends, making sure they were all safe. He liked to play and was a good church-going member of the community. He fit in large groups, yet somehow seemed a bit detached from them. So Marta thought he might understand the feeling of loneliness she felt, even in a crowd. The thought that he could protect her, understand her, desire her—combined with his masculine strength and physical beauty—drove her to distraction.

In order to see Phillip, Marta began attending the Catholic services. She arranged to take classes for converts. When she went to mass, she always tried to find a pew near him.

Over time, Genero noticed Marta, and their relationship ignited.

Within six months, Marta had converted to Catholicism and accepted Phillip's proposal, all on the same Sunday. In her heart Marta was still Amish, but her people had shunned her and turned her out. She could not imagine a way back. Although driven primarily by her desire to tighten the bond with Phillip, she took the classes seriously, and tried to find grace and beauty that she could hold for herself. She loved the feeling of belonging to a community once again.

The night that Marta revealed her feelings for Phillip to her married lover, he recoiled as if she had plunged a white-hot poker into his heart. Though he'd behaved like a cad in seducing her, he could not bring himself to stand in Marta's way. He quietly left her room and headed toward Alfie McDuff's to lick his wounds.

When Marta and Phillip traveled to Hagerstown to meet the Genero clan, her beauty, modest demeanor, kindness, and devotion to Phillip impressed the whole family, even though she was not Italian. The Genero clan could see that beyond her physical beauty, Marta was a twenty-carat diamond in the rough.

All of the Genero men, father and brothers alike, were smitten by this blonde goddess. Mama Genero pretended to be aloof, claiming the matriarchal right to reserve judgment. Secretly, mama was pleased that her bachelor boy had decided to settle down.

Phillip and Marta married a few months after the engagement and moved to a small farmhouse northwest of Carlisle at the base of the ridgeline under the road that connected Cumberland and Perry Counties. For Marta, the opportunities for intimacy, without the guilt of a forbidden relationship, were a marvelous release, inconceivable in her earlier life.

Marta loved Sunday afternoons after church. If the weather permitted, she and Phillip would cuddle together on the little wooden swing that they crafted for their tiny front porch. Once they were in each other's embrace, it was never long before the touching became more and more intimate, stimulating, and irresistible.

When they could no longer stand it, Phillip would sweep Marta's petite form up in his big arms and carry her into the house. Where they chose to consummate their love depended on how long they had been teasing each other on the swing. Many times, they never made it beyond the tiny foyer. While often sweet and tame, at times Phillip's desire swept over them both, exploring sexual depths not plumbed in catechism. When Phillip discovered Marta's enthusiastic responses, he felt liberated and honored that such a kind, gentle, and yet wantonly passionate beauty had chosen him.

The young couple continued to work for the Monarch family, but spent most of their free time alone, exploring their passion. It was an idyllic, extended honeymoon that world events would soon shatter.

In the spring of 1917, Congress declared war on Germany and America joined the allies in the Great War. The Cumberland County Draft Board selected Phillip in the fall of 1917. Genero reported for basic training at Camp Gordon, Georgia in October 1917, leaving a tearful wife at the Carlisle train station.

After Phillip's induction, Marta intended to keep working in the bookkeeping department at the clothing factory. Her immediate boss was the owner's son, Randall J. Monarch, Jr.

"Junior" was dissolute, lazy, and disreputable—an aberration from the otherwise respectable Monarch sons. He'd been a poor student in high school. He'd attended two Ivy League colleges but failed to complete even one semester.

As an adult, Junior acted like a spoiled and petulant adolescent. His father had given up on him. Now the two men could barely tolerate each other. Junior Monarch supervised the bookkeeping department at the company, because his father felt that Junior could do the least amount of damage in that position.

Junior fancied himself a great lover. For several years, even after she married Phillip, Junior had tried to seduce Marta. Abusing his position in the company, he attempted every trick and stratagem—to no avail.

Ever the amoral lecher, Junior had attempted to take advantage of Marta in Phillip's absence, but Providence interceded when she learned she was pregnant. As soon as she confirmed her condition, Marta left the clothing company. Phillip's brother Angelo and his wife moved to Carlisle, opened a small bakery near the college, and stayed with Marta in the farmhouse to help with the pregnancy. Expecting to stay home to raise her child, Marta began her new domestic life with no regrets.

Just before noon on October 8, 1918, Marta decided that she must name the baby boy after her husband. Due to her relationship with her former boss at the clothing factory, she could never use the word junior as any part of her son's name.

When the nurse arrived in Marta's room with the birth registration documents, the new mother wrote "Genero, Phillip Edward" in the appropriate blocks on the form. In order to distinguish her son from his father in the public record, she added the Roman numeral "II" at the end of his name.

At 1:30 p.m., the shift nurse carried Phillip Edward Genero, II, back into his mother's room for his second feeding. Holding her baby, Marta examined his features, cataloguing those that she thought were like her husband's.

*He really favors his father,* she thought. *He has my complexion, but looks like Phillip. It's too early to tell if he'll have his father's deep blue eyes.*

Marta closed her own eyes, and tried to picture her husband's handsome face. Marta couldn't shake the feeling that something bad had happened to Phillip. A cold chill ran through her body, followed by a sense of foreboding. Opening her eyes and gazing once again at the distant autumn colors, she began to pray.

# Chapter 2

0610 Hours
October 8, 1918
Argonne Forest
Near the DeCauville Railroad Junction
G Company, 328th Infantry Regiment,
82nd Infantry Division, American Expeditionary Force

While Marta Genero was in labor in Carlisle, Phillip was in France. He stood in a quiet glade in the Argonne Forest, preparing his squad for an assault on a well-defended German position, known to G Company as Hill 223.

G Company's mission was part of a larger attack against substantial German defenses in the Meuse-Argonne Sector. The staff officers had done a good job coordinating the offensive. So far, all had gone well.

This morning, elements of the 328th Infantry Regiment would sweep from their defensive positions, move over the top of Hill 223, and then infiltrate through a series of small valleys beyond. They intended to capture the vital railroad junction near DeCauville by the end of the day.

Cutting the rail line would deprive the Huns of a logistics link and make it difficult to resupply their forces. Unfortunately, nothing ever went as planned.

A corporal for only a week and nervous about leading men into battle for the first time, Phillip suppressed his nagging fear and kept busy attending to the pre-attack details of a new non-com. Responsible for 11 men, he worried about every issue to ensure that they were prepared and ready.

Genero hadn't been able to sleep. He'd been thinking about Marta. He wondered if the baby would be a boy or girl, though it didn't matter as long as the child was healthy.

Earlier in the morning, he'd said a final prayer for his wife and baby. Then, Phillip put them out of his mind. He concentrated on his duties so that he wouldn't leave Marta a widow and the new baby an orphan.

Normally affable and considerate, today he was all business. The soldiers in his squad understood. With a battle looming, they stowed their griping and complaining.

"Hey, Corporal!" jibed Private Koronopolis, a young Greek-American boy from New York. "Are we going to see the Kaiser this morning? I've come all the way from White Plains to this stinking forest. The least that son-of-a-bitch could do is serve us a little coffee and strudel on this chilly morning."

"Settle down, Steph," Phillip replied. "Save your energy. It'll be a long, difficult day. We'll need all of our wits about us."

The G Company commander decided that Genero would play a special role in the attack formation. Phillip would have a simple—but crucial—task.

After the artillery preparation, G Company would jump off and drive north. Genero would anchor the left flank of the lead platoon, as it moved out in skirmish formation looking for contact. As the last rifleman in that first line, he'd ensure that the Germans didn't turn G Company's left flank, by a surprise attack, enfilade, or ambush.

The captain had picked the right man for the assignment, since Genero had proved to be a steady and dependable man in combat. Sergeant Early, the platoon sergeant, thought highly of Genero's ability. The G Company platoon leaders agreed about the left.

Sgt. Early would take the center of the lead platoon in the company's three-platoon echelon. Corporal York would command the right squad. F Company would be to the right, beyond York.

Though well-trained and tested in earlier actions, the Yanks lacked the Germans' extensive combat experience. Undeterred, and sensing an end to the war, the Americans spoiled for this fight, so that they could defeat the Hun and go home. Imbued with a staunch fighting spirit, the feisty Americans prepared their equipment, hearts, and minds for the grim tasks that would lead them to victory.

Cpl. Alvin York was the unknown quantity in Early's lead platoon. Just over 30 and older than most of the other enlisted men in G Company, Alvin posed a troubling enigma. During his training, he'd established himself as the best shot in the regiment, maybe the entire All-American Division. Despite his age, he possessed a strong, wiry, and tough physique. With one glaring exception, he personified the ideal soldier.

York had changed his rowdy ways and found religion after a mysterious and traumatic event. By the time he joined the regiment, he was no longer a hard-drinking brawler. Sincere about his faith, he tried to live up to the teachings of a very strict, Christian sect.

No one in the 82$^{nd}$ Infantry Division quibbled with his religious views. Most of the professional officers and non-commissioned officers of that era belonged to established churches. But the commanders worried about York's earlier flirtation with claiming an exemption from combat as a conscientious objector.

York had argued that his religious beliefs precluded killing another person. This tenet created a serious problem for an infantryman, whose primary duty was to kill the enemy. No one at Camp Gordon doubted York's commitment to his religion or his courage, but some officers admitted that they were leery about trusting him. They wondered how he would react when he found himself in the unforgiving crucible of combat.

Hesitation in combat could spell disaster and death, not only for York, but also for his fellow soldiers. In the All-American Division, each man treated his buddy like his life depended on it, because it actually did. After a personal epiphany, York recanted and made a commitment to his unit, but his company commander confessed a vestigial doubt. One never knew how it would go with someone as conflicted as York, when he had to make the decision to kill another man. Some soldiers had no problem. Others could never cut it. Most did their difficult duty, the best they could.

An experienced hunter with uncanny intuition, York learned his field craft as a boy in the mountains of South Tennessee. If G Company were hunting deer, elk, or turkey, York would have been the first choice for the left flank.

This morning the regiment hunted men—veteran German combatants. In light of the danger, the G Company commander felt better about Genero watching the left.

Everyone in the company knew that Genero had a beautiful wife in Pennsylvania. She had a baby on the way. Desperate to survive and see his family, Phillip would do whatever it took to get home alive. No one doubted that Genero would pull the trigger.

Though unmarried, York claimed to have a girlfriend back home. A girlfriend wasn't the same thing as a wife.

At 0600, when the planned artillery preparation did not materialize, the commander postponed the attack. At 0610, and without one howitzer round downrange, Genero's platoon moved forward into the assault.

At first everything fared well—better than the staffers at division anticipated. Although the enemy fired sporadically at the Americans, G Company made good progress for the first few hours.

The Americans took Hill 223 in short order. That objective secured, they poured into the valleys between Hill 223 and their ultimate objective, the railroad junction at DeCauville.

Once the Americans moved beyond the hill, the situation deteriorated. German machine gun and rifle fire increased in volume and accuracy. American casualties increased dramatically. The Boche were everywhere.

Early's platoon lost five men as the German bullets snapped through the trees and brush like a swarm of angry bees, cutting small branches, tearing leaves from the hardwoods, and ending the lives of brave American boys. The worried sergeant noted that the enemy concentrated his fire

on the platoon's center and the right flank squad commanded by York.

"Alvin, watch your flank! Don't let those Heinie bastards
get between us and F Company," Early barked at York.

Blessedly, Genero's squad seemed far enough to the left
to be out of the enemy's range.

With the increased German resistance, the 328th Infantry
Regiment found itself in trouble. Short of the DeCauville
junction, it encountered a steep hill to its front, with a strong
German defensive position, comprising a series of trenches,
bunkers, and several heavy machine gun emplacements.
Hundreds of veteran German soldiers manned the fortifications.

The Germans maintained intense defensive fire, and
American casualties continued to rise. Without reinforcements from division, the regiment could not conduct a
frontal attack on the German emplacements. The colonel
would never countenance such folly, no matter how many
American reinforcements arrived.

In order to break out of the deadly bowl, the G Company
Commander ordered Sgt. Early to take 16 men, including Cpl.
York and Cpl. Genero, around the left flank. He wanted
Early's force to circle around the fortified hill and to ap-
proach the enemy defenses from their rear.

Genero, at the far left of the line, became the point man
for the group. Pvt. Koronopolis moved in four yards behind
Genero and a yard to his right. Koronopolis comprised the
one-man support element of the point team. He'd use hand
signals to relay data from the point man to Sgt. Early.

The rest of the men formed up behind the point element
in a skirmish formation of two lines with Sgt. Early and Cpl.
York in the center and between the two lines. York commanded the first skirmish line, which was to stay 30 yards
behind the point element.

Early commanded the second line 20 yards further back.
By design, he'd be able to see and control the whole force.

Sgt. Early directed Genero to move out and loop to the
left in a long, wide arc. This track took the point element

through a series of small ravines and rises, out of sight of the top of the fortified hill, where the Germans had established their right flank squad.

The men, except Sgt. Early who had a Colt .45, carried the 1903 Springfield, a .30 caliber, five-shot, bolt-action rifle. As a precaution, in the densely wooded battlefield, the men fixed bayonets.

After Genero and Koronopolis had traversed 500 yards, and moved safely past the right of the German lines, they stopped and waited for Sgt. Early and the other 14 men to advance. When they assembled, Sgt. Early held a brief council.

"Genero," Early began hastily. "Two hundred yards back, one of York's men spotted two Fritzes on the right. He shot at them but missed, damn it! Now, the enemy has to know that we're out here. They could send a large force down that damned hill and overwhelm us. We need to immediately reform, pivot right, and probe up the hill. At least we'll be facing them if they come down this way in force."

"Sarge, we've got less than twenty men. We're too few if we hit them on their flank. We'll do much better if we can get behind them. Maybe they'll think they're cut off. If we go up the hill now, most of us won't come back," Genero advised.

"Maybe you're right. The hill looks too steep anyway," Early conceded.

"Sarge, if we expose our position before we get to the top of the hill, we'll be under their guns, and defenseless. Our only hope is to infiltrate their rear in a surprise attack," Genero added.

"OK, we'll do it your way. Genero, take the point again. Let's move out another six hundred yards then swing right hard. Let's see where that gets us," Early directed. "York, move your people out, same as before."

It was a gamble, but worth the risk. If they surprised the Huns, they had a chance of success. If they failed, the enemy would cut them off and slaughter them. No help could reach them so far behind the German lines.

After the council, Genero again took the point and moved forward 600 yards. He and Koronopolis made another wide swing, first to the left then sharply to the right. At this point in their maneuver, they made good use of the heavy cover and concealment. Genero could barely see ten yards ahead.

After 15 minutes, Genero approached the rear of the fortified hill on which the Germans had placed the machine guns blocking the advance of the 328th. He heard the guns firing from the far side of the German position. Phillip knelt down behind a row of bushes to listen for enemy activity. He signaled the Greek boy to stop behind him.

There were Germans directly in front on the other side of a small brook, but because the forest was so thick, Phillip couldn't see where they were. His anxiety rising, Genero fought to keep control as he looked back, past Koronopolis. Somehow, he and the Greek had advanced too far ahead of Early's force. Genero could not see the first line of skirmishers under Cpl. York.

As he searched for a sign of the patrol, Genero detected movement from a large hedge behind Koronopolis. While Phillip focused on the movement, a tall, burly German soldier suddenly rose up from his concealed position.

Cpl. Genero spun around, and brought the butt of his Springfield to his face in an instant cheek weld. Try as he might, Phillip could not get the German in his sights because Koronopolis had misunderstood Genero's actions and moved the wrong way, positioning himself between Genero and the German soldier. It was a fatal error.

In less than a second, the tall German leapt behind Koronopolis. Genero tried to get off a shot, but his buddy was in the way. Phillip couldn't fire without hitting the Greek.

In a lightning-fast move, the German thrust his bayonet through the back of the soldier's neck. He impaled the blade to the hilt, causing the sharpened tip and several inches of the serrated blade to come out of the front of the young Greek-American's throat with a loud, wet, sickening pop.

A long thick stream of blood shot forward in a high arch for almost four feet. Stephan's eyes bulged like round white balls, spun in rotation, and rolled back into the top of his head. Unable to yell, scream, or choke, Koronopolis slumped lifelessly to the ground, still impaled on the German's bayonet.

The German stabbed the boy with such force that the bayonet on his Mauser remained stuck in the Yank's body. The German could not pull it free. With his weapon lodged in this macabre predicament, the German soldier began to frantically pull and twist to recover the use of his weapon.

Sensing a different danger, Genero spun back around in time to parry the bayonet thrust of a young, thin German soldier, who'd crept up behind him. The blade from the new threat slashed Genero's right thigh.

Motivated by primal rage, Genero parried the thin German's second thrust, countering with a horizontal butt stroke. Phillip aimed the butt of his rifle at the center of his young attacker's face. Genero's powerful stroke connected with a satisfying crack, breaking several bones in the German's face, knocking him back.

Cpl. Genero squared his body, kept his feet shoulder-width apart, weight forward and balanced on the balls of his feet like a dancer. He brought the Springfield back, parallel to the ground, muzzle up and pointed at the German. With his whole body—motivated by a hatred that he'd never before known—Genero thrust his bayonet into the young German's abdomen. As the blade sank into the enemy's stomach, he twisted the blade cruelly, 90 degrees to the right.

The Hun dropped his weapon onto the ground and reached with both shaking hands for the American's rifle, now firmly planted in his stomach. Genero was at full strength and too fast. The German was spent and dying.

Phillip pulled his rifle back before the German soldier could get purchase on the barrel of the weapon. The enemy soldier screamed in desperation, through a formerly boyish face, now crushed and bloodied by the earlier butt stroke. Tears from his eyes mixed with the blood on his cheeks.

The Hun slumped and fell to his knees, struggling to stay up. As he did, Genero brought his rifle to modified port arms.

A half-second later, he swung his Springfield around and down in a short, but powerful, arc.

The finely sharpened edge of Genero's bayonet made contact with the young soldier at the point on his right shoulder where the neck connects to the truck of the body. The bayonet sliced through the neck of the German, partially cleaving it. The wound extended from the boy's right shoulder to the middle of his chest.

Like Koronopolis, the enemy died quickly. The open wound pumped large volumes of dark, red blood into the air, covering Genero with a ghastly red mist.

After dispatching the young soldier, Genero spun around, turning to face toward Koronopolis, whose body lay prostrate on the ground. The burly German had placed his large boot on the Greek boys back. Thrusting, and extending his left leg, while holding the Mauser, the older Hun finally gained enough leverage to pull the bayonet from the dead boy's neck.

During the exertion, the German had lost track of Genero. He ended up facing toward the skirmish line commanded by Cpl. York, which had just emerged from the tree line.

Genero watched the burly German bring his Mauser to his shoulder and aim it directly at Cpl. York. York didn't see the enemy soldier. The Hun came within a hair's breath of shooting Alvin dead.

Instinctively, Genero raised his Springfield, firing it at the German. Before the German soldier could pull the trigger of his Mauser, a .30 caliber steel-jacketed bullet, moving at over 2,700 feet per second, pierced his skull just behind his right ear. The bullet made a large hole in the German's forehead and careened off into the forest.

Most of the soldier's brain landed on the ground more than five yards beyond the German's body. The rest of his body pitched forward and rolled in a bloody somersault, coming to rest in front of Cpl. York and his men, who advanced toward Genero.

Sensing extreme danger one more time, Genero turned back to face in the direction of the German lines. Genero focused on the opening in the forest on the other side of the brook in front of his position. He perceived movement, quite a lot of movement. Germans!

Genero worked the bolt on his Springfield, chambering another round. He heard Cpl. York coming up behind him. Phillip did not turn, but focused his attention on the danger from the enemy to his front.

In a moment, York knelt beside him and peered into the woods. Neither of the corporals looked at the other. The men in the first skirmish line took defensive positions among the rocks and trees on either side of the non-coms.

"That Hun had me dead ta rights. Ya saved my life! I'll be thanking ya, Phillip," York whispered, as both men peered in the direction of the Germans.

"That son-of-a-bitch got Koronopolis. I should have seen him first," Phillip complained, feeling responsible for the death of the young soldier.

"Couldn't be helped, boy! Ya done the best ya could."

Genero had just killed two men, violently and at close range. Adrenaline coursed through his body. His head throbbed from the elevated blood pressure. His whole body trembled, a reaction to the natural chemical imbalance. He watched as York took over.

York observed the tree line on the other side of the little creek for a long moment. He sniffed the air a few times, narrowed his eyes in concentration, focusing on some object. After a bit, Cpl. York smiled a cold, brittle smile. He looked over at Genero.

"I reckon those German boys are fixing a little bite to eat. I do believe I smell some bacon and sausage frying there in that holler," York said, a wry, insincere little smile replacing a very hard expression.

Genero simply nodded. York was an incredible woods-man, with uncanny powers of observation. It was possible. Even in a battle, the Germans had to eat.

At that moment Sgt. Early came up with the other seven men. He looked around, noting the bodies of the Germans and Koronopolis. He dispersed his skirmishers to various fighting positions and set a rear guard. He approached the two corporals.

Early looked them over. He saw Genero breathing rapidly, covered in blood. York was calm and assessed the situation competently.

"Report!" Early ordered, directing it to both corporals.

"Ma friend, Phillip, got both these Huns. As ya can plainly see, he stuck this one and blew the other's head clean oft," York explained.

"That big Hun over there stuck the Greek boy in his neck. He was just about to get me too, when ma friend shot him clean through his head. Saved ma life!"

"Good work, Genero!" Sgt. Early praised. "What's the situation to the front? We need to get moving." Early feared that they might lose the initiative—if, indeed, they'd ever had it.

"Alvin thinks the Boche are eating a meal in that glade over there. He says he can smell sausage frying," Genero said.

York sniffed the air again. He turned to Sgt. Early and with a conspiratorial wink briefly explained the situation. A number of Germans were having a meal, just on the other side of the creek in a small glade, beyond the thick tree line.

Sgt. Early made a decision. The group would move out in two skirmish lines. York and his men would be in front. Genero looked a little shaky, so he and one of the skirmishers would bring up the rear.

"Genero, you've done a good job. But we need to spell you. Take Private Davis and follow my line at a ten-yard interval. Don't let any of those bastards get in behind us. Understand?" Sgt. Early asked.

"Sarge, I can take point," Genero offered, still game, but not sure that he could keep his hands from shaking if he did go out in front.

"Don't need a point for this. I need a good man to keep us from getting jumped," Early responded.

Early turned toward York and gave a series of directions, punctuated by precise hand gestures.

"York, take your line across the creek. Move to the right as you enter the tree line. My line will follow, but we'll go to the left. Watch out! We'll be behind you and to your left. Genero and Davis will be behind both of us. The line will be extended a bit, so don't let your boys get trigger happy, or we'll be shooting each other in this thick stuff. When you break out into the glade, be ready for anything. If we get into a fire-fight, make the bastards pay!"

With the order to move out, the two lines reorganized. York started off with his seven men in less than 15 seconds. As York's skirmishers entered the tree line, the second line followed. Then Genero, wiping the German's blood from his eyes, motioned to Davis. They joined the assault.

Genero was less than 20 seconds behind the lead element commanded by Cpl. York. Crossing the creek and moving into the trees, he heard a commotion up ahead. He could make out shouts in English and German, but no firing.

Genero and Davis broke into a run, rifles at the ready, fingers near the trigger. They passed through the trees into the glade. Genero saw an astonishing sight.

At least 30 German soldiers of all ranks, including two or three officers, had been sitting and lounging in a meadow. Some were preparing a meal, when York's men stormed into the glade. Genero, 15 yards to the rear, saw the whole group with one glance.

It was pandemonium. The Americans shouted at the Germans to put up their hands and surrender. The Germans responded slowly.

Though American combatants were on the other side of the hill, these 30 *soldaten* ate and lounged in the open glade. Genero could not believe that a German officer would allow such cavalier behavior in the face of the enemy.

The scene rapidly deteriorated into confusion. The small American force didn't anticipate stumbling over so many Germans. The Germans refused to follow orders given in English.

As the situation became more perilous, one of the German officers stood up and shouted, "*Alarm! Amerikanische soldaten hinter unseren linen!*" Phillip did not understand the words, but noticed that several of the German soldiers turned in the direction of the reverse slope of the hill, less than 30 yards away, and looked up. A chill erupted down his spine.

*My God! That's the back end of the hill we're supposed to attack. There must be hundreds of Germans up there!* Genero thought.

Phillip saw one of the German sergeants standing behind Corporal York reach into his field coat with his right hand. Genero knew that the German would pull a gun.

Once again that morning, Genero saved York's life. Genero yelled a warning to York. York heard it, ducked and spun in the direction of the German at the same instant.

Before the enemy could extend his arm with the 9mm Luger in his hand, Genero shot him in the center of his chest. As the sergeant staggered back from the force of the bullet, York shot him in the forehead at point-blank range. The force of York's shot picked the German up horizontal to the ground and three feet in the air, carrying him back five or six feet and dumping his lifeless body on the rocky glade.

York looked over at Genero. He shook his head. "I reckon I'll be thanking ya again, boy."

Genero nodded his head in tacit recognition, one brave soldier to another.

Unbeknownst to the small American force, a German soldier on the hill above had seen Cpl. York and his skirmishers emerge from the tree line. He watched as they tried to capture his comrades in the glade below.

The soldier raised the alarm. Americans had infiltrated the rear. After a moment, a German lieutenant came to the soldier's position, observed the Americans, saw the difficulty that they encountered, and noted that there were fewer than 20 in their band.

The lieutenant raced over to his commander, an experienced Prussian major. He explained the situation. The major directed 80 German riflemen and machine gunners to turn around, face the rear, and fire into the Americans. The German commander perceived that the biggest threat from the Americans was now to his rear. He brought the bulk of his firepower to bear on Sgt. Early's modest force.

The major didn't have the luxury to forget about the Americans to his front. He left 50 other soldiers in their original positions to continue to deal with them. He felt a reinforced platoon would be adequate for the time being, since the American frontal attack had stalled.

The German commander knew he was in a tight spot, but in the last few weeks he'd done well against these American newcomers. The Prussian was a professional soldier from a very long line of distinguished military men.

The Prussian was not impressed with these Yanks. He was surprised that they'd found the initiative to infiltrate his rear. He'd deal with them quickly and brutally, and then return to his primary duty of repelling the attack of this so-called All-American Division.

After he'd reconfigured his force, the major gave the signal with a wave of his hand and the Germans focused a large volume of fire at the Americans in the glade. In the first few seconds the German assault killed or wounded seven of the Americans. It was the slaughter that Early had feared.

Since the Americans were interspersed among their prisoners, the German gunners were unable to discriminate. In their zeal to attack the Americans, they killed and wounded many of their comrades. One German machine gunner framed Sgt. Early directly in his sights. With skill honed by years of experience, the German riddled Sgt. Early with more than six direct hits.

Genero and Davis were only ten feet from the tree line when the shooting began. They hit the ground and crawled back among the trees for cover. As soon as they found fighting positions, they returned fire on the hill. Two bolt-action Springfields against the powerful German weaponry proved to be grotesquely inadequate.

Genero almost panicked as unimaginable horror and peril unfolded before him. Fighting to maintain control, Phillip understood that he'd never get back to Pennsylvania and his beloved Marta. For the next few seconds, he bid goodbye to his wife.

He prayed that she would find happiness with someone who would love and care for the new baby. Reloading his Springfield with a stripper clip from his belt, he consoled himself with the thought that his family in Hagerstown would help raise the child.

Neither Genero nor Davis ever considered crawling away in the woods to save themselves. They were scared, but they would never leave their buddies—who were bleeding and dying in that awful glade. They would stay and fight as long as they had a breath in their bodies.

At the bleakest point in the battle, Genero saw Cpl. York 35 yards away, moving like a man possessed. He crawled, ran, and dodged through the bodies of the dead soldiers, broken equipment, fallen trees, and other impediments. He was tracking to the far right, toward the Germans on the hill.

At this point, only Genero and Davis could fire at the Germans. The Boche could not see the two Americans because the Yanks had found adequate cover in the tree line. Since the American ammunition incorporated a smokeless powder and the din of the battle was overwhelming, the act of shooting in broad daylight did not give them away.

York scrambled to the American right and into the enemy's sight. The Huns focused a tremendous amount of fire on him, but nothing could stop him. Although Genero saw bullets impacting by the scores, even hundreds, all around the Tennessean, none found him. He remained unscathed.

*God must surely love that man*, Genero surmised, as York continued to struggle around to the right. *Might be something to his preaching.*

Eventually, York moved so far to the right that Genero couldn't see him. It was a difficult angle and Genero tried to get off shots at the Germans on the hill.

Genero was a good marksman, though not in York's class. He should have been hitting some of the Germans up on the hill. In the smoke and haze, he couldn't make out individuals, nor could he see where his bullets impacted.

In no time at all, Genero had used up eight stripper clips of ammunition. He would run out of bullets in a few moments if he tried to keep up this volume of fire.

Genero called over to Davis, who'd crawled to a position in the tree line, eight yards to his left. Genero asked how he was doing for ammunition. Davis thought that he had over 70 rounds left. Davis rolled over on his back, so he could check the ammunition pouches on the front of his web gear.

One of the German gunners on the hill spotted Davis moving in the tree line. The enemy soldier sighted in his Maxim machine gun on the spot where Davis thought he was concealed. The German gunner couldn't make out what the movement was, but he wouldn't leave anything to chance.

A second later, the Hun let loose a long burst, more than 40 rounds, on the suspicious spot. Satisfied, he swept the whole tree line with the balance of the belt. He sprayed bullets for 20 yards in both directions.

Without knowing it, the German hit Davis twice, once in the right shoulder and once in the left arm. The arm wound was minor, but the shoulder wound was serious. Davis lost consciousness.

The German also hit Genero three times. All three shots struck Genero in the left leg. One bullet passed through his thigh, another took a big chunk of flesh from his calf, but the last one hit right above the ankle, breaking both his tibia and fibula.

Since Genero was prone, he bounced hard, from the shock of the impacts. He remained still to assess his wound. He didn't want to draw more fire from the Germans on the hill. He felt shock and nausea. Despite his best efforts at control, he vomited.

The wounds hurt. Phillip bled profusely. He worried that he might lose too much blood. He struggled to remain calm.

The nausea passed, but not the pain. Phillip gathered himself, made a decision, and disregarded his wounds. He crawled along the tree line, to a spot with more cover.

Phillip cut a long piece of cloth from his blouse with his trench knife. He tied it above the thigh wound. He removed the metal cleaning rod from the chamber in the stock of his Springfield and slid it between the cloth on his leg and his uniform.

Once the rod was in place, using it as a lever, he twisted it three times to tie off the blood flow. His leg throbbed dreadfully, but the tourniquet slowed the bleeding.

Now in a better tactical position, Phillip turned his rifle over to examine it. He pulled back the bolt. The chamber was empty. He reached into one of the pouches on his belt and secured another stripper clip of five rounds.

His hands shaking, he fit a clip into the slot, stripping the bullets into the fixed magazine of his rifle. Phillip threw the bolt forward sending a round into the chamber.

"Just one of you sons-of-bitches, show yourselves, you Hun bastards," Genero said in an icy calm tone, through tightly clenched teeth, a small tear of frustration rolling down his dirty, blood-stained face.

Genero knew that he'd never leave this battlefield alive, but he wanted back in the fight so he could help his boys. The fear began to fade and knowing that he could not survive the battle, a spiritual calm enveloped him.

He brought his rifle up, rested the front of the barrel on a small flat rock. He looked through his metal sights at the German positions on the hill. He marked a possible target, brought the sights to bear, held his breath, and slowly began to squeeze the trigger in the way that Alvin had taught him many months before at Camp Gordon.

Despite the fire from the Germans, York had worked his way to the right of the glade. He found additional cover and concealment so he could begin ascending the hill.

As York moved toward the Germans, he stood astride the Huns' defensive trenches. From the corporal's perspective, the German positions stretched out in front and above him in a long, narrow line.

York had the angle on the enemy. He saw the top left profile of two German helmets. The helmets belonged to a soldier and an *unteroffizer* manning one of the Maxim machine guns firing into Early's men.

Cpl. York brought his own Springfield up to his right shoulder. As with all natural marksmen, he held his breath.

Focusing on the front sight, Alvin squeezed off a round. The first shot passed through the left side of the head of the German soldier. York chambered a second round. He immediately fired at the *unteroffizer*—a headshot, dead center, left side.

The two Huns slumped in death in rapid succession, almost simultaneously. As the dead men fell away from the machine gun, they exposed another Boche. York immediately killed him with another headshot.

With five shots from his first clip, York killed four German soldiers and one non-commissioned officer. York reloaded, and continued up the hill. Crouching low, he entered the trench near the bodies of the men he'd killed.

Stepping cautiously over the body of one of the non-commissioned officers, York un-holstered his own Colt .45 automatic pistol. York checked again to ensure that it was loaded. He stowed the pistol in the left side of his web belt as insurance, if he got into a close-quarters scrap.

At a slight bend of the trench, York saw more Germans manning machine guns and firing rifles down into the glade. Cpl. York began again. Using the same tactic, he coldly and calmly shot and killed several more Germans. He continued, reloading and firing.

The Germans on the hill realized that some number of Americans had flanked their trench line. At least one of the

Yanks was a hell of a shot. Whenever one of the *soldaten* raised his head, a sniper's well-placed bullet killed him.

The Prussian major beckoned a veteran sergeant. He ordered him to take five of the terrified men around through the back of the trench system to see if they could flush the sniper.

The officer addressed all six men at once. "Be careful, this American sniper is very dangerous. You must destroy him. If you fail, do not return alive! Understand?"

The German sergeant acknowledged the order. He'd fought on the Western Front since he left his farm in Bavaria in 1915. He'd received an Iron Cross for his exploits on the field. Sergeant Muller was one of the best soldiers in this regiment. He'd killed many French and British soldiers.

The sergeant deployed his men around to their left, using connecting trenches and keeping low. He had a hunch where the American sniper might be. Within three minutes, he'd maneuver in position to kill this Yank bastard, who'd shot several of his comrades. Like most field soldiers, he despised enemy snipers. *I will take great pleasure in killing this son-of-a-bitch. I want to do it close up, painful, and personal*, he thought.

He checked his Luger. It was loaded, safety off.

From Genero's position in the tree line below, the silence from the German position was miraculous. He heard the occasional report of a Springfield, off to his right. It had to be York.

*I'll bet Alvin is giving those Huns the devil.* Genero thought, with satisfaction, as he scanned the line of German trenches.

The pause in the German firing gave Genero the opportunity to visually inspect the gruesome meadow. He saw broken, bleeding corpses of both his buddies and the enemy. Genero understood that the Germans had shot their own men to kill Americans. Genero put the carnage out of his mind. He focused on what might be happening with York.

At that moment from the top of the hill on the right, Genero heard the familiar report of a Springfield, followed immediately by seven pistol shots. In the chaos, Genero couldn't tell if the pistol shots came from an enemy pistol or an American Colt.

Genero's heart sank. He imagined that York fired his rifle and while he reloaded, a German officer emptied his pistol into him. The few survivors of Early's small force were goners for sure.

Phillip was wrong. York had just killed six more Germans.

The German sergeant had maneuvered his squad through the trenches without compromising their presence. They'd found a place in the earthworks, just 20 yards from the place where York was waiting to take another shot.

The German non-com had worked out a viable plan. He whispered the instructions to his men, "When the American sniper fires his next shot, go over the top of the connecting trench and rush down the hill toward the American. Fire as you move! If you get a good shot, kill him! If you don't, I will finish him off."

Only a few yards away, York paused for a moment to scan the enemy line. York saw a slight movement to his left, near a makeshift emplacement. He saw only a sliver of metal, the very top of a helmet.

Cpl. York aimed and fired. The .30 caliber bullet from York's Springfield penetrated the enemy helmet at its apex, tearing off the entire top of the soldier's skull. The Hun flopped dead in the trench among a dozen terrified comrades, spurting blood and shaking from nerve spasms.

The German sergeant gave his men the prearranged command. All six sprung up from their trench, firing their weapons. They rushed York from his right side.

Cpl. York saw the attack developing out of the corner of his right eye. He reached into his webbing. With a graceful sweep of his arm, he pulled the Colt .45, extended his arm, and aimed the automatic at the last man in the group.

The Germans were not running abreast, but were strung out in an angled line. Alvin York began his deadly task by shooting the man last in line. He then worked forward calmly and accurately.

York did not want any of the Germans to see the man in front fall. It could spook them and cause them to go to cover. With seven shots he killed the German sergeant and all five of his men.

Several of the soldiers in the enemy trenches saw their comrades die as they charged the sniper. Not one of the terrified soldiers dared to raise his head. The whole German line deteriorated.

A German jumped from the trench and raced back up the hill. York shot him through the back of his head. Another soldier tried to crawl into a narrow depression, which led away from the trench. York killed him with one shot.

That was it. First one or two, then by threes and fours, they raised their hands over the top of the trench in surrender, yelling "*Kamerad!*" Several soldiers produced pieces of white or light colored cloth, waiving them in the air in total defeat.

The Prussian major felt utter despair. He considered shooting some of his own men to stop the wave of capitulation. If he did, the survivors might kill him. He tossed his pistol into the trench and raised his own hands in surrender.

York was more surprised than anyone on that hill when the Germans began to surrender in large numbers. He stood up. "You boys git down here, now! Drop yer guns! Keep yer hands were I can see them. Don't try nothing funny! Get along!" York ordered in a clear angry voice.

Only a few of the Germans spoke English. Even those who did were not able to understand much of York's South Tennessee accent. It didn't matter. York's bearing and their fear of him overwhelmed the enemy soldiers. One by one, they filed down the mountain, over 110 prisoners from the top of the hill.

From his place on the front edge of the tree line, Genero observed the long procession of German prisoners. He was stunned. The bloody glade filled with scores of unarmed Huns with their hands in the air.

Only a few moments ago, 17 Americans had difficulty controlling 30 Germans. Now, many of the Americans were dead, and there were only a half-dozen Americans trying to organize over 100 enemy soldiers.

Genero grabbed onto a tree branch. When he got the right angle, he used the limb for support. He stood up gingerly. Phillip hopped over to Davis, who'd regained consciousness. Despite his wounds, Davis was able to stand.

Genero took the bayonet from his rifle, and appropriated the one on Davis' Springfield. While leaning against the tree, Genero fashioned a crude splint, using the bayonets as the support pieces. He secured them to the lower portion of his left leg by wrapping them with a short piece of webbing.

Though the pain was intense, Genero hobbled forward to help the men who were trying to control the horde of German prisoners. Genero first checked the American casualties. Most were dead.

Of the 17 American soldiers who entered that glade at Chatel-Chehery on October 8, 1918, six were dead. Four were wounded and seven—including York—were unscathed. Two of the wounded, like Genero, could limp. Two, including Sgt. Early, were in critical condition.

Cpl. Alvin York, of Pall Mall, Tennessee, had killed 26 German soldiers and had fired his weapons 28 or 29 times. Genero estimated that York had forced the surrender of more than 130 Germans, including 20 who'd survived the German fusillade in the meadow.

Cpl. York was the last man off the hill. It was no longer a hindrance to the American advance on the DeCauville railroad junction.

York looked over the prisoners and assessed the options. He walked over to Genero, who stood with the weight on his right leg, using his rifle for support.

"Alvin, this is unbelievable. It's amazing!" Genero stammered.

"We had better look after Sgt. Early, and some of the other boys, if we're going to help them make it outta here."

"Alvin, most of the boys are dead and wounded," Genero explained softly.

Understanding, York looked directly at Genero. Phillip saw a deadly rage burn in Alvin York's eyes. He watched as the knuckles on York's hands turned white from the power of his grip on his weapon. For a moment York struggled with control. Then the rage passed.

"Phillip, can ya walk, boy? I'm going to need some help with these Huns. I'm fixing to take them back to the colonel."

"I can't move very fast, but I can hobble a bit. Maybe we can get these Huns to make litters for the wounded. They can carry them as we move the lot of them out of here," Genero replied.

"Good idea. Let's git along as quick as we can. Some of these boys won't be with us much longer if we dawdle," York observed.

"Alvin, you saved our lives. You are a real hero."

"Phillip, I reckon we've been friends about a year. It seems a bit longer somehow. I ain't no hero. Don't want to be one, never did! I hope my Savior will forgive me for what I done to all these Huns. Phillip, I jest couldn't figure no other way to stop them from killing us. Know what I mean?"

Genero could see that York was serious and he was touched by York's humility. They had wounded to care for and prisoners to turn in. They had to go.

York started giving directions to the ambulatory Americans and German prisoners. Soon, the whole long column was pointed back to the American lines.

Genero limped along. When he could go no further, York had two of the bigger Germans carry him the rest of the way.

Genero went to an aid station at the rear of the American lines. A day later, the medics sent him to a military hospital near Paris, where the surgeons tried to save his left leg—and his life.

# Chapter 3

Limping noticeably, Cpl. Genero walked through the Army hospital's outpatient processing office at the southeast corner of Carlisle Barracks. He knocked on the hospital administrator's office door. When the Medical Services Corps lieutenant acknowledged him, Genero entered.

"Corporal Genero reporting as directed, sir."

"Oh, Corporal Genero, good to see you! Stand easy. There's no need to be formal. How are you?" The officer said in a concerned tone.

"Fine, sir. Not much pain. The leg is a little stiff. Won't be running any races, but I can get around all right."

"That's very good. Glad to hear it. You've done well in your rehabilitation. I have your Army discharge papers right here."

Genero, walked over to the desk. Examining the documents, he noted that his discharge depicted his service as Honorable. Phillip was proud of his record, but never thought of himself as a career soldier. Good thing; his wounds wouldn't permit it.

"Corporal Genero, your separation papers reflect that you were wounded four times, once with a bayonet. You were shot in your left leg three times. You're entitled to recognition on your Certificate of Merit. Since the wounds come from two separate actions, the Army's awarded you two Wound Chevrons to wear on the right cuff of your Class A uniform," the medical administrator explained.

"Phillip," he continued. "I'm sorry. We're all embarrassed here. There's been no official action on the recommendation for the Distinguished Service Cross. It's a shame, considering all you've been through. I'd have thought that they'd push it along before we discharged you."

"Sir, it's OK. I'm glad to be home. I don't need chevrons or a medal to remember what I did. I'm alive and I've got the best wife and son that a man could have. Frankly, I hope to forget most of what I've seen and done. Better that way, sir. Believe me."

"Well, you have every right to feel that way. It's still a damn shame! Your friend, Sergeant York, sure got a lot of credit. He received the Medal of Honor and a Distinguished Service Cross. I believe he got awards from France, too. York's quite the celebrity. Invited to dinner at the White House, tickertape parade in New York, all the trappings. I'll bet he loves every minute of it, huh? I understand that Hollywood wants him to be a movie star," the officer expounded with wink and a smile, implying the lascivious, fringe benefits of being a hero.

"Sir, I'm sure Alvin's miserable. I can't imagine him in New York or with the President at the White House. He'll never be in the movies. My guess is that he'd rather be hunting along the Wolf River. Sir, if ever a man didn't want fame, it's Alvin C. York."

The officer and Phillip chatted for ten more minutes. Feeling uncomfortable, Genero asked to take his leave. He had family obligations.

The officer completed the paperwork, organized the copies that were Genero's, and placed them—and the balance of Phillip's military pay—in a large brown envelope. Neatly bundled, he handed the service record to Phillip.

Cpl. Phillip Genero snapped to attention, saluted—for the last time—and turned slowly, unable to execute a proper *about face* due to his leg. He walked out of the hospital and looked around the lovely, park-like grounds of Carlisle Barracks. As he took a deep breath of the warm, sultry summer air, Genero felt satisfaction knowing that he was now a small part of the history of this place.

Phillip Genero had spent nearly six months in hospitals in France, ships in transit, and medical facilities in New York and Philadelphia. After he made it back to the United States, Marta and Phillip's father traveled to see him in the hospital in New York.

The Generos had a tearful and joyous reunion limited by the fact that Phillip's injuries had not properly healed. Since the Argonne, Army doctors had operated on his leg five times.

The broken, shattered bones near his left ankle had caused complications. The bullet had damaged the muscles and blood vessels in his lower leg. The Germans had shot him twice more in the same leg. The infection that set in did not help.

Hobbling along the Meuse-Argonne battlefield with the now famous Sergeant York with a makeshift splint and a rigged tourniquet almost cost Phillip his left foot. The doctors would have amputated the foot, were it not for Genero's stubbornness.

Since Genero was a participant in the one of bravest feats of arms in American history, he was a minor celebrity. The doctors gave this wounded corporal more latitude than they normally allowed to an enlisted patient.

In May, the chief surgeon in Philadelphia decided that they'd done all that they could without taking the left leg below the knee. Genero was not ready for full release. Since he was a minor hero and lived near Carlisle Barracks, the doctor shipped him to Rehabilitation Hospital No. 31 for several weeks of outpatient care.

When Genero arrived in Carlisle, a huge crowd from the town assembled to greet him. The presence of family and friends overwhelmed him. As the medics helped him off the train, he glimpsed the beautiful ridges surrounding Carlisle for the first time in a year and a half. When Phillip saw his handsome baby son in the arms of his lovely wife, standing framed against the spectacular green hills, his eyes filled with tears.

In the Argonne, Phillip had resigned himself to his own mortality. He never expected to make it back to his valley alive. Yet here he was.

He remembered Pvt. Koronopolis. Like all survivors, Phillip felt pangs of guilt. When he looked into Marta's gorgeous brown eyes and saw the love she had for him, the guilt passed—for the moment.

The lively and boisterous crowd loved that a man from Carlisle had acquitted himself so gallantly. The mayor of Carlisle gave a fiery speech. Father Callahan spoke to the crowd in a more solemn tone. Friends and family enjoyed a fabulous welcome home party.

The mayor finally loaded Phillip, Marta, and their boy into a 1916 Model T hack. He considered it an honor to accompany this war hero and his tiny family home to their farmhouse near Waggoners Gap.

Phillip's first view of his farmhouse caused a second bout of intense emotion. As the hack approached their home, Phillip balanced his son in his lap. Marta held Phillip's hand in a powerful loving grip.

Once home, a neighbor stopped by to pick up little Phillip for the night. Marta made this arrangement because she wanted a very special homecoming. When they were alone, they held each other tenderly and began to slowly share their intimacy. The passion and the need brought them to a culmination too quickly.

Lying together in their bed, they laughed and giggled at their awkwardness.

"Honey, that was way too fast. I guess we'll just have to practice more," Phillip said.

"Phillip, I've missed you so. I need you so bad. Sometimes, since the baby was born, I thought I'd go crazy thinking about you," Marta said, fondling her husband and renewing his great passion for her.

"When, exactly, will Mrs. Rice bring little Phillip back?" Phillip asked slyly.

"I hope you don't mind, honey, but I wanted you all to myself this first night. She'll bring him back tomorrow morning. Is it OK? I know you love little Phillip," Marta said as she ran her tongue slowly along the inner surface of Phillip's left ear. "But I have needs too."

Marta's tactics had the desired effect on her husband. Phillip began to gently touch her and stroke her, in all the ways that intensified her passion.

Marta's eyes dissolved into that sexy, dreamy, far-away look, the one that drove him wild. Without stopping for an instant, Phillip brought his lips very close to Marta's sensitive right ear. As his tongue began tracing little, wet lines, he whispered, "Baby, I love that you named little Phillip after me, but we have to find something else to call him. It's too confusing."

Marta was almost over the edge, her eyes were closed, and she concentrated on the pleasure that Phillip's fingers were giving her. She moaned deeply. "Anything, baby— anything! I'd do anything for you!"

# Chapter 4

10:00 AM
November 11, 1927
Armistice Day
Indian Treaty Room
Old Executive Office Building
17<sup>th</sup> Street and Pennsylvania Ave.
Washington, D.C.

To the nine-year-old boy, the Old Executive Office Building was the largest structure he'd ever seen. The government building reminded him of a spooky German castle, or a fancy, multi-layered birthday cake with piles of blue-grey icing and lots of candles. Young Mr. Genero couldn't decide.

The place felt peculiar. He didn't want to stay inside the building waiting with the grown-ups in the Indian Treaty Room. Although he was an aggressive boy in Carlisle, on the grounds of the White House he was shy and intimidated.

The old steward, who drew the short straw and had to mind Phil and his sister, removed the children from the crowd gathering for the ceremony. He spirited them to a small side-garden just outside the building. The steward waited patiently as the Genero children preyed upon each other. They chased each other back and forth on the steps of the north portal of the office building, opposite the White House military mess.

Little Phillip, known to family and friends as "Gin," liked his baby sister. She could be a pain, but normally she was pretty neat. For her part, Karen barely tolerated her brother's existence. If you asked her, he was the epitome of inconsequential.

Karen, who was almost eight, was more sophisticated than this Huckleberry Finn. She found Washington, the monstrosity of a building in which they had to wait, the reception in the Indian Treaty Room, and her older brother's incessant banter totally boring.

She wanted to get on with it. The ceremony honoring her dad was supposed to have happened an hour earlier. *Something always happens with these grown-ups,* she thought. *Why couldn't they be on time? Don't they care about me at all?*

Karen, or Kari—as her dad called her—was a beautiful little girl with long, almost white, blond hair and a very fair complexion.

Physically, she looked like her lovely mother, except for the stunning light blue eyes that she inherited from the northern Italians on the Genero side. Her features added to her allure and made her appear very Nordic.

As the Genero children played outside, a large crowd congregated in the Indian Treaty Room to honor the former Army corporal. According to protocol, Mr. and Mrs. Genero would meet the President in the Oval Office. After the formalities, they'd go into the Indian Treaty Room and Calvin Coolidge would preside at the ceremony to pin a medal on Mr. Genero.

The steward had heard that the famous Sergeant York—the hero from the Great War—was a special guest of the President at this ceremony. Sgt. York would help the President and the Army bigwigs honor this simple man from Pennsylvania.

*I wonder what Mr. Genero did to deserve all this fuss?* The steward thought. *I hear that he runs a bakery in Carlisle. That's no big deal.*

Genero couldn't be in the same category as Sgt. York. The steward had heard that Sgt. York killed hundreds of Germans with his bare hands. *Didn't he personally capture thousands of enemy soldiers and even the Kaiser himself in Berlin? Whatever he did, it must have been pretty impressive,* the steward concluded.

Just as the steward was about to separate Gin and Kari for the third time, he saw a group of folks walk out of the White House and make for the back entrance of the office building. Even from this distance he could identify the figure of President Coolidge.

Walking next to the president was a very handsome woman with blond hair, all done up in a tight bun. This woman was obviously the little girl's mother.

She wore a simple, long blue dress and a matching bonnet with a small feather, cocked slightly to the right, as was the fashion this fall. For a married lady with two small children, she looked stunning.

Two men followed the president. One was a tall, rough-looking gentleman in his late thirties with brown, thinning hair and a thick mustache. That had to be Sgt. York. The other man was the same height, about ten years younger, and not so well fed. The younger man walked with a pronounced limp.

The steward gathered the children and brought them into the corridor, outside the reception room. Once inside the room, he found a little spot near the front of the large crowd, where Kari and her brother could see the ceremony and not be in the way.

A moment later, an Army officer announced the President. The reception room fell into a respectful silence. All turned to face Mr. Coolidge as he strode to the lectern. As usual, he was all business.

A conservative and careful man, the public knew Calvin Coolidge to be somber in his personal habits and moods. In his daily routine, he appeared distant and remote from the public. Renown for his economy of speech, if not his sense of humor, wags claimed that when a woman bet that she could get more than two words from him at a social gathering, he had responded, "You lose."

Ironically, no leader donated his presence more generously for special occasions. Coolidge understood the importance of his role as President and Commander-in-Chief.

He recognized that Americans craved a spot of color in the grays and blacks of their leaders.

Today, the ninth anniversary of the Armistice with Germany, the president had a pleasant chore. He would formally recognize ex-Corporal Phillip E. Genero of the All-American Division for his gallantry in that desperate battle in the Argonne, so many years earlier.

From the sound of the citation, Genero had earned his award, and more. *I don't understand why it took the Army so dang long to get the records straight on this business,* Coolidge thought. *If it hadn't been for Sgt. York—now there's a hero for you—the Army might never have given Genero this recognition.*

*Not that the public would much care any more,* Coolidge decided. *The Great War ended long ago. Its lessons, if any could truly be learned, have been forgotten by the average American citizen.*

Even York, the greatest hero of the war, had established a foundation for peace in Tennessee. He often preached the sensible philosophy of American Isolationism.

On that point Coolidge and York were in complete agreement. America must never again sacrifice and squander its wealth and blood, its treasure, and its sons in the squabbles of the corrupt Europeans. With any luck, in the future this type of ceremony would occur rarely or not at all. *Wasn't the Great War supposed to be the conflict that ended all wars?*

Coolidge believed that most Americans felt the same way. Folks were more interested in having a good time. They wanted to enjoy the economic benefits of the fabulous prosperity that he and his party had created. These were the Roaring Twenties, after all.

Sure, some of his constituents complained about Prohibition. The President knew that anybody could get a drink, if they really wanted one. Not that they should, of course.

He conceded that there were other excesses. *What about those floozies, or is it flappers? What about that behavior? Well, I guess there's no point in getting stirred up about that.*

*Best thing is to attend to the proceedings at hand,* Coolidge decided.

"Ladies and Gentlemen," the president began. "We are gathered here today on the anniversary of the Armistice to honor a gallant citizen-soldier. He is now a baker by trade from the great Commonwealth of Pennsylvania, former Corporal Phillip E. Genero. Brigadier General Adams will now read the official citation."

President Coolidge signaled to the officer from the Army staff, a one-star general who was a combat veteran of the Great War. The general stepped forward. In a clear voice General Adams announced the award of the Distinguished Service Cross, and read the citation that accompanied it.

"On October 8, 1918, in the Argonne Forest, while assigned as a squad leader in the 1st Platoon of G Company, 328th Infantry, 82nd Infantry Division, Corporal Phillip E. Genero, at great personal risk, volunteered to take the point in a hastily devised American attack on the rear echelon of a strongly fortified hill, manned by a reinforced German heavy machine gun company. After leading the American forces safely around the German defenses and into their rear elements, Corporal Genero personally engaged two German soldiers in difficult and bitter hand-to-hand combat. He personally vanquished both soldiers, while suffering a bayonet wound to his right leg.

"Moments later, during the capture of scores of German officers and men, Corporal Genero foiled a cowardly attempt by a German soldier to shoot Sergeant Alvin C. York in the back. At this point, a general battle in the rear of the fortified hill ensued during which Corporal Genero received three more serious wounds. Disregarding these wounds and suffering from shock and loss of blood, Corporal Genero continued to fire his weapon at the main German force to provide support to a flanking movement, then underway by Sergeant York.

"Corporal Genero's actions, in support of the attack led by Sergeant York, assisted Sergeant York's courageous efforts to silence the threat posed by the Germans to G Company and the 328th Infantry. Corporal Genero's fidelity to duty, gallantry, and heroic conduct above and beyond the call of duty materially contributed to the success of the attack. His courage and selflessness have brought great honor to himself, his family, the 82nd Infantry Division, and the United States Army.

"Signed and Executed at the White House, this Ninth day of November, in the Year of Our Lord, One thousand, nine-hundred and twenty-seven. Calvin C. Coolidge, President of the United States, Commander-in-Chief of the Armed Forces."

When General Adams completed the reading of the citation, an Army major handed the President a new Distinguished Service Cross for presentation. President Coolidge motioned to Phillip and Marta, who respectfully approached the Commander-in-Chief. With an efficiency borne of many award ceremonies, the President pinned the DSC to the left pocket of Phillip's gray civilian suit coat. The President shook Phillip's hand and then turned and smiled for the photographers.

Young Genero stood quietly during the brief ceremony and he heard the citation clearly. He had no idea that the loving and gentle father that he'd known all of his life was such a hero. To make it truly unbelievable, these events all happened on his birthday, or more accurately, the very day he was born.

Although the boy would not admit it, he was a little scared. He had difficulty accepting that his own dad could do all of those brave and violent things that the general said he did. He could not envision it. He saw his dad as the guy who did all of those undesirable chores around the farmhouse, or around the bakery that the Genero brothers operated in Carlisle, near Dickenson College.

The President ended the ceremony abruptly. He strode out of the reception, ostensibly to handle grave matters of state. He wanted to get back to the Oval Office, and as far away as possible from all these professional glad-handers. Though a professional politician, President Coolidge did not relish meeting people at these public events and sought refuge behind the mantle of his executive responsibilities.

The stewards served coffee, tea, and cakes. After a bit, the politicians and Army officers filtered out of the room and back into streets of Washington in pursuit of their lives and jobs.

Marta gathered the children and told Phillip that she'd walk them back to the Willard Hotel. The exercise would sap some of the energy from these two little hellions.

"Phillip, we'd better head back to Carlisle tomorrow morning," Marta said. "You know how your brothers are."

In 1920, with money that he and Marta saved from working at Monarch, Phillip and two of his brothers expanded the small bakery in Carlisle that Angelo had opened. In the last years they'd achieved a modest success, owing to Phillip's energy, business sense, and standing in that small community.

Phillip left the baking to his brothers while he managed the business affairs. He bought three Ford trucks, converted them into delivery vans, and set up routes throughout the little town into the farming community all the way through Mechanicsburg to Camp Hill. He brought the bread and baked goods to the customers in their homes.

The whole project was labor intensive. With a respectable number of customers, he paid all of the business expenses and provided the non-family employees with a decent wage. He and his two brothers made a very nice living.

The best part was that Marta didn't have to work at the factory. She could stay at home and watch over the kids. Phillip didn't want her near Junior. Monarch was a very slippery character.

*I don't trust Junior's intentions with Marta. If Junior ever touched her, I know I could kill him.* Phillip thought, though he seldom worried about Junior and Marta anymore. They'd had no contact these last years.

As the guests took their leave, they tried to buttonhole Sgt. York. Everyone wanted to be able to say that they had met the hero. Alvin York had changed in the last nine years, but he was still uncomfortable with strangers. These denizens of the dank Washington political scene made his skin crawl.

York was present in Washington for only one reason. He considered it a debt of honor to secure recognition for Sgt. Early, Cpl. Genero, and the boys who'd served in that deadly glade. Alvin recalled sadly that many of the boys on that mission did not leave the battlefield alive. Some were still over there, buried, and resting in neat rows in French cemeteries.

After an hour, York and Genero got their first opportunity to talk. They started out slowly, exchanging pleasantries.

"Alvin, I understand that you finally got that piece of land that you've always wanted. How's it going? Is it different now that you actually own the farm?"

"It's hard work, boy. I worry all the time. Bank's been after ma hide twice this year. But I surely love it! There's nothing like watching something grow. It's sure different from what we had to do in France. How about your business? Are you doing OK?"

"It's difficult, all right. Working with my brothers is a blessing and a chore. We squabble and fight a lot, but I wouldn't have it any other way."

With discomfort and a little awkwardness, the two old Army buddies loosened up and reminisced. They chatted that way for almost 30 minutes. In their whole relationship, it was the most they'd ever said to one another at one time. The hour nearing for York's return to Tennessee, he started for the door of the Treaty room.

"Whadda ya say we take us a little stroll?" York suggested in a weary tone.

"Sure, Alvin, let's walk back to the Willard. It's just down the street."

After they were finally alone, walking up Pennsylvania Avenue, Phillip stopped opposite Lafayette Park. He looked hard at his former comrade.

"Alvin, you worked hard behind the scenes with those generals to get this medal for me. The Army would never have gotten around to it. I'm grateful," Genero began. "I owe you my life. I think about what you did for all of us, stuck in that bloody meadow. I think about it all the time. I've had so many wonderful things happen in the last nine years, things I'd have missed, except for what you did. I don't have the words to thank you."

"I expect I've told ya many times, we're friends! Always gonna be! I won't never forget that ya saved ma sorry hide two times that day. God was with us for sure!" York responded.

Both men had deeper feelings of gratitude and camaraderie for the other than they could articulate. They recognized that they were—in the truest sense—brothers. They had bonded to each other by a baptism of fire. Only those who experienced it could ever hope to understand

York changed the subject.

"Well, ma friend," York began, "you surely have a handsome family. Your bride is pretty as can be and your kids are sure something!"

"Thanks, Alvin. It's tough raising a family in these times. Things have changed. People act a lot different than when I was a kid. I worry about how that might influence Gin and Kari."

"Phillip, I know you. You'll do the best ya can no matter what. You're a good man. Listen, I have an idea. Why don't you and Gin come down to Pall Mall and see me next year? It's about time Gin learned to hunt, don't ya think?"

Personally, Phillip never wanted to hold a gun in his hands again. Still, a hunting trip with Alvin might be nice. He agreed. The two men then took their leave, shaking hands warmly. Phillip watched silently as Alvin turned away with a wave and a smile. York headed off for Union Station to catch a train back to Tennessee. Phillip watched Alvin walk slowly and wearily down Pennsylvania Avenue.

*Thank you for my family and my life, Sergeant York. See you in a few years, my very good friend,* Phillip thought, unaware that he would never see Alvin York again.

# Chapter 5

3:00 PM
June 3, 1936
Chapel of the Sacred Heart
St. Ignatius College Preparatory
Camp Hill, Pennsylvania


T he 127 seniors of the St. Ignatius Class of '36 squirmed
and fidgeted in the mahogany pews in the front of their
alma mater's ornate, cruciform chapel. The chapel's
architecture created a bright and airy space, lit by a row of
translucent, clerestory windows under the domed ceiling.

The largest windows in the church framed imported
stained glass. Afternoon shafts of multicolored light illuminated the young men who had assembled to participate in
this most important rite of passage.

Tight as drums, the boys bristled with energy, pent up
from four grueling years. Bright young men and fortunate
survivors, they maintained a respectful silence. They knew
better than to test Father Nachen's patience.

In 1936, graduation from secondary school amounted to
a remarkable feat, considering that the economy suffered
from the Great Depression. Owing to the grave economic
times, less fortunate boys or girls never possessed the opportunity to finish high school. To the majority of American
middle class and working class kids, a college education
remained out of reach and seemed an inconceivable luxury.

Father Nachen, the vice-principal, threatened the graduating Ignatius boys with retaliation for the slightest aberrant
behavior during the baccalaureate mass. Father never made
an empty threat. He'd brook no challenge from his boys.

Father Nachen had a special gift for contriving just the
right punishment for any offense and for any offender. Since

no two disciplinary situations ever presented identical circumstances, Father never devised the same penalty twice. He never used physical punishment. If circumstances deteriorated to the point where he would have needed to use force, Father chose instead to expel the offender from St. Ignatius, permanently and without recourse. Cross the ultimate disciplinary line, you packed up and left forever.

For less than capital offenses, Father Nachen employed the institution of "J.U.G.," short for "Judgment Under God." Father used JUG to explore the parameters of his considerable intellect and imagination.

Father Nachen did not act sadistically. He did see humor in some of the predicaments that he created for his charges, when they had the misfortune or bad judgment to land in JUG. Fortunately, none of the graduates challenged Father Nachen's resolve. They understood the importance of matriculating from a Jesuit prep school and going off to college.

The boys pondered their luck as they waited for the Bishop to arrive so that the ceremonies could begin. Only the valedictorian and salutatorian remained absent from the pews. These top students sat with the faculty in the row of chairs to the right of the large dark blue marble altar.

The valedictorian, Terry Wandsworth, was a strange lad with a narrow face, small green eyes, and wild red hair. His family owned an interest in the manufacture of chocolate in the small town of Hershey, just north of Harrisburg.

Wandsworth possessed impressive intellectual gifts. None of the other talented boys at St. Ignatius operated on his cerebral plane. Even if he hadn't been so wealthy, he would have earned scholarships to many of the exclusive Ivy League universities.

The Wandsworth family possessed a singular spirit of generosity. Their contributions played a critical role for the financial wellbeing of the school, especially in these grave economic times.

The depression had hit St. Ignatius hard. Usually, the graduating class contained 180 souls. The difference in the number of students—and the decrement in the tuition proceeds—made things tight for the school's comptroller.

Jesuits comprised the entire faculty at St. Ignatius. All lived in a cloistered residence. The complement included 25 priests and scholastics, with three brothers thrown into the mix by the Provincial. All of the priests, scholastics, and brothers took vows of poverty, obedience, and chastity. The school administration didn't worry about salaries.

For 500 years, Jesuit education had succeeded as a first-class academic exercise. At S.I., the physical plant might be modest, but the boys always possessed the things they needed to pursue one of the most challenging curriculums in the Commonwealth of Pennsylvania.

The Wandsworth family made it possible for deserving boys from modest economic backgrounds, like the salutatorian, to attend and succeed at St. Ignatius. Matriculation at St. Ignatius provided less fortunate boys with a better chance at college scholarships.

Father Nachen admired the salutatorian. Not that Father would ever tell him, not while the boy remained under his care and protection.

The salutatorian, Phil Genero, had blossomed at St. Ignatius. He'd come up from Carlisle, still roughly hewn. He'd evolved into a polished academician with a sophisticated and operational moral compass. He was also one of the best linebackers in the history of the school's football team.

The Jesuits wanted to attract boys like young Genero. Intelligent, athletic, and a born leader, he seemed destined to be a prominent and successful luminary in the central Pennsylvania community.

The Jesuits had learned many lessons over five centuries of educating young men. They knew that one way to insure the viability of their order was to train—some said indoctrinate—leaders of communities all over the world. Father Nachen rejected that cynicism. He took pride in the contribution that St. Ignatius had made to the Commonwealth.

Phil demonstrated real potential. Father Nachen had hoped he would find a vocation in the priesthood. Unfortunately, Genero never showed a glimmer of interest in that quarter.

The young ladies at the girl's catholic school across the river in Harrisburg liked Phil far too much. Father Nachen had no doubt that Genero returned the interest three-fold. Father understood completely. Before his entry into the order, he'd fallen in love with a beautiful and sensual young woman.

They'd enjoyed a deeply passionate and satisfying relationship, yet he ended their engagement only days before they were to be married. The pull of his vocation sealed the fate of these star-crossed lovers.

After seeing so much misery, destruction, and death during the Great War, Father Nachen learned that the true path for him was the priesthood. Even now, he realized that he still loved Beth. He often wondered if she had ever married, if she had children, if she was happy.

Since he would have no biological children, Father adopted a boy, or a few boys, in each class. If they merited it, he gave them special attention. He took vicarious pride in their growth and accomplishments. Phil had become one of his adopted sons.

Father Nachen knew that the Ignatius boys often referred to the local Catholic girls' school—The Virgin Mother of Perpetual Hope School for Girls—as The Mother of Perpetually Hopeless Virgins. In the last year, to expand Phil's social horizons, Father had allowed him to spend considerable time at Hopeless.

Phil was about to graduate and go off to Pennsylvania State University on a number of different academic and athletic scholarships and grants, which amounted to a full ride. The scholarships had been a godsend, since the Genero family no longer possessed the resources to send him on to college.

The Generos had once been relatively affluent. Mr. Genero had owned and operated a successful bakery in Carlisle. He had lost almost everything in the panic and bank failures of 1930, following the stock market crash in 1929.

The family bakery survived because both of Phil's parents had gone back to work in the clothing factory in Carlisle. To Father Nachen that business seemed a bit of a miracle, since the Monarch Company had suffered its own reverses. In early 1930, Randall Monarch permanently laid off a third of his employees.

Father didn't know what intrigue might have acted as the catalyst for the rehiring. Perhaps it was because Phil's dad was a war hero. It might be that Phil's mother was one of the most beautiful women that Father Nachen had ever seen. Mrs. Genero always appeared to be proper and modest. But—and there was no denying it—she generated a sensuality that a man, even one committed to celibacy, could feel 20 feet away.

On balance, Father concluded that Monarch hired the Generos because Phil's dad had served with Sgt. York. *The Monarch family couldn't allow a war hero to starve, or to stand in a soup line, could they?* Father reasoned.

Father Nachen understood war. He'd served as 1st Lieutenant Evan R. Nachen, United States Marine Corps. He'd fought in France during the Great War. He'd seen—and caused—a lot of suffering and death.

Though in combat he never suffered even a scratch, three enlisted Marines died in his arms. The death of one young Marine still haunted him. He often flashed back to that awful episode.

In October 1918, his company had dug into a defensive position on the edge of an unnamed wood line in north central France. During one bloody day, his platoon fought ferociously on the company's right flank to blunt a vicious infantry assault by crack German troops. When the enemy attack finally faltered, a wounded German tossed a grenade into Danny Newman's emplacement. Before the Marine could find it, the grenade detonated, killing Danny's best friend and mortally wounding the eighteen-year-old from Etna, Pennsylvania.

When 1Lt. Nachen got to Danny's position, there was nothing that he could do. The explosion shredded the boy's chest and abdomen. Danny suffered horrible agony and had only moments to live.

"I'm sorry. I did the best I could," Lance Corporal Newman whispered to his platoon leader as the lieutenant cradled him in his arms.

"Danny, it's OK. We beat the piss out of those Boche bastards. You were very brave today. I'm real proud of you," Eddie Nachen said, trying comfort the boy.

"Lieutenant, please find the Padre! I need to confess. I don't want to die with these sins. I got to get it right!" Danny pleaded.

"OK, Danny, I've sent for the Chaplain. He'll be here any second," Nachen assured his wounded subordinate.

"Thanks, sir! I'm real scared. I've tried to be brave. Don't want to burn in hell, sir!" Danny confided in a voice so low and shaky that only the lieutenant could hear it. "Sir, don't let the others know I was scared. OK?"

"Danny, hold on!! The Chaplain's coming! He'll be here in a second. I promise you, you won't burn, Danny!"

"Swear to God? Swear to me, sir!" Danny asked, his voice failing.

"Corporal Newman, I give you my word as a Marine. You will not burn!" Eddie Nachen pledged as Danny's life force left his body.

Recognizing the familiar death rattle in the young Marine's throat, Eddie gently lowered Danny's body to the bloodstained ground. Nachen stood silently over his fallen comrade for moment. He then snapped to attention and— despite the danger on an unsettled field of battle—rendered a respectful hand salute.

"Semper Fi, Danny! Our just and merciful God will always take a brave Marine into His heart. Put in a good word for us with the Lord," Eddie said sadly, as he turned to resume command of his platoon.

The Navy Chaplain never got to Eddie's platoon that day. Nachen never learned why. Motivated by a building rage, in subsequent engagements, Nachen personally killed more than a dozen Germans.

The death of his enemies, the loss of his men, and his own metamorphosis changed the course of his life. A fearless, merciless, and competent leader in battle, in the rear he transformed into a considerate and caring father, though he was barely older than the Marines in his unit. The men in his platoon would have followed him anywhere. His experiences in France led him to the priesthood. The austere, highly disciplined, quasi-military life of the Jesuits drew him like a magnet.

Father Nachen brought his leadership skills to St. Ignatius. These boys represented his life now. Despite his role as school disciplinarian, the Ignatius boys, like the Marines he once commanded, admired him.

In the span of an hour, these young men would begin to pursue their adventures in a dangerous world. The Great Depression had spawned much suffering. Villains and demagogues had taken control of powerful countries. The few remaining democratic governments appeared to be alone and impotent.

What role would the St. Ignatius Class of '36 play in these future events? Father Nachen didn't know. He prayed that he'd prepared his boys for the challenges awaiting them.

Nachen understood only one thing. The Great War hadn't lived up to its billing. It was not the war to end all wars. There would be another and before many more years had passed.

Conflict and violence plagued people in Asia, Africa, and Europe. *Look what transpired with those monsters in Germany,* Father Nachen thought as he sensed the battles that were coming. He had an intuition that young Genero would do something important. He knew for certain that Genero would serve. The scholarship in the ROTC Nittany Battalion at Penn State guaranteed that.

Genero would do fine in the military. He possessed a tough, disciplined, and courageous character. Then again, because of his gift, Phil might never see a shot fired in anger.

Genero had an incredible talent. In all of his years as an educator, Father Nachen had never seen a young man with a greater innate talent for languages.

By the time he arrived at St. Ignatius, Phil spoke Italian like a boy from Milan, the result of interacting with his extended family. And, though he was very competent in all of his subjects, Genero excelled in the language courses.

In addition to Latin, Phil had studied French and German. He had done so well in French studies that he placed third in the statewide language competition for high school seniors.

Father Nachen could personally attest to Phil's fluency in German. Genero seemed to be able to hear a new language, determine its structure, cadence, and rhythm, build a vocabulary and start to *think* in it.

In the military, an officer with Genero's talent could avoid dangerous assignments and find a cushy job on some general's staff. Knowing his protégé, Father Nachen doubted that Phil would ever take the safe path.

A week before graduation Genero informed Father Nachen that he wanted to major in French at Penn State. Father counseled against it.

Father advised that Phil should pursue a major in science, engineering, or math, something practical. With his equally impressive affinity for math, he should study to be an engineer. Young Genero would have to find a job once he graduated and finished his military commitment. In a depressed economy, Father didn't see a market for French scholars.

As the ceremony was about to begin, Phil mentally reviewed the brief address that he'd prepared. Being the salutatorian, he would go first. The valedictorian was next. Then the Bishop would give the baccalaureate speech.

While waiting, Phil allowed himself to be distracted. He thought of his folks. He recognized that his family had managed to stay intact and healthy. His mom and dad were well. While neither liked working at Monarch, they felt fortunate to have jobs at all. Though the family didn't have much luxury, they had a good home, adequate food, a car, clothes, and a bit of security.

On the downside, an indefinable tension had grown between his mom and dad. For most of his life, he'd witnessed their obvious love for each other and their outward demonstrations of affection. These days, Phil didn't see much of that. His parents didn't fight a lot, like some folks, but the anxiety affected the entire family.

Phil suspected that the tension had to do with work at the factory. His dad and mom had gone back to work there over four years earlier. His father didn't like the fact that he'd lost control of the bakery and had no other economic choice. His dad hated that his mother returned as the private secretary for Linda's father.

Phil and Linda Monarch had dated since the 7th grade at St. Francis Xavier Elementary School. Beautiful and smart, Linda tried to hide a highly manipulative personality. Phil's sister, Kari, hated Linda.

"Brudder, Linda's a selfish bitch!" Kari argued to him a few days earlier. "She'll never stick with you. You'll never be able to give her the life she wants, even with your college education. You'll never be anything to her but a poor boy from Carlisle, whose mom worked for her dad."

Though Kari was a year younger, the girls were rivals. Linda was wilder and more destructive. Folks back in Carlisle thought Linda favored her father. The acorn didn't often fall far from the tree.

"I'm telling you, Gin, Linda's just toying with you. Experimenting. Once she goes off to Radcliffe, she'll forget all about you and find some Harvard guy from a wealthy Boston family."

Phil argued with Kari, but he worried that she might be right. As graduation approached, Linda acted differently toward him.

Phil and Linda had shared a sexual intimacy for over a year. Since the beginning of high school, they'd engaged in normal teenage behavior. But once he and Linda began to drive, they found opportunities to get away and be totally alone.

If they could wrangle Mr. Genero's Model A Ford or Junior Monarch's new Caddy, they'd drive up to Waggoners Gap. Phil's dad had shown him a special place, a half a mile from the main road at the top of the ridge, in a saddle between two peaks.

Situated off the beaten path, and away from the road, the lovers found lots of privacy. Linda never grew to appreciate the special charm. She thought of it this way: *How much beauty can there be, when all you can see is the ceiling of the car?*

The kids from Carlisle parked much closer to town. A few years earlier, the power company had fenced off the Gap and posted "No Trespass" signs. Power company employees rarely went up to the Gap. One could drive around the fence. You just had to know how.

Phil and Linda routinely consummated their propinquity in the back seat of one of their parents' cars, almost always at the Gap. Their lovemaking was enthusiastic and passionate. They practiced a lot.

Linda did not love young Genero, and she knew it. Phil happened to be the best option for her at this particular place and time in her life.

As graduation approached, Linda still made love to Phil, but showed him no affection. And, when they weren't making love, the only thing that Linda wanted to talk about was her plans to attend college in Boston.

Linda would experience less stress at college than Phil. Her dad would pay for everything. He'd get Linda a brand new car. She'd major in Social Science, a discipline that Phil thought was useless.

Genero's scholarships would cover all tuition, books, and room and board. There would be no money for clothes, travel back to Carlisle, or social life. Mom and Dad Genero had saved a modest amount, so they could help a little. To make up for the rest, Phil would work in the clothing factory all summer for 50 cents an hour, a princely sum in the Great Depression.

Genero would not have a car at the university. He'd travel back and forth to Carlisle and State College on the train.

Though his life was about to change, though his circumstances at Penn State would be difficult, and though he suspected that his long standing relationship with Linda was about to end—rather than be unhappy—Genero saw that the world had become a dangerous, enticing, and exciting place. He wanted to move on to the next stage of his life and prepare for the exploration into the unknown. He felt both trepidation and profound excitement at the thought of taking the first steps in fulfilling his destiny.

Carlisle was small and provincial. It was insular, even incestuous, especially if you believed all those strange stories about the folks in Perry County on the other side of the Gap. The idea of going out into the world and experiencing what lay beyond the horizon appealed to Phil.

Father McDermott, his Western Civilization instructor, had discussed with Phil's class the recent events in Europe, Africa, and Asia. Father Mac predicted that the next few years would test of the mettle of Western democracies. Individuals in the capitalistic societies had to sacrifice their own short-term best interest for the vital, long-term wellbeing of the larger community.

Father Mac believed that a Catholic gentleman would put the welfare of others before his own needs, especially in times of international crisis. Would there be enough altruism—doing something for someone else with no thought of reward—to carry the day? Father Mac's concept impressed Phil. When he prepared his comments, he decided to make altruism the theme of his speech.

At that moment, Father Dodd, the principal at St. Ignatius, walked to the chapel's pulpit to address the graduates and their assembled families and guests. He introduced the Bishop and made brief comments about the school and the

Class of 1936. Father Dodd turned his attention to the program and introduced the Salutatorian, Phillip Edward Genero, II.

Phil got up from his seat, carefully arranged the robes of his blue graduation gown, and walked up the steps of the pulpit. He set his notes on the small lectern and quietly looked over the assembled congregation.

He smiled at his mom and dad, his sister, Linda, and several other relatives and friends. Junior Monarch was absent. No surprise there and just as well. This speech would have no meaning for him.

Genero began, "Class of 1936, we're about to embark upon our adult lives in an era of great danger and even greater challenge. To help our society to succeed and to survive, we must be willing to make great personal sacrifices, perhaps even the ultimate sacrifice. We must learn the true meaning of altruism and to implement its tenets in our lives. We must become men who are not chained to our own selfish interests. We must learn to become 'men for others'..."

# Chapter 6

11:55 AM
July 21, 1936
Office of the Chairman and President
Monarch Clothing and Apparel, Inc.
Carlisle, Pennsylvania

Nearly noon on a sweltering, midsummer day, the sun burned white-hot in a cloudless sky. Muggy, without a whisper of a breeze, the mid-day scorcher muted all progress in downtown Carlisle. At the Monarch business offices, the poor design of the stone structure failed to moderate the misery caused by the summer wave.

To deal with the stifling heat, the Monarch clerks had opened the great windows in the offices, hoping that the banks of overhead fans might draw in and stir the soggy air to give them a bit of relief. Though uncomfortable and hard-pressed, no one complained. The clerks and secretaries knew they had it better than the laborers in the clothing plant, where the air was just as heavy but thick with suffocating dust and irritating bits of processed textile.

Upstairs in the Front Office, Junior Monarch stood behind the ornate maple desk in his lavishly appointed office. With a smug grimace, he surveyed his domain. For him, life was good.

Junior's white business shirt sported several yellow sweat stains below the left pocket. As usual, he'd left his collar unbuttoned and his bow tie askew.

Junior tossed his shoes over by the couch, under the faux masters-style portrait of his great-grandfather, Harold, the founder of the Monarch Company. Junior's immense girth determined that the wide leather belt, too small to span his waist, hung in slovenly lines along his wrinkled cotton pants.

Out of breath, he sat down in the antique chair and propped his shoeless feet on the credenza, near the half-empty bottle of expensive French cognac. Squirming to find a comfortable position, he balanced a snifter of the cognac on his stomach.

Junior watched Marta move around the outer office. This morning she wore a pink and white floral-patterned summer smock. It did nothing to hide her beautiful body. Certainly the most handsome woman in Carlisle, she had the best ass he'd ever seen, especially for a woman with two grown kids. Did she ever stir the demon in him!

Usually cranky at work, today Junior was in a fine fettle. He sipped his cognac and gazed out of the immense east window onto the street traffic two stories below. Despite the heat, townspeople walked slowly by his building, on the way to lunch, or to perform routine chores.

*Keep it up, you worthless peons,* Junior mused. *Work hard and earn your pathetic little wages, so you can save to buy my shirts, pants, and suits.*

Junior chortled as he reached into his center desk drawer. He wanted to celebrate. He selected a very expensive Cuban cigar.

He set his snifter down on the desk and rolled the large cigar up and down in the palms of his hands. After examining the Cuban, he snipped its end and ran the flame from his gold plated lighter slowly over the tip.

When the tip burned to an orange hue, he put the cigar to his lips, leaned back and inhaled, experiencing the first essence of the smoke. His lungs full, he removed the cigar from his mouth, extended his arm, and casually examined its length.

He admired the cigar as he exhaled. Junior began to cough. He coughed so hard, that he could not catch his breath. For a moment his lungs burned with an intense fire. Water ran from his tear ducts like a waterfall. He felt faint.

Junior coughed a lot lately. This morning, the coughing continued and he felt disoriented. Although worried about what it might mean, he didn't want to give up smoking cigars, especially this brand of Cuban.

Junior didn't enjoy smoking cigars that much. Inhaling the smoke did nothing for his lungs. But smoking the big phallic cigar added to his image. He liked to think it was one of virility, power, wealth, and success. He tried to generate that image around Marta.

Junior had become the chairman, president, and treasurer of the company in 1930, when his dad died and his Uncle Dan retired. Thinking about his father, he recalled how much he hated that old fart.

*Dad never gave a hoot in hell for me. Figured I'd fuck everything up,* Junior thought. *The son-of-a-bitch never gave me the sweat off his balls. I'm running things now. Everybody in Carlisle has to kiss my ass, whether they like it or not.*

Junior heard the chime of his pocket watch ring twelve times. He pulled the solid gold timepiece with the Monarch Family Crest engraved on the cover from his vest pocket. He opened the cover and examined the face.

*Oh, shit! Look at the time.* Junior thought.

He had business to conduct. Junior placed the cigar in a small crystal bowl that he used as an ashtray. He coughed hard again, six or seven times. He wiped the moisture from his face with his embroidered handkerchief.

Confirming the time, Junior closed the gold cover over the face of the watch. He replaced it in the pocket of his vest. He was careful with this heirloom. It was irreplaceable, his other trademark.

Almost a hundred years earlier, a master Swiss watchmaker personally crafted the timepiece for his great-grandfather. Every chairman in four generations at Monarch had carried it in his vest pocket. Eighteen karat gold, satisfyingly heavy, and well engineered, it kept time precisely. The heirloom was a beautiful, priceless work of art.

The gold pocket watch and his other ostentatious possessions demonstrated that Junior Monarch was a powerful economic force in Cumberland County. They showed that he was a capitalist, a man of means, and not the incompetent fuckup that his dad had believed him to be. While things were not as good for the company as they had been in the Twenties, at least he still had a company. He wasn't selling apples on the street corner.

Junior had 200 employees working like serfs to do his bidding under miserable conditions, for low pay, ten hours a day, six days a week. Junior didn't worry about bankruptcy. He had a plan. It was a very good plan for him.

*How many businesses had gone tits up in the last six years? Not Monarch. I've kept her afloat, and will for a bit longer,* Junior congratulated himself. *All we need is another war, some government contracts, and we'll be good to go for another generation. Too bad the country is full of isolationists.*

For the time being, until war brought more diverse opportunity to Carlisle, everybody in town would have to fall in line with his plans. That included that snotty Phillip Genero, who now worked for him.

Life could be so sweet. Wasn't Genero the best buddy of Sergeant York? Now that skinny wop had to do what Junior told him to do. It gave him a hard-on, just thinking about it.

*Speaking of hard-ons, where is the war hero's lovely little wife? She smells particularly good this morning,* Junior gloated.

Thinking of the twist of fate that caused Marta to be back working at Monarch caused Junior to laugh. It was too rich for words. Junior loved watching her body as she moved around the room, waiting on him and performing menial tasks. She had no choice. The Generos needed the money.

Conversely, Monarch had always disliked Phillip Genero. *I have no love for the son, that fucking Gin, either. Gin's an arrogant whelp! That shit had better be careful with Linda, if he knows what's good for him.* Junior swore. *I'm putting an end to that madness.*

Junior had disliked the older Genero from the first time they met. Phillip personified everything that Junior was not. He despised Phillip for being the better man. Monarch had been counting on making Marta his mistress, just as he had two other farm girls who'd once worked in the bookkeeping department. He'd seduced at least a dozen female employees since.

He'd been so close, too. Marta had succumbed, or very nearly did.

In his zeal to seduce her, Junior had cornered Marta a couple of times, years earlier, during the war. It was always late at night when no one else was in the office.

Marta always protested, then struggled or wiggled out of his meaty grasp. On those occasions she immediately left the office, once without her coat and on a particularly cold night.

As far as he could tell, Marta never told anyone about the sexual advances. And if she had, he'd have thrown her beautiful Amish ass out on the street. Once he understood that Marta would not tell, he increased his scurrilous assaults.

There was that one time. It still drove him crazy, even after all these years.

He'd told Marta that she had to work overtime to file a large volume of financial documents. That excuse was pure bullshit. He wanted her alone. Her husband was still in basic training in Georgia, so Phillip wouldn't be a factor.

Junior had been drinking cheap brandy all afternoon. On the slave wages his dad paid him, he couldn't afford the fine cognac he now enjoyed every day. Drinking always made him randy and considerably more aggressive.

Watching Marta move around the room that night, he planned his attack. He gave her the final set of papers to file and pretended to leave the office. While she was occupied with the files, he crept up behind her and pinned her between the filing cabinet and the wall.

Caught in his surprise, Marta struggled and fought ferociously, biting his hand in the process. Try as she might, she could not get free. In those days he was in better shape, and he outweighed her by 100 pounds.

Squashing Marta against the wall, Junior reached under the hem of her dress and ran his hand all over her firm body.

He discovered that her legs, hips, and groin were hot. Physically hot.

Driven by his lust, he put his hand inside her underclothes and started to fondle and probe her lasciviously. At first, she fought back hard. Then after a moment, she stopped.

As Junior ran his tongue over her neck, he swore he heard her moan. Surprised, he looked at her lovely face, and was momentarily shocked to see that her eyes were glazed. She had a hot, sexy far away look. He felt ecstatic.

Marta not only stopped struggling, but for the next several seconds seemed to respond to his probing by leaning against him. She began moving her hips rhythmically with his probing, while she pulled his arm very hard against her chest.

Just then, O'Malley, the old janitor, stumbled in and startled them. Marta let out a little yelp, and forcefully pulled Junior's hand out from under her dress. She stomped hard on his foot, and it was Junior's turn to yell. In the confusion, she broke away. She ran directly out of the office, down the stairs, and into the street.

Junior lit into the janitor in a terrible rage. He threatened to fire the old Irishman on the spot. Junior recalled that the janitor wet his pants in fear. But it was Junior who was afraid that night.

He feared that when Genero came home, he might come into the office and kick his ass, or worse. He knew that his own father would disapprove and call him depraved. Surprisingly, the next day Marta was back at work, prim and polite as usual. Not a word was said about the night before.

She never worked late or performed any overtime after that. In the end, Marta left the company before he got another chance to ambush her. The old janitor knew enough to keep his mouth shut.

A few months later, Junior learned that Marta was pregnant and probably would not return after she gave birth to her child. At the time, it was good riddance.

Now Marta was back. Junior was the big boss. She worked directly for him.

Her act didn't fool him. Despite her airs and protestations, Junior believed that Marta was just another little slut. The only difference was that she tried harder to hide it. She worried that she'd lose the war hero if Genero ever found out what she really wanted.

Junior knew Marta needed it. And Junior thought that he was just the man to give it to her.

*She only requires the right stimulus,* Junior chuckled, *like keeping her job. The fuckin' war hero can't save her. She'd bailed him out. If it weren't for her pleading with me, I'd never have let that guinea back in the place.*

Junior had no sympathy for Marta. *If she can't get beyond that good-girl, Amish-guilt shit, it's not my problem.*

Junior had a little house, out by Boiling Springs. He called it his little love nest. It was a rustic cabin up in the hills, very isolated. He liked to take some of the factory girls there, just before payday. He gave them a chance to earn their bonuses, so to speak.

He liked it when they competed to see who could please him the most. He enjoyed it when they begged. He wanted Marta to be part of that competition. It was only a matter of time. He had to get the war hero out of the way.

Junior's wife, Donna, never knew about his trysts and indiscretions. Even if she did, she'd never leave him and the economic safety of the Monarch money. She enjoyed the good life and his wine cellar too much to care if he was screwing the help.

But Marta was the one who'd eluded him because of the war hero. Junior hated Phillip. He'd brook no more interference with his plans for the little blond.

*Who'd that dago prick think he was dealing with?* Junior ranted. *Genero was nothing more than a guinea, without two nickels to rub together. If I hadn't bailed him out years ago, he'd be running numbers in Hagerstown with the rest of those ignorant wops. That bakery on High Street is a joke. Phillip has no business being married to that fine piece of*

*Dutch pastry. She needs a real man. One who knows what she really wants, and can give it her.*

"Marta! Come in here, I need you," Junior called. "I want lunch sent up immediately. I have a meeting with the buyers at one o'clock. Get your ass moving! Did you hear me?"

Marta Genero heard Junior the first time. She was adjusting the stockings on her very shapely legs, and trying to get the seams straightened. She'd had more of Junior this morning than she cared to see for a lifetime. The sound of his high-pitched squeaks sent little spasms of revulsion radiating through her chest into the pit of her stomach.

Every minute of the day she spent with Junior disgusted her. If she'd any other choice, she'd never have returned to Monarch. She knew what she'd be getting into if she returned. She'd been right, and now it had become intolerable. Her husband had no idea that she had begged Junior to hire them both back.

She loved Phillip and her children. There was nothing that she wouldn't do to protect them. Nothing.

If working with this subhuman and parrying his amorous advances would help her family, then she would endure. She could withstand anything for them.

"Junior, I called for your lunch twenty minutes ago. It will be here in five minutes," Marta responded.

"When it gets here, bring it in. I want to talk to you, understand?" Junior directed.

The porter arrived from the small executive dining room with Junior's lunch. He'd tastefully arranged it on a lovely silver service with iced tea in an antique crystal pitcher. Today, the porter delivered a mixed salad, a generous bowl of thick mushroom soup, a large steak with fresh asparagus, and a baked Idaho potato. For desert, he included an obscenely rich slice of German chocolate cake.

There was enough food on the tray to feed a small family for an entire day. Junior would inhale the whole meal in less than ten minutes.

Marta rearranged the service in the way that Junior liked, ensured the silverware was free of stains, folded the linen napkin, hefted the service in her hands, and carried it into Junior's office. She set the meal on his side table.

Marta turned to leave and Junior stopped her cold. "I told you that I want to talk to you," Junior barked.

"What do you want now, Junior? I've real work to do!" Marta snapped.

"Look, you had better do exactly what I say, and no fuckin' lip. I won't put up with much more of your shit. There's only one reason that I keep you and your husband on the payroll. And it ain't your clerical skills, darlin'. Do you understand?" Junior shouted.

"Yes, Junior," Marta responded, feigning a meeker demeanor.

"I've a number of important things to tell you," Junior explained. "First, I'm going to end the romance between Linda and your boy once and for all. I don't think it's appropriate for Linda. They're getting too close. I'm sending my daughter to tour England and France for the balance of the summer. I'll tell her it's a surprise graduation present. She'll be gone until just before her class starts at Radcliffe in the fall. She's leaving in two days."

Marta was not surprised and she was relieved. Like her daughter, Marta never thought much of Linda Monarch. She did not view this revelation as bad news.

She didn't know how young Phil would take it. He would be sad, but he would get over it. There were girls at Penn State. "Yes, Junior, I understand. I'll support your decision," Marta responded, still acting the part of the meek subordinate.

At that moment, Marta had an epiphany. She knew Junior had always wanted her sexually, but sexual gratification wasn't the key. Marta understood that her difficulties with Junior weren't about sex at all. It was all about power.

Junior was a fat, sadistic, selfish, and stupid man who had none of the fine qualities of his father, a man much respected until his death. Junior could never win the admiration of others by the quality of his character or accomplishments. He had to bludgeon people by demonstrating his economic power over them.

"You'd better support my decision, or you'll regret it, Marta," Junior retorted. "And that's not all. The company has had two very slow quarters this calendar year. We're going to lay off more people, maybe fifty or so. One of them will be Phillip."

Marta was instantly sick. Phillip's wages were critical to their family. She had Kari in a private school in Harrisburg, a mortgage, and family expenses. They couldn't survive if Phillip didn't have a job. There weren't any other jobs in Cumberland County. Lots of people here were in desperate straits.

"Junior, why are you doing this? You promised if I came back to work for you, that both Phillip and I could have job security here," Marta said.

"I'm not satisfied with your attitude. You know exactly what I mean. Don't you?" Junior interrogated.

"Yes, Junior," was all that Marta could say.

"There is a way out of this. I have a new opening for a factory representative. It would be a promotion of sorts. If you want, Phillip could have the job and a nice raise. Would you like that Marta?" Junior asked in mock concern.

"Yes, Junior," Marta said, fearing what he had up his sleeve. "But if you're upset with me, why would you give Phillip a promotion and a raise?"

"The truth is, I think he'll do a great job. Most of the pukes in this town and the buyers from the department stores seem to love him. I can see that he's popular. The best part is that I'll give him the Midwest territory, so he'll travel to Chicago, Minneapolis, Kansas City, and Denver on a routine basis. Your boy's going off to Penn State, and your daughter is a senior in high school. So it should be no big deal for you."

Marta got it immediately. Junior would promote Phillip and put him on the road. He would be gone more than at home. With young Phil away at college, Marta would be alone, except for Kari. Kari would be doing high school things up in Harrisburg most of the time. Marta would effectively be isolated and available once again for overtime.

"Take it or leave it! I'm serious. Either Phillip takes the factory rep job, or I'm going to lay him off. You have ten seconds to decide," Junior growled.

"Junior, I'd like to talk to Phillip first, just to see how he would feel about it."

"Bullshit!" Junior exploded. "I don't give a fuck what your dago husband wants. I only care about what I want and whether you understand who's in charge here. And it ain't you. What's it going to be?"

"You won't lay him off, if he takes the new job?" Marta pleaded. "I need the truth. You'll give him a nice raise? You'll treat him with respect, and act like a decent man around him?" Marta asked.

"Sure, darlin', anything you say," Junior replied oily. Junior grabbed Marta and pulled her close. His right arm snaked around her shoulder in a seemingly supportive half-embrace. In reality, it was very menacing.

"I don't want to make it harder for you, Marta. I want you to be real nice to me. Know what I mean?"

"Yes, Junior," Marta responded woodenly. "I'll convince him to take the new job," Marta said in a tone of total resignation.

"Don't worry, darlin'! I'm not such a bad person. Your family will prosper by this decision," Junior explained. "Now, I need to eat my lunch before the meeting. I'll call your husband up from the plant, and announce his promotion to the buyers. Some of his contacts are here this afternoon. He can begin arranging his trips. You'll see. It will all work out."

"Yes, Junior," Marta responded, totally flat.

"Get your cute little ass out of here and get ready for the meeting," Junior directed, as he ran his hand slowly down her back, resting on her bottom.

Somber and dejected, Marta walked out of the office. Junior noticed. It made him happy.

*It's about time that this little bitch got the picture,* Junior decided. *It'll be so sweet. In a few months, when Phillip is on the road, Marta will learn a thing or two about the Monarch men. I can't wait for her to earn her first bonus.*

Marta moved slowly into her office, and over to her small desk. Light headed, she leaned against the row of filing cabinets. She knew where this was heading, and she couldn't figure a way to derail the impending train wreck.

*I've never wanted to hurt a soul in my life,* Marta thought. *I think that I could kill this awful pig. I'm sure Phillip would. Oh my God! I could never let that happen.*

Then Marta had another epiphany. She put her face in her hands and wept silently.

*Is this my punishment for abandoning the religion of my family? Would God really do this? Phillip would kill Junior if he knew what Monarch's planning. Phillip's a good man. He's been a loving husband and a fabulous father to my children. I have to protect Phillip and the kids. I'll deal with Junior myself. There has to be a way.*

# Chapter 7

9:00 PM
August 10, 1936
The Genero Farm
Cumberland County, Pennsylvania
One Quarter Mile Southeast of Waggoners Gap


Phil's dad walked through the back door of the rambling farmhouse. He picked his way in the dark, negotiating the narrow dirt path beyond the high fence that separated the family compound from the pasture. He continued toward the ridgeline, until the distance muted the sound of the party.

High above the eastern hills, the quarter-moon cast a pale glow on the pasture and surrounding trees, all the way to the hills to the northwest.

Phillip needed a quiet moment alone. He didn't want to embarrass his son. Not tonight. He'd always known that this day would come.

Phillip understood that his son needed to grow, prosper, and learn how to make his way in the world. He also realized how much he would miss him. He'd focused on his children for so long that he couldn't remember his life before them.

In a day, young Phil would go off to college. The family would get together to celebrate holidays, birthdays, and special events, but Phil's room would remain empty. Phillip would no longer hear the comforting sound of his son's breathing when he made his nightly rounds, ensuring the security of the home.

Young Phil intended to start for school in the morning. At Penn State, the freshman football players had to report for conditioning drills at Beaver Field the day after tomorrow.

Phil planned to take the train to State College, so he could arrive by the afternoon.

With Phil's departure imminent, Phillip reflected on his son's accomplishments. Phil had evolved into a great student and leader at St. Ignatius. He'd worked hard to get all of those scholarships to Penn State.

Phillip cherished those important achievements, but he took the most pride in young Phil's strength of character. He predicted that his son would be the best of men and accomplish difficult and important things for himself and his country.

Tonight Phillip felt depressed because he'd failed at his business and didn't have the economic means to pay the full tariff for his son's college education. He regretted that his boy needed the ROTC scholarship.

Lately, Phillip had experienced haunting flashbacks to that savage fight in the Argonne. A week ago, he woke shouting from a dream, soaked in sweat. Marta held him close and asked him what he'd dreamt.

Phillip lied and told her that he couldn't recall. But he could. It was awful. In his dream, he stood helplessly watching the face of Stefan Koronopolis as the German soldier bayoneted the Greek boy. In excruciating detail, he saw the utter surprise, the horror, the great pain and—worst of all—the death. Then, Stephan's face had dissolved into the face of his beloved son. It terrified him.

Thinking of the dream made him queasy. The flashbacks had returned because his boy was off to school, to earn a degree and to learn to be a soldier, an officer.

World events had conspired against Phillip's peace of mind. The violent civil war that had erupted in Spain over the summer resurrected his fear. Italy's fascist government had been bellicose for years. *Look at what Mussolini and his black shirts did to the poor Ethiopians,* Philip reasoned.

The Germans had occupied the Rhineland with two new infantry divisions in March, flaunting the Treaty of Versailles. Hitler had re-annexed the Saar the year before. Bitter tension defined the relationship between the Nazis and the western democracies.

In Asia, the endless Japanese intrigues guaranteed a dangerously unstable relationship between them and warlords in China. In the five years since the Japanese had seized Manchuria, the situation had only deteriorated.

*The world is moving toward an Armageddon. How and when would America act? Would it be enough? Would it be too little, too late?* Phillip wondered. In his heart Phillip knew only one thing. *No international crisis could ever justify the loss of my son.*

Logically, Phil would remain safe for the next four years. Maybe what would happen in the world would occur before his boy could be a part of it.

*Most Americans don't want involvement in distant foreign wars, especially during this depression. Folks worry more about putting food on the table and heating their homes than what Italy, Japan, or those awful Nazis are doing to their neighbors.*

*If the coming war waits for Gin, then Gin will be an officer. That's not a good thing!* Phillip concluded.

He'd seen good officers come and go too quickly, wounded or killed, during the months that the 328th fought in France. Young officers faced a difficult and dangerous challenge, leading more experienced and older men into combat.

Tonight, Phillip had to put all of these doubts and fears out of his mind. Dozens of happy people wanted to celebrate and to wish his son a *bon voyage.*

Besides, he'd managed a surprise for the party this evening. The financial fortunes of the family had improved quite a bit. A few weeks earlier, Phillip had received a promotion and a significant raise.

He could give his boy a terrific going-away present. A month ago, this gift would have been impossible. Thanks to Junior Monarch's generosity, he could do something special for his son.

Junior had shocked Phillip with that new raise. Phillip never expected that Junior would do anything beneficial for him. He suspected every one of Junior's motives.

For the last few years, Phillip worked as a foreman in the plant. He knew all about Junior's philandering. Some of the women confided a little about the 'bonus' program at the Boiling Springs cabin. He'd pieced the rest together by himself.

Junior never forced the girls to do any particular thing. He did make it financially attractive to bend to his will. The man had disgraced his entire family.

If Junior tried any of those things with Marta, Phillip would make sure that the fat toad never drew another breath. Now that he'd be on the road, Phillip worried. *I know my Marta. She despises Junior. I'm not concerned about her, just that obese slug.*

Marta had come out of the back door, and was looking for him. She saw him off in the distance standing in the pasture. She hurried over.

As she approached, Phillip saw how lovely she looked in the pale glow of the moonlight. Beautiful as always, that gorgeous blond hair framed those soft brown eyes.

Marta personified an incredible incongruity—the innocent, angelic beauty—and the wanton sexual need. His addiction spanned 20 years.

In a year or so, when Kari left for school, they'd be alone in the house again. They used to have some pretty wild Sunday interludes, when they first got married. Maybe they could pick that up again. An empty nest provided some advantages.

"What are you doing out here, all by yourself? Want a little company?" She asked coyly, running her arms sensuously around his back.

"I'm thinking about our children and what it will be like from now on," Phillip said.

"I'm sad, too. Don't worry, honey, it'll be OK. Gin can take real good care of himself. You taught him well. He'll do fine," Marta counseled bravely. "He'll be so surprised tonight. We'll have to peel him off the ceiling. When will you give it to him?"

Phillip looked down at his wristwatch and responded, "I'm having Bill drive it up in fifteen to twenty minutes. I had the paint touched up, and it's cleaned and waxed. It looks brand new."

With the income from the raise, Phillip and Marta had used their modest savings to find a bargain on a used car for their son. A local mechanic, Phillip's friend, Bill, provided the car. It was a real beauty. Earlier in the month, Bill discovered a damaged blue 1931 Ford Model A Roadster with a tan leather bench seat in the front, a tan ragtop, and a rumble seat in the trunk space.

Its former owner had plowed into another car at a dangerous intersection in Wormleysburg, on the west shore of the Susquehanna River. The owner survived without a scratch. The accident nearly totaled the automobile. Unwilling to spend the money to fix it, the owner offered it for sale. He eventually sold the car to Bill for a fraction of its worth.

Bill worked hard all week on the car. He'd repaired the damage, repainted the chassis, and tuned the motor, linkage, and transmission. When he finished, the car ran like a top.

The Roadster looked sporty and very sexy. Marta thought the rumble seat on this model was impractical, but she conceded that young college boys would like it.

"Let's go back to the party. I want to watch Gin's face when Bill comes up the driveway," Marta said, pulling on Phillip's arm.

"First, I want a kiss," Phillip said, pulling her back to him.

They came together in a hot embrace, feeling the old passion returning. After a long moment they broke apart, but not before promising to pick it back up later that night. They turned and walked back to the house arm in arm, both smiling.

When Phillip and Marta returned, the party was in full swing. Most of Phil's friends had managed to attend. Several of the family retainers made appearances. Phil's uncles entertained the crowd with tuneful renditions of classic Italian songs. Uncle Angelo played the mandolin like a master. Everyone thoroughly enjoyed the show.

Phil seemed disappointed that Linda was not there. He tempered his grief by basking in the attention of a couple of attractive local girls, who paid a lot of attention to him.

Now that Linda had gone to Europe, one of them might get lucky. At the party, Phillip had allowed the young graduates to drink beer and a spiked punch. There was Chianti for the adults.

Young Phil, who had wine with the Generos whenever the extended family got together, could drink a gallon of the punch. The girls felt a little tipsy and the alcohol muted their inhibitions.

As he sipped his punch, listened to the singing, and flirted with the girls, Phil remembered the hundreds of days that he spent at the Gap dreaming about his future travels. Now, by God, he would start. The road ahead appeared to be limitless.

Phil looked over the party and watched his mom and dad dancing together in a slow waltz. Despite his bad leg, Dad negotiated the slow songs, as he held Marta real tight. They always looked so good together on these social occasions. Young Phil felt an immense sense of relief.

Everything seemed good between his parents lately. In the last week, he saw them getting back the old romance. Their devotion to each other gave him a sense of stability, which he needed as he was about to leave their care.

While his parents were dancing, Phil heard a commotion outside. Someone had driven up, raced a car's engine, and honked the horn in a loud irritating way. He hoped it wasn't one of his pals from the football team.

Everyone at the party stopped and listened to the honking. Phil noticed that his dad and mom hugged each other, turned, and walked over to him.

"What do you suppose all that racket is, son?" Phillip asked. "Let's go see what's going on."

Phillip and Marta took their son out through the large carved wooden door and into the small circular driveway in the front of the house. Parked directly in front of the house, Phil saw the most beautiful and sensual automobile, a dark, iridescent blue Ford Model A Roadster. Bill had taken the top down and tucked it away. He had opened the rumble seat in the back. The Roadster reeked with sex appeal.

Bill sat in the driver's seat with the biggest grin on his grizzled old face. What was Bill doing with a car like this at his party? Phil began to sense that something was up. He looked at his father and his mother. Both had tears in their eyes. He knew at once.

"Mom, Dad, is this for me?" Phil asked in a voice cracking with emotion. "I can't believe it. Oh, my God!"

At that moment, Bill opened the door, exited, and walked directly over to Phillip. He handed Phillip the car documents and the key to the Roadster. Phillip hugged his friend warmly, and thanked him for his help.

Phillip turned and looked up at his son, who was three inches taller. He grabbed young Phil in a great bear hug, squeezed him hard, and held him for a moment. Phillip slowly released his boy and gently pushed him back a foot or two. Marta stood next to her son, holding his hand.

"Gin, we're proud of you," Phillip said. "What you accomplish at Penn State will make us even prouder. We understand that it's a trek from the Cumberland Valley to State College by train. If you have this car, we might get to see more of you than if you relied on old Casey Jones to get you back here. Having the car will give you other advantages, as I'm sure you know. Promise your mother and me that you'll be the responsible man we know you are. Enjoy this fancy jalopy, son!"

It was Marta's turn to hug her son. He was much bigger than her and had to bend over to allow her to reach around his neck. She held him and whispered conspiratorially in his ear.

The partygoers moved around the car, admiring it. Stunned, young Phil walked to the car and stared at the console, fantasizing. He felt a tug on his elbow. When he turned, Kari gave him a dazzling smile, hugged him and planted a kiss on his cheek. Kari surprised him with her affection.

"Brudder, I'll miss you. It won't be the same around here without you. As brudders go, you ain't half bad."

"You take care of mom and dad for me, OK? They'll be a little lost when we both leave home," Phil pointed out.

"Gin, I'll be here for another year. I've decided that I'm going to nursing school. I might even meet a handsome doctor," Kari explained. "I'll watch out for the folks while I'm here, but they'll be fine. You take care of yourself and stay away from the damn Lindas."

Phil asked his parents if they would like to take a spin in his new car. They politely declined. He turned to Kari and asked her to be his first passenger.

"Brudder, how much of the punch have you had? Take Mary or Liz. They'd be willing to show their gratitude, if you took them up to the Gap."

"Sis, you can be a pain in the ass, but you're the best sister in the world. There's not one diplomatic bone in your body, but I know you love me. Get your butt in the car, and let's go. Liz will stick around."

Kari ran around the car and jumped in. Gin started the engine, shifted into reverse, and backed around the yard until he was pointed out toward the road. He shifted into first gear, lightly popped the clutch, and gave the engine just the right amount of gas. The roadster responded gracefully, but powerfully. The force of the acceleration pushed Phil and Kari back into the overstuffed leather seats. Phil drove down the driveway and out onto the state road toward Waggoners Gap on the first leg of his life's adventure.

# Chapter 8

November 12, 1936
The Virgin Mother of Perpetual Hope
School for Girls
Harrisburg, Pennsylvania

Dearest Brudder,
      I'm in Sister Erin's typing class. I'm pretending to work on our assignment. It's really stupid, so it made me think of you. Ha, Ha! Guess I'll write to you instead.

Gin, I'm having a hard time concentrating on any of my senior work. I'm ready to graduate, right now!

I've met a handsome intern at St. Teresa's. Of course, he is sooooo busy, he barely notices anything other than his patients. But I sure have noticed him. What a dreamboat!! His name is Mark Hansen. He went to Med School at Johns Hopkins, and wants to be a surgeon. I know he's too old for me, for now. I'm more certain than ever that I want to go to nursing school next year.

Dad enjoyed going up to State College to see you play in the freshman game against Syracuse two weeks ago. Tell me, if the varsity players are the Nittany Lions, are the freshman the Nittany 'Cubs?' That's sooooo cute! My big brudder is a cuddly, little cub.

Dad said that you were very aggressive. Did you really make five unassisted tackles? Were they players or cheerleaders? Ha Ha!! Just kidding!

St. Ignatius didn't have a good a season this year. The boys were upset when they lost to St. Mary's. Ugghh!! The Franciscans were a little smug. It's been years since they won, right?

The St. Ignatius priests were polite, but you could tell that Father Dodd and Father Nachen were XXXXXX upset. The Jesuits are not good losers, especially to the Franciscans.

Dad goes on the road at least half the time since you left. He's traveled to Chicago and St. Louis. Dad seems unsure about the job. He likes the money, but he hates the travel and leaving mom alone. Mom hates it too. She's not herself when he's away.

Dad's doing very well. He set some sort of sales record for Monarch shirts in October in St. Louis. He really impressed the sales manager. Not bad for a guy who is brand new on the job.

Speaking of Monarch. Something very strange happened to Mr. Monarch. Mom and Dad aren't talking about it, but last Thursday night, Mr. Monarch got involved in an incident with a female employee at a house in Boiling Springs.

There's a nasty rumor (the kind I like best) that the husband of one of the female employees caught Mr. Monarch and his wife together at the house. According to the rumor, she wasn't sewing the buttons on his shirt. Steamy stuff for boring old Carlisle, don't you think?

Some people say that the husband, who's a steel worker from the Bethlehem mill, beat the crap out of Mr. Monarch. Other people are saying that the guy STABBED Mr. Monarch. What a scandal that would make!

No one has seen the boss man since last Thursday. There hasn't been a hint of the story in the Sentinel. So nobody knows for sure.

Mom and Dad aren't confirming, but they're not denying it either.

I never liked Mr. Monarch. He's the biggest jerk I ever saw. I never had much regard for his daughter—the bitch—either, but you know that.

Mom told me that you'll be home for Thanksgiving. I never thought I'd say this, but I miss you, brudder. With you and Dad gone, I have no one to pick on.

Sister Erin is getting suspicious, so I gotta go. Drive home safely. I'll see you in a few weeks.

Love,
Kari

# Chapter 9

12:00 PM
November 18, 1936
Office of the Chief Physician
Communicable Disease Ward
Public Health Department
Dauphin County Hospital
Harrisburg, Pennsylvania

D ead tired, Dr. Simmons had managed three hours sleep in the last two-and-a-half days. Glad to be back in his tiny office in the Communicable Disease Ward, he needed to think through this awful Monarch business before he met with the family.

*The meeting with the Monarchs promises to be tricky. Knowing them, I'll have to handle it just right,* Simmons realized.

The doctor walked across the worn Persian rug on the floor in front of the small desk that he'd cluttered with his papers, patient files, lab reports, health notices, and technical books. The doctor bent over the top of the desk and examined the materials. After a frustrating five-minute exercise, he located Junior Monarch's chart. He scanned it and tucked it under his arm.

Called out of a dead sleep at 2 a.m. that morning, Dr. Simmons now needed coffee to stay awake and prepare for the afternoon meeting. After he re-read Junior's chart, he'd go out to the nurse's station and see if he could talk them out of a cup or two.

Relieved about last night, Simmons felt that it was better to lose sleep running down a false lead than to face an epidemic in an unprepared population.

The previous evening, a bright, young doctor at St. Teresa's had encountered a patient who seemed to have the outward clinical signs of typhus. Once a treating physician made a preliminary assessment of typhus, as the chief county health official, Simmons determined the accuracy of the diagnosis. He then ordered the appropriate public health precautions, if he confirmed the judgment.

Fortunately, the event turned out to be a false alarm. Not that Doctor Hansen made any mistakes. After running tests and further clinical observations, the doctors ruled out typhus.

Resolving that case at St. Teresa's took most of the morning. Back in his own hospital, he wanted to finagle coffee from the stingy nurses and get background on the diagnosis of tuberculosis while trying to plan a strategy for dealing with all of Junior Monarch's other healthcare issues. This guy was a mess.

The head nurse, Miss Elizabeth Landry, unexpectedly walked into the doctor's office with a steaming cup of black coffee in her hand. Tall, thin, and attractive for an earthy, worldly-wise, thirty-seven year old spinster, Nurse Landry wore her dark hair in a tight bun, tucked under her round nursing cap.

Even in the nurse's uniform, she transmitted a unique allure. She had a way of looking at men, sending the message that if they measured up, they might win the jackpot. Dr. Simmons always wondered why such a saucy wench had never gotten married.

At work, she could be mean as a snake. Blunt, direct, and completely candid, she proved to be the most competent nurse in the hospital. Simmons had worked with Landry for ten years, ever since she'd moved to Harrisburg.

Landry stood on the rug, three feet from Simmons, critically analyzing his pathetic, unkempt condition. The doctor appeared dead on his feet. She handed him the steaming cup. The doctor took the coffee gratefully but avoided her gaze.

Dr. Simmons knew he was in for a lecture. He had no patience for drama. He didn't like his women to be bitchy. He liked them to be nurturing, compliant and—if possible—horny.

"Betty, my innocent darling, you read my mind. I need this elixir to sustain my tortured spirit. How did you guess my secret?" Dr. Simmons asked, using his best Boris Karloff impression, as he bent over and gazed at her with one wide eye, mimicking the great actor's ghoulish countenance.

"I saw that fat butt of yours dragging up and down my ward. Be serious!" Landry responded, recognizing the theatrical technique as a tactic designed to distract her. "I figured you needed some help. You're like a child. If we didn't watch out, you wouldn't get your fluids, your solids, or your sleep.

"Listen Jim," she continued, "we've got to talk about Junior Monarch. He's the biggest pain in the ass I've ever seen. The staff wants to rebel."

Doctor Simmons raised his right hand, palm outward, fingers extended. He closed his eyes in the universally recognized gesture of painful resignation.

"Betty, please. I've been up all night," Simmons began. "Can I have my coffee and read Junior's chart before you verbally disembowel me? I know what a moron Monarch is, but the guy is very sick. We should show some compass ..."

"Spare me the Hippocratic bullshit!" Landry interjected angrily. "Junior got caught hiding the sausage in the wife of a deeply disturbed man. He's lucky he's alive, and a *man* for that matter. That steel worker stabbed him eight times with an ice pick in his chest, abdomen, and groin. If he hadn't been so fat, the husband might have been able to get at a vital organ. Come to think of it, not all of his organs are fat, if you know what I mean."

Dr. Simmons laughed at her remark about Junior's manhood. Since he had a mouth full of coffee, he drooled some onto the right breast of his white clinician coat.

"Calm down. I was trying to tell you that I'm working on the solution to your problem."

Betty Landry cut him off again, "It's not my problem, Jim. It's our problem. No, it's your damn problem. You're the chief of this service."

"OK, Betty! Sit down. We'll discuss the whole thing. I'll straighten the mess out by this afternoon," Simmons responded, pleading with Nurse Landry, who was madder than a rabid dog.

Nurse Landry sat down in the chair next to the doctor's desk. Simmons pulled up another chair to a position directly in front of the incensed head nurse. His tactic allowed him to look at her shapely legs, which she crossed and uncrossed as they talked.

"Junior is a prick, but he almost died on us. You've seen the chart. His heart stopped on the operating table, but the surgeon revived him. If the incident hadn't happened, he would've died in a year or so. He suffers from serious heart disease. We would not have learned of the TB until he'd spread it all over Cumberland County. Ironically, that beating he took saved scores of folks in Carlisle from contracting TB," Jim Simmons reflected.

"Where do you suppose he got the TB?" Betty Landry asked, genuinely curious.

"We don't know. We have difficulty tracking TB in cases like this," Simmons responded. "Junior likes to travel in South America, especially Brazil. He could've picked it up in Brazil while he was on a trip and we're just learning of it.

"I'm required to commit Junior to a course treatment and isolation in a sanitarium," Simmons continued. "I have the option to transfer him to a more favorable climate. I'll suggest Arizona, where we have reciprocal agreements with a number of institutions. There are promising new anti-TB drugs. With a sensible diet, exercise, and a regimen of fresh air, he has a chance at a recovery. With TB it's a very long process. It will take him longer, since he's in such horrific shape. He has to lose over a hundred pounds. He has to stop smoking and drinking."

"Where will you send him?" Nurse Landry asked.

"I was thinking of the Maricopa County Sanitarium. If he wants, there's the Andrews Institute in Sedona, Arizona. I'd go to Andrews," Simmons explained.

"What's the difference?" Landry asked.

"Sedona is a beautiful, spiritual place. Think of haunting red rock formations, dark green pines, deep blue skies, clean air, and fat white clouds. It's amazing. Sedona's temperate all year round. Andrews Institute is nicer than the place in Phoenix. It's more isolated, but Junior can get an individual bungalow. The accommodations are first class. The food is good, simple, and healthy. There's no drinking and no smoking. The staff is first rate," the doctor continued.

"Sounds way too good for the likes of Junior Monarch," Nurse Landry responded.

"The man has to go somewhere. We got him in time. We've been running skin tests and other exams on the people closest to him. So far, the results have come back negative, but he contracted TB for sure. TB is strange and unpredictable. You can get it by coming into contact with the bacilli and the symptoms remain dormant for years, until your immune system weakens. That's what happened to Junior. He started showing the first signs of the more advanced condition. He's a very lucky man."

Junior Monarch yelled at his wife and Uncle Dan. "I want to be transferred to a decent hospital! The people here are imbeciles. Look what they've done to me!" Junior continued angrily, raising his gown to show the stitches from the comprehensive surgery. The sight caused Junior's wife and uncle to turn away.

"Junior, these people worked hard to save your life!" Daniel Monarch yelled back.

Junior's wife and Uncle Dan wore sterile gowns, gloves, caps, and masks to lessen the chance of exposure. Although there was a seat on the other side of the bed available for Donna, she chose to pace back and forth in front of his bed.

She didn't want to get any closer to this awful, disgusting man.

"I'll make this short and sweet," Uncle Dan continued. "I retired from the business when your dad died because I thought you could handle things. I was wrong. Since this incident, I've had an accounting. I'm shocked, and—I must add—bitterly disappointed in you. You are quite dishonest. Even if you weren't so sick, I'd replace you. I still own thirty-five percent of the family stock. My sister owns ten percent. Your mother owns ten percent. That gives us fifty-five percent, and control. You're out. Do you understand me, you selfish, lying, little pervert?"

"You can't run me off, Uncle Dan. I own forty-five percent of the business. I can talk to mother. I'll convince her that she needs to support me. We'll see who wins this battle!" Junior responded.

"Junior, if you don't listen to your uncle, I'll get the best fucking lawyer in Philadelphia to sue you for divorce. You're an adulterer. I can get a large share of the stock that you own. Even if I only get half, or a third, that'll more than make up for your mother's share. You'll be disgraced *and* replaced. If that's what you want, just let me know!" Donna Monarch bellowed.

For the third time in as many weeks Junior felt fear. The first time was when Irene's husband burst in on them, while Junior screwed her on the tiny kitchen table in the Boiling Springs cabin.

Junior had worked up a head of steam as he pounded into his pliant employee. Irene lay on her back with her legs wrapped around his neck. Junior stood on the floor, his manhood imbedded in Irene to the hilt.

Irene moaned, groaned, and begged him to give it to her harder. Just then, the kitchen door flew open and a gorilla of a man burst through the opening. He tackled Junior and knocked him to the floor with a tooth-rattling jolt.

Junior landed squarely on his back and head, with his pants caught around his ankles and his organ rapidly receding.

Enraged, Irene's husband knelt on Junior's chest and punched him hard in the face. Before Junior lapsed into unconsciousness, he saw the light reflect off a thin, needle-like object as it arched and descended in a terrifying blur toward his chest.

Junior could not stop the assault. He felt a sharp, searing pain in his groin. Then he remembered nothing until he awoke after surgery.

Today, Junior learned that Irene saved his life by bashing her husband over the head with some blunt object that she grabbed from the kitchen. Junior realized that he should be grateful to Irene, but he could not believe that she let her husband pummel and stab him eight times before she got around to clubbing him.

The second time that Junior felt fear was when he learned that he'd contracted a virulent strain of tuberculosis. When they transferred him to the communicable disease facility, he panicked. This morning Dr. Simmons told him that state law required commitment to a sanitarium. Junior would remain in isolation indefinitely. What a nightmare!

Now, he'd endure the disgrace and lose his business. His uncle had hired auditors to examine the company's books. If they learned of his plans and his special accounts, he could face ruin.

He didn't care if Donna divorced him, but he didn't want to lose his interest in the Monarch Family business or the considerable funds that he'd hidden in Brazil.

"Junior," Uncle Dan began, "we can keep a lid on this shameful business. It's in everybody's interest. My lawyers have obtained a stipulation from Irene and Max Stevens, exonerating you from liability. They've agreed to keep the story of your debauchery a secret. That'll cost you $10,000.00. I'll deduct that amount from your share of the Monarch profits, if the company has any this year. You're to be committed for your TB. There's nothing you can do about it. I agree with your physician. You would have died if we hadn't learned of your advanced condition. You could have caused great suffering in Cumberland County."

Uncle Dan spoke more forcefully. "Randall, I've never been fond of you, nor did I fathom the depths of your depravity. You've disgraced the standing of a family that's worked hard for a hundred years to establish a reputation for honesty and generosity in this community. I'll not permit you to sully our name further. You have two options: you can follow the doctor's instructions, go to Phoenix, participate in the course of treatment and regain your health, or you can oppose me!"

Dan took a breath. "If you behave like a responsible gentleman, I'll allow you to return to the business in some lesser capacity whenever they give you a clean bill of health," Uncle Dan explained in a more moderate tone. "If you oppose me, I'll see that you lose your entire interest in the Monarch Company. Which will it be?"

Junior loved giving ultimatums. He despised receiving them. Junior understood that he'd lost the battle. *No matter what, I have to convalesce. I do not want to die,* he thought.

As he pretended to listen to his Uncle, Junior formulated his plan. Uncle Dan would rue the day.

"Uncle Dan," Junior relented, "I've lost. I'll do as you say. But you'll keep this quiet? Will you promise not to divest me of my business interest?"

Turning to his wife and trying to look sincere, Junior asked, "Donna, no divorce, right?"

Donna and Dan Monarch looked at each other. They had doubts about entering into any arrangement with Junior. They sighed and nodded in agreement. Uncle Dan assured Junior that he'd made the right decision.

Junior warmed to his ruse. He felt ghastly, but he enjoyed the subterfuge. This might take awhile, but he would get even with a lot of people in Carlisle.

"Uncle Dan, Donna, I know I don't deserve this kindness. I'll try not to disappoint you. Just one thing, it would be better for the whole family, if I went to that place in northern Arizona instead of the county institution in Phoenix. Would that be all right?"

Neither Dan nor Donna could think of a legitimate reason to balk at Junior's request. The Sedona option cost more, but offered far more isolation. Everyone benefited. The further away he was from Carlisle, the better. They all agreed.

Junior watched them, as they stood there in their gowns, caps and masks. They looked absurd. He'd enjoy destroying them.

Donna Monarch walked through the front door of the Dauphin County Hospital. She looked up and down for the car. Raymond should have been parked it in the circular drive, outside the exit.

She saw the large, highly polished, pearl-white Cadillac turn from the road into the entry. The chauffeur drove it to the spot where she was waiting. He stopped the engine, ran around the front, and opened the rear passenger door for her.

An impressive, well-built man whose family had worked for the Monarchs for three generations, the chauffeur offered his hand, and helped steady her. She stepped into the passenger compartment and arranged herself on the plush seat. Raymond carefully closed the door, walked around the car and reentered the vehicle.

"All well with Mr. Monarch?" Raymond asked politely, as he negotiated the exit route from the hospital grounds.

"Junior isn't coming home for many months, Raymond," Donna explained. "He's very sick. They're sending him out west to Arizona in a day or two."

Donna Monarch reflected that Junior's illness, forcing him to leave indefinitely, could prove to be the best thing that happened to her in ten years. She reached into her purse and found her little flask of cognac. She took a long pull, enjoying the taste of the liquor and the slight burn in her throat as she swallowed.

Raymond turned southwest and entered the bridge over the Susquehanna River. Donna noticed how competently Raymond handled the caddy. He possessed a lot of talent.

"Raymond, would you mind if I stopped by to see you tonight? I miss you! I think we'll get to spend a lot of time together from now on," Mrs. Monarch teased, giggling out loud.

"No, ma'am. I don't mind at all. I'll be looking forward to it. I always do," Raymond responded, a huge smile spreading on his dark, handsome face, as he watched Donna Monarch in the rear-view mirror.

In the tradition of his family, Raymond dedicated all of his efforts to the service of the Monarch family. He'd work hard to ensure that Mrs. Monarch got exactly what she needed.

# Chapter 10

D ue to the heavy snowfall, Phil drove slowly up College Avenue away from Atherton Hall, past the Mall toward Burrowes Road. Approaching the intersection he downshifted, gently tapped the brake, and negotiated a smooth right turn onto Burrowes.

A quarter mile down the road, he made a skittish left onto Pollock Road and left again into the ice-covered driveway of the SPO house. As the chapter vice-president, he used a designated parking space in the rear of the old house. He slid the roadster into it, turned off the big engine, and set the parking brake.

Phil buttoned up his coat, pulled his cap over his head, folded up the large maroon and gold wool blanket with the Sigma Pi Omega Crest, and stowed it under the rumble seat.

He stood next to the roadster for a moment, looking southwest toward the golf course. The tempo of the falling snow increased, causing the fat, wet flakes floating out of the black night to settle ponderously on the cold ground.

He had plenty of time this evening to find some of his brothers, chew the fat, and brag about his latest conquest. They'd be at it for the rest of the night.

Genero walked across the parking lot, toward the rear entrance of the fraternity house. He ambled through the obstacle course of slippery sidewalks, garbage cans, bicycles, boxes, and other detritus.

Camouflaged by a cover of white snow, the piles of jetsam took on a neat, pristine but surreal appearance. In the spring, when the snow melted, the thaw would reveal the rusty and deteriorated trash heap.

Safely on the SPO back porch, Phil opened the old screen door. Using his big shoulder, he pushed hard on the heavy wooden door. It stuck on the first attempt. After giving it another shove, it swung inward with an irritating creak.

Entering the utility room, he pulled off his coat and sweater. He could make out the sounds of a radio playing in one of the rooms upstairs. The local station transmitted a rendition of Artie Shaw's *When You Begin the Beguine.* Phil shook his head. He preferred Glen Miller's band to anything Shaw did.

The music convinced him that some of his brothers were still awake, and mixing it up on the top floor. He'd follow the sound. It probably came from Paul's room. Paul would play that swing station 24 hours a day.

By the time he got to Paul's floor, Shaw's ballad had ended, and a Cole Porter tune, *You're the Top*, had begun. Phil liked this song a lot better. He had a hard time hearing the lyrics because Paul and Tim were having one of their arguments.

When he got to Paul's door, Genero entered without knocking. He encountered four fraternity brothers and a pledge.

The room belonged to Paul Reilly, a junior and a mechanical engineering major. Paul's roommate in SPO, Tim Sullivan, also studied engineering, but he majored in fucking with Paul.

Two seniors, John Koslowski and Patrick Kelly, reclined on a bearskin rug that Paul had thrown on the wood floor at the foot of his bed, next to the large window. John and Pat had gone drinking at the Nittany Inn. They sported the silly, vacuous expressions of the inebriated. Pat watched with amusement as Paul and Tim went at each other.

They focused their argument on Tony Lupinacci, the SPO pledge, who hailed from Pittsburgh and played tackle on the freshman football team. Tony was doing pushups for Tim because of some infraction. When he finished 50 repetitions, he sprang to his feet and stood at the prescribed position for an SPO pledge.

"Sir, thank you for tolerating my behavior! May I do more pushups?" Tony asked.

"Lupinacci, are you brain dead? Did you actually drink the water from the Monongahela? Maybe that's why you're such an idiot! Sit down and shut up. I'll deal with Mr. Sullivan," Paul directed.

"It's not seemly for a pledge to suggest that a brother of Sigma Pi Omega is less than a man," Tim chided Tony. "Your big brother is from the Main Line west of Philadelphia. He's used to the finer things in life. You walked into our room in the middle of Paul's favorite story and interrupted him with a mean-spirited remark. You misunderstood the gravity of his achievement. Do you have any concept of how difficult it was for Paul to satisfy so many Betas with just his tongue?" Tim asked.

Genero interrupted, "Paul, what did Tony say?"

Paul noticed Phil for the first time. He rolled his eyes and sighed as he nodded. He looked back to Tim and raising his voice said, "Mind your own fucking business, Tim. I can discipline my little brother, you prick!"

Tim and Paul argued about everything. Paul had gotten angry because Tim messed with Tony. Tim's tactics had a diabolical way of screwing with both Tony and Paul.

"I repeat, what did Tony say?" Genero asked.

Tim responded gleefully, enjoying the trouble that he caused, "Mr. Genero, Pledge Tony is not only a football player, but a serious student of psychology. He's completed the entire first semester of the introductory course. When he heard Paul describe how he ate the four lovely Betas—all to orgasmic bliss—after the dance at the Armory a few years ago, Pledge Tony suggested that a man who was orally fixated on the female genitalia might be compensating for inadequacies in other important anatomical departments."

Phil laughed heartily. He enjoyed the camaraderie of life in the fraternity. He loved refereeing the exchanges between brothers.

It wasn't long after Paul pledged the SPO House that the legend of his tongue evolved. Like most adolescent myths, it originated from pure fantasy. Since Paul actually possessed an unusually long tongue, the legend had bona fide genetic support. The rumors and exaggeration created a misleading air of truth.

Years earlier, after a dance at the Armory, Paul had driven five drunken sorority girls back to their house. Later that night, when asked by his pledge brothers what liberties he'd taken in exchange for his courtesy, an inebriated Paul exaggerated his sexual conquest. True to his Irish heritage, Paul never let the truth get in the way of a good story.

Paul had actually driven around campus with the Betas for about 30 minutes, making a public spectacle. After their tenth pass through campus, Paul dropped off the Betas at their sorority house—all but one, a lovely girl named Debbie.

Debbie had substantial sexual experience. She'd maintained a sexual liaison with one of the professors in the History Department for nearly two years.

As Paul drove, she coyly suggested that they go to the golf course. She offered that they had time before the Beta curfew. They could park on the maintenance road near the eighth fairway, a remote and private place on campus.

Paul agreed. He was nervous, but interested. He despaired that he would remain a virgin for the rest of his life.

Ten minutes later, Paul and Debbie situated themselves in the back seat of Paul's old Buick. Debbie lay on her back, with her skirt bunched around her waist and her panties discarded on the floor. Paul knelt on the floor, with his head between Debbie's legs, his face buried in her wet and swollen vagina, her dark pubic hair rubbing against his face.

Debbie wrapped her legs around Paul's neck. Her hands grasped the back of his head with a force borne of intense lust, pulling him tight against her. She moaned and shuddered as Paul slowly and sensuously explored her intimate secrets using his considerable physical talent.

Debbie felt the rush begin. A moment later she experienced the strongest orgasm of her young life. A few moments later, she had another, even more powerful. So it went, one after the other, until she lost count.

Twenty minutes later, reasoning that she could not stand another thrill, she asked Paul to stop. She spent the next hour showing Paul everything she'd learned from her older, married lover. Around midnight, Paul lost his virginity.

There never was a bevy of satiated Betas, not that night and never all at once. The truth notwithstanding, the legend of Paul's tongue grew to epic portions. He found the legend to be advantageous. His reputed prowess made him notorious.

Earlier in the evening, Paul retold the old legend, supplementing it with newly created facts. Everyone knew he was fabricating. After Phil arrived, the five brothers and the pledge swapped stories of sexual conquests that were more imagined than real.

Tim finally asked Phil if he'd hit a home run while on his date with the new girl, Mary Jean. Genero responded that, unlike his ignoble brothers, he was a gentleman. He added that gentlemen never bragged about the intimate details of their relationships with women.

The SPO brothers used baseball metaphors to describe their success, real or imagined, with the Penn State co-eds. The late-night tradition possessed a flawed and profane logic, since baseball was a game of progression.

Tim had only hit two home runs in his whole life. Both of those occurred with a professional in Erie, Pennsylvania. In the last three years, Tim rarely got to first base with the any of the girls who lived around State College.

Conversely, Phil had earned the reputation of a being a serious batter, with an unusually high batting average, especially among the new crop of female students who entered Penn State in increasing numbers.

Phil had seduced five young women in the last two years, a large number for an era in which casual sex had many negative consequences. He had become colder, less empathetic, and more self-centered than he'd been when he arrived on campus. Genero recognized the change in his attitude. He understood the catalyst for the change in his life. He still smarted from it.

On his first Christmas home in December of 1936, Phil ran into Linda Monarch on High Street, near the Hamilton Restaurant.

After inhaling a couple of "hotchee dogs" at the restaurant and hanging out with high school friends for a few hours, Genero decided to pack it in, head home and spend the rest of the night visiting with the folks. When he left the restaurant and turned the corner onto High Street, he saw Linda, looking beautiful and sexy.

Reflecting back, he believed that the encounter was anything but chance. Linda had waited for him. At first, they made small talk. Phil asked her how college life was treating her. Linda responded with similarly mindless banter.

After a brief exchange, Linda asked him for a ride in his new roadster. Once in the car, they jumped all over each other in a lustful embrace. Less than 30 minutes later, Linda and Phil made passionate love on the bench seat of the roadster up in the snow-covered saddle at Waggoners Gap. Phil took his time and catered to Linda's every need. When she felt totally satiated, she helped him to a long and powerful release.

Over the next several days, Linda confided to Genero about her father's predicament and the medical treatment that he'd endured in an isolated sanitarium in northern Arizona. She related the intra-family intrigue regarding the Monarch business interests. In response, Phil happily gave Linda emotional support.

To the consternation of his mother and sister, Phil allowed Linda to monopolize his free time during the holiday break. The couple spent part of every day at the Gap. On New Year's Eve, as 1936 turned into 1937, Linda convinced Phil that they should continue on as a couple. To cement the bond, he should visit her in a few months in Boston.

Linda told Phil that on the weekend in March, when he came up to visit her, she'd sign out of her dorm, as if she were going home to Carlisle. Instead, he should reserve a room at the Wellington Arms in Boston. Linda would meet him there. They'd spend the entire weekend in the room using a real bed for their lovemaking.

As soon as he returned to State College, Phil started making the arrangements. While his family was better off financially than they'd been in years, he had to save and scrounge for the trip.

Genero left a day early on the train from State College to Philadelphia. He caught another through New York to Boston. Even with the inevitable delays, he arrived at the hotel several hours before Linda expected him.

Genero anxiously entered the hotel on that blustery day in March. He approached the desk clerk. In the most sophisticated voice he could muster, he asked the older man if the Wellington Arms had the Genero reservation.

The clerk had worked in the hotel for over 15 years. He realized something was up, but he recognized that the most valuable trait of a hotel clerk was the ability to mind one's own business.

The clerk told Genero that his sister "Karen" had already registered and would be waiting in the room. Phil and Linda had planned this little deception to throw off the hotel's management in case they became suspicious.

Phil grabbed his bag, declining the offer of a bellhop. Filled with anticipation and excitement, he rode the slow-moving elevator, which stopped at every floor.

When he got to his room, he used the key instead of knocking, wanting to surprise Linda. He got his wish.

Opening the door, Phil was shocked to see Linda with a special guest, a small unattractive man. His girl friend and her guest lay on the bed in the missionary position, totally naked and deeply in the throes of coitus. Linda had wrapped her long, beautiful legs around the guy's waist. Considering the sweat on their bodies and the condition of the room, they'd been at it for some time.

Genero froze, just inside the door. Then a horrible anger rose within him. He charged the couple, not 15 feet away.

Linda and her paramour, Evan T. Collingswood, realized that they were not alone. Evan, still atop his lover, spun around to face the assailant, just in time to catch Genero's fist squarely on his long patrician nose. Phil sent him sprawling senseless over the bed, halfway across the room.

With just one powerful punch, the fight ended. Collingswood seemed content to lie in a nude, obscene heap on the floor two feet from the radiator. Other than a screech and a series of pathetic moans, Collingswood did not utter a word.

Phil and Linda looked at each other for a long moment. All of Kari's warnings about Linda proved prophetic. They rang out like a series of gunshots in his ear.

Linda scooted up on the bed, and put her back against the ornate headboard. She pulled the damp bed sheet around her body to hide her nudity. She shook with fear.

Linda could see the mixture of bitter disappointment, pain, and sorrow in Phil's eyes. For the first time in all the years that she'd known him, she saw his eyes fill with tears. Finally, she realized that he wouldn't hurt her.

"What did you expect?" Linda asked in an exasperated tone. "Did you think, I'd hang around Boston pining for you for four years? Did you think I'd marry a soldier and live on some godforsaken Army post? Did you think you'd be the only boy I ever slept with in my whole life?"

Before Linda could say another word, Genero spun around, picked up his bag, ran out of the room and down the hall. He fled down the five flights of stairs, through the lobby and out onto the street.

Genero walked around Boston for hours. He lost track of the time. Eventually, he found himself at the Boston train station. He purchased a ticket for Philadelphia, and boarded a train leaving for New York City.

Genero took a day and half to get back to Penn State. Numb from the encounter, he decided that he'd put the sordid mess out of his mind, and never dwell on it again. He failed countless times. The experience made him more cynical and less considerate of the women that he dated. He became far less understanding, tolerant, and kind.

Phil never said a word to his family. When he stopped talking about Linda, his mother and sister concluded that something had happened.

Rather than driving the young co-eds away, Phil's new bad attitude drew young women like a magnet. His notoriety as a football player, his considerable good looks, his calculated distance, and an unresponsive demeanor made him more attractive to the girls at school.

Between his first and second years, Genero took a part-time job as an assistant to the chairman of the language department, a tenured professor of French. As a bonus, he traveled to Quebec and Montreal with his mentor for two weeks in July 1937.

In the summer of 1938, Genero won a special fellowship sponsored by the State Department. With the money from the government grant, he traveled to France, Germany, and Northern Italy with members of the Penn State faculty for over eight weeks. The faculty members were so impressed with him that he could have gone to Europe again in the summer of 1939, but Phil needed to complete his ROTC summer camp to get his commission upon graduation. He would have to pass on the second trip.

Tonight, Genero found himself in a warm and comfortable room while Tim playfully interrogated him about the raunchy details of his sexual conquest of the fair Mary Jean. Tim wheedled and cajoled until he was ready to drop a juicy detail or two.

"Did you give Mary Jean the famous Genero blanket treatment? I swear, once you graduate we'll fumigate that thing and give it to the Smithsonian," Tim joked.

"Well, guys, all I'm willing to tell you perverts at this time is that Miss Mary Jean Davis is a very demanding and vocal young co-ed," Phil explained.

"What you're saying is that she's a screamer! Right?" Tim shot back.

Phil looked at Tim. "That's a very indelicate, but not wholly inaccurate, description."

Tony tired of the discussion and went to bed for the night. John fell asleep on the bearskin, and Tim dozed in a chair. The conversation among Pat, Paul, and Phil began to wind down. Then Pat got serious.

Pat would graduate in a few months. He worried about world events. He believed that a general war was around the corner.

A cadet in the Navy ROTC contingent at Penn State, in June Kelly would receive a commission as an ensign. He'd serve on active duty in the Navy for two years.

Pat believed that events would drag the United States into a shooting war. He'd find himself aboard a destroyer out ahead of the fleet in harm's way. A German battleship would steam into sight, limbering up its sixteen-inch guns, finding his range with a course of fire.

"I'm telling you guys, a year from now we'll be at war. The Germans are greedy bastards. They've swallowed up Austria and the Sudetenland. It's only a matter of time before they grab the rest of Czechoslovakia. The Japanese are killing millions of Chinese. The Italians and the Germans helped Franco conquer Spain. They'll eventually try to come here," Pat predicted.

"I know you're Army green, Phil, but the Army's only a tactical force," Pat asserted. "You dogfaces won't play much of a role in the next war, except to defend the continental United States. The Navy's a strategic force. We project power through our fleet to every corner of the world. In the next war, the Navy will carry the lion's share of the load."

"I understand your point, Pat," Genero responded. "So explain to me how you'll get your destroyers, battleships, subs, and carriers up the Rhine River, or into the Chinese interior. The whole American Navy could sail into the Baltic Sea, where the German Luftwaffe would blow you out of the water. You're selling the Army and the Air Corps short. They'll be major players, if we ever go to war again."

"What do you mean, if?" Pat challenged. "I'm telling you boy, it's just a matter of time. Sooner or later we're going to war and the naval officers will play our part. You dogfaces will be home digging slit trenches and awaiting invasion."

"Neither of you is right," Paul interjected. "Congress passed the Neutrality Act to make sure that we stay out of the European and Asian political entanglements. We can't sell war materials to hostile powers, let alone join alliances or go to war. Whatever's going to happen with these madmen will happen without the Americans getting involved. We won't be going over there again. It's just as well. It's none of our fucking business."

"The only thing that Neutrality Act is good for is to make sure that America doesn't do anything until it is too late. Then, by God, we'll be shit out of luck. Guys like me will get fucked," Pat countered angrily.

"If you feel this strongly, why did you join the NROTC?" Phil asked.

"Service in the Navy is a tradition in my family. My great-grandfather was an immigrant from Ireland. He served as a petty officer during the Civil War. My grandfather was a commissioned officer with Admiral Dewey at Manila. My dad graduated from Annapolis and has spent twenty-five years in the fleet. The family wanted me to go to the Naval Academy, but I wanted to come here. The trade off was that I had to take NROTC," Pat explained.

"Gin, your family has a long military tradition too, doesn't it?" Paul asked.

"Not really," Phil responded. "My dad was a corporal in the infantry in the Great War. He was wounded in the same battle where Sergeant York got the Medal of Honor. Years ago my whole family went to Washington. I met Sergeant York and watched President Coolidge pin the DSC on my dad. As far as I know, my dad was the first on either side of my family to serve in the military. My Italian grandfather immigrated to the U.S. to avoid military service. None of my dad's brothers served. My mom's dad was Amish. Neither he nor any of his people ever served in the armed forces."

Genero continued more seriously. "The Genero military tradition goes back only one generation, but my dad set a hell of a standard. I'll be happy if I do my time and get an honorable discharge. The Army will be fine for a few years, but I'd like to try for the diplomatic corps. I had a great time in Europe last summer. The Foreign Service would be a perfect fit. Languages come easy to me."

"You went to Germany? What did you think of the Nazis?" Paul asked.

"I liked France better than Germany. We spent three weeks in Germany. I wasn't prepared for what I saw," Phil expounded. "The average Germans seemed normal. I wasn't surprised by what I saw in the small villages."

Genero continued more deliberately, "What we encountered in the large towns and cities shocked me. The militarism overwhelmed us. Swastikas hung from every possible place. You couldn't get away from it. The attitude of the young men defied logic. They were aggressive and confrontational. On occasion, the storm troopers assailed us, once they learned we were Americans. The Nazis really hate the Jews. It's unbelievable. If the Nazis don't get what they want from the other Europeans, they intend to take it by force. They believe they're entitled to most of the eastern part of the continent. They claim they need *Liebenstraum*. That's 'living space' in German."

"What can America do about it?" Paul asked. "Gin, you just said that Pat's Navy couldn't sail up the Rhine or operate in the Baltic. I read in the Saturday Evening Post that we have less than two hundred thousand men serving in the Army. Is that right?"

"It's far less than that, but that doesn't count the reserves or the National Guard. Still, your point is valid. The Nazis don't worry about the American Army," Genero conceded.

"We don't have the manpower in the Army, the Navy can't do the job and there's a law that makes it illegal to get involved. We should just stay out of the whole fucking mess," Paul contended.

Genero didn't answer Paul. He understood that America was not psychologically, economically, or militarily prepared for a European debacle of the first order.

It was 1:30 a.m. Phil told his brothers that Mary Jean had worn him out. He had a class in the morning and needed some sleep. As he took his leave, Pat and Paul continued to debate the issue of American isolationism.

Walking down the hall, Phil mused that the isolationist preferences of his countrymen amounted to a dangerous luxury in the modern world. Maybe the dictatorships and the democracies would find a way to accommodate each other. Maybe Prime Minister Chamberlain was right last October, when he returned fresh from Munich, declaring that he'd ensured "peace in our time."

Genero wondered how the non-Germanic residents of the Sudetenland felt about becoming the lost pawns in the chess match of European power politics. He couldn't imagine a single positive result from the concessions at Munich. *I'd better get some rest,* he thought, *if I'm going to solve all of the world's problems.*

# Chapter 11

June 28, 1939

From: Mrs. Marta B. Genero
Special Assistant to the President
Monarch Clothing Company
Carlisle, Pennsylvania

TO: Cadet Phillip E. Genero, II
Baker Company, 2d Battalion
Reserve Officer Training Brigade
Camp A.P. Hill, Virginia


Dearest Gin,
      Your dad and I were glad to get your letter yesterday. I know you're busy and the training is hectic, but your letters are very important to me. Write more often and I promise to stop nagging you so much.

I miss you, sweetheart. Your dad and I are looking forward to your trip home at the end of July. I hope you can find a way to spend more than a few days. This could be your last vacation as a student. Next year you'll get your commission. It would mean so much to me if we could all get together for at least a week before the end of this summer.

Kari's been home from nursing school for two weeks. She's working at St. Mary's Hospital in Carlisle to make extra money. As you know from her letters, she's excelled as a nursing student. She'll get her diploma and R.N. at the same time you graduate next June. I can't believe how fast you two have grown.

Kari is going steady with that charming Doctor Hansen. Mark is about half way through his surgical residency at St. Teresa's in Harrisburg. Dad thinks he's too old for Kari, but it's only seven years. I don't see that as a problem. I was already married to your father when I was Kari's age.

We've spent time with Mark and Kari this spring. He's a wonderful young man with a great sense of humor. I'd never have expected that in a surgeon. I assumed that practicing that kind of medicine would make him very serious. Not Mark; he's really funny. He cares for your sister very much. She'll be a handful for Mark to manage.

It sounds like you're playing the field and haven't found anyone special at Penn State. Have you? You'd tell your mom if you had a special girl, wouldn't you? You'd better!

Your dad and Kari think that since you'll be going into the Army that you shouldn't get serious about anybody just now. I'm different. I want you to find a nice girl, settle down, and be happy. It doesn't matter that it might not make sense. I don't have to be logical. I'm your mom!

Dad's doing fantastic. He got promoted again, and is now the sales manager for all of the Monarch marketing efforts. The Monarchs might make him a vice president of marketing. He got another raise, and all of the salesmen and factory reps just love him.

Dan Monarch is impressed with your dad because he negotiated a lucrative contract with the Army for the new lightweight fatigue uniform. Dan told me that your dad would get a nice bonus at the end of the fiscal year (two days from now). I want to surprise him with a little getaway to the Maryland shore. Don't worry! We'll be back in Carlisle in time for your heroic return. So, don't try to use that as an excuse not to come home.

On a sour note, Dan also told me that his nephew has made a recovery out west. Junior's lost an enormous amount of weight and has recovered from his heart and lung ailments. The Monarch family is thinking of letting him come back as the chief operating officer, or something. God help us!

Dan Monarch assured me that he'd stay in charge of the company. I dread the thought of Junior coming back, especially now that things are so good for our family. It's been so refreshing to work for Dan. He's a real gentleman and a good friend.

Your dad and I are in good health, and except for the news about Junior, things couldn't be better. I'll go to St. Francis on my way home this evening and light a candle. I'm grateful for all that we have. I hope God will protect us all in the future.

My darling son, I love you very much. Be safe, and come home to see us soon. I promise to bake a huge lasagna and have plenty of Chianti to celebrate.

Love,
Mom

# Chapter 12

Junior Monarch stood in the shower stall under the steaming cascade, absorbing the therapeutic effects and allowing the water to flow over his new lean physique. He felt rejuvenated.

That morning, Dr. Johansen had given him the best possible news. They'd cured his tuberculosis. The drug treatment and the pristine environment had done the trick. Junior's pulmonary condition no longer threatened the general public.

Junior's heart condition had also improved. He'd lost over 130 pounds. He could return to the land of the living.

Dr. Johansen warned Junior that since he'd mistreated his body for so many years, his cardiovascular system had permanent damage. Even with modern surgical techniques and medical treatment, they could give no guarantees that Junior would not have a deadly relapse some day.

It could happen suddenly, and be over in—well—a heartbeat.

Unless he took specific steps to maintain the dramatic change to his lifestyle, Junior would remain at serious risk for either stroke or cardiac arrest. Under no circumstances could he go back to his life of utter dissolution. Junior should refrain from any business enterprise.

*What a crock of shit*, Junior thought, as he toweled off. *The last thing that I'll do is retire to some fucking nursing home. I've got scores to settle.*

Junior had come perilously close to dying a number of times since he suffered the humiliating assault in his cabin in Boiling Springs. He'd seen the reports.

Even after the doctors had managed to stabilize Junior, he had relapses, some quite serious. Fortunately, the medical staff at Andrews included a first rate cardiac specialist.

Despite the dire medical warnings, Junior planned to return to Carlisle and work at the Monarch Clothing Company.

Thanks to Uncle Dan, he no longer had the power to exact revenge. Junior needed to be patient. He'd convince his uncle that he'd changed. If he wanted back in the business, with the opportunity to take it over again, he'd have to bide his time. Junior had learned a great deal about patience in Sedona.

Junior felt invigorated by his time in northern Arizona. Sedona possessed an unparalleled beauty. The monument-like red rock formations created a dramatic geological backdrop for his rehabilitation.

Over time, Junior had adapted to his surroundings. When he'd progressed sufficiently in his rehabilitation, he exercised by hiking up and down the miles of breathtaking mountain trails surrounding the institute, all the way to the Mogollon Rim.

At Andrews, Junior learned that he had a primitive talent for painting. He spent time every day learning the art. Over the last several months, he'd created a respectable portfolio, which depicted the dramatic local beauty.

Miriam Johansen, the director's wife, had once pursued an art career in Southern California. She abandoned it to marry the good doctor. To escape the boredom of life in rustic Sedona, Miriam volunteered her time and talent to help with the rehabilitation program at the Andrews Institute.

Miriam became Junior's mentor. Over the last year they'd worked together every day. Miriam and Junior often walked off with their painting equipment to do another still life up among the red rocks.

Life at the Andrews Institute had been better than Junior expected. He'd known that the institute would be isolated. He wanted it that way. The isolation would work both ways. He'd remain out of touch, but he'd be harder to watch and harder to catch if he had to leave suddenly.

In the first six months of his isolation, Junior lived in constant terror that the accountants would uncover his secret bank account in Rio. After all, they'd noticed many of the irregularities that he caused.

After several months, when the deputies from the Coconino County Sheriff's Office failed to materialize, he began to relax. Later, when they allowed him to go into the little town of Sedona, he used the telegraph office to make discrete inquiries.

Eventually, Junior concluded that the Brazilian account was safe. Uncle Dan's accountants must have missed the obvious clues. Knowing that he'd safely hidden several hundred thousand dollars in Rio gave him a more positive mental outlook. *The next time I go to Brazil, I'll be more careful about whose wife I screw,* he promised himself.

As Junior dressed for the day, the realization that he'd be leaving Andrews began to hit home. He looked around the bungalow with a new perspective. The room seemed comfortable and safe. He could rest here. He could relax.

Junior reached into the pocket of his painting pants. He pulled out his great grandfather's solid-gold pocket watch, a vestige of his former power. He opened the cover and looked at the time without really seeing it. The concept of time did not seem as important in Sedona as it had in Carlisle. He would miss that aspect of life here.

Junior would miss a lot about the Andrews Institute. He heard a quiet tapping on the rear door of the bungalow. He smiled a nasty little grimace.

Junior walked over to the back door and opened it wide. Miriam Johansen stood on his small back porch, looking expectant. Although she lived a relatively primitive life in this bucolic setting, Miriam had found the resources to maintain her youthful good looks.

"Where's the good doctor, my dear?" Junior asked. "You're early for our painting therapy session."

"Bill went up to Flagstaff for a luncheon. He's got some business for the institute afterwards. He won't be back until suppertime," Miriam explained. "Bill told me that your test results are all negative and that you've almost completed the course of rehabilitation. You're leaving soon. Aren't you, Randy?" Miriam asked as she walked into the main room.

"Mir, I haven't received my release. Nor did your hubby tell me when he was planning to let me go. I do think I'll be gone in a couple of weeks," Junior said.

"Randy, are you going to pack up and leave Sedona, and that'll be it?" Miriam asked with emotion in her voice. "What about me?"

"What about you, Mir?" Junior asked. "You're married to the great Doctor of Oak Creek Canyon. He needs you in his work. What did you expect would happen? You knew that I would leave some day, or have a heart attack and die."

"I thought, after all I've done for you, that you might fall in love with me and take me with you. You told me that you're married in name only. Your wife has never visited you here," Miriam argued. "I thought you liked the things I do for you. I'm sure that you haven't met anyone like me before. If you don't care about me, then I can go and you can plan for your new life," Miriam said, tears welling in her eyes.

"Baby, I'm sorry. I was only teasing," Junior lied. "I would've gone mad here without your kindness. I look forward to our little sessions. I've been thinking about you all morning. Why don't you come here? I have something that needs your personal attention. When we're done, we can talk about our plans."

Junior's oily explanation didn't fool Miriam, but she was desperate. She'd lived at the institute for ten years, all through the worst days of the Depression. She'd traded her marriage to Bill Johansen for economic security. With Randy Monarch she might have another opportunity. Life in Arizona bored her.

Miriam looked at Junior for a long moment. She knew he was a bastard, but he represented the only chance she might ever get.

She smiled a sexy smile, as she looked Junior directly in the eye. She began slowly unbuttoning her blouse. When she'd taken off all of her clothes except the special shoes and stockings that Junior liked her to wear, she walked over to him, and fell to her knees. She unbuckled Junior's belt and unzipped his trousers.

Miriam reached into Junior's shorts and began to stroke his manhood. As she exposed him, she took him deeply into her mouth. She had developed a special technique. With Randy Monarch, she practiced it a lot.

# Chapter 13

1:30 AM
December 25, 1939
Outer Courtyard
St. Francis Xavier Church
Carlisle, Pennsylvania

Early December 1939 had been unseasonably warm in central Pennsylvania. When the winter solstice passed, the weather turned cold, but remained very dry. The residents of Carlisle could not look forward to a white Christmas.

The new war had erupted in Europe with the German invasion of Poland in the predawn hours of September 1, 1939. In response, France and Britain had declared war on Germany, but otherwise did nothing to help the Poles. The Nazis made short work of the once proud Polish army.

Unable to resist the modern combined arms onslaught, the Polish government bowed to the inevitable. The Poles capitulated in early October, after being vivisected by the Germans and the Soviets. The Poles suffered a medieval fate in the middle third of the 20th Century.

In August 1939, in a diplomatic coup of historic proportions, representatives of Hitler and Stalin had surprised the western powers by signing a non-aggression pact. In addition to promising not to fight each other, the Nazis and Russians agreed to divide up the conquered Polish territory. By Thanksgiving, Poland ceased to exist as a political entity. The suffering in both zones of occupation defied description.

Central Pennsylvania contained a large population of Polish-Americans. Almost every Polish family had lost a relative or friend, as a consequence of the *Blitzkrieg*—or lightning war.

For the Polish-Americans and their friends, the holiday season in Carlisle was somber. Despite Poland's chaotic and often violent history, nothing prepared them for the death, destruction, and complete dismemberment of their homeland. Since many had dreamed of becoming successful in America and returning home in heroic style, Poland's political eradication in an unprecedented bloodbath—and the worldwide military calamity that it portended—eclipsed the darkest economic reversals of the Great Depression. The gloom spread like a virus from the Poles to other European immigrant enclaves in the Cumberland Valley.

Many Americans concluded that the United States was unprepared for what might come to pass. The spirit of isolationism, which was in no way extinguished in late 1939, had insured that America remained unprepared to react to the looming crisis.

Despite the march of totalitarian armies across the face of Europe, a plurality of Americans attempted to maintain a normal life. These folks still deluded themselves that, despite the unbridled aggression of the Axis powers, America could avoid the wars in Europe, Asia, and Africa.

By Christmas, in response to German belligerence, England, France, and their colonies had mobilized, but did not attack Germany itself. Instead, they chose to deploy hundreds of thousands of soldiers along the French and Belgian borders in a defense in depth. Though hostilities technically existed, the warring powers remained in a state of pseudo-confrontation on the Western Front in what became known as the "Phony War." While the Western Front was quiet, the lack of fighting created an ominous tension.

The Generos always got together for a huge feast on Christmas Eve. After dinner, they attended Midnight Mass. This Christmas, the Genero family included a new member, one who had romantically petitioned for membership in the boisterous clan.

Dr. Mark Hansen surprised almost everyone at the family gathering. While they sat at the traditional Christmas Eve dinner, Mark turned to Kari, took her left hand in his, reached into his vest pocket with his other hand, and produced a very lovely gold ring with a perfect marquis stone.

Nervously clearing his throat, Mark waited until the family quieted down, then spoke up loud enough for everyone at the table to hear him: "Kari, the first time I saw you, you were a candy striper, delivering newspapers and magazines to the patients in the surgical ward at St. Teresa's. My first thought was that you were the cutest girl I had ever seen. Later, when you came to the nursing school, we worked together in the clinic and I got to know you. I came to realize that your real beauty was not your good looks, but the kindness of your spirit and the warmth of your soul. You are simply the best person I know. We've been going together for months. I realize that after knowing you, I could never get along without you in my life. Before dinner I spoke to your father. I have his permission to ask you to marry me. I love you very much. Will you be my wife?"

Mark slipped the ring on the third finger of Kari's shaking left hand. The entire table erupted in applause and cheers.

Kari tried to speak, but Mark's gallant request was her most cherished wish. She had been in love with him since their first meeting. Despite an heroic attempt, all Kari could do was croak out an emotional: "Yes, darling!"

Still somewhat bewildered, Kari stared at the gorgeous ring. The jeweler had set the perfect marquis diamond in an unusually wide gold band. Inside, he'd engraved a caduceus symbol along with Mark's very private sentiment.

Finally, overcome by the romantic gesture, Kari's blue eyes filled with tears. She wrapped her arms around Mark's neck, and gave him a kiss so wantonly passionate that Uncles Angelo and John began to whistle and shout. Everyone cheered again.

Kari's dad stood up from the head of the table, and raised his wine glass. "Everyone knows how much I treasure my children. I've prayed for them to find happiness. All of you have come to know Mark. You understand what a fine man he is, and how much he loves our Kari. I would just like to say—like to say—like to..." Phillip stuttered, as he began to choke up from the wave of emotion.

Phil immediately stood up and walked over to his father. With a wide grin on his handsome face, he put his arm around Phillip's shoulder. With seamless ease, he finished his father's toast, "Mark, we—my father, mother, uncles, aunts and cousins—want to say that the Generos are honored that a man of your character would want to join our family. We will never part with Kari, but we welcome you into our clan. As for me, I've always loved my sister, but I always wanted a big brudder. Now I have one. All of our love to both of you!"

After dinner, and a number of glasses of Chianti, the clan bundled up and set off for St. Francis. The priests said a solemn high mass, and wore their most treasured holiday vestments in honor of the sacred ceremony. With all of the pomp and ceremony, the celebration would take hours.

Mark was not a Catholic. As a boy, he'd occasionally attended Lutheran services with his parents. As he got older, he became less religious.

He studied at the University of Maryland, where he excelled in the sciences. Mark decided on medical school late in his college career, which seemed a natural progression. Eventually, he graduated third in a class of 250 doctors.

As a surgeon, Doctor Hansen ruthlessly adhered to the scientific method. He mistrusted the concept of faith. He did not connect with the spiritual side of his personality. As a scientist, Doctor Hansen retained confidence in the vitality and strength of the human spirit. He interpreted humanity's technological and scientific accomplishments as evidence of a moral and sociological evolution.

Hansen understood that if Kari agreed to marry him, he'd be joining a family that had strong religious sentiments. He didn't care. He was crazy for Kari and would have proposed to her if she had been a druid.

By early Christmas morning, Mark Hansen had endured the complex rituals of a solemn high mass because it made his gorgeous, sexy fiancée happy. When the mass was over, he basked in the cold brisk air in the church courtyard.

Although it was nearly 2 a.m., some of the stalwart members of the congregation stood in the cold and continued to chat, sharing last minute holiday sentiments. Kari and Marta took this early morning opportunity to visit with some friends.

Kari's dad and uncles went to warm up the cars and to have a nip of Christmas cheer from Uncle Angelo's flask. Mark stood off to one side, shivering slightly as he watched his wife-to-be proudly show her engagement ring to everyone in Carlisle who she could buttonhole.

Phil noticed Mark standing by himself in the courtyard. Mark was whistling what sounded remotely like Glenn Miller's "In the Mood."

Phil walked over to Mark, taking this opportunity to have a private word. He admired Mark and felt relieved that Kari had found someone like him.

"Mark, you survived the endurance test. You've passed the point of no return. You're trapped like a fly in a web. You'll never get free of the Generos," he teased, as he put his arm around the shoulders of the smaller man.

"Gin, I don't want to get free of this family. You guys have emotional energy that my family would envy and never duplicate. I feel lucky to be a part of it."

"Have you and Kari set a date?" Phil asked. "Where are you two going to get hitched?"

"Some time in June, I think. I understand my place. I'll have no say in the planning of my wedding. I'm sure that Kari and Marta will decide exactly when, where, and how our sacred union will occur. I'll be patient and go along for the rollercoaster ride."

"Just make sure that you take into consideration that I get commissioned in June and may have to report for duty almost immediately," Phil reminded Mark.

"I hadn't thought of that. I need you at the wedding. I'd like you to be one of the groomsmen," Mark explained. "My brother will be the best man."

"Doctor, it will be my honor to serve you," Genero said in mock formality, punching it up with a very low bow from his waist, and a gallant sweep of his sword arm. "You may call upon me to do your bidding at any time, sir."

Mark became very serious, "Gin, I'm worried about you. Europe's at war again and you're about to get commissioned. Do you have any idea what you'll be doing?"

"The Professor of Military Science informed me that I've drawn the Infantry as my branch. This summer I'll go to Fort Benning in Georgia for the basic course for new infantry officers. That'll take eight weeks. I'll report by the end of June for a class date in early July. After that, who knows? I'll get more specific information as I get closer to graduation."

Phil continued, "The cadre at school is interested in my language skills and my travels to Europe a year and half ago. Since I can speak Italian, French, and German, I might land an intelligence billet in some command. I'd like that. Infantry types serve as intelligence officers in staff assignments at all levels. The running joke is that any infantry officer has to be a moron, and an infantry officer in an intelligence billet is an oxymoron," Phil said.

Mark laughed at Phil's self-deprecation. He liked the younger man. He respected the impressive intellect and obvious moral fiber.

"Gin, I'll keep my fingers crossed. In spite of the awful things that happened in Poland, there's a chance that the war may not expand further. Perhaps you'll be spared the dangers of a war in Europe," Mark observed.

"You can't be serious, Mark. What makes you think that the war in Europe won't get much larger?"

The passion of Gin's response surprised Mark. The younger man might be tense because he would be one of those compelled to face the dangers.

Dr. Hansen responded carefully. "Well, Gin, I admit that I haven't focused on the situation in Europe, certainly not the way someone in your circumstances might. I've noticed that since the Polish capitulation there hasn't been a lot of activity among the so-called combatants. From what I've read in newspapers and magazines, the Germans and the French aren't fighting. Some experts don't think they ever will. None of the Europeans want to get involved in that awful trench warfare again. Maybe they can make peace."

"Mark, as a surgeon, you use logic and scientific principles in your work, right?"

"Sure, of course. What's your point?"

"If you examined an unconscious patient, you wouldn't think he was OK just because you didn't see any symptoms right away. You'd look further, until you knew why he was unconscious, right?"

"Of course," Mark responded. "Certain conditions are hard to diagnose. You have to investigate pretty thoroughly in some cases."

"You would never simply accept the easy, superficial explanation, would you?" Phil asked again.

"No, and I think I see your point. You're suggesting that I've accepted the superficial explanation for the debacle in Europe, right?"

"Yes, sir. I am," Genero admitted, and then elaborated his own analysis.

Mark listened carefully. Caution, not optimism, was the watchword.

"Gin. I'd no idea you were so passionate about your convictions. You make a good case, but it's pessimistic. I try to think positively."

"Mark, the politicians of this world—men like Neville Chamberlain—are not the people who have to fight the wars in order to fix the mistakes. Chamberlain thought he was being optimistic at Munich, when he tried to buy 'peace in our time,' by compromising the freedom of the Czechs and Slovaks. With the onset of war, we'll find out what the cost of Chamberlain's optimism and appeasement will be," Phil said somberly.

"I hope you're wrong," Mark responded.

"I hope to God I'm wrong too," Gin conceded.

"God help us all!" Mark responded, unaware that for the first time in his adult life he'd called for divine intercession.

# Chapter 14

11:15 AM
May 29, 1940
Sigma Pi Omega House
Pennsylvania State University
State College, Pennsylvania

Unable to hide his rage, Tim Sullivan stood at the window and fumed at his roommate's incredible stupidity. The arguing and shouting had caused his voice to become hoarse and raspy. Angrier than he could remember, he forced himself to look away as Paul packed. Tim stared out the window in the direction of the golf course.

The leaves on the trees surrounding the course had grown the full complement of spring regeneration. The fairways looked lush and well maintained. Normally, Tim appreciated the ambiance. Today he barely noticed.

"Tell me something, roomie," Tim said angrily. "What kind of idiot leaves college after four years, with less than two weeks to go before graduation?"

Tim turned to face his roommate and continued, almost shouting, "You're on a track to graduate with honors in Engineering. You've a little more than a week, and you'll be set for life. You're a top student. How can you throw all this away on an idiotic, wild goose chase?"

"I have to go now, Tim. I might not have this opportunity again," Paul responded gently, understanding that—despite their years of arguing—Tim genuinely cared about him.

"That's fuckin' ridiculous. You'll have endless opportunities to throw your life away. I'm sure your parents don't realize that you're leaving school. I have half a mind to call your dad," Tim rasped.

"Mind your own damn business. It's my fuckin' life. I can do whatever I want with it. I'm 21 years old. If I want to do something stupid, I can. But this isn't stupid, Tim. It's the best thing for me in the long run," Paul tried to explain.

"Paul, this makes no sense. You've always been an isolationist, a pacifist. Last year you were telling everyone that Congress and the President would keep America out of war. So far, the Brits and the Frogs have been fighting the Krauts for nine months, and you were right! America is still at peace. Why would you want to go to England and fight for the damn British? You're not English. You're Irish-American for God's sake! What have the limey's ever done for our people, except exploit them? You don't have any family in Britain," Tim argued.

Paul looked at Tim for a moment, trying to find the words to describe his dilemma. "Tim, sit down and take a deep breath. Let me explain, will you?"

Tim fell heavily into the old, overstuffed chair, and glowered at Paul.

"Tim, a few years ago I tried to sign up as an Air Corps cadet. I had the two years of college. I passed every written and physical exam, but one. The Air Corps rejected me because I have 20 - 40 vision. They wouldn't waive that requirement. I never got to go to Alabama."

"I remember," Tim said. "You were trying to impress your old man. He's a pilot. The only time he pays any attention to you is when you guys are flying that old bi-plane of his. I never thought that you were serious. I thought that you were relieved that the dogfaces turned you down."

Paul smiled and nodded his head in affirmation. His roommate was a pain in the ass, but Tim knew him well.

"You're absofuckinglutely right!! I was relieved. I didn't want to go into the Army. I didn't want to be an Army pilot. I knew I didn't have a chance in hell of going to flight school. I figured I might score some points with my dad, if he thought I'd tried."

"Yeah, I remember. Your mom got hysterical. Your dad was amazed that you had the balls to try to be an Army pilot,"

Tim recalled. "What's your point here? Are you saying that the whole thing was a stunt to impress daddy? Is that what you're doing here?"

"Tim, shut up!" Paul interrupted. "Two years ago, I thought that America would be able to remain neutral, no matter what happened in Europe. I had a feeling the Germans would get Europe into a shooting war, the same way the Japs are in a real war with the Chinese. I stupidly thought that the French, British and Russians would be able to contain the Nazis, and that we'd never have to get involved. I didn't anticipate the German/Soviet pact, the fall of Poland, or the conquest of Denmark, Norway, Belgium, and Holland."

"Two days ago," Paul continued, "the British started evacuating their expeditionary force from Dunkirk. France is totally fucked! The Krauts will overrun France in two or three more weeks. Britain and its colonies will soon be fighting the Axis alone."

"So what? That's their problem. Didn't you tell me a thousand fuckin' times that the good old USA shouldn't bail out the English and French ever again?" Tim inquired sarcastically. "Were you bullshitting me? What's changed?"

"Tim, I never thought that the Nazis would be so powerful or unstoppable. This time next year they could be in London. I don't care for the Brits, but, I'm convinced that President Roosevelt does," Paul explained.

Paul continued without a breath, "Roosevelt's an anglophile. He'll never let the King, Chamberlain, this guy—Churchill—or anyone on that island fall to the Nazis without American intervention. Roosevelt wants America in this war."

Tim took a very deep breath. He looked up at the ceiling for a moment. He counted slowly to ten. He didn't want to admit it, but—other than his mom—Paul was his only family.

Tim composed himself and then continued his angry dialog with Paul. "So, Paul, if we're going over there again, why do you have to go now?" Tim asked, barely able to keep his voice down. "How can you go from isolationist-intellectual to Royal Air Force volunteer? I don't get the logic."

"It's simple. Our old friend, Ensign Pat Kelly, was right. America will fiddle fuck around 'til it's too late," Paul responded. "If I wait, I'll get called up in this new draft that Congress is debating. The Army won't ever let me be a pilot. I'll be lucky to get a commission in any service. I could end up as a private in the Infantry. I'd rather take my chances with the Limeys."

Paul paused for a moment to compose himself before continuing. "My dad's got a pal in London. His name is Chuck Sweeney. Mr. Sweeney is doing everything he can to attract American boys into the Royal Air Force, or the Royal Canadian Air Force. Mr. Sweeney's agent wired me yesterday. With my seven hundred hours of logged flight time, I qualify for pilot training in the RCAF. The Canucks have different standards. My vision's not an impediment. I'm confirmed for a class date. I have to be in Ottawa in seventy-two hours. Tim, I'm going. There's nothing you can do to stop me."

Overwhelmed by the reality of Paul's decision, Tim Sullivan realized that he might never see his friend again. Paul had been the closest thing to a real brother that he'd ever known. Tim could not imagine a more frightening scenario than Paul running off to this fucking war in Europe.

Paul had obviously thought the whole scenario through, and his choices made sense, in a weird, convoluted way. Tim began to wonder how the wars in Europe, Africa, and Asia might eventually affect him.

"Tim, don't worry about graduation. I only needed six hours to get my degree. I took twelve this semester to stay busy. I have A's in all my courses. Even with F's on my finals, I'll still have enough credits to graduate in two weeks. I won't be able to get the *Magna Cum Laude* on my diploma, but that doesn't matter to me."

Now more seriously, Paul addressed Tim, "Do me a favor, like a good and loyal SPO brother. At the graduation ceremony, accept my diploma for me. Send it to my folks. I'd really appreciate that."

There was nothing Tim could do to change his friend's decision. He had the sense that a great train wreck was about to occur. He wondered if he could get out of the way of that train. It didn't seem possible.

Tim wouldn't be a passive witness. He and all the people he knew would participate in an event of cataclysmic proportions. The disaster would spare no one. He looked down at the floor, shook his head slowly and sighed. "Paul, do you have enough money to get to Ottawa? Weren't you overextended in your allowance last month?" Tim inquired.

"Now that you mention it, I only have $16 dollars to my name," Paul offered. "I owe you $20 bucks. I'll pay you eventually."

Tim cut Paul off. He raised his hand, made a fist and extended his index finger directly up, and put the finger to his lips. "Shush!" Tim commanded humorously, as he walked over to his chest of drawers. "I've been saving this for our graduation. I planned to get us drunk and laid at the roadhouse. I think I should donate your share to the Paul Reilly Transportation Fund."

Tim reached into his top drawer and counted out a number of bills. He turned back to Paul, walked over to him, and extended his hand with $150 dollars. "Paul, you can use this to get to Ottawa. We'll settle up the next time we get together," Tim said.

Paul accepted the money, folding it and putting it in the pocket of his jeans. Too emotional to even say thank you, he just looked away.

"Paul, why don't I drive you the station when you finish packing. There's no hurry, we have a few hours before the train leaves for Philly," Tim offered.

"No, let's go now! I don't want to change my mind. We can grab a few drinks at the bar. Maybe celebrate graduation a bit early. You might have to pour me on that train."

The two young men looked at each other fully realizing that they might never see each other again. Tim was on the verge of an emotional outburst, instead he said, "Paul, if you try to hug me, I'll punch your fuckin' lights out!"

"I'd rather have the clap than touch a maggot like you," Paul responded, barely able to speak.

# Chapter 15

10:30 AM
June 25, 1940
State Highway 74
Waggoners Gap, Pennsylvania

Phillip sat in the front seat of Phil's blue roadster, as his son negotiated the sharp turns and switchbacks of the old state road up to Waggoners Gap. Phillip looked around the interior of the car. Phil had maintained it beautifully over the last four years.

The roadster didn't look or act its age. The engine purred like a hungry tiger, making short work of the steep grade. This buggy had a few good years left in her.

Phillip watched as his son shifted the gears up and down, working the brake and clutch in perfect synchronization. Phil knew this baby's idiosyncrasies.

Phillip would ask Bill to give the roadster a good tune up before Lieutenant Genero left for the basic class at the Infantry School next week. *I'll feel a lot better about Gin driving all the way to Georgia if the car's in top shape,* Phillip thought to himself.

*Lieutenant Genero!* Phillip contemplated affectionately, as he considered how far his son had come in so short a time. *Until a few years ago, I never thought anyone else in the family would ever serve in the Army, let alone be an officer! And in his uniform, my son looks every inch the infantry lieutenant.*

A few weeks earlier, the Genero clan had traveled to State College to participate in Phil's commissioning. At his son's request, Phillip wore the Distinguished Service Cross that President Coolidge awarded to him 13 years earlier.

After the adjutant read the commissioning order, the Professor of Military Science swore in the graduating cadets. Marta and Phillip pinned the shiny gold bars of an Army second lieutenant on the shoulder straps of Phil's tailored Class A uniform. Looking at her son, Marta cried like a baby.

Uncle Angelo gave his nephew a bear hug that would have broken a lesser man's back. He embarrassed Phil by kissing him on the cheek in the traditional way of Italian men.

Phillip gently hugged his son. He spoke quietly to him, "I'm so proud of you, Gin. I know you will serve honorably and well."

Kari hugged her brother and said, "Brudder, you look almost as good as an usher at the movies in Harrisburg. Could you get me a bag of popcorn and some Jujubes?"

As they neared the Gap, Phillip recalled that he'd tried to convince Phil to major in a hard science or engineering. Instead, Phil had studied romance languages. To no one's surprise, he'd graduated Summa Cum Laude with a Bachelor of Arts degree in both German and French.

Weeks earlier, troubled by the prospect of his son serving in the infantry, Phillip sought Father Nachen's counsel. Father Nachen had been a Marine lieutenant in what people now called World War I.

*God, help us! How many of these abominations will there be?* Phillip thought when he first heard the term.

Earlier in the year, Uncle Dan had promoted Phillip to Vice President of Marketing for the newly incorporated Monarch Industries. His salary doubled and he received a number of important perks, including a brand new Cadillac.

The new job gave Phillip more flexibility. He didn't have to travel so much and could take an afternoon off now and then. He'd received the promotion based upon his golden touch with the military contracts. In the fall, Phillip had negotiated with the Navy for the largest uniform contract in the company's history.

Dan Monarch realized that the company owed Phillip Genero a debt of gratitude for its new prosperity. Junior

Monarch, recently returned from Arizona, offered no opinion.

Uncle Dan and the other owners had restructured the company into Monarch Industries to meet the new business challenges and economic opportunities. The Board of Directors appointed Dan as President and CEO. Marta remained his special assistant and received a tidy raise. Dan selected Junior to be the Chief Operating Officer.

So on a brisk day in April, it was not a problem for Phillip to take an afternoon off to drive up to Camp Hill to meet with Father Nachen. In the intervening years, the Jesuits had elevated Father Nachen to be the Principal at St. Ignatius.

Phillip took Father Nachen to an Italian restaurant in Camp Hill for lunch. To lubricate their discussion, they split a bottle of fine red wine from the Piedmont.

"Father, I chose a Barolo for our meal. It's considered one of the best red wines in Italy. It's very strong, but it will go well with the dish I've ordered for us. I hope you enjoy it."

"I rarely have anything alcoholic at lunch. This is a real treat for me," Father responded with a smile.

After the waiter decanted the bottle, he offered Phillip an opportunity to taste the first pour. Phillip declined, passing the responsibility to Father Nachen. The priest swirled the wine in his class, allowing it to breathe. He brought the tip of his glass to his nose and sniffed the bouquet as he examined the wine's color and texture.

"Well, it's pleasantly fragrant. The color is bit lighter than I would expect from a wine that's reputedly so strong. Hmmm, it does have strong legs. Let's have a small taste," Father said happily as he brought the glass to his lips.

"Very tannic! Is that cherry and a little vanilla?" Father asked, not sure that his unsophisticated palate met Phillip's standards.

"Very good, Father! Now wait until the veal arrives. You'll experience a completely different sensation."

Over an exquisite meal, Phillip brought Father Nachen up to date on Phil's accomplishments. Tentatively, Phillip began discussing his fears over his son's pending assignment in the infantry. Father understood and listened intently.

"Father, I've never admitted this to another human being. I can't even share this with my wife. For years now, I've had nightmares about the death of one of my men during the fight in the Argonne," Phillip revealed to the priest—relieved to finally unburden himself to a friend.

"What happened, Phillip?"

"Stephan covered my back, while I walked point for our platoon. We tried to flank a large, heavily entrenched German position. Obviously, I had to focus on our front. Somehow, I must have walked right by that damn Hun. The Boche had done a very good job concealing his position, but—in any event—I never saw him. Once we passed, he jumped up behind Stephan—a nice Greek kid from New York—and stabbed him through his neck and throat. I saw the whole thing in horrific detail. I can still see the boy's face as he died. It was awful! Father, it was my fault!"

"OK, I know what you saw. What did you do?" The priest asked.

"Turned out there were two Germans. I killed one with my bayonet and shot the guy who stabbed Stephan. I blew his brains out."

"I'll let you in on a little secret, Phillip. I've killed men in combat, too. I remember every grisly detail. I don't think you ever shake it," Father conceded. "Phillip, I've seen your citation for the Distinguished Service Cross. You were very brave. Nobody can control everything in combat. You can't blame yourself."

"OK, Father, but over the last few years in the dreams, Stephan's face always becomes Gin's face. It scares the hell out of me. I feel so responsible. Maybe if I'd done things differently, Gin wouldn't have to be a soldier when the whole planet is about to lose its mind—again!"

"I see," Father observed, as the waiter poured each man a full glass of the Barolo.

After picking at his food and listening to Phillip for another hour, Father suggested that Phillip do three things. These strategies would help Phillip to achieve a sense of peace.

"Phillip, you've got to come to terms with the fact that Gin will be an officer in the Army during a time of great danger. You must understand that there is nothing you could have personally done to change history or to affect your son's fate. That's in God's hands."

Father paused, took a sip of his wine and continued. "Even if Gin hadn't sought a commission through ROTC, he'd be subject to the draft that Congress is planning. If it's God's will for Gin to serve, it's pointless for you to fret about it. Look, you're a good Catholic. Look to your faith. I know it's strong."

Finally, speaking as a combat Marine to a highly decorated combat infantryman, Father advised that Phillip should address the issue with his son. Phillip should explain the dangers Phil would encounter.

The two men spent the afternoon discussing the problem. They finished the bottle of wine, another equally good bottle and part of a third before they formalized the plan. The next time young Phil came home, Phillip would implement it.

Today, Phillip and his son would take the first steps in executing the strategy that he'd concocted with Father Nachen. The only place to do that was their sanctuary at Waggoners Gap.

Phil pulled off the main road and onto the dirt path that led to the fence line that encircled the special hideaway. He drove several hundred yards until he encountered the locked fence that the power company had erected.

Phil turned sharply to the right and followed the fence for 80 yards until it ended at the base of a moderate incline. He shifted into first gear and drove up the slope of the hill. When he passed the end of the fence, he simply turned left and then sharply left again, now driving down the hill on the other side of the fence. Other than the tracks left by his tires in the wet grass, he left no evidence of his entry into the fenced-off area.

Phil continued to drive for another quarter mile, until the path became too rough for the car. At that point the two men got out of the roadster.

Phillip walked to the back of the vehicle and unfastened the latch of the rumble seat. As the seat unfolded, it revealed a long wooden case and two metal containers, each about 12 inches long, 12 inches high and six inches wide. Someone had stenciled Ammunition on the sides of both metal boxes.

"Dad, what's this all about?"

"Son, I've been thinking about this for several months. I want to talk to you about what you might face in the future. I thought I could give you some pointers," Phillip explained.

"I learned how to shoot from one of the best riflemen in the history of the Army," Phillip continued. "Until a month ago, I hadn't touched a rifle in over twenty years, so I was pretty rusty. I've been coming up here to practice my marksmanship for the last few weeks. You never really forget. I think I can help you improve."

"Dad, I'm an officer. They'll issue me a Colt .45 semi-automatic pistol. In some units, that's all I'll get, especially if I'm an S-2 on somebody's staff. Even if I'm a platoon leader in a rifle company, it'll be my job to direct fire, not to provide fire. I'm supposed to shoot my weapon as a last resort in self-defense. I don't have to be an expert rifleman to do my job."

"Son, I'm not talking about doing a job. I'm concerned about your survival in combat. That business about directing fire is fine for the textbooks and the classrooms, but it isn't how it always works in the field," Phillip responded, thinking of Sgt. Early, as he lay wounded in the glade so many years before, armed only with a .45.

"The better you're trained, the better you can defend yourself. I hope to God it never happens, but if you find yourself in a predicament that you didn't anticipate, I want you to be able to extricate yourself. You have the brains and the courage. I'm not worried about that. I want to assure myself that I did everything I could to prepare you," Phillip responded.

"Dad, there's obviously a rifle in that case. I don't mind shooting it with you, but you must know that I qualified as a sharpshooter at Camp A.P. Hill last summer," Phil explained, quite proud of his achievement.

"My recollection is that sharpshooter is good, but it's not expert. In addition to helping you to learn to shoot better, I want to talk about your state of mind in combat. I want to help to prepare you for what you might have to face. Knowing when and what to shoot is as important as knowing how."

Phillip continued, "I want to suggest ways of dealing with the prospect of killing, or directing your men to kill, another human being. I was only a corporal and you're a fancy new lieutenant, but humor me for the rest of the day. Doing this with me will help me deal with the fact that you may some-day be in a desperate battle for your life."

Phillip turned away from his son, reached into the rumble seat and took the long wooden case out of the roadster. He placed it on the ground and opened it. Inside was a military surplus 1903 .30 caliber Springfield bolt-action rifle. In the spring, Phil's father had purchased the rifle from a surplus outlet in Harrisburg. It was the same type that Phillip had used in France. The Army's tight budget through the depression ensured that it was also the same type issued to his son in training, almost 21 years later.

Phillip cradled the rifle in the crook of his arm, the muzzle pointed safely away. The two men walked about 25 yards from the car toward the crest of the hill. Turning a bend in the trail, Phil could see that his father had constructed a makeshift target range in their sanctuary. The hill on one side of the saddle served as the backstop. Across the way, about 75 yards, as the ground began to rise to the opposite peak, his dad had established a series of firing positions.

For the next few hours, Phillip demonstrated the skills that he'd learned from Alvin York. After only three stripper clips of ammunition, the son could see that his dad was a far better shot than he was. Impressed, Phil concentrated on the lessons that his dad tried to teach.

By late afternoon, after shooting hundreds of rounds, using the sighting, breathing, and concentration techniques that Phillip demonstrated, Phil improved significantly. "Let's take a break for the day and talk," Phillip suggested.

The men walked back to roadster. Phillip removed a compact cleaning kit from the back of the car. Phil went to the front, reached under the seat and found his SPO blanket. He returned to a spot behind the car and spread the blanket on the ground.

"Gin, I don't want to make a mess on your fraternity blanket," Phillip said.

"Don't worry, Dad. It's seen far worse," Phil said, and smiled lasciviously.

"That falls into the category of things that I don't want to know," Phillip chuckled. "I'm sure you were quite the Romeo. There must be a line of broken hearts from State College to Philadelphia."

Phil didn't respond, but continued to smile as his Dad began to arrange the equipment. Chortling over his son's shenanigans, Phillip sat down on the blanket and crossed his legs.

Phillip spread the cleaning equipment out all around him in a neat little arch. Phil noticed a toothbrush, a dental pick and shaving brush among the items from the kit. These everyday devices would make the job of cleaning the weapon much more efficient; another lesson learned.

The rifle that Phil carried into battle would serve as his truest ally. A soldier had to treat his rifle with great respect. Those infantrymen who failed to take proper care of their weapons would pay a costly price for their folly.

As Phillip disassembled the Springfield, he explained, "Gin, it was always our practice to clean our weapons after every fire-fight, no matter where we were or what we'd done. The only time I neglected that important chore was the day I got wounded in the Argonne."

As the two men cleaned the various parts of the rifle, Phillip began to tell his son the details of the battle in the Argonne. His dad punctuated the tale with periods of silence, when he needed to stop in order not to lose his composure. Phillip became more deliberate when he got to the circumstances of Stephan's death. The son could see that those events still deeply troubled his father.

As he listened, Phil stood in awe of his father. In his ROTC classes, he had examined several of the important battles of World War I, as well as selected engagements from the Spanish American War, the Indian Wars, the Civil War, the war with Mexico, and the Revolution. He'd never heard a combat veteran describe his experiences so poignantly.

Phillip stopped for a moment. He looked over at his son. With a passion his boy had seldom heard, Phillip said, "We're not at war, but I'll be surprised if we don't find ourselves in one very soon. France has fallen and signed an armistice with the Nazis. England is alone. We may be in a shooting war before you finish your term of service. If it's your fate to follow in my footsteps, you have to make certain commitments.

"When you are in the field, promise me that you'll focus on your duties. Put our family, Carlisle, the Gap, and any of your girlfriends out of your mind. You can't afford to be distracted. Combat is primitive. It's life or death. You must be mentally prepared to do whatever you have to do to come home."

"Dad, I won't forget how much you care about me. I can't tell you how much it means to me, that you would do this to help me survive. I promise I won't let you down," Phil said.

Phillip smiled at his son and added, "I know you won't. I have a feeling God will be with you. I will pray for you every day that you're away."

Phillip let out a heavy sigh. Then putting his fears in a hidden place in his heart, he smiled and looked up at his son.

"Let's get back and start helping your mom," Phillip suggested. "Marta's been driving me crazy with the details of Kari's wedding. Uncle Angelo is tuning up the mandolin and the rest of the family is getting excited. We're going to have a great time.

"One other thing, Gin," Phillip said. "Did you know that Linda's back in Carlisle? Did you know she was married? Junior hired her husband, Evan Collingswood, to work as a salesman in my department. I just thought you should know."

"Yeah, Dad, I heard. Kari told me three or four days ago," Gin responded. "Don't worry, Dad. Linda is ancient history. I haven't laid eyes on her in over three years. She doesn't mean a thing to me. I don't expect we'll see her at Kari's wedding."

Phillip laughed out loud at the thought, "That'll be the day."

Still laughing at the absurdity, the two men packed the car with the freshly cleaned rifle, ammunition, and equipment. They closed the rumble seat and walked around to the front of the vehicle.

Gin tossed the keys playfully to his dad. "Dad, you're such a good instructor, maybe you could give me another driving lesson."

"No, thank you. I don't ever want to repeat that painful experience," Phillip chuckled, as he tossed the keys back to his son. "You drive!"

The two Generos jumped into the car and, still laughing together, started down the road toward the fence.

# Chapter 16

The Infantry School commandant considered personnel and finance to be support functions. Though important, he declined to house these operations in the main building of the celebrated Infantry School. Instead, the commander situated the personnel and finance offices in less desirable quarters in 'temporary' buildings in the rear of the headquarters.

Perhaps in revenge for their predicament, administrative non-commissioned officers took pleasure in harassing the new second lieutenants from the basic course. These green young officers knew only enough about military protocol to be dangerous. They were vulnerable to the sadistic machinations of the bureaucrats.

This morning, they'd receive their final assignments, draw their regular pay, and receive a stipend to cover the costs of travel, rations, and lodging until they reached the next post.

All of the young officers felt relieved to depart Fort Benning to begin their regular duties. Potentially, they could receive assignments to Army units throughout the United States, Alaska, Hawaii, Panama, or the Philippines.

As they lined up, the officers organized themselves in alphabetical order. Phil Genero stood in the first third of the group sandwiched between Second Lieutenants Rich Garvey and Tom Gilbert.

Garvey, a strapping lad from Boerne, Texas, had graduated from Texas A&M where he'd led the infamous "D" Company of the Corps of Cadets as their student commander. Their notoriety had come from the company's antics and practical jokes, some of which were so macabre that the administration considered disbanding the group. Under Garvey's leadership the pranks became so weird that the Corps of Cadets began to refer to his company as "Spider" D because the more disciplined Aggies considered spiders to be creepy and peculiar.

Garvey loved to tell stories about Spider D on Friday nights at the Fort Benning Officer's Club. He was especially proud of the time his men kidnapped a fraternity president from the University of Texas, got him drunk, and then tied him to a cross in a ritualistic crucifixion on the quad on the night before the A&M-UT football game. He wasn't shy about stealing the credit for their bizarre shenanigans.

Because of his long-winded stories about D Company, his classmates in the Infantry School called Garvey "Spider." He liked the nickname a lot and even used it when he referred to himself.

In the weeks of training, Phil and Spider had spent time together on those occasions when it was necessary to stand in line. In the Army, standing in line became a way of life.

Although they were in the same basic officer's class, Garvey and Genero served in different training sections. They never interacted during the classroom work or in-the-field problems and live-fire exercises. Over the last eight weeks, given the Infantry School's unique organizational imperatives, which demanded a rigid alphabetical order when the class formed up as a unit, they'd spent several hours waiting in line next to each other. On those occasions they formed enough of an acquaintance to counteract the boredom of attending upon the whims of the bureaucracy. They used the time to share their own impressions of the training.

Second Lieutenant Gilbert stood in line behind Genero on these administrative occasions. Since they were in the same section, they'd actually trained together and grew to be friends. Gilbert hailed from a little beach town south of Los Angeles. He'd attended UCLA, where he'd studied history and majored in chasing co-eds.

Gilbert bragged about his accomplishments at UCLA. He surely would have won the Distinguished Military Cadet Award, if it weren't for the irritating fact that out of the class of 21 students, 20 cadets graduated ahead of him in the military order of merit.

Tom Gilbert cut an impressive figure. He'd wrestled at UCLA and had been a weightlifter since high school. Though he was of average height, he possessed a massive, highly muscled upper body, with huge arms.

As the lieutenants waited in the sultry morning air, the three young officers discussed the possibilities of their assignments, and what they planned to do, if any got leave in transit to the next post.

"I'm hoping ta get stationed at Fort Bliss. That's about 450 miles from our ranch in Boerne. I got a girl back home and I'm hoping ta marry her, soon as I settle in to ma assignment," Garvey explained.

"Spider, are you sure that you want to get married right away?" Gilbert asked.

Garvey responded enthusiastically, "My momma didn't raise no fools! Ann's the prettiest thing you ever saw. She's a real sweet girl and lots of fun. I know she's crazy about the Spider, but she ain't going ta wait around until I get done being a soldier. She wants ta get married right away. She thinks traveling round with a lootenant and seeing the world could be exciting."

"What if you get sent overseas?" Phil asked Spider.

"That could be a problem," Garvey admitted.

"What about you, Gilbert? What do you want to do?" Spider asked.

"Don't think it matters what I want, does it? The Army's going to send me wherever it wants, right? If I ask for something, they'll send me somewhere else, just for spite," Gilbert answered. "If they want to know what I'd prefer, I'd like to get into the Airborne Test Platoon. Unfortunately, they've got all the officers they need for now."

An experimental unit, the Airborne Test Platoon explored the concept of using paratroopers in combat. The Russians and the Germans had worked with paratroopers for many years. The Soviets and Nazis called the employment of these forces in battle *Vertical Envelopment.*

The Germans had successfully employed paratroopers and glider-borne soldiers in the spring of 1940, during their conquest of Western Europe. The instructors at the Infantry School believed that the Germans could not have achieved the important tactical surprises and stunning battle successes without the use of their airborne forces to capture bridges and strong points in the Low Countries, ahead of their mechanized forces. The dramatic assault and capture of the impregnable Fortress Eben Emael in Belgium by a handful of daring German paratroopers, using specially configured gliders, had deeply impressed both the Army instructors and their students.

To an American military that had no viable airborne force even in the planning stages, it was sobering. Senior planners all the way to the Army Chief of Staff expressed concern. After some thought, the Army established an embryonic airborne test unit and stationed it at Fort Benning.

Phil had heard of the small unit of volunteers that trained in an old hanger down by Lawson Field. Phil liked the idea of parachuting from a plane and descending gracefully to earth. It reminded Phil of the eagles, hawks, and falcons at Waggoners Gap. If he got the chance, he'd volunteer.

In the middle of Gilbert's discussion about the Army's attempt to field an airborne force, a personnel clerk interrupted and called for Lieutenant Garvey. A few moments later, Phil got his turn. He walked inside and took a seat next to Sergeant Carlson's desk. The middle-aged buck sergeant greeted him enthusiastically. "Good morning Lieutenant Genero. I'll bet you're glad that this day finally came."

"No question about it, Sergeant," Genero replied, smiling. "Don't keep me in suspense. Which regiment did I draw?"

"Sir, you ain't going to a regiment at all," Sergeant Carlson responded matter-of-factly. "Seems the Army has unique plans for you. You're going to Washington, to a special assignment at the War Department, War Plans Division. You're going to work for Colonel Moses in the European Section. You'll be rubbing elbows with the top dogs in less than a week."

Phil had expected to go to an infantry regiment or to a training post, to help with the massive training mission that the new draft would generate. He had secretly hoped for a unit in Hawaii or the Philippines. Instead, he had these astonishing orders to Washington, D.C.

"Lieutenant, take a tip from an old soldier. This assignment will be difficult at first. You're a brand new butter bar. Everybody in Washington, including the janitor at the War Department, will out rank you. Every shit detail that comes down will be your responsibility. Just keep your sense of humor and you'll find opportunities to advance your career, sir."

I'll try to keep my nose clean. Thanks."

Sgt. Carlson directed Phil to the next station, where Genero would get his final pay and travel advance. Genero offered his hand to the non-com. Sgt. Carlson wished the young officer good luck. Phil sped through the rest of the process. As soon as he had his files and orders organized into a manageable pile, he carried them outside to see what had befallen Spider and Gilbert.

Both of his comrades stood in the shade, waiting for him. They'd received orders to Fort Bliss. Spider was very happy. Gilbert was not. Gilbert vowed to return to Benning as soon as the Army would allow him to volunteer for the paratroopers.

"Genero, your orders seem mighty strange! What business does a second lieutenant have on such a senior staff? Boy, I'm glad it's you and not me," Spider observed.

"Just make the best of it. Who knows? You could make some great contacts. Besides, what other choice do you have?" Gilbert asked.

The three officers walked together toward the orderly room, where they'd wait in line, again. This time they'd sign out of the unit, and begin their travel to the next station. Phil had the roadster packed.

It would normally take two days to get up to Washington, but Genero had arranged for a three-day pass in route. He'd promised his dad that he would take a detour into the Valley of the Wolf River, if his assignment permitted. After all these years, Phillip Edward Genero, II would pay his respects to Sergeant York. Maybe they'd go shooting.

# Chapter 17

2330 Hours
December 5, 1940
Shannon Seaplane Terminal
Shannon River Estuary
Foynes, Eire (Southwestern Ireland)

E xhausted from the trip, Phil sat quietly in a corner of the quaint Irish Seaplane Terminal, between the small bar and the roaring fire. He'd been awake for 20 hours.

He'd danced very close to the edge of a career-ending precipice.

His chest throbbed with pain. His ribs felt like they did when he'd cracked them playing football against Pitt in his junior year at Penn State. *God, I hope I haven't broken my ribs again. The colonel will never understand,* Phil worried.

Genero turned awkwardly in the winged-back leather chair, trying to find a more comfortable position. Scraped and swollen, his right hand wouldn't clench into a fist.

*Damn, I might have broken my hand, too!* Phil thought. As a precaution, he kept his damaged hand covered by the file folder in his lap, no point in advertising the injury.

Worn out from their long sojourn, the senior Army officers and State Department officials had dispersed among the small terminal's tables and booths, where they read, smoked, chatted, or snoozed.

The older men took full advantage of this rest stop to belly up to the well-stocked bar. Not that there was any shortage of booze on the flying boat. On this mission, the Boeing aircraft had certainly proved that it was the way to travel.

In the last half hour, the group's activity level had dropped dramatically. Genero could afford to take a little break. After checking around the room to ensure that everyone was occupied, he closed his eyes for a moment, ignoring the pain in his side and hand. With his good left hand, Phil balanced a pint of Guinness on his knee, his second of the evening.

The diplomatic entourage would rest once they reboarded the clipper. Even now, the crew labored to make up the sleeping quarters. The Americans had a very long flight to Botwood, Newfoundland, the next stop on the clipper's itinerary.

As Phil tried to reestablish his equilibrium, he recounted the events of the mission. Through both elation and dread, he recognized that a rookie second lieutenant had no business on an assignment like this one. The opportunity that had once seemed so fortuitous now threatened to be his undoing. *I just hope that I haven't fucked it up for good and all,* Phil thought as he recalled the encounter in Marseilles.

In spite of his trepidation, Phil couldn't help but smile at his overall good fortune. A year before he'd been a college student. He'd only been with the European Section of the War Plans Division for eight weeks, when he learned that he'd make this trip.

Tonight, he was traveling back to Washington aboard a chartered, ultra-luxurious, Boeing 314 flying boat, operated by Inter-continental Airlines on its North Atlantic route. For the last few weeks he'd accompanied the State and War Departments' mission to negotiate with Henri-Philippe Petain, Marshall of France, and head of the vestigial French government.

A hero of World War I, Marshall Petain became the Premier of what was left of the French government after the Nazi conquest and the Armistice. Currently, French civil authority in unoccupied France resided in the picturesque spa town in Auvergne Province, known as Vichy, 400 hundred kilometers south of Paris.

In 1940, in light of the stark and unforgiving geopolitical realities, President Roosevelt quietly pursued a strategy called the Two France Policy. Phil had assumed that this policy reflected a plan for dealing with occupied France, controlled entirely by the Nazis; and unoccupied France, controlled by the Nazis with a puppet government headed by Petain and his deputy, Pierre Laval. In reality, the President's policy simply recognized that the Vichy Government retained titular control of the French colonies all over the world. Since the United States needed certain vital resources, like rubber from Southeast Asia, the American government made accommodations with Petain's regime at Vichy. The Americans did not deal directly with occupied France on any issue.

The second French entity, the Free French government-in-exile, had situated itself in London, a city still reeling from the German air assault that the *Washington Post* called the Battle of Britain. Though unelected, General Charles De Gaulle had proclaimed himself to be the leader of the Free French contingent. Until the conquest of his homeland, he'd fought the Nazis as a commander of a division of the French armored forces.

President Roosevelt never trusted De Gaulle. He declined to endorse the general's ambitions. Ever the politician, Roosevelt did agree to provide limited support to the Free French. The President wanted to cover his bets in the event that De Gaulle ever assumed power in a liberated France, a proposition that in 1940 seemed very remote.

Roosevelt played one French entity off the other when it advanced American interests. For his part, De Gaulle understood and deeply resented the American practice.

On this trip, American distress over recent Vichy concessions to the Japanese in Indochina motivated the discussions with Petain. In the summer of 1940, the Japanese government took advantage of Germany's overwhelming victory in Europe and France's weakened position in its colonies in Southeast Asia. Through extortion and force, Japan controlled Tonkin, Annam, and Cochin-China, the three most precious jewels in the crown of French Indochina.

The Japanese allowed the French to maintain their colonial garrisons. Although thousands of French and colonial troops remained at their posts in Indochina, the Japanese preserved firm control, establishing air and naval bases in strategic locations throughout the three colonies. Their military build-up pissed off the Americans, who saw the change in the region's geopolitics as a threat to critical supplies and trade.

Tens of thousands of Japanese soldiers in Indochina threatened the Nationalist Chinese forces of General Chang Kai-shek in China. The Imperial Japanese Navy's presence in Cam Ranh Bay menaced the American military position in the Philippines across the South China Sea, and threatened British forces to the south in Singapore and Malaysia.

In early November 1940, Roosevelt won his controversial—and unprecedented—third Presidential term. Now safe from political backlash, President Roosevelt dispatched a team of State Department diplomats to Vichy to evaluate the Indochinese question. The President directed them to negotiate and cajole the French into retracting some of the concessions that they'd made to the Japanese.

After Election Day, the diplomats embarked upon a trans-oceanic liner, flying the neutral American flag. They sailed across the U-boat infested Atlantic, bound for the Mediterranean port of Marseilles.

The President's envoy and political crony, Ambassador Frederick T. Curtis, took his team halfway across the ocean, where they met in a conference room on their ship to discuss the details of their negotiations. Realizing that their mission would benefit from the participation of military experts, they requested representatives from the War Department's Asian and European Sections, a supply expert, and a tactician.

The envoy used the ship's wireless to radio a message to the Army Chief-of-Staff, General Marshall. He recommended that the Army personnel travel by air immediately in order to meet the State Department negotiating team in Lyon to plan for the conference with the Vichy diplomats.

Marshall considered the request for a day. Though he viewed the mission as a fool's errand, he supported President Roosevelt without question. He chose one of his best men: Colonel Harold T. Moses, Chief of the European Section's French Department. A Rhodes Scholar and a West Point graduate (Class of 1916), Moses would act as the officer in charge of the Army element.

Moses selected three of the European section's best field grade officers to accompany him to Vichy. He coaxed his counterpart in Asian to lend him a bright major, one of the few Army officers who knew anything substantial about Indochina.

While making his plans for the trip, Moses had an epiphany. *I could use an aide-de-camp, but I'm only a colonel. A special assistant would come in handy, even if all he did was carry the bags and run errands for my officers and the friggin' diplomats from Foggy Bottom,* Moses thought to himself.

Moses had just the right young man in his own section. A new lieutenant, big, strong, and capable of carrying baggage, he'd proved to be smart as a whip—a very impressive lad.

Three months earlier, Moses received notice that Army Personnel wanted to assign a second lieutenant, fresh out of the basic infantry course, to War Plans. Worse, the new officer would work in his department.

Moses could see no justification for such an unusual assignment, other than the young man possessed remarkable linguistic gifts in German, Italian, and French. Since most of his officers spoke at least one foreign language, Col. Moses did not view Genero's unique ability as critical or even necessary to the European Section.

Col. Moses ran an efficient operation and had no time to babysit a boy officer. New lieutenants weren't called shave tails—referring to the results achieved by the old cavalry practice of severely trimming the tail on Army mules—for nothing. For over 160 years, the U.S. Army had thrust freshly commissioned lieutenants into leadership positions where they routinely screwed up while they learned the complicated and deadly business of the profession of arms.

*It would have been a hell of a lot better if the geniuses in J-1 had assigned Genero to an infantry regiment. He'd have an opportunity to learn the ropes and make mistakes without causing too much damage or compromising his career. It's like a fishbowl here. If he screws the pooch at War Plans, everyone including the Chief of Staff will hear about it,* Moses reflected as he considered how he might use Phil to complete this new mission.

Officers who'd served since World War I bitterly remembered a peacetime Army severely constrained by budget limitations, the depression, and political intrigue. During those lean times, promotions came slowly. Moses had struggled to rise from second lieutenant to major—a climb that took him 20 years. Because of the expansion of forces brought on by the international emergency, he'd risen in temporary grades to full colonel, and only because he was a protégé of the Army Chief of Staff.

After watching Phil for two months, Moses concluded that Genero had real potential. At first, Colonel Moses rode Phil hard. Genero responded with a positive attitude, discipline, maturity, and a keen sense of humor. *This lad is greener than grass, but damn, he's got real promise,* Moses concluded.

Though not critical to the mission, Genero's linguistic abilities did impress Moses. Moses spoke German, French, and Russian fluently. He'd fought in France in the Great War as a young lieutenant. Later, he'd served as an exchange officer with the French armored forces in the late twenties. Because of his diplomatic skills and proven military achievements, he secured a post as a visiting professor at the French Military Academy at St. Cyr. Moses spoke French like a true Parisian.

Genero did not speak French as well as the colonel. He had minor difficulty with some pronunciations, causing him to sound more like a provincial from North Africa. Still, Genero understood virtually everything that he heard spoken in French. Genero processed information faster, and translated to English more accurately, than anyone Moses had ever met.

After thinking it over, Moses decided, *I'm going to take Genero along. I can use this big strapping farm boy. He'll carry bags, run errands, and scoop up the ground balls that get past my infielders. He'll also keep his highly trained ear to the ground.*

With this in mind on November 14th, Col. Moses called Genero into his small office to have a little chat.

"Sir, you wanted to see me?" Genero inquired, upon reporting to Col. Moses.

"Yes, I do. Have a seat. I have something I want to talk to you about," Col. Moses responded, directing Phil to the only other chair in his small space.

"Lieutenant, I have an important assignment for you. I've decided to take you along on the trip to Vichy. We'll be gone between three and four weeks. We're leaving on Saturday, the sixteenth, which is the day after tomorrow. It's not much notice, but you'll have to make do. Any problems?" Moses inquired.

"None, sir! But...why me?" Phil asked.

"Mister Genero, we've had very little warning that we'd be going on this State Department boondoggle. We're making it up as we go along. I've accounted for every contingency, but there's always the unexpected gremlin in the machinery, isn't there?" the colonel asked. "You're coming along precisely because you are neither a diplomat nor a military expert. You'll play *rover* on our diplomatic military team. You'll do everything that I direct you to do. Feel up to it?" Moses challenged.

"Sure, sir. I'm your man!" Genero responded.

"Good answer! The next question I have is whether you have guile and the soul of an actor?" Col. Moses wondered.

"I have no idea what you're talking about, sir."

"Listen up, and I'll tell you what I expect from you. The day after tomorrow we'll take the train to Long Island. At Port Washington, we'll embark upon the Yankee Clipper for Lisbon. The flying boat stops in Bermuda and the Azores. Better check on the itinerary for me.

"The French government will send a military transport to Lisbon to pick us up and fly us to Lyon. From Lyon we'll take a train ride to Vichy. Those details are settled. Confirm them for me. We know where we'll link up with the State Department folks in Lyon. Are you with me so far?" Moses asked.

"Yes, sir. I understand," Phil responded.

"On the first leg of the trip, you'll be the errand boy. You make sure every one of my officers has everything he needs. You insure that the luggage makes every connection. Got it?" Col. Moses asked pointedly.

"Yes, sir."

"I'm sure you're wondering why I don't take an enlisted man or non-commissioned officer to do this. Usually I would. I don't need a lieutenant to carry the bags, but you have special talent," Moses explained.

"What special talent is that, sir?"

"You have the doe in the headlights look about you. You are the epitome of a second lieutenant. If I wrote to Hollywood, I couldn't have gotten a more perfect specimen from Central Casting. Do you understand?" Moses asked.

"Sir, I haven't a clue what you're talking about," Gin answered.

"And, you're honest, too. Great! Well, here's the scoop," Moses continued. "You speak French very well, but you don't speak it perfectly. I'll fix that, given time. I've noticed that you have no trouble with most of the metropolitan dialects. On this trip, you'll act—pretend, really—that you're a stupid boy officer who's along to wait on the senior men. You'll keep your mouth shut and your ears open. You'll listen to everything.

"If I know my Frenchmen, once they think you can't speak their language, they'll talk openly in French in your presence," Moses explained. "They'll say things, many of them insulting, while you're standing around looking hopeless. Some of that might prove useful for the envoy and I to know. Now do you understand?"

"You want me to feign that I'm not francophone to lure the Vichy folks into a false sense of security, so that they'll make admissions, like while I'm running some errand. Right, sir? I report those statements to you."

"That's about the size of it," Moses replied.

"I can easily do that, sir."

"We'll practice from this point on," Moses said. "I'll speak to you in English, German and French. You're to respond only to directions and commands in English. I'll have Major Jardine do the same. If you act like you understand the German or French, I'll hand you your head. Get it?"

"Yes, sir. It's quite clear. No problem," Gin responded.

"Then get moving, my young friend, and find out the Yankee Clipper's itinerary. Report back to me when you have the information," Col. Moses directed in perfect French with a friendly smile.

Lieutenant Genero gave the Colonel a vacant, puzzled look, and shook his head slightly from side to side. Phil continued to look at the Colonel with a little smile.

"You ignorant whelp, you'd better move when I give you an order, or you'll find yourself back in Georgia, commanding a detail of yard birds shoveling shit for whatever mules we have left in this man's Army!" Col. Moses barked angrily in French.

Phil reacted to the angry shout by flinching, and demonstrating a very concerned demeanor. He gave the Colonel a troubled look.

Genero responded haltingly, "I'm sorry, sir, but I don't... how do you say...Parleez Vow Francois. Do you speak English?"

Col. Moses broke into a wide grin, and laughed out loud despite himself. Phil's acting had impressed him.

"Well done, lad. That's better than I expected from you. You'll do well. Now get moving. That will be all," Moses said in German, with a slight Bavarian lilt.

Genero did not move. He just sat in his chair. Then he began to fidget uncomfortably. Finally, after a pause, Phil responded in pidgin German, "No spriken mine heroine."

Once again Moses laughed out loud. "Genero, you are an actor out of work. This is better than I expected. You passed the first test with flying colors. Jardine and I will be setting traps for you, so don't let your guard down. If you would be so kind, get your ass moving and find out about the itinerary. Be quick about it. I've got lots for you to do this morning."

Phil did as the Colonel bid. The Yankee Clipper's itinerary would take the team from Port Washington to Bermuda, then to the tiny village of Horta in the Azores. Counting rest stops, necessary maintenance and flight time, cruising at considerably less than 200 knots per hour, that part of the trip would take almost two days. From Horta, it would require nearly half a day to reach Lisbon.

Genero confirmed with the French consul in Washington that the Vichy government had arranged to have a military transport pick them up in Lisbon and fly them to Lyon. Additional arrangements would have to be made to get the Army team from the Lisbon port facilities to the commercial air terminal. Phil started making inquiries.

Counting the flight to Lyon and the train trip to Vichy, the trek from Washington would take at least three days. That was much faster than going by boat.

Bright and early on November 16, 1940, the six Army officers assembled at Union station and embarked on the train for the first leg of the journey. Phil arranged for two staff cars and a small truck from Fort Hamilton to meet them at Penn Central Station in order to ferry them to Port Washington in Long Island. By late afternoon on the 16th, Genero had loaded the luggage and the Army personnel had boarded the Pan Am flying boat.

Once airborne, they cruised gracefully across the Atlantic toward Bermuda. The Army staff settled into the accommodations, which exceeded first class.

Inter-continental divided the passenger section, situated on the lower deck of the two level aircraft, into several separate and spacious compartments. Each compartment contained ten comfortable seats, situated in two rows facing each other, in the style of European train accommodations.

At mealtime, the large room in the center of the lower section became a formal dining room. At each sitting, an accomplished and attentive staff served a gourmet meal on genuine china and crystal. Between meals, the crew attended to the passengers, providing them with all manner of libation and snacks.

Traveling in this manner, the time passed acceptably for all of the Army officers, except Col. Moses who could not shake a sense of foreboding. *If the diplomats aren't able to get the concessions that the Japanese extorted from Vichy, President Roosevelt will convince Congress to pass sanctions against the Japanese Empire. That will lead to war,* Col Moses thought as he pondered the basic dilemma. *Roosevelt will never let the Japs establish their Greater East Asian Co-prosperity Sphere in Southeast Asia. That would amount to an economic monopoly over vital raw materials. We have serious interests there, too. It's beginning to look ominous.*

While Genero and the other officers enjoyed the trip, Moses fidgeted and obsessed the entire time. Even the gourmet meals failed to lighten his demeanor. Only the fine wines, and then only the full-bodied and aromatic Bordeauxs, mellowed his somber mood.

The Army officers planned to meet with the diplomats in Lyon for two days of briefings before the reinforced entourage traveled the remaining distance to Vichy by train. The Army element arrived at their destination 36 hours *before* the diplomats, who were delayed in their disembarkation at Marseilles.

Col. Moses' group received new instructions to proceed to Vichy. They had to make preparations for the arrival of the State Department diplomats.

Since Phil had no diplomatic role, once the soldiers reached Vichy his only non-clandestine job required him to attend upon Maj. Jardine and follow his instructions to the letter. Genero gave the appearance that he was not conversant in French or German, and was along on this diplomatic enterprise to run errands for the bigwigs.

The Vichy government billeted the soldiers and diplomats in a comfortable hotel that in simpler times catered to tourists who traveled to Vichy to take its famous waters. The Army team assumed that Vichy agents surreptitiously monitored all of their rooms. They would attempt no conversations of any consequence at the hotel, or at the Vichy government offices.

The American government maintained a small consulate in Vichy. Once a grand town home for a well-to-do vintner, it rested close to the hotel where the Americans were staying.

A five-story building, constructed in the French classic motif, the architect had set the town house back in a small private cul-de-sac, off the main street. To fulfill its new role, the State Department had converted many of its rooms into offices and meeting facilities.

A senior Foreign Service professional, Mr. Jean Montenegro, managed the consulate and its diplomatic affairs on behalf of the United States. Montenegro had served in France for 20 years. For the current negotiations he provided a small, completely secure conference facility for the American team.

Vichy had experienced war shortages of most necessities and all luxuries. Montenegro prided himself on his ability to obtain the hard-to-get. As a sideline, Montenegro made a small fortune on the black market, which had blossomed in unoccupied France over the last six months.

When the State Department diplomats finally arrived in Vichy, Genero observed that these men appeared to be starkly different from the officers in the Army contingent. The diplomats had an irritating habit of never saying what they meant. They mastered the art of talking around, but never addressing, an issue. To Phil, it seemed like a lot of equivocation.

Phil noticed that nearly all of the diplomats were well fed. He hadn't anticipated that the State Department team would include so many fat and sloppy men.

When he mentioned this to Maj. Jardine, the older officer snickered. A career officer who'd served in World War I, Daniel Jardine had not graduated from the Military Academy. Born and raised in Louisiana, a place that he described as Looseeanna, after high school, he had decided to pursue a career in the military.

In 1912, Daniel Jardine had passed up the opportunity to attend the Naval Academy, choosing instead the Virginia Military Institute. Although promotions had been slower for him than other officers of his year group, his superiors held him in high regard as a consummate professional. Now that the Army Chief-of-Staff was a brother rat, the West Point Protection Association might not network so effectively, and the promotion picture for VMI grads might improve.

Jardine liked his new protégé. He loved Phil's enthusiasm, and his naiveté. Phil's assessment of the diplomats amused the older man.

In response to Genero's observation, Jardine explained tongue-in-cheek, "Genero, these diplomats do a lot of their work at dinners, banquets, parties, and conferences. The ambassadors try to out-do each other by laying on lavish spreads and serving gourmet meals of the finest quality. As you know, the Lord blesses soldiers with a life of discipline and privation, while the poor diplomats are forced to serve their country by attending grand balls with champagne, cocktails, and exceptional wine. So, you see that fine china and lead crystal are to Foreign Service men what the rusty mess kit and leaky canteen with treated water are to the field soldier."

Fully understanding the sarcasm, Genero pressed his mentor, "Sir, I'm sure it's a real sacrifice for the diplomats to have to eat and drink so well, but why do all of the State

Department men, especially the envoy, treat all of the Army officers, including Col. Moses, in such a condescending and patronizing way? It's really pathetic, sir."

Major Jardine had an explanation for this as well, "Oh, that's simple. They're all assholes, pricks, and prima donnas."

Jardine vented further, "Every arrogant diplomat from Foggy Bottom—and in my career I haven't met another kind—thinks that the military was invented to provide the State Department with fancy uniformed lackeys. That's why they like the Marines. The leathernecks have those pretty dress blues. It's the best looking uniform in the entire American arsenal. Gotta admit it, Genero, the Marines do make a superb impression standing guard outside a major embassy."

Jardine paused in the hotel lobby, where they were talking, to take a Lucky Strike from the well-worn gold cigarette case that he kept in the inside pocket of his uniform blouse. After searching his pockets for a match, he put the cigarette to his lips, bent over slightly, and allowed Genero to light it for him with the new gunmetal grey Zippo lighter that Phil now carried full time for just such an exigency.

Jardine took a long, slow drag into the depths of his lungs. As he removed the cigarette from his lips, with fingers stained slightly yellow, Jardine continued his mentoring. "Get used to it, Mr. Genero. There's nothing we can do about it. As far as you're concerned, you are a fancy uniformed lackey."

Seeing that Genero was taken aback, Jardine continued with more camaraderie. "Genero, why do think that God created second lieutenants and posted them to senior planning staffs? To fetch for their betters and to teach them a little humility, of course," Jardine said, with a paternalistic little smile, as he patted Genero on the back. "It'll be OK, Lieutenant. Do what Colonel Moses instructed. Keep your eye on the prize, your mouth shut and ears open."

Finally, the major concluded, "Also, see if you can get some decent American smokes from the consulate. I didn't bring enough to last me, and I definitely don't want to smoke those awful French coffin nails."

For the balance of the time in Vichy, Genero acted as concierge, errand boy, and luggage handler. He had no time for himself. At Col. Moses' behest, he accompanied Maj. Jardine and LtCol. Edison on their regular sojourns to the local nightclubs. Moses wanted to insure that somebody would assist the senior officers to find their way back to the hotel.

Phil didn't attend the official negotiations at the Vichy government offices other than to bring items in or take messages out. He traveled to the site each day and stood around outside in the vestibule looking vacuous and hopeless, waiting for some menial chore or errand to run.

As Col. Moses predicted, once the French officials and security men got Genero's measure, they concluded that he was a harmless young dolt. At first, they addressed him in French, to test his knowledge of their language.

When Genero didn't respond, or assured them in primitive French that he couldn't speak even a modicum of the most cultured language in the history of western civilization, the Frenchmen treated him with unflagging disdain. After a time, they ignored him. All of the Vichy officials spoke English well, but they believed that it was beneath their station to converse with a servant, and especially in so barbaric a tongue.

Through the ruse that Colonel Moses affected upon the French, Genero found himself in a position to pick up an amazing amount of interesting, but mostly irrelevant, gossip. The Frenchmen could be very bawdy and deeply profane.

Some of their profanity and ribald jargon confused Genero, young and inexperienced as he was. Fortunately, Maj. Jardine had made a lifelong, personal study of the tawdry side of French culture. He could usually explain the gritty nuances to Phil.

After the official negotiations began, it took Phil a little more than a week to conclude that French diplomats were cut from the same cloth as their American counterparts. They just worked the other side of the street.

As the days wore on, Genero learned a lot about which French officials were screwing which wives of other Vichy bureaucrats. Phil observed that such behavior was apparently OK with everyone, and within acceptable moral limits in that community. He also heard that some of the French officials might occasionally dally with a colleague's mistress. In contrast, the Frenchmen considered that conduct to be insulting and totally unforgivable, providing grounds for a duel to the death.

Phil became so good at eavesdropping on the French conversations that he could work at other menial tasks while listening to two or more French officials insulting the Americans as they waited outside the conference for a car to take them to some local bistro. He understood that the Frenchmen thought he was an imbecile.

By the end of the first week, an unusual pattern in the French conversations emerged. In addition to the gossip, the officials felt comfortable enough around Genero to drop the odd comment about the geopolitical circumstances that formed the underpinnings for the negotiations with the Americans.

These admissions amounted to gold nuggets panned from tons of tailings in a cold, fast-moving river. Phil reported them to Moses at the evening debriefings that the team conducted in the consulate's third floor conference room. Col. Moses allowed Phil to attend those meetings to get instructions on what errands to run for the next day.

Phil eventually concluded that the envoy realized that the Vichy government could not change the nature or extent of its concessions with the Japanese in Indochina. That circumstance appeared to be a *fait accompli.*

Phil surmised that the real goal of the American diplomats was to use the Indochina negotiations to determine if Vichy would remain a puppet vassal of the Third Reich or become an active ally in the Nazi plan for world domination. The possibility of a French and German alliance caused grave concern in the State and War Departments.

France had considerable economic, industrial, and financial resources in Europe. Thousands of its soldiers remained prisoners of war in Germany, and the Nazis could reorganize them quickly under a joint German/Vichy command structure. The French colonies could supply substantial manpower and resources to the German war effort.

Conversely, the Vichy government had cause to resent their former British allies. Four months earlier, on July 3rd, the British Navy had attacked several French ships of the line. The surprise assault occurred while the French warships were moored at the port of Mers-el-Kebir, Algeria. The British justified their preemptive strike as an act of self-defense, designed to keep the world's fourth largest navy from falling under the control of the Nazis.

The British attack caused an appalling loss of life and destruction among the French forces and capital ships. Not one British sailor, marine, or airman suffered injury.

After the British attack, the Vichy government broke off diplomatic ties with England. France came within a hair's breath of declaring war on its erstwhile ally. By late November 1940, the passage of time had done nothing to assuage the outrage and anger that the French felt toward the treachery of their former ally.

As Phil learned from his eavesdropping, an influential lobby in the French government fully supported a formal military alliance with Hitler. Deputy Prime Minister Laval spoke with the most important pro-Nazi voice.

The current American military establishment did not impress French Officials. France saw itself as a continental power. Though the French diplomats conceded that the *Amis* had an impressive navy, they believed that the small and ill-equipped Army of the United States could not fight a modern, mechanized war in Europe.

The French knew that the United States could mobilize sufficient force to defend itself. It didn't seem likely, in light of the isolationist sentiment, that the Americans would stick their necks out again, especially for a former ally that Germany had defeated in less than six weeks.

Each evening, Col. Moses would receive Phil's report at the end of the debriefing. Phil gave sharp, crisp, insightful, and professional nightly summaries. He even managed to impress Ambassador Curtis.

"Harry, the boy's a natural," the ambassador observed, as he chatted with Moses after Genero provided a juicy report concerning one of Laval's assistants, who was sleeping with the wife of the Romanian consul. "He's got a real nose for intelligence gathering. He's smart, patient, resourceful, and careful. He knows his place. He'd go far in the State Department."

"You can't have him, Fred. He's Army. Besides, he's like a bull in a china shop. He's got great potential, but he's got a lot to learn, and a bunch of dues to pay."

Formal negotiations with the Vichy officials started on Thursday, November 21st. In 1940, due to a controversial executive order issued by President Roosevelt; Americans would celebrate Thanksgiving on the third Thursday, the 21st of November, rather than the traditional fourth Thursday.

True to their duty, the negotiators simply ignored the holiday, and focused on their work. That is, all of the Americans except Genero.

During one of his conversations with Consul Montenegro, Phil mentioned that he disagreed with the economic justifications, which the administration used to move the Thanksgiving holiday up one week. Montenegro agreed.

Montenegro offered to arrange a true Thanksgiving feast for all of the diplomats, including the French officials, on the traditional date, which would have been the 28th. Through his black market connections, Montenegro produced two big turkeys, a fat goose, a respectable ham, a large beef roast, sweet potatoes, fresh cranberries, pumpkin pie, and some superb French ice cream.

Montenegro advised Genero that he would supply a case of inexpensive, but very drinkable, Chardonnay. After some consideration of the tastes of the Vichy officials, Montenegro thought the 'Chard' might prove to be too buttery for turkey and goose. So, to insure that the French wine snobs were not offended, he decided to include six or seven bottles of his favorite Viognier, which was drier, but equally fruity.

The idea of throwing an official Thanksgiving party on the 28th, despite the executive order, so delighted Montenegro, that he covered most of the cost of the affair from his slush fund. The team's administrative account easily resolved the balance.

Late in the afternoon of the 28th, the negotiators broke early and repaired to the American consulate for traditional Thanksgiving festivities. Everyone enjoyed the occasion. Throughout the celebration, with generously filled glasses of the white wine, they toasted each other, the heads of their respective governments, and their eternal friendship.

After several glasses of the Viognier, Ambassador Curtis spoke to Maj. Jardine. "Danny, your boy, Genero, is a wonder. He worked his ass off to make this celebration a success. I've been thinking. I could use him, his enthusiasm, and his special skills when we return for the second round of negotiations next spring. Speak to Colonel Moses and see if you can spare the lad."

The following week, the negotiations concluded after accomplishing exactly nothing. Most of the diplomats and soldiers spent part of one day doing a little sight seeing. Afterward, they made preparations for the return.

Anxious for the debriefing, President Roosevelt took the uncharacteristic step of authorizing the Secretary of State to charter an entire Inter Continental Boeing 314 for the joint team's return. The administration needed to plot its next move in the geopolitical chess match.

Moses tasked Phil to arrange the details. While he made the calls, Curtis spent time with an old flame, the wife of the Romanian envoy. Col. Moses chose to prowl around the hotel terrorizing the Army staff and huffing at everyone in sight.

Genero arranged for the entire team to leave Vichy for Lyon on the Fourth of December. They'd layover in a nice pension in Lyon, and take the train to Marseilles early on the Fifth. The Americans would arrive in Marseilles in the afternoon, travel to the port, and embark upon the chartered flying boat by early evening. The Boeing would fly them to Ireland, Newfoundland, Nova Scotia, and then New York, carefully avoiding the continuous air battle over England.

The Seaplane Terminal in Southwestern Ireland lay along the Shannon River Estuary. A route well to the south and west of England would probably keep them out of danger with the Luftwaffe.

By late morning on December 5, 1940, the entire party of diplomats and soldiers traveled peacefully along the French rail system approaching the southern coast of France. That's where the serious trouble began.

While the accommodations on the train to Marseilles proved to be satisfactory, they were nothing special. The Americans filled two first-class compartments, and spilled over into a third.

All had gone well until two hours short of their destination on the south coast of France. The train stopped at the tiny village of Montelimar, on the east bank of the Rhone River.

That same morning, an earlier train had experienced equipment problems with an ancient coal-fired engine. Unable to continue, the French controllers sidetracked it for repair at the maintenance facility. The conductors required the passengers to unload and await a later train to continue their journey.

The complement of passengers from the stranded train included German officers and enlisted personnel from the Wehrmacht and Luftwaffe, stationed as garrison forces in occupied France. A few, highly decorated veterans of the uniquely named Waffen SS regiment, *Liebstandarte Adolf Hitler*, found themselves among the stranded passengers.

When the Germans boarded the new train, two Waffen SS officers—a *hauptsturmfuhrer* (captain) and an *obersturmfuhrer* (1st lieutenant)—decided to sit in the same passenger car as the Americans. The third compartment, in which Maj. Jardine, 2Lt. Genero, and a diplomat were situated, contained the only available seats.

The senior SS officer, Klaus Muller, hailed from Munich. He'd followed Adolf Hitler and served as a member of the Nazi party for over eight years. Muller, an intelligent, handsome man, held a degree in advanced mathematics from the Ruprect-Karl University at Heidelberg.

While a student in the late 20's, Muller captained the intercollegiate fencing team. Consistent with the bizarre rituals of the time, Klaus had fought two actual duels in addition to the more controlled, highly structured college matches. His face proudly displayed the dueling scars, which ran in two mostly parallel jagged lines from his eye to his chin on his left cheek. He considered the scars to be a badge of his demonstrated courage and stoicism.

Several months earlier, in the late spring, Muller had commanded a company of SS panzer grenadiers in Holland. On the second day of battle, his company received the mission of relieving the German paratroopers, who'd parachuted over a bridge on the Maas River in advance of the German armored thrust. Meeting more serious resistance than expected from the unprepared Dutch Army, Muller commanded his unit bravely and with great skill.

Although he suffered significant casualties in his force, he'd followed his orders to the letter, succeeded in his mission, saved the airborne force, and preserved the vital bridge as a conduit for other German mechanized units. Muller's company entered Rotterdam with the *Fallschirmjaeger* commanded by General Kurt Student.

For his courage in May 1940, the SS awarded Muller the coveted Knight's Cross, one of Nazi Germany's highest awards for gallantry. Along with the honor, he'd received a week's furlough at a villa near Monaco on the south coast of France. Muller had been traveling there to begin his holiday.

Karl Richter served as Muller's lieutenant and their unit's executive officer. In May, he'd fought as a platoon leader in Muller's mechanized company. The death of the company's first executive officer opened the door to Richter's advancement.

Much younger than Muller, Richter had become a committed Nazi. A product of the Hitler Youth program, Richter demonstrated all the traits of a highly indoctrinated, brainwashed hard-liner.

Richter fought more ruthlessly than his commander in the same battle in Holland. His subordinates knew him to be a man who took the fewest number of prisoners, no matter how many enemy soldiers wanted to surrender.

Richter had attended college, but not for very long. In the mid 30s, just after graduation from the local gymnasium, he studied for two semesters at a small Lutheran college. Richter's limited academic experience convinced him that the Nazis were right to burn the books of the American authors like Twain, Melville, and Hemingway.

An accomplished amateur middleweight boxer, after dropping out of college, he worked as a bodyguard to a major Nazi party functionary. His skill and willingness to use violence eventually resulted in an appointment to Heinrich Himmler's *Schutzstaffel* (SS), which initially devoted its efforts to providing armed security for Adolf Hitler.

By 1938, Richter had obtained a commission in the infant Waffen SS and an assignment to its first panzer regiment. During the reorganization in the *Liebstandarte Adolf Hitler*, the regimental command assigned Richter to Muller's company.

For his acts of heroism in the relief of the Fallschirmjaeger, Richter received the Iron Cross, First Class. He wore it proudly on the left pocket of his black tunic. He also traveled to Monaco on holiday.

When the SS officers entered Genero's compartment, they sized up its occupants immediately and made their introductions. The tone and tenor of the Germans' behavior hovered between patronizing and condescending.

Both officers could be very charming, even disarmingly so. When they found themselves in a train compartment with two American Army officers and a civilian, they thought that the experience would be interesting and mildly amusing.

Neither German thought the American military posed the slightest threat to their Fatherland, which was now the undisputed master of Western and Central Europe. Not in the nearly 1600 years—since the fall of the Roman Empire—had any nation been so successful in its conquests. They saw no problem with discussing the details of their combat activities and the capabilities of the German paratroopers with the impotent Americans.

Although the SS men bragged shamelessly, Phil found the details of the German assault to be fascinating. The exploits of the German paratroopers enthralled him.

The SS officers considered that it was cosmopolitan for them to educate the American officers for a few hours. The big, dumb-looking American lieutenant appeared so young, clumsy, and inexperienced that he had nothing to offer the Nazis other than comic relief. The civilian seemed inconsequential and beneath their contempt. Consequently, they addressed all of their comments to Maj. Jardine.

Both Germans spoke sufficient English to communicate with the Americans, though both had very thick accents. Genero understood their German perfectly, though he was still under orders to feign ignorance.

For the most part, the ensuing conversation among the five men in the compartment took place in a slow, halting manner. The Germans would routinely stop and speak to each other in German to discuss how to express an idea in English.

After a bit, convinced that none of the Americans spoke German, they began to boldly share their impressions about the men in whose company they found themselves. Their views were anything but complimentary.

Thirty minutes into the conversation, Capt. Muller produced a bottle of schnapps from his bag. A drink or two would loosen up the Americans, who seemed to be wound very tight.

Over the next hour, the Germans tried, with their limited English, to explain the difference between the elite Waffen SS, the more mundane Wehrmacht, and the unique Luftwaffe infantry formations, like the airborne *Fallschirmjaeger*. They eventually suspended their efforts. They deduced that the Americans were too stupid to understand the German military genius or to grasp the order of battle of a sophisticated, modern field army.

Things probably would not have deteriorated had Muller not produced another bottle of schnapps, and had Col. Moses simply remained in his own compartment.

As the train neared the last hour of its journey, Col. Moses set aside the first draft of the after action report that he was preparing for Gen. Marshall. He wanted to discuss the arrangements for moving the entourage from the train station to the port.

Moses entered the third compartment. He wasn't surprised to see two German officers sharing a bottle of schnapps with his men, since the train crawled with soldiers and airmen of the Third Reich.

He hid his surprise when he saw the twin runic lightning bolts that formed the symbol of the SS on the collar tabs of the two officers. He immediately noticed the piping, bearing the stylized signature of Adolf Hitler, on the cuffs of the left sleeve on both uniforms. These items identified the Germans as members of the elite SS Liebstandarte Adolf Hitler Regiment.

Throughout the summer, Army J-2 had supplied senior staff at the War Department with intelligence about the Waffen SS formations. War Plans had been aware of armed SS units for a couple of years.

These SS formations had originally served as security teams and guard units for the political prisoners at the concentration camps. Until the last two years, no one at J-2 had identified any of the SS elements as military formations, and certainly not as an elite combat unit.

Colonel Moses knew that in the fall of 1939, the Waffen— or armed—SS had taken the field with the Werhmacht against Poland's army. The armed SS regiments had fought very effectively. The J-2's sources reported that the Waffen SS proved to be a merciless bunch, especially with regard to political or ethnic enemies of the Reich. Sitting in the compartment, smiling and drinking with Jardine, these two examples of the master race didn't seem so threatening.

When the men noticed Moses standing in the doorway, the American officers stood up out of respect. The diplomat, who was lost in thought, remained crumpled in the corner, oblivious to the whole scene.

Maj. Jardine made the proper introductions, pointing out that this American colonel was the officer in charge of the Army element on this diplomatic mission. The two German officers stood, bowed slightly, clicked their heels together, and raised their right hands in a salute while uttering the standard, "Heil Hitler."

Col. Moses snapped to attention, and rendered a regulation hand salute, though he knew that under these circumstances U.S. Army protocol did not encourage a formal salute. It just seemed to be the respectful thing to do.

"Gentlemen, it's good to make your acquaintance. I hope that my officers have not made your trip too unpleasant by talking your ears off," Moses offered in polite salutation.

"Colonel Mosely, the honor is ours. Your officers have been a fascinating distraction from an otherwise boring journey. We are fortunate to have met them," Capt. Muller responded.

"I'm sorry Hauptsturmfuhrer, my name is Moses," the colonel corrected politely, but looking directly into the Nazi's eyes.

The older German officer thought for a moment, and then a light went off in his head. He looked over at his subordinate with disbelief and uttered but two words, dripping with animosity, "*Juden...untermenchen!*"

At first the German lieutenant did not understand the reference to something so vile as a Jew in the context of the conversation with these pathetic American officers. He needed clarification.

"Vas ist los, herr Hauptsturmfuhrer?" The obersturm-fuhrer asked his commander.

"Richter, the fucking American colonel is a despicable, lowlife Jew! Can you believe it, Karl? The Amis are so hard up for officers that they allow Jews to command their soldiers. These people are pathetic. They're no better than the French swine," Capt. Muller confided to his lieutenant in High German.

Though shocked and angry at these words, one glance at the colonel standing in the doorway told Genero to be cool. For his part, Col. Moses acted like he could not speak German. He simply smiled a cold, brittle grimace and told everyone in English that he had better get back to his duties.

As he left the compartment, he directed Genero to follow him in to the passageway. Watching Genero leave, the German captain poured another hefty shot of schnapps into his own glass and drained half of it in one noisy gulp.

"Yes, sir?" Genero said, when he and Col. Moses walked down the passageway about twenty feet.

"Mr. Genero, I saw you react to the comment that the SS captain made about me. You'd better stay calm! We are in the middle of unoccupied France, and I don't want you to compromise your cover. Do you understand me, mister?" Col. Moses said.

"Yes, sir. But..." Genero responded, trying to explain.

"There are no buts, Mister Genero!" Col. Moses inter-rupted angrily. "I don't owe you an explanation, but you've done a good job on this trip, far better than I expected. Ambassador Curtis wants you to go along with his team in April, when he plans to return. You will do nothing that would compromise your usefulness to this diplomatic team. Am I clear?"

"Yes, sir. I understand," Genero responded.

After obtaining the information from Genero about the transfer to the seaplane terminal, Moses returned to his compartment without another word. Outwardly he appeared nonplused and professional. Inwardly, he seethed with anger. He hated these anti-Semitic Nazi bastards, but he wouldn't give them the satisfaction.

Phil returned to the compartment with the Nazis. He'd received a direct order, and he had every intention of obeying it.

Neither of the SS officers could hold his liquor. Normally, Muller and Richter managed to hide their true qualities through practiced subterfuge. On this occasion, the effects of the alcohol subdued the thin facades that the sociopathic SS men constructed to allow them to interact with normal human beings.

For the next hour, Genero listened as the Germans alternately patronized Maj. Jardine in bad English, then insulted Jardine, Col. Moses, and Franklin Roosevelt using the worst German profanity imaginable.

The philosophical views held by the Germans were superficial, and so stupidly stereotypical, that Phil had to resist laughing at them. Then their game got personal. It made him angry, despite the warning from Col. Moses.

Richter started it. According to the SS Lieutenant, he believed that all Jews were subhuman, like communists, intellectuals, and homosexuals. In fact, most Jews, Richter suggested to his company commander, were homosexual. Muller agreed. At least, that's what the Nazi party held to be true.

According to Richter's logic, if most Jews were homosexual, then it followed that Col. Moses had to be one. Moses probably brought the lieutenant along on the trip to France to gratify his perverse sexual needs.

The more the SS officers drank, the more detailed their speculations became regarding what acts Phil might be willing to perform to satisfy his colonel. At first Phil thought it was strange that the Germans seemed so fixated on the homosexual thing, as if they protested too much. Eventually, as the speculation took a particularly raunchy twist, Genero became livid.

As Muller and Richter droned on and on, the encounter with the Germans became painfully interminable. Mercifully, the train began to slow for its arrival in Marseilles. All passengers gathered their belongings in preparation for leaving the train.

The Americans headed to the port. The SS men had to transfer to another train for Nice. That should have been the end of the encounter.

Phil had made arrangements for the luggage to be transferred to the port. The station porters located all of the bags, except a small trunk belonging to Ambassador Curtis. They loaded the rest into waiting taxis.

After accounting for the personnel, Genero sent them on their way. In order to locate the missing trunk, Phil remained behind with Maj. Jardine to talk to the stationmaster's representative.

After 15 minutes, the assistant located the trunk, as it was about to be loaded on the train to Nice. After retrieving the luggage, Maj. Jardine, with the ambassador's trunk in tow, headed for the street to hail another cab. Genero needed to stop in the latrine in order to relieve his very full bladder.

When Phil entered the small lavatory near the platform for the Nice-bound train, he noticed two things at once. The men's room appeared to be the filthiest privy he'd ever seen, and he was alone.

Phil stepped into a stall, closed the door and urinated for over a minute. When he finished, he took several additional moments to insure that his uniform appeared professional.

While he straightened up, Genero heard two men enter the room. They acted boisterous and drunk. They spoke to each other in German. Phil recognized the voices: the two SS officers.

*Great,* Phil thought, *that's all I need, another run in with the two supermen.*

According to their chatter, the Germans had stopped for a quick drink at the station's small bistro. Richter, now obviously intoxicated, entertained his commander with a horrific vignette concerning an incident that had occurred in Poland, sometime after the capitulation in the fall of 1939.

"Sir, you may recall that you sent my platoon to a village to arrest and transport a half-dozen Jewish families to the holding center south of Warsaw," the lieutenant reminded his superior.

"I do, Karl. That was a very fluid time for us," Muller recalled.

"Well, it turns out that the Jewish vermin had relatively attractive wives—for subhuman scum. My men had fought for three days straight without rest or food. You could see how exhausted they were. You know how the morale of my men comes before anything, except the mission, right sir?" Richter asked.

"Sure, Karl. Your men respect you and would follow you anywhere."

"Herr Hauptsturmfuhrer, I knew I couldn't do much for them. We had no rations. Water was low. I had very few options to reward them, so I improvised," Richter bragged.

"The mark of an effective leader is his ability to improvise," Muller slurred slightly.

"I lined up the husbands, then told their wives that they would sexually gratify all of my men, or I would personally shoot their husbands," Richter explained coldly.

"They must have been terrified!" Muller responded supportively.

"Yes, sir!" Richter acknowledged. "But a couple of the women seemed skeptical. So, I walked over to the oldest male Jew in the group. I took out my pistol, pointed it at his head and reiterated my demand."

"He must have been pissing in his pants," Muller chortled.

"Yes, sir! I could see by his eyes that he was petrified. I smiled at him. He relaxed a little. Then I shot him right between the eyes. The back of his head exploded, blowing blood, brain and skull fragments all over some of the children. The wives and children screamed. The Jewish men just stood there. It was hilarious. I spun around and screamed at the women that if they did not obey my orders instantly, I would do the same thing to their husbands and their children," Richter continued.

"What happened then, Karl?"

"My actions definitely motivated the wives. For the next few hours, I allowed the husbands to watch as my men had their way with the Jew bitches. When the grenadiers finished, I simply walked down the line of men, shooting each one in the head with my Walther. The women seemed too exhausted to cry, wail, or complain. We loaded the rest of the Jews into the transport and motored over to the holding center."

"Good work, Karl. No wonder your men respect you," Muller praised.

"Thank you, sir. I left the bodies of the husbands on the road to rot like the vermin that they were. Let that be an object lesson to the enemies of the Reich. We left the Jew whores with transport forces, who continued to ravage them until they shipped them off to Dachau."

"Well done, Karl! You will go far in the SS," Muller predicted.

Phil could see that Muller thought this story was hilarious. He'd punctuated Richter's rendition with supportive comments of all kinds.

Nothing in his life in America had prepared Genero for the horror of such a story. Despite his attempts to control himself, Phil became incensed. Richter's story provided evidence of inconceivable depravity.

Angrier than at any time in his life, Phil lost his resolve to follow the colonel's orders. Knowing that the mature decision would be to wait until the Germans left the latrine, he opened the door and stepped out anyway. As Genero expected, he encountered Richter, who recognized him immediately.

"Look at what we have here, sir. It's the Jew's butt-boy. Hanging around in the men's room, like all of these queers do," Richter said to Muller in German, slightly slurring his words.

"Be careful, Karl! Don't touch that sissy! You don't know whose cock he's sucked today," Klaus Muller advised.

The last comment from the Nazi did it for Genero. Despite the order from Col. Moses, Phil would give the Germans a nice little surprise.

Phil thought about how he would provide it for ten seconds. He remembered something he saw Tony Lupinacci do in a bar in Pittsburgh during an Easter break two years before. Genero decided that approach would be the soundest.

As he walked toward the two Germans, he smiled the same vacuous smile that he'd used on the train over the last few hours. He reached into the inner pocket of his uniform coat and extracted a pack of Lucky Strikes. He'd carried American smokes so the diplomats could bum them from him.

He put a Lucky to his lips, reached into his pants pocket and pulled out his grey Zippo lighter. As if he'd had an afterthought, he looked at both Germans. He motioned with the pack, offering them a cigarette.

In 1940, in any part of France, the residents considered American cigarettes to be an incredible luxury. Because of the U-Boat war in the Atlantic, the French experienced shortages in American products.

Both Nazis eagerly accepted the cigarettes. They continued to insult Genero in German, assuming that he did not understand. As they each put a Lucky to their lips, Phil raised his Zippo, flicked the flame and offered to light their cigarettes.

 Genero purposely held the lighter chest high and equidistant between the two Nazis. As they bent over to accept the light, the heads of the two officers were separated by only 30 inches. Then, Phil intentionally lowered the lighter four or five inches, forcing the Germans to bend over a little more toward each other, significantly narrowing the distance between them.

Richter commented that the American queer was as clumsy as he was stupid. Muller gave an irritated huff, and muttered an insincere *Danke*.

Genero smiled a cruel smirk, and said in his very best German, "Think nothing of it, you fucking evil ignorant Nazi swine.*"*

Even through the alcoholic haze, those particular words, spoken to them in perfect German, caused tremendous shock and surprise. Before they could react, in a lightening fast move, Phil dropped the lighter to the floor, moved both his hands behind the heads of the German officers, and without further warning, using all of his considerable strength and leverage, savagely smashed the heads of the SS men together very, very hard.

The last thing either German expected was a brutal attack. As Genero bounced the heads together, Richter's forehead smashed into the left front side of Muller's chin, at a point right between his dueling scars.

Both officers saw stars. Muller sagged noticeably, swooning as he staggered back from the tremendous blow.

Phil planted his left foot toward Muller. He hit him hard with a powerfully sharp left jab, right on the point of his chin. Phil quickly followed up with a strong right hook, catching the German captain on the left temple with his best punch.

The force of the punch slammed the SS captain against the wall, where he hit the back of his head. The collision with the wall was of no consequence, since Muller was unconscious seconds before he hit. Muller simply bounced hard, and slid to the dirty floor in a heap.

Richter reeled from the savage blow. He'd been drinking, so the alcohol had muted his senses, but he had trained as a fighter. Phil did not expect to confront a skilled boxer.

Although Richter never recovered enough from the first brutal shot to put the contest in doubt, he gave a decent account of himself in the next 20 seconds. He stepped into Phil and swung hard for the American's mid-section.

Richter proved to be an excellent puncher. He hit Phil five or six good blows in the solar plexus and ribs. The last punch was so solid, that Genero could actually feel his rib cracking. He moaned aloud in pain.

The floor was so filthy that Richter could not find his balance on the wet surface, slippery from God knows what. Genero was considerably bigger and much stronger than Richter. Phil managed to push the SS man backward where he had the advantage with a longer reach.

When the German came on hard, Genero—bouncing on the balls of his feet on a relatively dry spot—kicked up hard with his right foot, catching the SS officer squarely in the groin. The kick caused the younger SS officer to cry out in intense pain. If Phil had done nothing more, Richter would have fallen forward on his face. He teetered seconds from unconsciousness as it was.

As the younger Nazi began to fall forward, Phil stepped forward and hit him four solid times in the head and face. After absorbing the full force of each blow, Richter too fell to the floor unconscious, bleeding profusely from his nose and mouth.

Genero watched mercilessly, as the SS officer pitched face first into the slime of the men's room floor. He could muster no sympathy for these inhuman monsters. Then, Genero began to realize the magnitude of his folly.

*Holy shit! What have I done?* Phil thought. *I've just kicked the crap out of two armed Nazi officers! Man, I could go to French prison, or worse.*

*It's hard to feel sorry for these inhuman bastards. Compared to the way they treated those Poles, these fuckers got off light. They should be horse whipped,* Genero reasoned, as he looked down on the two men lying unconscious on the slime-covered floor.

As the fear passed, Phil felt unusually calm. He thought about what he should do for a long moment. He walked over to the SS captain, grabbed him by the collar and dragged him into the nearest stall. Although the officer was dead weight, Genero easily pulled him up and sat him on the commode, leaning him back against the wall.

Next, Phil walked over to Richter. Genero intended to do the same thing to the younger Nazi, but the other stall didn't have a door. Genero improvised.

Phil pulled the lieutenant into the stall in which the German captain sat. He deposited the lieutenant in a kneeling position, facing his unconscious commander. He dropped Richter on the Captain. Genero balanced the younger man's chest on the older man's lap. Gin stuffed the lieutenant's arms under him, so they wouldn't dangle to the wet floor.

Genero finished his work and closed the stall door. He stepped over to the old mirror on the opposite wall, to assess the damage to his uniform. While he examined his appearance, two middle-aged French men entered the rest room.

The older and more robust of the two walked across the room in an obvious hurry. He was about to enter the stall when his alert companion informed him that someone occupied it. It was someone who wanted and needed privacy.

The old, fat Frenchman took a step back, peered at the limited sight that the space at the bottom of the stall provided. He saw what seemed to be a man in a German uniform, on his knees in front of another German in uniform.

Despite a heroic effort, he erupted in a huge guffaw. The old man decided that he could delay his business. Better yet, he would find a more attractive venue to conduct it.

The skinnier Frenchman simply looked at Genero, rolled his eyes in Gallic disgust, shook his head back and forth, and clicked his tongue as he turned to go. Phil made out a faint insult about German perversity, as the two men left the room.

Looking up from the mirror, Genero noticed that his right hand might be broken. He'd sprained it badly, and it started to swell. He felt an intense pain from his left side. Not that old rib injury, he hoped.

Inspecting himself in the mirror he looked flushed, but generally OK. He'd calm down and get his natural color back by the time he met up with Maj. Jardine.

When Phil got to the cab, Jardine showed only mild signs of irritation. The major didn't seem to notice anything and said nothing on the way to the port.

Colonel Moses had executed the exit visa paperwork by the time that Genero and Jardine arrived at the terminal. The crew made a final flight check, loaded the ambassador's trunk, and boarded the two American officers.

An hour after Phil and Maj. Jardine arrived at the port, the flying boat embarked on its circuitous route south and west of Britain, bound for Western Ireland.

Cruising over the northern slope of the Pyrenees, Phil watched the sun set toward North America and pondered his fate. He alternated between concern for his career and exhilaration for giving the two Germans the beating they deserved.

When the Inter-continental flight landed several hours later, no Irish police officials turned up at the terminal to throw him jail. An hour after landing at Foynes, Phil realized for the first time that he had forgotten his grey Zippo lighter on the floor of the latrine. This revelation caused Phil to spend time in Ireland fretting, but that too passed. The Guinness helped sooth his nerves, but his conscience remained absolutely clear.

When the team re-boarded the flying boat for transit to Newfoundland, Genero went about resolving all details for the team. Satisfied, he went to his bunk in the third compartment, and slept the sleep of the just for over seven hours.

The entourage arrived in New York late on December 7, 1940. Again, no police officials waited to take him in tow. By this time, Phil decided that his hand was not broken, but it had swelled considerably. Unfortunately, Richter had cracked his rib for sure.

When Ambassador Curtis noticed and asked about his hand, Phil quipped that he had a lot to learn about handling baggage. Curtis accepted the explanation without comment. By the time that the military men made their train for Washington, Genero began to believe that he'd gotten away with his retaliatory strike.

# Chapter 18

1430 Hours
December 20, 1940
Office of the Chief
French Department, European Section
War Plans Staff, War Department
Washington, D.C.

C olonel Moses walked into his small, windowless office, sat down at his worn, Army-issue desk, and leaned back on two legs of the armless chair. Long hours of sitting at his infernal desk had caused his lower back to act up. Stress added to the discomfort. Today, he felt particularly stressed.

Moses had suffered a serious wound in World War I from the powerful shockwave of a close impact of a high-caliber German artillery shell during the very last week of the war. The explosion picked him up and threw him against something solid.

Moses couldn't remember any detail of the trauma. When he awoke at the hospital three days later, all he could recall was the whine of the incoming round, and thinking that it was going to be close.

Balanced on the back legs of his chair, Moses looked around the office. Two inches of paperwork covered the top of his desk. Despite his dedication and efficiency, he had such a backlog that he routinely worked six long days every week.

Earlier this morning, the colonel's secretary had placed a State Department folder concerning the trip to Vichy on his desk. Moses picked it up the moment he walked in.

Moses didn't expect such a rapid response. The entourage had returned to Washington less than two weeks earlier.

Normally, the Foggy Bottom diplomats liked to ruminate about their positions for at least a month, so they could have time to check the direction of the wind of official opinion before they took a stand.

Even this file wouldn't be finalized until after everyone had reviewed it to ensure that it posed no threat to State Department reputations. The enclosed rough draft of the after action report would only be signed by Ambassador Curtis after he approved the waffling, which was his trademark. Naturally, the self-serving report praised the hard work, dedication, and fidelity of the diplomats and military advisors.

After reviewing the draft, Moses consigned it to the seat of the only other chair in his office. Then Colonel Moses noticed that there was a second report in the folder. In this second and more troubling item, Consul Montenegro summarized a serious incident that Vichy authorities from Marseilles had been investigating.

According to Montenegro, three or four days after the Americans departed Vichy, a police investigator—Detective Bruno Abelard from Provence—made an official inquiry of the American Consul. Detective Abelard asked questions about the State and War Department's team, wanting to know the number of men, their names and histories, and their itinerary during their travels in France.

Consistent with the diplomatic arrangements that the United States had with Vichy, Montenegro provided all the data that he possessed. The consul promised to make his own inquiry to see if he could find additional facts for the French police.

When Montenegro asked why the police wanted the information, Detective Abelard wouldn't say, explaining that it was official business. Over a generous glass or two of the buttery Chardonnay, Abelard became more cooperative.

The detective revealed that on the evening of December 5th, the Marseilles police found two German SS men unconscious in the latrine of the Marseilles train station. Someone had brutally beaten the Nazis. The older man, a captain, had a serious concussion. The younger man suffered a broken nose and a shattered jaw.

The authorities admitted both men to a local hospital. The captain couldn't remember details of the assault, probably due to traumatic amnesia as a result of the concussion.

The younger SS man, talking through wired teeth, told authorities that he and his commander intended to use the men's room before boarding the train to Nice. According to the SS lieutenant, as the two Nazis entered the latrine at least eight hooligans viciously assaulted them without cause or warning. Though the SS officers fought valiantly, the attack happened so quickly and the hoodlums so outnumbered the Germans, that Richter never got a good look at any individual before the villains overwhelmed them.

A couple of witnesses vaguely recalled seeing a soldier with a foreign uniform in the latrine earlier in the day. It could have been an American, but they weren't certain.

When the police examined the latrine, they found an American-made Zippo on the floor, likely dropped at or near the time of the assault. As it was covered with a nasty wet substance, the police tried to avoid direct contact with it and managed to wipe away any possible latent prints in the process.

Abelard related that the police discovered the two Nazis crammed into the same stall, suggesting that their relationship was much more intimate than most armies permit between a commander and subordinate. Two restroom patrons had seen one of the officers kneeling at the feet of the other over an extended period of time. This highly suspicious circumstantial evidence caused the French police to doubt the German's version of events.

Detective Abelard had done his research, and while there were American naval personnel on liberty from a United States Navy destroyer in port at the time, the only soldiers who were in the vicinity of the Marseilles train station had been advisors to the diplomatic mission to Vichy. That lead seemed an obvious dead end.

The detective told Montenegro that it was ludicrous to believe that a group of senior American Army officers, on a trip of such sensitivity, would hide out in the men's room in order to ambush two SS men that they'd never met. Ultimately, the authorities had found no evidence to corroborate any detail of the younger SS officer's version of events.

Abelard had to run down every lead, no matter how silly. The German military government in occupied France threatened retaliation. His superiors wanted an answer, or at least a scapegoat, before the incident spun out of control, and the Gestapo or SS took reprisals against the local population.

Detective Abelard admitted frustration because somebody obviously beat the snot out of the two Nazis. He did not believe the Germans and could not explain why they would not be more forthcoming.

Conversely, the detective conceded to Montenegro that the residents of southern France had no love for the Germans, especially the SS. Marseilles had a well-deserved reputation for being a tough port of call. Abelard knew scores of local thugs who would have happily thumped the Nazis, just for the sheer joy of it.

The Frenchman would run down all leads in a professional way. Ironically, if the mundane version were true, Vichy would never risk making the Germans angry by laying the blame on Frenchmen.

Curtis attached a draft response to Montenegro in the copy that he sent to Col. Moses. In the cover letter, Curtis asked Moses for his endorsement. If Moses executed the document, that would be the end of it.

Moses planned to concur with the envoy. Neither he nor any of his men lurked around the latrines at the Marseilles train station in order to beat up homosexuals. If some group of Americans waylaid the SS men, it couldn't have been his staff.

Moses remembered his run in with the SS officers in Jardine's compartment on the train, but couldn't recall their names. The names on the report sounded right, but he couldn't be sure. Col. Moses called Maj. Jardine into his office to discuss the matter with him before he executed the paperwork requested by State.

Ten minutes later, Jardine arrived. He knocked and took the seat next to the desk. Although Moses outranked Jardine by two grades, the two were old comrades. They'd served together in the Philippines three years earlier. Both had been staff officers on Corregidor.

Since his return from Vichy, an Army board had selected Jardine for promotion to Lieutenant Colonel. It was about time. He'd been in grade over ten years.

"Dan, you look at the report from Consul Montenegro?" Col. Moses asked.

"Sure did, Harry. What a bizarre allegation. I agree with Ambassador Curtis, it definitely wasn't us," Jardine explained. "We didn't have eight men in uniform in the whole entourage. It must be some other group of vigilantes."

Jardine leaned forward, and lowered his voice, suggesting that he wanted to make an off-the-record comment. Col. Moses nodded, accepting the offer.

Jardine continued quietly, "I remember the names of the two SS supermen from our train compartment: Muller and Richter. It's the same two guys who got their asses kicked in the French crapper. Not that they didn't deserve it."

Moses looked up, slightly shocked at Jardine's last comment. "What do you mean, Dan? Nobody deserves to be beaten half to death by a mob, even if they are Nazi storm troopers."

Maj. Jardine responded, "I'm not advocating vigilante justice, but I spent over two hours listening to those two pricks. They are evil, evil men. I'm just saying that you reap what you sow in this world. Harry, I understood most of what those two assholes were saying about me and Genero, and all of what they were saying about you," Jardine revealed conspiratorially. "If these SS men are an example of their peers, we're in for a horror show this time around. Mark my words."

"Then you agree with Curtis that none of our staff could be involved in this incident, right?" Col. Moses asked in a semi-official tone.

"Exactly right, sir. Everybody went directly from the train to the port facilities, except Genero and me. We spent ten to fifteen minutes locating the Ambassador's trunk, the one that contained all the black market champagne. That's the luggage that the great ambassador smuggled through customs, claiming diplomatic status, so he wouldn't have to pay the tariff," Jardine recalled sarcastically, remembering his irritation at being the bagman in the Ambassador's little smuggling operation.

"After we got the trunk, we headed directly for a cab. Genero was never out of my sight for a second," Jardine lied. "I can tell you this, Harry. I never laid eyes on either Nazi after they left the train. I never put a hand on those SS men or saw anyone else do so."

"Well, that's good enough for me. I agree. This allegation is bullshit," Col. Moses said, as he scribbled his endorsement on the report from Curtis to Montenegro. "I hope that's the end of this nonsense."

# Chapter 19

An institution in the nation's capital since the late 1880s, the Army and Navy Club catered to the needs of a small clique of men. It filled a vital niche in the political and social life of the District, providing a suitable venue for active duty and retired officers to network, entertain, and conduct government business.

In light of the looming international crisis, a dedicated officer assigned to the War Department would still be chained to his desk, working late, and shepherding some official action through the bureaucratic maze. Instead of burning the midnight oil on this very cold evening, Genero had traveled to the Army and Navy Club.

Phil sat—alone—at the end of the long, ornate mahogany bar in the room that the club reserved for junior officers to do their drinking. The club's trustees knew that young officers needed a place to relax without having to worry about the colonels and generals watching their every move.

Genero nursed a cold Schlitz draft. He'd been in the bar about 15 minutes, and had barely touched his drink. Recent developments prevented him from enjoying his beer.

Since Christmas was around the corner, the bar attracted fewer patrons than normal. Under the circumstances, Phil didn't want to socialize with anyone, anyway. He avoided making small talk with the habitués, or the friendly and considerate bartender.

Ironically, everything had gone so well over the last two weeks. The older officers had begun to accept him as a competent staffer. He'd received invitations to their homes for the holiday celebrations. He finally felt like a part of the team, instead of like everyone's goofy little brother.

Late this afternoon, Maj. Jardine had walked into Genero's tiny cubicle, tossing the Montenegro report onto his small desk. The major directed him to read it carefully, and then meet him at the Army and Navy Club at 1930 hours to discuss it.

Since Genero's assignment to the Vichy trip, Jardine had become his mentor at War Plans. After a rough start, they'd established a friendship of a sort.

Genero read the report as soon as Maj. Jardine left his cubicle. He immediately understood its meaning. The reference to the Zippo lighter sent a chill down his back.

*Damn it! I never intended to hurt those Nazis so badly. Shit. Nobody will believe that. They won't care about my intentions. They'll only concern themselves with what I did. I'll get raped at a court-martial. None of the court members will buy my story, or be moved by my motives. I'll lose my commission for sure. I could get dismissed and serve time in Leavenworth. Mother of God! What did I do?* Phil lamented as he reviewed the report.

Oddly enough, while someone could place an American near the incident, no witness could—or apparently would—provide evidence or testimony about Phil. The Germans had feigned amnesia and lied to the French investigators.

*I can't figure these Nazis. Why would they claim that eight gangsters whipped them? Maybe they're too fucking arrogant to admit that just one American lieutenant kicked their collective butts,* Phil thought.

*Major Jardine never even entered the latrine at the train station. He can't actually testify against me. All the major can do is provide a court-martial with something the French police already know: an American was in the vicinity when the phantom hooligans struck.*

*I could admit being in the latrine. Obviously, I could claim that I lost my lighter there. I could insist that my presence was a mere coincidence. I could probably convince a court-martial that I had no knowledge of the beatings. I could express sympathy for the injuries that the Nazis suffered,* Genero pondered as he sipped his beer. *If I lie to the Major, I could get away with this. If I admit the truth, I'm through. Geez, real life is a lot more complicated than school.*

By considering a course of conduct that involved these lies and prevarications, Genero crossed a fundamental line. He'd never see himself in the same idealistic terms again.

When Jardine arrived, Phil's fragile hope evaporated. Genero could sense that his mentor was livid. Phil had seen that look only two or three times in his life, when his own father had to punish him for some serious misdeed

Walking up to Phil, Jardine jerked his thumb over his shoulder, motioning to an empty booth at the far side of the room. "Let's go sit over there, mister. We'll have more privacy," Jardine directed.

A moment later, they found their seats in a booth. Jardine reached over, put his glass to his lips and drank his beer in three noisy gulps. The major glanced over at the bartender, and signaled for a refill.

Jardine examined Genero critically before he began to speak. Phil steeled himself for the trip to the wood shed.

"Mister Genero," Jardine began. "I know about your family, your education, and your training. I'm convinced that you're aware of the definition of integrity."

Maj. Jardine continued, "Integrity, Mister Genero, is the watchword of the officer corps. Subordinates must be ruthlessly honest with their superiors, even when the truth will harm them or their careers. If a subordinate lies or leaves out material facts in our business, the lives of soldiers and innocent civilians can be lost and wasted. You know this, right?"

"Yes, sir," Phil responded.

"Today, Mr. Genero, and for the first time in twenty-eight years, I deceived a superior officer, someone I care about, trust, and deeply respect. I'm telling you that I violated my oath as an Army officer. Would you like to know why?"

"Sir, I don't know what you mean," Phil responded honestly.

Jardine passed Genero a mimeographed copy of the endorsement that Col. Moses had provided to Montenegro's inquiry. Phil read it. Then read it again.

Phil understood that the colonel's endorsement, along with the skewed facts given by the Germans, gave him complete cover. He looked up from the document and directly at Maj. Jardine. Genero's expression revealed emotions that ran the gamut from relief for the cover, to shame for considering a plan of fabrication and deceit.

"Sir, I'm sorry," Phil conceded respectfully.

"Son, the minute I read the report I knew it was you who beat up those fucking Nazis. The Zippo on the floor of the latrine sealed it for me. I knew that if Colonel Moses or—God forbid—General Marshall ever found out, you'd face a court-martial so fast, your eyes would pop out," Jardine explained. "You'd be dismissed and do time in the disciplinary barracks for sure.

"This afternoon, I told Colonel Moses that you were never out of my sight, even for a moment, while we were getting the Ambassador's trunk full of champagne. I reminded the good colonel of the Ambassador's smuggling operation because any inquiry into this business will bring that little fact to light as well," Jardine said smugly. "After all, no one wants to cast an aspersion on the ambassador. He's a personal buddy of the President.

"Genero, for some indefinable reason, I believe that you are worth a shit. I got a horrific glimpse of the future on that train to Marseilles. Those Nazis are more dangerous than any enemy in our history. This country will need you and thousands of decent, brave, courageous, and resourceful men, like you, in order to fight those German madmen," Jardine explained. "As your mentor, I've arranged—at the expense of my personal honor—to give you another chance to become a real soldier."

After a pause, designed to allow this to sink into Genero's thick skull, Jardine continued in a deadly serious tone. "Son, I promise you, if you blow this one, I will personally tear out your heart and feed it to you in tiny little pieces."

"Sir, I don't know what to say."

"Well, you won't get off scot-free. I have a difficult little chore for you to perform and it'll ruin your Christmas leave, to say the least," Jardine informed Phil.

"I'll gladly do anything you say, sir," Genero responded.

"That you will, son. That you will. Make no mistake!" Jardine repeated unkindly.

By way of explanation, Jardine continued in a less angry tone, "I got a visit yesterday from Major Bill Lee. He's the action officer for the Chief of Infantry on the airborne project at Fort Benning. This paratrooper thing is Marshall's pride and joy. The Chief-of-Staff has taken a special interest in developing airborne capabilities, and getting them ready as soon as possible. The staffers are so pleased with the paratrooper tests to date that they've approved a number of airborne battalions. I don't have all the details, but the units will comprise both paratroopers and glider-borne forces."

Genero had read everything available concerning the German use of paratroops and gliders in their attacks in Scandinavia and Western Europe. He agreed that the Americans should seek an airborne capability to effectively fight the Nazis.

"Sir, what does all this have to do with me?" Phil asked.

"Mister Genero, our intelligence resources have been working overtime in the glorious Fatherland. They've gotten their hands on several German training manuals, and even a bona-fide Nazi training film depicting the details of turning German youth into *Fallschirmjaegers*. How about that?" Jardine chortled,

With a conspiratorial smile, Jardine continued, "The material is all in German, of course. Some German linguists in J-2 gave it a quick review and summarized the material in English. Bill Lee and Major Miley, the commander of the new 501st Parachute Infantry Battalion, want someone to take a more careful look at the stuff and give them a more accurate translation. That's you, bub! They want it done immediately.

"Tomorrow morning you'll receive specific orders to proceed to Fort Benning. You'll arrive no later than 1600 hours, December 27th. You'll report to the headquarters of the 501$^{st}$, near Lawson Field. Your contact is First Lieutenant William Yarborough, a bright young officer on Miley's staff. He'll show you all the Fallschirmjaeger materials, and tell you what to do. You'll stay down there and give them your complete cooperation, until they have no further use for you. I've already squared this with Colonel Moses, who—by the way—thinks that this is a great opportunity for you to learn something about the Army. Any questions?" Jardine requested.

"Actually, none, sir. Other than, shouldn't I leave immediately?" Phil asked.

"And break your mother's heart?" Jardine asked affectionately. "*Gin*—I know that's your nickname—you don't remember, but I was at your dad's award ceremony back in '27. I'm a veteran of the 82$^{nd}$ Infantry Division, though I was never in your dad's regiment. By November of '18, I was working at the division staff in the G-3 shop. I never knew either York or your dad during the war. I was in Washington, in another staff assignment as a captain in '27.

"A week before Armistice Day, we got a memo that the President, with Sergeant York's assistance, would present a Distinguished Service Cross to a former corporal of the 82$^{nd}$ Infantry Division. The Chief-of-Staff strongly encouraged all veterans of the 82$^{nd}$ to attend, even though it was otherwise a rare day off. I was there. I must say that you acted far more maturely in the Indian Treaty Room than you did on portions of our last trip together. I recall speaking to your dad. He's a charming and decent man. Your mom is very lovely. You must be very proud of them," Maj. Jardine said.

"I am, sir," Phil affirmed.

"And some day, bub, they will have the right to be proud of you. Just no more stupid, fucking, self-righteous, impetuous acts, right, Lieutenant?"

Phil nodded, agreeing with his savior, a man far more complex than he ever imagined.

"Gin, as soon as you get your orders, take a few days leave with your family. This may be the last opportunity for quite a while. To get to Benning on time, you'll have to leave your home on Christmas day, by noon at the latest. This gives you Christmas Eve and Christmas morning with them," Jardine said.

"Thank you, sir,"

"If you do a good job at Benning, I'll arrange to get you reassigned there. You've screwed up an unprecedented career opportunity here at War Plans. It's probably fate. I'm sure that you're cut out for better things than baggage handling, cigarette lighting, and champagne smuggling. Go down to Benning and help those brave men. And don't ever let me down again!"

"I give you my word, sir!" Phil said.

"As someone I deeply respect said to me earlier today, 'That's good enough for me'," Maj. Jardine replied, remembering the last words Col. Moses uttered on the Montenegro report.

# Chapter 20

5:00 PM
December 23, 1940
Genero Farm
Carlisle, Pennsylvania

As the daylight turned to dusk and the sky filled with multi-colored streamers, Marta sat in silence at the breakfast nook's small rustic table on the west side of the spacious farm kitchen. Stunned, she stared—unseeing—out of the nook's window, oblivious to a stunning view of the Allegheny Mountain ridgeline and a gorgeous winter sunset settling over Waggoners Gap.

Unable to appreciate the celestial beauty, tears welled up in her doe-like eyes and rolled down her pretty, now red and puffy, cheeks. Propelled by gravity, the tears fell to the surface of the table where they formed a small, salty pool between Marta's outstretched arms.

Marta muffled a sob and took a jagged breath. Her right hand gripped a large mug of untouched coffee, her knuckles white from the vice-like grip that she had on the handle of the cup.

Phillip sat next to Marta. He stroked her hand, trying to comfort her.

Since their two children had grown and left home, Marta and Phillip took all of their meals together in this cozy nook, a comfortable place nestled between the hearth and the dining room. After Kari's decision, no amount of heat from the roaring fire could chase the bitter chill from Marta's spirit.

Yesterday, their son Phil returned home with the news of his temporary assignment to Fort Benning. He'd provided few details, not mentioning his duty with the paratroopers. As far as Marta knew, her boy would head to Georgia to put his language skills to good use.

*Dear God, I remember that awful time when Phillip was in France. I didn't know from day to day if my husband was alive or dead in some French field. He had such a close call. I almost lost him. It was a miracle that he came back to me. I never thought I would have to live through that pain again. I know we're facing a national crisis and my son must do his duty, but Georgia sounds like a safe enough assignment. Maybe the Army will leave him there,* Marta hoped.

While her boy's new assignment caused her no serious concern, Kari's news had stunned Marta.

Ever since Congress passed the draft law last spring, Marta had worried about what might happen to her son-in-law, Mark. Government officials now planned to induct hundreds of thousands of soldiers. They'd want a proportionate number of doctors to care for them.

It was only a matter of time until the Harrisburg board realized that the Army Medical Corps needed this young, capable doctor. Marta hoped that when that happened, Mark might be able to train at Carlisle Barracks or get a permanent instructor assignment.

*I figured that Mark would get drafted. I just never expected that Kari would get caught up in this awful business too,* Marta thought.

Not wanting to serve in the Army, Mark had spoken to the Navy recruiter in Harrisburg. He obtained an application for a commission as a physician in the Navy. Without discussing it with Kari, Mark submitted his paperwork to the Navy Department. The Navy approved his basic application in early December, giving Mark a direct commission and two choices.

Dr. Hansen could report for active duty immediately, at the rank of Lieutenant, Junior Grade, the equivalent of an Army or Marine First Lieutenant. If he chose that option, Mark would train for several weeks, and then receive an assignment as a general medical officer at a Naval station, or a billet on board a cruiser or battleship.

As an alternative, the Navy would allow him to await the results of his general surgical boards. If the state certified him, the Navy would bring him on active-duty as a full Lieutenant. The state would publish the board results in February and Mark would report afterward. This option would not only guarantee a higher rank, but would insure that Mark could serve as a surgeon in a larger naval medical facility, a hospital ship, or on an aircraft carrier.

Mark wanted to be a surgeon. He would not let a little thing like national military mobilization interfere with that dream.

*If America can't avoid this conflict, the experience that I'll get from treating the wounded will be irreplaceable. Peacetime medical practice can't compete with the opportunities to treat serious wounds, traumatic amputations, and life-threatening cranial or orthopedic injuries. Doctors in Harrisburg don't encounter these problems as often,* Mark had reasoned. *If America does go to war, the weapons, bombs and killing technologies will be very hard on our boys. Look at what the Nazis and Japs have done to their enemies. The experience that I'll gain will allow me to help our men, and make me a far better surgeon.*

In early December, Mark revealed his decision to Kari. At first, she reacted angrily. Married life had turned out to be far better than she'd anticipated, and her expectations had been high. Every bit her mother's daughter, she'd inherited the same set of intense passions.

Doctor Hansen had demonstrated enthusiasm in his husbandly responsibilities. The thought of Mark sailing away on a Navy vessel for months, maybe years, defied logic. Kari had never considered the possibility. It frightened her.

Kari was more independent than her mother. She contacted the same Navy recruiter and volunteered to be a nurse.

Every bit as good a scrub nurse as her husband was a surgeon, Kari's abilities as an assistant in the operating room matched Mark's skill as a physician. The Navy Department approved her application in less than two weeks, according her the equivalent rank of Ensign.

*I don't care about rank. I love Mark with all my heart. When he deploys, I will miss him, but I will not be left behind! If the whole world is at war and my husband sails into harm's way, I will be as close to him as possible,* Kari decided.

At first, Marta refused to believe the news about Kari. When she finally accepted it, she wept.

The revelation devastated Phillip. He'd been hoping for grandchildren.

"Sweetheart," Phillip turned to Marta, "our children are grown. They have lives of their own. We have to love them and support their decisions. When you think of it, we have a lot to be grateful for. We have two children and a son-in-law who are selfless, decent, and patriotic souls. We can't be upset when our puppies act on the principles that we tried so hard to teach them."

"I know, baby," Marta responded. "It's not that I'm not proud. I'm just scared. Phillip, I don't know what I'd do if anything ever happened to Kari. She may think that she's all grown, but she's still my little darling."

Phillip took his hand off Marta's. He put his arms around her and pulled her into his chest. He nuzzled his bride. "Sweetie, I love you with all my heart. I'm worried too, but I'm pretty sure everything will be OK. I'll stop at St. Francis tomorrow and light a candle," Phillip whispered.

Phillip and Marta held each other for an hour or more. They didn't speak. Lost in their own thoughts, they wondered if their family could survive the cataclysmic events that seemed so inevitable.

Marta fell into a deep sleep in Phillip's arms. When he was sure that she was out, Phillip picked her up, and carried her to their bed.

"Dear God, I swear that if you protect Gin, Kari, and Mark, I'll never ask You for another thing," Phillip prayed as he covered his beloved wife.

# Chapter 21

The 501st Parachute Infantry Battalion Commander kept his S-2 office in a new two-story white barracks next to his headquarters. The wooden building sat on the edge of a ridge overlooking Lawson Field at Fort Benning. The intelligence officer and his staff worked on the first floor, down the hall from the supply cadre of the S-4. Other support staff had the run of the second floor.

Hard at work in an office that he shared with three other soldiers, Genero had until 1500 hours to complete his portion of the staff intelligence estimate for the commander's briefing. If he kept his focus, he could make it.

Major William M. Miley, the feisty commanding officer, maintained his headquarters in an identical building next door, along with the S-3 operational staff and the S-1 personnel experts. Maj. Miley recognized the importance of the S-1 and S-3 functions and chose to keep them handy.

Not that Miley stayed in the headquarters building very much. Miley exemplified the hands-on commander, who believed that his place was with the troops. Since he led his men from the front, the enlisted men and officers held him in high esteem.

Miley graduated from the Military Academy in 1918, but had seen no combat in the Great War. When Maj. Miley received his orders to establish and train the first American parachute infantry battalion, he'd been working at a dead end job as the post athletics officer.

With the assistance of the alumni of the Parachute Test Platoon, Miley had trained a combat-ready battalion of paratroopers. The tidal wave of enthusiastic volunteers had undergone the difficult selection process and brutal training. They could now stand toe-to-toe with any elite military unit on earth.

To address the needs of a rapidly growing American Army, the Chief of Staff decided that despite their combat effectiveness, he would cannibalize the $501^{st}$ officers and non-commissioned officers. He would turn them into cadres for additional paratrooper battalions. If these new units proved successful, the battalions would grow into regiments. There would be artillery, engineers, and service troops in the formations.

Gen. Marshall toyed with the concept of an airborne division, with three regiments of paratroopers or glider-borne forces with indigenous artillery. As a result of persistent shortages in supplies, equipment, and aircraft, only Gen. Marshall, with his boundless optimism, thought the Airborne Division was feasible.

While Gen. Marshall fine-tuned his plan, on May 16, 1941, President Roosevelt asked Congress for emergency military appropriations. To justify his request, President Roosevelt catalogued the menace that the ultra-modern Nazi military machine posed to the only remaining western combatant, Britain. Roosevelt claimed that he needed vast sums to counter the menace of enemy airborne forces, which could strike without notice and create unimaginable havoc. In an eerily prophetic statement, the President expressly noted that, "Parachute troops are dropped from airplanes in large numbers behind enemy lines. Troops are landed from planes in open fields, on wide highways, and local civil airports."

Four days after Roosevelt's speech, the Luftwaffe struck its boldest stroke since the war began 20 months earlier. Leapfrogging over the British Royal Navy in the eastern Mediterranean, Gen. Kurt Student sent three regiments of *Fallschirmjaeger* along with a mountain division and glider troops to drop zones along Crete's northern coast. Student assigned 1,000 aircraft, including fighters, bombers, and transports to support these forces.

Facing the Germans on Crete, Britain mustered an impressive 32,000 Commonwealth troops and 10,000 Greek soldiers. Many of these men, some from as far away as Australia and New Zealand, had evacuated Greece in late spring after a disastrous campaign. The soldiers were still full of fight, but were also tired, haggard, and poorly supplied.

On May 20, 1941, a great bloody battle ensued. Combat losses among the German airborne force shocked Student and the German Command in Berlin. The *Fallschirmjaeger* suffered staggering casualties in their first line troops because the British Command expected an airborne attack and had done its best to defend against the tactic. An outraged Fuhrer ordered an immediate cessation to large-scale German airborne assaults, reasoning that this strategy had outlived its usefulness. Crete would be the last German regimental airborne assault during the war.

After the bitter fighting, the Germans managed to get the upper hand. Through British miscommunication, German tenacity, and blind luck, the *Fallschirmjager* were able to capture Maleme airport on the northern coast of Crete. In possession of an airstrip, the Germans air landed additional troops, including a mountain division. These reinforcements made the difference in the battle.

A week later, after suffering substantial losses of their own, the remnants of the British forces withdrew from Crete, leaving the last bastion of the Greek nation in German hands.

The Third Reich had executed the world's first large scale airborne invasion. The Germans had taken a substantial risk. From the American perspective—not cognizant of the huge Nazi losses—the venture had paid handsome dividends. As a result of Gen. Student's bold gamble, the strategic situation in the eastern Mediterranean strongly favored the Germans.

The U.S. Army struggled far behind the airborne power curve. The apparent success of the German invasion of Crete silenced the skeptics on the Army staff who had criticized the concept of the airborne division. In light of the peril created by the Nazis conquests throughout Europe, on May 27, 1941, in an address made from the White House, President Roosevelt declared a national emergency and finally began the process of putting America on a war footing.

While the action on Crete unfolded, German message traffic came through the S-2 shop in the 501st. Genero translated the data for the S-2, so that Captain Smith could brief the Major. Genero processed the data quickly. More than satisfied with Phil's performance, the S-2 and the battalion commander concluded that Genero was a good man to have around.

Phil had worked hard to gain the respect of the officers and men of the 501st. He started by driving straight through to Georgia from Carlisle in late December 1940. He departed in the afternoon on Christmas Day. He would have left earlier, but his mother was depressed about Kari's decision to join the Navy. He waited impatiently for his dad's signal that he could leave.

After kissing his mom goodbye, young Phil and his father walked to the roadster, already packed for the journey south. Nearer to the car, the older man stopped. He had something to say.

"Son, remember everything that we've talked about," Phillip began. "After what you told me last night, I doubt that you will ever see your staff job in Washington again."

"Well, Dad, I'm just going down there to translate."

His dad cut him off with a wave of his hand. "Gin, I have an idea what this airborne concept involves. In my day, the infantry walked everywhere. If we could hitch a ride on a wagon, a truck, a train, or a boat, we were happy. I read an article about the paratroops while I was in the barbershop at Boiling Springs. It sounds dangerous. I know you, son. You'll march to the sound of the guns every time. Don't try to play me the way you're playing your mother. I know better."

Phillip reached into his pocket and pulled out a small white box. He handed it to his boy. His son pulled the lid off and examined the contents.

In the box lay a gold medallion, the size of a quarter, attached to a simple gold chain. The medallion's face depicted a triumphant Saint Michael the Archangel, brandishing a broadsword in his right hand while stepping on the throat of a vanquished Satan. Turning the medal over, he saw the engraved words: "Phil, *AD MAJOREM DEI GLORIAM*, Love, Dad."

The older man took the gold medal and chain from the box. He stepped forward, and draped the chain over Phil's head, centering the medallion on his son's chest. Once in place, the father tucked the medal inside his son's sweater, and then gave Phil a hug so powerful that it took his son's breath away. As he released his boy, the dad looked up at him and began, "St. Michael is the patron saint of soldiers. He's an archangel. No doubt he'll extend his protections to paratroopers. I'll pray every day that St. Michael protects you. The sentiment on the back is a phrase you learned at St. Ignatius. Remember it. Ensure that everything you do for our country is also for the greater glory of God. I've given an identical medal to Kari. I had them both blessed by Father Nachen."

With the medal safely around his neck, Phil drove without sleep right through to Fort Benning, arriving on the night of the 26th. He reported to the officer-of-the day and the charge-of-quarters at the 501st. Though they didn't expect him until the next afternoon, they found a billet for him in the bachelor officer quarters.

Phil managed a few hours of fitful sleep. He reported for physical training with the battalion staff at 0530 on December 27th on a cold, dark, and blustery morning. The eager—but apprehensive—airborne volunteers had nicknamed the new barracks buildings *The Frying Pan*. They knew they soon would be leaving the Frying Pan of their billets and jumping into the fire of paratroop training.

Genero breezed through the five-mile run. Afterwards, Bill Yarborough introduced himself, and the two men chatted as they walked back toward the bachelor quarters to clean up.

"Genero, you got off to a good start. The Major appreciates officers who show enthusiasm, initiative, and dedication. Keep it up. You'll do well here. When you're cleaned up, report to the S-3 shop and I'll get you started on the materials we've gotten from the Germans. We're not just interested in a translation. We want you to help us decide what about their airborne program works and what doesn't. We don't want to copy the Krauts. We want to do it better, faster, and more efficiently."

"Sir, I could be more effective on the qualitative analysis if I had a frame of reference," Phil responded.

Yarborough laughed. "OK, Genero! You've been here less than twelve hours, and already you want to be a paratrooper. That's fabulous!! I'll tell the C.O. Major Miley will like that. Remember, this training has its dangers. You get all of these materials translated and I'll guarantee that you go to jump school."

Then, after looking Genero over, Yarborough added, "You look a bit bigger than six foot two, and you must be nearly two hundred pounds, though it looks like all muscle. You're in great shape. You're a bit over our maximums, but I believe—since it's my call—that you can get a waiver for the training. Do the translations first, then we'll make you into a paratrooper."

Genero worked hard translating the documents, manuals, equipment instructions, and the training film. The 501$^{st}$ had more data than he'd anticipated, but Phil completed the project in less than a week.

Remembering Yarborough's remarks about improving on the German training, Genero created two lists. The first list included items that Phil thought could safely be eliminated. The second list reflected his thoughts on processes that could be improved.

Recognizing that he was a second lieutenant and considered a rank amateur, Phil proposed the changes from a trainee's perspective, thinking that point of view would give him more credibility.

For a newcomer to the concept of vertical envelopment, Genero produced a pretty good report. Miley found some of the suggestions to be intriguing. He called Yarborough, the S-2, Captain Smith, Genero, and the battalion sergeant major into his office for a discussion of Phil's recommendations. The meeting went so well that three hours passed before Maj. Miley realized it.

In early 1941, the War Department intended that in addition to losing officers and men to act as cadres in the new formations, the remnants of the 501$^{st}$ would function as the training unit to provide basic airborne instruction for the vast echelons of paratroopers on their drawing boards. Maj. Miley realized that he had a diamond in the rough with young Genero. He quietly pled his case to LtCol. Bill Lee, so he could keep the youngster in the airborne at Fort Benning.

When Lee floated the proposal by Major Jardine at War Plans, he learned that a permanent assignment would not be a problem. Lee, who'd spent a lifetime in the Army, wondered whose pooch Genero had screwed to be so expendable. By the end of January 1941, the Army transferred Lieutenant Genero to the 501$^{st}$.

The same afternoon that Phil received his transfer orders, he made his first jump from an airplane. Since Phil had become permanent party with the 501$^{st}$, Yarborough decided that he could skip the weeks of preliminaries and get directly to the jump training. Miley needed Genero for other duties.

By early March, Phil had qualified as a military parachutist. During the training, he'd made 12 additional jumps. Phil discovered the adrenaline rush of leaping out of a perfectly good airplane. He loved being part of the pioneer airborne effort. He would have done anything to stay in the 501$^{st}$.

The pride of being a paratrooper defied lucid explanation. Jumping took guts. Soldiers had to be special to make the grade. The men who passed muster took pride in their accomplishment. They protected their insignias with intense jealousy, using violent methods to enforce its exclusivity.

The uniform and qualification badges of the paratroopers evolved over time. In early 1941, the paratroopers wore Corcoran jump boots instead of the shoes and leggings prescribed for the regular infantry. To provide the airborne with a special élan, the Army permitted the parachutists to wear these boots, always polished to mirror-like shine, with their Class A uniforms. The paratroopers bloused their uniform trousers into the tops of the boots. Both officers and enlisted men also wore a round hat patch, depicting an open, white parachute on a field of blue on their overseas caps. If paratroopers caught anyone wearing these items without paying the dues, they exacted brutal retribution.

Paratroopers called the soldiers in the rest of the Army by the derisive term *legs.* By regulation, a leg had to wear the trousers of his Class A uniform neat and straight, down to his low-quarter shoes. Legs were never permitted to blouse their boots. If a paratrooper caught a leg wearing paratrooper insignia, the trooper would assault the other soldier, beat him senseless and physically confiscate the offender's unearned uniform items. Paratroopers considered this behavior to be a question of honor. If an enlisted or non-commissioned leg got caught wearing jump boots, the airborne vigilantes would cut them down to low quarters, while the soldier was still wearing them.

In its wisdom, the War Department decided that the larger airborne units would include both paratroopers and glider men. There were no plans for special insignia for the glider forces. In fact, though the world had seen the Nazi's effectively use gliders to carry elite troops into battle in Holland, in 1941 the Army Chief-of-Staff had no firm idea how he would implement the glider concept and meld it into the airborne regiments.

Enlisted paratroopers received an extra $50.00 per month. Officers got $100.00 in addition to their pay. The Army paid a buck private $45.00 each month. Jump pay more than doubled a private's monthly salary. Glider men would receive no special hazardous-duty pay.

In the spring, Maj. Miley sent 1Lt. Yarborough to Washington to win approval for a parachutist badge, which Yarborough had designed. When Lt. Yarborough returned to Fort Benning in April, he brought several hundred newly minted sets of silver jump wings, which Bailey, Banks and Biddle had fabricated for him in Philadelphia.

Each set of wings bore a number and the initials "BBB" on the reverse. Phil, assigned as an Assistant S-2, received set No. 173. As was the practice in the 501$^{st}$, Genero wore his wings above the left breast pocket of his uniform tunic, over an oval cloth backing of artillery red with an infantry blue border.

After he completed two months of intense training, Phil settled into the slightly less strenuous pace of a junior officer on the battalion staff. He had a little more time to socialize with the other cadre at the Officer's Club. The jump wings attracted the local Georgia girls like a magnet. Phil had been in the 501$^{st}$ less than six months, and he'd already broken the hearts of two attractive young women.

Tonight, if he could get everything done by 1900, he would meet Ms. Laurie Bowman at the club for drinks. Tall, blond, and beautiful, she was a real stunner.

Bona-fide southern gentry, Laurie's dad came from money so old that she had no idea how the family made it in the first place. She didn't care. All that did matter to her was getting this big great-looking officer to pay a little attention to her.

Laurie could have had any man at Fort Benning or anywhere else in Georgia.

*I surely don't know why I waste my time with that big, Yankee farm boy!* Laurie thought. *I could have fifty dates on any weeknight, and a hundred on Saturday. I'm used to men who want to show me a little appreciation and affection. Phil acts so distant and even disinterested sometimes. It drives me crazy! I swear that I'd give him his walking papers, except he's sooo sexy!*

In the three weeks that they'd been dating, Laurie had given Genero a cherished little thing that she'd been saving all her life—her virginity. She surrendered that item in the front seat of the roadster, ten minutes into their third date.

Phil enjoyed the attention of this 20-year-old debutante. With a little more practice, the sex would be fantastic. He didn't mind the lustful looks directed at his date by all the horny young officers whenever he squired Laurie on a date at the club.

Undistracted by his fellow soldiers in the S-2 Office, Phil finished putting the final touches on the intelligence estimate for the briefing at 1500. Bill Yarborough stuck his head around the room divider in the S-2 office. He had a cat-ate-the-canary look on his face.

"You almost finished with that estimate, lad?" Yarborough asked.

"Not quite, sir," Phil responded.

"I've got some news for you," Yarborough explained, leaning casually against the room divider. "All of us will become cadre for the new battalions. It'll start happening right after Independence Day."

"Where am I going?" Genero asked.

"All in good time, lad, all in good time," Yarborough teased. "By the way, you're talking to a captain. I'm to be promoted later this afternoon. I'll be wettin' down the tracks later at the club. You bring that sweet Laurie with you and I may buy her a drink. Now that I'm finally rising through the ranks, you'll have to show me the proper level of respect for a change."

"Yes, sir!" Phil barked. "My compliments, sir, and would the Captain please be telling me what the hell my next assignment is."

"It'll be the guardhouse, if you don't learn to treat your superiors with the respect!" Bill joked. "Actually, you're to be the Assistant S-2, for the 504th Parachute Infantry Battalion."

"No shit? Who's going to be the S-2? Who's going to be the C.O.?" Genero asked.

"Those details have not been ironed out. You're an intelligence officer. You figure out the answers. I don't know where the 504th will assemble to train. So don't get too comfortable here. Don't make any promises to the fair Laurie," Yarborough warned.

Bill Yarborough smiled, showing all of his teeth. He reached into his pants pocket and pulled out a small silver bar, the insignia of an Army first lieutenant. Bill tossed the bar to Phil, who caught it in the air.

"Miley got selected for lieutenant colonel. He's in a generous mood. He received authorization to promote you. He'll do it at the same time he promotes me. Now I can get rid of that silver bar and get you to help pay for the drinks tonight, First Lieutenant Genero. The Colonel told me to fetch you about 1600 hours. Think you can make it, lad?"

Astonished, Phil sat frozen to his desk. He stared at the brightly polished, solid silver, first lieutenant's bar in the palm of his right hand.

*There's no way that I deserve to be a first lieutenant after barely a year on active-duty. The guys who spent ten years as second lieutenants must be pissed to see rookies like me advance so fast. But the Army's growing exponentially. Experienced officers are in short supply. I'll just keep my mouth shut and do my job, as a first lieutenant! Holy shit! It's my first promotion!* Phil thought as Yarborough teased him.

"Captain Yarborough, my respects to the Colonel. I'd be honored to accompany you to his headquarters at 1600. I'll be honored to share the expense at the club tonight."

Yarborough smiled at Genero again. "Phil, I'm glad you're a part of this. I don't know where it's going to end up, but we're in for a wild ride. Just remember your jump training. When the ground is coming up fast, and you've forgotten everything else, just keep your feet and knees together, your head tucked, chin down—and relax."

# Chapter 22

Kari Hansen, resplendent in her new Navy uniform, stood in the receiving line with her arm intertwined with the arm of her husband, Naval Lieutenant Mark Hansen. The line formed inside the double oak doors of the stately Lafayette Room in the Officers' Club at Carlisle Barracks, the venue for Kari's Bon Voyage Party.

Marta and Phillip Genero stood next to the Hansens. Marta looked stunning, as usual. Still, the stress of Kari's overseas assignment had taken its toll. To provide comfort, Phillip held Marta's hand.

First Lieutenant Genero stood next to his dad, looking sharp in his tailored Army officer's uniform with the glittering silver wings pinned above the left breast pocket. He exchanged pleasantries with the guests as they filed by.

The whole Genero clan had gathered for Kari's party. Half of the town of Carlisle attended, including members of the dysfunctional Monarch tribe. Earlier, Phillip had explained to Kari that because of his status as a vice-president of Monarch Industries, he couldn't invite the whole town to a big party and exclude the Monarchs.

Anticipating trouble, Kari spoke to her brother before the party. "Linda Collingswood is coming tonight. She's a bitch on wheels. She treats that pipsqueak of a husband of hers like a galley slave. Brudder, stay away from her! She's still attracted to you and self-destructive enough to try to do something about it."

"Don't worry, Sis, I have no interest in Linda."

"We'll see!" Kari snapped. "She's trouble with a capital T."

Genero had no plan to court trouble. He was up to his ears in work at Fort Benning. For months Phil had labored seven days a week, trying to help the Army make up for two decades of neglect in preserving its military power.

He kept so busy that it was hard for him to get away from his new assignment with the embryonic 504th Parachute Infantry Battalion, a progeny of the 501st. When he explained to his boss that his sister, a Navy nurse, had to ship out for Subic Bay in the Philippines, the battalion executive officer relented and gave Phil a precious 96-hour pass. The major understood reality. Genero couldn't predict when he would see his sister again.

The assignment to Subic Bay disappointed Kari. She'd hoped that her first duty station would be Pearl Harbor, in Hawaii. She wanted to be close to her husband. The Navy posted him as a surgeon on the Enterprise, an aircraft carrier under the operational control of the Commander in Chief of the Pacific Forces (CINCPAC), and home ported out of Pearl Harbor.

When the oily personnel officer at the Navy Department wrote to inform Kari that the Navy would send her to Subic Bay on the island of Luzon, he included some encouragement to soften the blow: "Considering the Fleet's current mission, the carrier task force to which your husband has been assigned can be expected to visit the Philippines almost as often as it puts into its home port. On those occasions, duty permitting, you and Lieutenant Hansen should be able to take advantage of the travel opportunities in that part of the world. I served in the Pacific Fleet for five years and can personally assure you that there are dozens of exotic locales that are ideally suited for romantic interludes."

Always pragmatic, Kari thought the personnel officer's observation was wildly optimistic. Still, she would hope for the best and take advantage of every opportunity with Mark. With a little luck, the time would go by quickly.

After their discharge, the Hansens planned to return to Harrisburg. Mark would open his surgical practice and Kari would start the family. Everybody would live happily ever after.

Outwardly supportive of Kari's plans, Phil actually felt pessimistic. His duties as an intelligence officer had forced him to focus on the war in Europe, which had taken a bad turn three months earlier with the German invasion of the Soviet Union. The last reports he'd seen before traveling to Pennsylvania documented rapid, sweeping advances by the German forces through the vast eastern European battlefield.

Russian losses numbered in the hundreds of thousands, perhaps millions. The Germans had surrounded Lenningrad earlier in the month. Less than a week before Kari's party, the Nazis captured the Ukrainian capital of Kiev.

Two weeks earlier, the President had signed an executive order directing American naval forces to take an aggressive posture while patrolling in the North Atlantic along the convoy routes. Roosevelt needed to keep the sea-lanes open so that he could continue to send war supplies to England.

Genero had also seen intelligence regarding the Japanese. The Imperial leadership fumed at Roosevelt's recent embargo of American strategic materials to the Japanese Empire.

Three days earlier, 1Lt. Genero spoke with his S-2. "Sir, I'm not sure that the Japanese Empire is stupid enough to start an actual shooting war with us. Their anger at the embargo demonstrates a fundamental vulnerability. Colonel Moses explained to me during our trip to Vichy that the Japs don't have enough raw materials in their home islands to maintain a war footing for very long. They would be hard-pressed to withstand our overwhelming naval power in the Pacific."

Both Phil and his boss conceded that the Japanese navy was first-rate, but they believed that it couldn't stand up to the American force that had been dispersed and forward deployed from the West Coast to Hawaii. If the Japs tried anything radical in Asia, the American Navy, with the best battleships and aircraft carriers on earth, would give them a major thrashing.

*In light of the geopolitical realities, Kari's assignment to Subic Bay is far better than anything in the Atlantic Fleet, which—because of President Roosevelt—is officially on a war footing.* Phil thought as he watched his sister greet the guests. *My guess is that we'll be at war in the Atlantic soon. Kari will be safer at a sleepy post in the Far East. General MacArthur is back on active duty. He commands a large force in the Philippines. Kari should be OK.*

As the line of arrivals started to thin, Phil noticed that another Navy nurse had arrived. Quite a bit older than Kari, she seemed very attractive in a worldly-wise, older woman sort of way. The newcomer wore the two-and-a-half stripes of a lieutenant commander.

A moment later, 1Lt. Genero met Lieutenant Commander Betty Landry, recently employed as a nurse at the Dauphin County Hospital. The Navy had appointed Landry to be the assistant head nurse of the hospital facility at Subic Bay. She also had orders to travel to Luzon.

According to the scuttlebutt that Kari shared with her brother, during Landry's prior service after the last war she'd been engaged to a highly decorated Marine officer. She'd been wild about him. Inexplicably, the jarhead backed out of his commitment right before the wedding. According to Landry, the Marine went off on some weird personal goose chase. Kari hadn't been able to wrestle the details from her new boss.

Landry never got over the Marine. Though she'd earned a saucy reputation over the years, she'd never married. Lacking a personal life, Commander Landry devoted all her energy to her profession.

"So, you're the famous Gin," Betty Landry said, her voice filled with levity. "I expected you to be eight feet tall. Are all the paratroopers as good lookin' as you? If they are, I might have to transfer to the Army."

"Ma'am, I'm the runt of the airborne litter. Back in Georgia I'm considered downright homely compared to the other officers and men of my battalion," Phil kidded back, feigning a deep southern accent.

"Is that a fact, sir? I do declare that the thought of all you handsome men gives me the vapors. I might just swoon into your strong, manly arms!" Landry responded in kind, using her best southern belle accent, while fanning her face with her right hand and batting her eyes.

"Listen, Lieutenant," Landry continued in a normal tone, "When your duties as greeter are over, introduce me to some of the local folks. I don't see a lot of familiar faces."

"Yes, Ma'am. I'll be happy to show you around the glittering Carlisle social scene. I'm bored and I really need a beer," Genero explained.

"When you find that beer, be a gallant paratrooper and bring me a scotch. Make it a double," Betty Landry requested.

Phil remained at his post long enough to note the arrival of Junior Monarch's entourage. Greeting the Monarchs posed a challenge. Phil thought that he'd seen Linda's husband Collingswood before, but he couldn't place it. Collingswood seemed reticent. He offered Genero a weak, sweaty handshake.

Linda acted bubbly and vacuous. Phil hadn't expected this silly behavior.

When they greeted, Linda held Phil's hand a second too long. He shrank back from her in mild Pavlovian revulsion.

"You look very chivalrous in that uniform, Gin," Linda remarked as she appraised him, looking him up and down. "Life in the Army suits you."

"Thank you, Linda. You're looking well, too. Would you excuse me? I've been given a task to perform for a damsel in distress. I should attend to it," Phil responded, as he left the receiving line and headed across the room to the bar.

When Phil stalked away from the line, he noticed that Kari had been glowering at him. His decision to walk away from Linda in mid-greeting caused Kari to nod at him and smile wickedly.

A few moments later, armed with a large glass of Genesee and a double single-malt scotch, Genero found Commander

Landry. They began to chat as they drank to each other's health.

"Who were those folks who just went through the line? Forgive me, Gin, but you seemed uncomfortable talking to that young woman. Are you OK?" Betty Landry asked.

"Oh, that was nothing. Those are the Monarchs. They own half of Carlisle. The rest of us are their vassals and serfs. My dad's a vice president in the company. I used to date the daughter several lifetimes ago."

"Which branch of the Monarch family do those people represent?" Landry asked. "I've met some of them. They're a unique clan, to say the least."

"That short, thin man bellying up to the bar is Randall Monarch, more commonly known as 'Junior.' The bored matron is his wife, Donna. The younger woman is their daughter—the debutante from hell—Linda. And the squirrel look-alike is the son-in-law, Collingswood. He works for my dad in the marketing department."

"That skinny man can not be Junior Monarch. I've met the S.O.B. and Junior Monarch is at least a hundred pounds heavier than that runt over there."

"It's the same guy, ma'am," Genero explained. "Junior got sick a few years ago, ended up convalescing out west. He managed to lose a ton of weight."

"Then it is the same man! Wow, the marvels of modern medicine! I know all about his illness. Some of his difficulties came from sipping from the wrong gourd, if you know what I mean," Landry responded, while rolling her eyes.

"That's what we heard. Although it was mostly rumor. Funny, nobody felt the least bit sorry for him," Phil responded.

As Betty Landry looked past Phil toward the receiving line, her eyes suddenly got wide as saucers. The color drained from her face, as if she'd seen a ghost, because—in a fundamental way—she had.

In a shaky voice, Landry asked Phil to turn around and identify the man in the black suit, who was coming through the receiving line. Genero spun around to reconnoiter, determined to find the reason for Landry's reaction.

Phil recognized Father Nachen talking to his dad. He hadn't seen his old mentor in three years, since he'd gone up to Camp Hill during a vacation from college. He'd hoped that Father would make it to the party. He wanted to show off his accomplishments to one of the finest men he knew.

Phil turned back to Landry and reported, "Ma'am, that's Father Nachen. He's the Principal at St. Ignatius in Camp Hill. He's an old teacher of mine. He's a friend of the fam...."

"Edwin Nachen! Is his first name Edwin?" Betty Landry interrupted, her eyes filling with tears.

"Yes, ma'am. How did you know? Have you met him before?"

Commander Landry's hand trembled. She seemed scattered. Genero asked if she was all right. Landry didn't respond, but continued to stare at Father Nachen only 15 feet away.

At that moment, Father Nachen turned to look in Genero's direction. He recognized Phil, and nodded in recognition, giving his former charge a smile and a friendly wink.

Surveying the gathering, Father gazed past Phil, focusing on the senior Navy nurse for a second. Father Nachen looked away. Then, Father Nachen lost his legendary composure. He did a double take that might have injured the neck of a lesser man. He could not believe his own eyes. "Beth? Beth Landry, is that you?" Father Nachen asked.

"Holy Christ. Eddie, it is you! My God, Eddie. You're a priest? A god damned Jesuit priest! Holy shit," Landry blurted.

Father Nachen and Commander Landry stared at each other in total silence for an interminable 30 seconds. Everyone around them believed that they were witnessing something momentous.

The roman collar and priestly habit on Father Nachen, and the Naval officer's uniform worn by Betty Landry, created an aura of authority so imposing that no one dared interrupt—at least, no one who had respect for personal privacy.

Junior Monarch, standing 20 feet from the couple, possessed no such reverence. He couldn't resist inserting himself into this difficult private situation. He rudely broke the silence.

"You two know each other from somewhere?" Junior asked.

As one, both the priest and the nurse turned toward the sound of the voice and scowled at the interloper. After a few deafening heartbeats, they looked back at each other. Father Nachen spoke first. "I suppose you could say that, sir," the priest admitted, looking at Betty Landry.

"Yeah, I'd say we knew each other in a former life, huh, Father?" Landry added in a voice that was soft and affectionate, unable to tear her eyes from this specter from her youth.

Phillip had observed the phenomenon from his wife's side.

"What's that all about?" Marta asked Phillip.

Phillip shrugged.

Kari, who'd been watching the whole scene, leaned toward her mother and whispered, "Father Nachen was a Marine, right? I'll bet you a thousand bucks that he's the jarhead who stood Miss Landry up all those years ago. Wanna bet?"

"Nooo! Really? Are you sure?" Marta asked. "Do you really think so? That would be wild, almost unbelievable."

Cautiously, the two old friends walked toward each other until they were only a foot apart. For another 30 seconds, both Father Nachen and Landry looked one upon the other. Both began to smile.

Betty looked up in the face of her old lover, cocked her head to one side, smiled, spread her arms, and said, "Eddie, do any of those vows you took keep you from hugging an old friend?"

"I don't believe they do, Beth! It's good to see you," Father said, stepping closer and embracing her.

The anticlimactic hug broke the spell on the crowd. The guests began to mingle again, convinced that nothing exciting—or worth reporting tomorrow—would occur.

"This is amazing. It's been so long. I never thought I'd ever see you again," Edwin Nachen continued, still hugging his former sweetheart.

Betty's emotions ran from joy in encountering her true love after 20 years to confusion over the circumstances of their unexpected reunion. "That makes two of us, Eddie. I can't believe this is happening after all of these years, and you a priest! Why didn't you tell me?"

"Beth, just a minute," Father said. "Let's take a breath, find somewhere to sit down, and get a drink. We'll sort this out. Do you have time?"

"I have thirty-six hours 'til I catch a train for San Francisco, then a boat for Manila. I suppose you can explain all of this to me in the next day-and-a-half, Father," Landry said, gesturing at Father Nachen's roman collar and black habit.

Phil had been so close that he couldn't help but overhear all they said. He went to the bar, got another single-malt and a large glass of red wine for Father. He walked back over to the couple and offered them the drinks.

Both looked at him vacantly as he handed them the glasses. They were distracted, interested only in each other. Father Nachen took a sip of the wine, swallowed, and closed his eyes for a moment to get his bearings, disoriented for the first time in many years.

"Gin, I'm happy that I got an opportunity to see you tonight. I'm very proud of what you've accomplished in the Army. And, look! You're already a first lieutenant. The cream always rises to the top," Father said as he looked Phil over and examined his uniform.

Wanting to give the reunited friends a little space, Phil took his leave, shaking Father Nachen's hand in a powerful grip.

"That's a pretty impressive young man, Eddie. I suppose you had something to do with his development," Landry said, watching Phil extract himself from their presence.

*My God! If things had worked out between Eddie and me, we could have had a boy almost the same age as Gin,* Landry thought. "Do you want to find a table over in the corner, so we can talk?" Landry continued aloud.

"I suppose we should. We have a lot of catching up to do," Father agreed. "But even though this might seem scandalous, I would rather take a walk with you."

"Doesn't seem scandalous to me," Landry offered. "I walk around with men all the time. This is my first time with a priest, though. Eddie, I need to powder my nose and compose myself. I'll meet you on the front steps in ten minutes."

Father Nachen nodded. He watched as Betty Landry walked in the direction of the ladies' room. He finished his wine, took a deep breath, and stepped over to the bar to fetch another glass.

As Father Nachen passed Junior, the obnoxious calculator couldn't resist putting in a jibe at the priest's expense. "Old girlfriend, Padre?"

Father Nachen stopped cold, turned 90 degrees, and faced Junior squarely. He gave Junior an evil look before leveling him with a scathing rejoinder, "Mr. Monarch, I'll thank you to mind your own business. You, least of all in this community, have the moral high ground to judge another person. If you have the slightest glimmer operating in that pea brain of yours, you'll know that it's best to refrain from any contact with me."

With that insect crushed, Father Nachen walked to the bar and asked the attendant for another glass of wine. The bar tender poured one for the priest from his best bottle of Chianti.

Glass in hand, Father walked through the crowd, making polite conversation. Though several tried to engage him in long harangues, he extracted himself in order to move toward the door that led to the stairs at the front of the club. He wouldn't miss meeting with Beth, not this time.

Linda and Donna, Junior's daughter and wife, had seen his exchange with the priest. Linda had heard the priest's none-too-subtle warning. Donna had missed it.

"Linda, what did that priest say to Junior?" Donna Monarch asked her daughter.

"Father Nachen thinks Dad has a pea brain," Linda Collingswood responded.

"Well, there's a headline for the Sentinel! Geez, everybody in Pennsylvania knows that!"

The bon voyage party continued for several hours. Long before Uncle Angelo broke out the mandolin, Kari and Mark slipped away.

Mark planned to travel with Kari as far as San Francisco. They had less than ten days to be together before Mark flew off to Hawaii and Kari sailed for the Philippines. They didn't want to spend any more of their precious time apart.

Phillip and Marta would stay at the party in order to give their daughter and son-in-law a little privacy at the farmhouse. Before leaving, Kari instructed them to keep Gin away from Linda, and vice versa.

Marta observed that Linda spent no time with her husband, Collingswood. Instead, she followed Phil around until she realized that she would not get an opening. At that point, Linda grabbed her husband and pulled him to the exit in an obvious snit.

Marta caught Junior staring at her. His wife either didn't see him doing it, or didn't care. *Thank God for Dan Monarch!* Marta thought. *I hope he gets here soon. Junior usually behaves a lot better when Dan is around.*

By the time Kari left, Marta had consumed four glasses of wine. Phillip tried to cut her off from a fifth glass. She knew that he was right, but the effects of the alcohol helped to numb the pain of her baby's leaving for Manila.

After a bit, Uncle Angelo played a slow Italian love song on the mandolin. Phillip pulled Marta over to the dance floor, and the two began a slow waltz. Everyone thought they made a great couple. Everyone—but Junior.

When Edwin Nachen stepped out of the club and onto the front stairs of the officers' mess, Betty Landry waited for him on the sidewalk. He walked over to her. They spent several seconds staring at each other and assessing how much each had changed.

Though he had gotten older, Betty thought her old flame was still a handsome devil. He appeared more distinguished and—even with a roman collar—just as sexy. No man had ever stirred her or satisfied her the way he had.

For his part, Edwin Nachen thought that Beth still looked as beautiful and sensual as the day he first saw her. Just gazing at her made him remember why he fell so hard for her, and never got over her.

After a moment, Betty grabbed Father Nachen's arm. They turned to walk, arm in arm, down the tree-lined street toward Thorpe Field. They walked along in silence for a few moments.

Betty felt very comfortable on Eddie's arm. As they walked, she had a flashback to a similar stroll they took in Annapolis, one early fall day, a lifetime before.

Although she had thought about Eddie every day since he broke off the engagement, the passage of time had blurred her recollection of the intensity of her love for the man. Tonight it all came flooding back in a deluge of conflicting emotions: Glad to see him—yet furious at the same time.

Father Nachen also felt the intensity. His choice in following the priestly vocation didn't occur because he lacked great love and strong passion for Beth. He took his vows because he believed to his core that it was God's will for him to be a Jesuit in spite of his love and passion for this wonderful woman.

Edwin Nachen yearned for the physical life that he'd shared with Beth. He recognized that its loss was a genuine sacrifice that God wanted him to make in His service. If sex were unimportant to a priest, then giving it up through a vow of celibacy would mean nothing.

Father Nachen had faith that God answered prayers and directly affected the lives of human beings. He wondered how his meeting with Beth would affect the fabric of the universe. What part could it possibly play in the Grand Plan?

Approaching the bleachers at Jim Thorpe Field, Betty Landry broke the silence first. "Eddie, what happened? Why didn't you tell me what you were going to do? Didn't you trust me enough to share your secret with me?"

Father Nachen responded, "Beth, the only way I can explain this is to tell you the truth. You may not accept it, but it will be the truth. OK?"

"Go, ahead, Eddie. I'm all ears," Betty responded.

"Betty, do you remember how we first met?" Father asked.

"Of course; how could I forget? We were at a dance at the Marine Barracks in Washington. You walked in out of the night, looking so dashing in your dress blues with all of your battle ribbons from the Great War. You were irresistible to a young girl right out of nursing school."

"I'm glad you remember. You were breathtaking, the most beautiful and sensuous young woman I'd ever seen."

"Eddie, I was yours from that moment on. I'd have done anything for you."

"I felt the same for you. Though even then I was terribly conflicted by the death and destruction I'd seen, and the mayhem that I personally caused."

"Yeah, I do recall that. The irony is that nurses are particularly vulnerable to troubled men. It's the caregiver in us. Eddie, your angst was never a problem for me."

"I knew that, Betty. It was never about you. It was always about me. I don't think that I was more sensitive or frightened than the average Marine. That wasn't it."

"Well, what was it? Eddie, you changed two lives when you made your decision. Don't you think I have a right to know why the man of my dreams chose celibacy over a life of love and passion with me?"

"Yes, I believe you do. First, I always thought that our intimacy was profoundly satisfying. Frankly, I miss it to this day. Second, what troubled me and made me feel guilty—besides the utter inhumanity of combat—was that I found the violence so exhilarating."

"Are you telling me that you enjoyed killing other men?" Landry asked.

"No, not at all. But, Betty, I did find it satisfying, and it gave me a profound sense of accomplishment to lead other warriors in battle against a vile enemy. War is primitive and there is a barbarian hidden in my soul, who revels in the victories that we won at a terrible cost. I ask for forgiveness everyday because I am not sorry that I killed those Germans, and given the same circumstances I would do so again today without hesitation."

"Eddie, I don't get it. You did what you're supposed to do. The Marine Corps gave you the Navy Cross, didn't they? What does this have to do with us?"

"Perhaps if I tell you what actually happened to me, you'll understand better."

"OK, Eddie. I told you. We have a day and a half."

"Beth, it was late spring in 1918. My platoon led our company in a sweep through Belleau Wood. Due to casualties, we were under strength with a little more than twenty Marines. We'd gone past our maps, so we didn't understand the ground in front of us. When we got to the top of a hill, we realized that it was a false crest and that the hill still continued up above us, but at an easier angle. The Germans had dug in above the false crest. Suddenly, we were committed and in among the Boche infantrymen. All of my men engaged in bitter hand-to-hand combat with the enemy."

"Eddie, it must have been terrifying for you." Beth offered.

"No, it wasn't. That's my point!" Father Nachen said. "And for some reason, known only to God, none of the Germans attacked me. I was armed with a hunting knife and a Colt .45 automatic pistol. I was able to walk through the melee, completely untouched—like some Angel of Death—and shoot the Germans who were fighting with my men. It felt surreal."

"You weren't afraid, Eddie?"

"No; not really. I was more concerned about hurting my own men as I shot the enemy soldiers who were struggling with them. Believe it or not, I had the presence of mind to shoot most of the enemy soldiers in the head, ensuring that my rounds would not go through them and into my own Marines. I remember feeling very calm as I blew the brains out of more than a dozen Germans. It was amazing. I even reloaded twice during the fight."

Father Nachen explained that he'd personally killed 14 German soldiers. His presence of mind and coolness under pressure saved the lives of a half-dozen Marines. As the battle shifted in favor of the Americans, the Marines under his command slaughtered the rear guard. Only four prisoners, all wounded, survived.

"Beth, as I said, to this day I've not felt the slightest remorse. I enjoyed the praise and adulation from my men. It wasn't until after the admiral pinned the Navy Cross to my tunic that I began to question my role. Frankly, by the time we'd met, I had already decided to leave the Corps and investigate the Jesuits."

"I guess that was bad luck for me, Eddie!"

"I know this will make you angry, but as I see it now, meeting you was the great test of my commitment to a priestly vocation. I came as close as one can come to abandoning my quest. I know I loved you without question."

"Eddie, I believe you. But you could have still married me and been a good Catholic man, devoted to his faith."

"Beth, you have to admit that even from the beginning I told you of my doubts. I just wasn't honest about the why."

"I suppose that's true enough. I never said that you were a liar, only that you broke my heart, Father Nachen. You still haven't explained all the secrecy. Why didn't you tell me?

Why am I finding all this out twenty years later, for God sake?"

"Betty, about two weeks after I...," Father began before Beth interrupted him.

"Before you walked out on me and broke my damn heart!" Beth inserted.

"Two weeks after I 'walked out on you and broke your damn heart,' I entered the Jesuit novitiate. A condition of my entrance was that I would not contact you in any way. The Jesuits assured me it would be better for you as well. Looking back on it, I concede that not telling you was cruel and unnecessary."

"Eddie, why didn't you tell me in the two weeks before you went into the novitiate? Certainly, you could have said something, anything, rather than disappear from the face of the earth, right?"

Elizabeth Landry's observation stunned Father Nachen. He stopped and thought about her comment during a pregnant pause in their conversation before he continued.

Finally, he began again, "Beth, during all of these years, I guess that I soothed my guilty conscience for the way I treated you by blaming the Jesuits and their rules. You're right. I should have told you before I left. I had two weeks to explain my decision before I promised no contact. There's no denying it. I just didn't have the courage to tell you. Now that I confront it, I know it's because I was afraid that you would try to talk me out of trying to be a priest, and I was sure that you and your loving ways would be able to do so," Father Nachen confessed. "At the time, I consoled myself into thinking that a wonderfully passionate woman, like you, would easily find love with another man, someone who would appreciate you."

"Just goes to show you how wrong a priest can be! Eddie, I'm not a nun and I've tried to lead a full life, but there has never been—and will never be—another man for me. Period."

As a scholastic and later as an ordained priest, Father Nachen had spent most of the last nine years in Maryland,

Pennsylvania, and New Jersey. As they continued, Eddie told Beth all about his life since he'd been an instructor, the Vice-principal and, now, the Principal at St. Ignatius.

Betty Landry listened as the true love of her life explained, in terms that she believed were honest and accurate, why he had chosen the priesthood over a life of passion with her. She didn't like it one damn bit.

"You know, Eddie, I believe you, but in a way it would have been easier for me if you'd have run off with a floozy. At least I could accept that. Our love had a quality that I've never been able to recapture, no matter how many men I've lured into my bed."

*God,* she thought to herself, *I must be the most pathetic mess in Christendom. Why don't I just tell him off and get the hell back to the party, where I can get soundly toasted? There are men in there who would love to have a go at me.*

Instead, Betty sat for more than two hours and discussed the minutiae of her life over the last 20 years with her old lover. Father Nachen asked Betty if he could write to her after she arrived in the Philippines.

"I don't know, Eddie. This whole episode has been such a shock that it will take time for me to deal with it. I know how to contact you. I'll write you if I feel comfortable with this whole soap opera."

Walking back to the club, knowing it was wrong but unable to resist, Betty Landry stopped Eddie, hugged him tight, kissed him on the lips and told him how she felt.

"Eddie, there hasn't been a day that's gone by that I haven't thought about you. In the early days, I wanted to strangle you. Other days I remembered how good you loved me, and I longed for you. Eddie, I wouldn't care if you were the Pope. I will always love you with all of my heart. Nothing can change that."

"Beth, I know this sounds unbelievable, but I've never stopped loving you. You are the only woman I've ever loved or will ever love," Father Nachen admitted.

"Well, that's some consolation, I suppose," Landry responded. Then in an almost affectionate tone Betty added,

"Since you broke up with me, I have learned that all men are bastards. Now I realize that includes you, dear Father."

"I've haven't been called a bastard to my face in many years," Father Nachen said, smiling broadly.

As she turned to leave, Father Nachen said, "Be careful, Beth! Have a safe trip. May your journey bring you fair winds and following seas. God bless you! I will say a prayer for you and your shipmates."

Father Nachen heard a faint "Thanks, Eddie," as Betty Landry walked alone toward her car.

# Chapter 23

Doctor Hansen entered the ship's wardroom, nodding at Petty Officer Second Class De Peralta, the Filipino steward, who went to fetch him coffee and juice. Hungry this morning, Mark thought bacon and scrambled eggs would be the ticket.

Mark hoped that they were close enough to Pearl that the ship might be able to receive commercial radio transmissions. If operations allowed, the Captain permitted Sparks to broadcast popular stations. Music would go well with breakfast.

The ship's vibrations had kept Mark up for a good portion of the night. On its warships, the Navy provided austere accommodations for its sea-going personnel. A blue jacket might bunk with 19 other shipmates. A chief petty officer might share the same space with five other senior men. Ensigns and j.g.'s slept four to a stateroom. On a Yorktown Class carrier like the *Enterprise*, the design allowed enough space in officers' country that full lieutenants in the crew had to share with only one other officer.

A lieutenant's stateroom contained two utilitarian bunks, two desks, and two lockers, all built into the bulkheads. The ship's pipes and electrical lines passed through the room, exposed in the overhead. Depending on the location of the stateroom on the ship, it might buzz, hum, or vibrate with the vessel's engine, machinery, or air operations.

Mark bunked in one of the worst officer staterooms with Lieutenant Jimmy T. Nolan, a Baptist chaplain from Pendleton, South Carolina. Situated three decks below the hanger deck and near the stern, the room absorbed every vibration caused by changes in engine speed.

This morning, the *Enterprise* steamed east toward Pearl Harbor after delivering a squadron of Marine fighter planes to Wake Island, a small but strategically vital spit of land in the middle of the vast Pacific Ocean. The Carrier Task Force had been operating west of Hawaii since the last week of October.

On duty, Mark had settled into a dull and mindless routine in the ship's sickbay. Though a highly qualified, board certified surgeon, he primarily supervised the hospital corpsmen as they performed first-level contact with sick and injured crewmen.

Though most of their work seemed mundane, the enlisted hospital corpsmen and their work ethic impressed Mark. These young men practiced a level of medicine that would not have been permitted in a civilized place like Harrisburg. An experienced, first-class bunch, after only a few weeks all of them agreed that Lt. Hansen was the best surgeon they'd ever seen.

Dr. Hansen's surgical skill saved the life of a petty officer second class from the air wing who had come into the dispensary, delirious and in great pain. Mark diagnosed acute appendicitis. He helped the corpsmen prep the man and then performed the emergency surgery, quickly and efficiently.

Lieutenant Commander Cohen, the senior physician on board, told Mark and the rest of the assembled staff that he'd never seen finer, nor more professional, work.

The lead corpsman, a crusty old chief, gave Mark his highest accolade: "You'll do, Lieutenant! You'll do!"

On the *Enterprise*, the Skipper, Captain Murray, encouraged his officers to take their meals in the wardroom. The communal life aboard the carrier required a special camaraderie among the ship's company and the officers of the air wing. The time spent in the wardroom fostered that solidarity.

The stewards had painted the bulkheads in the wardroom a light blue, in pleasant contrast to the gunmetal gray of the rest of the ship. The Skipper furnished the room with long wooden tables, spotless white tablecloths, simple china, respectable silver, and glassware embossed with the ship's name and designation, "Enterprise CV-6."

Mark felt that the food in the wardroom was first rate. A staff of well-trained Filipino stewards served each meal to the officers, who viewed this service as a perk. The dining experience in the wardroom far exceeded the more routine messing facilities provided to the petty officers and enlisted men.

If the operational status permitted, after evening mess on Saturday night the Executive Officer, Commander Jeter, allowed a movie in the wardroom. The stewards prepared coffee, lemonade, sugar cookies, and popcorn for those who attended.

The Captain originally planned to get the carrier back to Pearl by Saturday afternoon, December 6th. The men hadn't been on shore leave in quite awhile. They'd done a good job at Wake. It wouldn't hurt any of them to have a Saturday night liberty in Honolulu.

On the return leg, the "Big E" ran into bad weather. For two days the headwinds created difficult navigational conditions. They couldn't make it into the harbor before Sunday night. As a consolation, the Captain and the Exec authorized double features on the Saturday night movie at the various locations throughout the ship.

In the wardroom, the attendees got to see *Sergeant York* with Gary Cooper and Walter Brennan, as well as *The Road to Singapore* with Bing Crosby, Bob Hope and Dorothy Lamour.

Mark had seen the road movie with Kari before they joined the Navy. A night at the movies had been one of their favorite dates. Watching these two shows reminded him of his beautiful wife and how much he missed her.

Ever since their tearful goodbye in early October in San Francisco, Mark had asked himself a thousand times if he'd made the right decision. He always came to the same conclusion after he thought it through. He'd have been drafted in the Army, had he not gone into the Navy.

Kari would have joined the Army Nurse Corps. The Navy in the Pacific seemed a far safer bet for Kari than where Mark thought the Army would end up.

The war in Europe had gone badly for the English and the Russians. That appeared obvious from the newsreel Mark had seen last night, which was only a few weeks old.

Throughout the fall, the Germans had beaten the Soviets forces to a pulp. The Nazis and their unstoppable army had penetrated deep into Russian territory. The Wehrmacht held positions within sight of Moscow. The Krauts could make out the gingerbread towers and multicolored spires of St. Basil's at the Kremlin. Strong German forces surrounded Leningrad. The siege had caused much suffering in the civilian population. Across the entire Eastern Front, Russian soldiers fled in retreat.

Mark concluded that it was just a matter of time until Stalin's utter capitulation. The only thing that seemed to inhibit the Nazi blitzkrieg was the onset of winter, Russia's historical ally. If Russia left the war, it could spell the end for England. After a little over two years of war, the Fascists controlled virtually all of Europe, a good bit of North Africa, and were close to making the Mediterranean their private lake.

Mark had heard rumors that America was only a depth charge away from war with Germany. Its destroyers had engaged the German wolf pack in several incidents near Iceland.

A brutal air war still raged between the RAF and the Luftwaffe. No place in Britain was safe from aerial bombardment.

Last night, the newsreel had featured a human-interest piece on the American Eagle Squadron in the RAF. It included a short interview of a young American flying officer, Paul Reilly, from Philadelphia.

The newscasters interviewed Reilly of the Eagles' 71<sup>st</sup> Squadron because he'd shot down his fifth German aircraft, an ME 109, over the English Channel. This air victory made Reilly the third American in the three Eagle Squadrons to become an ace.

To Mark's surprise, Reilly seemed uncomfortable, shy, and humble. He'd noticed that among the Navy pilots aboard the *Enterprise*, humility was a trait in short supply.

At the end of the newsreel, Reilly mentioned that he'd attended Penn State University before joining the Eagles. Of all things American, he missed his family and the Nittany Lions' football games most of all.

Mark wondered if his brother-in-law had known Reilly while he was at Penn State. They seemed about the same age. In fact, one of the scout pilots, Mr. Sullivan, had gone to Penn State, too. The next time he saw the airdale, he'd ask Sullivan if he knew Reilly.

The steward brought Mark his bacon and eggs, along with toast and grape jelly. While the petty officer served Mark, Jerry Thomas, a Supply Corps lieutenant, junior grade, walked over to the table and asked to join him.

Mark grimaced a bit, but smiled. He gestured for the younger officer to take a seat.

Thomas had proven to be a serious pest. Whenever they ate together, Thomas took the opportunity to get as much medical advice from Mark as possible. Mark had never seen a more committed hypochondriac.

A few moments later, other officers joined them. They began a spirited debate over which movie star, Linda Darnell or Dorothy Lamour, would be the best date for an uninhibited, three-day liberty on the big island.

Mark voted for Linda, since she was a blond. He was very partial to blondes.

The men at the table had been at sea for weeks. They were all horny as hell. Twenty-four hours after this meal, most of the men would take the opportunity for liberty and all things sexual and alcoholic.

Mark noticed that none of the pilots seemed to be having breakfast this morning.

"Where are the airdales?" Mark asked Jerry.

"Most of Scout Six is on its way to Pearl. The rest of the brown shoes are getting ready to unass this ship. They'll fly to Ford Island and Ewa Field. The shore mechanics will do maintenance on the planes that we can't do on the hanger deck. Those mothers'll be downtown, screwing the best whores, before we get within fifty miles of the harbor." Thomas complained.

"Don't worry, Jerry; there'll be plenty of whores in Honolulu. The airdales are fast on the draw. They'll be there and gone before you know it," Mark kidded.

As the officers laughed at his joke, the steward came to Mark and told him to report to the captain's sea cabin immediately. PO2 De Peralta looked concerned, which caused Mark to wonder what could be up.

"Hey, Doc! The Captain probably has a hemorrhoid that needs checking so you'd better hurry," Lt.(j.g.) Thomas offered.

"Thomas, the only hemorrhoid that the Captain has to worry about is you. He can excise that by sending you to a merchant scow," Mark shot back.

That exchange caused the whole table to guffaw. The officers continued to exchange jibes as Mark hurried toward the bridge, several decks up, and forward in the vessel.

When Mark got to the captain's bridge cabin, a grim Marine gunnery sergeant was waiting for him. The gunny, one of the senior non-commissioned officers said, "The skipper wants to see you, Doc!"

"What's up, Gunny?" Mark asked, very concerned.

The gunny looked around, leaned closer, and confided in a near whisper: "Doc, our own people are shooting at our planes, over Pearl! We've already lost radio contact with one of scout planes over Ford Island. Something very bad is happening! I'm not sure what."

At that moment, Commander Jeter stuck his head through the hatch of the captain's sea cabin and said, "Hansen, in here, now! Gunny, zip it! No scuttlebutt, 'til the captain decides it's time. Get me?"

"Aye, Sir!" The gunny responded.

As Mark entered the cabin, Capt. Murray was giving his final instructions to the exec and LtCdr. Cohen, the Chief Physician. A moment later, the captain left for the bridge, brushing right past Mark without acknowledging him. He wondered what caused the skipper to be so brusque.

Before the exec could get started with the doctors, the ship's claxon sounded the shrill tones of the preliminary call for battle stations. The bos'n mate of the watch announced the order on the 1-MC shipboard public address system: "Now hear this!! Now hear this!! All hands, man your battle stations! All hands, man your battle stations! This is not a drill! Repeat—this is not a drill! All medical personnel report to sick bay!"

Commander Jeter looked directly at Hansen, appraising him. "Well, Doc, you'd better be as good a surgeon as Dr. Cohen says you are. We've got a wounded pilot and a gunner who may already be dead, trying to make it back to the *Enterprise*. If they land safely, you'll have to operate. Understand?"

"Actually, sir, I don't understand at all. What's happening?" Mark responded, confused, and more than a little shaken by the news.

"Son, we're at war!" Cdr. Jeter said simply. "The Japanese snuck an entire fleet, including carriers, within striking distance of Oahu. They've given Pearl an awful shellacking. Several of our battleships have been bombed and torpedoed. The Navy and Army airfields are under aerial attack right now! We're all in the shit and that's for sure!"

The exec, feeling great emotion but maintaining a professional demeanor, continued: "Who'd have thought those bastards could use torpedoes in a harbor as shallow as Pearl?

If it weren't for the god-awful weather, we'd have been tied up in port, like a sitting duck! Our first flight of scout aircraft stumbled on the Japanese attack about twenty or thirty minutes into it. Our own people shot down one of our planes, while the pilot was trying to land on Ford Island. We presume that the crew has been killed in action."

"Oh, my God!" Mark groaned. Kari was thousands of miles away, right in the path of the Japanese Imperial Navy.

Ensign Tim Sullivan began to fidget. He hadn't relieved himself in a while, and his bladder was full.

Sullivan had been cruising in his scout ship at about 12,000 feet over the Pacific Ocean, for a little over two boring hours. As his flight began to near the northwestern tip of Oahu in the Hawaiian Islands, his most important military decision would be whether to pee in the bottle that he stored in the cockpit or wait until he landed at the Ford Island Naval Air Station to relieve himself in the officer's head.

Time was of the essence. If he were going to use the bottle, he'd have to undo his flight suit and juggle the bottle and his manhood with his left hand. He would keep control of the aircraft with his right hand on the joystick. He'd have to accomplish this gymnastic feat while maintaining the trim with his feet on the rudder pedals.

Tim wanted to complete this ultra-complex military maneuver before he broke radio silence, contacted the Ford Island air controller, and got into the pattern for his final approach. Ensign Sullivan had turned out to be an above-average scout pilot, but he was not capable of landing a Douglas SBD-2 while taking a leak.

*Why does this always happen to me? I used the head right before take-off. I must have the smallest bladder in the friggin' fleet. I've got to be careful. I don't want anything on my flight suit. I'd never hear the end of that. I'm not feeling that bad. I'll wait,* Tim concluded.

Since he had taken off from the carrier and formed up with his wingman, Ensign Eric Wheeler, they'd flown a carefully plotted course. The first leg off the *Enterprise* had been 040 degrees to the northeast. Ninety minutes after takeoff they'd turned to 135 degrees heading at 160 knots, flying directly toward Pearl Harbor on the south side of Oahu.

As scout ship pilots, Sullivan and Wheeler flew specially modified, long-range versions of the Navy's Dauntless dive-bomber. Their job, along with other pilots in Scouting Six Squadron (VS-6), was to create an aerial screen, well ahead of the *Enterprise*, to let it know what lay ahead as it steamed east toward Oahu.

This morning, they expected nothing out of the ordinary. They'd seen the signs of mounting tension between the Americans and the Japanese Empire. Why else would the Navy have reinforced the Marine Corps air assets on that god-forsaken Wake Island?

Nobody believed that the Japanese would start any trouble this far to the east in the Pacific. If the *Enterprise* had been operating in the Philippines, it would've been another story. Still, for the last ten days, by order of the captain, every flight took off with its guns loaded.

Like all scouts, Tim and his radioman/gunner formed a crew of two. They flew in tandem in the cockpit, with the gunner facing the rear. The gunner had twin .30 caliber Browning machine guns, which he could unleash on any miscreant who dared challenge the mighty force of American naval aviation.

The SBD-2 had two fixed, forward firing .50-caliber machine guns that the pilot controlled. The designers provided these weapons more for defense than anything else. The Navy never intended the Dauntless to be a dog fighter.

Tim could carry a 500-pound bomb under the fuselage, or two 100-pound bombs on carriages beneath the wings. These bombs could be used on sea-going targets of opportunity. Tim had ranked first in his class in bombing technique when he went through the transition to scout ships. This morning, he anticipated no targets, so the bombs remained stored in armored magazines on the *Enterprise*.

Everybody in Scouting Six expected this trip to be a routine hop. Take off from the "Big E," fly your piece of the arc, turn southeast toward Pearl, land at Ford Island Naval Air Station. After the short debriefing, have breakfast, and then prepare for a terrific 48-hour liberty.

Tim planned to take full advantage of this liberty. He'd get a room at the beach in Waikiki. He'd have no problem on a Sunday night. The *haoles* and mainlanders did not visit Hawaii in large numbers in December.

*I'm going to have a real Sunday dinner at a nice little restaurant. I want five or six cold bottles of beer, too*, Tim fantasized as he fiddled with the rudder controls. *Before dinner, I'll take the longest shower in the history of Hawaii. After dinner, I'll sack out for ten hours or more. Of course, if I can interest a cute little number in a three-hour interpersonal adventure in my room, then it really will be paradise in Hawaii!*

*Damn, if I want to get laid I'll have to wear the uniform. I've never had much luck picking up girls without it. But then I'm not a genetically enhanced mutant like Paul, or handsome and athletic like Gin. Didn't Pat Kelly tell me that Gin is now a paratrooper?*

*Goddamn!* Tim thought. *Why would anybody with a brain, let alone anybody as smart as Gin, want to jump from a perfectly good airplane?*

Like most pilots, Tim Sullivan had an inherent mistrust of parachuting. It was to be done in an actual emergency and then only as a last resort. It seemed too perilous an undertaking.

*Yeah, come to think of it, 'undertaking' was the right word for it,* Tim thought, giggling at his own stupid pun.

As for Paul, Tim hadn't received a letter from him in months. The last time he wrote, Pilot Officer Reilly had destroyed his third German. It was a Luftwaffe bomber of some type that was attacking a target southeast of London.

*What a hot shot! Paulie gets to fly Spitfires, while I have to fly the slower dive-bombers. Oh well, life is not always fair.*

*Paul is in real combat, fighting the Nazis in war-torn Europe. I'm about to have a great meal, get laid, sleep for ten hours then lie on the beach and drink cold beer for two days. We're even! Except that deadbeat still owes me a hundred and fifty bucks. Or, is it a hundred seventy? I can never remember the exact amount.*

Tim had missed the movies in the wardroom the night before. He had drawn the mid watch on the hanger deck. This morning at pre-flight, he'd heard from another airdale that the newsreel featured some American from Pennsylvania who'd become an ace with the American Eagles in the RAF. Tim wondered if it might be Paul.

*If we still have that reel, maybe I can get a private viewing from the morale officer. I'll ask the black shoe after my liberty. It's funny—I was so opposed to Paul's decision, and it turned out well for him so far. I know one thing. I wouldn't be flying around in this kite with a bladder ready to burst if it wasn't for Paul.*

When the hangovers dissipated after graduation, Sullivan had knocked around for a month. Eventually, Tim had decided to become a naval aviator. Navy flight training had been a long road. He almost washed out on three separate occasions, but somehow he'd made it.

After he completed the flight training, Tim received his assignment to the air group on the *Enterprise*. In the last few months, through a lot of commitment and dedication, he'd established himself as one of Hopping's best scout pilots.

Tim turned his flight to the south, southeast. He allowed himself to get distracted again by the possibility that he might get laid. A benefit of being a naval aviator was that girls definitely liked pilots. The ladies were interested in a good time with an exciting guy. They were blinded by the gold wings on his white uniform, and ignored his plain features and average physique.

While Tim was contemplating his liberty tactics, he and Wheeler pulled through the dense cloudbank and saw Oahu beneath them off to the southeast. They realized that something was dreadfully wrong.

Off in the distance, where Ewa field would be, at least four large billows of thick black smoke rose thousands of feet in the air. Beyond Ewa, toward the east, the smoke looked even more black and dense. That had to be Pearl Harbor.

At that moment, Eric's shaken voice came over the RT set. "Scout Six-S-One-Eight look out! At your ten o'clock, low. Angels four. *Japs!*" Not wanting to give the enemy their altitude, he used the term 'angels' for a thousand feet.

Looking south of due east, and down toward the deck, Tim recognized a line of around ten Nakajima Type 97 torpedo bombers. Tim and his shipmates called these Japanese carrier attack planes the 'Kate.'

Tim did not see any Zekes, Japanese fighters, anywhere in the sky. Where could they be?

"Clark, go from radio silence mode. Acquire the local frequency for Ford Island." Tim directed Petty Officer Third Class Clark, the radioman gunner in the back seat of his SBD.

"Sir, Ford Island reports that it's under attack from a strong force of Japanese bombers. They identify the Aichi carrier dive-bomber," Clark reported less than 30 seconds later.

"Scout Six-S-One-Six, this is Scout Six-S-One-Eight, those Japs have attacked the fleet at Pearl! That's what the smoke over to the southeast is all about. They must be hitting Ewa, too."

Since Ensign Sullivan was senior to Mister Wheeler by six days, he acted as the flight leader.

"Scout Six-S-One-Six go to a heading of one-eight-zero degrees. Try to raise the Big E. First priority is the ship. If after three minutes you have not raised the Big E, go down on the deck, turn to two-seven-zero degrees magnetic, and make all possible speed back. Once you do make contact, ask the CAG how you should proceed," ENS Sullivan ordered ENS Wheeler. "Be careful, Eric. It's critical that you warn the skipper without giving away his position. Good luck!"

"You too, Tim! Don't do nothin' stupid! Out!" Wheeler transmitted as he peeled off to starboard and executed his orders.

Sullivan turned his own ship east to reconnoiter. As Tim charged his weapons, he peeled sharply to port, diving on the long Japanese formation.

As Lieutenant Hideki Tanaka piloted his Kate toward the Japanese carrier force northwest of Oahu, the last thing that he thought about was the possibility of an American dive-bomber coming out of the west. In the last 40 minutes the Japanese pilot hadn't seen a single American plane in the air. He'd observed the Japanese fighters and bombers obliterating American planes as they sat idly on the airstrips at Hickham, Ewa, and Ford Island airfields.

Tanaka witnessed the massive destruction of the American Naval and Army Air Corps facilities before and after he made his attack on his target vessel moored alongside the USS *Maryland*. After he pulled up from his torpedo run on the USS *Oklahoma*, he looked hard, but couldn't see a single undamaged American aircraft on Ford Island.

Tanaka felt a profound satisfaction. All the months of training to deploy special torpedoes in these shallow waters had paid off.

After dropping his torpedo and clearing the row of burning American battleships at an altitude of less than 100 feet, Tanaka's gunner reported that their torpedo exploded amidships on the dreadnaught, along with massive secondary explosions. Their attack had destroyed the Oklahoma's bridge.

If the next wave achieved the same level of success, the American fleet would be shattered with one possible exception. Tanaka had seen no carriers in the harbor. Admiral Nagumo and Commander Fuchida would deal with those ships later. Tanaka doubted that American carriers could operate effectively against the great Japanese Imperial Fleet when their escorts were sitting at the bottom of Pearl Harbor.

Tanaka had difficulty maintaining his course. As he turned to a heading of 345 degrees, he kept sneaking glances back to starboard to see the vast smoky ruin that had once been the pride of the American Navy.

Unexpectedly, Tanaka heard his radioman yell out a warning, followed immediately by tremendous shudders, teeth-rattling vibrations, and terrifying explosions in the fuselage and cockpit of his torpedo bomber. Tanaka's elation evaporated with the impact of high velocity, steel-jacketed, and tracer rounds all around him. After targeting Tanaka's ship, Sullivan had maneuvered so he could fire the forward guns of his scout ship as he bore down on Tanaka's bomber.

Recognizing that he'd get only one pass on the line of Jap torpedo bombers, Tim waited until he was less than 200 yards away from the plane he chose to attack. At emergency war speed, Tim only had time to get off three short bursts— no more than 70 rounds.

When he fired his .50 caliber machine guns, Tim was so close that two-thirds of his shots struck the fuselage and wing root of Tanaka's bomber with thunderous force. Sullivan pulled hard on his stick to avoid a mid-air collision. His action caused the remaining bullets to work upward from the midline of the Japanese craft, through the cockpit.

The American's assault killed both the torpedo control officer and the radioman/gunner instantly, the huge bullets riddling and shredding their bodies.

A split second after Tanaka realized that his ship was under attack, he absorbed three .50 caliber bullets in his left leg, abdomen, and chest. Sensing his death, the Japanese pilot looked down and saw a piece of his intestine protruding through the outer wall of his abdomen.

*I will miss the celebration in the wardroom, when the squadron assembles to express gratitude to our ancestors for this great victory. Karma!* Tanaka thought as his breathing became difficult.

Tanaka's seat began to fill with his own blood. Now, the victory at Pearl Harbor did not seem so glorious.

The last thing the Japanese pilot saw was his bomber's control panel disintegrating in a fiery blaze. After he said a prayer to his ancestors, he lost consciousness. Tanaka did not live to see the American SBD-2 streak over his burning aircraft by the thinnest of margins at over 220 knots.

Tim watched as the Kate disintegrated in mid-air. After one pass, and less than one minute of air combat, Sullivan had scored his first aerial victory.

Sullivan continued at his top speed toward the airstrips on Southern Oahu. The Japanese attack had achieved startling success. By the time Tim flew over the southern part of the island, the surviving defenders manned every anti-aircraft gun, machine gun, and light arm on the island. They trained every weapon on any incoming aircraft.

When he neared the naval air station on Ford Island, Tim heard a shipmate, Ensign Vogt, warn the Navy gunners not to shoot. Then he heard the awful silence of a radio transmission cut short by gunfire.

After Vogt's experience, landing at Ford Island seemed like suicide. Ewa Field burned like a torch. Tim had few options on southern Oahu. He would have to try for Hickham, a mile or so further to the southeast from his flight path.

In order to adjust to his new objective, Sullivan turned his scout ship to the north, flew evasively on the deck for five miles. He executed a tight bank at 700 feet, until he was flying almost directly to the south. Tim thought this would give him the best angle for an unguided approach to Hickham Field.

As Sullivan got closer to the Army Air Corps facility, he could see the smoke rising from targets all over the southern and central part of the island. The American military facilities had absorbed an awful pasting.

Tim's gunner scanned the skies for enemy Zero fighters. They had to be around somewhere. He tried to raise the air traffic controllers, but had no success.

As Tim dropped below 300 feet, not two miles from Hickham, he began taking hits from anti-aircraft batteries and small arms of all sorts. Flying low and slow on final approach, and not in a steep dive at emergency war speed, he became an easy target.

Despite his gunner's efforts to warn the tower, the profile and configuration of his Dauntless looked too much like a Japanese bomber, especially to the frightened and trigger-happy gunners below. The hornet's nest of soldiers and sailors on the deck shot at everything. As he flew into range, they concentrated their fire on him.

Before Tim got to within half a mile of Hickham Field, the ground fire pounded his aircraft relentlessly. The bullets and shrapnel tore through the fuselage, and wounded Sullivan and the radioman/gunner. Sullivan took a shot in the right thigh and left shoulder. A large piece of shrapnel pierced the gunner's right knee and several smaller pieces tore into his groin.

As the rate of fire increased, Tim decided to break off the landing attempt at Hickham. He descended 200 feet, until he was less than 100 feet off the ground.

Tim increased to maximum speed. He twisted the Dauntless in a wingover sharply to starboard, and sped out of his flight path in a generally southwesterly direction. Below safe minimum altitude, and at over 220 knots, the scout ship took a few more hits before it cleared the tip of the island, and continued out to sea on the south side of Oahu.

On board the Dauntless, the gunner sweated in agony. The petty officer tore a long wire from some damaged equipment in the back of the cockpit. He tied off his wound above the knee to control the bleeding.

As they streaked away from the island, Clark kept trying to raise someone—anyone—on Oahu, but was not successful. He faded in and out of consciousness from the loss of blood and intense pain in his knee and groin.

Sullivan realized that in a way he and Clark were fortunate. The scout configuration of his Dauntless included special long-range gas tanks. He could make it back to the *Enterprise* with his remaining fuel.

He had to ensure that he and Clark did not bleed to death in the interim. ENS Sullivan knew he could try to land on other fields on Oahu, like Kaneohe or Haleiwa in the north, or try for another island in the chain.

Sullivan didn't like either of those options. PO3 Clark needed immediate medical attention.

Sullivan chose to go back to the *Enterprise*. He could be on the flight deck in 40 minutes. Sullivan would have to use his ship's maximum speed. He and Clark would need better luck going back to the Big E than they had coming to Oahu.

Tim turned the scout starboard to 272 degrees, barely north of west, and headed out, away from Oahu at emergency war speed. He kept the craft at 100 feet over the ocean, since he didn't want to signal which direction the Japs could take to find an American carrier. He had no margin for error. Despite the pain from his wounds, Ensign Sullivan had to concentrate on keeping the aircraft level.

Ten minutes after Sullivan set the scout on the new course, Clark regained consciousness. Tim instructed him to try to raise the *Enterprise*. After two tries, Clark got sparks on the line, and gave him a full report.

Twenty-four minutes later, the arresting wire on the *Enterprise* caught the tail hook of Sullivan's scout. An emergency medical team rushed out to the flight deck to pull them out the aircraft, and to hustle them down to sickbay where Doc Hansen was scrubbed and waiting.

Unconscious again, Clark had the pale grey look of death about him. Sullivan had lost a lot of blood, but just made one of the better carrier landings of his career. Like the excellent officer he'd become, he insisted that the corpsmen care for Clark first.

As his shipmates pulled him from the damaged scout ship, Tim observed 30 large holes on the starboard side of the plane. The fuselage resembled a slice of Swiss cheese, and the triple A had severely damaged control surfaces. Tim wondered if the crate could still fly.

*If I can absorb half the punishment that my ship can, I'll be fine*, Tim thought as he began to lose consciousness from the shot of morphine that the chief corpsman jammed into his right arm.

The medical personnel rushed Sullivan down to sickbay. The lower portion of the ensign's flight suit was soaked with both blood and urine. The corpsman took out his surgical tool and cut the bottom part of the suit away, discarding it.

PO3 Clark remained on the flight deck. The corpsmen correctly triaged his condition and gave priority to Sullivan in this medical emergency.

They had no need to get Clark to sickbay. He died seconds after they gently laid him on the flight deck. As PO3 Clark lay in peace on a light tarpaulin, Chaplain Nolan ran to attend to him. The minister noticed that Clark was very young. The petty officer had a calm, serene expression in death.

With some difficulty, Reverend Nolan began his prayer for the beloved dead. He feared that it would be a long war.

# Chapter 24

O ver 220 years before Genero arrived in the sand hills of North Carolina, a small band of hardy Scots navigated their flat-bottomed boats up the Cape Fear River to establish the tiny villages of Cross Creek and Campbellton. The dense forests of loblolly pine, the well-drained soil, and the convenience of a navigable river for shipping produce and lumber to the small town of Wilmington on the Atlantic coast inspired the colonists' pioneer spirit.

Fifty years later, the original sites merged into a single town. The citizens named the new municipality Fayetteville, in honor of the French Marquis, who'd become a hero in the American Revolution.

In 1789, North Carolina ratified the American Constitution in the State House in Fayetteville. A fire destroyed the State House in 1831, and the town folk replaced it with the Market House a year later.

For 110 years, the Market House had served as the geographic, commercial, political, philosophical, and social epicenter of the Fayetteville community. Before the Civil War, the town folk sold all manner of produce, including human beings, on its premises.

By the turn of the 20th century, Fayetteville evolved into a typical southern town. The population, mostly white, enjoyed a slow, safe and comfortable lifestyle. A smaller subset, mostly black and Lumby Indian, worked hard but did not share in the benefits that accrued to the more affluent group.

In 1918, the Federal government purchased a vast track of land 12 miles north and west of the Market House, stretching all the way west to the towns of Southern Pines and Aberdeen. The vast, unpopulated forests and rolling hills would make ideal impact sites for the artillery testing necessary for victory against the Kaiser's forces.

The government named the new federal reservation Camp Bragg. Its namesake, General Braxton Bragg, had been a hero of the Confederacy. The bureaucrats felt that honoring a native son might assuage the sensibilities of the locals, who'd welcome the commerce that a new encampment would bring. The same folks would resent the consequences of a military installation in their midst, especially the influx of outsiders.

The peacetime draft in 1940 changed Fayetteville, Cumberland County, and Camp Bragg forever. The number of soldiers at the newly designated *Fort* Bragg increased from 5,000 to over 67,000 in a few weeks. Before the American participation in World War II was a few months old, the number hovered around 100,000 active-duty troops.

The units at Bragg included thousands of raw recruits, draftees in training, artillerymen in separate brigades, tankers from the 2d Armored Division, infantrymen from the 9th Infantry Division, and the legion of support personnel necessary to supply, feed, administer, and control such a large armed force.

War Department planners situated Colonel Bill Lee's new Airborne Command at Fort Bragg. Elements of the expanding airborne force, including the newly designated 503d Parachute Infantry Regiment, trickled into Fort Bragg throughout February of 1942.

Phil had reported for duty at Bragg 12 days earlier, with the leading elements of the cadre from the former 504th Parachute Infantry Battalion. In the continuing evolution of the airborne forces, the Army had reconstituted the 504th into the 2d Battalion, 503d Parachute Infantry Regiment, or

"2/503d PIR." Genero had served as a paratrooper for only a year, and this would be the third unit to which he'd been assigned.

Gin's old mentor, Colonel Miley, would command the Regiment. Major Edson Duncan Raff would take the reins of the 2/503d. Phil had served with Maj. Raff at Benning and knew him well. Though early in the history of the Airborne, Raff had already acquired a reputation as a tough, pugnacious officer who tolerated no fools. The enlisted troopers called Raff *Little Caesar* in reference to both his physical stature and the considerable force of his personality.

The non-coms admired him and felt that Raff ran the battalion competently. Phil would do fine with such a C.O.

In central North Carolina, the growth spurt of military forces put a strain on every service and commodity that the town had to offer. Everything that the soldiers needed was in short supply.

The limited number of apartments, hotel accommodations, and motel rooms could not meet the overwhelming demand. Soldiers and recruits clogged the two railroads that serviced the Fayetteville area.

When the railroads weren't ferrying passengers, they transported millions of board feet of lumber and large quantities of other products necessary to the complex construction projects that the government initiated to house and support the massive influx of troops at Fort Bragg.

Following the Japanese attack on Pearl Harbor, the government employed 31,000 civilian workers at Fort Bragg. These men, hardened by the depression, traveled from all over North and South Carolina to labor at well-paying jobs that the construction contractors offered to any man willing to work.

In early 1942, end-of-the-month payday created a dynamic event in downtown Fayetteville. The thousands of soldiers, recruits, civilian laborers, testy local citizens, manipulative bartenders, impatient whores, violent pimps, dishonest gamblers, scam artists, and crooks—along with large quantities of alcohol—always proved to be a sure-fire recipe for trouble in the bars along Hay Street. To this volatile cocktail, the Army added the nitroglycerine of airborne forces.

Col. Lee, Col. Miley, and the other airborne pioneers worked like yeomen to find the best possible young men to fill all the ranks of the airborne units: superbly fit, smart, aggressive, independent, self-reliant risk-takers. The Army intended that service in the Airborne would be different from traditional soldiering.

The young paratroopers developed into a tough, arrogant, and cocky bunch. They always spoiled for a fight, especially with straight leg soldiers.

By 1942, in Phenix City, Alabama and Columbus, Georgia, the violence caused by the paratroopers on Saturday nights and paydays had become legend. Many a bar brawl erupted into a small riot with serious injuries meted out to military policemen and airborne soldiers alike.

The post commander at Fort Benning had learned that the feisty and inebriated paratroopers would react more docilely if the authority figures confronting them were also airborne. Once he had this epiphany, he added temporary military police duties to the long list of undesirable responsibilities for airborne officers.

Brigadier General Kennedy, the Fort Bragg Commander, had discovered the lessons of Fort Benning's travails. As soon as the paratroopers started arriving at Fort Bragg, he required their officers and non-coms to pull temporary military police duty in Fayetteville on payday.

On his second Saturday night in North Carolina, Phil found himself in the front seat of a poorly maintained Jeep that the MPs had loaned to the Airborne for crowd support. Genero ordered his driver to park the Jeep in the small traffic circle outside the Market house at the end of Hay Street. In this way, the three temporary airborne MPs could keep watch on the whole street and respond if called by the regular constabulary.

Along with Genero, two enlisted paratroopers comprised the special detail. Maj. Raff had selected two large and bulky specimens of the non-commissioned officer corps. Phil had directed Corporal Tomas Echeverria to drive, while Staff Sergeant Bob Mason, an old veteran and a cool head in any crisis, would operate the radio.

Their mission: wade in when called. Soothe the offending paratrooper until he could be restrained. They might save the violator a concussion from the ravages of a nightstick wielded by a sadistic leg MP.

By 2130 hours, things started to sizzle on Hay Street. The bars jumped and so did the crowds of rowdy, intoxicated soldiers. Phil and his men remained alert: slightly tense, but motivated. They knew that trouble was brewing.

A few days earlier, Cpl. Echeverria had celebrated the end of his first year on active duty. Before the war, Tomas had spent two years in a Texas National Guard unit near his home in San Marcos. During the national emergency before Pearl Harbor, his entire unit volunteered for the Airborne.

After he completed jump school, Col. Miley selected Echeverria for Officer's Candidate School (OCS), which trained thousands of young men to be officers in the rapidly expanding Army.

Echeverria had a class date beginning in April. His time with the 2/503d grew short. Unfortunately, when he completed the 90-day course and received a commission as a second lieutenant, he might not return to the 503d PIR.

The Army usually didn't permit new shave tails to go back to their old units. The conventional wisdom among the top Army brass held that mustangs, officers who came up from the enlisted ranks, could not expect the same level of respect from the men who had served with them.

To bide the time, the three temporary airborne MPs sat watching and waiting, chatting calmly about the corporal's predicament. Tomas admitted that he wanted to be an officer. He did not want to serve with 'fucking legs.'

"Lieutenant, I don't really mind leaving the 503d. It would be OK, so long as the Army assigns me to be a platoon leader in one of the other airborne units that they're forming in Georgia. I worked hard for these jump wings. I don't want to serve with no fucking legs! Sir, it's only a matter of time until we're in combat in Europe or Asia. I want to be around men I can depend on. I don't want to lead a bunch of unmotivated draftees."

"Corporal Echeverria, my advice to you is to go to OCS, work your butt off, get the award for distinguished graduate, and ask for reassignment to the Airborne." Phil counseled, as he looked down Hay Street, and noted that the crowd outside the Town Pump had grown larger and rowdier.

"Sir, do you think I've got a chance of getting back on jump status?"

"The way the airborne is expanding, I have a hard time thinking that they'd turn you down. They need qualified officers too much. You're already airborne. How many jumps do you have?" Gin asked.

"Eleven, sir," Tomas responded.

"That's great. You'll have no problem whatsoever."

S/Sgt. Mason chimed in from the back seat, "Tommy, I've got an idea. When you get your butter bar, tell them that the last place in the world you want to go is the 503d PIR. I've been in the Army almost nine years. I can tell you that if you if want to go someplace, the best approach is to tell them you want to go someplace else. See, there's this rule in the Adjutant General's Corps that they can't give no soldier or officer any assignment that he asks for. So, you've got to trick them into sending you where you want to go."

"I wish it were that easy, Staff Sergeant," Phil responded, with an unusual edge to his voice. "I sure as hell know where I want to go right about now."

"Where's that, Lieutenant?" Mason asked.

Mason had kicked around the Army since the summer of 1933. He'd met a lot of officers. Most of them acted like giant pains in the ass. Genero seemed different. He carried his own weight.

"If I could, I'd leave for the Philippines tonight," Genero said.

"Sir, I've heard from the grapevine that you've got a brother with MacArthur on Bataan," Mason offered, regretting it the moment he uttered the words.

Phil turned in his seat, until he could face S/Sgt. Mason in the back of the vehicle. He looked him dead in the eye. "Actually, I've got a sister there." Genero said.

Everyone knew from the papers and the radio that the Japanese had MacArthur's forces trapped on Bataan. If President Roosevelt didn't send relief soon, and none seemed to be on the way, the Japs would destroy the American forces on Luzon.

"The situation on Bataan is scary," Tomas observed. "If we had the ability to send reinforcements, wouldn't they have done that? We're all airborne. If the President abandons the Army in the Philippines, what will happen if we get surrounded and cut off? Will the Army come for us?"

"Sir, what's your sister doing in the Philippines?" S/Sgt. Mason interjected, ignoring Echeverria's rhetorical question.

"My sister is a Navy nurse. She was stationed at Subic Bay, near Manila. When the Japs attacked the Navy installations, they spared the hospital complex, but pretty much flattened the place. Kari got out of Subic and over to Bataan with the help of the leathernecks in the 4th Marine Regiment. My dad has only had two letters from her since the war began. So right now I don't know exactly where she is, or how she's doing." Phil explained.

While Gin was sitting in a Jeep waiting to roust a bunch of drunks outside a sleazy bar in Fayetteville, his baby sister was hunkered down on Corregidor, a small island in Manila Bay. Kari had a ringside seat as the Japanese 14th Army under General Homma squeezed the American and Filipino forces under Wainwright, Parker, and MacArthur into a shrinking perimeter on the Bataan peninsula.

"I'm scared for my sister, guys," Gin admitted. "I think she's OK, for now. The other problem is that my mom's taken this very hard."

Phil continued, "My dad's written me every week since Pearl Harbor. I haven't gotten one word from my mom. Dad says that she's deeply depressed, cries a lot, and tries to blame herself for everything that's happening."

Cpl. Echeverria tried to console his lieutenant. "*Mi momacita* is very emotional too, sir. She went crazy when she heard I'd become a paratrooper. She's frightened for me. Moms are like that. Your mom'll calm down, sir."

"I'm not so sure, Corporal. My mother's a wonderful woman, but she has a dark side. I never saw it when I was a kid, but I've seen it lately."

Phil couldn't criticize his mom for being scared, when he felt terrified that something bad might happen to Kari.

Genero had reasoned that America didn't want to be in a war. Most families came to the United States for the express purpose of avoiding the repetitive wars in Europe. Americans weren't like the Germans or the Japanese. Americans wanted to be left alone to live their lives, protected by the two vast oceans from the excesses of the Nazis and other fascists in Europe, and the intractable imperialism and militarism in Asia.

Despite the geographic advantages, despite the peaceful intentions, despite the committed isolationism, America found itself at war. It was a war for its very survival.

At the moment, Americans seemed to be losing. Much of the main line of defense in the Pacific smoldered at the bottom of Pearl Harbor with thousands of dead Americans still trapped aboard the derelicts.

America had lost Guam. America had lost Wake Island. The Japanese Empire would kick America's butt out of the Philippines.

The Brits had lost ground all over the world too. Singapore had fallen. The Brits had evacuated all of Malaysia. The Germans had placed Egypt in peril. The Japanese controlled the Dutch East Indies, with all of its resources. Burma, then India would be next.

The Japanese had landed on the north side of New Guinea. The Japs threatened all of northern Australia. They had bombed and damaged the city of Darwin.

Phil thought, *if we ever manage to extricate ourselves from this horrific mess, I'll devote my life to ensuring that my country is never unprepared, surprised, and left vulnerable again. God, please protect my sister! I'd gladly sacrifice my own life in her place.*

A call came in on the radio that S/Sgt. Mason tended in the back of the Jeep. Mason listened on the headset, and then clicked the switch, responding that he understood. "Sir, they want us up by the Town Pump. Some tankers are not impressed with the elite nature of our comrades. A big fight broke out. They want us up there now!"

"OK, men. Let's get this over with," Gin said, meaning far more than resolving the evening's events outside a grimy gin joint in the little southern town of Fayetteville, North Carolina.

# Chapter 25

0300 Hours
April 21, 1942
Hospital Corridor
Malinta Tunnel,
Fort Mills, Corregidor,
The Philippine Commonwealth

Ensign Kari Hansen shuffled away from the operating room, negotiating the stacks of boxes and crates blocking the exit of the surgical theater in the medical lateral in Malinta Tunnel. As she passed through the theater's outer door into the dank cavern, she pulled off her surgical mask and tossed it into the large cylindrical hamper with the mound of other soiled gowns and dressings.

In any civilized medical facility, the staff would incinerate linens and materials as bloody and filthy as these. Buried in a cavern on Corregidor, the orderlies didn't have the luxuries of a stateside hospital. Japanese bombardment had created havoc with their precious medical supplies.

Instead of destroying the dressings, Army medics would gather the pile in the morning and take them to what was left of the laundry. The staff would salvage the dressings, washing and sterilizing as best they could. Although the reuse created the probability of cross infection, the volume of wounded men and the lack of proper supplies mandated this desperate measure.

Throughout the entire shift, both Kari and the surgeon had operated on some of the most seriously wounded and injured men that Kari had ever seen. No matter how hard they tried, it didn't seem to be enough. Kari and the doctor barely made a dent.

Though he was an able physician, Kari's surgeon had lost the second young man in a disturbing night. The fact that the last dying soldier looked a little like her older brother unsettled her.

The ceaseless Japanese naval and aerial bombardment had destroyed the aboveground structures on Topside, Middleside, and Bottomside. Shells from navy destroyers, antipersonnel explosives from 'Betty' bombers, and rounds from land-based artillery—now situated on the high ground of the Bataan peninsula—killed and wounded any American who ventured from a fortified emplacement.

The whole exposed infrastructure of the once-proud bastion of America's military might resembled the ruins of a lost city. Few of the Americans, who manned the defensive positions on Fort Mills, had prepared for the horrible circumstances that they encountered during the siege of Corregidor. In contrast to the pre-war garrison life, their current circumstances seemed surrealistic. Unfortunately, they would not awaken from this particular nightmare.

For Kari, her family and life as a doctor's wife in Harrisburg seemed like ancient, irrelevant history in this sticky and badly lit tunnel deep in Malinta Hill.

About 20 yards down the tunnel from the operating room, Kari found a metal bench and plopped herself down. Leaning against the tunnel wall, she closed her eyes and thought of Mark. Kari wondered where he was and what he was doing. Mark remained the one constant in her universe. *I only hope Mark is still all right. No one knows where the Enterprise is operating, or if—God willing—she's still afloat. Lord, please watch out for Mark. Make him be careful. I don't care what you have in store for me, so long as Mark survives this awful war,* Kari prayed.

News of the war beyond Corregidor arrived in a garbled form to those few thousand Americans who still held out on the Rock. Rumors covered the whole spectrum from dire reports of a complete American defeat in the Pacific to hopeful claims of scattered allied victories.

*War Plan Orange*, the strategy designed over decades to defend the Philippines, had proved to be disastrous. Bataan had fallen two weeks earlier in one of the most appalling military catastrophes in American history.

All the surviving American and Filipino forces on the peninsula had surrendered. Most of the Army nurses—and three Navy nurses—evacuated to Corregidor. The rest of the Americans, including most of the Navy nurses, became prisoners. After two weeks on the Rock, Kari had made peace with the notion that she and her comrades would not live to see the next month.

As she half-dozed on the metal bench, Kari thought that the first days of the war. Though frightening, they were child's play compared to what she'd experienced as the Japanese tightened their vise around the island and increased the bombardment.

In early November of 1941, after a 31-day cruise with stops at Midway and Guam, the ship carrying Kari and Betty docked at the port in Manila. To a girl who'd not seen much of the world until she joined the Navy, the Philippine Commonwealth seemed an exotic and enchanting place.

After her arrival, Kari and Betty Landry rode through the busy streets and densely populated warrens of old Manila in the staff car that the Navy sent to fetch them. Kari marveled at the unusual sights, foreign sounds, and unique smells, especially the beautiful fragrances of oriental plants and flowers.

The image of the slow-moving carts filled with goods and produce, pulled by carabao, painted a quaint picture, as they shared the busy streets with a wide variety of cars and trucks. The market's hustle and bustle created an atmosphere unlike anything Kari had ever imagined.

After her first few hours in P.I., Kari began to panic, feeling the ground shifting under her, as Manila had nothing in common with Carlisle. Kari was tired from the sea voyage.

She was halfway around the world from her mom and dad, and thousands of miles from her husband.

After allowing them a day to get their bearings, the brass in Manila directed the two nurses to a briefing at the Navy hospital at Cavite to give the women time to acclimate to the tropics and the Navy way of doing things in the Far East. During this respite, the two women had the opportunity to take short trips through Manila and to socialize at the Army/Navy Club.

At the end of their first week, the nurses boarded a local steamer for passage to Olongapo, the little Filipino town next to the Navy installation at Subic Bay. Although the schedule suggested that the steamer would leave promptly at 1600 hours, it was nearly 2300 hours before they left the dock for the short trip west, past the mouth of Manila Bay. When they passed into the South China Sea, they turned north for the quick jaunt to Subic Bay. Owing to the weather and the ten-knot speed of the steamer, Kari got her first view of Corregidor that night as they sailed past on their way out to sea.

Fog obscured the light of the crescent moon on the water. From the rail of the steamer Kari could only make out a dark, hulking mass in the distance. She had no idea what lay in store, or the importance that the Rock would soon play in her life.

In her first days at Subic Bay, Kari enjoyed her assignment. Filipino custodians kept the nurses' quarters clean and well maintained. For just a few dollars a month the houseboys cleaned her room, made her bed, did her laundry, and shined her shoes. Each duty day, all Kari had to do was get up, shower, dress in a fresh set of starched whites, eat a hearty breakfast at the officer's mess, and report to work.

When she returned to her quarters after lunch, everything would be shipshape. Since their small hospital was quiet, Kari and Landry could take some afternoons off. Her assignment to Subic felt more like a vacation than the usual pace of a surgical scrub nurse from a busy stateside hospital like St. Teresa's.

In the afternoons Kari could swim, play tennis, read, explore the market in Olongapo, play cards, and get ready for the round of social events that the base provided all through the week. The shank of the day seemed like total indolence.

Kari wished that Mark could be there with her. Life at Subic Bay could have been the honeymoon predicted by the Navy personnel officer, except that her husband was 2,500 miles to the southeast in Honolulu.

American men outnumbered the women on the base by hundreds to one. The nurses got a lot of attention from the male officers who were actual or geographic bachelors. Though some young Filipino women were exceptional beauties from a culture that permitted the world's oldest profession, American nurses remained very popular with the guys.

Though the most beautiful American woman on the installation, because of her personality, Kari had no clue. Being modest, she chalked up the attention she got to the fact that there were very few American women around. Unfortunately, having inherited her mother's passionate nature, she became desperately randy. Kari made a commitment to ignore her desires and the naval officers and Marines who openly lusted after her.

*The next time I see Mark, we'll have a reunion that he might not be able to walk away from. Poor dear, I'll find ways to comfort him,* Kari thought.

Kari's insistence on fidelity did not keep her from boating, fishing, bicycling, shopping, card playing, dining, partying, or dancing with the single men on social occasions. She always participated in these events in the company of Betty Landry.

Betty had a more pragmatic approach to the demographic advantages in Subic Bay. She took full advantage of them.

Landry's meeting with Eddie Nachen less than two months earlier had opened old wounds and caused a lot of pain. That evening had shaken her.

It took Landry several weeks to deal with it. By that time, she had traveled halfway across the Pacific Ocean. In Subic

Bay, she could do nothing about Eddie Nachen. After all, he lived in a cloister. He'd taken a solemn vow never to do all of those sensuous things that he once had done so well.

Betty Landry, a classic Type A personality, wanted to understand the Grand Plan. If there was a God, as she believed, how could He be so callous with her feelings? How could an omniscient and all-caring Being cruelly dangle the thing she wanted most in life right before her eyes, then pull it back out of reach?

Landry had divined no answers to these great questions by the time she got to Subic Bay. One look at the good looking men lining up to entertain her caused her to consider one question: Why the hell not?

While Kari remained faithful to Mark, but otherwise had the time of her life, Betty Landry felt miserable about Eddie Nachen, but tried to find solace in the arms of a very fit major with the 4th Marines.

The 4th Marine Regiment arrived at Subic Bay only days before Kari and Betty. These tough and experienced Marines had served for ten years in Shanghai. They'd evacuated to Subic because of the deteriorating relations between the United States and the Empire of Japan.

More than a 1,000 strong, the 4th Marines were a welcome addition to the Navy's defenses at Subic Bay. Tensions with the Japanese soared and the possibility of war increased daily.

In late November, Betty Landry began spending her nights in the bachelor quarters of Major Ted McTagert, USMC. A short but powerfully built man, McTagert had devoted 28 years to his beloved Corps, mostly as a fleet Marine or a grunt in China.

Though 44 years old, Ted had the stamina and strength of a man in his early 30s. While stationed in China, Major McTagert had studied various forms of Chinese martial arts. He'd become proficient in Wushu—or Kung Fu—and Jiao Di. These served him well since he dearly loved to fight.

Maj. McTagert's men respected him because he was a competent leader. It didn't hurt that he could beat the snot out of anyone who had the bad judgment to challenge one of his orders. Once in a while, just to prove a point, he did.

Incredibly fit, Ted had the stamina to keep up with Betty's physical needs, which proved to be considerable. While stationed in Shanghai, Ted had employed a young Chinese girl as a concubine. The girl often complained to her family that the Marine officer's sex drive wore her out and made her very sore.

Betty had no complaints. She liked his prowess and enthusiasm. Betty thought it ironic that the only other man who could do that was also a Marine. *Whatever did the DIs teach these boys in that Boot Camp on Paris Island?* Betty thought.

Of course, she actually *loved* her first Marine. As time wore on, Betty recognized that she still did.

In Subic Bay, the first week of December came and went without real significance. On Sunday, December 7, Kari, Betty, Ted, and a young Marine officer in McTagert's battalion spent the balmy afternoon playing doubles on the base tennis courts. Later in the evening, the same group, along with a few other nurses and officers, got together for Sunday dinner at the club. After dinner, the group played a robust local version of pinochle.

That night in her quarters, Kari slept fitfully. She woke several times in a cold sweat, thinking about Mark.

In the early morning hours, when she could stand it no longer, Kari relieved her sexual stress. She thought of the first time that she and Mark had made love in his apartment near the hospital. That became the first delicious episode in a satisfying series that, until the peacetime draft, had seen no threat of interruption.

The fantasy of Mark's gentle lovemaking raised Kari's heart rate and temperature. Her flawless skin broke out in small goose bumps. Out of control, Kari's own manipulations intensified as she fell over the edge. She punctuated her relief with a series of high-pitched squeaks and moans, as she came in a quivering wave.

While Kari lay alone in her bed retreating from her sexual high and dreaming of her husband, Betty Landry awoke with a plan to screw Ted's brains out. Landry always performed her best in the wee hours.

To her delight, Ted also enjoyed a morning interlude. Landry believed that good sex was the only civilized way to start the day.

McTagert enjoyed Landry's version of reveille. He'd been a Marine since he lied about his age to escape an abusive stepfather in 1914. If his relationship with Landry lasted, 1942 might be the best year of his career.

McTagert had seen bad times. As an enlisted Marine, he'd fought in limited engagements in Central America. Later as a corporal he'd served in France during the World War I.

In the 20s, the Corps stationed Ted in China. In 1924, while on leave in Hong Kong, he killed an Englishman in a vicious bar fight.

The confusion of the British colonial constabulary allowed him an opportunity to slip out of the jurisdiction on a boat to Macao. Ted had started the fight and intentionally killed the man for insulting his tattoo of the Eagle, Globe, and Anchor.

All through his career, Ted trafficked with scores of local women. Betty was the first woman he might be able to really love.

Ted looked forward to his intimate interludes with Betty. The most responsive and vocal lover he'd ever had, when Betty got wound up, she let him, and everyone in the vicinity, know that he had pleased her.

In the past, Ted didn't care whether he satisfied his partner or not. With this saucy, outspoken vixen, pleasing her became his paramount concern.

At 0400 hours on Monday, December 8, 1941, Ted woke up from a contented sleep to find Betty hard at work stimulating him. As strong and powerful a man as he was, he enjoyed it when Betty took charge.

Betty threw her shapely leg over Ted's body, straddling his waist, and positioning him for their lovemaking. With a needy moan, she took him inside.

Betty moved faster and faster, up and down, rotating her hips in sharp, sensual ellipses. Several minutes later, she increased the tempo again. She noticed Ted had a far away look, as she focused on the pleasure in her sexual core.

Sooner than she wanted, she felt the rush of her impending climax. She redoubled her efforts. She wanted Ted to come with her. Unable to resist the stimulus of a truly wanton lover, Ted moaned as he lost control. Spent from their passion, Betty collapsed on top of Ted.

McTagert sported a silly and vacuous expression. He remained on his back with his lover on top of him. He closed his eyes, wrapped his arms around her and enjoyed Betty's weight, while she lay satiated and stretched across his chest. On the downside of his hormonal rush, Ted drifted off into a light sleep. For an officer who had no home but the Corps, this was as good as it would ever get.

Ted hadn't been asleep for more than ten minutes when something disquieting caused him to wake with a start. Betty had slipped off to his right side, but dozed softly with her arm draped over his massive chest.

Ted didn't move, but listened for several seconds. At first he heard nothing out of the ordinary for a busy military base in the hour before reveille. As he started to relax, he again heard the sound that had startled him.

Off in the distance, but growing louder and closer, he heard the shouts. Thirty seconds later, the base siren began its awful wail. McTagert jumped out of bed and started to dress. They had a problem. It couldn't be good.

The siren startled Betty, who sat up and watched in some confusion as Ted moved like a human blur around his bachelor quarters.

"What's happening, Ted?" Landry asked. "Why is the siren blaring? What in the hell is going on?"

"Don't know, but you should get moving, too! Sounds like an alert to me," Ted explained.

Betty had gotten into the habit of bringing her uniform to Ted's quarters so she could dress before walking out his door. This tactic avoided needless explanations, if she ran into other officers on the way back to her own room. Of course, everyone on Subic knew that McTagert and Landry had shacked up.

While Landry broke starch on her white nurse's uniform and put the last touches on her hair, a Marine buck sergeant ran up and started pounding on McTagert's door.

"Stop that pounding. I hear you. Who is it?" McTagert asked in an irritated tone, as he laced and tied his low quarters.

"Sir, it's Sergeant Hall. The Colonel wants you down at HQ, now! The fucking Japs have bombed Pearl Harbor! We're at war, sir!" The sergeant yelled through the door. "The regiment is at Condition Red. All officers are to report..."

Maj. McTagert strode to the door and opened it, cutting Sgt. Hall off in mid sentence. Ted smiled at the non-com. "That was a dumb ass thing for the Nips to do, don't you think Sergeant? All that means is that now they'll have to fight us. The 4th Marines will make those crazy bastards wish that their blessed ancestors had never been born, right?" McTagert asked in a calm, confident tone, designed to spin the younger man down.

Up until that moment, Sgt. Hall had been scared. A tough young man from Spokane, he'd never fired a shot in anger. He'd already concluded that he would rectify that problem in short order.

He stood in Maj. McTagert's doorway, watching over the officer's shoulder as that sexy nurse straightened the seams of her silk stockings. She might be older, but she was still hot.

Maj. McTagert noticed the sergeant's voyeurism. He gave the younger man an obvious wink, a gesture by one Marine who'd gotten lucky to a less fortunate comrade.

"Sergeant, I've got the word. Move out and alert the other officers. Tell Captain O'Dowd that I want him to meet me at the battalion CP in fifteen minutes. He and I need to talk before we report to the Skipper."

"Aye, sir!" Sgt. Hall responded, rendering his superior a crisp salute, then executing a perfect about face.

*I actually feel bad for those dumb Jap fuckers. They'll have to tangle with the fighting 4ᵗʰ Marines,* Sgt. Hall thought as he moved out smartly to alert the other officers.

The Americans on Luzon did not fare well over the next few months. Their plight became a tragedy of historical proportions.

The Japanese conducted air assaults against vital American assets. Despite the lessons of Pearl Harbor, the Japanese caught American aircraft on the ground on two separate occasions.

Faced with an invasion by General Masaharu Homma's 14ᵗʰ Army at Lingayen Gulf on the west coast of Luzon and a dire threat from Lamon in the east, Gen. MacArthur declared Manila to be an open city. To avoid being surrounded, and consistent with War Plan Orange, MacArthur ordered all of the American and Filipino forces on Luzon to retreat to the Bataan Peninsula to set up a line of defense.

Throughout January and February, the Americans and Filipinos fought a series of brutal and vicious engagements with the invaders. Despite the fact that they lived on half rations, the defenders battled the Japanese units to a standstill.

The Japanese invasion force fared poorly. As a result of combat losses and disease, the bulk of the 14ᵗʰ Imperial Army became ineffective by late February. Gen. Homma suffered much loss of face with the Japanese high command. He suspended offensive operations until reinforcements arrived to assist him.

The Americans had based War Plan Orange on a complete fallacy. WPO-3, as the staffers called the strategy, assumed that the American forces would have the manpower, logistics, and tenacity to last six months on Bataan until the Navy could muster a force in America and Hawaii to relieve and reinforce them.

For the plan to have any hope, the allies had to move their military supplies from Luzon to Bataan and the land and air forces had to achieve tactical successes. Even then, the Navy still had to bring overwhelming force into the Philippines by the late spring of 1942.

In execution, the American commanders failed. The logisticians could not transport vital stores from sites on Luzon to Bataan. The Japanese destroyed the American aircraft on the ground, and had gained tactical air superiority in the local theater of operations.

Aside from submarines and small PT boats, American vessels could not operate for long in the waters off the Philippines. Re-supply slowed to a trickle.

By March President Roosevelt realized that America would lose the war of attrition on Bataan. Much of his Pacific Fleet lay at the bottom of Pearl Harbor. America could not muster a relief force for the men who called themselves the *Battling Bastards of Bataan*, because they had *no mama, no papa, and no Uncle Sam.*

Kari saw the war through a garish kaleidoscope. In December, from sandbagged emplacements on the base at Subic Bay, she watched as the Japanese air forces bombed her installation. Subsequently, she helped the Navy surgeon, Lieutenant Cambridge, operate on the wounded sailors who'd manned the anti-aircraft emplacements.

After the initial air attacks, the American command decided that the Navy defense of Subic Bay was hopeless. MacArthur transferred the 4th Marines from Subic Bay, making them part of the defense of Corregidor.

The Navy evacuated the rest of their personnel to Bataan, south of the Hermosa-Dinalupihan line. Two U.S. Army Corps, commanded by Generals Wainwright and Parker, established their defense south of this line. To avoid being cut off by the Japanese advance, the Navy abandoned Subic Bay right after Christmas.

On December 26, Ted McTagert and Betty Landry bid each other an affectionate farewell. Though they promised to find each other when the emergency was over, it was the last time that they would ever be together.

Maj. McTagert moved his men in small amphibious craft down the coast to Bataan, and then overland to the southern tip of the peninsula, where the 4th Marines motored across the straight to Corregidor and Fort Mills.

As part of the evacuation from Subic Bay and Olongapo, LtCdr. Landry moved all of her nurses to a small Army Hospital at Camp Limay on the Bataan peninsula. Kari went along with the other six nurses.

The entire group remained at Camp Limay until the vicious fighting pushed the American lines further south. In late January, the medical entourage moved to Little Baguio, closer to Corregidor.

While on Bataan, Kari worked as a scrub nurse, and always in tandem with Doctor Cambridge. During her tour, the Japanese air force bombed the medical facilities on Bataan twice. The Japanese perfidy wounded and killed many Americans, who'd already been wounded in the defense of the peninsula.

Several weeks before the American lines collapsed on Bataan, the Far East Command sent Ens. Hansen and Lt. Cambridge to the coastal town of Mariveles, where they waited for transportation to Corregidor. Kari never learned why they singled her out from all the other Navy nurses. She suspected that it was because she was part of a surgical team.

The last time Kari saw Betty Landry, the older woman was triaging several severely wounded soldiers, who'd been sent back from the heavy fighting. Neither woman had much time to talk.

Kari had to leave immediately, and Betty had to make critical decisions about life and death. Kari stepped forward, embraced her friend and mentor.

"Commander, I'll see you on Corregidor." Kari offered.

"Sure, Kari. Listen, stay safe and when you get a quiet moment, say a prayer for us, OK?"

"Betty," Kari responded—her eyes filling with tears, "I promise that I'll pray hard!"

"OK, kid. Get moving! Keep your pretty head down," Landry directed as she turned to attend to a soldier who was missing most of his left shoulder.

Five weeks later, several Army nurses and two Navy nurses made it to Corregidor. Betty Landry never got away from Bataan.

The survivors presumed that Landry was alive, and part of the force that the Japanese had overrun after the general collapse of the last line of defense on April 8, 1942. If she were still alive, the Japs would intern Landry in one of their prison camps.

By the time Kari made it to Corregidor, the Japanese had bombed the place back to the Stone Age. While the artillery batteries on the Rock remained effective, all support facilities above ground ceased to exist. The command moved everything that wasn't shooting back at the Japs inside Malinta Tunnel.

Kari spent almost all of her time assisting Dr. Cambridge in the endless cycle of surgery. In her first four weeks on Corregidor, Kari assisted in more operations than she might have in three years at busy St. Teresa's.

Around the middle of March, Gen. MacArthur and his family evacuated Corregidor by PT boat. The general's departure left many demoralized. In light of his actions, none of the men left behind thought much of MacArthur. Many of the embittered Army grunts, and even the highly disciplined Marines, reflecting on his caution while on the Rock, called Gen. MacArthur: *Dugout Doug.*

By the end of the third week of April life on Corregidor looked bleak and hopeless. The rumor around the hospital was that MacArthur had made it safely to Australia, where he promised to return to the Philippines.

MacArthur's promise gave little comfort to the grunts and nurses on the Rock. Not many of them expected him to come back, since he left them to their fate in the first place. If he did return, only the most optimistic expected to be alive to see it.

Toward the middle of April, Gen. Wainwright, who succeeded MacArthur in command, began evacuating small groups of personnel from Corregidor. He gave these fortunate people precious space on the submarines, Navy PBY scout planes, and PT boats that braved the waters of the South China Sea.

Kari never understood what criteria the command used to make the decision regarding who could leave. Dependent wives, officers' children, and nurses had a chance.

Just as Kari nodded off to sleep on the metal bench, someone began shaking and pushing her. Exhausted and cranky Kari awoke fighting mad.

At first, Kari didn't recognize which asshole in the Malinta Tunnel had the brass to wake her up. As her vision cleared, she recognized Second Lieutenant Ann Stevens, an Army nurse who was assigned to the orthopedics ward. Ann bunked near Kari in the nurse's dormitory further down the laterals.

"What in the hell do you want, Ann?" Kari asked. "Can't you see that I'm trying to get a little sleep?"

"Sorry, Kari," Ann responded. "I have to talk to you. I got orders to evacuate on the PBY coming in tomorrow night. I didn't know when I'd see you again. I wanted to return your wallet, watch, ID card, ring, and St. Christopher medal."

"It's a St. Michael's medal, not a St. Christopher medal!" Kari snapped, irritated that Ann didn't know the difference.

Lieutenant Stevens ignored the outburst. She didn't give a damn which saint in the endless Catholic pantheon was depicted on Kari's little gold medal. She wanted to make sure that Kari got it back before she left. Kari had entrusted her valuables to Stevens, since she couldn't take them into surgery and she had no other safe place to store them.

Stevens handed over the little cloth bag, containing Kari's most prized possessions, but she could not meet the Navy nurse's eyes. Ecstatic about her good fortune, she did have a tinge of guilt about leaving her comrades.

With the battle news so fluid, no one knew who would be the last person to get off the Rock before it fell into Japanese hands. Ann might be talking to a person whom the Japanese might kill in only a day or two. Ann believed that every other nurse would jump at the chance to escape from Corregidor.

The women had much to lose. The Japanese could brutalize them in ways that men seldom endured. Stevens knew that the Japanese in China raped the local girls. The enemy had nothing to keep them from treating American females the same way.

"Kari, I'm not leaving for eighteen hours," Ann said. "If you have letters you want to get out, I'll take some with me, and see that they get posted when I get to Australia."

Still irritated, and a tinge jealous at Ann's good fortune, Kari accepted the offer. She feigned a smile and thanked Ann.

Recognizing that Kari was out on her feet, Ann offered to help her back to the nurse's dormitory. Ann would get Kari into bed.

Walking back up the lateral toward the billets, Kari wondered whom she would entrust with her precious ring and medal when she woke up this afternoon for her next surgical shift. One of the ward nurses should be responsible enough to trust.

Kari wanted to sleep. She needed to awaken with enough time to write a letter home to the folks before Ann's departure.

Kari took the cloth bag with the trappings of her former life, and put them in the pocket of her surgical gown. She made sure to button the flap. These items were far too precious to lose.

# Chapter 26

1530 Hours
June 4, 1942
Scouting Six, Second Sortie
120 Nautical Miles West/Northwest of Midway Island
2,920 Miles West of San Francisco

Lieutenant (junior grade) Tim Sullivan pulled back on the joystick of his new scout ship. Scanning the horizon, he enriched the fuel mixture and tapped the throttle forward. Not satisfied, Tim continued to fiddle with the controls until he gained 80 feet in altitude and ten knots forward speed.

When the altimeter registered 15,000 feet, he kicked the rudder and crabbed to starboard. Sullivan battled to maintain his course of 305 degrees in the face of the shifting headwind, now blowing fitfully out the northwest.

Tim looked out of his cockpit to the northeast and then to the southwest, examining the configuration of the other three planes in his flight. They made quite a picture, framed against the light blue sky and the deep blue water.

Sullivan had never imagined that a battlefield, especially one this deadly, would be monochromatic. At altitude he could distinguish the difference between ocean and sky only by azure shades and tones.

Sullivan observed that his wingman was in the right position to support their assault. He noted that the other two bombers had pulled in tight in the formation. In about five minutes, all hell would break loose for the second time in one incredible day.

*Man!* Tim thought. *It's a miracle that we're all still in one piece and combat effective. I can't believe what we've been able to do to the Japs today.*

Sullivan credited much of his good fortune to the newer version of the Dauntless dive-bomber. The third iteration of the SBD—known affectionately to its pilots as the *slow but deadly*—proved to be a major improvement over the former model.

For one thing, the SBD-3 had a more powerful radial engine. It gave the fully loaded bomber an increase in top speed. The "3" sported a bullet-proof windscreen, larger self-sealing fuel tanks, four .50 caliber machine guns, a larger reservoir of ammunition, extended armor protection, and better hydraulics.

With these changes, the SBD-3 flew faster and more reliably with a more destructive bomb load. As for survivability, Tim's new kite had demonstrated that it could absorb punishment like a dry sponge soaking up water.

*If I'd been flying the old scout ship this morning, I'd be dead at the bottom of the Pacific Ocean,* Tim thought as he peered at the horizon. *Damn! At least eighty good pilots and crewmen are with Davy Jones. Thank God! I've been lucky.*

Sullivan was a flight leader on this second sortie from the *Enterprise* against the pride of Admiral Yamamoto's fleet. His own flight trailed Commander McCluskey's. Since Sullivan didn't have to worry about the navigation, he monitored his bombers and scouts, maintained the interval with the squadron leader, and played a deadly game of follow the leader.

This afternoon, the *Enterprise* mustered six flights of dive-bombers, an amalgam of scouts from VS-6, and the dedicated bombers of VB-6. The CAG put 24 SBD-3s in the air. They'd make their next bombing run on the only remaining undamaged Japanese heavy carrier in this part of the Pacific: the *Hiryu*.

After scanning the sky to the northwest for the thousandth time, Tim concluded that the Japanese had no Zekes in the vicinity. At least, he couldn't see any.

*Where are the damn Zekes?* Tim wondered, becoming more edgy. *We're supposed to have fighter support, not that the Wildcats are having much luck against those fucking*

*Zekes! The op order called for them to link up with us over the Enterprise. So much for the damn plan!*

*Jesus,* Tim recalled. *Those Zeros from the Kaga were unbelievably fast and maneuverable. Very dangerous!*

For the first time since clearing the flight deck of the *Enterprise* that afternoon, Tim looked down at his right leg. It was sore and throbbing. The discomfort came from a wound that Tim received in his right calf during the squadron's first attack on the *Kaga*.

When he returned to the Big E after the first attack, Doc Hansen and the corpsmen managed to stop the bleeding, and stitch him up. With the intense preparation for the second attack, they hadn't been able to check him out more thoroughly. There hadn't been time.

When the crewmen refueled and rearmed his kite, Sullivan had to go. After the beating the Americans had given the Japs in the morning, nothing could keep him from the second round.

Besides, the American carriers still faced grave danger. By early afternoon, the *Yorktown* had taken several hits from Japanese aerial and submarine attacks. Her gallant crew fought to keep her afloat.

Upon close examination, Sullivan could see that his leg wound was bleeding again. The bloodstain on the flight suit grew slowly, but surely. Tim didn't care. He only had to make it another few moments. After he dropped his next bomb load—hopefully on some Jap admiral's head—he'd leave his fate in God's hands.

Sullivan had first realized that he was wounded five hours earlier. He felt the pain in his leg right after he pulled out of his high speed, dive on the *Kaga*.

Starting at 20,000 feet, Sullivan came boiling down directly over the Nip flat top. Waiting 29 seconds, he armed the ordnance and then pressed the red button on the top of his joystick to initiate the release. As soon as he hit the button, he felt the big bomb pull away on the steep trajectory created by his dive.

The release of 500 pounds of high explosives changed the aerodynamics and handling characteristics of his aircraft. If he'd waited a second longer or had more weight, he wouldn't have been able to pull up in time. Despite the wall of orange flak and the volume of anti-aircraft fire, Tim placed his high explosive dead center on the *Kaga's* flight deck ten yards aft of the symbol of the rising sun.

*A little payback on the Pearl Harbor account, you sneaky bastards!* Tim thought, hoping that the destructive force that he'd unleashed would blow the carrier into the afterlife, and incinerate the sailors of the Rising Sun.

Unfortunately for the Japanese, the Americans could not have timed the attack better if they had tried. The American dive-bombers from the *Enterprise* found the *Kaga* and *Akagi* while their crews tried to refuel and rearm the flight wing for their second attack on Midway and Sand Islands.

Due to this foul up, the Japanese couldn't launch other aircraft in support of defensive air operations. Worse, the flat tops had become floating ammunition dumps.

Even more fortuitous for VS-6 and VB-6, when the American pilots began their runs against the *Kaga* and *Akagi*, the Zekes were thousands of feet below decimating the American torpedo bombers. At the expense of the lives of their shipmates, the *Enterprise* dive-bomber pilots lined up at altitude, focused on two of the carriers, and attacked in detail, unmolested by enemy fighters.

The attack by the *Enterprise* dive-bombers destroyed the *Kaga* and the *Akagi* and all of their aircraft. Both ships blazed out of control, doomed to destruction and dereliction at the bottom of the Pacific. As the pilots from the *Enterprise* attacked their targets, dive-bombers from the *Yorktown* destroyed the *Soryu*.

While Sullivan had managed the very best run of his career, after he dropped his bomb on the *Kaga*, two Zekes pounced on him. After his run, he'd leveled off 60 feet off the deck. He flew at less than 180 knots.

For the next 30 seconds, Tim and his gunner engaged in a frantic battle for their lives. Twisting and turning like a flying corkscrew, Tim tried every trick and crazy maneuver in or out of the book to try to lose the two Zekes. The gunner, Petty Officer Second Class Lembke, kept firing his twin .30 caliber Brownings, trying to get a piece of either of the Zekes. Despite Lemke's efforts, the Japanese pilots stayed glued to their tail.

Tim and his gunner survived because Sullivan had the presence of mind to realize that he would never outrun or out fly the Zekes. Instead, he engaged the Swiss cheese dive brakes, pulled back on the throttle, and abruptly slowed the dive-bomber to a crawl—a notch above stall speed. The first Jap pilot hadn't expected the move. He flew past Sullivan's SBD at over 260 knots.

In what Tim's fellow pilots later described as, "the luckiest fucking deflection shot of all time," Tim fired his four .50 caliber Browning machine guns in a wide pattern to the Zeke's port quarter. The Japanese pilot juked up and, for reasons best known to his ancestors, turned his fighter into the pattern of .50 caliber rounds that Tim fired.

The Japanese pilot's fighter absorbed 60 direct hits. A few seconds later, the Zeke caught fire in its engine, and lost most of its port wing.

No longer aerodynamic, the little Mitsubishi spun down for 100 feet, inverted, and crashed into the ocean. The craft disintegrated as if it had hit a brick wall. The debris skidded across the sea, like a sack full of burning hockey pucks dumped on an ice rink.

After the Zeke spun in, PO2 Lembke reported that he'd damaged the second Zero. The Jap broke off the attack on their six. A moment later Sullivan noticed the blood stain on the lower portion of his flight suit.

Tim had registered a sharp pain in his right leg after the Zekes initiated the attack. Sullivan had been too busy trying to out-fly the best dog fighting aircraft in the Pacific with this glorified washing machine to check himself out.

Out of bombs and ready to rearm, Tim formed up with another scout and a bomber. Acting on the order of the squadron leader, Sullivan set a heading for the *Enterprise*.

For Lt.(j.g.) Sullivan, the first attack had lasted less than 15 minutes.

As he got closer to the carrier, Sullivan realized that the corpsmen would try to ground him in order to care for his leg wound. He would not let that happen.

*My shipmates and I have a huge fucking score to settle with these meatballs,* Tim thought. *I'll pay those bastards back and avenge all of my buddies, if it's the last thing I ever do.*

*Geez, I miss Pat Kelley.* Tim remembered. *He was such a nice guy and a great fraternity brother. Pat was such a card. He had the driest sense of humor in Happy Valley. What a clown! He was Paul's big brother. If he hadn't been so funny when he hazed us, Paul and I might not have made it through hell week at SPO.*

*Pat really helped me adjust when I first got to Pearl. It was comforting to have him stationed nearby. He was such a decent guy. Those fucking assholes blew him to pieces on the Oklahoma. He was standing watch for God's sake. He was helpless. He never got to fire a shot. God, how I hate those rotten, sneaky, motherfuckers!*

*Jesus, Pearl Harbor used to be so beautiful. Now it's littered with the remnants of our fleet. Some of our boys—good men—are still entombed on those ships. It was Sunday morning. Some of the white hats were still asleep. Dear God, please give me the strength to go back! Don't let the medics ground me. Lord, I swear that I will fight them if they try. They don't have enough jarheads on the Enterprise to keep me there.*

As he suspected, when he landed, the deck crew began patching, repairing, refueling, and rearming his kite. The corpsmen and Doc Hansen pulled him over to the side and examined him.

They wanted to operate on Sullivan to get the metal out of his lower leg. Tim would have none of it. He threatened the chief corpsman. "Chief, if you or your fucking corpsmen try to keep me on board, I'll blow your goddamned heads off!" Sullivan promised as he menacingly tapped the butt of the

.38 colt revolver that he kept in a shoulder holster on his left side.

Doc Hansen listened to Sullivan. Mark ordered the corpsmen to stitch Tim up and get him back in the fight.

*I guess even Doc Hansen changed after Pearl Harbor. No! It had to be Corregidor. That was a tough blow,* Sullivan thought as the corpsmen stitched up his calf.

"Don't worry, Mister Sullivan. We'll let you go back. We can't give you morphine for the pain. It would adversely affect your flying abilities," Doc Hansen explained with no hint of emotion.

"That's OK by me, Doc. The pain's not that bad. When it gets bad, it'll give me one more reason to be pissed at the Japs."

This afternoon, on the second sortie as the first Japanese picket ships hove into view in the blue distance, Sullivan remembered the first time he'd really noticed Doc. It was right after the corpsmen got him down into sickbay after those Army gunners had shot him and his crewman over Hickham.

*Doc was a cool customer. Everybody said he was a great surgeon,* Tim recalled. *The chief doc at Pearl told me that Hansen saved my leg. I'd never have made it back on flight status, if Doc Hansen hadn't been so good. Still, it took me four months to fully convalesce. With the therapy, rehab, and that damned review board, I was lucky to get back to the Big E by April.*

When he did return, Tim was not only several months older, he was a newly promoted *j.g.* He had a row of new ribbons, a Purple Heart and a Distinguished Flying Cross. He also had the right to paint one meatball—a Japanese war flag—on the fuselage of his aircraft to demonstrate to the world one victory in aerial combat.

Tim missed the raid on Wake Island. Worse, he was still in rehab during the Doolittle raid on Tokyo. He understood that Scout-6 had flown a lot of air cover, but it had only seen a small amount of action against picket ships on the day that Admiral Halsey launched the B-25s from the deck of the *Hornet.*

Tim reported back on board the *Enterprise* in time to ship out to the Battle of the Coral Sea. He noticed new faces aboard and a lot of old ones. He felt good to be back with his shipmates. They seemed glad to see him.

Coral Sea proved to be a nasty business. The Japs got the *Lexington*, an older carrier. Tim didn't have firsthand knowledge of the battle because the *Enterprise* arrived on station one day after the battle ended.

The Battle of the Coral Sea proved that the Americans could actually stop the Japs. The Empire would not take Port Moresby this time around.

This afternoon, as Tim and his flight closed with the main fleet, the Japanese pickets and larger Japanese ships hove into view ahead. Tim reached over and charged his .50 calibers. He prepared the 1000-pound bomb for release. Using the intercom, Sullivan alerted Lembke, cautioning him to be vigilant.

Sullivan knew he should focus on the attack, but he felt very tired. His thoughts went back to the day that he reported back on board the *Enterprise*. After he met with his squadron leader and got squared away with the CAG, Tim made a point to go down to sickbay to see Doc and the guys. He wanted to thank them for saving his leg.

Tim had smuggled two bottles of Scotch on board, a present for the corpsmen. "Gentlemen, I know that alcohol is prohibited on this ship. I'd never condone a violation of standing orders. So, this scotch is only for medicinal purposes, right?"

"Sure, sir. We'll save this for medical treatment, right, Chief?" the senior corpsman assured, as he took the bottles from Sullivan.

"That's right, Lieutenant. Medicinal purposes only!" the chief agreed, as he snatched the bottles from the corpsman and passed them to Doc Hansen.

Prior to reporting, Sullivan had never had a private conversation with Lieutenant Hansen. That morning, Hansen chatted with Sullivan for a few moments, touched by the young pilot's gratitude. Then, as Hansen was about to make an excuse to break off the conversation, the doctor remembered something he wanted to ask Sullivan.

"Mister Sullivan, I recall that you went to Penn State. Is that right?" Hansen asked.

"That's right, Doc. How'd you know?"

"Some brown shoe told me. I was curious. Before the attack on Pearl Harbor I saw a newsreel about a kid from Pennsylvania named Reilly, O'Reilly, or something like that. He'd gone to Penn State and flew in the RAF. Just got his fifth Jerry. Since both of you are flyers, you might have known each other in college. My brother-in-law went to Penn State. I had a funny premonition. With all that's happened in the past several months, I don't know why I remember it," Doc Hansen explained.

"Oh, yeah. I know the guy! His name is Paul Reilly. He was my roommate and fraternity brother. I could tell you stories that would make your head spin. That RAF war hero and 'ace' pilot is the biggest pervert on the eastern side of the Atlantic. I'm sure he is very popular with the English girls, and not because he's a hot pilot," Sullivan said, a smile on his face for the first time.

"No kidding?" Doc responded, finally lightening up. "What a coincidence! Were you as big a football fan as Reilly?"

"Nobody was as big a fan as Paul. We had several players in the house. They were all great guys. We had lots of reasons to cheer for the Lions."

"Maybe you know my brother-in-law? He was a linebacker on the team, graduated in '40. Phil Genero? Ring a bell?" Doctor Hansen asked.

The question stopped Tim Sullivan cold. While he had genuine respect for Doctor Hansen's professionalism, with this news the man became a demi-god in his eyes.

"Are you telling me that you are Gin's brother-in-law? You get to be both a doctor and the husband of Kari Genero? How can one man be so lucky?" Sullivan asked, intending some levity.

Hansen's expression changed. For an instant he looked angry, then sad. Tim knew that he'd said something terribly wrong, but he couldn't figure what it was. Doc Hansen excused himself and walked out of the sick bay.

Sullivan looked around and realized that the two corpsmen, sitting by the admissions table, were averting their eyes. What ever it was, he'd fucked up for sure.

"Petty Officer, what did I say wrong? What's going on?"

The petty officer looked down at the table for a moment and played with a stubby pencil for five or six seconds, gathering his thoughts. Finally, he decided what to say. He turned in his seat to face the pilot.

"It's not your fault, sir. You couldn't have known. Doc's wife was a Navy nurse on Corregidor. Doc got word a week ago that his wife was killed four or five days before the island surrendered. Doc took it pretty hard. He blames himself. He thinks if he hadn't joined the Navy, she'd still be in Philadelphia…"

"Harrisburg, Joe, they were from Harrisburg, not Philly," the other corpsman interrupted, as if this detail was somehow important.

The first petty officer gave the second a look of exasperation. He continued with Mister Sullivan. "OK, Harrisburg! Sir, you didn't do nothing wrong. You didn't know no better."

Tim realized that he couldn't be held responsible for an innocent jibe that went unbelievably wrong because of the megalomaniacal aspirations of the Empire of the Rising Sun. Still, he felt miserable. Two days later Sullivan found Hansen in the wardroom at dinner. "Doc, please forgive me. I had no idea about Kari. I was just trying to be funny. I'm very grateful to you. I'm sorry if what I said made things worse," Tim offered.

"Mister Sullivan..." Mark began, before Tim cut him off.

"Doc, please call me Tim. I'm a friend of your family."

"OK, Tim, I'm sorry too. I didn't mean to be rude. I guess I'm still in shock. I feel so responsible. Kari would not have been on Corregidor if I hadn't joined the Navy!"

"Look, Doc, I know you're hurting bad. If you want a friend to talk to, I'm here for you."

The two men chatted through dinner. They began the process of becoming friends.

In the days that followed, the two officers spent much of the time together talking about neutral, unemotional subjects, like Phil's athletic prowess at Penn State. For his part Doc told Tim a lot about the Generos that Tim had never known.

In the next several weeks, Sullivan worked hard to help Doc Hansen deal with his enormous loss. Yet, in truth, he felt a deep sense of melancholy with the death of Phil's sister.

Tim had met Kari several times. He had a modest crush on her. In addition to being drop-dead gorgeous, she seemed to be a wonderful young woman.

Nothing romantic ever developed between them because Tim was too shy to pursue her and Kari was already smitten.

*I guess every woman they kill is someone's daughter, sister, mother, or friend.* Tim thought.

On takeoff for the second sortie, the bright crimson stain on Tim's right calf approximated the size of a silver dollar. Now it covered an area the size of a pie plate. The hastily stitched wound had popped a gasket.

Sullivan would not bother about it. He'd used up all the luck any pilot could ever hope to have. He had no right to expect any more.

*In combat I've been wounded about once every thirty minutes. Shit! At this rate, I'll be dead in another twenty minutes flying time. With what we have to do this afternoon, my little leg wound won't mean a thing, not a Goddamned thing,* Tim reflected.

On the horizon, Tim could make out the billows of smoke rising from the burning hulks of two of the first three carriers. A few minutes at this speed and they should be able to see the *Hiryu.* Until today, Tim would never have guessed how quickly the fortunes of war could turn. One minute you're down, the next you're up, way up.

At 1000 hours on June 4, 1942, the Japanese had become the irresistible conquerors and military masters of the Pacific. By 1030 hours, the course of the war in the Pacific had changed in America's favor.

In 30 minutes, American forces had destroyed and sunk three of the most important ships in the enemy fleet, the *Kaga, Akagi,* and *Soryu.* The dive-bomber pilots destroyed irreplaceable Japanese carriers with hundreds of planes and—more importantly—the best and most experienced Japanese naval aviators in the Empire on board.

At 1000 hours, the Americans seemed to be losing the battle at Midway in a most convincing manner. In futile, uncoordinated attacks, the Americans had sacrificed over 40 warplanes, and hadn't struck a blow against even one ship in the vast Japanese fleet.

By 1030, the American Navy had delivered a decisive and strategic blow to the Japanese. The enemy would have to go on the defensive.

Less than 40 dive-bombers—and a hand full of pilots and gunners—made the difference, all of the difference between victory and defeat. While courageous men in slow and obsolete planes made the ultimate sacrifice, the Dauntless bomber/scout pilots and gunners, mostly from the *USS Enterprise*, had won the morning.

In about 30 seconds, the pilots would win the afternoon, or they would die trying. The Americans had no other choice.

They fought a war for the very survival of their country and their way of life.

Tim put aside his thoughts of home, his family, his friends, the *Enterprise*, and his shipmates. He warned Lembke and the other three planes in his flight.

There it was! Sullivan could see it. Five miles out, he spotted a long sleek flat top with the flag of the Rising Sun painted gaudily on the fore deck. The *Hiryu* steamed west at flank speed surrounded by a cloud of angry, buzzing Zekes.

*May God have mercy on your fucking souls, 'cause I'll give you none!* Tim swore.

Sullivan watched as Commander McCluskey's flight went to emergency war speed, peeled off in starboard wingovers, and began their steep dive patterns. Seconds later Tim Sullivan led his flight down on the *Kiryu* through a wall of flack, triple A, and machine gun fire.

Tim never flinched or changed the course of his attack dive, even as the last SBD bomber from McClusky's flight blew up and disintegrated into a cloud of small metal fragments and human parts.

Despite the fact that Tim's scout ship began taking savage hits in the fuselage and undercarriage, Sullivan kept the cross hairs of the small 3x power gun sight directly on the control tower of the *Hiryu*.

Tim's SBD-3 had a new and improved bulletproof windscreen. Though good protection, it was not designed to protect a pilot from a direct hit by a Japanese 40mm antiaircraft artillery shell.

When just such a projectile struck Sullivan's aircraft, it blew out a jagged piece of the windscreen nearly a foot in diameter. The impact sent shards of glass aft into Sullivan's face at nearly 500 miles an hour.

A two-inch long glass shard stuck Tim on his right cheek, slicing inward and severing the skin and sinew for several inches, just above and to the right of his lip. The shard missed his eye and the major blood vessel in Tim's face, but the other small veins provided an adequate supply of serum.

Streams of very red blood began to run freely down his chin and neck, soaking the top of flight suit.

Tim ignored the intense pain, but did notice that he'd have trouble talking with half his lip missing and his mouth filled with blood. Good thing he didn't have to talk. All he had to do now was press the little red button and put the bomb right into the lap of a faithful servant of the glorious emperor.

Five seconds from impact with the carrier, Tim released his bomb. Feeling the shudder in the superstructure, Sullivan pulled back as hard as he could on the joystick. He dropped the flaps and kicked the rudder into a tight turn to port at over 220 knots.

The tremendous 'G' forces consequent upon such a maneuver and the pain from both his wounds conspired to help Sullivan lose consciousness. Tim avoided blacking out by the thinnest of margins.

Tim never did see his 1000-pound bomb strike the *Hiryu* just forward of the tower on top of the ship's elevator, exploding a refueling truck brimming with aviation fuel. The explosion from Sullivan's bomb, assisted by the sympathetic detonation of the fuel truck, set off a destructive chain in the confined space of the hanger deck. The resulting fire incinerated the irreplaceable Japanese pilots and officers in the ships' company.

All air operations on the *Hiryu* ceased. The United States could claim the fourth large carrier destroyed in one fortunate day.

For Sullivan and Lembke, the battle continued. The anti-aircraft shells had damaged their dive-bomber. Sullivan bled profusely from two painful wounds and the Zekes filled the sky with no place to land. It was a long way back to the Big E.

# Chapter 27

2030 Hours
September 15, 1942
The Road between Saffron Walden
and Debden Village, Essex County
35 Miles Northeast of London, England

Stretching from the Thames River estuary in the south to the Suffolk coast in the north, the landscape of south-eastern England began along an irregular coastline thrust into the turbulent currents of the North Sea. The terrain continued west as the flat, featureless marshes of East Anglia. In Essex County, foggy lowlands gradually evolved into verdant hills, knolls, and glades. Yeomen, through the labor of a hundred generations, had transformed the shire's primal forests into picturesque farms and pastures.

From time out of memory, the soil in western Essex County had been fertile and well drained, supporting the industry of farmers, shepherds, and dairymen. The farms of western Essex County were small and labor intensive, but efficient and highly productive.

The worldwide depression of the '30s and the ravages of total war in the early '40s changed the economic landscape. The farmers and herdsmen found themselves in difficult circumstances. The war with the Nazis brought about significant modifications to the land, the economy, and their lifestyle.

The residents of Essex County couldn't blame their own politicians for this predicament. Neville Chamberlain's government had tried everything—including abject ap-peasement—to avoid armed conflict with the Germans. With Churchill as Prime Minister, the Brits would fight this war.

Since old Winnie was in command, they would win it or they would keep fighting 'til the last man was no longer standing.

On a rainy Tuesday evening in late summer, driving far faster than good judgment would dictate, Captain Phil Genero tried to negotiate the diabolical switchbacks and curves of the old country highway south of Saffron-Walden. Genero's circumstances became even more precarious, since he drove too fast on the left side of the narrow road in a Jeep built in America for right side operation.

Genero was late. He'd taken too long to extricate himself from an intimate liaison with a British Wren in Chelsea. He'd lingered too long in her bed that afternoon and took his leave at teatime to begin his trip to the Royal Air Force fighter base at Debden.

To avoid killing himself or harming some innocent pedestrian or stray cow, Phil had to concentrate on driving the Jeep. Due to his earlier propinquity in Chelsea, he did not leave time to fully appreciate the substantial charm and beauty lining the Essex County roads. Genero did note that the countryside reminded him of the area surrounding Lancaster, where his mother's family still had property.

Earlier in the day, Captain Genero had finagled a rare pass from his assignment at American II Corps Headquarters in London. This evening he had a personal mission.

By the time Phil found himself on the road between Saffron-Walden and the village of Debden, he'd been in the British Isles for three months. Along with the 2/503d, he'd made the Atlantic crossing on the refitted ocean liner, the *Queen Mary*.

The voyage had been an adventure. The threat of German U-boats, the cramped conditions, and the roiling ocean made the journey a challenge. Travel on that boat convinced Phil that his decision to go into the Army was the right one. He'd never make a good sailor.

The organization and execution of the seaborne transfer of the first airborne combat unit to leave the United States had been a complicated operation. The passage had been so tedious that every paratrooper in the unit was happy to finally settle into their base on an estate near Chilton-Foliat, west of London.

From the middle of June until the beginning of September, Genero and every paratrooper of the 2/503d had trained hard with the British 1$^{st}$ Airborne Division. Although each American had passed rigorous challenges in Georgia and North Carolina to get his jump wings, the exercises and drills in England were difficult and dangerous.

At Chilton-Foliat and other venues in the English countryside, the American paratroopers engaged in live fire exercises, extensive field problems, forced marches, tactical training, and combat equipment jumps from very low altitudes at night. The British spared no effort to provide the most realistic experience possible, short of actual combat.

The training had been intense because the allied command had selected the 2/503d to be the first American force to participate in a battalion-sized combat jump, supporting a large-scale allied raid along the French coast. The planners had scheduled the raid, known as *Operation Jubilee*, for July of 1942.

The planners intended the raid to be executed by Canadian, British, and American forces. The focal point would be the French resort town of Dieppe.

Other than to kill German soldiers, the goals of the raid remained murky and ill defined. The motive to risk such a valuable force was to make the German high command feel vulnerable along their Atlantic flank.

The allied planners thought that if the raid were successful, Hitler would move substantial German units back to France from the eastern front. A reduction in German troop strength in the east could bring relief to Stalin's army, which recoiled from the German offensives along a Russian battle zone that was more than 1,000 miles wide.

The operational planners scrapped the airborne element of *Operation Jubilee* when they postponed the Dieppe raid in July and rescheduled it for mid-August. At first, this decision angered the American paratroopers. The Yanks wanted to get into the war. The sooner they opened a second front against the Germans, the quicker the allies could defeat Hitler.

After the Dieppe raid failed, the paratroopers realized how close they'd come to witnessing the demise of their unit. The details of the ill-fated assault and the allied losses were sketchy and mostly classified. What few facts the paratroopers did learn alarmed them.

Despite air cover flown by several squadrons of the RAF, including the American Eagles, the Canadian and British forces—sprinkled with a few American Rangers—encountered a strong and determined German defense. The Nazis decimated the main Canadian force, which never secured its objectives.

American airborne planners realized that had the 2/503d actually jumped into the proposed drop zone near Dieppe, the German defenders would have chopped up, killed, and captured most of the paratroopers. The revelation tempered their eagerness and provided a sobering lesson.

Two weeks after the news of the failure of the Dieppe raid, recently promoted Lieutenant Colonel Edson Raff, commander of the 2/503d, sent for Genero in order to give him a new assignment.

"You wanted to see me, sir?" Phil asked as he walked into LtCol. Raff's office at the rear of a Nissan hut at their small base near Chilton-Foliat.

"Genero, come over here. I want to show you something," Raff instructed.

As Phil walked over to Raff's desk, he saw his commander toying with a dark, maroon-red beret, the primary headgear worn by the British paras. The American paratroopers envied their British counterparts. The beret was more than just headgear. It symbolized the elite nature of the airborne mission.

Raff looked up at Phil and smiled. Raff's cordial demeanor surprised Genero.

"Captain, what do you think of the British paras? We've been training with them for two months. You're one of the intelligence officers. You should have made observations and formed opinions about our allies. I'd like to hear them," LtCol. Raff directed, motioning Genero into a nearby seat.

"OK, sir," Genero began as he sat down. "I'm impressed with the conditioning, level of preparation, efficiency, *esprit de corps*, and commitment of His Majesty's paras. I'm glad they're on our side. I wouldn't want to fight these guys. They're a first rate bunch. Major Frost's raid on the radar station at Bruneval was particularly impressive."

"My thoughts exactly, Captain," Raff expounded, spinning the beret on his finger. "I spoke with the 1st Division commander, General Browning. He was most complimentary about our progress. He intends to tell II Corps that the 2/503d is ready for combat. There are big plans looming. Browning thinks we're up to the challenge.

"General Browning wants the 2/503d to become honorary members of the British 1st Airborne Division. He presented this beret and told me that the members of my command were officially qualified to wear it, whenever I decided that it was appropriate," the colonel said. "What do you think of that, Captain?"

Capt. Genero had been on active duty for 27 months. He'd received his last promotion while embarked upon the *Queen Mary*. Everyone who counted in the battalion trusted his judgment. He'd given an excellent account of himself since joining the Airborne.

Phil excelled because he was tough, smart, intuitive, and highly suspicious. Suspicion was a necessary trait in an intelligence billet.

Genero had worked with Browning's intelligence staff at 1st Division. Phil respected the Brits and their capable leaders, but he had a bad feeling about the general's offer. The Anglo-American alliance, cobbled together out of a mutual need to fight Hitler, comprised a union of competing forces. The alliance often operated at cross-purposes for separate— and frequently irreconcilable—goals.

Genero liked Gen. Browning. Browning had married well and was a very gallant gentleman. Browning possessed an exemplary war record from World War I. No honest man could question the general's right to be called a soldier.

All the same, Phil didn't trust Boy Browning's motives. He was ambitious and had the clout and political connections to realize his aspirations. He counted Winston Churchill, Lord Mountbatten, members of the Royal Family and several members of Parliament among his close, personal friends.

Soon a tidal wave of American soldiers, commanded by newly promoted American generals, would inundate the British Isles. These new generals would be officers who'd labored for a generation in a pre-war, military sweatshop, as lieutenants, captains, and majors. For the last two decades, most would have considered themselves a success to retire as a lieutenant colonel.

While none of these men wanted another global conflict, the war created an opportunity for advancement. Few of them would squander the windfall.

These capable and ambitious American officers would hate Gen. Browning. They'd resent any attempt by Browning to intrude upon American military prerogatives. Senior American airborne officers would see Browning as an upper class rival.

The Brits had begun their airborne experiment far earlier than the Americans. They had a big lead on the Americans in fielding airborne divisions. In the late summer of 1942, the Americans were still wrestling with the basic airborne concept, and how to implement it.

Some advisors in Washington recommended to the Chief of Infantry that airborne units should be no larger than battalions, or at most regiments. These units would be suitable for special operations of the sort that made the *Fallschirmjaeger* famous during the conquest of Western Europe.

Other planners believed that airborne regiments should be combined into airborne divisions and transported into battle in large aerial armadas. The apparent success of the German assault on Crete seemed to vindicate this approach.

General McNair, who commanded all of the Army's ground forces, had approved the basic design of American airborne divisions. He'd decided that each division would follow the classic 'triangular' concept. Each airborne division would include three infantry regiments, two glider-borne units, and one regiment of paratroopers.

Only a few weeks earlier, the Army leadership picked the 82nd Infantry Division and the 101st Infantry Division to be the first to pursue the airborne experiment. Genero reasoned that it would take many months to fully train these units. Neither of these divisions would be available for combat until halfway through 1943 at the earliest. An awful lot could happen in the next year.

Browning could take advantage of this temporary vacuum in the American force structure. The British general recognized that power in the Anglo-American alliance would eventually have to be parceled out and shared. Gen. Browning had begun his campaign to become the top commander of all allied airborne forces. This offer to make the 2/503d honorary members of the British 1st Airborne was the opening gambit.

"Sir, I'd find some way to politely decline the honor that General Browning has offered you," Phil responded. "Let me give you an example of the issue that you are facing. The British commandos offered Major Darby the opportunity to train a battalion of American volunteers as commandos up in Scotland. The American leadership agreed and some Americans have completed the difficult training regimen. These soldiers have exactly the same combat preparation as the British, but II Corps refused to allow the graduates to be called Commandos. Consequently, Maj. Darby has fielded an American Ranger battalion."

"What's your point?" Raff asked.

"Sir, we've got a good thing going with our British cousins. We should do everything to keep the relationship close. That is, everything short of professional suicide. Sir, you start wearing that beret, which most of our men would love, and

General Clark at II Corps will think that you've gone over to the Brits."

"You're exactly right, Genero. We're the first airborne unit to leave the U.S.A. We'll be the first to jump into combat. It would be nice to avoid the pettiness and get down to planning the details for killing the enemy, don't you think? I'll ruminate about this beret thing. But I will not sacrifice something as precious as the morale or esprit of my men because some politician at II Corps would be offended. If wearing this red beret would give my men a boost, so that they would kill more enemy soldiers, then I'd personally buy each and every one a beret tomorrow. And, let the politicians stuff it, you know where!

"Genero, I've picked you for a special assignment," LtCol. Raff continued—changing the subject. "The II Corps staffers have cooked up an interesting plan. It includes a bold concept for the utilization of the battalion. I've reviewed the operational model. I'm convinced that we can do it. Go to London and be my liaison with Clark's airborne advisor. He's your old pal, Major Bill Yarborough. Do you think that you'll be up for a week to ten days in London?" Raff added sardonically.

"Yes, sir," Phil responded. "When do I leave?"

"As soon as you can pack a bag. But understand this is an operational planning job. Normally, I'd send the S-3. The fact that I'm sending one of my smartest S-2 officers to perform this special detail is an item that I hope you've not overlooked," Raff explained.

"The Dieppe fiasco was a near thing for us," Raff continued. "I don't know why they cancelled us, but thank God that they did! Otherwise, the Krauts would have destroyed our battalion. The Brits made assumptions they had no right to make. They didn't understand the enemy, his strength, his determination, or his fighting skill. A lot of Canadian boys are dead, wounded, and captured because rear echelon commandos screwed up."

LtCol. Raff stood up, walked over to Phil, and put his hand on the younger man's shoulder. "I trust you, Captain.

You're suited for this assignment. Your language skills will come into play. You're a suspicious man. So, question everything. Don't let the staffers at II Corps get us into another Dieppe! Understand?"

"Sir, I promise, I won't let you or the battalion down." Phil offered.

"Good; that means I won't have to rip your throat out."

Just as it began to drizzle, the front gate of Debden Airdrome finally sprang into view. Genero came barreling over a slight rise in the road and passed the base without a backward glance.

When they'd spoken, Paul Reilly had given Phil directions to a public house in Debden Village where they would meet. The pub let rooms. Paul assured Phil that he'd make all the arrangements. He'd have a nice pint of Guinness waiting for Genero at 1930 hours.

When Phil arrived at the village square, he saw the pub right away. A bit more than an hour late, Genero pulled his Jeep to the south side of the Fox and Hound Pub. Phil jumped out of the Jeep and walked toward the front of the building, avoiding the puddles and muddy paths to preserve the immaculate polish on his jump boots.

The front of the pub looked like others Phil had seen in his travels throughout the British Isles. The door was heavy dark oak. Above the portal, a faded sign bore the images of a sleek red fox leaping over a fence, chased by a hound on steroids.

Phil opened the wooden door and entered the establishment. Since it was dark, it took a few seconds for his eyes to adjust. When he could focus, he noticed a gaggle of flyers crowded around the bar, engaged in several separate animated conversations.

One of the pilots observed the American interloper and alerted his mates. The conversations ended abruptly. Everyone turned and stared at Genero. After a pregnant pause, one of the pilots spoke up.

"Well, as I live and breathe, a bloody Yank!! An 'onest to goodness Yank, isn't he? I've 'eard that the Yanks were coming to Britain to lead us to victory in the bleeding war. I 'aven't actually seen one, until now, have I? Not until this bloke strolls in," a tall, thin, and freckled man in the uniform of an RAF pilot officer decreed.

The RAF pilot leaned against the bar sipping a dark beer. He watched Genero, who stood self-consciously in the doorway.

"Evan, you insufferable snob! The Yanks have been over here for years. We've been bailing your limey asses out of the fire since the Battle of Britain," a smaller man with a prominent mustache responded. He was seated at a table between two of the most beautiful women Phil had ever seen.

The larger man turned to address the second fellow seated behind him.

"Paul, you ain't no bloody Yank! You came 'ere before it was fashionable, didn't you? You're our mate, now. This great ox is obviously a bleeding conscript, forced at gunpoint into the service of 'is country, after the Japs destroyed his bloody Navy in 'awaii."

Recognizing Paul, Phil waved at his old friend. Paul Reilly had changed since the last time they'd been together. He looked much older than his 24 years. The facial hair made his face appear fuller, and it bore the evidence of immense stress.

As Paul was about to answer Evan, Phil stepped over to the bar and smiled at the large red-haired man. "Well, mate, I'm no draftee. I am glad to be here so that my wiser, more experienced, English cousins can teach me how to fight the Jerries."

"As it 'appens, mate, I'm a Welshman, aren't I? I don't know if I could teach ya anything about the bleeding Jerries, other than to shoot a few of them down. But, if ya like, I've 'alf a mind to teach you about manners," Evan said menacingly.

Phil hadn't been in a fight since he landed in Britain, but a few of the men in the 2/503d had. The British soldiers viewed the Americans as an overpaid, loutish, womanizing horde of invading colonials. Though the Yanks were in Britain to help them whip the Germans, the American soldiers had an unfair edge in competing for the available women. Even though the alliance stood on solid ground, individual allies often punched each other's lights out—especially when alcohol was involved.

Phil hadn't wrangled his pass so he could brawl with the RAF, but he wouldn't let a Welsh flyboy try to intimidate him. Genero had trained hard for months. For the last few weeks he'd worked on the boldest, scariest war plan he could imagine. Phil's tension and frustration levels soared. Three months hence, he might not be alive. If the Welshman wanted a go, he'd accommodate him.

Before the two allies could exchange another word, Paul got up from his table, winked at the two ladies, and walked over to the bar—inserting himself between Phil and Evan. With an authority that Phil had never seen during their years at Penn State, Paul squared himself with Evan. Paul suggested that if Evan couldn't show more hospitality to his friend, Paul would find some way to resolve it.

Evan looked at Paul hard, but he obviously respected him. For three seconds Evan weighed his options. Finally, the Welshman visibly relaxed and nodded his head up and down a half-dozen times, smiling at Paul. He looked directly at Phil. With twinkling eyes and a friendly expression, Evan offered Genero his hand.

"Sorry, mate," Evan said. "We 'ad a bit of a rough rhubarb out there today. I suppose I'm acting the fool. Fancy a bitters?"

"Thanks," Phil responded. "I'd appreciate that."

While the bar man poured Genero's drink, Paul shook his old pal's hand, clasping it hard and firm. The men looked at each other like the long lost friends that they were.

Paul introduced Phil to the other pilots who were habitués of the Fox and Hound. Seven or eight were Americans assigned to the Royal Air Force 71$^{st}$ Squadron at Debden. The 71$^{st}$ was one of the three American Eagle Squadrons in the RAF.

When Phil had his drink in hand, Paul guided him to the table where the two beautiful English women were seated. One of the women, a gorgeous blond, looked familiar, but he couldn't place her.

"Captain Phillip Genero," Paul began formally with a hint of levity as he gestured at the stunning woman with long auburn hair, seated to his left. "I have the honor to present Lady Cynthia Devereaux, daughter of the Earl of Royston."

Cynthia offered her hand, while she pierced Phil with her stunning green eyes. In her liveliest voice she offered, "Very pleased to meet you, Captain. Do sit here, next to me."

"*Enchante, Mademoselle Devereaux,*" Genero responded in his best French, while taking her hand, and brushing his lips along the topside of her fingers.

"What was Evan thinking?" Cynthia Devereaux said to Paul. "Your friend's manners are impeccable!"

"Must be something they taught him in jump school. I don't remember him being this charming," Paul quipped, turning to the other, stunning woman at the table.

"Gin, I want you to meet my fiancée, Katherine Thomas-Lindsey," Paul explained as he gestured with real affection to the petite blond on his right.

Once he heard the name, Phil recognized Paul's fiancée. He was stunned. Paul had just introduced the newest darling of the British cinema, Katherine Thomas-Lindsey, as his fiancée!

*Holy shit!* Phil thought. *Paul's going to marry a movie star! My God, who would have thought that back in the SPO house in Happy Valley?* "I'm glad to meet you," Phil began. "I just saw *Trafalgar* at camp up at Chilton-Foliat. You were very good!" Genero offered, a genuine admirer of Katherine's fine work in the movie.

Thomas-Lindsey was born in Rhodesia in 1921. She went to private school in South Africa in her teens. In 1938, at the behest of her father—a large Rhodesian landowner—she traveled to Britain to attend university. While at the London School, she dabbled at dramatics. Later, when a director cast her as an extra in a small play, her incredible beauty caught the eye of a famous English producer. Within a year she became his mistress and a budding young star with two small film credits for her resume. Since *Trafalgar,* Katherine had larger parts in two motion pictures. Her studio expected her star to continue to rise.

Her liaison with a flight leader in the American Eagles had begun in April of 1942 after she dumped the older patron. Being the fiancée of an ace pilot in the Eagle Squadron had not damaged her career in the slightest.

The British public adored the American Eagles. From the last days of the Battle of Britain when a trickle of American pilots entered the fray until the Japanese attack on Pearl Harbor, the three American eagle squadrons became the embodiment of every Briton's hope of logistical assistance from—and eventual military alliance with—the United States.

Ironically, in a week the RAF would disband all three of the American Eagle squadrons. All of the Eagle pilots would transfer into the American 8th Air Force as constituent parts of the 4th Fighter Group. A page in the history of a gallant band of fighting men was about to turn.

Phil pulled up a chair next to Lady Devereaux as she gave him her most dazzling smile. There was definite chemistry.

During their brief phone call Paul hadn't said anything about a fiancée. The women at the pub were a surprise. Phil took his time sipping his bitters, looking Paul over carefully.

"Paulie, you've changed," Phil began. "With that mustache, and the weight you've gained, I might not have recognized you. I never imagined you in a uniform, but you look every bit the gallant pilot. All you need is long, white silk scarf."

"Thanks, Gin," Paul responded. "You're exactly what I'd have imagined back at Penn State."

"After Tim told me that you left for Canada, I was shocked. You were always the voice of reason and restraint. I couldn't picture you shooting people out of the sky or strafing troops on the ground," Genero said.

"Tim's my old roommate," Paul explained to the two ladies, as they listened with interest to the two friends catching up. "Tim's a pilot in the Navy. He was at Pearl Harbor and the Battle of Midway. He was seriously wounded in the face, and may never fly again. He wrote me a month ago from a hospital in San Diego. He almost lost an eye and was lucky to survive. Tim's commander recommended him for the Navy Cross for helping to sink two Jap carriers."

"Paul is a British hero too, you know," Katherine asserted to the discomfort of her fiancée. "He has credit for eight and a half Jerries, two probables, and four destroyed on the ground. He has a Distinguished Flying Cross, a Distinguished Service Order, and has been mentioned in dispatches. Paul's the number three ace pilot in all of the Eagle Squadrons."

"Paul, these last two years must have been difficult," Phil observed.

Paul looked away to compose himself. When he was over-fatigued, he got emotional. All the pilots did. Most were too proud to admit it. Phil's comments made Paul think of all the British and American pilots who'd not been as fortunate as he.

During the pause, Cynthia Devereaux took the opportunity to question Phil. "Have you and the American paras seen much combat, Captain?"

"Actually, Lady Devereaux, none of us have seen any yet," Genero responded, feeling guilty that his fraternity brothers had made important contributions to the war, while he'd been safe. "We trained for Dieppe, but they cancelled our drop a few days before the raid."

"Dieppe was a very bad show. Turns out it was one of the most bitterly contested air-to-air contests in the war so far. I was there. It was obvious, even at altitude, that the raid on the ground would fail," Paul reflected.

"You haven't seen combat with the Jerries?" Katherine asked.

"Unless you count a brawl I had with two SS men in the loo of the Marseilles train station nearly two years ago," Genero offered as a lame joke.

Several of the pilots, including Evan, had been eavesdropping on the conversation at Paul's table. Evan couldn't resist. He asked for clarification.

Phil immediately regretted that he'd mentioned the incident. He'd taken pains to hide it after his talk with Major Jardine. But when pressed by the crowd, he told the whole story, including how it almost resulted in his court-martial and caused his transfer from Washington to Fort Benning.

"You suckered two Nazi storm troopers into bending over, so you could bash their bleeding 'eads together? Right?" Evan asked.

"They were drunk. I admit that I took advantage of that too. It wasn't a fair fight at all. I'm not very pro..." Genero tried to explain as Evan cut him off.

"It ain't like them blokes to know a bloody thing about the Marquis of Queensbury rules, is it? That's rich! I'd give a month's pay to bash a storm trooper. Yank, you're a bit of all right! How about another?"

While Evan ordered up another round for his new American pal, Paul explained to Phil that by the end of September, the commander of the 4th Fighter Group would assign all of the Eagles to the 334th, 335th, and 336th Squadrons.

"I'm going to be the exec for the 334th. I'm getting a direct commission to Major," Paul elaborated. "Gin, you can't believe the difference in pay. What with flight and combat pay, I'll make three times the salary of an RAF flight leader. With the increase, Katherine and I can get married and live in Debden.

"Gin, the wedding will be in early October. I want you to be the best man. I know I'm dropping this on you suddenly, but in war there isn't a lot of time to plan ahead. You're one of my best friends, and have been like a real brother to me. If you can arrange it, we'd consider it an honor. I'd have asked Tim, but he can't be here. I want you to stand in for Tim and stand up for me."

Phil was genuinely touched. It was the last thing he'd anticipated.

"Of course, I'll do it, Paul and Katherine. It will be a privilege," Genero responded.

"I'm to be the maid of honor," Cynthia Devereaux piped
in. "I have the thankless job of making the arrangements for
the love birds and their friends. If you can tear yourself away
from the war, we can meet in London to discuss the details."

Genero had a hunch that Cynthia wanted to discuss more
than the details of Paul's wedding. Phil would not disappoint
her.

With the preliminaries settled, the two women excused
themselves in order to powder their collective noses. They
left Paul and Phil alone.

"Cynthia has the hots for you. I've seen it before," Paul
confided conspiratorially. "She has a terrific flat in London.
You'll be spending time there in the next few weeks, duty
permitting, of course."

"Duty always comes first," Phil agreed with an obvious
smirk.

"Gin, Tim wrote that one of the physicians on his ship is
your brother-in-law. He also told me about your sister. I'm
very sorry! It must be very difficult for your mom and dad,"
Paul offered to his friend.

"Paul, I try not to think of it. Over a month ago, an Army
nurse contacted my mom and dad in Carlisle. The command
evacuated her by submarine three days before the surrender
in May. It took her a week to get to Australia, and then a
month to find her way back to the U.S. on an empty returning
troop ship. She discovered my sister's remains after a Jap
artillery shell exploded in the midst of a half a dozen Americans. My mom doesn't know this, but the explosion decapitated Kari and pulverized her body.

"The nurse found my sister's wallet, her wedding set, the
St. Michael's medal that my dad gave her, and her identification card in a small bag in Kari's pocket. The nurse personally
delivered Kari's things to my parents. There was part of a

letter that Kari hadn't gotten to mail. My dad re-copied it and sent the copy to me," Phil continued.

"My parents were glad to get Kari's personal items, but the visit re-opened some deep wounds. My mom—you remember how she was—has taken this hard. Dad is worried sick about her."

Paul tried to comfort his old friend, but the genie was out this bottle.

"Paul, a few weeks ago, the family held a memorial service for Kari. They buried some of her personal items, but kept the ring set and St. Michael's medal as keepsakes. My old teacher and vice-principal, Father Nachen, said the Mass for Kari.

"My dad told me that Father Nachen has convinced the Jesuits and the War Department that he should be an Army chaplain. I guess he had to pull some strings, but when he learned that an old friend had been captured on Bataan, he decided that he couldn't sit out the war in Camp Hill."

"I don't think I ever met your old mentor, but I know exactly how he feels," Paul responded.

"Yeah, I guess you do," Phil conceded.

Unbeknownst to Phil, Cynthia stood behind him and had overheard the whole story. As a British subject in a country in its third year of total war, she'd seen the consequences that her country's policies of the 30s had wrought. As a survival tactic, many Brits became callous to the suffering. Cynthia couldn't do that.

Her heart went out to this big, good-looking American para, who might be sharing his sister's fate in short order. She made a commitment to make his nights in the British Isles as pleasant as possible. She would chalk it up as her little contribution to cementing the Anglo-American alliance.

# Chapter 28

3:30 PM
October 30, 1942
Office of the President
Monarch Industries
Carlisle, Pennsylvania

D
an Monarch sat behind the big mahogany desk
staring at the silent telephone. He'd finished the
most important call of his long and distinguished life.
After receiving the news, the current patriarch of the Monarch dynasty had placed the handset down in its cradle.

Dan had expected this call for several weeks. He thought
he was ready. But can you ever prepare for the end of the
world? The cancer had metastasized. It was only a question
of time and not very much of that.

His doctor said that he had eight or nine weeks, maybe as
many as 12 to 15, before they'd begin sedating him so strongly that he'd cease to function. He'd be dead in six months. If
he survived longer, the pain or the medication would inca-
pacitate him.

Today, he could manage. With just a touch of good fortune, he'd be able to function as the President of Monarch
Industries long enough to tie up all of his personal and
business loose ends.

Dan hit the button on the intercom and asked his secre-
tary to find his administrative assistant. Normally, Marta
Genero would come to his office in less than five minutes.
Lately, there was no telling when Marta might respond.

Dan had seen this sort of behavior before, but always in
other, less reliable, employees. Monarch understood that
Marta's behavior was a symptom of a deep depression over
the loss of her daughter. In its way, Kari's death affected Dan

as profoundly as Marta. Dan regretted that Kari wasn't his own daughter.

Fifteen minutes after being summoned, Marta appeared in the doorway to Monarch's executive suite. She looked ravishing, but seemed a little disoriented and scattered.

"You sent for me, Dan?" Marta inquired.

"Yes, Marta, I did. Come on in, and take a chair. I have some important things to discuss with you," Dan directed.

"Dan, if it's about that report on the Navy denims, I'll have that on your desk by tomorrow. The contracts were more extensive than I thought," Marta began, before Dan Monarch waived her off, his face contorted by a tight smile.

"Marta, I don't want to talk about those things now. I have some news, bad news. I want to discuss the implications with you. I feel I owe it to you for all that's happened over the years," Dan explained.

"Dan, what's the matter?"

Monarch waited until Marta took her seat at the side of his desk. He pulled his chair around, so the great wooden monstrosity would not interpose between them.

"Marta," Dan began, "I have to leave the business. It will be for good this time."

"Are you all right?" Marta asked, panic rising in her voice.

"I'm very sick, but there's hope," Dan lied. "I don't have the option of trying to lick the cancer and run this company at the same time. I'm giving up the reins."

"What's your prognosis?" Marta asked, not sure whether she should believe her old friend.

"I have a chance at recovery, if I quit soon, and concentrate on the course of treatment," Dan lied again.

"Oh, Dan. I'm so sorry. I'll do anything to help you. You know that, don't you?"

"Marta, I think that it's time that you left the company."

"Why, Dan? Who will replace you as the chief executive?"

"My nephew will be the next president, Marta. In my absence, he has enough votes on the board to secure the position."

"I see, Dan. That's too bad!"

"Marta, there's no time to beat around the bush. You can't stay on after Junior gains power. You're a sick part of his lust for revenge. Junior's been unable to pursue it, because I'd have destroyed him. If I'm not around, and I won't be forever, he'll make you and your family miserable."

"My family? Dan, where is my family? My daughter was killed on Corregidor. My son is in England. I have no idea where he'll be next week. Gin's a paratrooper, for God's sake! What chance does he have? My husband travels around more than half the time. When he's home, he pities me! Can you believe that? He feels sorry for me. He thinks that I'm becoming an alcoholic. I haven't seen my own brothers and sisters in twenty-five years. I have no family!

"Marta, I knew you were suffering, but I'd no idea," Dan responded. "Now, it's more imperative that you leave the company when I do. You and Phillip have been saving your money. You're fairly well off. I've made it a point to give you both every fiscal benefit I could."

"Dan, you've been very generous. It's not a question of money. Phillip and I have a tidy nest egg. Thanks to you, we don't have to worry about the future."

"Marta, you know how I care about you. I always have. I want to ensure that you're provided for after I'm gone. I plan to leave you $150,000.00. That's more than ten years' salary for Phillip. That should be enough for you and your husband to walk away from Monarch without risking your nest egg. Maybe Phillip could go back into the bakery business, which was always his first love," Dan offered, his voice taking an uncharacteristically emotional pitch.

Marta was stunned. $150,000.00 was an unbelievable sum in 1942. Marta and Phillip could do a lot of good with that kind of money.

"Dan, how would I explain such a generous bequest from you to me? Don't you think that it might make Phillip a bit suspicious, about us?" Marta asked with uncharacteristic coolness.

"Marta, I've always loved you. You know that. I've loved you since you were the nanny to my children. I treasured our intimacy and always wanted us to be together, but you refused to break up my marriage. I promised you twenty-five years ago that I would never stand in your way. When you decided to leave my home, and take a job in the company, I supported you. When you fell in love with Genero, I was devastated, but I supported you. I've been your friend, and only your friend, since the day you got married. I want to make sure that you don't have to deal with Junior and all of his evil machinations."

"Dan, you mean well. I can't stop you from leaving me the money. I'm sure that your other heirs will hit the roof if you do. I don't know what my reputation is in Carlisle, but it will be ruined if you leave me a vast sum of money. Please think about that before you do anything," Marta requested.

"What will you do?" Dan asked. "You wouldn't seriously consider staying on here and continue working for Junior?"

"Dan, you worry about getting well. I'll be fine. I've been here more than eleven years this time. I'm not the babe in the woods that I was when you first took me under your wing. Junior's mellowed out a bit. He's not as bad as he was before he got sick. I think I can handle him now. I don't want to be by myself every day, waiting for another telegram from the government. The people of Monarch are the only real family I have left. I don't want to leave them. So, even if you give me a million dollars, I intend to stay right here, and make my little contribution to the war effort."

Dan Monarch looked at Marta with a combination of un-requited love, frustration, and fear. He'd envied Phillip Genero every day over the last 25 years, and now he felt sorry for him. Dan would consider Marta's concerns about the money. He wouldn't make the decision today. He still had a few more weeks.

# Chapter 29

A steady drizzle soaked the three men as they slithered through the muddy North African field in a night as black as Junior Monarch's heart. Genero, Captain Louis Anton, and Staff Sergeant Taylor crawled from their camouflaged position to the edge of the low ridgeline, located five miles south of the Berber village of Feriana.

*Of all the surprises in the last two weeks, the one condition that I did not expect to see was mud. Sand, yes. Rocks, sure. Desert, unquestionably. Heat, of course. But oceans of mud and torrents of rain in a record cold winter! That's been a total surprise,* Phil thought, as he struggled through the mud.

A small community south of the ancient Roman ruins of Thelepte, the village of Feriana lay along the improved road equidistant between Gafsa in the desert south and El Kef in the temperate north. Feriana represented the last outpost along the western edge of the French Protectorate of Tunisia.

Feriana sat 2,400 feet above the level of the Mediterranean and 100 miles from the sea. Though the Sahara Desert began 65 miles to the south, the hilly terrain around the village was semi-arid, covered in hardy grasses, small thorny bushes, dwarf trees, and several varieties of cactus.

Kasserine, another Berber town at the western end of an important pass in the Dorsal Mountains, was 21 miles north of Feriana. In Central Tunisia, the Kasserine Pass formed a bottleneck, canalizing commercial and military traffic from the Tunisian east coast through the Dorsals to the western frontier with Algeria.

The highways intersecting at Feriana and Thelepte south of Kasserine created a tactically important crossroads. As the allies struggled to move west from their victories in Algeria into the bitter fighting in Tunisia, the commanders decided that Thelepte would be an ideal spot to base fighter aircraft. The area also had immense value for the tankers, paratroopers, artillerymen, and engineers of the ad hoc group that had become known as the *Tunisian Task Force*, or—more frequently—*the Raff Force*. The Raff Force included orphan units, numbering 3,000 American, British, and French soldiers.

Earlier in the day, Genero's scouts reported that a strong German and Italian motorized battalion had cut the main road between LtCol. Raff's troops and the main allied effort to the north. In light of the threat, Phil needed to know the enemy's true strength and disposition.

The presence of axis armor north of their area of operation could be disastrous for the Raff Force, whose primary mission had been to protect the right flank of the Anglo-American units along the coast. For the last few days, the British 1st Army and the American II Corps had moved eastward in parallel columns, advancing toward Bizerte and Tunis, the two strategic targets along the Mediterranean coastline.

On the previous day, Capt. Genero's command had encamped at the base of Hill 2817. The hill formed the dominant terrain feature for 100 square miles. A steep slab of sandstone, the hill stuck out of the plain like a bent thumb along the improved road ten miles south of Feriana.

Genero and Anton had been planning a different mission when they learned that three companies of German armor and one company of Italian mechanized infantry had arrived in the vicinity of the villages of Feriana and Thelepte. A force that size could mean that 500-600 enemy soldiers had passed through the Kasserine Pass and had cut them off from the main allied body in the north.

Genero immediately presided over a council of war. Capt. Anton; six British, French, and American lieutenants; and ten senior sergeants of mixed pedigree attended the council.

One week earlier, LtCol. Raff had placed these officers and non-coms under Phil's command. Raff ordered Genero's unit to act as the rear guard for the larger task force. Raff intended the rear guard to be a reinforced company. With the addition of elements of the French Foreign Legion and British engineers, Phil commanded 280 men.

The Raff Force rear guard included two platoons of infantry from the 2/503d, a reinforced platoon of M-3 tank destroyers, two platoons of British combat engineers, two platoons of anti-aircraft artillerymen, and two platoons of French Foreign Legionnaires, who had appropriated a heavy weapons squad from the 3d Zouave regiment at Youks Les Bains in Algeria.

Raff directed Genero to shield his task force at all costs. In the event of trouble, Phil had to eradicate any threat as the colonel executed a bold reconnaissance-in-force to the south and east.

Above the platoon level, none of Genero's men had served together. Other than the Legionnaires and the Brit engineers, the men had seen only a glimpse of actual combat in the last two weeks, since their airborne or amphibious entry into Western Algeria.

A strong enemy contingent now imperiled the mission of the Raff Force, and the II Corps' southern flank. Genero had to act before first light. After personally reconnoitering the enemy position, Phil had less than eight hours to devise a plan. He had to find a way to use his small, multi-national unit to defeat a numerically superior, better-equipped, more homogenous force—one that undoubtedly had significant combat experience.

Genero could not risk allowing the Nazis to catch his men out in the open after dawn. Nor could he permit the Germans to cut Raff's lines of supply and communication, leaving him out on a perilous limb.

As Phil studied the enemy positions, he reminded himself that he was a paratrooper. He had trained to be bold. He expected to be surrounded and outnumbered. He committed to the fight that was coming. He and his men would prevail. Genero would consider no other option.

For millennia, Tunisia had been an incomparable land with an ancient culture. A thousand years before the Christian era, Berber tribesmen roamed the plains and Mediterranean coastline hunting, gathering, and herding. Eight centuries before Christ, the Phoenicians disturbed the pastoral life of the Berbers by erecting a new city among the tribes.

For the site of this new city, which in Phoenician became Carthage, the colonists chose the northeastern shore near the Gulf of Tunis. To the east, Cape Bon jutted into the Mediterranean to form the northernmost point of the vast continent of Africa.

In the 4th Century B.C., Carthage became the undisputed ruler of the western Mediterranean. In three separate wars the less cultured Roman barbarians defeated the more civilized Carthaginians. At the end of the last Punic war, the Romans eradicated all traces of Carthage. For the next 600 years, the Romans controlled the Tunisian countryside as an important North African province in their empire. The vast wheat fields of central Tunisia became the breadbasket for the Italian peninsula.

After the Romans, the Vandals ruled Tunisia until displaced by the eastern hegemony known as Byzantium. Later, the followers of Mohammed roared westward out of Arabia and conquered the land for Islam. Eventually, the Ottomans absorbed Tunisia into their empire. Finally, the French took control of the administration of the Tunisian government in the last 12 years of the 19th Century.

Tunisia had been the focus of conquerors over thousands of years because of its strategic geographic location. Cape Bon was separated from the southwestern shore of Sicily by a narrow passage known as the Sicily Straits. This line marked the ancient east/west division in the Mediterranean.

In 1942, Tunisia became the epicenter of a major military campaign. The Anglo-American alliance needed a second front in the hemisphere. They had to relieve pressure and bleed resources from the epic battles raging in the Soviet Union.

Winston Churchill sold the western alliance on the theory that the southern European nations, especially Italy, would offer a "soft underbelly" for the allied conquest of the continent. Churchill argued that the Anglo-American alliance could exploit this underbelly with relative ease to liberate Europe from Nazi occupation.

Except for the Battle of Midway, 1942 had been a very bad year for the Americans. In the European Theater, American land forces needed to get into the shooting war as quickly as possible in order to chalk up victories.

Since late 1940, the British 8th Army had been fighting the Italians and Germans in a great seesaw campaign along vast tracks of desert in eastern North Africa. A large Anglo-American armed force in the west would create a strategic pincer, which would be a disaster for General Erwin Rommel and the famed *Deustches Afrika Korps*. Until their defeat at Al Alamein, the DAK had held its own against the British and their Commonwealth troops in extensive and bloody fighting in Egypt and Libya.

The conquest of Western North Africa, including Tunisia, would give the Allies a jumping-off point for an invasion of Sicily. Success in North Africa would provide them the opportunity to begin to feast on the soft underbelly of Europe.

Churchill and Roosevelt agreed that the invasion of Morocco, Algeria, and Tunisia would be a viable and attractive alternative to another incursion into France. Ironically, these three target countries had no significant German or Italian garrisons and remained colonies of the Vichy puppet government in unoccupied France.

During the planning phase for what became *Operation Torch,* no Anglo-American leader knew if the Vichy armed forces in North Africa would oppose a landing by allied troops. Bad blood persisted over the British attack on the French naval forces in Algeria in 1940. If the British invaded alone, planners believed that the Vichy forces would fight like hell to repel them.

Since a cordial relationship still existed between the Vichy French and the Americans, using American forces in the initial assaults might elicit a more peaceful response from the Vichy French. Still, there were no guarantees.

In order to test the sentiment of the Vichy forces in North Africa in the summer and fall of 1942, the Americans and the Brits attempted many stratagems. Spies in France made contact with military leaders. General Mark Clark landed in North Africa by submarine in order to have a clandestine meeting with important Vichy commanders.

Despite serious efforts, the Americans could reach no accord with the French. Consequently, the allied command drew up two totally separate schemes for the implementation of the armed incursion into North Africa. Until the date of the invasion, the planners pursued two inconsistent versions of *Operation Torch*: the war plan and the peace plan.

On the eve of the invasion in November 1942, the allies didn't know which plan they would implement. At worst, it was madness. At best, it was naive.

Phil learned of *Operation Torch* in September when he reported to Major Yarborough at II Corps Headquarters at Norfolk House in London. North Africa was the last place he expected the allies to attack, especially if much of the operation would be staged in Britain. The distances between England and the airborne targets stretched to the very edge of allied logistical capabilities.

The mission required the 2/503d to chute up, load themselves and their equipment onto C-47s, and take off from

Land's End in England, the southernmost point of the British Isles. The aircraft, loaded with paratroopers, would fly south, southeast 1500 miles across the Atlantic, through Spanish air space—without permission—and into the Mediterranean—without refueling. About 12 hours after takeoff, assuming that the pilots found their way to North Africa, the Air Corps would drop the Americans near the French aerodrome at Tafaraoui, south of the city of Oran in western Algeria.

In the brief history of vertical envelopment, the airborne assault portion of *Operation Torch* was unprecedented. Though the Germans used the equivalent of two divisions in their airborne invasion of Crete, the distance from Greece to Crete was far shorter than the distance from England to Algeria.

If the Vichy forces did not fight, the American airborne forces would land at the La Senia aerodrome, several miles from Tafaraoui. If the French resisted, the Americans would jump on pre-designated drop zones and engage the French in combat operations.

The two plans were mutually inconsistent. Genero perceived the duality as a dangerous threat. After reviewing all options, Genero concluded that the American paratroopers should jump the night before D-Day, ready to fight. If the French resisted, the Americans would engage them on the spot. If the French didn't fight, then little would be lost in the extra effort.

Phil didn't believe that any French commander would allow the Americans to waltz into his territory without at least token resistance to save the notorious Gallic pride. When his superiors asked for his views, Phil gave them the unvarnished version. Maj. Yarborough had to explain to the offended planners at II Corps that Capt. Genero was impetuous and high-strung.

Despite his initial concerns, LtCol. Raff embraced the invasion plan with unbridled enthusiasm. Consistent with the force of his personality and depth of his commitment, he prepared his men long and hard for the operation.

For two months, Genero worked day and night on the planning in London. He also helped to supervise the training at Chilton-Foliat. The press of his duties required him to shuttle back and forth, sometimes three times each week.

In October, Phil managed a few nights with Cynthia Devereaux at her flat in London. They would meet for a late supper, have drinks at her father's club, and end the evening with a passionate encounter.

Lady Devereaux represented the product of the British system of "public" schools. This meant that she'd spent her adolescence in the finest private schools that her father's influence could arrange. Her family had groomed Cynthia to be part of an elite class, destined to govern an empire upon which the sun was to never set.

Cynthia subscribed to the doctrine of the British ruling class. Although she was the least snobbish young woman in her circle of friends, she believed that she would marry well and live a life of comfort, luxury, and privilege.

Lady Devereaux had traveled throughout the empire and had explored the parameters of her sexuality. She especially enjoyed the various techniques that Phil employed to please her. Disturbingly, this Yank had become special to her.

Early in the relationship she calculated that the Phil's chances of survival, given the dangerous nature of his branch of service, were effectively nil. He would be fortunate to be alive this time next year.

*It will be a miracle if the allies win this bloody war, though our chances are definitely better with the Yanks as our allies,* Cynthia thought. *So far, the Jerries have only suffered one significant set back. That was in Egypt at Al Alamein. I can't really see how that changes anything in Europe. I fear this war will end in another armistice.*

*I cannot allow myself to fall in love with a working class Yank, especially one who will probably die gallantly behind enemy lines in some far-off battlefield.*

Cynthia's resolve disappeared early one morning after she and Genero finished a session of vigorous sex. If she'd been more satisfied, she couldn't remember the occasion.

Instead of rolling off her tight little body and going to sleep, like most of her lovers, Phil pulled her close, spooning their bodies together. He ran his hand up and down the side of her thigh, calling her the most delicious pet names.

While whispering some interesting suggestions in her ear, Phil called her Cindy. Formerly, Cynthia would have disemboweled anyone so impudent. But, Genero's sweet demeanor and the way he spoke the name caused her to shiver and glow with contentment. Lady Devereaux's breeding could not overcome basic chemistry.

Notwithstanding her common sense and better judgment, she fell in love. Cynthia recognized her hopeless emotional state. She decided that it would be best if she kept the unfortunate news to herself. *I simply will not stand on a train station platform like a common shop girl, wailing and sobbing, as Phillip's troop train chugs out of sight bound for eternity,* Cynthia swore.

While Phil planned for war, Cynthia kept busy by making the final arrangements for Paul and Katherine's wedding. The ceremony would take place at the chapel at Debden Aerodrome. Afterward, they would host a reception at the officer's club.

Normally, LtCol. Raff would not permit Phil to take precious time away from the pre-invasion planning to participate in a wedding. However, the 8th Air Force and II Corps press officers saw Maj. Reilly's marriage as a significant human-interest feature and natural morale-boosting event for the folks back home.

An ace fighter pilot, former RAF Eagle, and current Air Corps major would marry a gorgeous British movie star. One of the groom's best friends, a big strapping American paratrooper, would serve as best man. The maid of honor was the eldest daughter of an important British peer, who happened to be a vocal member of the stodgy House of Lords. The wedding party mirrored the Anglo-American alliance.

Both of the men had dangerous assignments. Both risked death in the service of their country. More than one magazine wanted to do a feature story on the wedding. It would make a big splash throughout the United States. In the future, if anything dire happened to the fighter pilot or the paratrooper, it would be melodramatic grist for follow-on stories. In the cynical world of the press, it seemed like a natural.

The press officers prevailed on Gen. Doolittle and Gen. Clark to influence LtCol. Raff. Realizing that he'd been outmaneuvered, Raff gave Phil permission to be Reilly's best man.

Early on Friday, October 17, 1942, Phil and Cynthia traveled to Debden in a Rolls Royce driven by the Earl's personal chauffeur. Although he didn't realize it, Genero possessed the last pass that he'd see for more than eight months.

Cynthia sensed that the relationship was ending. She tried to convince herself that her feelings were the product of the natural drama of the times. She never succeeded for more than a few moments, and never while Genero was within arm's length. Cynthia took full advantage of the drive up to Essex, sipping champagne and cuddling with Phil in the luxurious back seat of the limousine.

When the couple arrived at Debden, they took two rooms at the Fox and Hound. It was a waste. Over the whole weekend, Genero spent less than ten minutes in his own room.

The rehearsal on Friday evening went well. Threescore British and American fighter pilots—who out did each other trying to get drunk—attended it. There was almost no violence, but some furniture and a few glasses did get broken.

Paul's bachelor party became the stuff of legend and a turning point for the new American fighter group. For years thereafter, pilots who attended the party would regale the regulars of the Debden officer's club with exaggerated and sensational versions of the events of that evening.

Over time, attendance at the bachelor party became the mark of a 4ᵗʰ Group veteran. If a pilot attended the bachelor party, his peers recognized him as an old timer. If a pilot were assigned to the 4ᵗʰ Fighter Group after October 18, 1942, the vets would label him a junior birdman.

Phil presided over the festivities. During one of his monologues, between featured entertainers imported from London, Genero amused the allied pilots with an embellished version of Paul's encounter with the four Betas at Penn State. The crowd went wild, until one skeptical British pilot demanded corroboration.

A wag from the newly formed 4ᵗʰ Group publicly suggested that the fact that a beautiful British film star would marry so plain an American peasant supported Phil's story. To the commentator, for the first time ever, the match made sense.

The American's logic did not convince his cynical British comrade. The British officer would settle for nothing less than a demonstration. One of the more attractive entertainers valiantly offered to be a test subject for such a demonstration. Once again, the crowd went wild. Despite his affection for Genero, Paul considered shooting his old fraternity brother.

Paul had matured two decades over the last two-and-a-half years. He now held the rank of major in the Air Corps and served as a fighter squadron executive officer. He would not compromise his position in the group by engaging in a ribald display.

When the hooting and hollering of the crowd threatened to get out of control, Paul thought of a clever alternative. He raised his hands as if to surrender. He shook his head up and down, feigning affirmation. Paul called for the volunteer to come to him. As she strutted across the room, Paul swiveled a chair in her direction.

With a lascivious look, Paul startled everyone by sticking his tongue out very far and licking his lips. The men began to whistle and holler.

Once the entertainer sat in the chair, she hiked her skirt, exposing her beautifully formed calves and thighs. The room fell into an unnatural hush. Some of the men could be heard breathing very hard.

"Paul, you'd better 'urry. Evan's going to blow a bloody gasket over 'ere!" Another RAF pilot warned.

Paul winked and pretended to get down on one knee. Instead, he genuflected, and took the volunteer's head in his hands. He turned it to the side, exposing her left ear. For the next two minutes, Paul demonstrated his unique genetic talents. At the end, Paul received a standing ovation from all the guests.

The girl claimed to be disappointed. She gave Paul her number in London in case things didn't work out in the marriage.

The next day, an Anglican chaplain preformed a simple ceremony in the chapel. At the reception at the officer's club, Phil offered a nice toast to the young couple, which the *National Weekly* reported ten days later.

By 1800 hours, the newlyweds marched under the arch of swords. They jumped into Catherine's Aston-Martin and sped away on their honeymoon, which would last only three days because of the war. The reception over, Phil and Cynthia repaired to the room at the Fox and Hound and sequestered themselves for the night.

As a follow up, American reporters found Tim Sullivan in San Diego, convalescing from his wounds. He'd undergone several operations on his face, and had lost some of the feeling on the right side of his head.

Tim had successfully opposed a move by the hospital administrators to give him a medical discharge. Instead, he received permanent orders directing him to a billet in the Navy Department in Washington where he would fly a desk for the duration. In the interview, Tim wished the couple every happiness, but swore to the reporters that he'd be back on flight status in a few weeks.

Cynthia saw Phil one last time in London after the wedding. Phil seemed distracted, and more nervous than she'd ever seen him.

Despite her best intentions, Cynthia became emotional. She'd never cared so deeply for another person. She could not bear to think of what lay in store for her lover.

After a pleasurable session of lovemaking, Phil cuddled her in his usual fashion. Later, Cynthia would recall that Genero's genuine affection created the ultimate aphrodisiac.

For reasons that Cynthia could never explain, as Phil held her, she began to cry. She not only wept, she cried hard for the first time in her entire life. She had no frame of reference for the spectrum of emotions that she felt.

She experienced immense joy in her love for the man and abject fear for what was sure to come in his future. She knew that she would gladly trade places with him, if it would mean his survival. Knowing that it was impossible to swap her fate for his, Cynthia felt such sadness that she questioned whether she would want to know this kind of love again.

Phil tried to console her, but nothing seemed to work. "Cindy, you know how much I care?" Phil asked.

"Phillip," Cynthia began, using his formal first name as was her habit, "I know you care, but I'm afraid that I've gone and fallen in love with you, haven't I? It's a mistake, but there it is. There's apparently nothing I can do about it!"

Genero was stunned. He was not in love with Cynthia. He enjoyed her company. He looked forward to the intimacy, but he didn't feel true love for her. Early in his training, Phil decided that he wouldn't allow anything to distract him from the war. He understood that his chances of getting through the war unscathed were remote. At first, that realization frightened him. Later, he accepted the situation, and made peace with the fact that each day might be his last.

"Cindy, I'm going away. I was hoping that you'd write. I'd cherish your letters. It would be a way to stay in touch, to stay close. Who knows what will happen? If we don't loose this thread, when it's all over we could see where it goes," Phil offered in his most unpretentious tone, not revealing to

Cynthia that he'd given the same speech to Laurie at Fort Benning and Patti at Fort Bragg.

*He hasn't even said that he loves me, but I know he does. He's a man, isn't he? He'll never admit how he feels,* Cynthia thought as she listened to Phil.

Cynthia accepted the small consolation that Genero had offered, and promised to write him every day. She reached up, wove her arms around his neck, and pulled him down to her. She'd make sure that he never forgot what was waiting for him in England. It might give him a reason to survive, and if he did, to come back to her.

During the first week in November of 1942, while he was in isolation at the RAF aerodrome at Land's End with the rest of the 2/503d, Capt. Genero fantasized a lot about Cindy. He thought about Laurie, Patti, Linda—of all people—and a half-dozen other girls with whom he'd shared an intimacy.

Phil thought of his family in Carlisle, especially his mom. His dad's letters arrived regularly and they always included a message from his mother. Marta's notes made it obvious that she was deeply depressed over Kari's death.

Phil thought about Kari every day. He'd been blessed to have her as his sister. He regretted that he'd not told her more often how much he loved her.

He wondered how his Uncle Anglo was doing with the bakery. He thought about all the Generos. He regretted never getting to know the Brumbachs.

Before America had completed its first year in this Second World War, his sister had made the ultimate sacrifice for her country. His fraternity brother, Pat Kelly, had died horribly on the bridge of the *USS Oklahoma*.

Phil's brother-in-law had seen action in the Pacific. Tim had fought, suffered serious wounds, and received important decorations in two major battles. Paul had been in combat for over two years and was now an ace pilot with the 4th Fighter Group.

Other than training with the Airborne, brawling in men's rooms, and seducing willing young women, Phil couldn't recount a single significant thing that he'd done since the war in Europe started. It was about time that he made his own mark.

Genero's contribution to actual combat operations began in the evening of November 7, 1942. At 2100 hours, he and 555 of his comrades loaded on board 39 Air Corps C-47s for the long flight to North Africa.

Until 1630 in the afternoon on the day of departure, the allied command held them in suspense. As the paratroopers loaded their equipment on the aircraft, LtCol. Raff informed all of the officers that the 2/503d would follow the peace plan. Many of the paratroopers seemed relieved.

Genero had a bad feeling about this development. All of his knowledge of the French, all of his experience, all of his considerable intuition and suspicion screamed that the 2/503d would be flying into a trap.

There was nothing that Phil could do. He boarded his aircraft with the rest of the team and waited for the take off. After the whole battalion was airborne, Phil settled in for the long flight. He was the senior officer on his C-47 including the two Air Corps pilots up front.

Phil checked the other 14 paratroopers in his stick for the tenth time and tried to get a little rest. Even with the peace plan, he would not have much time for sleep after they landed at Oran. He dozed for several hours before waking up in the early hours of November 8th.

After he stretched and got the kinks out of his neck, he went forward in the aircraft to get a situation report from the pilots. That's when the shit hit the fan. As soon as Phil stuck his head into the cockpit, he could tell that something was dreadfully wrong. The young pilots seemed anxious and confused. During the night, the flight of C-47s had dispersed after the aircraft entered a cloudbank while over the Pyrenees in Spanish air space.

The pilots had continued on the proper heading, but neither of the planned navigation aids materialized. Phil ran over every emergency scenario in his mind from ditching in the sea to a crash landing in the desert. These were two real possibilities, given the circumstances.

When Genero thought his anxiety could not get higher, the sky began to lighten on the port side of the aircraft. Thirty minutes later, Phil's C-47 broke through the cloud cover into open sky with a brilliant dawn exploding in the east.

Capt. Genero received the shock of his life. Of the 39 aircraft that left Land's End, only five remained in the formation. Though shaken, his pilots insisted that they were on the right heading. By their calculations the Algerian coastline should come into view in minutes.

The plane's fuel gauges read nearly empty. The head winds had been brisker than the optimistic II Corps planners had contemplated. As the tension reached its zenith, the North African coastline hove into view. When the co-pilot saw it, he let out a huge whoop!

Genero made a very public sign of the cross and said a brief Hail Mary for their deliverance. The C-47 crew chief saw Phil's religious demonstration and smiled at Genero, while conspicuously wiping the back of his hand across his forehead in a silent demonstration of his own relief.

Before they crossed the coastline, the little flight of five linked up with one more C-47. Then, the pilots received bad news. They'd drifted too far to the west. Their small flight of C-47s had made landfall over Spanish Morocco, not western Algeria.

American aircraft could not land in Spanish Morocco. The Spanish government was neutral, but fascist. It would intern the aircrew and all paratroopers for the duration.

"Gentlemen, turn this crate east! Get us as far into Algeria as possible before we run out of fuel," Genero ordered the two young pilots.

"Captain, the pilot of that last transport to join up says that your colonel is on board his aircraft. The colonel is assuming operational control of what's left of this flight," the co-pilot responded.

"Understood," Genero said. "Tell your buddy to inform Lieutenant Colonel Raff that we're standing by for instructions."

The flight of six C-47s turned to a heading of 105 degrees magnetic and flew without incident for nearly ten minutes. As the Americans passed deeper into Algeria, the radio on Phil's aircraft began to crackle.

"Captain," the co-pilot addressed Genero, raising his voice slightly. "We're receiving transmissions from the missing aircraft. They're ahead of us. Sir, about twenty transports made it to the aerodrome at La Senia. Unfortunately, the Frogs fired on them when they tried to land. So, the fucking peace plan is out the window. Since they couldn't land, the planes flew about thirty miles northeast of the aerodrome and landed on the surface of the dry lake bed."

"Any instructions from Lieutenant Colonel Raff?" Phil asked the pilot.

"Yes, sir! We're hearing that French tanks are on that lakebed and have attacked the transports. Your colonel wants your men to prepare to jump to assist your buddies."

"Inform the colonel that I've received his orders and will comply."

Phil had known that something like this would happen. "What a fucking mess! How could the rear echelon commandos have been so stupid?" Genero asked the pilots, rhetorically. Neither of the pilots responded. They simply shrugged and stoically accepted the hand that fate had dealt them.

In response to Raff's order, Genero went aft and briefed the other paratroopers. They reacted quickly and professionally. They had nine minutes to station time.

Five minutes later, the loadmaster opened the port side cargo hatch. Encumbered with his equipment, Phil knelt on the deck of the aircraft and stuck his head into the wind stream, facing in the direction of flight. Holding onto to the doorframe and craning his neck, he looked out toward the jump point. A few miles ahead, he saw several American planes on the ground. The paratroopers were spreading out to form a perimeter around the parked aircraft.

Confident that his C-47 was on the correct heading, Genero stood up and gave his 14 paratroopers the standard jump commands. When the last paratrooper yelled "OK," Phil directed his men to move aft toward the hatch. Phil took the door position. Despite his training, he ignored the horizon and watched the ground carefully.

As the nose of Genero's aircraft crossed the first of the parked aircraft, the pilot rang the bell signaling that it was time to jump. When he heard the bell, Phil sprung into space like an angry rattlesnake making a strike.

Genero tucked into a tight body position with his chin pressed against his chest, his elbows in close, hands on his reserve, and the trunk of his body bent at the waist. He began his count. Before he could get to 3,000 he felt a surprisingly strong opening shock. After bouncing in the air like a human yo-yo, Phil looked up at the inverse side of his canopy. Two of the gores in the shroud were blown, an indication that the chute had opened too hard.

After checking his rate of decent, Genero concluded that the tear wouldn't be a problem. A few seconds later, Phil landed hard on the rocky drop zone. *Welcome to North Africa!*

Five of the sticks came down close to Genero. He soon had 70 paratroopers setting up around him. The colonel landed 90 yards to the north.

Coming down too fast, Colonel Raff tried a forward roll, but struck a large rock and broke a rib on the rocky hillside. The injury caused the colonel to cough up a prodigious amount of blood.

Within minutes of his own landing, Phil approached Colonel Raff. "Sir, Captain Genero reporting!"

"Genero, I want you to stand by to take command. I may have punctured a lung. I'm coughing up too much blood," Raff said. "In the meantime get this group in a tactical formation and move them toward the C-47s immediately. Put men with Thompsons and anti-tank rifle grenades on point. Tell them to stay alert. Looks like we've got to fight the French."

As Raff's jumpers approached the American perimeter, one of the scouts ran back with a stunning report. "Sir, those tanks out in front of our perimeter are American! They're Grants. They have a platoon of mech infantry with them."

Within a half hour Raff established a link-up between the paratroopers and the armor force that had made an amphibious landing several hours earlier. After ensuring that everything was secure, Raff sent for Maj. Yarborough, who had come along as an observer for the II Corps commanding general and had landed with the contingent of C-47s. He'd been waiting for Raff.

Raff asked Yarborough for a report.

"Colonel, as our flight of C-47s attempted to land at La Senia, French gunners opened up on us unexpectedly. We didn't suffer serious damage or casualties, but we realized that if we landed we'd be very vulnerable out there on the airstrip with no cover. So I ordered the flight to head northeast and land on this dry lakebed. Since we had less than half our men, I wanted to take stock before we assaulted the airfield," Yarborough explained. Yarborough's briefing shocked Raff. He never expected the peace plan to go without a hitch, but he never contemplated that it would fail utterly.

Since Raff was too injured to lead the men to La Senia on foot, Genero and Maj. Yarborough prevailed on him to ride in one of the Jeeps used by the command element of the armored force. With Maj. Yarborough in technical command of what remained of the battalion, they started off on a forced march toward La Senia. As he trekked along with his comrades, Phil prepared a mental after action report on the fiasco.

Two hours into the march, Raff received the news that other allied mechanized forces had taken La Senia. Their commander wanted to move out toward Tafaraoui, but had too many French prisoners to guard to continue with his combat mission.

Raff decided to have a few of the C-47s that were parked back on the edge of the lack bed cannibalize gas from other parked aircraft. Once refueled, the selected C-47s would take off, fly the short distance to the task force and land nearby.

Raff would load a company of paratroopers on these aircraft and ferry them to La Senia immediately. A company of paratroopers could lend the tankers a hand with the French prisoners, and free them up to liberate the aerodrome at Tafaraoui.

An hour later several C-47s landed near Raff's temporary lager. The colonel dispatched E Company for the mission. The planes hot-loaded the troopers for the short hop to La Senia.

Raff decided that Yarborough would lead E Company to La Senia. Genero and several other officers were to stay with the remaining paratroopers and continue the long road march to the aerodrome.

Three hours later and 11 miles farther, the colonel called Genero and his other officers for a staff meeting. Raff gave the battalion a short rest from the arduous road march.

"Men," LtCol. Raff began, after gathering the officers around him out of earshot of the enlisted paratroopers, "French fighter pilots attacked the C-47s that were ferrying E Company to La Senia. They killed or wounded several of our comrades. The French didn't shoot any of the aircraft down, but they damaged all of them. None of the C-47s got to La Senia. They've landed short of the aerodrome."

Raff continued in a somber tone, punctuated by an occasional cough in which he spit up blood. "Major Yarborough is OK, but Doc Moir is seriously wounded. Lieutenant Kunkle is dead. It looks like six or seven dead, and fifteen to twenty wounded.

"Yarborough got to the objective on foot and made arrangements to ferry the remainder of E Company. He'll take them overland for the balance of the distance to La Senia. Once E Company is at La Senia, Yarborough will send the transports out for us. You company commanders and platoon leaders, make sure your men are ready for anything."

Phil was livid. Their circumstances bordered on disaster.

*My God!* Phil thought. *The whole battalion is struggling to get to an aerodrome that the tankers have already captured, so we can guard prisoners! This was not our mission. It's a waste of time for elite paratroopers. Worse—the fucking Vichy fighter pilots shot up E Company. Damn!*

*I swear that if we make another jump, I won't let the commander underestimate the enemy and make another tragic mistake.*

Phil didn't have long to wait for his second jump. Within two days of their arrival at Tafaraoui Aerodrome, Raff called for Capt. Genero.

"Genero," Raff began. "I've been called up to Algiers. We're to make another jump in a few days, by the fifteenth for sure. I'm going to H.Q. in Algiers to get a briefing on our target. I want you to come along with the S-3."

"Sir, that's only five days from now. We haven't accounted for all of our boys. Some are in French Morocco. Some are interned in Spanish Morocco. If you include the decrement in our force due to the casualties, we can field barely three hundred paratroopers in the whole battalion. It took us ten weeks to get ready for the last jump. Does Corps think we can plan and execute an airborne assault in less than five days?"

Raff gave Genero a very hard look. The colonel still suffered from his broken rib. He had less patience than usual.

"Genero, I don't care what those idiots at Corps think! I believe that we can do it. And we will plan and execute the operation by the fifteenth, or I'll cause some heads to roll. Get me?" Raff barked.

Genero snapped into a position of attention, and said, "Yes, sir. I fully understand. I'll get my equipment, and be ready in five minutes."

Raff had achieved the desired affect. The colonel had knocked around the Army for more years than Genero. Raff had graduated from West Point, but he'd developed no skills as a politician.

Raff knew that the concept of vertical envelopment had many detractors. Many of these were senior officers who were salivating to get battalions of elite paratroopers into straight leg formations that they could command. Raff would not let that happen.

LtCol. Raff understood that in the Army, as in life, impressions defined reality. No matter how badly you executed an operation, if higher headquarters was satisfied, then their favorable impression trumped your bad operation. Conversely, if you did well, but made a bad impression with the generals, you were screwed.

If the senior commanders ever got the impression that airborne operations were too costly, too complicated, or too difficult, they'd stop using them. It wouldn't matter that the operations were successful.

The quickest way to create a negative impression would be for Raff's own staff officers to bad-mouth the results of the operation. He jumped on Genero to stop the whining.

"Genero, you're a good man. We're on the spear point of a new concept for the Army. Accentuate the positive. Stop the carping. Now! OK, you've got bragging rights. It was foolhardy to rely on the peace plan. You were right. Feel better?"

"Actually, I don't, sir. I don't want to be whiner. You can rely on me, sir!"

"I know I can," Raff responded. "What we're doing is far too important. I need your help with the next operation. We'll fare better with you doing your part. No more negative thinking, OK?"

"All the way, sir!" Phil responded, hoping that what was left of the 2/503d would not be thrust into another boondoggle.

Early in the morning, on November 12, 1942, Genero traveled with LtCol. Raff, Maj. Yardley, and the remnants of E Company to Maison Blanche Airfield on the outskirts of Algiers. Raff reported to higher headquarters, situated on an American war ship anchored in the harbor.

Before leaving, Raff directed Phil to scare up as much intelligence as possible about the Germans, Italians, and Vichy French in northeastern Algeria and northwestern Tunisia. Raff wanted the whole picture, as accurately as possible.

Maison Blanche was a busy airport, with allied aircraft of all kinds staging operations. Genero located the air ops folks to see if they understood what the allies were facing, as they sorted themselves out for an aggressive move to the east.

Phil found the operations center and entered the tent. He encountered an Air Corps major and two lieutenants. They tried to help him understand the tactical and strategic situation. They explained that the port city of Bizerte and Tunis, the capital, were the critical targets for the next phase of the operation. Both of these cities were situated along the Mediterranean coast.

Based on the Air Corps ops briefing, Phil assumed that the next mission for the 2/503d would be a jump to seize a vital target in advance of the allied northern thrust. That would be the classic implementation of vertical envelopment.

After a few hours with the operations staff, Genero visited with the Air Corps S-2. He wanted more information about the threat along the Mediterranean coast, between Bone—which Boy Browning's 1st Airborne had just seized in a fabulous coup de main—and Bizerte.

While gabbing with the Air Corps spooks, Genero learned a number of important things. First, General Montgomery's 8th Army had been pushing Rommel and the DAK west through Libya. If Rommel behaved as predicted, which he had a nasty habit of not doing, it was a good bet that he would set up a defense in depth in southeastern Tunisia, near the town of Mareth. Reconnaissance flights had detected

German engineer units working on defensive positions in the Mareth area.

The Air Corps S-2 had bad news for Phil regarding northern Tunisia. The Germans had been airlifting huge numbers of troops into an airhead around Tunis and Bizerte. The Germans had flown many of these reinforcements in by glider. Intelligence detected substantial numbers of *Fallschirmjager*. The German paratroops could be relied upon to fight to the last. If they came over from Sicily in strength, they could stall the Anglo-American offensive drive toward Tunis.

The Germans had also transshipped several battalions of armored forces into Tunis. The Air Corps identified specific units, all of which were equipped with the Panzer IVs. No tank in the Anglo-American arsenal in North Africa was its equal.

Even worse, the Germans had fielded a new giant tank that no one had seen. Initial reports revealed that the Germans referred to these tanks as *Tigers*. German troops arriving in the northern Tunisian airhead also included several battalions of artillery, which employed the German 88mm cannon. The Nazis had originally designed the 88 as an anti-aircraft weapon.

The British 8th Army in the east had learned the hard way how effective the 88 could be against armored forces. The 88 gunners could engage the allied tankers before the tankers got into range to use their main gun against the German artillery. The Nazi artillerymen had created a lot of death benefits for Commonwealth widows.

Armed with this important information, Genero returned to the large hanger that Maj. Yardley secured for E Company and the staffers from the 2/503d. He wanted to get working on his intelligence assessment for the colonel. The situation did not look good.

By the time he got back to the unit, Raff was already there. The C.O. stood inside the giant hanger door, surrounded by a gaggle of officers from the battalion, who'd flown in from Tafaraoui. The colonel was jubilant despite the fact that he was still hurting from his injury. He sported a huge smile.

As soon as Raff spotted Genero, he called him over. "Genero, I've got our next target. It's an airfield near Tebessa, which I'm told is a small town to the east."

When Genero heard the name, he pulled out his map, and looked for the town. He found it located 25 miles west of the frontier with Tunisia.

Tebessa had a significant rail operation. It was the largest population center in the entire region. During his debrief by the Air Corps, Phil had taken notes. As was his habit, he'd annotated his map with comments about garrisons, roads, trains, resources, water sources, and population centers. He'd focused so much on the north, where he predicted that they would go, that he almost failed to gather data about Tebessa.

When he examined the map, Phil noticed that the Air Corps S-2 had identified a much larger airfield ten miles north of Tebessa, adjacent to the village of Youks Les Bains.

As a strategic target, Youks Les Bains seemed more attractive than Tebessa. It had the infrastructure to support forward based allied fighter aircraft like P-38s and Spitfires.

*Obviously, the J-3 planners at II Corps don't realize that they're sending the battalion to the wrong aerodrome. These goddamned oversights get paratroopers killed!* Phil recalled.

Phil knew better than to say anything negative. When the colonel finished briefing him, Genero folded his map so the east central portion of Algeria was isolated and obvious to the reader. He told the colonel that he had an observation about the selection of the target for the battalion's airborne assault. He used the map as an illustration.

"Sir," Genero began, "The Air Corps has discovered a more important airfield ten miles north of Tebessa. It's near the village of Youks Les Bains. If we seize it, the flyboys could begin operations from it immediately. I don't think the smaller facility at Tebessa is as useful for allied purposes. Perhaps the planners at Corps meant Youks Les Bains when they gave you our mission. Perhaps they were not aware of the Air Corps recon efforts. This intelligence is only a few hours old."

"You think we should jump on this Youks Les Bains place, right?" Raff asked.

"No question, sir," Genero responded. "The only catch is that there's a Vichy French Zouave unit at Youks Les Bains. They're at battalion strength or more. Figure three hundred fifty to four hundred fifty men."

Genero watched as the colonel digested this information. He could almost hear the wheels turning. There might be a fight at Youks Les Bains, but the 2/503d had a score to settle. If the Vichy French resisted, Raff's boys would take the airfield from them.

Raff looked over at his S-3 and gave him immediate instructions. "Contact your counterparts at Corps," Raff directed. "Advise them that Youks Les Bains is a better target. Get the orders changed, if possible. Tell them that after we secure the larger airfield, I'll send a company on foot to liberate the aerodrome at Tebessa."

In advance of the airborne assault, Genero worked around the clock gathering information about the military facilities at Youks Les Bains. Ultimately, II Corps agreed with Captain Genero's assessment of the military value of the Youks Les Bains. They informed Raff to switch the target.

Phil had been right about another thing. For the assault on this new target airfield, the battalion could muster only 300 men.

One week after their first combat jump, on the morning of November 15, the 2/503d chuted up and enplaned in C-47s. After takeoff, they began a circuitous flight from Maison Blanche toward Youks Les Bains. This time II Corps assigned a strong fighter escort to defend against attacks by German, Italian—and Vichy French fighters. On this jump, the S-3 manifested Genero on the same aircraft as Raff. As soon as

Phil found his seat, he fell fast asleep. He didn't wake up until Sergeant Long shook him, 30 minutes before action stations.

The S-3 hadn't selected Genero to be the jumpmaster on this flight. Phil volunteered to lend a hand. He'd assist Raff by making one last minute in-flight inspection of each paratrooper's equipment.

On this jump, Raff designated Genero to be the last man out, and 'push' the stick. The last man was in the aircraft longer. The longer he spent in the aircraft, the longer he'd be vulnerable to the ground fire that the paratroopers expected on every combat jump.

The danger motivated the last man to push the men in front of him to get out of the plane as fast as possible. With practice, 15 fully loaded paratroopers could get out of the one door on the C-47 in five seconds. It took a dedicated man at the end of the stick.

As the planes got closer to the target area, the pilots illuminated the red lights on the door panels, signaling that the paratroopers should get ready. The loadmaster opened the jump door, and prepared the bundles of equipment for release.

The interior of the plane got colder. Genero's assessment of the temperature over the DZ had been correct. Tonight, the guys would thank him when they wrapped themselves in the blankets that he had them carry on this jump.

Before Raff began to issue the standard jump commands, the loadmaster shouted a message to the colonel. "Sir, the fighters have buzzed the DZ. They saw some French soldiers near the airfield, but they didn't act hostile. The aircraft received no ground fire."

Genero had finished his in-flight inspection and stood next to the colonel. He'd heard the news from the loadmaster. "Sir," Phil began. "We should be cautious about this news. The French might be playing possum and hold their fire until the sky is filled with our battalion."

Raff nodded in silent agreement. A moment later the colonel ordered all of the paratroopers in his aircraft to stand up. Loaded down with his equipment Genero waddled forward in the aircraft and found his place at the end of the stick, where he faced aft. Once situated, Phil hooked his static line to the cable that ran the length of the C-47.

After the final equipment check, Phil signaled, "Fifteen OK, "simultaneously smacking rump of trooper number 14. Receiving the correct response from each paratrooper, Raff gauged that they were seconds from the green light.

Raff gave the order to stand in the door. Despite the pain from his injury, the colonel took the door position. A second later the entire stick automatically closed up on him, to lessen the distance and shorten the overall time for the exit.

On this jump, Genero never did hear the jump bell ring or notice the green jump light. It didn't matter. As the colonel jumped, the stick lurched forward as one man. Phil didn't have to push hard. The men were anxious and pumped.

Phil shuffled toward the door, careful to maintain his balance in a plane that pitched and yawed from port to starboard. Three seconds into the exit, half the men in the stick were out. Only a handful remained between Genero and the door.

A heartbeat later, Phil saw the fourteenth jumper framed in the door for half a second. Beyond the soldier, Genero got a brief glimpse of a difficult and mountainous countryside.

Genero sprang out far enough that the prop blast caught him squarely, shooting him aft at 90 knots for a lateral distance of 60 feet. In three seconds Phil's chute opened hard.

This time, the opening shock did not blow any of the panels in the canopy. The force of the prop blast spun his chute around like a top as it deployed from the bag. His risers—the four webbed supports that connected his harness to the shroud lines from the canopy—were twisted from the skirt to the top of Phil's helmet.

Genero and all of his attached equipment spun in a circle like a puppet on a fouled string until all the twists could work themselves out. He grasped two risers in each hand and pulled them apart, increasing the speed of spin and clearing the lines faster. By the time Phil straightened out his chute, the DZ was coming up fast. He concentrated on his landing.

Despite the equipment he carried, Genero made a passable roll without injuring himself. On the ground, he made a quick sign of the cross, grateful for another successful jump.

The jump had scattered the battalion across the drop zone. While they were still shrugging off their chutes, Corporal McLaney called over to Capt. Genero and pointed to a nearby ridgeline where several men observed the airborne operation.

Phil took out his field glasses and studied the men. All were French soldiers. Four of the men on the hill wore the unique steel helmets utilized by French in North Africa. Two of them wore the white kepi, the distinctive symbol of the French Foreign Legion. One of the men wore a darker kepi. He might be an officer.

Captain Genero looked around the drop zone until he located Raff. Grabbing his equipment, he moved out to join the colonel. He heard Raff order the E Company's executive officer to march the unit to Tebessa, since the company commander had broken his leg in the jump. The rest of the battalion formed a perimeter and dug in to await the pleasure of the local Vichy commander.

Once Raff felt satisfied with the immediate circumstances, he turned toward Genero.

"Sir, do you see the French soldiers on the ridgeline?" Genero asked.

"Where?" Raff responded, as he followed in the direction of Phil's finger, as it pointed toward to the observers.

"There, sir! I make seven Frenchmen. Looks like both Zouaves and Legionnaires from their headgear. See the two with the kepis? I had no G-2 that the legion might be here," Genero explained.

"Any of them look German or Italian?" The colonel asked, wanting to know if committed enemy combatants were on the hill.

"No, sir," Genero answered. "The DAK is too far to the east at the moment. They're still in contact with British 8th

Army in Libya. The new group of Nazis that's air landing around Tunis and Bizerte is moving cautiously south and west. We're too far southwest for them to have reached this point. We beat the Jerries here."

"Hmmm," Colonel Raff thought out loud. "Maybe, but didn't you tell me that the Nazi forces around Tunis included *Fallschirmjaeger*? There's nothing to stop them from jumping in here, just like we did. Right, Genero?"

"Yes, sir! That's correct. I guess we'd better be prepared to defend against a German airborne assault," Genero agreed.

"First things first. I'll make sure we're hunkered down here. Take Sergeant Le Blanc with you and parlay with those men on the ridge," Raff directed. "I want to know if we are welcome here."

Phil acknowledged the order and moved out looking for a place to stow his equipment. He located Sgt. La Blanc in the perimeter. He was hobbling around on a twisted ankle.

Sgt. Le Blanc acted as a squad leader in D Company. The American son of French immigrants originally from Bordeaux, Le Blanc's dad had worked in the wine business. In the early 20s, an upstart vintner lured him to Northern California. Le Blanc grew up in the little town of Santa Rosa, California.

At his mother's request, he'd gone to two years of high school in France. He spoke French as well, perhaps a bit better, than Phil.

Genero, Le Blanc, and two corporals set out to approach the French contingent on the ridgeline, a quarter of a mile from the newly established American perimeter. Once the Frenchmen realized the Americans were moving toward them, they set out in the direction of the American lines.

Phil carried a .45 Colt automatic on his right hip in a standard issue, flapped holster attached to his webbed pistol belt. He also brought his M-1 Garand, which he slung over his left shoulder.

Genero had settled on the M-1 because it was a reliable, highly accurate, easily maintainable weapons system. Based on his dad's tutoring and his own dedication, Genero had become one of the best marksmen in the battalion and the finest of all the officers.

As with the non-coms, both of his weapons were loaded. However, the safety on the M-1 was engaged and the hammer of the .45 was on half-cock notch.

Phil wanted to be prepared if the meeting with the French got ugly. As the French contingent approached, he noted that it had blossomed into 12 men. He wondered where the other five had been. Perhaps they'd been waiting just beyond the ridge.

The Vichy force included three officers, three non-coms, and six privates. When they drew to within 150 yards, the officer in charge gave an order.

The enlisted men slung their rifles over their shoulders, mimicking the Americans and reducing the level of confrontation. This first meeting would start out friendly. Two minutes later, the two groups drew together. Though wary, both committed to a non-violent contact.

"Good day, Colonel," said Genero in his best French, while giving a sharp salute. "I am Captain Phillip Genero, American Parachute Infantry, at your service." Noting the insignias and badges on the senior officer's uniform, Phil had recognized that the Frenchman was a full colonel in the Zouaves.

"Good day to you, Capitan Genero. I am Colonel Berges. I command all of the French Army forces in this sector. Allow me to introduce Capitan Anton of the *Légion Étrangère*. He and his men are temporarily attached to my command."

Col. Berges was an older, experienced officer. Though he seemed friendly, Genero could see that he was all business. As Phil sized up the colonel, the French officer did the exact same thing to him.

Capitan Anton, the Legionnaire, looked like a 17$^{th}$ century pirate. He was as tall as Genero, but noticeably thinner. The French captain's bearing was impressive, as were the three rows of ribbons on the left breast of his impeccably tailored battle tunic. Phil did not recognize all of the decorations, but did note that one was the *Croix de Guerre*. The French captain must be a brave man.

Anton had a black eye patch over his left eye and a deep, jagged scar that ran in a cruel arch from his mouth to his ear on the left side of his face. When the captain smiled, the scar extended the grin in a most disconcerting manner. In addition to brave, the foreign legion officer must be one tough customer.

Adding more drama to his appearance, Anton's one good eye was a startling light shade of blue. Phil had never seen that shade. It must be a unique genetic trait.

Anton's kept his one blue eye riveted on the Americans. Anton evaluated and assessed their capability. Genero added smart, experienced, and observant to his assessment of Anton.

"Capitan Genero, I would be honored if you would convey my respects to your commander. Please ask him if he would permit a counsel. There are many things that I would like to discuss with him," Col. Berges explained.

"But of course, Colonel. I will do so immediately. If you, Capitan Anton and one sergeant would accompany me back to the perimeter, I will arrange an audience with our commander, Lieutenant Colonel Edson Raff. If you please, would you have the rest of your men wait here with Sergeant Le Blanc?"

The French colonel gave the appropriate commands, and nine of his men stood easy. Genero left them with Sgt. Le Blanc and one corporal.

Fifteen minutes later, near his command post inside the American perimeter, LtCol. Raff conducted a counsel with his French counterpart. Present were Capt. Anton and Sergeant Major Villiers of the Third Zouaves. In addition to

Raff, the battalion XO, Maj. Yardley, and Capt. Genero represented the 2/503d.

Using Genero as an interpreter, the French colonel welcomed the Americans to east central Algeria. He told Raff that his own sources had informed him that American paratroopers were coming. He expected the Americans yesterday. When he heard the interpretation, Raff shot Genero a look that could kill. Phil guessed that the old man was pissed about an obvious—and potentially disastrous—lapse in operational security.

*Fortunately, that will be the S-3's hot potato,* Genero thought.

Before Raff could ask Col. Berges where the leak in American security was located, the French commander dropped another bombshell. Col. Berges had learned that German airborne troops planned to come to Youks Les Bains in force.

"Ask Colonel Berges when he expects the German Airborne?" Raff directed.

"Please inform your commander that they could arrive at any time. At first, we thought you were the Boche, until we recognized the markings on your aircraft," Berges responded to Genero in French.

Phil observed a genuine smile of anticipation on Raff's face. The American colonel had spoiled for a real fight.

"Tell Colonel Berges that we must make immediate arrangement for the mutual defense of our positions from German attack. We may have very little time," Raff warned through his interpreter.

Col. Berges seemed nonplused. In the most affable manner possible, the French commander explained that all necessary steps had already been taken. "Capitan Genero, please tell your commander that the only possible spot in these hills for an airborne assault is this very airfield. If the Boche come, they will be committing suicide. Any assault on this position will result in the utter destruction of their forces."

"Genero, are you translating the colonel's words accurately?" Raff asked, somewhat irritated when Phil finished interpreting the French officer's confident statement.

The French colonel's assertions did not make sense to Raff. After all, the Americans had jumped into the DZ without incident.

"Actually, Colonel Raff, I speak English. Perhaps you would be more—how you say—comfortable, if we continued in your own language?" Col. Berges offered, causing Raff to do a double take.

Raff gave Phil another killer look. This one directed at an S-2 officer who embarrassed his commander. Genero should have ascertained that Berges spoke English before he brought him back to the command post.

"If you wish, sir, we'll speak English," Raff responded in a clipped voice.

"Colonel Berges, it's my duty to protect this air head from attack by Axis forces..." Raff began before Berges interrupted.

"Colonel Raff, I've been anticipating a German airborne assault for a week, ever since the Hun started bringing in reinforcements into Tunis. I've taken all necessary precautions," The French commander explained.

Raff looked at the Frenchman in utter disbelief. If the Americans could gain this ground so easily, how did the Frenchman think he would stop a German assault?

Col. Berges saw the look of disbelief on Raff's face. He understood exactly what it meant. *These foolish Amis*, the colonel thought, *they are arrogant and naive. Did they think we are so inept that we could be pushed over by a feather? These Americans might be brave, but that's not enough. They have a lot to learn before they will be able to defeat the Germans.*

"Colonel," the French commander began, "if you would be so kind as to humor me, I have a few things to tell you. Let's begin by taking a look around."

At that moment, the commander of the Zouaves gestured at the nearby hills with his walking stick, holding it in both hands over his head and pumping it up and down three times. On a hillside, several hundred feet above the DZ—500 yards distant—the Americans saw movement, quite a lot of movement. Hundreds of French soldiers stood up from their camouflaged positions, and waved at their commander.

"Colonel Raff, as you can see, half of my regiment—nearly one battalion—is deployed above you on that hill to the south. They have heavy machine guns and light mortars trained on this spot," The Frenchman explained smugly.

Pointing to the west, on a smaller hill, one that was less than 350 yards from the command post, Colonel Berges asked Raff to follow the tip of his walking stick as he pointed at an area that appeared to be scrub trees, thorn bushes, and cactus. The Frenchman repeated his earlier signal and again the Americans saw scores of men exposing their position to the startled Americans.

"Monsieur, that strong point to the west is a full battery of 75 millimeter artillery, which has zeroed into this position. We have four operational cannon and several heavy mortars," Col. Berges added with a sly smile.

As the French Colonel pointed to the other cardinal points of the compass, he explained how he'd deployed his forces in those zones, creating a trap for airborne forces of incomparable lethality.

For once in his life Raff was speechless. Although the French colonel had the good taste not to point it out, the American commander concluded that had the Vichy forces resisted, they would have slaughtered his 300 paratroopers in the air and on the drop zone.

Phil watched the whole scenario unfold in slow motion. It felt like a horrible dream. Genero had personally convinced his commander to deploy the battalion here at Youks Les Bains. If the French had fought them, his recommendation would have been the catalyst for the destruction of the 2/503d.

When Raff said nothing, but simply turned 360 degrees, and looked again at the Vichy force that ringed his position, the Frenchman decided that he'd better say something. He'd made his point. Now he wanted to make another.

"Lieutenant Colonel Raff," Borges began, "you and your paratroopers are welcome in my command as allies. If you would be so kind, I hoped that you and your officers would accompany my staff to my headquarters in the village. There is a brief ceremony that I would like to conduct to celebrate our new friendship."

Raff accepted the French commander's offer. The Zouaves brought up an armored car. The American officers got in for the short ride to the village. On the way, Genero tried to talk to Raff, but the colonel remained quiet and introspective. He waved Genero off, indicating that he wanted to sort the whole thing out first.

When the Americans and the French officers reassembled in the village of Youks Les Bains, the atmosphere became very cordial. Col. Berges broke out several bottles of good French wine. He poured all of the American officers a generous glass.

Berges toasted the new American-Free French alliance. He thanked the Americans for their efforts in driving the Nazis out of eastern Algeria. Col. Berges became emotional. He asked the Americans to use their vast resources to begin to liberate all of the French possessions in North Africa and— eventually—France, itself.

As a mark of his respect for the American airborne forces, the colonel gave Raff his crest of the Zouave regiment. In return, Raff presented the French colonel with an American flag.

During the impromptu reception, Phil had an opportunity to chat with Capt. Anton, and was intrigued by the interesting Frenchman. As the two officers discussed military matters, they made a connection. They had begun to form a friendship.

Capt. Anton was 30 years old. Though his parents were French, he'd been born in Saigon and raised on a rubber plantation in southern Annam in Indochina.

Anton's natural father had been a career soldier in the French Army stationed in Indochina. Upon retirement, Sergeant Major Anton took a position as a manager in a Michelin Rubber warehouse in the Cholon section of Saigon. Between his pension from the Army and the wages that he received from Michelin, Anton's father supported his family and a beautiful mistress.

Anton's father died of malaria in 1923. Shortly after the death of her husband, Anton's mother married the wealthy owner of a vast rubber plantation in the central highlands, 40 kilometers west of the Annamese village of An Khe.

The planter's home was a palace. Servants and retainers abounded. For young Louis Anton it was a big, unfamiliar, and scary place.

After she remarried, Anton's mother never raised a finger to do a domestic chore. She focused her energy on pleasing her rich husband. She had a lot of competition. Henri de la Cort maintained at least one young mistress among the Vietnamese girls who lived in the hamlets that ringed the plantation.

Over time Anton made friends with the Annamese children from the local villages whose parents worked at various tasks around the property. After two years, Louis could speak Vietnamese like a native.

When he turned 13, Monsieur de la Cort sent Louis to a French boarding school in far off Hanoi, the seat of the French government in the Indochinese colonies. Four years later, Anton matriculated near the top of his class of 120 students.

Louis' performance in secondary school qualified him for admission to a proper university in Metropolitan France. Monsieur de la Cort pulled a few strings, securing for Louis admission at the prestigious Sorbonne.

After an early graduation from college, Anton entered the competition for an appointment to *L'Ecole Speciale Militaire de Saint-Cyr.* With his own excellent qualifications and the substantial assistance of his stepfather's money, Louis secured a commission in the French Army and an appoint-ment to the corps of cadets.

Louis Anton positively sparkled at St. Cyr. In 1934 he graduated third in his class. Louis could have secured a posting to any number of politically advantageous units in the French Army. Instead, he chose the Légion Étrangère—the French Foreign Legion.

He hoped that someday he could get posted to Indochi-na. The Legion seemed like the best bet to facilitate his plan.

Genero and Anton were sipping their third glass of wine as the French officer summarized his career. Over the last eight years, Anton served four of them at various duty stations in Morocco, Algeria, and Tunisia. In 1938, the Legion posted him to French Guiana, where he helped the colonial government suppress a small rebellion by a primitive jungle tribe.

In the spring of 1940, Anton fought bravely against the German invasion of France. He'd been wounded twice in small, frustrating engagements. Anton's personal nadir occurred in the last week of fighting. He lost his eye when a German tank shell blew up the machine gun position that he'd been manning.

The force of the explosion shredded his body and knocked him unconscious. Louis expected to die in that battle. Instead, he woke up in an intensive care unit of a German field hospital. The Germans had wiped out his entire platoon in that engagement. He was the only Legionnaire left alive to tell the tale.

After the capitulation in 1940, which Anton viewed as an act of abject cowardice by a feeble, corrupt, and ineffective government, Vichy posted him to Algeria. He obeyed these orders only because he'd developed a strong sense of duty. Over time, he regretted his decision. He should have joined Charles de Gaulle in Britain.

Two days before the American invasion of North Africa, the Legion sent him from Algiers with two platoons of infantry to reinforce Col. Berges. By the time of the American assault, his men had been dug in on the west side of the drop zone for 24 hours.

"I pledge my sacred honor that I will devote the rest of my life to the liberation of France. Hopefully, that will be the first step in expelling the Japanese from Indochina, my true homeland," Anton pledged to Phil.

Genero gave Anton the abridged version of his own, far shorter and far less illustrious career. The Frenchman smiled at Phil's humility.

"*Mon ami*, this war has been going on for many years, but it is far from over. You will have many opportunities to do your duty. Be patient, my young and enthusiastic American friend," Capt. Anton advised.

Anton offered his hand to Genero in a gesture of friendship. Phil grasped it warmly, not fully realizing the significance of his gesture or the consequences he would face because of it.

# Chapter 30

1640 Hours
November 23, 1942
Rear Guard Command Post,
Tunisian Task Force
8,000 Yards South of Feriana Village
French Protectorate of Tunisia

As the light began to fade in the overcast sky, the din of the battle slowed—muting the shock of the last several hours. A tenuous calm settled over the field, interrupted by the distant cries of wounded soldiers, the sporadic explosions of incoming artillery shells, and the staccato report of small arms fire.

From his command post, Captain Genero surveyed the battlefield and the shattered remnants of several once-proud military units. As far as he could see along the Feriana road, there was carnage.

To his north, smashed and demolished trucks, armored cars, halftracks, tanks, and Jeeps burned steadily despite the intermittent rain. The wreckage and devastation of the battlefield overloaded his senses. Rifles, machine guns, bayonets, helmets, soft caps, pieces of uniforms, canteens, webbing, maps, twisted pieces of metal, shards of glass, and odd shapes of lifeless—formerly-human—tissue littered the field on both sides of the road.

The smell of smoke, cordite, oil, gasoline, human waste, and burning flesh permeated the air. The sickly-sour stench overwhelmed him. As the adrenalin drained from his body, he felt exhausted.

Genero suddenly realized that he was thirsty. Despite the cold wet clime, his throat was parched.

With his bandaged left hand, Genero groped around his back for the canteen attached to his pistol belt. His hand throbbed with pain. Phil hadn't looked at the dressing since the night before when the medic treated his wound. He didn't want to examine it again, since it was likely that he'd lose some fingers.

Genero forced himself to ignore the pain. After two awkward attempts, he found the canteen's canvas cover and unsnapped it. He removed the metal water bottle, unscrewed the cap with his good hand, and held the canteen to his parched lips. He took his first mouthful of water of the day. A moment later, he took another long pull. Gulping and swallowing the treated water slowly, Phil looked to the northwest and wondered how Anton and his Legionnaires had fared on Hill 2875.

The Legionnaires had taken a defensive position on the eastern slopes of the tall and imposing hill situated 1,000 yards to Phil's northwest. Its heights created the western boundary of this bloody battlefield.

For the last two hours, all attempts to raise Anton's force on the radio had failed. Genero decided that before dark he would send a squad of paratroopers across the valley and up the hill to try to establish contact with the French survivors.

First things first. Phil needed more information about the allied casualties on this side of the valley before he could make reasoned decisions about how to deploy what was left of the rear guard.

Genero called for the medics. Within minutes, six of them arrived at his temporary CP.

"I want each of you to find a couple of unwounded soldiers to accompany you out into the battlefield," Capt. Genero began. "Disperse and don't bunch up. You'll cover more ground that way. Check our men first, but go beyond our defensive perimeter to examine the German and Italian casualties. Give them whatever treatment you can, then cart them back to the aid station."

"Sir, are you sure that you want us to check the Jerries and the I-ties?" A senior Army medic asked.

"That's right, Sergeant. Those dark specs out there represent what may be a human life. I don't care what uniform the wounded man is wearing. I don't want any living veteran of this battle to suffer through a long, cold night as he slowly bleeds to death on this godforsaken Tunisian plain. But use extreme caution—be ready for any trick."

Satisfied that he'd done all he could for the dying soldiers, he sent his runner for Master Sergeant Thomason, his senior enlisted soldier. The runner responded, "Sir, Sergeant Thomason is dead. He got it from that panzer crew that almost breached our last line of defense. A round from the main gun took him out along with two artillerymen."

"Damn it," Genero swore, slumping his shoulders. "Danny, find Sergeant Hatch instead. Tell him to report to me immediately."

When Hatch reported, Genero saw that the sergeant was seriously wounded. His left arm hung limp by his side.

"Jack, how's that arm? Shouldn't you get that taken care of at the aid station?" Phil asked.

"It's not that bad, sir. Took two rounds. It was small arms. I can still do my duty. You wanted me, sir?"

"Yeah, Sarge. Thomason is dead. You're our top soldier now. I need you to give me an estimate of our casualties. I want to know who's present for duty. Can you do that for me?"

"No sweat, Captain. I'll get right on it. By the way, sir?"

"Yes, Sergeant. What is it?" Phil asked.

"Permission to speak freely, Captain?"

"Go ahead, Jack."

"You did real good here, Captain. A couple times, I thought we were goners for sure. You did fine, sir! I'm real proud of you, son," the much older man said, his voice cracking slightly, as he offered his good hand to his C.O.

"Thanks, Sergeant Hatch. Coming from you that means a lot," Phil responded as he firmly shook his sergeant's hand. "Now get me those estimates. Then tell the medics to look at that arm. By the way, that's an order, Sergeant."

"Yes, sir. I'll go to the aid station right after I get you the dope on our guys."

Standing at the CP at twilight, it was impossible for Phil to know if the Germans had withdrawn the remnants of their force past Feriana through the Kasserine Pass into the foothills east of the Dorsals. If they hadn't gone back across the mountains, the enemy might regroup north of Thelepte for a counterattack on his position. That could make for a long, dangerous night.

In the last 20 hours, Capt. Genero had vindicated all of the training and preparation of the last few years. He'd done an extraordinary job for an officer new to combat, commanding troops in their first major engagement. It had been an incredibly violent battle.

For Genero and Louis Anton, the combat had begun late the night before, as they scouted the extreme southern element of the German-Italian motorized infantry group that had inserted itself between the Raff Force in east central Tunisia and the American supply base at Tebessa, Algeria. From their hidden vantage, Genero, Anton, and S/Sgt. Taylor surreptitiously observed a small unit of Italian mechanized infantry.

"Louis, I make it five soldiers and one sergeant," Phil estimated.

"No, mon ami, I can see eight men," Anton corrected.

"Louis," Genero whispered. "Look at the way the Italians have set up their position. They're oriented to face an attack from the west and northwest."

"Yes, I agree. Phillipe, these Italians do not expect to find us so far to the south. It is so obvious, no?" Anton responded muting his voice. "That is why there is only one squad here."

"We've got to know what the Germans and Italians are up to," Phil said, stating the obvious as Anton and S/Sgt Taylor simply nodded.

"Phillipe, there is but one thing to do. We must take prisoners and question them. We can learn everything we need to know about their mission, strength, and dispositions to the north," Anton advised. "I've done this sort of work. I had to infiltrate the Boche lines in France. Phillipe, let me take Staff Sergeant Taylor and we will bring back prisoners for you."

As the commander, Phil knew that he should delegate, but he was reluctant to order S/Sgt Taylor to do something that he wouldn't do himself.

"Louis, you're right," Genero conceded. "We need to capture some of those Italians. The problem is that we have to neutralize the whole squad. I don't want to get one or two prisoners and leave any of their buddies up there to sound an alarm to the main force in the north. That would compromise the only advantage that we have and could be the worst thing we could do."

"Well, mon ami, we take two prisoners and kill the rest," Anton responded coldly.

"Hmmm, we might have to do that, but there are three of us and eight of them. We don't have time to get additional men up here. If we have to kill five or six Italians that means we'd probably have to shoot some. I don't know how far north the next listening post is located. We could wind up creating such a commotion that we compromise our own position. No, Louis, the trick is that we've got to capture that whole squad and do it very quietly. No shooting unless there is absolutely no other choice."

"That does not sound possible, Phillipe. But Taylor and I can try."

"Louis, you and I will take the prisoners. Taylor, you will remain here," Genero directed.

Anton smiled at Genero's decision to personally join the assault on the Italians. Though irresponsible, from a certain perspective it was courageous. Anton liked that.

Turning to the non-com, Genero explained, "Sarge, if anything happens to Captain Anton and me, get your butt back to Lieutenant Davidson and tell him to assume command of the rear guard."

"Yes, sir," S/Sgt Taylor acknowledged. "Sir, which one is Davidson? With all the new men, I don't know him."

"He's the short, blond, younger guy. He commands the reinforced tank destroyer platoon that just joined us," Genero explained.

"Oh, Jesus! Sir, he's just a kid, I'll bet he's not even twenty," Taylor complained.

"Well, Staff Sergeant, Congress, the President, and General Marshall have reposed a special trust in his dedication and fidelity to duty when they gave him his commission. After Captain Anton, he's senior. So he'll assume command. Let's just hope that his rise in authority won't be necessary."

"Sir, I'll pray hard for your safe return," Taylor responded, as he looked skyward hoping that a divine presence had noted the conversation and would intercede.

According to the assault plan, Louis and Phil would steal forward to the Italian position that was situated on the low ridgeline, less than 100 yards north.

They could see one sentry. The rest of the Italians appeared to be sleeping next to their armored car. Since time was short, the two officers decided to go immediately.

The ridgeline ran west to east with a slight bend to the southeast. Anton would head in the direction of the slight bend, targeting a small patch of cactus on the top of the ridge at the eastern edge of the sentry's perimeter.

On the western side, 140 yards from their current vantage point and 50 yards west of the cactus patch, an erosion rivulet that looked to be six feet wide ran from the top of the ridge to the valley floor 75 feet below. Phil would aim at that point and use the rivulet as cover to get to the top of the ridge.

The two officers disposed of most of their equipment. Genero surrendered his pack, helmet, webbing, and M-1 to S/Sgt Taylor. In place of his helmet, Phil donned his black stocking cap. Genero retained his .45, but he took off the pistol belt and holster since they rattled and squeaked far too much. He ensured that he'd chambered a round and that the hammer on the automatic was at half-cock notch. He shoved the pistol into his waistband. He took another seven-round magazine from his pistol belt and stuffed it into his left pants pocket.

Reaching down to his right jump boot, Genero felt for his 11-inch, razor-sharp Randall combat knife. A final gift from his dad, the Randall was well-balanced, bone-handled, full tang, and double-edged. Phil had spent hours honing it. He knew that someday his life might depend on the knife. That someday might be tonight.

Anton also dropped his gear. Instead of a cap, Louis chose to go bareheaded. His jet-black hair would not give him away.

By the time they got situated, it was 2234 hours. They estimated that it would take Genero 40 minutes to steal across the 140 yards that separated him from his target point. Anton had 100 yards or so. The Frenchman should be in position ten minutes before Phil arrived at his.

If things went right, Anton would make the first attempt on the sentry. After he'd quietly neutralized the Italian soldier, at 2320 hours the two men would rush inward, catching the enemy soldiers napping.

If any of the Italians awoke and resisted, the weapon of choice would be the knife. Anton produced a nasty looking dagger with an eight-inch blade. From the easy way that he handled the knife, he knew how to use it.

After disarming the Italians, Genero and Anton would walk them back to Taylor. The three soldiers would hustle the prisoners back to the CP for a quick interrogation.

Genero gave the order to begin. Louis nodded and without another word, the two men started out.

Genero made better time over the terrain than he'd predicted. The light rain muted most of the noise of his trek across the valley floor. Once he began, Phil found that he could move rapidly but still keep his profile down, if he used a low crouch.

Since it was raining, the rivulet had a steady stream of water that made the rocky crevice slippery. To get to the top of the ridge, Phil had to climb up a steep grade for 25 yards. He had to be careful about sound discipline. This close to the enemy, he could make no mistake.

Crawling up the rivulet took Genero another quarter of an hour. He arrived at his position on the low ridge, directly west of the Italians, more than seven minutes ahead of schedule.

Genero had expected the Frenchman to do the dirty work on the sentry, since he'd have the first opportunity. Phil was surprised to see the sentry walking slowly in his direction, not 25 yards away. Fate had given Phil the first crack at the guard. It was the moment of truth: Genero would have to kill another human being at close quarters.

As the Italian walked in a straight line from where his comrades were sleeping, Genero made his final plan. First, he evaluated his target. While he was well under six feet tall, he looked to be very strong with a substantial upper body. Though Phil was much taller, he didn't want to wrestle with the Italian, who weighed at least 200 pounds.

Genero's assault required stealth, lightning speed, tremendous force, and no hint of mercy. If they were to take the other enemy soldiers alive without a great hue and cry, the sentry had to die quietly.

Genero reached into his waistband and secured the Colt semi-automatic. He made a final check of his clothes and equipment. Nothing could clang, rub together, drop off, or tear.

Without taking his eyes from the Italian, now only 15 yards away, Phil reached down to the outside of his right jump boot where he'd secured the Randall's leather sheath with sturdy webbed straps. Genero unsnapped the band. To his nervous ears, the sound seemed like the firing of cannon. Fortunately, the light rain muted the noise.

Genero crouched low to diminish his profile in the rivulet. With the rain, the overcast skies, lack of ambient light, and dark stocking cap the Italian sentry did not see him.

Tired, cold, wet, and bored, the sentry approached the depression in which Genero hid. All the Italian soldier could think about was staying awake for another ten minutes, when he would alert his relief and get some sleep. To keep awake, he quietly hummed the tune to the popular German song, *Lili Marlene*.

Private Giovanni Ferrero had been in North Africa for ten days. Like thousands of his fellows, the Axis command had loaded him onto a German transport and flown him to Tunis after the Americans invaded Morocco and Algeria.

A former Calabrese farmhand from the extreme south of Italy, Ferrero had participated in the invasion of Greece, and had been severely wounded on the first day.

Giovanni had convalesced in an Italian field hospital for the duration of that misbegotten conflict. In early 1942, fully restored to duty, the Italian High Command posted him to an infantry brigade at Gela, Sicily. When the Germans and Italians realized the danger of the Anglo-American invasion of western North Africa, Ferrero's unit was one of the first to be transported to Tunisia.

For the last four days, Ferrero and a motorized company of his comrades had served under the operational control of a small Nazi *untergruppen*: a task force of mixed arms, designed to perform a specific mission.

Gruppe Gerhardt had specific orders from their high command in Tunis. In compliance with them, on November 21st, the gruppe had crossed the Dorsals, moving west on a battalion-sized reconnaissance.

The Germans and Italians passed quickly through the Kasserine Pass. Once on the western slopes, to insure security, the commander left a platoon of infantry at the Thelepte airdrome and proceeded rapidly southwest, occupying Feriana and setting up on the best high ground in the area to resist the Americans and British forces advancing from the west.

Lieutenant Colonel Gerhardt felt confident. Once the green Americans learned that there were Germans on their side of the Dorsals, they would come blundering out of the north and west. He would show them what it was like to fight real soldiers.

Earlier in the day, the Italian sentry's platoon sergeant sent one armored car and eight soldiers to the southernmost extreme of their operational area in order act as a listening post for the gruppe. The fascist sergeant wanted a little insurance in the unlikely event that any Americans or Englishmen materialized out of the south.

At this stage of the war, none of the Germans or Italians had encountered Americans on the field of battle. While they had a grudging respect for the British who'd recently gotten the best of Field Marshall Rommel, none of the axis soldiers considered the Americans to be worthy opponents. At best, the Americans were rank amateurs.

Ferrero believed that the Americans were far to the west, getting organized in Algeria. He thought that the only threats to the south were the Arabs, scorpions, snakes, cold wind, and continuous rain. He hadn't counted on one motivated airborne captain.

When the Italian soldier was only five yards from his position, Genero could see his face, even though the light was very poor. The Italian looked tired and haggard.

The sentry had slung his rifle over his right shoulder, indicating to Phil that the soldier was probably right-handed. That would be useful to know in the next 60 seconds.

The Italian carried a bolt-action rifle. It looked like a Carcono. He'd fixed a bayonet to the tip of the barrel, adding another 18 inches to the length of the weapon.

Getting the slung rifle off his shoulder and into action, even if he didn't have to work the bolt, would take two seconds. Carrying the weapon slung was sloppy and inexcusable. The sentry's carelessness sealed his fate and the future of his comrades.

*If I ever get out of this, I'll make sure my men learn the lesson of the Italian sentry,* Genero thought, gripping the Randall harder in his right hand and balancing on the soggy lip of the rivulet with his left hand, readying himself to spring.

Phil intended to wait until the sentry turned east. Then, he would climb out of the rivulet, creep up behind the sentry, and stab the Italian in the throat.

During his training, Phil learned to attack a man from behind by reaching around the target with his left hand, gripping the enemy's jaw, and pulling up with as much force as possible. Simultaneously, the tactic required the attacker to plunge a knife into the victim's throat and twist hard.

The goal of the assault would be the victim's main carotid artery. Sever that and you immediately interrupted the flow of blood to the brain, ruptured the large vessel, and caused fatal hemorrhaging. The assault would destroy the windpipe and artery. The victim would bleed to death, suffocate, or drown in his own blood. The force of the assault, the viciousness of the wound, and the position of the jaw would insure a silent death. That was the theory. Now Phil would find out how it worked in the real world.

Ferrero turned around and retraced his steps. With abject resignation, he began another 50-yard walk to the east. He'd lost count of his completed circuits over the last two hours.

When the sentry started to walk away, Genero climbed silently out of the rivulet.

Despite the steady drizzle and the cold wind, as he crept closer to the sentry, Phil felt hot, clammy, and unsteady. His breath came in shallow bursts. He struggled not to hyperventilate, as the fear-driven adrenaline coursed through his body. The big Randal quivered in his unsteady right hand. Though the muddy ground made it slippery, he closed with the Italian in an interminable four seconds.

When he got within a foot of the sentry, Genero swung his great bear paw of a hand around the sentry's left shoulder, missing his chin but managing to grab a hunk of the enemy's face and nose. He felt the unshaven bristles of the Italian's two-day old beard and the heat of his breath.

On impulse, the sentry swung his left hand upward, partially blocking Phil's left arm. Terrified that he'd lose the advantage, Phil groped wildly and barely managed to take hold of the narrow brim of the sentry's helmet, secured to the enemy's chin by a leather strap. With a desperate heave and as much strength as he could muster, he pulled the soldier's head skyward, while he savagely plunged his knife into the sentry's neck. He missed the carotid artery and showered them both in the sentry's blood from a large—but less vital—blood vessel.

Terrified by the vicious attack and the painful wound in his neck, the Italian began to wail. Fearing that the other Italian soldiers would hear the desperate struggle, Genero released the helmet and shoved his left hand over the sentry's mouth to stifle the sound. He stabbed the Italian again, harder and deeper, twisting the blade and interrupting the flow of blood to the man's brain.

Only seconds from death and knowing it, the sentry sank his strong peasant teeth through the skin on Genero's left hand, severing muscle, ripping tendons, and shattering the largest bone in Phil's ring finger.

Gritting through the pain, Genero managed to hang on as the Italian bucked and shook in his death throe. As the struggling slowed, an acrid stench billowed from the dying soldier's skin, face, and hair. It reminded Phil of the sweat-soaked parachute harnesses that he and hundreds of other acutely apprehensive paratroopers had used and reused in thousands of jumps at Fort Benning to qualify for the Airborne. In an inconvenient and unexpected epiphany, Genero understood that fear caused the unpleasant odor. Surprised by the revelation, Genero shivered.

Genero lowered the sentry's body to the wet ground. As he rolled the enemy soldier onto his back, he heard a final pathetic gasp. A small stream of blood from Phil's hand ran down the sentry's chin and mingled with the river of Italian blood, soaking into the wet, sandy soil.

With nothing to wrap his hand, Genero ignored his wound. Despite the clumsy attack and all of the commotion, the other Italians remained motionless. At this point, Genero felt entitled to a little good fortune.

Phil stood over the Italian sentry as he caught his breath. When he was sure the soldier was dead, he wiped the blood from his knife on the Italian's pants leg and checked his Army-issue watch. The luminescent hands indicated that it was 2318:42.

Phil had a little over a minute to prepare for the next phase of the plan. Knife in hand, he cautiously moved toward the sleeping Italian soldiers.

At exactly 2320 hours, Anton appeared on the edge of the ridge and moved deliberately toward the sleeping Italians. Ten seconds after Anton arrived at the rendezvous, Genero appeared from the west.

Anton could see that Genero was wounded. Louis would get details later. The first priority would be capturing the remaining Italians.

Waving to Genero, Anton approached the Italian soldier closest to him. The French officer produced his personal sidearm—a vintage Broomhandle Mauser automatic pistol with a five-and-a-half-inch barrel. Anton stepped over the sleeping soldier and stood astride his prone body. Crouching low, he inserted the long, thin barrel of his pistol into the mouth of the sleeping soldier as he snored softly. Startled by the placement of the foreign object, the Italian gagged and awoke with a start. When he looked up at Anton's cruel, scar-enhanced smile, he pissed himself.

By 0200 hours on November 23, 1942, based on the intelligence obtained from the Italians, Genero had a good idea of what the Raff Force rear guard was up against. It was not a pretty picture.

Five of the seven Italian prisoners proved to be cooperative. Two Italians resisted the interrogation techniques including the violent ones, conjured up by Sergeant Duvall, Anton's top Legionnaire. Genero watched Duvall's brutality for about five minutes before he put a stop to what amounted to torture. Phil had learned all the information that he needed to know from the cooperating soldiers.

The Italians revealed that Genero's command faced a battalion-sized task force of mixed arms, conducting a reconnaissance-in-force. The Germans had initiated the probe because they needed to determine how far south and east the Anglo-American forces had gotten into Tunisia.

According to the prisoners, the Axis troops in the Tunis/Bizerte airhead called themselves the Fifth Panzer Army. The Germans had recalled General Von Arnim from the vicious battle near Stalingrad and sent him to Tunisia to take command of the new North African force.

Four hundred kilometers to the southeast, Field Marshall Rommel still commanded remnants of the Afrika Korps in and around the town of Mareth. Between the two substantial Axis armies, the Germans controlled the entire eastern coast of Tunisia along with its improved roads, modern rail lines, and several usable airfields.

The Germans had to stop the Anglo-American force in the north before it could take Bizerte and Tunis. They needed to ensure that the Americans would not sneak around the Dorsal Mountains and attack the rear of Rommel's corps along the south to north lines from Mareth, through Gabes and El Djem to Sfax.

The German command had ordered Colonel Gerhardt to smoke out the Allied forces, so that General Arnim could deal with them directly and ruthlessly. The German colonel hoped that by taking the Feriana/Thelepte crossroads, he'd provoke the American II Corps commanders into doing something rash.

Gerhardt wanted to lure the Americans into a trap. He intended to give them a bloody nose and shake their confidence. After his victory, he intended to pull back to the eastern side of the Dorsal range.

A professional soldier, Oberstleutnant Gerhardt had been a panzer officer for 14 years. Gerhardt had no political agenda, and had no serious issues with Hitler, the Gestapo, the SS, or the Nazi party. His relatives had taken over a small chain of grocery stores from a once-rich Jewish family. Had he been able to choose, he would have happily cast his ballot for Adolf Hitler.

By November 1942, Gerhardt had served with great distinction in several campaigns. In 1939, he'd fought at the spear tip of the Nazi invasion of Poland.

In 1940, he commanded panzers in France, where he lost all of the toes on his right foot with a lucky shot from a French 75mm field gun. By the early fall of 1941, Gerhardt was back in command, this time leading a tank battalion during the invasion of Russia. His Panzer III was one of the first tanks to enter Kiev.

LtCol. Erik Gerhardt had personally seen the spires in the Kremlin from the front lines in the center of the German advance. Tantalized by those onion domes, Gerhardt and his men had given their total commitment to the fight. Despite their heavy sacrifice, the Russian capital remained out of their reach. They vented their frustration during the brutal Siberian counteroffensive.

Gerhardt and his men fought savagely in defense of their position. The high command awarded him the Knight's Cross after he ordered his men to counterattack, when by all accounts they should have retreated. The final engagement proved so vicious that for hundreds of square meters around the battle site, the snow was a deep crimson from the blood of the fallen soldiers.

Desperate Soviet infantrymen shot Gerhardt twice during the battle. It was a miracle—attributable to his fighting spirit—that he survived at all. After a seven-month convalescence, he received an assignment to command a small armored force in Sicily. After only a few weeks among the friendly, boisterous, and affable Sicilians, Gerhardt thought he would go mad.

So fundamental was his depression that he blessed the Allies' stupidity in invading North Africa. When he received orders for transport to Tunisia, Gerhardt was ecstatic.

With his brilliant record, the Wehrmacht would eventually promote him to *oberst*, or full colonel. While his family had served in the German military from before the reign of Frederick I, his forebears were line soldiers and sergeants, not officers. No Gerhardt had ever risen so high in the ranks as he had.

*I have a chance to be the first general officer in the family: I'm a junker, not a yeoman like my father and his father before him. I will not squander the opportunities that the Tommies and the Amis are providing in Tunisia. Maybe with a little luck, the blessings of the gods, and the will of the Fürher, I could be the first Gerhardt to carry a Field Marshall's Baton,* LtCol. Gerhardt thought when he received the alert for transshipment to North Africa.

Genero paced inside the narrow space of the small tent. The tent provided a dry, well-lit, and secure environment for his immediate purposes. His watch showed 0200 hours. It was November 23, 1942.

An enemy motorized task force of battalion strength, including at least one German tank company, had deployed immediately north of his command post. The southernmost element had entrenched only 1,500 yards away.

The Italian prisoners had been fuzzy about the total number of men in the enemy force, but they were certain that there were at least 600 combatants. The Italians accounted for 150 men. The rest were German.

The Germans called their task force *Gruppe Gerhardt*, after its Nazi commander. The prisoners didn't know much about Gerhardt other than he was an arrogant, Prussian son-of-a-bitch. They agreed that their German commander hadn't anticipated a strong allied force to their south. Assuming that the Anglo-American response would come from the west or north, along the improved roads, Gerhardt had disposed his troops to face an attack from Tebessa. In this configuration, he could easily fend off a probe from El Kef in the north.

The German had placed one platoon of infantry at the abandoned aerodrome at Thelepte. These German soldiers held the airfield and acted as an early warning if the allies came boiling out of the north.

His most powerful unit, a tank company, sat north and east of Feriana on the improved road's eastern side. It had a complement of 16 Panzer III tanks and various support vehicles, motorcycles, halftracks, and armored cars. The presence of so powerful a tank force worried Genero—but he was thankful the situation wasn't worse.

The Panzer III tanks in North Africa used a short-barreled 50mm main gun. While it was a very potent weapon, it was nothing like the Panzer IVs with their 75mm gun or this new super tank that S-2 called the *Tiger*.

Northwest of the crossroads, the Germans had assembled a motorized rifle company to act as the tripwire for allied forces moving east. Finally, the Germans relegated an Italian tank platoon to a position 3,000 yards south of the crossroads. The Italian tankers had four unremarkable obsolete M-14/41 tanks. These were slow, lightly armored, and underpowered.

The balance of the fascist company dug in on both sides of the Feriana road 800 yards or so south of the tank platoon. Genero's prisoners had come from the Italian infantry platoon, stationed one mile north of the Raff Force rear guard CP.

To counter the Nazi threat, Phil could muster less than half the enemy's strength. The backbone of Genero's force included two platoons of lightly armed, untested—but really pissed off—American paratroopers and two platoons of more experienced French Foreign Legionnaires. The rear guard could field 140 riflemen.

To support this force, Genero had a heavy weapons squad that Colonel Berges had loaned to Captain Anton. Phil also commanded two platoons of anti-aircraft artillery totaling six 40mm Bofors guns; a reinforced tank destroyer platoon consisting of five, totally outclassed, M3 halftracks with the improved 75mm anti-tank gun; and a platoon of British engineers and sappers. These included another 140 men. Genero's entire force, including staff and runners, numbered 290 effectives.

After discussing the tactical situation with the officers and senior non-coms, Genero arrived at some conclusions. *With the personnel and equipment that I have available, I cannot attack a superior, experienced armored force that's arrayed in a defense in depth and expect any of my men to live to tell the tale. Doctrine says that to attack, I need at least a three-to-one advantage. I have less than one-to-two. Though it would be madness to attack, I can't allow the Krauts to isolate Raff and the rest of the force in the south.*

When he first learned of the German incursion, Genero had sent a runner with a message describing the situation to LtCol. Raff in Gafsa. Raff's response directed Phil to take whatever action he thought prudent—as long as the rear guard neutralized the threat.

After reading Raff's order, Genero had thought, *I cannot attack the Germans in the north, so I have no choice but to lure them south into this valley and trap them. If I do this right and get a little air support to help with the Kraut armor, I might be able to pull it off. I'll have to disperse my forces into the hills and ridges around the valley. Dispersal is risky. It dilutes our power and could make us even more vulnerable, but I have no real option. If we're to succeed, it's especially important that I hold that high ground to the northwest. I'll send the Legionnaires there. God help us all!*

Genero then radioed a message to the Army Air Corps at Youks Les Bains. The flyboys had been there three days and were itching to catch some panzers out in the open. Genero had gotten his first lucky break. By first light, four P-38 twin-engine fighters and four A-20 light bombers would be available for close air support.

To prevail, Genero had to find a way to convince the experienced German commander to pull some or all of the 16 Panzer IIIs from their camouflage netting four miles up the road and rush south into the narrow part of the valley. *Piece of cake*, Phil thought.

Once in the ambush zone, the Krauts would have little room to maneuver. Phil's force would attack them from positions on the high ground and call in the P-38s and A-20s from Youks Les Bains. The flyboys would bomb and strafe the Jerries into the next life.

Genero had to give the enemy a good reason to be over-confident. He had to have some way of springing the trap, and then blocking a retrograde movement out of the valley.

Genero explained his plan to his senior staff. After listening intently for ten minutes, S/Sgt Taylor emitted a long whistle and looked warily at the other assembled soldiers. "Sir," Taylor began, "we're in a very tough spot. We'll do our best, but we're going to need a lot of luck and some help from the Man upstairs to pull this off."

According to Genero's plan, the rear guard—except for the M3 75mm tank destroyers—would deploy to positions around the high ground in the little valley and dig in. Genero, half of one platoon of the 2/503d, one halftrack, one gun Jeep, and one towed 40mm Bofors gun would be the bait.

Once Phil had lured the German forces—including any of the 16 Panzer IIIs—into his ambush, he would call for close air support from the pre-positioned P-38s and A-20s.

In the narrow valley, the massed fire from the American A-20 bombers should annihilate the axis tanks. If no German aircraft showed up, the P-38s could assist the allied infantry by coming down on the deck and strafing the German forces.

The 20mm cannon and four .50 caliber machine guns in the nose of each of the forked-tailed devils would devastate the Jerries. The lightly armored tops of the Panzer IIIs, the armored cars, the German halftracks, the trucks, and other light-skinned vehicles would be vulnerable to the fighters and small bombers of the American Air Corps.

If any German armor and motorized infantry survived the air attack, the British, Americans, and French would commence firing from their hidden positions on the surrounding high ground. They would destroy the German survivors with fire from a combination of heavy mortars, light mortars, the 40mm Bofors—cranked down below zero degrees elevation—machine guns, and small arms.

Genero had a special mission for four of the M-3s and two Jeeps. They would be the trap door, keeping the main German armor force in the valley after it entered the trap.

To implement the plan, Anton would place his Frenchmen high on Hill 2875 on the valley's western edge. The eastern escarpment of Hill 2875 was too steep for the German's motorized vehicles. Infantry could assault up the hill, but there was no cover. In the face of massed rifle fire and light machine guns, an assault by straight leg infantry would be suicide.

The British engineers and sappers would lay anti-tank and anti-personnel mines along pre-designated portions of the shoulders of the valley's improved road. The other platoon of the 2/503d, four of the Bofors, and all of the British engineers would take positions on two hills on the east side, north of the CP, directly across from the French forces on Hill 2875.

Four of the M-3s and two gun Jeeps would immediately proceed north until they were a few hundred yards beyond Hill 2875. Once in position, the halftracks and Jeeps would move west off the road into a deep draw. After pre-deploying into their fighting echelon, they would hunker down, camouflage their location, and remain hidden until the main body of German panzers came churning down the road from the north, passed them by, and committed to an assault into the valley.

The allied aircraft would begin strafing the Krauts. Three of the tank destroyers and one of the gun Jeeps would then emerge, turn south, and attack the German armor from behind. The American 75mm gun on the M3 tank destroyer could defeat a Panzer III with a close range, well-placed shot in the back of the hull or turret. To succeed the Germans had to believe that a small Allied reconnaissance patrol had come probing out of the northwest from Tebessa. When faced with a Nazi attack, the Americans would seem to make the fatal mistake of retreating to the south into the valley instead of back to II Corps in the northwest.

*If my plan works and the Jerries are overconfident, they'll assume that the recon patrol has screwed up. If they make that mistake, the Kraut commander will probably send some armor into the valley to destroy the patrol. At least that's how I hope this goes,* Phil thought as he directed his men.

The Americans would strip down one the halftracks and put 15 paratroopers onboard. Along with one towed 40mm Bofors and a gun Jeep, they would move west for a few miles and head toward the flat plain west of the valley. Upon arrival, they would turn right and proceed in a great circle to the west of Hill 2875, north of the valley, and opposite the Italian position. Then they would sit tight and wait for dawn.

An hour after sunrise, the faux patrol would move slowly east, directly into the Italian lines, as if they were on the anticipated reconnaissance from Tebessa and had stumbled into the southern part of the German trap. While Genero and 30 of the men acted as bait, the remainder of the first platoon paratroopers and the crew of one of the Bofors would prepare defenses at the valley's southern end.

Getting the balance of the rear guard—the Legionnaires, engineers, and paratroopers—in place would be fairly easy. Phil's challenge would be to get the small unit acting as bait in position by first light without revealing the ruse.

As Genero planned his first major action, he recalled his Army training. The instructors at Benning said that in battle luck always plays a part. *Look what happened to the Japanese at Midway. No matter how well I plan this ambush, the German and Italian tactics will force me to improvise.*

*Like Staff Sergeant Taylor said, some divine assistance wouldn't hurt either.* Genero hinted heavenward.

Oberstleutnant Gerhardt hadn't slept well. His old gunshot wound throbbed in his chest. Normally unflappable, this morning he was out of sorts.

Gerhardt had expected the Americans earlier. Their tardiness demonstrated that they were worse soldiers than he'd been led to believe. He finally received word from an Italian lieutenant on his southern flank: There might be a small patrol moving up. Gerhardt got excited—it was about time.

German intelligence suggested that an American recon team was moving southeast two miles south of the Tebessa road.

The location of the American force and the direction of their march surprised the Nazi commander. He'd expected the Americans to use the highway from Algeria. In anticipation of such stupidity, Gerhardt had ordered that every inch of the Tebessa road be zeroed in for a mile west of the crossroads.

Their location could mean that the Americans were smarter than they appeared. Or—just as likely—they could have gotten lost.

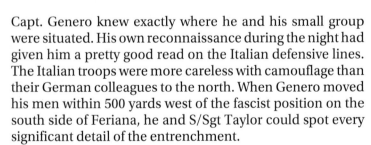

Capt. Genero knew exactly where he and his small group were situated. His own reconnaissance during the night had given him a pretty good read on the Italian defensive lines. The Italian troops were more careless with camouflage than their German colleagues to the north. When Genero moved his men within 500 yards west of the fascist position on the south side of Feriana, he and S/Sgt Taylor could spot every significant detail of the entrenchment.

At 400 yards Genero stopped the stripped down M3 halftrack in a little gully. He made a big show of lifting the engine's cover so it would appear that he'd encountered some mechanical problems. He ordered the driver to pour motor oil on the hot engine, creating a thick plume of blue-white smoke, adding to the illusion.

In anticipation of an enemy attack, S/Sgt Taylor dismounted the two teams of paratroopers so they could take up defensive positions along the low ridgeline that formed the gully, north and south of the M3. Simultaneously, Genero brought up the 40mm gun to cover the eastern approach. The halftrack, gun Jeep, and Bofors truck stood by ready for action, quietly idling.

When Gerhardt received a report about the American patrol's mechanical problems, he was hardly surprised. He'd heard that the American equipment was third-class trash. Gerhardt ordered Warrant Officer Klaus to take a squad of German infantrymen to the Italian lager, assume command from the Italian officer, and await further orders. Klaus was to inform the Italian commander that under no circumstances were the Italians to do anything until Gerhardt could get two or three Panzer IIIs into position.

Gerhardt would make quick work of these Americans. Still, he had to be careful. He assumed that these Yanks comprised the point element for a larger Allied force to the northwest. The panzer officer didn't want to give away his position or scare the other Americans away from his trap. He sent for the German tank company commander.

Further south, Captain Lanciano, the senior Italian officer in the task force, had become impatient with LtCol. Gerhardt.

"Where had the German martial genius gotten the Italian Army?" Lanciano confided to his executive officer, Lieutenant Gandolfo. "What military mastermind decided to allow the Americans, British, and the French—of all people—to squeeze us into this huge strategic vise?"

At the moment, Capt. Lanciano had an American patrol not one-quarter mile west of his third platoon. His scouts reported that an engine fire had immobilized the American halftrack. The Yanks were alone and unaware of his presence.

*I will not permit a German warrant officer to push us around and take the glory of this kill,* Lanciano thought. *I can't waste time, while the Panzers sneak south. I've got four perfectly good Italian tanks right here. They're more than enough to destroy a broken-down American tank destroyer.*

*I'm the senior officer in command of this sector. Gerhardt outranks me, but he's more than two miles away. He can't possibly have the same intimate grasp of the tactical situation. I have the discretion to modify orders as the fortunes of war and operational mandates dictate.*

"Gandolfo, get the tank platoon moving against the Americans. Do it now!" Lanciano ordered.

Lanciano's actions fit perfectly into Genero's plans.

In response to Lanciano's order, the four outmoded tanks moved out from their camouflaged positions, separated into a tactical formation, and swept to the southwest in an arc that stretched 80 yards wide. At Lanciano's direction, the Italian infantry platoon directly east of Genero attacked west with two squads abreast and one in support.

The Italian infantry charged downhill for the first 150 yards, then across open terrain for 250 more. Coming from the northeast, the Italian tanks had to negotiate open ground for about 500 yards. The muddy ground slowed the tanks down to less than ten miles per hour.

Genero's forces were just where he wanted them. The halftrack swung to the northeast. The 40mm Bofors swiveled its anti-aircraft gun to face the Italian tanks.

The paratroopers were ready. In addition to the .50 caliber in the gun Jeep, they'd brought one .30 caliber Browning light machine gun and one 60mm mortar in the halftrack.

Genero dramatically increased his firepower by arming four of the paratroopers with Thompson submachine guns. Two of the remaining riflemen had the Browning M1918 Automatic Rifle, known as the BAR. The rest of the airborne complement, including Genero and SSG Taylor, carried the M1 Garand.

The semi-automatic M1 fired much faster than the old Springfield. Its fixed magazine received an en bloc clip of eight rounds of .30-06 Springfield ammunition. A competent paratrooper could reload with a fresh clip in less than four seconds.

When the Italian infantry got to within 200 yards of the gully, Capt. Genero gave the order to commence firing, shocking the Italians. For a small unit, the Americans had produced devastating firepower.

From its defilade position in the gully, the M3 opened up on the lead Italian tank approaching from the left oblique. The first shot went wide, but the American gunner scored a direct hit with the second.

The force of the anti-tank projectile punched a hole in the Italian tank and detonated inside, killing the entire crew and exploding the unused ordnance. The sound of the explosion traveled all the way back to the German commander's CP.

Within 15 seconds, the American gunner in the tank destroyer damaged a second Italian tank by blowing off the vehicle's left track. The Italian tankers in the two remaining tanks began to fire their 37mm guns at the American position—too late, and poorly aimed. Before the Italian tankers could correct their aim, the crew of the 40mm Bofors got their range and started firing.

As bad as it was for the fascist tankers who lost half of their force in the attack's first three minutes, it was far worse for the Italian infantry. The Americans slaughtered them. Of the 42 Italian soldiers who came down the hill to support the tank attack on the seemingly stranded Americans, the paratroopers killed, severely wounded, or incapacitated 28 before the fascist non-com broke off the assault.

With the threat from the Italian infantry neutralized, Genero's force concentrated all of its firepower on the remaining fascist tanks and armored cars. Between the anti-tank gun and the Bofors, American gunners destroyed or severely damaged all four of the Italian tanks. They also put two armored cars out of the fight.

The Americans suffered few casualties. The fire from the Italian tanks slightly wounded four men, who remained able to fight.

When LtCol. Gerhardt learned of the Italian captain's defiance, he nearly had a stroke. He struggled to control his temper. He'd seen incompetence but never coupled with such rank insubordination. He ordered his headquarters staff and the reserve infantry platoon to move southwest and then set up at Captain Lanciano's command post. Too impatient to wait while they struck the camp and gathered their equipment, he immediately left for the Italian CP. The staff could catch up later.

Because of the difficult terrain and muddy roads, it took the German colonel more than 20 minutes to travel the 3,000 yards between the two HQs. Gerhardt, his driver, and an old veteran corporal—who spoke Italian—were the first of the headquarters group to arrive at the Italian mobile CP. Upon arrival they learned that the inexperienced Americans had somehow managed to destroy an entire platoon of Italian tanks and most of an infantry platoon.

Through his interpreter, the colonel asked an Italian sergeant for Lanciano's location. The sergeant, noting the vile mood of the German officer, avoided his gaze and simply pointed down the western slope of the hill.

LtCol. Gerhardt walked toward an Italian armored car that sat on the hill's western ridge. Lanciano and the earlier dispatched German warrant officer stood near the vehicle, observing the American position through field glasses.

When Lieutenant Gandolfo saw the German commander walking toward them, Gandolfo whispered something to the Italian officer. Capt. Lanciano looked past the lieutenant at the rapidly approaching German officer.

Lanciano was in deep trouble with the gruppe commandant. As Gerhardt stepped to within five yards of the vehicle,

Capt. Lanciano turned to face the German. The Italian popped to attention, saluted, and bowed slightly.

Gerhardt ignored the salute. Instead, he aggressively closed the distance to Lanciano.

Turning to his corporal, he directed, "Ask Captain Lanciano whether he received my orders to await the arrival of Stabsfeldwebel Klaus before he ordered the attack on the American tank destroyer." As the German corporal translated the question, Gerhardt stared at the Italian with open contempt.

The Italian officer listened patiently to the corporal. He pondered his answer for a long moment. "Corporal, please tell the colonel that I did receive his message, but as the senior Italian on the site I exercised my prerogatives and inherent command authorities in the best way that I could. I had no idea that the American gunners would be so effective."

The old non-com began to interpret Lanciano's excuse. Listening intently, Gerhardt turned to face the corporal, presenting his left profile to the Italian captain. Gerhardt grimaced and nodded his head several times.

When the corporal finished, LtCol. Gerhardt spun hard on his left foot and faced the Italian officer. Gerhardt extended his right hand, which now held a Walther P-38 automatic pistol and leveled the muzzle against Lanciano's forehead.

In shock, Lanciano took a step back, his eyes widening to the size of small saucers. "Sir, what is the mean..?" the Italian began before his words were interrupted by the savage report of single shot from the Walther.

An instant later the soft lead bullet from the P-38 smashed into Lanciano's skull. Lanciano's body jackknifed backward and over the side of the hill, landing with a sickening thud on the downward slope.

The other Italian officers and non-coms stood in silent shock. The summary execution of their commander was the last thing that they expected.

Gerhardt spun around, staring down all of the Italians. The pistol was still in his hand pointed safely, though menacingly, toward the ground.

"Gandolfo," Gerhardt began, directly addressing Lanciano's subordinate through the interpreter, "You are now in command of what's left of the Italian infantry. Are you prepared to obey my orders? Or would you like to follow Captain Lanciano into Guinea heaven?"

Staring in disbelief at the German commander, Gandolfo thought, *if I only had my pistol in my hand, I would happily shoot this Prussian bastard.* Instead, Gandolfo said, "Colonel Gerhardt, my men and I are under your authority until we return to the other side of the mountains. We will comply with your commands."

Satisfied that there would be no more insubordination in the Italian ranks, Gerhardt holstered the Walther and walked over to WO Klaus and asked politely to use his field glasses. Gerhardt focused the binoculars on the American position. The Americans had begun to move steadily toward the south, southeast.

"Klaus, why do you suppose the Americans are withdrawing into that valley over there? Why aren't they pulling back to the west?" Gerhardt asked.

Stabsfeldwebel Klaus was 28 years old. He was an experienced and battle-hardened soldier. By the time he found himself in the Tunisian desert, Klaus had served Germany for more than ten years. He was that rare veteran of the Spanish Civil War and wore the Spanish Cross on the right pocket of his field tunic, balanced by the badge of the Condor Legion and the Panzer Combat Badge on his left breast pocket.

In the Furher's service, Klaus had killed Spaniards, Poles, Dutchmen, Frenchmen, Englishmen, and Australians. The gruppe had no better soldier.

"Herr Oberstleutnant, the Americans cannot withdraw to the west. As you can see, sir, they'd have to move uphill over muddy terrain. We would slaughter them," Klaus explained matter-of-factly. "Their halftrack is smoking badly. You can see the bluish plumes. Perhaps a lucky shot from one of the

Italian tanks damaged the tank destroyer's engine. I've inspected a captured American halftrack. They're pathetic. That monstrosity could not get quickly over that muddy trail. The Americans probably decided to make a run for the improved road, there to the southeast. The map shows that the valley is short, only about two miles long. If they get to the far end, they can swing west again. It's muddy, but flat, all the way to Algeria."

"You're probably right, Klaus," Gerhardt conceded. "We need to make an example of them. I want that group destroyed. I want all of them killed or captured. If they won't surrender, kill all of them. Understand?"

"Of course, sir."

"Klaus, here's what I want you to do," Gerhardt began.

The warrant officer sighed. Once again, Gerhardt would micromanage the situation, as if Klaus had no idea how to run his unit.

"I don't want to lose the advantage that we have in the crossroads north of here. But I won't let those Americans kill soldiers under my command—even if they are Italians—and live to tell the tale. Organize an assault force with the German infantry platoon that I brought down, the infantry squad that accompanied you earlier, and the remainder of the Italians. That's three full platoons. I'll give you three of the Panzers and any Italian vehicles that can still run. Your orders are to overtake the Americans before they reach the southern end of the valley. Teach them a lesson! Put the Italian infantry at the front—in the event that the Americans are still interested in fighting."

"Yes, sir," Klaus responded.

In any Army in which advancement depended solely upon merit, WO Klaus would have been a major or—at least—a captain. Although he'd demonstrated courage and competence under fire countless times in several difficult campaigns, the realities of life in the German army dictated that he would never serve as a commissioned officer.

Despite the fact that he did not possess a commission, Klaus presently commanded German and Italian soldiers, including an Italian lieutenant who would normally out-rank him. Klaus intended to make short work of the small American force with the crippled tank destroyer.

The warrant officer was no fool. He could learn from other's mistakes. He would not go headlong into the valley, chasing blindly after the Americans.

Klaus had observed the last half of the skirmish between the Americans and the Italians. The amount of firepower that the Americans brought to bear against the Italian armor attack had surprised him. The Americans had an anti-tank gun, an anti-aircraft gun which could do double duty against light-skinned vehicles, a light mortar, a heavy machine gun, a light machine gun, two automatic rifles, two or three submachine guns, and new—very impressive—semi-automatic rifles.

There was something suspicious about the setup. To Klaus's experienced eye, the Americans had more firepower than one would expect from a simple patrol in reconnaissance. Were the Americans planning for a fight with a vastly superior force? Why would they do that?

Klaus would strike a balance. When the Panzers came down from their position in the north, Klaus would divide the three-platoon force into three mini taskforces, each with a tank as its main element.

The three groups would head south into the valley in an echelon. The center force would be the German platoon with one tank, and would use the improved road and try to catch up with the Americans as quickly as possible.

The right—or western—force would include one Panzer and half the Italians. Its mission would be to guard the western flank. Since the road ran 250 yards to the east of Hill 2875, there would not be much room to maneuver.

The left—or eastern—force would include one Panzer and the remainder of the Italians. The valley stretched much wider to the east. So that force would move off 300 yards to the left and 75 yards to the rear of the middle group.

Klaus thought of keeping a squad of Germans in reserve, as a precaution. However, he worried about the size and tactical value of Hill 2875.

Klaus had fought major battles since 1937. He didn't like having an unsecured hill with its imposing heights on his right flank. Klaus ordered the reserve squad *unteroffizier* to take his men up Hill 2875 to secure the high ground, coincidental with the three-echelon assault to the south.

Within ten minutes of receiving his orders, Klaus's force moved out to the south, taking Genero's bait—hook, line, and sinker. The Germans and Italians comprised an aggressive and experienced force on their way into a very deadly ambush.

Less than 15 minutes after Klaus began the southward chase, he spotted the small American force. The Americans had passed the southern end of Hill 2875, where Klaus had expected them to turn west.

Instead of turning toward Algeria, the Americans continued their slow, clumsy procession down the improved road, which curved to the southeast. The Americans were moving away from the Algerian frontier and deeper into central Tunisia. Something was wrong.

A moment later, the American force moved off the improved road. Instead of turning west, the Americans headed directly east toward a low ridgeline.

Klaus signaled all three groups on the valley floor to stop. He'd become very suspicious. He took out his field glasses and studied the Americans from a distance of 500 yards.

*Even these inexperienced Americans can't be so stupid that they would retreat in the wrong direction. No American officer could be so incompetent to allow—no, invite—his enemy to cut him off and surround his force,* Klaus thought.

As the German warrant officer watched, the American unit dismounted their vehicles and began digging into Hill 2653's ridgeline. *OK, maybe that ridiculous halftrack is on its last legs. If the Americans felt they could go no farther, that ridge could be an acceptable place to make a stand. No, that explanation is too easy. I've been in this business too long to accept an obvious ploy. Why would the Americans want me to follow them deeper into this little valley? Oh, shit!* Klaus thought, as he realized the danger. He had taken his force into an ambush.

Seconds later, Klaus heard the unmistakable popping of mortar rounds clearing their tubes. The sound sent a shiver through his body. Looking around from the turret of the lightly armored command vehicle, he could see that every one of his men had heard the mortars, too. They all recognized the sound of incoming explosive ordnance.

With a shout, the men scattered and dispersed. They maintained discipline; mortar attacks were old hat. If you kept your head and stayed low, your chances of survival were good.

The British engineers had done a meticulous job of mining the shoulders and ditches on both sides of that stretch of road, out to 25 yards on both sides. When the German soldiers left the road to find cover, they found death instead.

Klaus and his men, deafened by exploding mines, assumed that the mortars were with the Americans on Hill 2653. Before the Allied mortar rounds actually struck, the anti-personnel mines killed at least eight of the German soldiers, while maiming and wounding several of their comrades.

A second later, the first mortar round landed among the German troops and vehicles on the road. The third round scored a devastating direct hit on the top of the tank in the center group on the road.

The German tank exploded with such force that large pieces of the tank swept through the German force like scythes. During the mortar barrage, WO Klaus had stood his post in his command vehicle ten yards behind the tank.

A piece of the tank's turret the size of a baking pan smashed into the warrant officer's command vehicle, bounced off the hood, and split Klaus in two. The shrapnel severed muscle, ripped tendons, and cleaved bone. One second Klaus was issuing orders, the next the trunk of his body—less his head, left shoulder, and arm—plopped into the front seat of the command vehicle, pints of spurting blood soaking the wooden floor boards.

The driver panicked, shifted into reverse, and nearly ran over a half-dozen wounded comrades strewn on the road behind him. Once he cleared the blast zone, the driver stopped. He rested his forehead against the steering wheel. Glancing to his right, he examined the broken, bleeding body of the warrant officer. He felt a guilty sense of peace.

*I'm alive,* he realized, *at least for now.*

The Americans who had escaped to Hill 2653's ridgeline began firing their 75mm gun at the German's left flank. From prepared positions, the Americans used the Bofors, a Jeep-mounted .50 caliber machine gun, two lighter .30 caliber machine guns, and four BARs to engage the nearest elements of the Axis force.

The American fire killed or wounded the Germans or Italians who'd not found adequate cover. Unlike the center and eastern elements, the Axis force closest to Hill 2875's high ground escaped the devastation.

Crouched above the Axis position, the Legionnaires held their well-camouflaged positions and awaited their moment. They were itching to get into the fight but understood Genero's orders and did not engage.

Less than five minutes into the attack, the German reserve squad scaled the northern crest of Hill 2875. None of the Germans expected to find anything threatening on the top of the hill. They were wrong.

The Legionnaires ambushed them with vicious effectiveness, killing eight and wounding four more. The French attack lasted less than 20 seconds.

Lieutenant Gandolfo, in command of the small western element west of the road, realized that his position was untenable. He issued the rational order to withdraw. *Better Gerhardt shoot me than more of my men die*, he thought.

In anticipation of the battle, LtCol. Gerhardt had moved his CP to the same hill where Genero and Anton had captured the Italian squad the night before. His men found the Italian armored car and the body of the Italian sentry, and reported these findings to their colonel.

Before he could think the situation through, the Americans attacked Klaus's men after the Germans halted their advance 500 yards north of Hill 2653. Through binoculars, Gerhardt watched with mounting rage as the Americans destroyed two of his Panzers and ripped up his superbly trained infantry with mortars, anti-aircraft artillery, and small arms.

Even from his distant perspective, Gerhardt could see that the Americans had at least twice the firepower and manpower on Hill 2653 as they'd exposed when they first appeared out of the west.

Including the failed attack by the Italians, Gerhardt's gruppe had lost six tanks and the better part of three platoons of infantry, one of them German. In exchange, Gerhardt had achieved nothing of military value. Even worse, he had no actionable intelligence regarding the force with which he had engaged.

*How did the Americans get all that firepower, the ordnance, and crew-served weapons to that ridge on the south side of this little valley?* Lt. Gerhardt wondered. *Could the Americans and British have inserted a larger force to the south than German military intelligence had estimated? If so, that force could imperil the defense of Mareth and place the entire German plan for the defense of Southeastern Tunisia in jeopardy. I need to know what we are facing.*

*Mein Gott!* Gerhardt realized. *I've just made the same fundamental mistake as the Italian captain. I've underestimated an enemy, solely because I've never fought him.*

*I don't know the size or the disposition of the Americans to the south. I have the option to absorb these loses and withdraw back to the Kasserine Pass and then to the eastern side of the Dorsals. I could report that there are significant Americans in the central part of western Tunisia, perhaps as far as Gafsa. General von Arnim's staff could decide how to react to this news. Everyone would agree that I've done my job and performed my mission to the letter,* Gerhardt considered.

*My orders were to conduct a reconnaissance. Extended contact with the enemy, beyond what we've already done, is not within the spirit of my instructions,* the Nazi commander conceded. *On the other hand, I can legitimately continue the reconnaissance and move the men south to gather more data about the American threat to the southeast. If I'm forced to destroy that American strong point, so be it.*

*It's reasonable to assume that the Americans have tipped their hand. I have a good read on their capabilities. I'll handle them more carefully and apply much more force to resolve the problem. I'll be damned if I'll let these inexperienced Americans run me off this field,* Oberstleutnant Gerhardt decided finally.

The steep hill to the west, Hill 2875, seemed to be empty. None of the Germans had distinguished the brief firefight between the German infantry and French Foreign Legionnaires from the sounds of the rest of the battle.

Gerhardt concluded that Hill 2875 was not a threat. Otherwise, the Italian infantry and the only undamaged German tank west of the road would have taken fire. Once all the surviving Italians withdrew from the valley, he'd send all of them up Hill 2875 as additional insurance. Gerhardt had little regard for the Italians and did not plan to use them in the final assault.

Gerhardt looked up at the overcast sky. The ceiling was too low for Stukas. Maybe he could get the JU 88 bombers to come in and make a low run under the cloud cover. Gerhardt directed his executive officer to make radio contact and find out if the Luftwaffe was flying in this soup.

In the meantime, he had 14 Panzers left in his battalion. He decided that he could send 12 of them south to destroy the American position. Gerhardt also had four towed 88s. He would leave two tanks and two 88s at the crossroads. He would deploy the other two 88s so that they could fire down the valley. Both crews were experienced in providing both indirect and direct fire.

*Just before the tanks make their assault, I'll have the eight-eights fire twenty or thirty rounds of high-explosive shells at that ridgeline where the patrol has dug in. That'll soften up the goddamn American bastards,* Gerhardt vowed.

By 1000 hours, Genero's force had accomplished everything that he'd hoped it would. As he fidgeted in his foxhole on the ridgeline, he pondered only two questions: *Would the Germans bite and come down the valley? Was the cloud ceiling high enough for the American A-20s and P-38s to provide air cover? If the answer to the second question is no, I hope that the German commander has the common sense to believe that it would be wiser to fight another day.*

Should the German battalion come south in force, it could be a very long and bloody day for the Americans. The fate of their rear guard depended upon reliable air support—and it continued to rain.

The ceiling proved to be so marginal that Genero had to ask the Air Corps to stay away until the Germans deployed. There was no sense sending the aircraft in to test the ceiling and tipping their hand prematurely. Once the German armor committed, if the close air support could not materialize, Phil had left his men few viable options.

*Well,* Genero thought, *I've dealt this hand. We'll have to play it out.*

Master Sergeant Thomason, a grizzled old American non-com and the rear guard's top enlisted soldier, approached Genero. By the battle of Feriana Village, Thomason had served 29 years in the U.S. Cavalry. As a rookie, he'd chased Poncho Villa with General Pershing. Thomason had served with distinction in the infant armored forces in the Great War.

Thomason commanded the M3 that had looped around Hill 2875 with Capt. Genero. Thomason had been on the receiving end of artillery in World War I and didn't want to repeat the experience. He sought out Capt. Genero to give him a bit of advice.

"Sir," Thomason began after he plopped down next to Genero in the mud of the foxhole that passed for the CP, "after that last little unpleasantness, we pretty much identified our position and capabilities. If the Germans come down the valley in force, we will be on the receiving end of a nasty barrage."

"Sarge, I haven't seen evidence of German artillery," Genero responded.

"Captain, trust me! The Krauts got artillery. I'd bet the ranch on it. When the Jerries come down the valley, every one of the tanks will be firing their main guns at this position. It could get real hairy, real fast."

"What do you have in mind, Sarge?" Phil asked.

"Sir, let's be a little sneaky here. We can move our men and guns back about 100 yards, right up to that little streambed to the southeast. After the barrage ends, we can run like hell to our prepared positions, and we'll be here in plenty of time to take the Germans under fire. Hell, sir, we'll be back here before the Krauts get within five hundred yards, and there'll be a lot more of us when we do."

Genero thought it over for a couple of long minutes. Thomason was right. Phil ordered everyone to move back to the streambed.

The German air controllers on the eastern side of the Dorsals struggled with weather at least as bad as Gerhardt experienced locally. The rain and the fog at their aerodrome drove two decisions. The Stukas would not fly, but the controllers would try to help Gruppe Gerhardt with two sorties of JU 88 level bombers.

The trick would be to get the bombers over the Dorsal Mountains without crashing, finding the German gruppe in the overcast skies, and then getting the two-engine JU 88s low enough to strafe and skip bomb. Under these conditions, two sorties were all the precious air resources that the German air controllers were willing to risk on a reconnaissance mission.

It would have to do. Along with his planned barrage with the 88s, even one planeload of bombs on Hill 2653 might make the entire assault unnecessary.

Out to the west at the American Army Air Corps aero-drome at Youks Les Bains, the weather was significantly better. The Air Corps scrambled one flight of four P-38s and one flight of four A-20s.

Since Feriana lay only 60 air miles from Youks Les Bains, the controllers ordered the aircraft to fly south to a position along the Algerian/Tunisian border just west of Genero's valley. Once there, the two American flights took up station. They flew a series of long elliptical patterns, waiting for Phil's signal.

The American flyers had arrived on station at approximately 0945 hours. Both flights had sufficient fuel reserves to loiter for over two hours. Neither flight would have to wait that long to get into the battle.

No two soldiers ever witness a firefight in exactly the same way. The fear, rage and rush of adrenaline suspend the warrior's sense of time and severely limit his perspective, especially for the inexperienced fighter. Inside this fog of war, deceit and deception make useful tools to trick a foe into believing one circumstance exists, when quite another is real. So depending on the intensity of their individual experience and the subjective effects of the enemy's tactics, after a battle two surviving soldiers fighting next to each other may relate two starkly different episodes.

On the morning of November 23, 1942, Capt. Genero gave Oberstleutnant Gerhardt the false impression that the Germans had trapped a small unit of Americans at the southern end of a short, narrow valley. Although Gerhardt was suspicious, he had no idea that the French Foreign Legion had a strong force on Hill 2875 and that other strong elements of the Anglo-American alliance were waiting to ambush his forces on the two ridges across from Hill 2875 on the eastern side of the narrow valley.

Despite the fact that the isolated unit had an unusual number of crew-served weapons, Gerhardt thought that the Americans had dispersed in a manner that would be vulnerable to a German armor attack. The American mortars and .50 caliber machine guns would not pose a serious threat to Gerhardt's Panzers, especially if his tanks kept on the move.

By 1000 hours, with the rain continuing in a slow, cold drizzle, Gerhardt assembled his assault force. Once again, he divided his contingent into three elements.

Each section included four Pz IIIs and would be supported by a platoon of German motorized infantry. Scout cars and motorcycle troops would take the far western and far eastern flanks, just in case. The remnants of the Italians, a force a bit larger than a platoon would assault the heights on Hill 2875.

Before he launched the attack, Gerhardt would bring in the light bombers. Whether they were able to bomb or not, the German commander would follow up with his two artillery pieces. For good measure, Gerhardt decided to use 40 high-explosive rounds on the Americans.

At the end of the barrage, Gerhardt would launch the armored assault in three prongs. Each prong would use a route that was different from the earlier mission, in order to avoid the minefields.

He should have the Americans for lunch—literally and figuratively.

As planned, the German commander called in the two JU 88 light bombers. The lead pilot reported that the effective ceiling was 200 feet above the highest peak. Since there were several higher hills in the area along the Dorsals, the German pilots worried about flying too fast and too low, and crashing into a Tunisian peak. They had to be very careful and could only make three passes on Hill 2653.

They designed the first pass to get a good look at the target. On the second pass, the JU 88s came in as slow as possible. The absence of ground fire surprised them.

On the second pass, each aircraft dropped a stick of ten 100-pound bombs on the hill. Most of the German ordnance hit the hill as intended. Had Thomason not convinced Genero to pull back, the attack would have obliterated the Americans.

On the final pass the German pilots sprayed their 7.92 mm machine guns on the suspected positions. Once again, the pilots received no ground fire.

Between the second and third pass, Gerhardt had ordered his two 88 mm gun crews to begin their barrage. Each gun fired 20 rounds. All but the first two of the 40 rounds landed within 35 yards of the target.

As the JU 88s finished their third pass, Gerhardt launched the armored assault. Everything went fine for about two minutes, and then all hell broke loose.

Out of nowhere in the overcast sky, two American P-38 fighters jumped the second JU 88. As the German pilot tried to out-maneuver the Americans, his plane slipped and juked laterally to starboard, allowing the lead P-38 to unload two five-second bursts with its 20 mm cannon and four .50 caliber machine guns on the enemy plane.

The JU 88 disintegrated and fell to earth in thousands of pieces 800 yards east of the American position on Hill 2653.

Within five minutes of the launch of the assault, the three prongs of armor, led by the Panzer IIIs, had moved halfway down the valley. The lead tank in each prong repeatedly fired its main gun on the forward slope of Hill 2653.

As the Germans passed the point of no return, a number of things seemed to happen at once. The first thing Gerhardt observed was a group of three M3 tank destroyers, which mysteriously appeared on the improved road to the rear of the assaulting Panzers. Another tank destroyer and a Jeep took up a position on the road and started firing. Their attack didn't damage anything, but it did interrupt activity and did harass the German rear echelon.

The first three M3 tank destroyers turned south down the improved road and started firing at the rear of the German infantry and armor in the far western prong. None of the Germans in the assault echelons noticed the M3s until they scored direct hits on an armored car and one of the Panzers.

American two engine light bombers suddenly appeared overhead and started attacking the center and eastern prongs, with good success. In a matter of moments, the American A-20 bombers disabled or destroyed two tanks in the center prong and two in the eastern.

Gerhardt's surviving tanks passed Hills 2704 and 2720 on the valley's eastern side. His forces, including his elite motorcycle troops, began taking heavy casualties from enemy soldiers who'd hidden in fortifications on those hills and fired at the elements of his assault force.

Moments later, a heavy mortar barrage began again at a steady pace. With the overcast sky and the pandemonium from the three-sided attack, Gerhardt could not determine the mortars' location.

Gerhardt watched the Americans destroy half of his armored assault force in less than ten minutes. Despite their training, élan, and zeal, the German attack ground to a halt.

Stopped cold halfway down the valley, the far western element on Gerhardt's right flank reported accurate small arms fire coming down from the steep slopes of Hill 2875. The German casualties rose ominously.

Despite losing tanks and several infantrymen, the center prong tried to press the fight. At one point, the lead German tank got to within 45 yards of the base of Hill 2653, only to be beaten back by fire from a multitude of American weapons.

Gerhardt watched the allies cut his forces to ribbons. He went into a black rage.

The German commander ordered one of the 88 mm cannon to load anti-tank rounds. The crew took the halftracks under fire, starting with the tank destroyer on the improved road that had been firing rounds into his rear echelon.

Gerhardt directed the commander of the other cannon to use anti-personnel rounds on the southern ridge. The gun kept firing until it ran out of ammunition. The 88 gunners succeeded in inflicting heavy casualties on the Allies.

Genero lost three M3 tank destroyers and both Jeeps, but not before all of the German tanks and soft-skinned vehicles in the western prong met the same fate.

By noon, Genero's men had destroyed over three-quarters of the German force. Recognizing that it was futile to continue the attack on Hill 2653, Gerhardt began to withdraw.

Unlike his assault down the valley, Gerhardt's retrograde movement worked. Only 20 percent of the Axis force that started down the valley made it back to the starting point by 1415 hours. Four battered tanks, of the twelve that began the assault, left the infernal valley under their own power.

Two days earlier, Gerhardt had crossed the Dorsals with 20 tanks. Now he had a total of six, and two of those were on their last legs.

By 1500 hours, Oberstleutnant Gerhardt knew two things: He must retire to the Eastern Dorsals to report his failure to General Von Arnim—and he would never be a full colonel. Though he'd been wounded in France and nearly died in Russia, Feriana was Gerhardt's first defeat.

*If I had any honor, I would put the barrel of my pistol into my mouth and spread my brain across this cursed desert,* Gerhardt thought. After reflection, he rejected that plan—for the moment.

Oberstleutnant Gerhardt realized that if the Germans were to prevail in North Africa they had to return and defeat the British and Americans on this high plain. The Kasserine Pass would be the ideal path to initiate a winter offensive.

*I'll take what's left of my men to the other side of the mountains,* Gerhardt vowed. *I'll find a way to make amends for this disaster. I'll convince General von Arnim to give me another gruppe. Perhaps I can get Tigers. With those new Panzers, I could sweep west from the pass and make all of these American bastards suffer for my humiliation.*

# Chapter 31

1115 Hours
December 5, 1942,
Sick Bay, *USS Enterprise.*
Operating in the Coral Sea,
10 Nautical Miles Northwest of Noumea,
French Territory of New Caledonia

Doc Hansen had gotten out of the sack late, so he hadn't had time to take breakfast in the wardroom. His stomach's gurgling distracted him from the spontaneous game of hearts that had erupted on a dare from the chief. Since the medical staff rarely had free time, Doc and the corpsmen had jockeyed for sickbay bragging rights for most of the morning.

At the moment, Hansen had the fewest points. *It had better stay that way or I'll find a reason to neuter the fucking chief corpsman,* Mark thought, as he watched the senior petty officer. *I know that dickhead is cheating. He's too damn good! I just can't figure out how he's doing it.*

For the last several months, there'd been too much work to allow many card games in sickbay. Flight and combat operations had been so hectic on the *Enterprise* that no one could find a spare moment.

Today, the unexpected absence of combat put the crew and the medical team in a lighthearted mood. Although the men had begun to joke a little, the humor had a dark and ominous tone, more like the graveyard variety.

Since the battle at Santa Cruz at the end of October, the Big "E" had been the only American carrier left in the South Pacific. Tempered by the realities of combat, the crew believed that they were living on borrowed time. The *Enter-*

*prise* could follow the *Yorktown*, *Lexington*, and *Hornet* to a watery grave at any time.

Six Japanese bombs had struck the *Enterprise* during combat operations over the last several months. Three hundred crewmen had died as a result. Everybody had lost at least one friend.

The danger steeled their resolve. All of the crew might perish in this war, but they believed in an eventual victory. In November, to demonstrate their fortitude, they hung a banner on the hanger deck that simply said:

## *ENTERPRISE V. JAPAN*

The under-staffed medical team had been very busy during the campaigns. The physicians and corpsmen worked around the clock saving their shipmates' lives.

Today, the *Enterprise* steamed south of the Japanese operational area toward Noumea in the French Territory of New Caledonia. The Skipper did not expect to encounter the enemy. Except for the standard combat air patrol, he'd stood the air wing down.

Today, there would be no casualties. The doctors and corpsmen would have no broken bodies to mend. Shipmates would not be buried at sea. No limbs would be amputated. No wounds cauterized and treated. No fractured bones set. For a few hours, the whole crew could go about their normal routines.

The corpsmen kicked back a little. After the rigors and horrors of combat, routine sick call—which required the medical staff to attend to mundane illnesses and accidents—seemed anticlimactic. Even though the medical staff was present for duty, the absence of trauma and carnage made working in sickbay feel like a liberty in Honolulu.

"Sir, I'm starting to feel poorly," Petty Officer 2d Class Thurmond revealed for the first time that morning, as he folded the cards in his hand into a single stack. "I might be coming down with the grippe or something. I might not be able to finish our game."

"Me either, Doc! I'm starting to feel very faint," the other medic—Petty Officer 3d Class Johnson—chimed in, as he stared at his hand and pondered which card he should lay down in response to Thurmond's lead.

"Chief Jaslowski, what do you suppose could be the cause of this sudden grave epidemic among the corpsmen?" Doc Hansen asked, addressing the chief, while holding his cards defensively close to his chest.

"Sir, Thurmond's just trying to wheedle a shot of Mr. Sullivan's medicinal scotch," Jaslowski responded in a bored tone, designed to mask the fact that he had the Queen of Spades and was hoarding it so he could dump it on Doc Hansen at just the right moment.

"I'm not too sure there's any left, Chief. I think I gave the last of it to that airdale gunner whose foot we had to amputate after Guadalcanal," Doc Hansen explained. "Besides, it's a bit early in the day for a nip of scotch. Don't you agree?"

"Well, sir, I believe that you've over a half a bottle locked in the bottom left hand drawer of the desk in your stateroom. And, as for the time of day, a medicinal dose of scotch is not subject to the 'sun over the yardarm' rule, sir," the chief shot back.

Mark was surprised to learn that the chief knew the contents of his stateroom's locked drawer. *I don't think Jaslowki has ever been in my quarters. Why would a chief stalk around officer's country?* Mark thought.

Mark decided not to ask Jaslowski any questions. He knew he'd never get a straight answer. He didn't want to give the chief the satisfaction.

Mark and Jaslowski respected each other professionally, but over the last six months, each had taken perverse pleasure in screwing with the other's psyche. Mark had committed to winning the psychological war.

Chief Jaslowski had great affection for the much younger doctor. He played with Mark's brain to distract the young doctor from his grief over the loss of his wife. More often than not, it worked.

Continuing the banter, Mark shot back, "Chief, since you know how much medicinal scotch is left, you must also know that Navy regs do not permit alcohol on American naval vessels except where it is necessary for medicinal purposes or for operational imperatives—like alcohol-based hydraulic fluid. You would definitely not want to get the two types mixed up."

"No kiddin' sir! Last cruise before the war, I knew this airdale mechanic," Jaslowski said, beginning one of his long-winded sea stories. The two junior petty officers groaned, knowing these tales were at least half fantasy.

Jaslowski ignored their protests and continued: "This mechanic was a petty officer first class in the flight wing. His chief caught him drinking the hydraulic fluid. At Captain's Mast, the skipper took his rate and busted him to ordinary seaman. Gave him five days in the brig on bread and water. While he was in the brig, he went blind from the effects of the hydraulic fluid. He did!"

"Actually," laughed Johnson, "me and Thurmond were on that cruise and we don't remember no airdale going blind while in the brig."

"No, Bill, that's not true," Thurmond added with a straight face. "I remember a yeoman from the captain's staff going blind."

"No, Tom, you've got it wrong," Johnson explained in a faux-serious tone. "That yeoman went blind all right, but not from drinking hydraulic fluid. You remember! The master-at-arms caught him beatin' his meat in the head. He just whacked off 'til he went blind."

"You snotty sons-of-bitches better watch your step!" The chief warned. "You fuck with me—and next liberty I'll leave you on the duty roster. Worse, instead of getting' laid in Noumea, I'll get Doc to assign you to the penicillin patrol."

"Oh shit, Chief!! We're really sorry. We're just kidding," Johnson said, mustering his most respectful tone.

"I'd rather be keel-hauled than give those shots to the clap-ridden."

*I love this banter—it's like the arguments among the orderlies at St. Theresa's an eternity ago,* Mark thought. *There hasn't been much to laugh about this year.*

Mark still mourned his wife's death. He blamed himself for the circumstances that led to Kari's loss.

*If I hadn't been so set about the Navy Medical Corps, Kari wouldn't have been so stubborn about becoming a Navy nurse,* Mark thought. *It's my fault that she ended up in the Philippines right before the Japs decided to launch their sneak attack. It's my fault that Kari got stranded on Corregidor. She'd never have been in harm's way if it weren't for my selfishness. If I had waited for the Army to draft me, that beautiful, loving woman would still be alive. I'm the one who deserved to be blown to kingdom come, not her.*

*I don't want to die, but I will not allow myself to fear the prospect of dying,* Mark promised. *War with the Japanese Empire is a necessary evil. We must pursue it with every fiber of our bodies and not just endure it. No one will ever convince those sneaky Jap bastards to give up peacefully. They will stop only when we have them on the ground, our foot on their throat and the barrel of a gun in their face. Maybe even that won't be enough. Millions of Japanese and Americans will have to die before the world is at peace again,* Mark thought.

*If it's my fate to die in this war, fine! I only hope that I go quickly, like Kari. If Chaplain Nolan is right and there is a heaven, then Kari would definitely be there to meet me at the gates,* Mark hoped. *I'm sure that I'll recognize her loving spirit. I pray to God that her Catholic theology is not simply mythology.*

While Mark pondered the mysteries of the universe, Chief Jaslowski yelled at Johnson, "Play your fucking card before the war ends, bub!"

As Johnson pulled a card from his hand, the Bosun's Mate broke in over the ship-wide loud speaker with his irritating, "Now hear this! Now hear this!"

All of the card players had come to hate and fear the sound of the disembodied voice. True, he came on several times a day to make routine announcements about shipboard issues, but too often his voice first mustered them to battle stations.

The Bosun's Mate personified the ancient sirens, whose irresistible tones lured sailors to their doom.

Happily, today's announcement provided a wonderful gift.

"Now hear this, now hear this! By order of the Captain, off-duty crewmen will muster on the flight deck to render proper military honors to the captain, officers, and crew of the *USS Saratoga*, now steaming one-quarter mile off our port side."

Cheers and shouts echoed through the *Enterprise*. The *Saratoga* (CV-3) was a fast, Lexington Class carrier. She carried a complement of 81 planes. Her appearance in these waters meant that the Big E was no longer the only American carrier in the South Pacific.

Johnson and Thurmond threw their cards up in the air, jumped from their seats, and began to cheer. Jaslowski threw his hand down on the table in disgust. Though delighted with the news about the *Sara*, the chief had been counting on dropping the queen of spades on Doc.

While the petty officers danced around sickbay, Mark grabbed the chief's discarded hand. He examined the cards. When he found the queen, he admonished the chief with a knowing look.

Jaslowski smiled and said, "Fortunes of war, Doc. I'll get ya next time."

Smiling back, Mark told the petty officers to settle down and come back to the table. "Chief, I'm starting to catch that bug that Johnson and Thurmond have. Perhaps I should go to my stateroom and fetch Sullivan's bottle, so we can all have a shot—I mean a dose," he said with a huge smile.

"Don't trouble yourself, sir. I have the medicinal scotch right here," Jaslowski said as he got up from the table and reached into his personal kit. *Officers are like children*," Jaslowski thought as walked back to the table with the half-full bottle of scotch. *They think they run this ship.*

# Chapter 32

5:30 PM
December 15, 1942
Le Tort Brothers' Funeral Home
Carlisle, Pennsylvania

Winter had come early to the Cumberland Valley. It had been chilly and blustery since Halloween. The ridgelines surrounding Carlisle looked bare and lonely long before the winter solstice, and the somber note of nature's display sent a sad message to the good people of Carlisle, already dispirited by the war news.

Thanksgiving had been a wet, icy affair. Over six inches of snow had fallen in Carlisle the day after the holiday. War rationing limited highway travel, but even that became snarled on the slick, frozen roads.

Although the war reports had been bad for most of 1942, the hearty people of central Pennsylvania had persevered. When compared to the circumstances in France, Holland, Belgium, Denmark, Britain, Russia, China, and the Philippines, life in America—even with all the rationing and deprivations—was still good.

Though only half past five, it was past dusk when Phillip and Marta pulled their Cadillac off of High Street and into the diagonal parking space at the Le Tort Brothers Funeral Home. The dark, overcast sky added to the gloom of the mournful event.

Knowing his end was near, Dan Monarch's children had prayed for his peaceful death. On Sunday evening, God answered their prayers. Dan and his children wanted an intimate family gathering to mark his passing. The community had other plans. Dan had made such a mark that his children relented and agreed to a public viewing on Tuesday evening.

As he contemplated the viewing, the elder Genero felt depressed. 1942 had been an awful year for the family. Kari's death had been the worst news of all. He'd not gotten over it, and probably never would. He missed his beautiful daughter. Many nights he found excuses to walk in the hills behind the house, or hike up to the Gap.

While Phillip walked, Marta drank. Her despair and horror over the loss of Kari drove her to the distraction of rye whiskey, but her attempts to lose herself in the liquor only magnified her sorrow. Nothing made it go away. When Marta drank, she'd chase her own tail until it got numb, but her mind never turned off. She never found peace. She needed Phillip to pull her from her self-absorption, to be by her side, to share her heartbreak. Phillip thought he had to pretend to be strong for them both and to hide his own pain. Instead of standing by her, he walked the hills alone.

Phillip worried about his son. Phil was somewhere in North Africa fighting the Germans and the Italians. Phillip's nightmare about Koronopolis returned with unerring regularity. The dreams so troubled Phillip that most nights he was afraid to go to sleep.

He went to church every day, begging St. Michael to intercede with God to protect his son. Phillip wore Kari's St. Michael's medal around his neck as a constant reminder of his beloved daughter. It disturbed Phillip that Kari had not been wearing the chain and medal when she was killed.

For some reason that Phillip couldn't understand, she had carried it in a bag in her pocket with her rings, identification, and other personal effects. Kari treasured her ring set. It symbolized her marriage to Mark and the rings had become her pride and joy.

Ever since his brother Angelo and his wife Mary had moved to Carlisle to help with the bakery, the Genero brothers had become very close. That closeness also brought pain. Local doctors had diagnosed Angelo with liver disease. Although serious, his prognosis was uncertain. The bakery became their refuge. In spite of the rationing, the economy showed signs of growth, and they hoped they could make it viable again.

Though expected, the death of Dan Monarch saddened everyone. Dan Monarch had acted as a mentor for Phillip. Dan cared for the Genero family very much. Secretly, Phillip had suspected that Dan was in love with Marta. Phillip had seen it in Dan's eyes on countless occasions.

Phillip understood the intensity of being in love with Marta. He had been that way himself for over 25 years. He still loved her desperately. Phillip was not jealous of Dan's affection for Marta. She had never given him the slightest reason to believe that her relationship with Dan had been anything other than platonic.

Phillip assumed that Dan's love for Marta was unrequited. Dan and Marta were dear friends and, despite Dan's feelings, had never had been anything more. Phillip would have been surprised—but not really disappointed—had he known the truth. After all, Marta had chosen him over Dan decades earlier.

Junior Monarch, on the other hand, was a snake. Phillip knew better than to trust him or to believe that his physical recovery mirrored a moral improvement. Junior intended to bide his time until he could take over the company.

In the last year, Junior had created an ally in his son-in-law, Evan Collingswood. With his control of Monarch Industries firmly established, Junior appointed the unqualified Collingswood to chief financial officer ahead of 30 senior officers. Had it not been for the family ties, Phillip would have fired Collingswood two years earlier. When the new finance officer refused to fund the Cumberland little-league team with Monarch money, a community outreach program that had brought years of goodwill and publicity, it showcased his arrogance and ineptitude.

After parking the Cadillac, Phillip got out, walked around, and opened the door for Marta. She needed Phillip's arm to steady herself. They walked into the viewing room filled with a lifetime's worth of friends and neighbors. Dan's coffin lay in the front of the large room, at the foot of a marble-trimmed altar.

In contrast to the barren world outside, scores of bouquets in every color, size, and variety imaginable surrounded the altar and every square inch of free space. Framed by the floral beauty and the indirect light from cornices in the ceiling, Dan Monarch's body rested quietly. The morticians had left Dan with his trademark little half-smile. Marta and Phillip stopped at the coffin out of respect for their friend and benefactor. Phillip reflected on all of the good things that Dan had done for people throughout the valley.

As Marta gazed at Dan, she remembered the first day she ever saw him all those years earlier when she applied to be his children's nanny. Marta had been a girl then and Dan Monarch was a handsome, sweet, charming, rich, and powerful brother of the most prominent man in the Cumberland Valley.

Dan was such a contrast from the serious, dour men in her Amish community. Dan displayed a fabulous sense of humor and enjoyed life. She developed a crush on him. His affection and devotion to his children stoked the feelings of a young girl, starved for those very attributes in a man in her life.

Dan quickly picked up on Marta's feelings. Even though he was considerably older and Marta was just a girl, he could not resist taking advantage. Dan was the first lover Marta had ever known. He was a kind and sensitive lover, and she initiated their passion more often than not—but she could not continue and bear the weight of having destroyed Dan's marriage.

Still, he'd always been special to her, and in a final gesture, Marta reached over and touched Dan's hand. Startled by the cold and lifeless texture of Dan's skin, Marta choked back a sob.

After guiding Marta away from the casket, Phillip walked her through an archway to a small table in the next room. Phillip offered to get her coffee and a small sweet cake from another table nearby. Marta accepted.

While Marta was sitting at the table, Junior Monarch strode into the room. He wore an expensive light gray suit, which contrasted with the dark and somber attire of all the other visitors. Only the black strip of cloth on the left sleeve of his coat gave any indication that Junior mourned for his uncle. Without asking, Junior took the seat next to Marta.

Of all the people on the earth, Junior Monarch was the very last one she wanted at her table. Junior's rudeness had an unusual effect. Marta got irritated, distracted from her sadness, and she stopped weeping.

Expecting Junior to pick up where he had left off all those years ago, Marta steeled herself for some offensive comment. Instead, she was shocked by what she heard.

"Marta, I know that you think very little of me as a man. I suppose that with all you had to put up with for all those years, you have a right to think of me that way," Junior began.

"I know you're sad about the loss of your daughter. Now, the death of a good friend makes the world look like a very unhappy place. With the war, there's a lot to be sad about," Junior continued in the same surprising tone. "What I want to say is that Monarch Industries needs you. You're a dedicated and well-respected employee. I don't want to lose you, Marta."

"What are you talking about?" Marta asked, dumbstruck by Junior's behavior.

"Before he died, Uncle Dan told me that you might leave the company to devote more time to other interests. Based on the terrible way I used to treat you, I wouldn't blame you for leaving now that I'm in charge again.

Marta said nothing. She just continued to stare at Junior in disbelief.

Junior persisted, "Marta, I've changed a lot. I'm still rough around the edges, and no picnic. But I swear, my own brush with eternity helped me to find a different way. I no longer think of people as just chattel."

In all of the time she'd known Junior, this was the most self-deprecating behavior Marta had ever seen. She was very sad and had been drinking for a good part of the day. She had not properly calibrated her radar.

"As bad as I've been, Marta, you've got to admit that I'm not Adolf Hitler, right?" Junior said, making the first joke Marta had ever heard from him.

The source of the joke and the question were so outrageous that they caused Marta to laugh. It was the first time she'd laughed in months.

Halfway across the room Phillip was startled by his wife's gentle laugh. It was a rare sound these days.

Phillip looked over at Marta and was shocked to see that she had stopped crying. She seemed to be chatting amicably with Junior Monarch.

"Junior, you're not Hitler," Marta said at last, "but you were crude and offensive. I could never tolerate any of that garbage again."

Junior was stung by the last remark. *I hate people telling me what they won't tolerate,* Junior thought as he pretended to respectfully listen to Marta. *The assholes should just shut the fuck up and do what I tell them. I'd better be cool here. I don't want Marta to leave Monarch Industries. If she does leave, it'll be a lot harder to get even. If it wasn't for subservient little Miriam and my plans for revenge, I might not have been able to survive all those days in Sedona. I've got a lot of time and energy invested in this plan. I can't afford to blow it.*

*Speaking of Miriam, if I can get out of this damn wake at a reasonable time, I might be able to get over to Camp Hill for a quickie without raising much suspicion,* Junior decided. He'd allowed Miriam to join him two years earlier after she left the good doctor at the Andrews Institute.

Miriam traveled to Pennsylvania and, after several bouts of great sex, convinced Junior to make her his permanent mistress. With money from his secret accounts, Junior found Miriam a small house in a remote neighborhood and visited her several times a week.

Junior wasn't worried about his wife finding out. After all, he had photographic evidence of her philandering with the chauffeur. Junior had been more concerned about Uncle

Dan. *Uncle Dan is dead now, isn't he? The hour of revenge is getting closer*, Junior promised.

Junior focused back on Marta. "I don't blame you for feeling that way. I want to apologize now," Junior said. Then, with diabolical inspiration, Junior continued: "And, I think I should do it now, and publicly!"

Standing and addressing the assembled people, he pronounced, "Ladies and Gentlemen, as you know, the funeral for Dan Monarch is private. That request was among his last wishes. Of course, we will honor them. However, I would like to take this opportunity to do two things. First, I want to pay homage to a great man who, like my own father, was much respected and loved in the community. I am well aware that he will be missed."

People began to drift in from the viewing room to see what was going on. By the time Junior got going, nearly 70 important and influential people from all points in central Pennsylvania were listening to Junior's extraordinary speech.

"Second: I know that there is a legitimate concern that I'm going to cause pain, suffering, and economic difficulties for some of you. At one time in my life that concern would have been fair. I've hurt a lot of people. I've been selfish and arrogant. I've abused the power that my family entrusted to me. Well, I want to apologize to all of the directors, officers, and employees of the company for all of the things that I did. Most especially, I owe a sincere apology to Mrs. Genero, who for many years was my assistant and had to bear the brunt of my misconduct. Marta, I hope in time that you will come to forgive me for the past and rely upon me for the person that I've become."

With those words, Junior walked over to Phillip Genero and offered his hand. Other than Junior's footsteps, there was complete silence in the room. All eyes focused on Phillip, awaiting his reaction.

Phillip didn't trust Junior's sincerity or motive. He'd seen too many little things since Junior's return from Arizona. Phillip looked past Junior and for the first time in many months saw the liquid brown pools of his wife's eyes without tears. More than that, she was smiling. Marta nodded at Phillip in a clear sign that he should accept the very public olive branch that Junior had offered.

Despite his reservations, Phillip reached over and shook hands with Junior. The crowd, now numbering 80 or more, broke into a spontaneous applause, punctuated with supportive comments from dozens of men and women.

By 8:30, the viewing was over and only family members remained. Junior worried that it would be hard to get out to Miriam's place for a quick piece of ass.

Donna and Linda had just left. Only Collingswood and Junior remained to watch Bobby Le Tort close Uncle Dan's casket for the last time. Finished with the viewing, Bobby disappeared in the back to attend to other matters.

After ensuring that they were alone, Collingswood began, "Dad, did you really mean all those pathetic things you said this evening? I thought I would have to cry or puke if you didn't stop," he continued, baiting Junior.

"Don't call me Dad, you ridiculous piece of shit. I've told you that thousands of times."

"Oh my god; that apology shit was so moving. Half the people in here were eating out of your hand, including that fine Marta Genero," Collingswood responded.

"That's not all she'll be doing before I'm through with that bitch. The problem is that, like you, I was stupid when I was young. Now I've learned that raw power is not enough. Sometimes you have to be nice," Junior explained.

"Well, Dad, no one's going to think you're nice when they realize what you've done to this town," Collingswood observed.

"So what? I'll be long gone. I couldn't care less for these morons."

"What about me? I don't have an exit plan. I could get caught holding the bag for you on this little enterprise," Collingswood responded.

"I promised you a piece of this. You'll get a taste," Junior promised.

"I need more than a taste, Dad! I need to be a full partner. I'm running the same risks as you. I want a larger share or you could lose a lot more than I could."

The veiled threat angered Junior. He took two steps closer to Collingswood, grabbed him by his lapel, and pulled him roughly to within six inches of his face.

"You fucking weasel! You try to fuck with me, and I will have you killed. Make no mistake. You will disappear and they'll never find your body. I brought you into this because I need one other person to pull it off. You're the only shit head I know who was dishonest enough to agree to it. You are in this up to your scrawny little pencil neck." Junior threatened.

"Don't you ever call me Dad again!" Junior continued. "Don't ever try to cross me. Don't make the mistake of thinking that you're smarter than me. Don't give me a reason to show you what I am capable of. Get me, shit head?"

"Yes, sir!" Collingswood squeaked, barely able to breathe until Junior finally released his grip.

"All right, then; go get your car. You're going to drive me to Mechanicsburg," Junior directed.

# Chapter 33

E ven during war, the everyday life of the French constabulary in the remote tracts of west central Tunisia was dull. Corporal Henri St. Jacques liked it that way. When things were slow, he had less paperwork.

St. Jacques held a modest rank with the French Colonial Police. Due to the American invasion, he'd become the acting prefect for the entire west central territory. He'd assumed the post when the Vichy French Inspector hightailed it for the Nazi zone of operations. The Vichy collaborator got out ahead of Colonel Raff's task force with all the prefecture's money.

*I do not care for Colonel Raff,* St. Jacques thought as he sorted through the paperwork at his desk. *The man is unsophisticated and primitive. He treats my people with all the personal warmth of a sledgehammer. I couldn't believe it when he dressed me down in front of the constables and called me a liar. He has no respect for our culture and our traditions. If it weren't for his uncivilized demands, we wouldn't be at work at so barbaric an hour.*

The sun had barely broken the horizon and St. Jacques had to investigate a murder. The night before, curious villagers discovered a French merchant in the rear of his tiny shop with his throat cut. They found him *in flagrante delicto* in the arms of a notorious Arab woman. The woman had a small caliber bullet hole neatly drilled into her forehead. There was no exit wound.

After St. Jacques had shooed the villagers away and began his inspection of the crime scene, he observed the French merchant sprawled naked on top of the Arab woman, soaking her flawless white skin with his crimson French blood. He ordered the two assisting constables to separate the bodies.

As he carefully examined the merchant's corpse, he noticed that the Frenchman no longer had a penis. His entire scrotum was missing, suggesting that his penis had recently been attached but had been removed by involuntary trauma. Despite an extensive search of the premises, none of the constables could locate the Frenchman's organ anywhere.

*I knew something like this would happen someday,* St. Jacques reflected. *Farah's husband is a hot-tempered and violent bandit. He has been quite generous to the constabulary's retirement fund, which—since the Inspector fled—is now my province. I wonder how much Emil will pay for a favorable outcome.*

While St. Jacques contemplated the size of the bribe he'd demand from the Arab bandit, he spotted something unusual out of the east window of his tiny office. Off on the horizon, he spotted a dark dot moving against the rising sun. As the prefect continued to watch, the dot grew in size and multiplied in number.

*Those must be men,* St. Jacques deduced, *but they're not Arabs or Berbers. Three of them walk straight-backed and stiff like Europeans. I can't identify the fourth by his gait. It's strange to see men afoot approaching from the east.*

*There's nothing between the village and the Mediterranean except three hundred kilometers of desert, mountains, farmland and the coastal plain. The only Europeans in that direction are Germans and Italians on the other side of the mountains. These men could be German scouts, reconnoitering on foot ahead of an Africa Korps armored column. They might be coming to reclaim the village!*

St. Jacques immediately began buttoning up his tunic. It wouldn't hurt to make a good impression on the Axis liberators.

*How will I explain my cooperation with the Amis? Hmmm, I'll just lie and see how far I get,* St. Jacques decided.

Thirty minutes later, the four strangers were only 250 yards from the police station. Cpl. St. Jacques and one of the Arab constables went outside the tiny station to the dusty village street to greet their liberators. When the strangers got closer, their appearance startled him.

The men were not German, Italian, or Vichy French. They were four very tired, haggard, unshaven, thirsty, and starving Americans and Free French. St. Jacques had never encountered soldiers in such bad condition. *I guess the murder investigation will have to wait,* he thought.

When he reached the edge of the village, the tallest soldier gave a series of verbal instructions and hand signals to the other three. The other soldiers deployed quickly to defensive positions around the square where they could cover their leader and each other.

The leader strode toward the police station and did not stop until he was ten feet away from Henri. As he got closer, St. Jacques recognized him to be an American officer, wearing the tattered remnants of a jump suit—like those of Col. Raff's paratroopers. A sixth sense told Henri to keep his hands away from his holstered pistol.

The officer had a rifle in his hands, which he kept pointed at the ground. The American's left hand sported a filthy battle dressing, but the index finger on his right hand curled around the trigger of the rifle. St. Jacques could see that the safety was off. In perfect French, the officer addressed Henri, "Monsieur, I'm Captain Phillip Genero, American Parachute Infantry. Where are we?"

"Captain Genero, you are in the village of Hadjeb El Aioun, in the Anglo-American zone of operations. You must know the task force commander, Colonel Raff. I am Corporal St. Jacques, the acting Prefect of Police," Henri explained. "What has happened to you, Captain? Can my modest force be of some service?"

*The American appears to be a tough customer. He looks like he would shoot Halim and me without blinking an eye,* Henri thought.

While St. Jacques watched, Genero turned slightly to his right. Without taking his eyes off the two policemen and without removing his finger from the trigger of the rifle, he shouted to one of the men in French.

"Louis, come on over here. We've made it back to the task force. We actually did it!"

When Louis got closer, St Jacques could smell the acrid scent of stale Gauloises and recognized the tattered uniform as French. The acting prefect shivered when he saw the unusual scar, eye patch, and aquamarine blue eye.

"Mon ami," Louis Anton began in French, "who are these insects? They have the look of Vichy about them. What makes you think we can trust them?"

"Louis, I met this one several weeks ago," Phil responded as he gestured toward Henri. "He took over from a Nazi collaborator. He's Free French and reliable. Otherwise, Colonel Raff would have had him shot," Phil elaborated.

Looking past Anton and with a crisp series of hand signals, Phil directed the other two men to assemble on him. Both soldiers moved warily in the direction of their leader.

"Corporal, I am Capitan Louis Anton, Free French *Légion Étrangère.* You will find us clean water to drink and hot water for bathing. We require hot food to eat. Have your man do this immediately. While he is occupied with these tasks, arrange transportation for us to Colonel Raff's command post. We will leave within the hour. See to it now!" Anton commanded, intentionally using his rudest Gallic tone.

As the two policemen scrambled to obey Anton, Phil looked over and gave Louis a patronizing smile. *We've been through a lifetime's worth of shit since Christmas. Louis has been like a brother to me. I'd never have made it back without him,* Phil thought.

Whispering to his friend, Phil chortled, "Louis, you were rude to our hosts. Haven't you learned that you can attract more flies with sugar than you can with vinegar?"

"I will tell you this, Phillipe. I do not trust this Vichy-loving corporal—beyond what I can see with my one good eye," Louis responded. "He has the smell of collaboration about him. I have half a mind to come back in a few nights and cut his throat while he sleeps."

"Maybe you should," Phil thought out loud as he eyed the corporal. "First, let's get to the Colonel and report on our latest debacle."

"My friend," Anton began. "You are a brave man and a skillful soldier. It was not your fault that those pigs in pilot suits dropped us in the wrong place. The fact that even some of us made it back is a great victory."

"Louis, with a few more victories like this one, we just might lose this war!" Capt. Genero responded.

By late December of 1942, the newly arrived Germans and Italians had stopped the eastward Anglo-American advance on Tunis. In heavy fighting in the North of Tunisia, the German forces, sprinkled with the advanced Pz IV tanks and a few of the new Tigers, pushed the Anglo-American armies back toward Algeria. The strategic situation west of Tunis deteriorated into a stalemate. The hope of taking Tunis by Christmas faded to oblivion.

At the other end of the country, Field Marshall Rommel completed his epic retreat from Egypt through Libya. With the 5th Panzer Army holding the ground directly to his north, the Desert Fox was able to reorganize his Afrika Korps and establish a formidable line of defense near Mareth, where he would make his stand against Gen. Montgomery. To the consternation of Roosevelt, Churchill, and the entire Allied command, Monty's 8th Army continued to creep west along the Libyan coast.

Once the Germans had secured their Northern Tunisian airhead, they brought heavier supplies to North Africa by sea. The Axis ships ran a dangerous gauntlet of Allied aircraft stationed in North Africa and the Island of Malta. Allied bombers damaged some of the enemy vessels, but enough of the craft got through to keep the large German force adequately supplied.

After off-loading the vital war materials at the Port of Bizerte, the German supply corps used the locomotives, boxcars, and rolling stock of the Tunisian national railroad to ferry supplies down to the Afrika Korps on the Mareth Line. As long as the Germans and Italians could keep the supply stream coming into Bizerte and as long as they could distribute the supplies to the combat elements of the 5th Panzer Army and the *Deutches Afrika Korps*, the Axis soldiers could keep the Allies at bay.

Rommel had been in worse predicaments before. Despite the fact that the Allies had Rommel in a strategic vise, no allied officer would predict his defeat. Rommel had pulled the rabbit out of the hat too many times in the past for the Allies to assume anything.

Faced with a stalemate on two fronts, the Allies tried to break the logjam. The Tunisian railroad became a crucial target, especially the stretch that paralleled the Mediterranean coast between the cities of Sfax in the north and Gabes in the south. Between the two cities, the national railroad crossed a small ravine near the town of El Djem. A strategically vital bridge spanned the ravine.

If the allied bombers could knock the bridge out, the German command would be hard-pressed to supply the Afrika Korps in the southeast, making it easier for the British 8th Army to make headway. Success in the southeast would relieve pressure in the north.

During the first three weeks of December, 1942, the British and Americans threw everything they had at the bridge: B-25 Mitchells, A-20 Havocs, and P-38 Lightings in the fighter-bomber configuration. All tried without success to destroy the bridge at El Djem.

As Christmas approached, an Allied staff officer came up with the idea of dropping a paratrooper raiding party at night north of the El Djem Bridge. Once assembled, the raiding force would capture and destroy it in a *coup de main*. The paratroopers would bring hundreds of pounds of TNT and use it to blow out the superstructure underneath the bridge.

After destroying the bridge, the paratroopers would have to make their way back to the allied zone of operation, requiring them to evade all hostile forces through 80 miles of enemy-held territory.

In mid-December 1942, the Anglo-American command had selected Col. Raff's old battalion for the El Djem raid. In a move that confused every paratrooper in North Africa, the War Department officially detached Raff's battalion from duty with the 503d Parachute Infantry Regiment (PIR).

The Army Staff re-designated the paratroopers in North Africa as the separate 509th Parachute Infantry Battalion (PIB). The re-designation became official on November 7, 1942. No one bothered to tell LtCol. Raff until January 1943.

Changing designations was nothing new to Phil He didn't care what number the staff in Washington gave to his unit. Raff's men had served together since the early days on the frying pan at Fort Benning. They'd trained and bonded in Georgia, North Carolina, and England.

*The 509th is an experienced, bloodied, motivated, kick-ass force. These guys are stone-cold killers with solid unit cohesion and a great esprit de corps,* Raff thought when he first heard about the new designation. *And they'd be just as great if they were called the 1/435th Spoon Platoon.*

Eisenhower and Clark thought well of the 509th, too. Less than a week after the battle at Feriana, Eisenhower called Raff to Algiers where the general promoted Raff to bird colonel. The commanders intended the promotion to reward Raff for the fine work that he and the Task Force were doing in Tunisia, keeping the Germans off-balance and protecting the Anglo-American southern flank.

Though the 509th had fought gallantly in several separate actions, a few of the paratroopers stood above the rest. Even Eisenhower and Clark had heard about the spectacular fight at Feriana, where Genero secured an important tactical victory against long odds. For his courage and leadership Raff had recommended to Lt. Gen. Clark that Genero receive the Distinguished Service Cross.

Phil was at the 239th Field Hospital near Algiers, having the top half of his ring finger and the pinky finger on his left hand amputated, when he learned of the recommendation. He was shocked.

*Nothing I did at Feriana could ever equate with Dad's personal heroism in the Argonne. I don't want this award. It doesn't seem right.*

A few days after the amputation, a harried hospital administrator temporarily released Phil so that he could go to the capital to receive the Purple Heart and a Silver Star from Lt. Gen. Clark.

A medal like the Distinguished Service Cross would take months to approve. In the interim, Clark decided to award the Silver Star to Genero for his gallantry in capturing the Italian squad the night before the battle south of Feriana.

Phil thought that the award ceremony in Algiers was quite pleasant. Fresh from surgery on his left hand, he was still on pain medication when he stood before Lt. Gen. Clark to receive his medals. He was high as a kite.

When Mark Clark tried to engage Genero in polite, soldierly conversation, Phil responded in a flat, subdued manner. His answers to the general's questions were such non-sequiturs that Clark left the ceremony thinking that this young captain was very brave—and totally dense.

After his readmission to the hospital, Phil could not abide the 239th for long. The presence of the American Army nurses constantly reminded him of the death of his sister.

On December 3rd, without further medical consultation, Phil went absent without leave. He did have one quick tryst in the linen tent with an especially randy Army nurse from Denver before he went over the hill.

Hitching a ride on an Army deuce-and-a-half, Genero linked up with the 509th, which had been withdrawn from

Tunisia. It was then staging its operations out of Tebessa, Algeria.

By the time Phil reported back to his unit, Lt. Gen Clark had appointed Maj. Yardley the acting commander. II Corps had kicked Col. Raff upstairs. Little Caesar devoted all of his time to the Tunisian Task Force, of which the 509th represented only a small part. Raff was so busy in Tunisia that Yardley, Genero, and the men of the 509th rarely saw him.

On December 18, 1942, when the warning order for the El Djem Raid first crossed Phil's desk in the S-2 shop in Tebessa, he felt dumbstruck at its imbecility. Within the first 30 seconds, he identified ten reasons why the Army should not send a combat platoon of paratroopers on such a foolhardy mission.

Genero reviewed the plan in depth. Using all of his considerable influence, he convinced the S-2 to recommend to Maj. Yardley that the plan be tabled pending further intelligence analysis. For two days, Phil languished in the glow of an incorrect belief that he'd sidetracked the fiend at higher headquarters who thought that all paratroopers had "Expendable" stenciled on their foreheads.

On December 20, 1942, the final mission order came in. It made no mention regarding the objections made by the 509th S-2 and the S-3. In its final form, Maj. Yardley had tasked 2d Lieutenant Dan DeLeo to take 30 paratroopers, along with two Free French volunteers, to assault the El Djem Bridge. DeLeo and all of the raiders were 509th replacements, who had arrived in England in October too late to make the jump on La Senia.

These replacements had the requisite airborne training, but none of the raiders had made a combat jump. The El Djem raid would be a fitting test of their mettle. It was their turn.

By December 21st, higher command had overruled or ignored all of Genero's objections. The raid was on and scheduled to be executed on Christmas Eve. When he learned of the decision, Genero went ballistic. Then Genero learned of the second mission, the one that Maj. Yardley designed to piggyback on the El Djem raid. That one put him into the ozone.

Genero had been healing for nearly 30 days, and his left hand was doing well. He was back on full-duty status. He still wore a dressing on his hand, but that was just a precaution, designed to guard against infection.

On December 22, 1942, Phil learned that in addition to sending Dan DeLeo on a fool's errand against the El Djem Bridge, Sergeant LeBlanc and another French-speaking American private had volunteered to go with Captain Anton on a suicide mission.

The intelligence staff at higher headquarters did not have a clear understanding of the German and Italian order of battle in northeast Tunisia. In mid-December, the Axis forces had great success flying troops in by transport and glider. The Germans also managed to ship powerful armored forces into its beachhead near Bizerte.

New German formations appeared on the battlefield west of Tunis daily. The Germans fielded armored forces in ever increasing size and strength. Elite units, like *Fallschirmjaeger*, appeared in Tunisia in substantial numbers in both the north and southeast.

The Americans and British had a good estimate of the size of German and Italian units in the field. They had no good intelligence concerning how many more German armored and airborne formations were in reserve in the rear.

II Corps Headquarters decided to send in a special operations team to reconnoiter. Since DeLeo would jump into a drop zone three miles north of El Djem, an alert staffer thought it might be possible to send in an additional four men to jump with DeLeo's raiders.

Instead of heading south with the raiders, the special operators would move north toward Sfax and insert themselves into the pocket where the large formations of German reserves might be forming. The small team would all speak French and they would blend into the French Colonial culture.

The insertion team would take a special radio. If they succeeded in gathering the anticipated intelligence, they would send a coded message. If the conditions were right, a British submarine would extract the special team. The team and the submarine would rendezvous at an appointed time at a point along the east coast of Tunisia to be designated later.

"Sir," Genero began when he reported his findings to Maj. Yardley, "the insertion mission is even more ridiculous than the bridge raid. There are twenty-five reasons why this mission will fail. For example, Captain Anton is a brave Legionnaire, but he's never jumped from a plane."

"Anton's not airborne?" Yardley asked.

"That's right, Major."

"Well, Genero, give him some instruction and get him a practice jump. II Corps wants this intelligence and we're sending in a team. Do it now!" Yardley ordered.

Genero accomplished his mission early on December 23rd. As a precaution, Phil made two training jumps with Anton.

Phil need not have bothered. Anton loved jumping from airplanes. In fact, he liked it a lot more than Genero, who—with 42 jumps to his credit—had gotten over his initial infatuation with the process.

By Christmas Eve of 1942, Genero began to see the whole airborne concept in a larger context. *Jumping is simply a mode of transportation. It's an important one to be sure, but it's only a means to an end: moving elite Infantry into battle quickly to achieve a tactical advantage,* Phil thought as he helped prepare Anton for his mission.

Despite II Corps' insistence, late in the day on the 23rd, it looked like Col. Raff would scrub the intelligence-gathering mission. Then just before midnight, 24 hours before time over target in eastern Tunisia, Raff reestablished the covert insertion with one important change.

Raff insisted that Capt. Genero lead the covert mission and that Anton go along as the second-in-command. The colonel had sound reasons to make this alteration to the higher headquarters plan. Genero and Anton had worked well together in the battle south of Feriana. They were a proven team.

"Genero, I fully comprehend the tactical importance of getting reliable intelligence about the 5$^{th}$ Panzer Army order of battle. I just don't trust the French after only seven weeks of fighting in this Theater of Operations. I want an American to lead the mission. That means you, bub! Are you up for it?" Raff challenged.

Upon learning of his assignment, Phil put all of his objections aside and worked without sleep for the next 18 hours to put the mission together. Once again, Phil intended to sleep in the plane on the way to the drop zone.

During the flight to El Djem, Phil had a pleasant flashback to the last happy Christmas for his family. That was three years earlier at the end of 1939.

Mark and Kari had gotten engaged. The family had enjoyed a sumptuous Christmas Eve dinner. Uncle Angelo and Uncle John had been at the top of their game. The Christmas carols and traditional Italian songs had lent a perfect tone to the evening.

When he wasn't dozing, Phil wondered what his parents were doing in Carlisle. *It must be afternoon there. God, please take the pain of Kari's loss away for one night. Let mom and dad have a good Christmas,* Phil prayed.

A few minutes before midnight, the red light went on in the C-47. Genero and his team stood at the front of the stick on this aircraft. The rest of the men were in DeLeo's raiding party. Dan and the balance of his team had crammed into the other C-47.

The jump went fairly well. It was as routine as jumping at night onto a hard desert floor in country controlled by a skilled and dedicated enemy could be.

Phil brought a surprise for the Frenchmen. When Genero's team met at the assembly point, he pinned American jump wings on the left breast pocket flap of the two new Franco-American paratroopers.

Both Frenchmen kissed Phil on the cheek after he pinned the wings on them. The French practice of men kissing men on the cheek was awkward for Genero. Only his father, his uncles, and now these crazy Frenchmen had been able to get away with it.

Without further ado, the five special operators moved out to the north. Before leaving, Phil shook Dan DeLeo's hand and wished him well. Genero didn't envy Dan's raiders. They had a difficult march, a sharp fight, a tricky demolition, and a very long trek back to the American lines. In comparison to the El Djem raid, infiltrating Sfax would be a Sunday stroll.

After only ten minutes on the drop zone, including the ad hoc award ceremony, the five-man special operations team struck north along the railroad. Their plan required them to stay along the tracks for three to four hours, detouring only when necessary to avoid detection.

The team moved in a group of four with one man scouting 40 yards in front. All of the team members, including Phil, were to rotate through this assignment.

When the team reached a designated switching station along the track, 65 kilometers from Sfax, they would set an azimuth of 15 degrees and proceed north, northeast. The team would hide and rest up during the day. They would begin the trek again at night.

They expected to be north of Sfax in three nights. If everything went well—two or three nights later—a British submarine would pick them up in along the northern shore of the Gulf of Gabes.

Two and a half hours into the trek north, Sergeant Jean Chagny, acting as scout, brought the group to an abrupt halt. He'd seen something troubling.

Genero and Anton snuck forward to check out their latest predicament. This one turned out to be mind-boggling. The El Djem Bridge lay dead ahead.

Anton spoke first in whispered English, "My friend, it cannot be! This must be another bridge to the north of DeLeo's target."

"No, Louis, this is the fucking bridge! Even in the dark, I recognize it and the terrain features. It's the target bridge all right. Holy shit!!"

"Mon Dieu!!" Anton exclaimed softly in French. "This means that the sons of whores in your Air Force dropped us south of the bridge, not north. This also means that if your lieutenant has made the same assumption as we, he has marched with his entire team for several hours in the wrong direction," Anton added.

"Louis," Genero responded, "if De Leo continued on his course, that means he's at least five hours south of here. Even if he somehow recognizes his error, he can't get here in time to blow the bridge. If Dan doesn't realize where he is, he might run smack into the German garrison 20 miles south of the bridge. We noted a Nazi installation in the last intelligence analysis. Shit, he could be walking smack into the lion's den."

"Phillipe, is there anything that you think that we can do to the bridge?" Anton asked.

Phil thought about Anton's question. *We're the only allied force with an opportunity to blow this bridge. But what can we do with five lightly armed soldiers against this target?* Phil thought. *We don't have any explosives and there's no telling what we'll find near the bridge. Our mission is to go north to infiltrate Sfax and learn the order of battle of the 5th Panzer Army.*

"Louis," Phil began, "We're not prepared to attack the bridge. Our mission is in the north. We're duty bound to proceed on that assignment, even if we have to skulk around the bridge."

"I think you are right, Phillipe," Anton agreed.

"If DeLeo and his raiders realize the mistake and get here in time, fine. If they don't, it will be a monumental blunder to add the failure of the intelligence gathering mission to the failure of the assault on the bridge," Phil observed.

"Oui, Phillipe. We must move on to see what the Boche are up to in the north." Anton granted after considering the alternatives for 30 seconds.

"Men, gather around," Phil whispered. When the others had drawn close enough to hear, he continued, "We have to move north. We don't have time to skirt the ravine. We'll have to risk climbing down in darkness, crossing the stream, negotiating the other side, and moving across the plain. Sound discipline and stealth are paramount. We'll sacrifice speed for security. Everyone check your equipment. No mistakes! Let's go. Sergeant Chagny, lead us out."

*We're already hours behind schedule,* Genero thought. *This fucking detour will cost precious time. We'll be lucky to get across the ravine and a few miles north by daylight. We can't risk moving during the day, especially this far from Sfax. We'll find a spot. Dig in and cover up. No matter how you look at it, those bastards in the Air Corps cost us an entire day!*

As it happened, DeLeo would not realize the mistake for another two hours. Since the bridge was not where he thought it would be, DeLeo wasn't sure whether the Air Corps had dropped his raiders north of the bridge or south of it.

With dawn approaching, DeLeo decided to abandon the search for the El Djem Bridge and settle on blowing up a large section of the railroad tracks.

As dawn broke, De Leo's demolition experts rigged the TNT along a stretch of track about the length of a football field. DeLeo reasoned that the destruction of the tracks in this manner might not slow the Jerries for long, but it was better than nothing.

When the charges were ready, DeLeo sent most of the personnel west in two and three man teams to find their way back as best they could. Then he set the charges. He and five of the men ran like hell.

The resulting explosion destroyed a respectable amount of railroad track. It also alerted every Nazi in the local garrison, only a few miles to the south.

While the demolition experts rigged the charges, DeLeo got a fix on his actual position. His raiders were 20 miles south of the target bridge. In addition to the humiliation of missing the target, the trek south had added at least ten miles to their escape route. To rejoin the 509th, he and his men had to negotiate 90 miles of enemy-held territory.

By the time DeLeo blew the stretch of track, Genero and his team had traversed the ravine and were two miles north of the El Djem bridge and 400 yards west of the railroad track.

At dawn, Sgt. Chagny found a modest depression in the plain away from the track. The men dug in and covered up. An enemy would have to get within ten yards of the hidden position to see anything. In that vast expanse of open country, it was unlikely. Besides, it was raining like hell. While the rain gave Phil's team additional cover, all of the men were soaked and miserable.

Even though the special operations team was 20 miles north of DeLeo's explosion, Capt. Anton later claimed that he heard it. Louis Anton maintained that with only one good eye, he always slept with one ear open.

A few hours after dawn, Phil awoke from a very deep sleep by a firm shake from Anton. As Genero's eyes tried to focus in the dim light cast through the overcast sky, Anton's face was less than a foot away from his own.

"Be very quiet, Phillipe," Anton whispered. "The Boche are close. They seem to be looking for us. Stay very still."

Immediately understanding, Genero rose out of the shallow hole, now half full of water. Following Anton, he slithered through the mud to the lip of the depression. He raised his head only so that he could see to the east.

Sure enough, 400 yards away, 20 German soldiers patrolled along both sides of the railroad track. They moved slowly. Their leader kept looking at the ground, as if he were trying to pick up on sign or spoor.

*This doesn't make sense,* Phil reasoned. *If that faint explosion was DeLeo, he had to be several miles to the south. Why would the Jerries be looking for us this far north?*

Genero and Anton watched the German patrol's progress for three quarters of an hour, until the enemy file became a blur in the distance. Breathing easier, Phil looked around. As far as he could see, the ground was flat, open, and empty.

Feeling safer, Genero addressed Anton, "What were the Jerries doing? Why would they be tracking like that this far north? I guess it's a good thing that it's raining. That will make it harder to find our trail."

"Phillipe, by now the Boche know a great deal. I suspect that they know how many of us went north and the details and goals of our mission. Depending upon their techniques, they may even know our names and the name of the last woman each of us has loved," Anton commented bitterly.

Genero looked puzzled, so Anton continued, "My dear friend, if the German swine have captured even one of DeLeo's men, they have made him...how do you Americans say it...sing like a parakeet?"

"You mean pigeon, Louis. A guy who squeals on a buddy is a stool pigeon," Phil explained, as he began to understand Anton's point.

"What makes you think that one of our guys gave us up?" Phil asked in an irritated tone, feeling anger at the French captain for the first time since they met at Youks Les Bains.

"It's the reality of war, my young friend. If the Germans capture some of your paratroopers, one will talk. It is not that they are not brave. It is only that they are human. Any man can be broken. You must trust me on this. I know what I say is true," Anton responded.

"How can you say that, Louis? Could someone break you? Wouldn't you die rather than give the enemy information to harm your friends? Why, that's as bad as treason," Genero snapped.

"Thank God, I've never been put to the test, but I tell you that I have broken brave and resourceful men. I've done this thing personally," Anton stated.

"You have tortured prisoners?" Genero asked in disbelief.

"Don't sound so surprised, or so full of...how you say...rightness," Anton snapped back, becoming peeved at the naiveté of the man commanding the mission 90 miles behind enemy lines.

"You mean righteousness," Phil corrected.

"I mean that I have done what I had to do to protect my country. I took no joy in it, but, oui, I tortured prisoners. I saved the lives of some of my men by doing it," Anton said smugly in French, tiring of the dialog with Genero in English.

"Captain Anton, I did not permit your sergeant to abuse the Italians at Feriana. You will torture no prisoner while you are under my command. Is that clear?" Genero ordered.

"Phillipe, it is true. I am under your command. I will do my duty, and obey your orders. I will also do everything I have to do to complete this important mission and get all of us back to our lines. Is that clear?" Anton responded.

Though Genero understood the words that Anton had uttered, he couldn't be sure that the Frenchman was agreeing or disagreeing with him. Phil decided not to push it.

The team would need all of its resources just to avoid getting captured. There was no need to squabble with the brave French captain in the middle of the Tunisian plain, while they sat in a half submerged foxhole, soaked to the bone, far from the goal of the mission, and equally far from the relative safety of their own lines.

Consistent with their plan, Phil and his team laid up in the soggy depression all throughout Christmas Day. They saw no other German patrols or much of anything else.

In the early afternoon, they observed one military supply train chugging slowly south. The Axis commanders had posted Italian soldiers on the tops of the boxcars to act as guards.

After sunset, the five soldiers set out again. This time, they marched for almost four hours before they ran into trouble.

Only one of the infiltrators had received any training with radios. However, the special radio that they carried would be their lifeline on this mission.

Since no one knew much about the device, and its transmission time was limited, Maj. Yardley insisted that Sgt. Le Blanc receive a basic orientation on radio operations before the mission.

Le Blanc was the right choice since he was very bright and maintained a life-long love affair with all things technical. Unfortunately, over the last week Le Blanc had developed a serious cold.

By Christmas Day, the constant rain, the intemperate weather, and the long day spent in the shallow, wet depression caused Le Blanc to begin to cough. On Christmas Night, Le Blanc's cough became persistent, raspy, and loud. He had trouble controlling it.

Around 2200 Hours, Phil moved his team to the west, a few hundred yards farther from the track. The men needed a rest. There appeared to be a village or station up ahead. He asked Anton to scout it out. Louis moved out into the darkness.

Genero decided that if Le Blanc's cough continued, the sergeant would have to leave the infiltration mission and head west toward the American lines. Phil hated to put his loyal subordinate through that additional risk, but he had no choice. With all of the coughing, it was a matter of time until Le Blanc compromised the mission. Sgt. Le Blanc would understand the decision.

Since there wasn't a convenient depression or other terrain feature in which to take refuge, Phil ordered a stop and everyone took a knee. At that moment Le Blanc's cough became uncontrollable. While he made a heroic effort to suppress it, in the barren desert the sound of his coughing carried dangerously far.

Phil stepped over to Le Blanc in order to evaluate the non-com's condition. At that moment Genero spotted something unidentifiable moving to the northwest. Instantly, he gave a whispered order to freeze, and dropped silently to the ground.

The three other soldiers quickly obeyed. All remained completely still.

Even Le Blanc maintained control. He removed his stocking cap from his head and stuffed a corner into his mouth to help muffle his coughing.

The men listened hard and stared futilely into the black night. At first they detected nothing unusual.

Then they heard the distinct, military sound of a metal bolt chambering a round in a weapon. The resulting clang reverberated and echoed for hundreds of yards.

There was no question that some number of the enemy had crept up on them. From the sound of the weapon being charged, at least one of them had taken a position to the northwest.

Phil gave a series of hand signals and all of the men readied their own weapons. Genero pulled a hand grenade from his webbing. He made sure that the pin was ready to be pulled. Then he waited.

Phil was concerned for Anton. The French officer hadn't returned from his scouting mission and he might not be aware that the enemy was so close. Capt. Anton might stumble into them on his way back. The thought of Anton getting jumped by a bunch of Germans or Italians made Phil very tense. He could feel his own heart beat by the throbbing in his temple.

A moment later, Phil spotted more movement, perhaps 40 yards off. He saw several ghostly figures, ten or more, moving slowly and cautiously from the west directly to the east.

Apparently, the enemy soldiers didn't realize that Phil and his men lay quietly on their right flank. If the enemy soldiers maintained their present formation and continued on the same azimuth, they would miss Genero and his men by twenty yards.

*All we have to do is stay put and remain silent and calm,* Phil thought. *The Krauts will go right past us, hopefully all the way to the tracks. Once they've passed, we'll slip further west and resume our march north. The only catch is Louis. Where in the fuck is he? Well, there's nothing I can do. We'll just have to sit it out.*

As Phil waited and listened, he couldn't help but admire the professionalism of the enemy. Other than the sound of the bolt, they'd made no discernable noise for several moments. In fact, the only way that Phil could follow their movements was to lie flat on the ground and pick them out against the ambient light on the northern horizon.

After several more tense moments, the ghosts swept past the allied position. They'd moved 30 to 40 yards off to the northeast, when Le Blanc started to cough again.

The cough was barely audible, even to Phil who was no more than 15 feet from Le Blanc. The sound sent a cold chill down Genero's spine. He knew the enemy had heard it.

Phil silently readied the pin in the grenade in his bandaged left hand. Sgt. Chagny followed Genero's example and prepared a grenade.

*Throwing a grenade in this darkness will not compromise our position. Hopefully the explosions will kill or confuse the enemy. Hand grenades are definitely the right tactic,* Genero thought.

While he waited for the enemy soldiers to make a mistake, Phil concluded that he was facing Germans, not Italians. From what he had seen in the last several weeks, the Italians didn't have the discipline, field craft, or soldierly characteristics to move in the manner of these ghosts.

The German panzer grenadiers and motorized infantry-men couldn't have pulled it off either. They were good soldiers, but skulking around the desert at night was not their strong suit.

*These ghosts might be SS or Fallschirmjaeger,* Genero worried. *I haven't seen any reports that the German High Command has sent SS to North Africa. These guys must be German paratroops.*

Just then, one of the ghost-like figures materialized out of the darkness only 15 yards northeast of Phil's position. The German knelt on one knee, peered into the darkness, and pointed his weapon in the direction of the Americans.

Phil and his men were all prone. The German could not see them. Still, the German knew the Americans were there. It was as if he could sense their presence.

Genero watched the German for a full three minutes. The Nazi did not move or make a sound. He waited for the Americans to make a mistake.

Finally, the German point man crept three yards closer to the Americans. Phil had been right. The man was a Nazi paratrooper. Phil recognized the unique, simple round shape of the German airborne helmet, which looked distinctly different from the Fritz helmet with its flared bottom rim that the Wehrmacht and SS infantry wore.

Amazingly, the point man hadn't detected the Allied po-sitions. A moment later, another figure joined the first.

The two figures whispered hurriedly.

*Thank God!* Phil thought. *The soldier who makes the first mistake dies. I can barely hear their whispering, but it's definitely German.*

"Can you make out where they are?" The second Nazi soldier whispered to the point man.

"Be quiet! Stay still!" The point man whispered back, in a more urgent tone, "They're very close. I can smell them."

Fully understanding the brief exchange between the German paratroops, Phil thought, *maybe he can smell us. I noticed at Feriana that the Germans and Italians smelled very different from us. Must be the food, uniforms, and equipment.*

"Go back to Hermann; tell him to take two men and move to the right. You take two men and move to the left. I will move straight ahead with the other four," the point man directed.

*The point man is probably a senior non-com*, Phil thought. *He's good, seems to know what he's doing. If I permit them to flank and envelop us, we're done for. I won't allow the Jerries to surround us. We've got no choice. Show time!*

With a nod at Sgt. Chagny, Phil pulled the pin of the hand grenade and let the spring-loaded spoon fly off the grenade. Genero counted two seconds, and then he and Chagny threw their grenades directly at the two Germans.

It took an instant for the grenades to travel to the feet of the two Nazis. They both had exactly one second to react. Although both were veteran soldiers, neither could do a thing about the grenades.

Both grenades exploded in a deafening roar, blinding flash and with enough force to pick up the senior sergeant and throw him back 15 feet. He was dead before he hit the ground.

The second German paratrooper was standing over Chagny's grenade when it exploded. The force of the explosion tore off a great chunk of his right leg. He immediately went into shock and never regained consciousness.

The explosions caused two of the other Germans to fire their weapons in the general direction of the Americans. Genero and his men maintained their discipline and responded effectively with hand grenades.

The Americans did not open fire until the *Fallschirmjaeger* tried to rush forward. Fearing that the Germans would overrun them, Genero and his team fired point-blank into four of the Germans, killing two outright and wounding two.

One of the wounded Germans pulled his own hand grenade, a device that the Americans referred to as a potato masher. He tossed into the midst of the Americans. It landed between Le Blanc and his radio.

Later Phil could not determine if Le Blanc had seen the grenade or if he hadn't been able to find it in the dark. When the grenade exploded, it killed Le Blanc instantly. The explosion riddled his body and reduced the special radio into a pile of scrap.

There had been 11 German paratroopers in that patrol. Three were still effective. They decided to withdraw. They ran directly into Captain Anton, who calmly killed all three with well-placed short bursts of his Thompson submachine gun.

The entire firefight lasted less than three minutes. Genero and his men killed eight Germans and seriously wounded three. Though they had won the firefight, the destruction of the radio doomed their primary mission.

They couldn't go forward with the infiltration plan. Further incursion into Sfax was out of the question. There'd be no way to report what they learned and no way to arrange their own extraction.

Their only alternative was to follow the plan of the bridge raiders. They would escape and evade to the west toward the American lines, across enemy-held eastern Tunisia.

It would be a daunting task through a countryside already alerted and looking for American paratroopers on foot. Their chances were slim and none.

Then Anton came up with an idea. "Phillipe, I saw the transportation that the Nazi paratroops used to get here. There's an armored car and two motorcycles with sidecars," Anton explained. "We should take the motorcycles and head west immediately after we disable the armored car."

"Won't we be sitting ducks on those cycles?" Genero asked Anton.

"If we take the overcoats from the dead Boche and use their unique helmets, we'd look like German paratroops from a distance. If we show courage and have some luck, we might get away with it," Anton argued.

"Louis, driving those things at night will be dangerous, but if it works, we'll have a twenty-mile head start on the Germans who must be moving this way based on the sound of our skirmish. Let's fucking do it," Genero concluded.

An hour later, after burying Sgt. La Blanc in a shallow grave and caring for the German wounded, the Americans and Frenchmen sped off on the motorcycles, hoping to pass as harried German *Fallschirmjaeger* in the event that they encountered enemy forces.

Genero and his team used the motorcycles for two days. Phil estimated that they covered 30 to 35 miles before they abandoned the vehicles in a dry wash. The little band continued the rest of the trek west on foot.

The entire Tunisian countryside crawled with German and Italian patrols. The locals turned out to be suspicious and uncooperative at best, and downright hostile at worst.

Each of the paratroopers had a survival kit, which included gold and silver coins. Anton and Chagny had rifled the bodies of the dead German paratroopers and confiscated any money that they had. During the trek, the men used all of these resources to barter for food with the local Arabs and Berbers on those occasions when Anton thought it might be safe.

The rain and the cold continued unabated, but the bad weather was an ally. The rain made tracking the Americans very difficult. It also inhibited the team's progress. Some nights they made less than two miles. Some days they made more but had to double back to avoid detection. The days turned into weeks.

After the second week, it became obvious to Genero that the Krauts had built up substantial offensive forces east of the American lines in central Tunisia. These soldiers were not there to look for a handful of American paratroopers trying to return from a failed mission.

"Louis, we've been evading the Krauts for two weeks. We've seen more German units than I ever expected," Genero conceded to his French counterpart during a rare break in the trek.

"They're planning an offensive, Phillipe. There is no doubt."

"Where will they strike, Louis?"

"Somewhere to the west. Who can know for sure?" Anton answered.

"Louis, it's ironic. We were sent on one kind of intelligence gathering mission and we find ourselves learning something we didn't expect. If we can figure out this German build-up, our mission will not be a complete failure."

Eventually, the special operators found themselves in the eastern foothills to the Dorsal Mountains. If they could get across, the American and British lines were on the other side.

Because of the number of German patrols and the continuing bad weather, it took Phil and his men almost a week to get safely across the mountains. By the time that the four soldiers encountered Corporal St. Jacques, it was the middle of January.

All of the men had lost weight. Chagny had picked up an infection and was pissing a lot of blood. All of the men were exhausted.

They had important news for Col. Raff. The Germans were about to strike directly west, perhaps through the Kasserine Pass. The enemy armored formations were coming in strength. There wasn't much time to prepare.

# Chapter 34

1400 Hours
January 20, 1943
Washington Navy Yard
Washington, D.C.

Lieutenant Tim Sullivan looked up from the drawing board in the weapons research center and tried to uncross his eyes. He'd been staring at the technical drawings for the new dual-purpose gun for over two hours.

Tim glanced at his watch. *Damn it! I've missed lunch again,* he realized. *I'm too focused these days. When I concentrate on a project, I lose track of everything. Maybe it's just as well. I'm still not keen on eating in front of other people.*

*I've got to admit that the surgeons have done a great job on my face,* Tim thought. *Most people won't notice my wounds. You have to be close and look hard to tell that the Jap anti-aircraft artillery nearly tore off my lips. I wish I had more nerve function. I still don't have much feeling in the upper part of my right cheek. On balance, I'm very lucky! A couple more inches and the Jap Triple-A would've made me fish bait at the bottom of the Pacific along with scores of my shipmates. I should count my blessings. I still have my eyesight, sense of smell, hearing, and taste.*

By January 20, 1943, Tim Sullivan had been back to duty for months. He felt good to be out of the hospital, but his current assignment bored him.

Instead of the frantic and exhilarating life of a naval aviator, he now filled a mundane shore billet at the Washington Navy Yard. His present job required him to use his engineering skills to help get the bugs out of the prototype of the new rapid-fire 5-inch .38 dual-purpose naval gun.

*Who says the Navy doesn't have a sense of humor?* Sullivan thought as he rolled up the drawings to stow away. *A Jap gunner nearly took my head off and left me disfigured. Triple-A has all but ended my career as a pilot. Now the Navy wants me to help improve these guns, so that our sailors can shoot Jap pilots out of the sky. Very funny, indeed!*

Tim's new job provided professional rewards, like the chance to publish in technical journals. The assignment could be an opportunity to gain recognition with the clubby and exclusive northeastern engineering societies. Any tangible success in fielding the dual-purpose gun would almost certainly translate into a promotion to lieutenant commander and generate much-improved prospects for a civilian career after the war. Ironically, when he graduated from the Penn State engineering program—with honors— he'd dreamt of a job like this one.

*Though I never had the balls to mention it him, I always hoped that Paul Reilly and I would be partners in a blue-chip engineering consulting firm. Of course, the fucking war intervened. Now Paul's flying combat missions in Europe and I'm here, stuck in a shore billet.* Tim sighed as he looked around for his cover, so he could leave the building and scare up some good old Navy chow.

Despite these prospects and when he wasn't working on his engineering solutions, Tim manically plotted a return to flight status, a scenario that everyone—except Tim—thought unlikely.

Tim missed the wild adrenaline ride of the bomber jock. His former shipmates—and his old roommate—faced aerial combat's dangers every day while Tim enjoyed his safe job in the states. Although he'd been seriously wounded, he was ashamed that his life was no longer on the line when others were losing theirs. His dream assignment had become a nightmare. *I'm back here getting medals when I should be killing Japs,* he thought.

Before Christmas, in a formal ceremony in the office of the Chief of Naval Operations, Admiral King had pinned the Navy Cross on Tim's blue tunic. Tim's mother came down from Erie to attend the award ceremony. When the admiral's dog-robber read Tim's citation and his mother heard the details of her son's gallantry, she wept.

Before she returned to Erie, Tim's mom pointed out that an assignment in the District of Columbia had certain social advantages. Tim knew that she was hoping for a daughter-in-law with grandchildren to follow.

Most nights, when he was off-duty, there was a party somewhere, where he could meet beautiful young women who'd come north from small towns throughout the South to work as clerks and secretaries in the various bureaus, departments, committees, and offices in the Executive and Legislative Branches of the Federal Government.

Although his wound made him self-conscious, his Navy Cross, Distinguished Flying Cross, and three Purple Hearts revealed him to be a genuine war hero to the hordes of young women who'd traveled to Washington to meet a well-educated and dashing young officer.

For the first time in his life, Tim got laid regularly. He sometimes reflected that none of the men who died at Midway would ever again get to experience the sensuality of a woman's touch or experience the thrill of a long anticipated orgasm. He owed it to them to take full advantage of his newly discovered opportunities.

In Washington in early 1943, mores were vastly different than they had been in Happy Valley in 1940 or Erie in 1936. The young girls wanted to experiment and expand their sexual horizons.

The government had called up millions of young men and boys to serve in the military. All knew that they might die for their country. Young women and men lived for the day, since for some there would not be a tomorrow.

On the other hand, people hoped for better times in 1943. 1942 had proven to be a very difficult year.

The war news had not been all bad. The Navy had fought hard in the Pacific. The Japanese Empire no longer posed an imminent threat to the United States or to the Territory of Hawaii.

Lieutenant Colonel James H. Doolittle had led the first successful air raid on the Japanese Home Islands. The Navy had claimed victory in the close contest in the Coral Sea and had clearly prevailed at Midway. At the moment the Pacific Fleet fought the Battle for the Solomons and supported the Army's defensive campaign in New Guinea. The Marines had conducted the first offensive action against the Japanese with their landing at Guadalcanal and the seizure of a vital airfield. Unfortunately, the outcomes of these conflicts were still very much in doubt.

In Europe, the Army had finally gone on the offensive and invaded North Africa, but the contest was still anyone's to win. Thankfully, the tactical picture looked far better for the Allies than the Axis since British troops had recaptured Tobruk that November.

There had been two very promising strategic developments in the war. Montgomery had pushed Rommel out of Egypt through Libya and into a pocket in southeastern Tunisia. More ominously for the Germans, the Russians had—at long last—stopped the Nazi advance at Stalingrad on the Volga River. In the last few weeks, the Russians had surrounded an entire German Army. The prospects were very bad for the encircled Nazis. Stalingrad shaped up to be the first major setback for the German Wehrmacht in Europe in over three years of horrific fighting.

The encouraging developments in the Pacific, North Africa, and along the Volga River provided only limited evidence of a trend toward final victory. In fact, Winston Churchill had addressed this very issue, explaining: "Now this is not the end. It is not even the beginning of the end. But it is, perhaps, the end of the beginning."

There was still a lot of fighting to do. The war was far from won. Many difficult months, maybe several years, lay ahead.

On January 23rd, Tim attended a special party at the home of Alice Roosevelt Longworth. "Mrs. L," as she was known, was the most famous of the Washington celebrity hostesses. Her reign began before the Great War and continued unabated throughout World War II.

For decades, an invitation to a Longworth party guaranteed A-list status all over the District. In 1943, as she approached her 60th year, Alice Longworth had achieved the height of her power. Politicians from Foggy Bottom to Capitol Hill courted her support. Grown men groveled for the opportunity to attend a function at Mrs. L's.

The oldest child of Theodore Roosevelt and the most precocious, Mrs. Longworth had become an outspoken, self-centered, egotistical, highly influential power broker.

In addition to being Teddy's daughter, she was also the distant cousin of Franklin and Eleanor Roosevelt, the President and First Lady of the United States in 1943. Normally, a blood relationship would guarantee an insider's privilege with the first couple.

In Alice's case, she wielded tremendous influence with the Roosevelt Administration, despite the fact that she was not a democrat and had been openly critical, even contemptuous, of both Cousin Franklin and Cousin Eleanor.

Mrs. Longworth constantly hosted and attended the District's social functions. On this occasion she had invited to her home a number of young officers who all had one thing in common.

Each of the young men had, like her beloved father, distinguished himself in combat with a sworn enemy of the United States. To counterbalance the testosterone, Mrs. L invited an appropriate number of young women.

At her parties, Alice Longworth insisted on being the center of attention. She had a quick and acerbic wit, which she wielded with a rapier-like tongue.

Although Tim arrived fashionably late, was properly outfitted in his mess dress with all of his dazzling medals, and was the equal or better of any hero in the house, he felt uncomfortable. With her well-honed instinct for mayhem, and the skills borne of four decades in Washington, Alice pounced on poor Lt. Tim Sullivan the minute he appeared in her foyer.

As an interrogator, Alice had no equal since the Spanish Inquisition. Within ten minutes, she had Tim telling her the story of his life and relating all of his hopes and dreams.

"Mister Sullivan, it sounds like you're doing important work at the Navy Yard. Getting this project on its feet could materially assist the war effort and save hundreds, maybe thousands of sailors. Are you certain that you want to walk away from this project and go back to flying dive bombers?" Mrs. Longworth asked, after listening intently to Sullivan's story.

"Yes, ma'am," Sullivan replied. "I can't really explain to you why I feel this way. I know I have it very good here. I guess that I could claim to have done my part in this war. No one would quibble with me about that, not in the face of a Navy Cross, a DFC, and three Purple Hearts."

"That's certainly true, Mr. Sullivan," Mrs. L agreed. "You have already done your duty at Midway. Even if you went back to the Pacific, the chance of you sinking more Japanese ships is remote. However, it's quite possible, even probable, that you'll get wounded again or much, much worse!"

"That's very true. I think about that all of the time. Candidly, it scares the hell out of me! Sorry, ma'am. I didn't mean to curse," Sullivan apologized awkwardly.

"Mr. Sullivan, I'm no shrinking violet. I've heard much worse," Mrs. L replied while laughing softly. "My father liked to hang around with cowboys, boxers, and soldiers. I've heard it all. But I do understand your fears."

"Thanks, ma'am. It means a lot that you would listen to my tale of woe. I'll leave it at this: I wish this war were over. I don't want to, but I must go back. I will never rest easy if I'm in some plush shore billet, while what's left of my shipmates have to go in harm's way without me. It haunts me constantly. I'll do anything to get back out to the Fleet."

"What's the Navy's position?" Mrs. Longworth asked.

"The commander of the Navy Yard wants me to go on a tour selling war bonds," Tim responded. "I know that's important too, but—well—you know how I feel. I can't explain it any better, ma'am."

"Mr. Sullivan, I've been ignoring my other guests. I best be getting back to being the hostess of this little party. I have a hunch that things will work out for you. Excuse me, now. Be sure to come and visit me again."

Normally, Mrs. L would have dismissed Tim's circumstances as inconsequential and unimportant. After all, they could not possibly affect her life in any way.

Over the next two hours, she reflected on Tim's story; first about Pearl Harbor, and then about Midway. She knew that pushing for his reassignment—even though that was what he wanted—would put him in awkward political territory, but she didn't care. The fact that she would cause angst and consternation in the Department of the Navy was icing on the cake.

On Friday January 29, 1943, Captain Lewis K. Young, a special projects officer assigned to the Chief of Naval Operations, summoned Lt. Tim Sullivan to the CNO's office. He had a three-fold agenda.

First, Capt. Young wanted to inform Mister Sullivan that a special board of officers had met earlier in the week and selected him for promotion to lieutenant commander. Since his selection would not be final for three to four months, the CNO had decided to frock Mr. Sullivan.

The Navy custom of 'frocking' meant that the Navy would promote Sullivan in rank, but not advance him in pay grade until the Navy Department cut the final orders. Other than pay, he would have all the rights and privileges of a lieutenant commander.

Most officers cared far more for the rank than the pay. Rank, especially to officers like Captain Young who had been frocked twice since Pearl Harbor, meant everything.

Second, the CNO had decided to restore Mister Sullivan to flight status. Even more importantly, the Navy would assign Sullivan to the trials for the new Grumman F6F 'Hellcat' fighter. This plane was the fighter that Navy planners hoped would sweep the Japanese Zeros from the Pacific skies. By summer, the Navy wanted the Hellcat on at least three carriers in the Pacific Fleet. If the Hellcat lived up to its expectations, the Japs were in for a nasty surprise.

Third, Capt. Young needed to explain the political and professional realities to this newly promoted commander. There were perilous risks to using back channels to obtain plum assignments.

Using a back channel might achieve a near-term goal. However, if noted in the CNO's special file, it could irretrievably harm an otherwise stellar career.

*The fact that Sullivan fought at Pearl Harbor and Midway, had shot down two Japanese aircraft while flying dive bombers, had helped to sink two Japanese carriers, with hundreds of experienced pilots and thousands of irreplaceable technicians, had been wounded—seriously—both times, and been cited for valor only means that Mr. Sullivan is a hero,* Capt. Young thought as he prepared for the meeting. *Sullivan's gallantry is not the issue here. Heroics do not change Navy protocols. Valorous acts don't give Sullivan the right to flaunt the rules. Only the CNO has a right to flaunt the rules!*

Tim arrived at Capt. Young's office three minutes early. Young felt mildly disappointed because he liked to begin any meeting by raking an officer over the coals for not being punctual. A serious ass chewing could help to set the proper tone.

At exactly the appointed time, a chief yeoman ushered Mister Sullivan into Capt. Young's office. Sullivan reported smartly and correctly.

"Good you could make it, Mister Sullivan, especially on such short notice," Capt. Young began. "Please be seated."

Tim took the only other chair in the room, situated across from the captain. Sullivan uttered a simple, "Thank you, sir."

"Well, Mister Sullivan, I believe that I have some good news for you. Are you ready for some good news?" Capt. Young began.

"I can always use good news, sir." Sullivan responded, wondering why he had been called to the fabled inner sanctum of the Navy.

"Let's begin, shall we?" Capt. Young asked rhetorically. "You've been selected for promotion to lieutenant commander. Admiral King has a new assignment for you, so we're going to have you frocked on Monday at the Navy Yard. How's that sound?"

"What! I'm sorry, sir. What did you say, sir? I'm getting promoted on Monday?" Sullivan asked.

"That's right. Time is of the essence, here. The promotion is only part of the good news. Admiral King has decided to restore you to flight status; that is, if the medical board agrees, of course," Capt. Young said.

"I don't know what to say, sir," Tim responded.

"You might send a note to Admiral King to thank him," the captain suggested.

"Sir, why is time of the essence? You said that I have a new assignment, right? What might that be, sir?" Sullivan asked.

"We're assigning you to the F6F project. You'll help us iron out the engineering issues on this new fighter and you will help us with the air trials," Capt. Young said.

"What! The new Hellcat, sir? I'm going to fly the Hellcat?" Tim asked, not believing the news.

"That's right, Mr. Sullivan. You have to be in New York next week. So you can see why I said that time was short."

Tim sat across from the captain in complete disbelief. Had he not been seated in the CNO's suite of offices, he'd have assumed that the news was a well-constructed subterfuge, designed by the large contingent of practical jokers on the dual-purpose gun project.

Tim had not been privy to Mrs. L's decision to help him. Nor was he aware of any of Alice Longworth's machinations with her powerful political cronies. He was simply the unwitting beneficiary of her largesse.

Tim recoiled when the captain began to criticize him for going around the proper procedures for reassignment and warned him of the serious consequences of repeating this behavior. "Mr. Sullivan, let me temper this good news with some advice: it's perfectly fine for congressmen, senators, ambassadors, and cabinet members to use the influence of powerful friends to get what they want, but it's unseemly for a junior Naval officer."

*Damn it, I've done no such thing,* Tim thought. *I'd really like to tell this shore-based commando where to stick his promotion. God, what a pompous asshole! I suppose to him a junior officer is anyone without four stars on his flag.*

Tim struggled to hold his temper. It finally occurred to him that discretion here was the better part of valor. *I'll just keep my mouth shut and act like a respectful subordinate. After all, I'm back on flight status. I'm going to fly the fucking Hellcat. This motherfucker can keelhaul me for all I care.*

Through the balance of the meeting, Sullivan kept his own counsel and held his tongue through the trip to the woodshed. He concluded that the CNO and his high-ranking lackey were not his adversaries. In his mind, he had only two enemies: the entire armed forces of Japan, Germany, Italy, and their puppet allies—and incompetence.

In the first days of the war, incompetence and willful blindness, with their ally complacency, had caused Congress and the administration to place thousands of Sailors, Soldiers, Airmen, and Marines in harm's way with cheap third-rate equipment. American boys went into battle in 1941 and 1942 with tanks, planes, and cannon that could never meet the standards necessary to engage the sophisticated and experienced enemy. Even with the fiscal difficulties facing the Federal government during the Great Depression, the President and every experienced Congressman and Senator actually knew or should have realized that war with either Nazi Germany or Imperial Japan was a probability. Yet they hid their collective heads in the sand, pretended to do their jobs, and avoided making the tough political decisions that could have led to the development and fielding of better planes, tanks, and ships for the armed forces.

Many brave men died because of the incompetence, ignorance, and complacency. Sullivan could see no defense or justification for this monumental dereliction.

As the captain droned on, Tim flashed back to the Battle of Midway. He was flying high over the Japanese Fleet on his first run at the carrier group. *I'm adjusting the trim and I've armed my bomb. I look down on the deck and can see the fucking Zekes swarming all over my shipmates in those obscenely obsolete torpedo bombers. Those boys were virtually defenseless in the face of the Jap's advanced technology. The Nip bastards slaughtered them, almost to a man. I still feel guilty because if it weren't for their amazing courage and sacrifice, I would be dead and the Battle of Midway— and maybe this whole awful war—might have turned out very differently. Oh, God! Thank you for letting me go back.*

At that very moment, in the Office of the Chief of Naval Operations, Tim made a sacred vow: *If I survive the war, I will use my status as a war hero to gain political office. I will move heaven and earth for the rest of my life to guarantee that America will never be unprepared to face an implacable enemy again. So help me, God.*

# Chapter 35

C aptain Genero walked from the warm interior of the intelligence tent into the cold wet evening at the 509th's temporary headquarters. Phil looked carefully around the sandbagged defenses, noting the significant terrain features, like the normally dry wadi, now flush with the run off from the barren, sandstone buttes that dominated the encampment to the west.

*The Algerian frontier has to be the loneliest spot on earth,* Genero thought. *Only the Sahara Desert can compete with this place for sheer isolation.*

Phil pulled the collar of his jumpsuit tight around his neck as a defense against the wind, rain, and cold. The constant rain added to the situation's melancholy.

*I guess the circumstances are stabilizing to the east.* Genero considered the reports that he'd just reviewed for the commander's briefing at 1800. *Unfortunately, it's still awful.*

Capt. Genero was a witness, present on the outskirts of one of the most stunning and complete disasters in the long history of the American Army. So far in this war, only the loss of American forces on Bataan had eclipsed the severity of the Army's defeat on the rain soaked, gloomy battlefields near the Kasserine Pass.

Exact figures of the losses were not available. It was too soon.

*God help us! The Krauts have killed thousands of American boys. Even more are wounded or missing. The Afrika Korps must have taken thousands as prisoners. Whole battalions and most of some line regiments are gone. It's no consolation that Louis and I were right. If we'd been smart enough, we could have made the II Corps staff listen to reason.*

When Phil, Louis Anton, and the two non-coms returned from their difficult trek across Tunisia, Genero had reported the substantial German build up on the eastern slopes of the Dorsal Mountains. In his formal account, he had predicted that the Germans would try to punch through one or more of the passes in the mountains in order to attack the southern flank of the Anglo-American alliance in northern Tunisia to disrupt the supply centers in eastern Algeria.

II Corps and the British 1st Army were vulnerable. Genero had recommended that immediate steps be taken to counter the threat.

Though impressed with Genero's feat, crossing 90 miles of German-held territory and losing only one man, the allied command remained skeptical of Genero's report of a looming offensive. The Germans and Italians seemed to be in a weak position, caught in an immense strategic pincher. The generals and their staffs thought the Nazis and Fascists would stay behind their mountains and fight a losing defensive war. They recommended Genero for a citation. *Another booby prize*, he thought.

Despite their skepticism, when weather permitted, II Corps sent P-40s on reconnaissance flights along the eastern slopes of the Dorsal Mountains. The recon efforts disclosed Axis forces where Phil said they would be. However, the photographic evidence showed the German and Italian soldiers manning defensive positions. The allied commanders decided that the German troops posed no offensive threat to the Anglo-American southern flank.

Consequently, when Genero's prophecy failed to materialize by late January, 1943, the rear echelon staffers simply chalked up Phil's estimates to battlefield inflation. Genero's predictions were, no doubt, the product of fear and fatigue over a dangerous escape.

In mid-February, Rommel demonstrated why he richly deserved the moniker *Desert Fox*. He surprised even the most careful allied staffer by launching an attack at one of the most vulnerable points in the Anglo-American line. Boiling out of the east, he punched through the pass in the Dorsal Mountains east of Kasserine.

After the Nazi and Fascist forces raced through the Dorsals, they mauled whole battalions of unprepared Americans. In the first few days of battle, the Germans made short work of every American unit they encountered. It was a slaughter.

The Germans attacked in strength both west toward Tebessa, and north in the direction of the allied right flank. The Germans drove their armor toward Tebessa, since it had become a critical logistics center for the southern allied elements.

The American infantry did not suffer the humiliating defeat alone. Rommel and the Afrika Korps shattered British and Free French armored formations, artillery batteries, and engineer emplacements. They overran and captured forward air corps bases that were loaded with planes, fuel, ammunition, and vital equipment.

Phil hadn't personally seen or participated in any of the battle. He hadn't fired a shot in anger or observed anyone else do so. Until yesterday, this position on the border had been too far in the rear to experience anything but the distant sounds of the fighting.

Yesterday, forward elements of the 509th along with units from the 1st Infantry Division engaged the lead elements of the German thrust. In heavy fighting, the Americans finally repulsed the Germans. Similarly, the other German prong that had attacked to the north met stiff resistance and recoiled.

Twenty minutes earlier, Phil learned that the Germans were withdrawing to the east. The withdrawal was organized and orderly.

The Axis retrograde movement could not honestly be called a retreat. The Germans had soundly whipped the

Americans in the first division-sized engagement involving American and German land forces. The Germans were simply moving back to a more favorable tactical position.

*It's far too early to reach conclusions about this debacle,* Genero thought. *Still, it's pretty clear that our tactics, doctrine, and protocols were flawed—fucking fatally flawed! Much of our equipment is grossly inferior to the German materiel. God bless our armored troops; they might have gotten the worst of it.*

*At Kasserine, we got our noses busted—but good. Despite all these problems we've got to continue the fight. I just hope that the brass—all the way to Eisenhower and Roosevelt—learn something from this tragedy.*

*As soon as the smoke clears, they'll send us out to figure out what went wrong and piece together what actually happened,* Genero concluded. *The next few days will be critical. I already know one thing I'll put in my report: the Americans were green, inexperienced troops saddled with substandard equipment, forced to fight the best veteran forces that Germany could muster. We need to fix this problem and do better the next time.*

Phil took a deep breath and pulled his collar even tighter around his neck. He checked to make sure that all of the catches were fixed and tidy on his jumpsuit. Satisfied that he looked liked a paratrooper, he strode out into the night to make his way to Maj. Yardley's tent.

# Chapter 36

1400 Hours
March 13, 1943
Office of the Regimental Chaplain
187th Glider Infantry Regiment (GIR)
11th Airborne Division
Camp Mackall, North Carolina

Seated at the metal desk in the sparsely appointed, roughly hewn, tarpaper-covered room at the rear of the non-denominational military chapel, Father Nachen contemplated the sermon for Sunday's service. He'd developed a bad case of writer's block. He glanced over his office, longing for Divine inspiration.

The Army engineers had designed the regimental chapel to be multi-functional. It could hold up to 300 soldiers. During the week, company officers lectured on military subjects: field sanitation, the risks of venereal disease, the Articles of War, and military courtesy. On Saturdays and Sundays, the chaplains held religious services for the men.

The civilian construction crew had built the chapel in less than two days. They had thrown all of the other buildings in the regimental area together with similar wartime haste. One day, virgin forest covered the site; the next, 30 buildings and two full battalions of glider infantry blanketed the North Carolina red clay.

When the glider men and paratroopers of the 11th Airborne Division completed their training and preparation for combat at Camp Mackall, they'd either move on to another stateside post or ship out to one of the theaters of operation. Since the 11th Airborne had only been activated for a few weeks, it was too early for the strategic planners to decide whether the division would go to Europe or to the Pacific.

That simple logic did not keep the men from engaging in endless speculation. Like soldiers everywhere, they latched on to every rumor, no matter how absurd or ill founded. In the meantime, they had to prepare for jumping and gliding into combat. Over the next several months, the men would train 12 to 18 hours a day, six to seven days a week.

General Joseph Swing, the division commander, had decided to take an innovative approach with his command. He wanted all of his men to train as both paratroopers and glider men. Having a para-glider division would increase the flexibility of his force. If he cross-trained all of the men, he could deploy any regiment for any mission. The General's decision also avoided the morale-busting pay differential between the two specialties that had hurt both the 82$^{nd}$ and 101$^{st}$ Airborne Divisions.

Father Nachen applauded General's Swing's innovation, but silently criticized the Army's tradition of allowing its soldiers to become specialized into various elite formations. In his beloved Corps, every Marine was a highly trained, motivated rifleman. A Marine might spend a decade learning how to competently fire a howitzer, but if the need arose, any Marine could pick up a rifle and become an effective member of a rifle squad. The Army did not have this tradition.

Father Nachen had come into the Army with mixed feelings. After Beth Landry's capture in the Philippines, he felt guilt so fundamental that he could not sit out the war in Camp Hill.

When he served with the Corps during the Great War, he and his men looked upon the Army with unconcealed scorn. They believed that the Marines were elite. Anyone could be a dogface. It took someone special to be a Marine.

*Could the draft be the reason why the Marines seemed to accomplish more than the soldiers? It must be hard to generate esprit de corps in a group of men who had been compelled into military service. Then again, how would you explain Sergeant Alvin York or Corporal Phillip Genero? Both Army draftees; both heroes—even by the Marine Corps' high standards. So conscripted men could get the job done with the right training.* The question was more than theoretical to him, as he couldn't wear his Marine uniform any longer—since the Corps didn't have chaplains.

The Navy provided chaplains, corpsmen, and other support services to the Marines. Chaplain Nachen could have used his considerable influence to secure a commission in the Navy, but he didn't want extended sea duty, nor could he bear the shame of being a squid. *At least the Army has infantrymen, and that's where I belong. These are my men. My calling is to minister to grunts,* he thought with a laugh, e*ven if they do fall out of airplanes.*

His own war experiences, his Jesuit training, and his work as a teacher and principal had been ideal preparation for this assignment. Since meeting Beth at Kari's party, he had come to realize that breaking off their engagement was also a part of his journey back to combat.

*This whole episode is a demonstration of God's hand in my life,* Father concluded. *I've embarked on a course that God wants for me. I promise that I'll never let these wonderful boys down.*

Even though the priest was almost 47 years old, he'd stayed fit. After a few weeks of training, he could keep up with all but the most athletic para-gliders. Each day, Father Nachen fell out with a different company in the regiment. He made the morning run, did physical training, and went on the long forced marches.

The enlisted men loved seeing the old Padre out in the field. When they learned that he'd been a combat Marine and wore the Navy Cross, they idolized him. They teased him with good-natured, affectionate jibes about jarheads, leathernecks, and devil dogs. The former Marine teased them right back, lamenting the fate that tossed him in with a unit full of route-stepping dogfaces.

Father Nachen stood with the paratroopers and glider men of the 187th as they trained and maneuvered in the snow, sleet, and rain. He ate cold K rations. He slept on the ground. He bore their privations, comforted their misery, shared their joys, and inspired their courage. Just about everybody who spent any time with Father Nachen came to love him.

Shaking off his reverie, Father Nachen returned to his task, deciding what subject to address in his sermon the following morning. He wanted to make his homily interesting, stimulating, and inspiring.

St. Patrick's Day was only a few days away. It was an important holiday to most of the Irish-Catholic boys. In all of his years as a priest, he'd never met anyone, other than the Scots-Irish, who had anything bad to say about St. Paddy's Day.

Father Nachen toyed with using a lesson from St. Patrick as the theme for his sermon. As he contemplated the life of this great Saint, he had an inspiration. He hurriedly began making notes before the epiphany passed.

The next morning at the early mass, after reading the Gospel, Father Nachen stood in the small pulpit, adjusted his vestments, and gazed across the rows of assembled soldiers. Even in the muted light of the chapel, he could see each face clearly. These boys looked dead tired. They'd trained hard all week. Many nursed hangovers from Saturday night passes into town. Some had spent the last evening in the temporary beer hall run by the PX.

*God, they all look so young.* Father thought. *Most are young enough to be my sons. Many are still in their teens. They'll grow up before their time. Or they'll die in combat. Sad.*

"It struck me as important," Father Nachen began his sermon, "that this coming Wednesday is the day that we honor the Patron Saint of Ireland, St. Patrick. I know we have a substantial number of Irish men in the regiment."

Father Nachen had to pause because all of the Irish boys cheered. Others yelled "Airborne!" which was the universal response of affirmation among paratroopers and glider men.

Holding up his hand, Father Nachen smiled at the congregation. They quickly settled down. Not one of them looked like he might fall asleep.

"Well, men, on St. Patrick's Day, for this brief time of celebration—whether you come from Dublin, Boston, Philadelphia, or even Hoffman and Fayetteville—everyone wants to believe that they have a little of the Irish in them.

"You all know that what I'm saying is true. And it's more fundamental than pretending to be Irish so you can get free beer," Father continued, allowing the spontaneous laughter to settle down.

"Why do you suppose that is? What's so special about being Irish on St. Patrick's Day?" Father asked.

"There are many reasons, but let me discuss with you a few of the more important ones. And, by important, I mean: important for airborne soldiers.

"First off, you proud Irishmen should know that as a boy, St. Patrick was a Roman citizen. Irish pirates captured him in Britain, and sold him into slavery in Ireland. Although he was a citizen of Rome, he was probably Welsh by birth.

"The man who would become Patrick, a Catholic bishop of Gaul, was known as Malwyn Succat during the time that he served his Irish masters as a simple shepherd. Eventually, the slave boy grew tired of getting up before dawn, staying on guard all night in the rain, sleet, and snow, sleeping on the ground, having too little to eat, and facing danger constantly," Father explained, as some of the soldiers moaned audibly—relating directly to Malwyn's plight.

"Somehow, and history does not record how, this young Roman escaped from his master. He made his way to Gaul, where eventually he became a priest. After his ordination, he spent several decades in the service of the Catholic Church.

"During this period in his life, the middle-aged man, known by a Christian name—Patrick—felt an irresistible tug to return to Ireland. He perceived a special inspiration to try to convert the pagan Celtic tribes into Christians.

"We all know that Patrick eventually made it back to Ireland. Over a period of years, he converted a large portion of the population to what we now call the Catholic faith. We also know that, consistent with the blessings bestowed upon him, he performed many miracles for the benefit of the newly converted Celts.

"I want to talk about one of St. Patrick's most famous miracles because I believe that there is a great lesson, a parable really, for all of us Angels who wear the Airborne tab over the 11$^{th}$ Division patch. But before I do, I want to remind you that St. Patrick was a master of the symbolic. He made clever use of commonplace items to help him to explain the important tenets of our religion to a tough, primitive people. For example, to relate the concept of the Blessed Trinity, St. Patrick used the Irish Shamrock, with its three separate leaves flowing from a central stem in order to demonstrate how our Deity can have three separate persons in one God.

"The special miracle that I have in mind is the one in which St. Patrick climbed to the top of Mount Croagh. After fasting for many days, Patrick began to preach a sermon so eloquent that the force of his faith caused all of the serpents in Ireland to slither into the Irish Sea. Since today Ireland has no indigenous snakes, the Irish credit St. Patrick with ridding the Emerald Isle of the reptilian pests.

"Of course, there are many scientists who will tell you that the absence of snakes in Ireland is an easily explainable, naturally occurring phenomenon. They will point out that during the last ice age, a thick glacier covered Ireland. It would have been far too cold for snakes to survive. After all the ice melted, Ireland was too far from Britain for the snakes there to swim.

"Men, it is very possible that the scientists are right.

"St. Patrick did return to Ireland as a priest. He did dedicate the balance of his life to the conversion of the Celts. Among other miracles, Patrick did eradicate the serpents from Ireland.

"But the serpents that Patrick sent from Ireland were not mere reptiles. St. Patrick—through his dedication, courage, and faith in his cause—eradicated the serpents of paganism, idolatry, amorality, and evil from the hearts of the Irish tribesmen. Through his unparalleled commitment and love of God, he helped to guide the Irishmen into an era of enlightenment, education, religious fulfillment, and salvation.

"The lesson that St. Patrick teaches us, as paratroopers and glider men, is that in our own time, we too are faced with evil serpents. In our case, it is the evil of Nazism and Fascism, the scourge of totalitarianism, and the deadly plague of unbridled militarism.

"So to answer my original question about what is so special about being Irish on St. Patrick's Day: the Irish are heirs to a long and proud tradition of dedication to the ideals of St. Patrick, who helped lead a primitive tribe of pagans into a vibrant society of dedicated Christians.

"Like Patrick, we airborne soldiers must be willing to dedicate the rest of our lives to eradicating these serpents from our planet. I say: the rest of our lives in this pursuit, because some of us will not survive the future battles to see the end of the war. Our installation, Camp Mackall, is named for a brave paratrooper who died in North Africa fighting for his country.

"In the weeks and months ahead, we must all train relentlessly. We must dedicate our bodies, minds, and collective spirit to the goal of destroying the evil serpents that the Germans, Italians, and Japanese have loosed upon our world.

"Like Saint Patrick, who sacrificed the easy life of a Catholic bishop in Gaul to go overseas to fight the forces of evil in Ireland, we—American airborne soldiers—must leave our families, our homes, our friends, our jobs, and everything that is familiar to us, in order to fight the evils in this world in our own time.

"Saint Patrick knew fifteen hundred years ago—and it is still true today—that nothing worthwhile can be accomplished against a strong enemy without brave men and women who are willing to make a commitment to sacrifice for the welfare of the many. Private John T. Mackall made that commitment and he made the ultimate sacrifice.

"As airborne soldiers, you will be asked to carry the heaviest loads, over the longest roads, face the most dangerous circumstances, and fight the deadliest foes. With God's help and his blessings, we will prevail.

"We must succeed! We have no choice. Our failure would result in circumstances so horrible for our country that I will not even contemplate the possibility.

"As you go about your duties, and you feel fatigue or your spirits are low, say a prayer to St. Patrick or to St. Michael the Archangel to give us all a little more strength to drive on.

"If we sacrifice and dedicate ourselves in the way of St. Patrick, some individuals among us will be injured, wounded, and killed; but as a nation, with God's blessing, we will prevail. Airborne!"

Almost as one, the assembled soldiers stood and responded in the manner of the 11th Airborne Division, "All the way, Padre!"

"Now, my comrades, please bow your heads and let us pray. *Pater Noster qui es en coelis...*"

# Chapter 37

10:00 PM
April 12, 1943
Quarters No. 21
Debden Airdrome
Essex County, England

Katherine Reilly lay next to her husband as he slumbered in their small custom-made double bed. Even though Katherine could afford a much larger flat in Saffron-Waldon or a small cottage in sleepy Debden Village, she felt fortunate that Colonel Anderson had allowed her to live with her husband in what used to be enlisted quarters on the airdrome.

Katherine blessed the fates for any time that she spent with Paul. Tonight Paul slept soundly thanks to the flight surgeon and powerful sleeping pills.

Katherine rested her left arm around Paul's waist and wrapped her long shapely leg around his with satisfaction. Contact with Paul gave her great—almost maternal—comfort.

*Maternal is not the right word,* Katherine thought, as she reached up to stroke Paul's hair. *I suppose that Paul is a plain and physically unremarkable man, but no one has ever stirred me the way he does.*

Though they had been married several months, Paul still drove her wild. Her pregnancy hadn't diminished her desire for him. Although her swollen belly made some of their most athletic loving difficult, Paul's gifts made it possible to share intimate embraces without serious risk to the baby.

*Paul is such a jewel of a man. He will make the perfect father,* Katherine thought as she pulled him closer and felt the rise and fall of his chest.

*I think our child will be a boy. He's certainly been can-tankerous enough through this pregnancy. I can just imagine him with a cricket bat standing next to the wicket and facing off some determined bowler or running down a pitch in his cute little rugby togs, evading tacklers on his way to the winning try.* Katherine daydreamed. *Of course, my Paul knows nothing of cricket and rugby. He's such a fanatic, isn't he? He'll want his son to play American football or baseball.*

Fear began to creep into her thoughts, especially when she reflected about the birth of their son. *Paul's job is one of the most dangerous in the Empire. He's a fighter pilot, now with the American 4th Fighter Group. He's one of the very best in the world, isn't he?* Katherine reflected proudly. *He may look mild-mannered, but he certainly has testicular fortitude. Paul's so aggressive. On patrol, my husband is always where it's the most perilous.*

Maj. Paul Reilly had 12 air combat victories to his credit, four probables, five German aircraft destroyed on the ground, and was the 4th Fighter Groups' second-ranked ace. In the last month, Paul also had the added pressure of leading the transition to the new fighter aircraft, while still flying missions as the 334th Squadron's XO.

In early 1943, the 4th Fighter Group began discarding the sleek, wasp-like Supermarine Spitfires and began replacing them with the squat, thuggish, American-built Republic P-47 Thunderbolts, nicknamed the Jug. Like Paul, most of the American pilots of the 4th Fighter Group had been American Eagles with the RAF. All of them had flown the Hurricane and then the Spitfire. All had come to trust the agility, speed, and survivability of the Spit.

The Jug would be the fighter aircraft of her husband's future. Katherine felt nervous about the transition because—despite Paul's denials—she knew that he worried, too, and was powerless to stop the process. Colonel Anderson and the entire 8th Air Force hierarchy had mandated the switch. They thought the Jug was faster, more maneuverable, with better firepower.

Katherine suspected that the real reason for the change was that these great ponderous Jugs had more range. The Americans could not jury rig the smaller Spits to go further into enemy territory to escort the American Flying Fortresses.

*I hate the Thunderbolt! The very thought of a machine that will take Paul deeper in the enemy's lair frightens me. Nothing good can come from this transition. Nothing!*

At this stage in the war, none of Paul's peers thought much of American technology. They distrusted anything that came from an American factory. Paul's mates formed a small, very exclusive club of combat fighter pilots.

When they weren't flying, they loved to drink, party and talk endlessly about their one true love—high performance aircraft. While they clearly adored the Spitfire, they could be brutally honest and completely unforgiving with the many technical shortcomings in the American weapons inventory.

The conventional wisdom among the experienced pilots was that the P-40 was a dud. Word had seeped back to Europe from the Far East that the Flying Tigers had racked up impressive statistics with the P-40 because of the superior skill and daring of the volunteer pilots and in spite of the sever limitations of their grossly underpowered kites. Apparently, the P-40 simply could not dog fight with a Japanese Zero and General Chennault's boys had to use every trick in the book to stay alive. Everyone feared that the P-47 was the P-40, only more so.

No American pilot at Debden wanted to be the first to fly the Jug into combat. Since he'd been assigned to the transition, Paul knew he had to lead from the front. Over the last ten days, he'd flown the Jug on missions into France, escorting bombers. Called rodeos, these trips were long, arduous, and frequently deadly—especially for the bomber crews.

His latest rodeo had ended earlier in the day, before he came home to Katherine. After that mission's debrief, the flight surgeon gave Paul the little white pill. With luck, and the aid of modern medicine, he'd get a whole night's sleep.

By early evening, the weather in Northwestern Europe had turned foul. A storm front slammed the whole of Essex all the way to the North Sea. According to the weather officer, they'd be socked in for the next 48 hours. The grounded pilots of the 4th would avoid becoming casualties for two more days. Katherine reveled in the respite, brief though it would be.

Katherine learned that living with a fighter pilot who spent his days in combat and his nights with her could be a wild crazy ride. Before they knew that she was pregnant, she and Paul had agreed to take each day one at a time and to live for the moment.

Their pledge had been sane under the circumstances, but things had changed with the baby. A child meant planning for the future, assuming there would be one.

There was a glimmer of hope for them. Paul had nearly completed his tour of duty. Like all other flyers in the 4th Fighter group, he had to complete a total of 400 hours of actual combat before the group would relieve him from hazardous duty. As of this last mission, he had 340 combat hours, not counting all of the time that he'd spent with the Eagles in the RAF.

*When he completes his tour, Paul can stand down,* Katherine mused. *He could rotate back to the States. The Air Corps could make him an instructor pilot. If he wants to stay in England, Paul could get a desk job in London with the 8th Air Force staff. Some of the lads have already done just that, haven't they?*

*My Paul has nothing to prove. He's been flying in combat since the fall of 1940. He's paid his dues. The group decorated him for valor and honored him for that wound he received from the Nazi ground fire in the mission over Brest. I don't want him to press his luck.*

*The Eighth Air Force brass—all the way to General Doolittle—respect Paul. All he has to do is ask, and they'd snap him up in a minute. I've saved quite a bit of money from the movies. We could afford a nice flat in London near the headquarters. We'd be able to spend lots of time together and Paul would be able to be a real father.*

So far, Paul hadn't agreed to leave the 334$^{th}$ Squadron at the end of his tour. He was non-committal, even cagy, when she brought up the subject. Katherine suspected that Major Blakeslee and her husband intentionally forgot to log mission hours in order to extend their opportunity to fly in combat. For some of the men, the fight was everything. It was intoxicating and addicting.

After a time, Katherine became uncomfortable, and decided to roll over. She not only ate for two, she slept for two as well. Although she tried to move without waking Paul, he sensed her body turning and it caused him to awaken.

"You OK, baby?" Paul said. "You need anything?"

"No, Paul," Katherine responded. "I'm fine. I'm a wee bit uncomfortable with the baby."

Paul turned over and it was his turn to cuddle his beautiful wife. Laying on his left side, and spooning with her, Paul ran his hand over her swollen belly. Katherine began to purr contentedly as Paul stroked her. Then, very slowly, he ran his right hand down from her stomach into her still-moist folds.

"Ummmm, don't stop," Katherine whispered hoarsely. "That's delicious."

"Baby, you are so wet," Paul observed, his own voice husky with lust.

"You make me that way, Paul. I can't resist you," Katherine admitted.

"Tell me again how you satisfied all those little harlots at university," Katherine pleaded, seeking to lose herself in fantasy.

"Well, it was right after the big football game. The school sponsored a dance at the armory. The Betas had been drinking all day," Paul whispered softly in his wife's ear.

# Chapter 38

5:15 AM
May 4, 1943
Room 310
The Willard Hotel
1400 Block of Pennsylvania Avenue, North West
Washington, D.C.

In the late spring of 1943, the 5:00 A.M. hour could be hectic at the Willard Hotel. The morning shift always arrived before 4:30. The cooks, waiters, chambermaids, janitors, and maintenance men went about their duties, preparing to assist their guests to greet each new day. Important leaders staying at the hotel got their morning start with the able assistance of the Willard staff and then spent their days making critical decisions about the course of the war.

After almost a century, the Willard dominated Washington's political landscape. During the American Civil War, the Willard had been the hotel in Washington for the rich and powerful to congregate. In 1861, the Peace Congress met here in a final attempt to avert the Civil War.

That same year, Nathaniel Hawthorne observed that the Willard, "may be much more justly called the center of Washington and the Union than either the Capitol, the White House, or the State Department...you exchange nods with the governors of sovereign states, you elbow illustrious men, and tread on the toes of generals; you hear statesmen and orators speaking in their familiar tones. You are mixed up with office seekers, wire pullers, inventors, artists, poets, posers...until identity is lost among them."

By the time of the Grant Administration, the lobby of the Willard Hotel became a *de facto* extension of the White

House. President Grant often spent evenings there drinking at the Round Robin Bar. The president loved smoking expensive cigars and drinking brandy while discussing the issues of his administration with the other patrons.

Favor-seekers would approach Grant in the Willard lobby to buttonhole the president into indulgences and all manner of favors. Grant listened politely to the opportunists out of political necessity. Privately, he referred to them as *lobbyists*, a derogatory term which persisted right down to Junior Monarch's day.

In the middle of a much different—but equally devastating—war, the Willard Hotel drew Junior Monarch and his small retinue like moths to the flame. An amoral opportunist of the highest order, Junior clearly understood that the Willard had become the epicenter of political and financial power in the Capital. He never passed an opportunity to travel to Washington. He loved the Oval Suite with its elliptical-shaped living room, just like the President's office.

Following in the footsteps of two generations of lobbyists, Junior Monarch sought to advance his corrupt agenda to undermine the viability of Monarch Industries, embezzle funds entrusted to his care, and cheat his own government. Revenge for slights from old enemies was icing on the cake. To Junior, the Willard was the logical place to initiate his plan.

In the last few weeks, he'd gotten control of all the corporate financial books and records. Since the death of his uncle, Junior had siphoned millions from the corporation's accounts. He'd managed to open offshore bank accounts in the name of one of Monarch's biggest suppliers. After creating false invoices, it was simple to deposit Monarch's checks into the account that only he controlled. If his luck held, by August he'd be sipping champagne from a crystal flute on the wide veranda of a grand villa in Sugarloaf Mountain's cool shadows.

Through adroit manipulation, Junior had transferred and deposited most of the new money into confidential accounts throughout the Caribbean, Latin America, and Brazil. All of that money just sat there waiting for him.

*I can go to Brazil immediately. I don't need to take a single thing or person with me,* Junior thought as he sat with his back propped against several pillows on his suite's immense bed. *I've got more than enough money to live like a Roman emperor for the rest of my life, but I could use one more score from the War Department.*

*Another large contract for uniforms should do it. If I can convince the contracting officer that I need a large cash advance to secure raw materials, I'll be protected from a severe bout of South American inflation.*

*That just leaves the final piece—revenge.*

Uncle Dan was dead. Junior couldn't hurt him. Marta Genero, though—she was alive.

As Junior fantasized, he wound the stem of his pocket watch. Fidgeting with the antique gold watch calmed him. The weight of the gold watch comforted him. *I'll be the last of the Monarch line to possess this exquisite heirloom,* Junior thought smugly. *I'd never part with it.*

*With Uncle Dan out of the picture, who would run Monarch? Donna? Linda or Collingswood? Absolutely not!* Junior gloated.

*Maybe a court will appoint Mr. Phillip E. Genero, Senior, to be the receiver,* Junior thought. *That would be rich! It would be great to see the war hero saddled with the responsibility of cleaning up the massive economic mess that I'm going to make.*

*On the other hand,* Junior considered, *maybe I should muddy up the waters a bit. I could make it look like Genero had an active hand in the embezzlement. Even if the authorities see through and don't prosecute him, he'll never be able to prove that he didn't have complicity in or knowledge of my crime. The suspicion alone will ruin his saint-like standing among his admirers in the valley.*

*What about that $150,000.00 that Uncle Dan left Marta? What had she done to deserve that kind of money? She's not half as innocent as she wants people to believe,* Junior rationalized. *Maybe I can use that obscene bequest to help muddy the waters a bit about the embezzlement. Laying the blame for my little venture on Phillip and Marta is one of the sweetest things about this plan.*

*After last night, nothing at the Genero farm will ever be the same,* Junior chortled half-aloud to the woman sleeping next to him. She began to stir, and Junior looked down on her naked and gorgeous body—one more trophy for him to possess.

Junior pushed his pillows onto the floor, reached around the woman, and cupped her full breast with his right hand. He squeezed her nipple until it hardened between his fingers. He reached down between the woman's legs, and began to fondle and probe her. Still half asleep, the woman moaned and pushed her naked bottom against Junior's stirring manhood.

"That's it baby. Show me how much you want it. Tell me how much you need it." Junior moved against her. "C'mon baby," Junior insisted as he raised her leg and positioned himself, rubbing his manhood along the woman's wet folds.

Junior's hand actually trembled. He'd wanted this for so long.

"Tell me you want me," Junior continued. "C'mon Marta, darlin'! You don't get any of this until you say what I want to hear!"

Five days earlier, late in the afternoon on Friday, April 30, 1943, Junior Monarch called Marta Genero into his office in downtown Carlisle. He claimed to have several serious business conflicts and he wanted her to cover one of them for him.

Since Dan Monarch's funeral in December, Junior had been polite, kind, and even gracious to Marta. After five months without a single hint of his former behavior, Marta began to think that Junior had reformed. He'd finally decided to grow up.

Marta's husband had been gone from Carlisle for almost three weeks. He'd be away for at least two more. Phillip was in Hawaii to address a series of complaints from the Navy and Marine Corps to the government-contracting officer.

According to the Marines, entire production lots of tropical uniforms had arrived in the Pacific and Southwestern theaters with substantial defects. The Navy claimed that pallets of recently manufactured stock were useless. Since Phillip had negotiated the contracts, he was troubled by the charges.

*The Navy allegations are hard to believe,* Phillip concluded as he reviewed the paperwork on the train to San Diego. *Government inspectors have carefully examined each lot of finished uniforms in accordance with exacting protocols. The inspectors would not allow shipments from Monarch unless they were completely satisfied. The results of the inspection process undermine the claims of shoddy material and defective workmanship. I've worked with the Marine Corps reps in the past. They're tough and demanding, but ruthlessly honest. What's going on?*

Most troubling of all, Phillip had begun to have his own suspicions about the manufacturing process at Monarch Industries. Since he'd worked on the line for many years, he had experience in the level of effort and time constraints necessary for the proper manufacture of the tropical fatigues.

*Over the last six months, the production at the Boiling Springs plant appeared to be more efficient than I ever expected,* Phillip worried as he looked up from his work and out the window of the train. *Damn it! I've checked and double-checked the results of the acceptance tests, examinations, and inspections. They've all been good. Maybe a little too good!*

After winning a series of lucrative war contracts, Monarch Industries had increased its labor force to nearly 1,000 employees in three separate plants in the Cumberland

Valley. After the expansion, production increased dramatically. At first, the results were predictably bad.

*Bad results are to be expected in new production runs,* Phillip concluded. *They are not a cause for serious concern, unless they persist. Any new manufacturing process conducted by an inexperienced labor force is bound to have difficulties.*

Several months earlier, Junior and a handpicked team had solved most of the manufacturing problems. Subsequent inspections and examinations appeared to support Junior's claim that he'd found and exorcized the gremlins.

*Junior's fix at Boiling Springs did seem too good to be true. Now with these complaints from the Pacific, maybe they are.*

When Phillip had shared his concerns with Marta, she found them difficult to accept. While she wouldn't put such conduct past the old Junior, the reborn version seemed to have cleaned up his act. She argued that even if Junior had wanted to do such a vile thing as cheat the government, he would need the knowing assistance of other conspirators. Neither she nor Phillip could think of anyone else who would behave so despicably.

When she met with Junior on Friday afternoon, she gave him the benefit of the doubt. During the brief meeting Junior explained that he was in a real pickle. He hoped that she could help him out.

"Junior, I do want to help you. I think that you know that I'll do anything—within reason, of course—to help Monarch Industries," Marta said.

"That's comforting, Marta," Junior responded. "I have to be in Boston on business all next week. Everyone else is on the road, too. There's a series of meetings in Washington on Monday and Tuesday. Since I can't be there, would you go in my place and represent the company? The meetings will deal with the specifications for the new high performance flight suits for the Army Air Corps. If we want that contract, somebody from Carlisle has to go."

"Junior, I'd be honored to represent Monarch Industries."

Over the last few months, Junior had given Marta increased responsibilities on a number of projects. Junior's apparent trust in her and her enhanced workload had helped Marta battle her depression. She no longer felt scattered or inefficient.

"I'm sure that you'll do fine. If I didn't have faith in you, I'd never ask you to go," Junior acknowledged. "My secretary will give you the memo from the War Department, your itinerary, the agenda for the meeting, and the technical specifications. Be sure to familiarize yourself with the details before you leave for the Capital."

Junior's secretary had purchased train tickets for Marta. She would leave very early on Monday. She could return to Carlisle late on Tuesday night.

Since the meeting would be over two days, Junior's secretary had made reservations for Marta at the Willard Hotel on Pennsylvania Avenue. Junior gave her a number where he could be reached in Boston on Monday or Tuesday, in the event that anything came up that she couldn't handle.

"I'll get it done, Junior. You can count on me. I'll come home with good news for the corporation."

"I know you will, Marta," Junior responded. "Pardon my rudeness, but I have calls to make. Have a good trip. Knock 'em dead at the meeting and we'll talk when I get back from Boston."

"Enjoy your trip as well," Marta said sincerely.

*Oh, I will, Marta darlin'. I will!* Junior thought.

Junior never intended to go to Boston. He had planned to trick Marta into attending the War Department conference in Washington. The first phase of his scheme had gone like clockwork. Marta had agreed to go, and bought his ploy without reservation.

The second phase went equally well. Junior arrived in Washington early on Monday afternoon, just as if he had come down from Boston.

Junior had prepared to explain that he was in Washington because the government had cancelled the meetings unexpectedly on Monday morning. With no conflict remaining, he had taken the train down to Washington to check on the War Department meetings.

Without Marta's knowledge, Junior reserved the suite's optional second bedroom, with its own entrance and connecting door.

When Marta returned to the hotel on Monday afternoon, she found a note from the concierge informing her that Mr. Monarch wanted to meet with her in the bar. Marta desperately wanted a drink and she didn't want to drink alone. Although suspicious, meeting Junior in the public bar seemed safe enough.

Marta walked into the hotel bar just after six o'clock. As she looked around the room, several of the men noticed her. She looked stunning.

Marta spotted Junior at a table in the corner and walked over to him. Junior stood and pulled out a chair for her. Marta took the offered seat, as the last of her anxiety slipped away

A waiter quickly took her drink order and returned with a large glass of Amarone. With the war on, good Italian wine was in very short supply.

Junior nursed an expensive French cognac. He took a sip of his drink and smiled innocently at her.

*The Willard must have some impressive contacts to get wine like this with a war on,* Marta concluded.

"Well, Junior, what brings you to Washington? Did you get lost? You know Boston is considerably far to the north."

Junior responded by giving the alibi about the cancellation in Boston. He simply wanted to meet with Marta to get a report on the meetings at the War Department.

"Marta, you need to make those meetings tomorrow. I'll head down to Norfolk and check on the shipments to the Pacific," Junior lied with great skill, honed over a lifetime of deceit.

Marta relaxed and reported on the day's events. While they chatted, Junior made sure to behave correctly and he ensured that Marta's wine glass was always full. By 8:00 P.M, Marta had begun to feel a serious buzz. She hadn't been drinking as much lately and the excellent Italian wine had gone to her head.

"Junior, I've probably had too much of this excellent wine. I should go up to my room. I'll need my sleep if I'm going to be effective in any of the meetings tomorrow," Marta said.

"You had better get something to eat first. You'll feel worse tomorrow if you don't get something in your stomach. Believe me, I know," Junior said.

"I guess you would be an expert on hangovers. Frankly, during all those years that I worked for you, I never understood how you did it. Then you got so ill."

"I wasn't just ill, Marta. I almost died," Junior said with just the smallest hint of malice. "The experience did teach me some very valuable lessons."

"Well, you seem to have changed quite a lot. I never believed that you would," Marta admitted.

"Marta, I have changed. Now I hope that we can become good friends," Junior said with a deceptive smile.

"We'll see, Junior. There's a lot I could never forget. I may forgive, but that will take a lot more time and a lot more of this good behavior of yours."

"That sounds fair enough," Junior lied. "For now, let's grab a bite around the corner," Junior suggested.

Junior had made reservations at the old Ebbet's Grill, a block west of the hotel. Like the Willard, Ebbet's Grill was an important meeting place and watering hole for Washington insiders and power brokers.

Junior steadied Marta as they walked out of the front door of the hotel for the short stroll around the corner. As they walked arm and arm down Pennsylvania Avenue, Junior and Marta ran into Don Martin a competitor, who manufactured uniforms in North Carolina and who was staying at the Hotel Washington.

"Randy! It's good to see you," Don said insincerely, as he leered at Marta.

"How's business, Don?" Junior had no interest in Don's answer, but he noted Don's interest in Marta and savored that she was on his arm—and not on Don's.

"Obviously not as good as yours, Randy. I wondered if you were going to show up at the Air Corps contract meetings."

"I had other matters to attend to, but now I'll be able to tend to my business here," Junior responded with a wink and smirk that Marta missed. "I don't mean to be rude, but we've got important things to discuss, Don."

"I'm sure you do, Randy. I'll see you soon. Good luck in your business dealings," the older man said, delivering a sly wink of his own.

When they arrived at Ebbet's Grill, the staff had Junior's table ready. They quickly served the meal, along with two more bottles of wine. The wine steward could have saved the second bottle, because Junior saw to it that Marta drank most of the first. By 9:30, Marta was much more intoxicated and very disoriented. Unsure of Junior's intentions, she insisted it was time to return to the hotel.

"Marta, you're a bit unsteady to walk back to the Willard. I'll have the waiter call a cab. In the meantime, try this glass of Auslese. It's a sweet, German desert wine and will help settle your stomach," Junior said.

"Junior, do you only drink wines made by the enemy? I shouldn't drink this. I've had enough." Marta took the half-full glass of amber liquid and brought it to her nose. "It does have a very sweet, clean scent."

"It does, doesn't it?" Junior purred. "Go ahead; finish yours. The cab will be here in a few moments."

Marta sipped the chilled wine. "Oh, yes; that's very good. Thank you, Junior."

"Don't thank me, Marta. It's a pleasure making you feel good."

Marta simply smiled at Junior.

A few moments later, Junior got up from the table, offered Marta his hand, and assisted her through the crowded restaurant to the door. The cab driver waited right outside with the rear passenger door already opened. He noted that the gentleman had a gorgeous woman in tow. *Lucky old fart!* the cab driver thought. *He must be rich as shit. He's way too ugly to get a broad like that on the up and up.*

"Where to, sir?" the driver asked after he helped the woman into the wide back seat.

"The Willard," Junior said.

"Sir, that's just around the corner," the driver complained, thinking of the paltry fare. "You could walk there faster!"

"I don't think she'd make it," Junior responded, nodding at Marta as he passed a twenty-dollar bill to the driver. "Just be a good fellow and take us around the corner."

"Yes, sir!" The driver started the engine and let out the brake. *A twenty-dollar fare. This guy is in a hurry and that woman must be feeling no pain. The old fart is going to get very lucky tonight,* the driver predicted as he pulled up to the front door of the Willard. "Just a moment, sir. I'll give you a hand."

"Son, I don't need any help," Junior slipped another five-dollar bill into the cab driver's hand as he wrapped his arm around Marta's waist.

As they walked through the lobby toward the elevator, Marta tried to pull away from Junior.

"Marta, you'd better let me help you get to your room. You've had way too much to drink," Junior offered.

"I suppose so," Marta conceded. "I don't know what got into me."

By the time Marta and Junior arrived on the third floor, she felt ill. Junior helped her down the hall, unlocked the door to her room with his own key and pushed her roughly inside.

Marta wanted to protest Junior's presence in her room, but the room wouldn't stop spinning long enough for her to get the words out. A moment later, she found herself in the bathroom, throwing up her meal. Marta felt too dizzy to stand. She knelt on the floor next to the commode. When she looked over her shoulder, the last thing she saw was Junior's evil grin.

Junior knelt down, picked Marta off the bathroom floor, swept her up into his arms and carried her out of her room through the enormous oval suite and into the master bedroom. Junior dropped Marta unceremoniously onto the bed and began to undress her.

First, Junior removed her shoes. Then he turned Marta onto her stomach. He reached up and unzipped her dress, which he worked up over her head. Next, Junior removed Marta's short slip.

Marta remained unconscious and barely stirred even when Junior removed everything except her bra, panties, and wartime cotton stockings.

Lying helpless on his bed, Marta aroused Junior beyond belief. Almost drooling over his conquest, Junior slowly removed the rest of her clothes.

As Junior looked upon Marta's gorgeous body, he wanted to ravish her. He ripped off his clothes.

He moved to lie on top of her, contempt and desire mingling into a blossom of passion. The passive Marta roused him to a fury; he needed to punish her, he needed to possess her. As she lay on her stomach, limbs splayed to either side, he held himself up with one arm and used the other to pull her hips up and back, pressing himself against her thighs. The scent of her, the feel of her warm, pliant skin, the control he had over her, all combined into a sensation that overwhelmed him, heart and body, cresting into a wave that enveloped him.

The wave crashed before his first thrust. He dropped her back onto the bed and watched his seed trickle down her thighs. *Control,* he berated himself. *You don't have control over anything—not even yourself.* Marta had felt nothing of his power. She hadn't even woken up.

Marta's turbulent sleep that night had brought her no rest. She hadn't been dreaming much when her drinking was at its worst; these days, her mind seemed to be trying to make up for lost time. After passing out in the bathroom, Marta remembered nothing until she began to dream of Phillip, a Waikiki hotel room, and a long night of incredible passion. Somehow she must have made it onto the bed, at least in her dream, where she lay curled up against her husband. Philip woke first and began to fondle her in her sleep.

Phillip's touch was not as gentle and loving as usual. Instead, his hands pressed hard and rough against her flesh. She wanted to tell him to go easier. In her dream, she could not say the words, no matter how hard she tried to form them. All she could manage was a strangled moan. She pressed back against him to make him stop.

She heard a far-off voice. It was shrill, mean, and scary. It was not the voice of her husband. The nasty voice ordered her to "ask for it," and said she would not "get it" until she did.

Marta jerked awake, and for a few seconds she felt disoriented. She didn't know what day it was. She didn't know where she was. She did not know who was with her in bed or whose fingers were stroking her.

Marta had never felt more terrified. She reached down and pulled the unidentified hand away from her body. Released from the grip, Marta jumped out of the bed. She spun around and confronted her tormentor.

When she saw Junior naked in the bed and realized that it had been his hand that fondled her, she was sickened. Despite her hangover, Marta realized that she had just spent the night with Junior and she could not remember a thing.

"Junior, you son-of-a-bitch! What have you done?"

After his failure the night before, Junior had considered how he could snatch some victory out of his impotence. *She never woke up,* he thought. *So she doesn't know what happened—or what didn't happen.*

"Nothing that you didn't want, my little dove! Marta, you were magnificent!" Junior lied. "You were one of the best pieces of ass I've ever had. You wore me out. After last night, I didn't think I could get it up this morning. Then you started fondling me."

"You rotten bastard!" Marta cut him off. "You took advantage of me. You got me drunk. You...!" Marta shouted.

"I didn't get you drunk. There's a room full of people at the Round Robin Bar, diners at the Grill, a man on the street, and a cab driver who will testify that you were drinking and eating with me willingly. No one forced you to do anything, especially all those nasty little tricks you use in bed. You know, Marta, you're a passionate woman after you get started."

"Junior, is this your room?"

"Yes, it is," Junior replied.

"Where is my room in this God-forsaken hotel?" Marta asked.

"On the other side of the suite, through the living room. You'll like it. It looks just like the President's office. It was thoughtful of you to arrange for us to share this suite," Junior responded.

"What are you talking about? I didn't make the arrangements. I certainly didn't reserve a suite for you and me," Marta said, her voice becoming shrill.

"If you check with the front desk, they'll tell you that Marta Genero from Monarch Industries made these reservations for her and her boss over a month ago. The clerk will tell you that Marta Genero was very flirtatious and bold about the fancy Oval Suite."

"You set me up. Exactly how long have you been planning this?"

"I have been planning it for years. Good planning pays off in the end. Now get your beautiful little ass into bed and be a good little girl, or daddy will spank."

"Junior, I don't know what horrible thing I've done in my life to deserve this punishment, but I don't care what happened last night. If you ever come near me again, I'll kill you, I swear! I will kill you! You mean, evil son-of-a-bitch!"

Junior stretched his naked body over the hotel sheets. "Marta, if you don't do exactly as I say and do all of those sensuous things for me that you did last night, I'll make sure that your husband finds out about this. I can make him believe that you and I have been carrying on for months. What do you think your wop husband will think of you then?"

"Junior, I don't know if you can understand this, but Phillip is a fine man. He's everything that you're not. It's probably one of the reasons that you've tried so hard to hurt him over the years. So let me tell you, I'm on to your little scheme," Marta bluffed, thinking of the allegations involving the tropical uniforms.

She yanked open the closet door, grabbed one of the plush hotel bathrobes, and wrapped it around her body like armor. Her voice became cold as steel. "If you harm a hair on Phillip's head or cause him one minute of unhappiness, I will go to the Carlisle police. When they are through with you, I will kill you."

Junior mistook Marta's statement about the scheme to mean that she knew about his plans to embezzle millions from Monarch Industries. Junior was frightened; perhaps he'd overplayed his hand trying to seduce Marta.

"Marta, I thought this was what you wanted. If you're so offended, I'll leave you and the war hero alone. I don't need this crap."

"Go to hell, Junior! I've heard all I'm going to from you. Remember what I said. If you even hint that I slept with you, I will shoot you dead. If any rumors start, you are a dead man. Don't you ever even speak to me again! Understand?"

"Sure, Marta. Whatever you want," Junior conceded for the moment.

*I will never take another drink. I will destroy this beast if he ever tries to harm my Phillip,* Marta swore as she searched for her clothes. With a sigh that was part frustration, part rage, and part shame, she walked around the room, gathering her things.

Without looking once at Junior, she walked over to the door that joined the two rooms. As she passed through the doorway, she pulled the door so hard that it slammed, shaking the room for a full two seconds.

Junior sat on the bed watching Marta. His stomach clenched and his mouth went dry. Although he didn't want to admit it, Marta's threat frightened him.

*Jesus,* Junior thought. *I'll have to do something about her or I'll never be safe.*

# Chapter 39

1830 Hours
May 20, 1943
Commanding General's Mess
Headquarters, 82nd Airborne Division
Camp Kunkle
Oujda, Morocco

As the sun slipped below the western peaks, scores of ruby ribbons—woven with bright golden threads and studded with rose-colored flakes—flared in the blue-black sky. The officers of the 509th were too busy, too tired, or too distracted to pay attention to the gorgeous sunset. This evening, they gathered in the new division commander's mess to celebrate Phil Genero's promotion to major—and to say goodbye.

Phil's exploits, especially during the battle at Feriana, had become legend among the airborne troops in North Africa. No one questioned the wisdom of Genero's selection to higher rank. He'd earned his promotion the hard way.

Since the 509th had no billet for another field-grade officer, the Army would be kicking him upstairs. He'd move up to be an S-2 in one of the recently deployed regiments of the 82nd Airborne Division.

Though Phil felt a strong kinship with the paratroopers of the 509th, he was ready for new adventures. Unlike most of his comrades, the 82nd Airborne Division and its leadership had impressed him. Maj. Genero believed the airborne division was a grand notion with unlimited potential to defeat the enemy. Besides, his father had served in the 82nd Division in World War I. He liked the idea of serving in his dad's old unit. He'd spent time in this primitive new camp, plotting to find a way to get an assignment to his dad's unit. Now fate—and a generous promotion board—had taken a hand to help him.

The Allied command had placed Phil's camp near the small eastern Moroccan city of Oujda, an important and long-standing commercial junction between Algeria and the French Protectorate of Morocco. The allied command had established extensive air bases in and around Oujda to provide staging areas for allied operations all through the North African and Mediterranean battle zones. Since the terrain west of Oujda resembled the landscape in southern Sicily, and Sicily was next on the Allied target list, the American commanders chose this site to be the temporary home of the 82nd Airborne Division.

By May, the cool and damp spring weather had ended. The Moroccan summer had begun in earnest. The countryside dried up from the effects of the unusually wet winter. Instead of a sea of mud, the outskirts of the Oujda became a vast dust bowl.

In mid-May 1943, six battalions of highly trained—but untested—paratroopers of the 504th and 505th Parachute Infantry Regiments strutted into their unimproved bivouac. From their perspective, the command couldn't have chosen a sorrier site.

The 82nd Airborne's arrival at the temporary camp capped a difficult sea-borne journey followed by an uncomfortable trip from Casablanca in old French rail cars. With poor rations, overly ambitious training, primitive conditions, poor sanitation, oppressively hot weather, and dysentery from the local flies, morale among the paratroopers plummeted.

Before the 82nd Airborne had landed in North Africa, the Army had pulled a seventh battalion of paratroopers from combat in Tunisia for encampment near Oujda. These men, who were the first to arrive, named their new site Camp Kunkle to honor Lieutenant David Kunkle, the first officer of the 509th PIB to die in combat.

Unlike the men of the 82nd Airborne, the paratroopers of the 509th were victorious, battle-tested veterans. To the everlasting consternation of every single soldier in the 509th, some rear echelon ranger had decided to attach the veteran 509th to the inexperienced 82nd Airborne for operational control. For the foreseeable future, the division commander, Major General Matthew Ridgway, would decide their fate.

Like his comrades, Genero worried about the chain-of-command. Not only were the division's staffers not tested in combat, many were only legs. Even those All-Americans who were actually jump qualified had never been near a shot fired in anger. Unlike the other soldiers, Genero decided to wait and see—Ridgway had been an officer in China and Nicaragua, and had attended the Army War College. He would see the need for excellent staff officers, and Genero felt that he fit the bill.

When the time came for combat operations, the 82nd Airborne planned to deliver a large part of its staff to battle in gliders. Most of the division's staff officers had not received any form of jump training.

Early in the deployment, Maj. Gen. Ridgway had issued a controversial order, permitting the leg staffers who made one jump to wear the prestigious jump boots and parachute hat patch, even though they had not earned the jump wings. The men of the 509th considered this heresy to be a classic example of stateside anti-airborne chicken shit.

Though suffering serious privation at Oujda, the rookies of the 82nd, including their leaders and staff officers, were full of piss and vinegar. They were not impressed by the exploits of the 509th. The All-Americans made it clear that they intended to show the Geronimos how real airborne soldiers operated.

If the soldiers thought about it at all, they viewed the jumps on La Senia and El Djem Bridge to be abject failures. With all of the wisdom of the inexperienced, the newcomers believed that they would forge a new airborne tradition, unencumbered by the failures of the 509th.

Unable to coalesce with the division, the 509th PIB became Ridgway's redheaded stepchild. Like many of his men, the general did not admire the 509th's jump record. Nor did he have a high regard for its former commander, Col. Edson Raff.

At this stage of the war, Ridgway had not completed the requirements to be jump qualified and wore no jump wings. After only a few meetings in North Africa, he developed a serious personality conflict with Col. Raff, who wore his own wings proudly, and had made two of the three American combat jumps in the theater. Raff treated all the division's non-airborne senior officers with undisguised disdain—bordering on insolence.

Col. Raff had distinguished himself as an effective modern commander in innovative combat operations while commanding the Tunisian Task Force. By May 1943, the need for such a task force had passed. Because he was now a full colonel, Raff had become far too senior to return to the 509th and command a battalion.

By any reasonable analysis, Raff had earned the privilege to command a regiment, but all of the regiments in the 82nd Airborne were taken. Raff had no interest in commanding a glider regiment.

In the middle of May, Ridgway spoke privately with his chief of staff, Colonel 'Doc' Eaton. "Colonel Raff is too high strung to fit in well with our staff."

"Sir, the J-3 on Eisenhower's staff told me that Raff may be too mouthy, but he's a diamond in the rough. Eisenhower credits Raff with holding the entire II Corps southern flank with only a reinforced brigade task force of mixed arms and some ash-and-trash orphan units. It was really quite a feat. They think that had Raff's boys not turned north on their axis of advance and crushed Rommel's left flank, Kasserine might have been much worse."

"Yeah, Doc, I've heard that too," Ridgway said. "Still, I can't stand the guy. He's arrogant and insufferable. There's a rumor that he wrote a book or an article for the Saturday Evening Post about his brilliant feat-of-arms at La Senia. The smoke isn't even clear from that battlefield screw-up and Raff wants fame and fortune.

"Doc, we have no openings for a full colonel in our regiments and Raff's too senior and too poisonous for our G staff. Besides, he's too chummy with Boy Browning. He loves the Brits. I think he forgot whose uniform he wears."

"Sir, Eisenhower likes him. He personally promoted Raff to full colonel. It won't sit well, if Eisenhower thinks you can't get along with him," Doc Eaton advised.

"Doc, I don't care how you do it, but he's not coming here. We have no place for him."

"General, that could create a different kind of problem. If you don't find a place for him, he might end up on Eisenhower's staff, maybe as General Browning's assistant or something," Eaton predicted. "If you and Raff don't get along, if he's more loyal to Browning, and Eisenhower trusts him, we could end up getting the short end of the stick in Sicily and play second fiddle to the British Airborne."

"You're right, Doc. We have to find a way to send him and his loyal protégés home. If we have to permanently fold the 509th into our division somewhere, I'm eventually going to replace their entire command structure with men in whom I have more confidence. So, whatever we do, let's include those officers, too."

"Well, there is one protégé of Raff's that I've got my eye on. He's a very impressive young officer. Three days ago I pinned his oak leaves on for him, while you were in Algiers," Doc Eaton said.

"Who is he? What's so special about him? We're hip-deep in quality officers." Ridgway observed.

"Name is Genero. Works in the 509th S-2 shop." Eaton explained. "He was the commander of the Tunisian Task Force rear detachment that won that nasty battle at Feriana. He's very brave. There's a DSC pending. He knows special operations better than any of our guys. He and a Free French Legionnaire did an epic trek through German lines in January. They tried to warn everyone that Rommel had something up his sleeve. Genero's smart as hell. Speaks several languages and wants to come work for us in the worst way. Both airborne regimental commanders want him, but I'd like him to be an assistant G-2 and work for me under Whitfield Jack."

"No kidding? You mean he doesn't think that Raff is the center of the universe?"

"Oh, he's a Raff protégé all right, but he told me that his dad served in Sergeant York's company in World War I. His dad got the DSC in that same battle in the Argonne. He thinks it's fate for him to become a second generation All-American. Trust me, sir; he'll transfer his loyalty in no time. He's a very good officer."

"Look, Doc, if you want him, we can make an exception. He sounds too good to be true, though. Just get rid of Raff and his other boys. You can keep this Genero lad, but he'd better keep his nose clean."

"All the way, sir!" Eaton responded.

Ridgway could see the future battles looming on the horizon. Eventually, the 82nd Airborne would be sent back to England for the cross-channel invasion. Ridgway figured that before his division ever saw England, it would experience tough fighting in Sicily and Italy. If he and his men were to succeed and survive, he'd need lots of men like Major Phil Genero.

For the Sicily invasion, General Eisenhower had assigned the 82nd Airborne to the 7th Army. The planners intended them to play a vital role in the airborne assault. With the operation less than two months away, the Anglo-American leadership debated the details of the 82nd's participation. If Doc Eaton was right, this kid, Genero, could be a big help.

Only a week before Phil's promotion party, on May 13, 1943, the Americans and British had accepted the surrender of all axis forces in Tunisia. The surrender ended German and Italian organized resistance in North Africa.

The North African campaign was an overwhelming allied victory. It was a far closer contest than the result suggested.

Next to Stalingrad, the German debacle in North Africa proved to be its most startling and profound defeat to date.

The next allied campaign would begin on the island of Sicily, which was likely to be a tough nut to crack. Operation *Husky* would be the allies' first large-scale operation of liberation in the homeland of one of the major axis powers. The enemy resistance would be fierce.

As Ridgway had feared, the 509th demonstrated a closer kinship to their British cousins, with whom they had shared so much, than they did with their upstart brothers who were fresh off the boat from America.

As a token of respect, Gen. Browning had authorized the original members of the 509th to wear the British red beret. Gen. Ridgway expressly countermanded that honor. He despised the British beret and all that it symbolized, when worn by Americans. He fought any attempt to anglicize his command. He immediately humiliated any American soldier assigned or attached to the 82nd Airborne who dared to sport one.

Phil tried to avoid being caught up in the political intrigues and petty rivalries between the senior Allied officers. The arrival of the 82nd meant that the United States Army would deploy airborne operations on a large scale. Genero only cared about winning the war and division-sized airborne operations could help shorten it.

In preparation for his transfer, Phil received a briefing on the Sicily Invasion. The 82nd Airborne would make two successive night jumps near the town of Gela, to protect the American beachhead, which in turn covered the British left flank. He found the details of *Operation Husky* to be fascinating. The airborne assault onto Sicily was the American answer to the German airborne invasion of Crete. Only this time, the Germans would be among the defenders

In 14 hours, Phil would meet with the 82nd Airborne G-2. Tomorrow morning, he would learn which specific assignment he would get. He hoped that his next job would permit him to develop the Pathfinder Concept: sending small groups of paratroopers in first to secure drop zones for larger formations and set up electronic guidance for the Air Corps. After his three combat jumps Genero felt he had earned the right to be the first Pathfinder to land in Sicily.

Phil's 509th comrades had intended that his promotion party be a private affair. Genero had wanted Louis Anton to attend, but the Free French had suddenly reassigned him to their headquarters in Britain. They were planning something unusual. Louis would naturally be a part of it.

Phil had procured several bottles of the local wine to wet down his new gold oak leaves. His comrades from the 509th had broken out their stashes of contraband booze to toast his departure to higher staff assignments and to soften the blow of bidding their friend adieu.

After only an hour and a half, many of the officers had a noticeable buzz from the alcohol. It was all good fun and everyone had a great time regaling, retelling—and sometimes reinventing—their adventures in Algeria and Tunisia.

Phil's closest friends pitched in to obtain a few small parting gifts. Since gift shops were few and far between in eastern Morocco, the men made do with items that could be produced locally and adorned with paratrooper memorabilia.

One item that the officers of Easy Company presented to Phil was beautiful dark wooden plaque. The gift had been handsomely carved by local artists and served as a backdrop for an oversized rendition of the 509th's unit symbol—a stylized depiction of a paratrooper standing in the door of a troop transport, ready to jump. The word *Geronimo* was carved directly under the symbol.

Two of his friends bought Phil a souvenir red beret that they'd adorned with crests from closely associated American, British, and French units. Although they intended that he display it on his desk or eventually on a mantle-piece, and not wear it, after the presentation was made, several of the more inebriated officers started taunting. They convinced Genero to put it on so that they could take a few pictures.

Wearing a cover in a general's mess would break a long-standing tradition. As an officer and a gentleman, Genero knew and followed this convention. He'd also read Maj. Gen. Ridgway's directive prohibiting the All-Americans from wearing the British headgear. Even so, amid the informal party atmosphere, he relented to his buddies and donned the beret. It was a decision that would change his life forever.

During the party, a few of the division officers from the G-3 and G-4 staffs dropped into the mess tent. These men had been working feverishly on the plans for *Operation Husky*. Only a few moments earlier, Col. Eaton had released them to get their evening meal.

The staffers wanted to get some chow and head back to work. There were thousands of details to resolve, if the operation was to have any chance of success.

They went through the chow line, got their rations, and intentionally took seats several tables away from the tipsy revelers of the 509th. Since all of the officers were famished and tired, they focused on their food and engaged in little conversation with each other.

Later, Genero couldn't remember how the trouble started. The best he could recall was that one of the 509th lieutenants noticed that one of the 82nd Airborne staff officers wore bloused jump boots, but no jump wings.

Had it not been for the alcohol, the lieutenant would not have hectored the leg staff officers. Even after it began, it was fairly mild and mostly good-natured.

If the staff officers had not been so stressed out, tired, and cranky, they might have handled the harassment better. Unfortunately, a senior major from the G-4 staff lost his cool.

Major Andrew Williamson was a fine officer with an unblemished record. He was from Anderson, South Carolina and had obtained his commission in the Quartermaster Corps in 1938 after graduating from the Citadel.

While at the Citadel, Andy Williamson established himself as one of the best offensive linemen in the history of the school. He knew that he was tough. He took great pride in his physical strength.

Though not a bully, Maj. Williamson never permitted another man to give him any shit. He possessed zero tolerance for harassment, especially where snotty, young paratrooper lieutenants and captains were concerned.

After only a few snide comments from the 509th officers, Williamson pushed his plate of half-eaten G.I. chow aside. He got up from his seat—his 240 pounds rising to his full height of six foot four—and walked over to the corner of the mess tent, where the 509th officers were winding down the party.

Williamson had been with the 82nd since June of 1942, several weeks before the War Department designated the division to become airborne. From those early days in Louisiana, Williamson had focused on the unforgiving task of securing, organizing, protecting, and nurturing the equipment necessary to field an airborne division.

Andy Williamson would have taken more jump training, but the G-4 demurred. Williamson had become that rare commodity, the irreplaceable man. His work in logistics was flawless and too pressing to release him for further jump training. Williamson made one jump but never got to be a full-fledged paratrooper. Over the last year, he had suffered in silence as the jump-qualified officers harassed and criticized their leg comrades.

On the eve of the 82nd's debut into vertical envelopment in combat, Williamson could not bear the hectoring. He had worked too hard to make the mission possible to be left behind now, and was in no mood to listen to more crap. One look at the patches and unit insignia and Williamson understood why these guys behaved so badly. They were Raff's boys, the 509th.

Maj. Williamson had few heroes in his pantheon. Most were historical figures like Francis Marion and Robert E. Lee. If he had a live hero, it would be Gen. Ridgway—to Williamson's eye, the ideal officer. Ridgway was a soldier, scholar, and diplomat. Williamson considered it to be the highest honor to serve on the general's staff.

Williamson also sensed that Ridgway disliked Raff. Consequently, Williamson despised Edson Raff and everyone who acted like him. Since most of the men of the 509th admired Raff, Williamson had no use for any of them.

Williamson approached the revelers from the 509th burning with anger. He strode into the midst of the paratroopers and ordered, "Be at ease!"

Although the officers of the 509th were well trained and superbly disciplined, Williamson's action did not intimidate them. They got angry. They kept mumbling and acted disrespectfully.

A captain from the 509th's S-4 shop recognized Maj. Williamson. He was in no mood to show respect. "Hey, Major!" shouted Captain Clark. "What's this all about? You're intruding into a private party."

Clark's insubordination poured gasoline on Williamson's fire. The major took two steps over to the captain, got directly into his face, and began to dress him down.

"Captain Clark! I thought I recognized you. You better button your lip, mister! I don't care what kind of discipline y'all are used to in the 509th, but you're in the 82nd Airborne now and we don't tolerate this kind of bullshit from subordinates! If you don't start acting like a commissioned officer, you and I will be discussing this with Colonel Eaton before you can whistle Dixie!"

The whole exchange unfolded so quickly that Genero, who'd been talking to a small group of friends, hadn't noticed any problem until the logistics major gave the command to be at ease. After observing him for ten seconds, Phil decided that the staff major's behavior was appalling.

Phil didn't need any trouble with a senior man on the G-4's staff. To salvage his party, Genero decided to spin the major down a notch or two.

Forgetting that he wore the beret, Phil walked up behind Maj. Williamson. To get the major's attention, Genero put his right hand on Williamson's left shoulder and gently spun him 90 degrees to his left, so Phil could face him.

Williamson, overcome by his own anger, misinterpreted Genero's well-intentioned gesture and knocked Phil's arm away with a powerful sweep of his own left forearm.

For an instant, both men faced each other. Their eyes locked and neither man intended to look away.

Then Williamson did a stupid thing. He noticed that Genero wore the souvenir beret. After a spontaneous guffaw, he mocked, "Well, well, what have we got here? Son, you look like a clown who escaped from the circus! Don't you men from the 509th have any manners? In the 82nd we don't wear a cover in the General's mess." Williamson ground his teeth as he clenched and released his fists. "Are you bucking for a transfer to the limey army?"

Maj. Williamson's insult brought immediate and angry responses from the airborne officers.

Genero said nothing. He just continued to stare into Williamson's eyes. It began to dawn on Phil that he would have to kick the major's ass.

Williamson had always been bigger than the rest of the boys in school. He'd always been the strongest. He hadn't been in many actual fights—he hadn't needed to. His impression was intimidating enough.

Genero, on the other hand, had trained intensively in close combat. Gearing up for *Operation Torch*, Genero worked out with the hand-to-hand combat instructor almost every day. Phil had become far more formidable than he had been when he had kicked the shit out of the two SS men in the Marseilles train station. He might be a little smaller than the angry division staffer, but Phil was trained to kill.

Up to this point, Phil might have let the whole thing pass, but Williamson had concluded that these smaller men would back down, in the same way that smaller men had been backing down from him for most of his life. The logistics major made the serious error of trying to press an advantage that he didn't have.

"You men from the 509th better learn that nobody is particularly impressed with you. You all think that you're tough, 'cause you fought the Italians and a few Germans. Well, you're assigned to a real division now, one with real leadership. You're not serving with Raff anymore. You've got a real commander now, not a Little Caesar."

Williamson's use of Raff's nickname brought another round of disrespectful comments from the junior officers. The situation had deteriorated and it was about to get worse.

Genero spoke for the first time, without taking his eyes from the division staffer. "Major, you are out of line. Up until a minute ago, I'd have let this pass, seeing that it's my party and you are a guest—an uninvited guest—but still a guest. Paratroopers have manners. Unlike legs, we don't act like fucking assholes, trying to throw our weight around. As airborne officers, we respect the men who have the unenviable job of commanding fucking leg staffers like you. We'd never insult a man like Colonel Raff, who is a combat veteran and who's been recognized by the theater commander. You're fresh off the boat from America. You haven't paid your dues here.

"I'll tell you what I'll do, Major," Phil continued. "You apologize to my friends, and say you're sorry, and I won't kick your fat leg-staffer ass all over Camp Kunkle."

Thrown off-balance by Genero's condemnation, Williamson hesitated. *Shit, he's a major*, he thought. *Rank's no advantage here.* No one had ever spoken to him like this before. Genero continued to press him without mercy.

"Major, you've got five seconds to tell my friends that you're sorry that you interrupted my party and had the balls to cast an aspersion on one of the finest senior officers in the Army."

With those words, Williamson lost it. He closed the space between him and Genero, and with both meaty hands, tried to grab onto the lapels of Phil's blouse. It was a serious mistake.

As Williamson made physical contact, Genero shot both of his hands up and inside Williamson's arms, knocking them up and away from his body. Phil pivoted and punched Williamson hard on the left side of his chin.

Williamson dropped like a rock onto the floor into an unkempt heap. Genero stepped two paces back from the unconscious man. He looked over at the division staffers and barked at them to help their fallen comrade.

The paratroopers started to whoop it up. Genero silenced them with a stern look.

"Looks like the party's over, guys, everyone should grab his gear and head back to quarters. Let's see if we can forget this unpleasantness."

By this time, four of the division staffers had manhandled the big major into a chair. He was no longer unconscious, but he was groggy. His chin hurt like hell. He'd need treatment for the hairline fracture. A thin stream of blood ran from the corner of Williamson's mouth.

Genero walked over to the group that was hovering over Williamson. He stayed a respectful distance and tried to determine if the staff officer needed more attention.

Williamson noticed Phil standing nearby. "What are looking at, you fucking asshole?" the big major asked, the words mumbled through his swollen lips.

"Are you OK? Do you want a medic?" Phil asked sincerely.

"I don't need anything from you, you prick!" Williamson said, spitting blood.

Genero shrugged, and turned to walk away. He felt no remorse. His punch had been delivered in what was clearly self-defense. The leg attacked him first.

"You bastard, you haven't heard the end of this," Major Williamson snarled prophetically, as Phil left the mess tent in silence.

# Chapter 40

After finishing a six-mile run with Able Company, Father Nachen received notice to attend the Monday morning meeting of the Airborne Command's Health, Welfare, and Morale Committee. Colonel Drexler, a stickler for punctuality, chaired the weekly meeting.

Eddie Nachen had been at Camp Mackall for several months. Until today, he'd never been to one of the meetings. He didn't want to be late and make a bad impression on the colonel.

Father Nachen hurried over to his bachelor quarters and cleaned up in record time. Twenty minutes later, as he approached the headquarters complex, he realized that the meeting wouldn't convene for another 40 minutes.

Blessed with extra time, Father contemplated his options. He could get some chow or visit with the post chaplain, a Methodist minister, who was the senior military cleric at Camp Mackall. He decided that would be the best use of his time.

As Chaplain Nachen parked his Jeep outside the main post chapel, he noticed five or six officers loitering outside the headquarters building across the street. They were probably waiting for one of the command staff officers who was late returning from the officers' mess.

New officers were commonplace at Camp Mackall and arrived daily from Fort Bragg, Fort Benning, Camp Toccoa, or Camp Blanding. The Airborne Command had earmarked the new replacements for an airborne unit that it intended to field after it certified Eddie Nachen's 11<sup>th</sup> Airborne Division for combat.

The War Department had mobilized the 82<sup>nd</sup> Airborne, which had recently deployed somewhere overseas. The Army kept the actual location of the All-Americans a secret.

The 101<sup>st</sup> Airborne was fully manned, thoroughly trained, and on its way to being certified for combat. No one knew in which theater the Screaming Eagles would sink their talons.

The 17<sup>th</sup> Airborne Division was on the Airborne Command's drawing board. The Pentagon had chosen Brigadier General Miley to command. After the 17<sup>th</sup>, there would be a 13<sup>th</sup> Airborne Division. Hopefully, nobody in that unit would be superstitious.

All of the new men outside the headquarters wore the Airborne Command patch on their left shoulder and the 509<sup>th</sup> PIB's patch on the right shoulder. In the Army, a soldier had the right to wear the patch of the unit in which he had served in actual combat on his right shoulder.

*What are men from the 509<sup>th</sup> doing here?* Eddie Nachen wondered. *They must have been reassigned from North Africa. None of them appear to be convalescing or suffering from serious wounds. Why would half-a-dozen fit officers with combat experience be standing on the wrong side of the Atlantic?*

The post chaplain could wait. Curiosity got the better of him. He walked over to the men to see if they needed anything. New arrivals—regardless of their experience—always appreciated a kind word.

One of the officers was a full colonel. He was a small man, but judging by his robust mannerisms and bearing, he was in charge.

One of the other men—much taller than the colonel—seemed familiar. He was a major and looked very tough and fit. As he turned toward the chaplain, Father Nachen could see his ribbons on the left side of his green blouse.

*He has a Silver Star, a Bronze Star, a Purple Heart, and three stars and an arrowhead on his campaign ribbon. He also has a French Croix de Guerre. This officer has seen some serious fighting and has behaved gallantly,* Father Nachen thought.

*I wonder what that narrow rectangular patch means. It has three gold stars and was sewn on his blouse right over his silver jump wings. I've never seen that decoration before.* He looked back at the colonel and saw that the senior man only had two stars over his wings.

As Father approached the officers, they noticed him. They stopped talking to each other and turned politely in his direction. It was then that Father Nachen recognized the major. The chaplain saluted the colonel, and said, "Good morning, gentlemen, sir. Welcome to Camp Mackall. I'm Chaplain Nachen. Hello, Major Genero! Gin, it's been a very long time."

Genero had been chatting idly with the other exiled alumni of the 509th as the chaplain approached. Phil didn't notice him until Captain Rogers interrupted the conversation with a question.

"Who's the Holy Joe?" Rogers asked, as he nodded his head in the direction of the priest.

Phil glanced in the direction of Roger's nod. The Chaplain looked familiar. Genero didn't recognize him as his old mentor until Father Nachen addressed him.

"Father Nachen! How are you?" Phil responded, springing at the older man. Chaplain Nachen was the first person from Central Pennsylvania that Phil had seen in over a year. All of sudden, he was hit with the depth of his homesickness.

Father Nachen grabbed Phil by his shoulders and gave him a hearty smile. He reached down, and took Phil's great paw in his right hand and gave it a good shake. The other officers stood by and watched with some curiosity.

"Gin, you're about the last person I expected to see in North Carolina. I heard you were in North Africa, slaying the Hun. Obviously, some of those rumors were true," Father Nachen said, gesturing at the impressive row of ribbons.

Father Nachen's comments generated an unexpected series of disgruntled sighs and moans from four of the officers. Genero and the colonel did not react.

"Father, I'd like to introduce Colonel Edson Raff, former commander of the 509th Parachute Infantry Battalion and the Tunisian Task Force. The rest of these reprobates are my comrades. We've just returned from North Africa. All of us have been reassigned to the Airborne Command," Genero said, as he gestured first at Colonel Raff, then at his four friends.

"What are you guys doing back in the States?" Father Nachen asked innocently. "Shouldn't guys with your experience stay in the theater, where you might do some good?"

A couple of the younger men guffawed. One of them whistled and rolled his eyes. Only the colonel remained expressionless.

When Father Nachen saw the reactions on the younger men's faces, he realized that he had said the wrong thing. He'd hit a sensitive nerve. *What had happened here?*

"Father, we're in-processing into the command. We're to get our actual assignments this morning. We're waiting for the G-1 to arrive and reveal our fate," Phil explained, with more than a hint of frustration.

"Gin, I've got a meeting with the deputy chief of staff in a few moments. After that, I have appointments and responsibilities that will keep me busy most of the day. I'm the Regimental Chaplain at the 187th Glider Infantry Regiment in the 11th Airborne Division. I'd really like to talk to you. Perhaps you could meet me at the Officer's Club tonight?" Father Nachen inquired.

"Absolutely, Father. My dance card is totally open tonight. What time?" Genero responded.

"Let's meet about 1800. We can have a little drink and then some chow. We have lots to talk about. Bring your comrades," The chaplain offered.

"OK, Father. Will do! I'll be looking forward to it."

With that settled, Father Nachen released Genero's hand and hurried off to his meeting, wondering what in the hell had happened to bring so many decorated officers back from the combat zone.

Col. Raff now spoke for the first time. "Genero, who was that chaplain? How do you know him?"

Maj. Genero turned toward his mentor and said, "Believe it or not, sir, he was my high school vice-principal."

"No shit?" Raff asked.

"Absolutely none whatsoever, sir." Phil responded.

In 1943, the Camp Mackall military reservation included nearly 53,000 acres of prime North Carolina old-growth forest near the small, quintessentially southern town of Hoffman. Before the war, a northeastern steamship line had used the site as a hunting preserve and built a grand hunting lodge. After taking control of the property, the Army leveled much of the virgin forest, but preserved the lodge. The Camp Mackall commander wasted no time converting the hunting lodge into the officers' club.

Chaplain Nachen loved the O Club. The modifications had not affected the old lodge's rustic charm. Eddie Nachen often left the 187th and enjoyed an evening meal there.

At 1815 hours, Chaplain Nachen sat at the main bar, sipping on a scotch and water. The bartender, a long time native of Hoffman, knew the chaplain's tastes. While there were some molecules of water in the glass to dilute the scotch, most drinkers would have thought that the chaplain took his drink neat.

Nachen appreciated his scotch, although he wasn't particular about which brand he drank. When he became the principal at St. Ignatius, he had gotten into the habit of having one medium-sized tumbler before dinner. He would sip on it as the members of his order gathered in the paneled study, just outside their communal dining room.

The 15 to 20 minutes before supper were his favorite time of day. He loved interacting with the other priests, scholastics, and brothers. He listened to problems, suggested solutions, cajoled, directed, and inspired. Like the boys assigned to his regiment at Camp Mackall, the Jesuits at St. Ignatius had trusted and admired him.

When Father went to the O Club, he also tried to have one drink before dinner. Then, he would work the room, talking with the other officers from his regiment to address and solve problems.

As Father took the third sip from his scotch, he saw Phil arrive alone. His comrades were nowhere to be seen. Phil looked around, spotted Father Nachen at the bar, and walked over. Ten seconds later both men shook hands again.

The chaplain offered to buy Phil a drink and he accepted, asking for the coldest bottle of beer in the place. The bartender reached under the bar, and came up with a frosty Miller High Life. He popped the steel cap off the top of the bottle with an all-purpose can and bottle opener that he kept clipped to his belt.

Genero picked up the bottle of beer and gazed at it. "It's been a long time since I've had Miller's. And it's so cold! Funny what you miss when you're overseas," he mused.

Genero reached over and touched the neck of the bottle to the lip of the chaplain's glass in an obvious salute. "Thanks, Father," he said, as he took his first sip of the cold, amber liquid.

Father Nachen suggested that they get a table. The club was filling up fast. There would be a crowd tonight, and if they wanted to talk in private, they needed a table. They found a small one across the room, near one of the windows that had been carved out of the log wall.

"Gin, it's good to see you—and in such fine health. I'm very glad that you made it back OK. Your mother must be pleased. By the way, what happened to your hand?" Father asked.

"I got sloppy and put it where someone could take a bite out of it. I was very lucky, Father. A lot of good boys won't be coming back. Two fingers are a small sacrifice. And hell, I don't mind giving a finger to the fascists," Phil responded.

Father smiled at the pun. "Though they clearly deserve them, Gin, rude gestures won't faze those fiends. It breaks my heart each time I hear about the death of one of our boys in this war. The more time I spend with the paratroops and glider men in the 187th, the more worried I get. I know from my own experience in France that we'll lose many of these fine young men. I guess I don't need to tell you this, after your experiences in North Africa and the losses your unit suffered. The Army named this camp after one of your comrades, John Mackall. Did you know him?" Father asked.

"Father, we called him Tommy. He was a good kid. A Vichy fighter pilot strafed his plane. Killed Dave Kunkle, an officer I knew well, and several others. I wasn't there when the Vichy air force attacked. Kunkle, Mackall, and most of Easy Company had gone ahead of our main column in C-47s to get infantry forces on La Senia airfield," Genero said.

"I met Mackall's mother and two brothers when we dedicated the camp. Mackall's mom is a real lady. She has two other boys in the army. They're privates. Both were overwhelmed by all of the brass," Father Nachen replied.

"That's how it is, isn't it, Father? Every boy who dies in this war is somebody's son, brother, father, or uncle."

"No man is an island. Right, Gin?" Father Nachen asked.

"That's right, because 'Each man's death diminishes me, for I am involved in mankind. Therefore, send not to know for whom the bell tolls. It tolls for thee.'" You made me memorize John Donne's poem in JUG, when I was a sophomore at St. Ignatius, about two lifetimes ago. That must be nine or ten years. The world was a different place then, wasn't it?"

"Gin, the world was not so different ten years ago. Americans are just more familiar with reality now. For the Chinese, Ethiopians, Manchurians, and many others, this war has been going on for nearly a decade. For the French and British, it's been four years. America has lost a lot of her innocence since Pearl Harbor. We're not so self-centered anymore.

"Gin, why are you back stateside? I can see that something's happened. The Army wouldn't normally send a gallant, experienced man like you back home. Are you in trouble?"

Phil looked hard at his old mentor. He took a lot of time, mulling the answer over in his mind. "I guess the answer to that question depends upon your perspective. No, I'm not in trouble in the sense that I might be subject to court-martial. I'm not in jeopardy of being arrested," Genero explained. "But it's fair to say that my military career is in a shambles. The reassignment to Camp Mackall is the airborne equivalent of being exiled to Siberia."

"What happened, Gin? I know enough about the Army to conclude that whatever happened must have been serious."

"You'll get nowhere trying to apply logic. The situation is way too emotional and political for logic to play much of a role," Phil said.

For the next several moments, Phil explained the difficulties and petty rivalries that had sprung up among the senior officers in the Anglo-American alliance. As a protégé of Colonel Raff, Phil could not avoid being caught in the vise.

After listening to the whole story, which required a rare second scotch and postponed dinner, Father Nachen felt thoroughly depressed. He had no reason to disbelieve Phil's version of events.

"I suppose you handed the 82nd Airborne's CG a legitimate excuse to discipline you when you punched out his logistics star, notwithstanding any other petty motive the general or his staff might have entertained. After all, you don't have the moral high ground on at least two issues," the chaplain explained.

Phil was a bit taken aback. "What do you mean, two issues? I understand that I shouldn't have brawled with the major from G-4. What was my other lapse?" he said with a tinge of anger.

"Sorry that I'm reverting to my mentor role, Major Genero. However, I helped you through four of the most important years in your life and have been a friend of the family for years. Since your dad is not here, I feel fully qualified to talk to you like a father. We may have the same rank, but I'm a whole lot older and more ornery," Chaplain Nachen said.

A pregnant pause followed, while Phil looked down at the half full bottle of beer in his hand. He was being rude to one of the most important people in his life. He apologized and asked his mentor to explain the second moral issue.

"We both agree that field grade officers don't brawl in the CG's mess in front of the company grade subordinates. I'm not saying that fights don't occur. But they're rare and always in private. Agreed?"

"Yes, Father. I understand, but what's the other part?" Genero asked.

"Gin, I'm fortunate to be in the 11th Airborne. General Swing is trying to cross-train all of the division's soldiers to be both paratroopers and glider men. It's going slowly. Even though the command initially labored under the completely false impression that I was too old to jump, I've taken all of the ground training and have made three jumps. I sprained my ankle on the third jump and have been recycled. I'll go back over to Bragg in a couple of weeks to make two more jumps to get my wings," Father explained.

"Gin, I've been down to our glider facility in Laurinburg. I've made two glider assaults while I trained with our regiment. Let me tell you, sitting in a small, fragile, canvas and plywood glider as it is plummeting toward the ground is far scarier than jumping out of an aircraft with two parachutes.

"Paratroopers, with silver wings, shiny jump boots, hat patches, and special pay ought to be a little more respectful of their unheralded glider-borne brothers. Paratroopers who've been cross-trained hate the glider. It's small and fragile for an aircraft. Unfortunately, it's a great big, inviting target to an enemy machine gunner. It takes a lot of balls to get into those things and fly into combat. So, punching out the G-4 major, in part because he gets to the battlefield in a different manner, was silly and stupid. It's insupportable for a thinking man like you."

"You're right, of course," Genero admitted, now even more depressed than before.

"Gin, what's next? Did they give you your assignment?" Father asked.

"No. Both Colonel Raff and I are leaving for Washington the day after tomorrow. Raff has a chance at being an airborne advisor to the top-level planners in England. With his experience, he could help with the planning for the airborne phase of the channel invasion that we will mount someday. Nobody knows the details. It's top secret. Anyway, the brass at the War Department will explain it to him later in the week. He's very happy that he's going back to Europe. He wants back in the fight. So do I." Genero explained.

"What about you, Phil? What will happen to you? Are you going with the colonel? You'd be a natural with your language skills."

"I don't think so. Although I don't know for sure what they have in store for me, I have a hunch that I'm not going back to Europe. The G-1 asked me a lot of questions about my role as an intelligence officer in the planning for the three combat jumps that I made in North Africa," Phil said.

"You made three combat jumps? That must explain those three sewn stars above your wings," Father Nachen observed.

"That's right, Father. That piece of embroidery is a tradition that we've started in the 509th. Anyway, the G-1 asked me how well I know Major General Moses, who's on MacArthur's staff in New Guinea. They must know that I worked for Moses before I went airborne. I'm also a veteran of the 503d, which unofficial scuttlebutt says is in the Pacific somewhere, probably Australia. I have a feeling that they're planning something for the 503d. I think I might be able to help," Phil explained.

"How do you feel about going to the Pacific? With your experience fighting the Germans and with your language skills, that would be a complete waste."

"There you go, trying to apply that Jesuit logic again. Brigadier General Taylor of the 82nd Airborne speaks fluent Japanese and he's the assistant division commander in North

Africa. There's probably some guy who speaks Arabic in the Aleutians right now. Anyway, I'm anxious to go to the Pacific. I've got a personal score to settle."

"One last piece of advice, my young friend. I can imagine that you're very angry about your sister's death. Remember that this is not a private war. Don't let your desire for revenge cloud your judgment. I'll state the obvious. No Japanese soldier that you kill will ever bring Kari back from the dead. But you could end up getting some of your own men hurt and killed, if your judgment is affected by your desire to get even. Winning this war and ending the era of militarism in Japan is the best way to insure that Kari's death is vindicated as a worthy sacrifice in a just cause," Father assured Phil.

Although Genero listened to his old mentor and appeared to be calm, inwardly he seethed with anger. That morning, when he began to suspect that he might be sent to the Pacific to fight the Japanese, he felt elated. In an epiphany, he saw the exile from North Africa as miracle. *I don't give a damn if I never make Lieutenant Colonel. I only want to get to the Pacific where I can even the score. The Japs killed one of the three most important people in my life and I will make those bastards pay and pay and pay. No sermon from Father Nachen will ever change my mind.*

# Chapter 41

11:30 AM
June 18, 1943
The Genero Farmhouse
Cumberland County, Pennsylvania
Southeast of Waggoners Gap

On Friday morning, a prematurely graying Phillip Genero sat fidgeting next to the breakfast nook's open window. There was no cool breeze off the ridgeline to stir the stifling air. Phillip felt edgy as he nursed his second cup of black coffee.

Normally, the men in Phillip's family had aged well. After all, he was the product of hardy peasant stock. The death of his daughter, his fear for his paratrooper son in this awful war, the strange and inexplicable events of the previous night, and his wife's highly unusual behavior had taken a serious toll. This morning, Phillip felt much older than his 45 years.

Five days earlier, on Monday, Phillip's boy had returned from the war.

*I didn't expect Gin to come home so soon. Lord, he's full-grown. He's not my boy any longer. He's a changed man, burdened with crushing responsibilities,* Phillip thought as he took another sip of his coffee.

On Monday morning, Phillip and Marta had been sitting in the same breakfast nook enjoying their coffee and their time together. Phillip had been keeping Marta amused by reading to her from letters to the editor in the Carlisle *Evening Sentinel.*

Since their schedules had often conflicted, sharing breakfast had been a rare luxury. All of that changed a few weeks earlier when Marta announced that she'd quit her job.

Marta hadn't offered much of an explanation for her decision. Phillip didn't need one. He was only glad that his bride no longer worked for Junior.

*Besides,* Phillip thought as he looked as his wife, *ever since she quit and stopped drinking our relationship has taken on a new lease. It's almost like the old days. I should have paid more attention. That job, working for Junior, and Kari's death took such a toll on her. I should have insisted that she leave Monarch a long time ago.*

Marta was still wearing the top half of Phillip's pajamas and not much else. She tried to distract her fully dressed husband by running her sexy foot up and down his leg.

"Honey, you have to behave," Phillip offered half-heartedly, as Marta's tactics had the desired effect.

"I don't think you want me to behave. Do you?"

"Yes," Phillip lied. "One of us still has a job. If you keep that up, I'll be late for work."

"You mean that your tired, old wife can still make you late for work?" Marta asked as she got up, pulled the newspaper away, and sat on Phillip's lap. She ran her hands around his neck, pulled him close, and moved her tongue over his ear. "Come back to bed, honey, and I'll show you how I behave!"

Phillip picked his wife up in his arms and moved toward the stairs. He made it to the first landing when they heard a car pull up in front of the house.

"Who could that be?" Marta said, an impatient scowl spreading on her pretty face. "Maybe they'll just go away."

When they heard a car door slam and a male voice, Marta sighed. Phillip set her down on the step above the landing.

"It's too early for visitors," Marta said. "I guess I better make myself more presentable."

"I'll see who it is and get rid of him," Phillip promised.

"I won't change then. I'll be waiting upstairs." Marta teased, as she sauntered up the stairs.

Before Phillip could get down the stairs and through the living room to investigate, the front door flew open and—morning light framing him like a halo—his beloved son filled the opening.

Phillip was stunned. Although his boy had sent a card from Camp Mackall, the post office had not found time to deliver it before Phil's arrival in Carlisle. In the card, his boy had explained his unexpected reassignment to the States. He promised to get home as soon as he could. As it happened, young Phil was able to keep his promise to his folks, one day before he could communicate it to them.

Phillip ran over and hugged his son. Phillip tried to yell to Marta, but only managed to croak and bleat the wonderful news.

"Marta, Marta! Get down here right away. Gin's home! Honey, your boy's here. Thank God. He's down here with me!" Phillip managed.

Marta heard someone calling out her name, but she couldn't make out the rest. Then she heard Phillip yelling her son's name.

Her blood ran cold. *Oh, God! What if it's a telegram? Please, God, don't let my baby be hurt!*

Marta made out two separate voices and more shouting. Although she couldn't understand the words, she realized that something good had happened downstairs.

Marta threw on a robe and ran out of the bedroom and turned right to negotiate the stairs. She was barefoot and the hardwood steps stung the soles of her feet as she took them two and three at a time.

Arriving near the bottom of the stairs Marta collided with her son. Phil swept her petite frame in his powerful arms and smothered her with his embrace.

Standing cantilevered on the third and forth stair, captured in Phil's crushing bear hug, Marta craned her head and neck to get a glimpse of her son's handsome face.

"Phil! Oh, Phil; thank God you're home! I've been so worried about you," Marta shouted. She grasped her son's head and kissed both of his cheeks and forehead countless times.

"Mom, it's been such a long time. I've really missed you and Dad. It's good to be home," Phil said, his voice cracking.

The first day of Phil's homecoming went well. Phillip cancelled his appointments for the balance of the week. Nothing was more important than being with his son.

Marta and Phil spent two hours together in the kitchen nook, where she refused to let go of his hand. When Marta first noticed that he'd lost most of two fingers, she wept.

The family had a lot of catching up to do. It was a bittersweet moment but the Genero family found their equilibrium. The balance of the week went well, although awkward interludes and sad vignettes punctuated each day.

The Generos had lost a cherished daughter and sister. They'd never grieved together as family. Over the next few days, they did so by recalling some of the most poignant and humorous events in her life.

Phil was now a grown man. He was used to commanding men in combat. He could not revert back to being his momma's little boy. When Marta and Phillip tried to discuss his next assignment, his evasiveness made both parents anxious.

Despite their grieving and Phil's reticence, the family was on track, until it all unraveled on Thursday night. On Friday morning, as Phillip finished his third cup of coffee, he shivered when he recalled the circumstances of the night before—and how life for the Generos would never be the same.

Phil should have told his parents about his assignment to the Pacific when he first got home. Bad news never gets better with time. As Thursday rolled around, Marta began to press her son for details.

*I just know that Gin's going back overseas,* Marta thought. *Those damn Russians want our boys to open a second front in Western Europe. Everybody knows that. Gin's a paratrooper. He'll be one of the first on the ground in any invasion. Dear God.*

Since he had to leave by Friday afternoon, Phil told his mom and dad of his new assignment late on Thursday morning. "Mom, the Pentagon has posted me back to my old unit, the 503d. I can't tell you exactly where that is, but I can tell you that it's in the Pacific."

*Maybe that's not so bad,* Marta thought as Phil chatted on with his dad. *I wish they'd given Gin an assignment to train paratroops at Fort Bragg. That would be much better than combat. Maybe the Pacific will be safer for him than Europe. We don't seem to hear as much about the Japanese as we do the Germans.*

Phil's dad did not view the reassignment as good news. Phillip had toured the Pacific. He'd seen a lot of boys, mostly Marines, badly shot up from the Solomon Campaigns, especially Guadalcanal.

By early evening, things became emotional at the Genero farm. "Gin, why don't you take the Cadillac and drive into Carlisle?" Phillip suggested. "Your mom needs some time to digest your news."

By 7:30 on Thursday night, Phil stood in his parent's kitchen, resplendent in his tan trousers and forest green uniform blouse, known as the 'pinks and greens,' with all of his ribbons, badges and accouterments properly displayed. Giving his mom a hurried peck, he walked out of the house, got into his dad's caddy, and drove off toward town to see if he could scare up some company at old Alfie McDuff's.

The bar in the basement of McDuff's on High Street had been around since before the American Revolution. It always had a coterie of regulars. The patrons at McDuff's would be glad to see young Phil, now that he was back from the war.

Phil spent a few pleasant hours leaning against the long, copper-trimmed mahogany bar, sipping from several cold bottles of Genesee, while he held court with McDuff's habitués. None of the locals would permit him to pay for a drink, so long as he told them about his adventures in England, Algeria, Tunisia, and Morocco.

Popular legend had it that George Washington had lifted a tankard at this very bar after reviewing the troops who went off to quash the Whiskey Rebellion. Recalling the story, one of the local women teased Phil about becoming a general, just like George Washington.

Phil assured her that he would never be a general. Examining his medals and jump wings with three stars for his combat jumps, the woman chose not to believe him, chalking up his pessimism to a sense of modesty.

All of the attention embarrassed Phil and he hadn't had this much to drink since Bill Yarborough pinned his jump wings on him at Fort Benning. Normally, Phil was a happy drinker, but his experiences in combat had brought out a sadder and more introspective tone when the alcohol depressed his defenses.

"Folks, I've been very lucky," Phil said, as he recalled his friends who had died in North Africa. "The real heroes are the boys who will never come back to share a drink with friends and family at a local bar."

John Hatch, a manager at the Masland textile plant—Monarch Industries' biggest rival in Carlisle—was the oldest and most respected man in the room. Moved by Phil's modesty, he stood up and cleared his throat to get everyone's attention. When the bar fell silent, he raised his glass and began.

"Gin, I've known you all your life. All of us in Carlisle, whether we work for Randy Monarch or the Masland Brothers, are extremely proud of you and the man that you've become. We share your grief for your fellow soldiers and for your own beautiful sister, who died tending to our wounded countrymen on Corregidor.

"Gin, like your dad, I fought in World War I. To honor your comrades and your sister, and with apologies to Major John McCrae, I would like to quote a part of his famous poem from my war, because his words say it better than I ever could:

'We are the dead. Short days ago
We lived, felt dawn, saw sunset glow.
Loved, and were loved, and now we lie
In Flanders Fields.
Take up our quarrel with the foe.
To you from failing hands we throw
The torch; be yours to hold it high.
If ye break faith with us who die,
We shall never sleep, though poppies grow
In Flanders Fields.'

"Ladies and Gentlemen, to all of our brave men and women who have given their lives so that the rest of us can live free, please raise your glasses and reflect on their sacrifice for a quiet moment."

When the moment passed, Mr. Hatch said, "Gin, you must take up the torch for the fallen. Though you've already made us proud, we know you will continue to do your duty. God bless you and keep you safe!"

The crowd at Alfie McDuff's uttered a unanimous "Hear, hear!" Then they continued on the more upbeat tone, especially after Hatch ordered a round for the bar and told the bartender to put it on Frank Masland's tab.

While the locals crowded around the bar to get their drinks, Phil turned away and stared unseeing at the exposed brick wall. *I know I've had too much to drink,* Phil thought. *Only a few days ago, I was in North Africa, helping to plan the invasion of Sicily, where more of my friends will die. Now, I'm home and these folks have no idea what's happening out there. I feel so angry. I can't let them see what I'm feeling. I'll take up the torch all right. I'll take it and shove it down the throat of every fucking Jap soldier I can find.*

Reenergized by the free round, the patrons began to pepper Phil to give his views on the war's progress. Everyone agreed that success in North Africa was just the beginning. There was a long and treacherous road ahead before the war was won. The conversation changed into a spirited debate, as the entire bar argued—each patron advancing his or her own back-seat general theory.

Later in the evening, Phil's uncle Angelo came into the bar. He'd just closed the family bakery, which was only five blocks away. Earlier, when he made his daily call to his brother, he'd heard that his nephew might be at McDuff's. Angelo had made it a point to see Phil every day since his return from the war.

Around half past ten, Uncle Angelo decided that his nephew had enough to drink. Angelo suggested that he and Phil walk over to the bakery. He was proud of his business. He wanted Phil to see the improvements he'd made before his nephew left to go overseas. Besides, he'd warm up some fresh Italian bread and make him a sandwich to counteract the beer.

Reconnecting with the folks of his hometown had been important to Phil, and he'd enjoyed the banter at McDuff's. It was getting late, and he was ready to leave with his uncle. Phil and Angelo made their exit after a more hugs and handshakes.

As the two men walked west on High Street, they encountered friends at the town square. After exchanging greetings, they continued west on the short walk toward Dickenson College and the bakery, passing by the Hamilton Restaurant. Their timing was jinxed.

As a boy, Phil was addicted to the Hamilton's signature hot dog. During his trips home, Phil made it point to go to the grill and have a couple of the hotchee dogs.

On this particular trip, he'd spent most of the time with his family and hadn't had the opportunity. It had been more than a year and half since he'd last indulged. As Phil and his uncle passed by the grill, the pungent aroma pulled them into the Hamilton.

Late at night, the grill catered to customers who, like Phil, had been drinking at one of the Carlisle bars and who wanted something to eat to help sober up.

While Uncle Angelo had never acquired a taste for the Hamilton's fare, if his inebriated godson wanted a couple of chilidogs, he was all for it. They entered the grill together.

There were eight couples and 20 other patrons in the restaurant, some of whom recognized Phil. They greeted him with friendly shouts.

After Phil and his uncle found an unoccupied table near the front, a few of the customers came up to welcome Phil home, to thank him for his service, and to wish him good luck.

Neither Angelo nor Phil noticed the couple sitting in far corner in one of the four booths located against the back wall. The occupants of the booth had not missed Phil's entrance.

Linda Monarch-Collingswood eyed the Generos as she stirred her second cup of coffee. Phil had matured into one of the most handsome and virile young men she'd ever seen. Despite the fact that she was married to Evan Collingswood, Linda had sampled several young men in Pennsylvania and New York.

To survive in the dysfunctional Monarch Family, Linda had developed a sophisticated personal façade with ten inches of armor plate. Any attempt Linda made to obtain affection was rejected, criticized, or crushed; she searched endlessly for it outside her home. She quickly learned that men would trade affection for her sexual favors. Unfortunately, no one source of affection was ever adequate.

Even though she had cared for Phil—after a fashion—her needs were intense and immediate. Linda would never be satisfied with a long-distance relationship. So, when she went to school in Boston, she found a local source to satisfy her needs, at the expense of Phil's broken heart.

*It's amazing, really,* she'd thought at first. *Just by letting these men think I can be had, they'll trip over each other to pay attention to me. They're such fools.* She admired them for their power, and disdained them for their passions.

Months earlier, Linda had begun to notice that her husband was up to something nefarious. She didn't know if it was another woman, something at work, or if he'd simply grown tired of their loveless relationship.

*It really doesn't matter,* she had thought at the time. *I'm going to end this charade with Evan. But I don't want to be alone. I just need to find a suitable replacement.*

Once she made the decision to dump Collingswood, she'd redoubled her sampling efforts. Earlier in the evening, Linda had been out drinking with Richard Madison, one of Consolidated Steel's junior executives. He'd avoided military service because he was 28 years old, married with children, and held an industrial job critical to the war effort. He was a rising star with a secure future. *Too bad he's such a crappy lay,* Linda thought.

Linda had taken Madison for a tryst in the back of Dick's Pontiac. They tried to go to the special place at Waggoners Gap, but the Pontiac was too big and clumsy to negotiate the fence line, so they parked outside the locked gate. They spent a heated hour before Linda's boredom and the muggy weather forced an end to their lovemaking.

On the way back through town, they stopped at the Hamilton for coffee so that Dick could drive home to his wife and family in Bethlehem. While Dick babbled about boring fiscal issues facing the steel industry in wartime, Linda kept remembering how sweet it had been with Phil when they were kids. Even after the interlude at Waggoners Gap, Linda was still horny.

Seeing Genero for the first time since Kari's going away party got her juices flowing again. *Hmmm,* Linda thought. *Gin would make the ideal replacement. He's respected in the community and he's a great lover. I'll bet I can generate a little interest, just like the old days.*

Linda excused herself from Madison, saying that she needed to use the ladies' room. Instead, she left the restaurant and walked through a connecting corridor to the front desk of the Hessian Hotel, which sat next door to the Hamilton. She knew the night clerk well.

Mr. Anderson had worked at the hotel for 15 years. He was a quiet man, cautious, intelligent, and discrete. From time to time, in exchange for his good judgment and discretion, Linda provided him with a cash-filled white envelope.

Without a word, the clerk passed Linda a special key. It belonged to the door on the corporate suite that Linda's father had rented over the last four years. After his near-death experience in Boiling Springs, Junior Monarch had decided that a remote farmhouse was not the best or safest venue for his illicit affairs.

Two years earlier, Linda had learned of her father's love nest. With Mr. Anderson's complicity, she used it from time to time without her dad or husband finding out. Linda hadn't taken Dick Madison to the suite, as she reserved the room for special occasions and not run-of-the-mill infidelities.

Linda walked away from the front desk with the key in her hand. *Maybe tonight I'll renew an old friendship,* she thought.

Linda encountered Phil as she passed the rest rooms on her way back to the restaurant. When he exited the lavatory, Phil collided with Linda. His eyes widened in surprise.

"Well, well! Fancy running into you. What do we have here? The hero, home from the wars!" Linda said, trying to flash her most alluring smile.

"Oh, hello, Linda," Phil responded without enthusiasm. "Here with your husband?"

"Actually, "I'm having coffee with an old friend of the family. Would you like to join us?"

"Not really. I want to be with my family tonight because I'm leaving tomorrow."

"Gin," Linda interjected as she stepped in close giving him a whiff of her expensive perfume. "This guy that I'm having coffee with is a little pushy. I'd feel better if you'd stick around and discourage him. Afterward, you can go home to mommy! I won't bite you. If you can deal with the Germans, I should be no challenge."

"Linda, I don't think that's a good idea. Why don't you tell the guy to shove off? The grill's full of people. He won't start anything. I've got to get back," Phil explained, as he inhaled Linda's perfume.

Phil hadn't been with a woman since his last night in Cindy's flat in London. That was almost eight months earlier. This evening, Phil had consumed more beer than he was used to drinking. He was drunk and he was randy. Linda's proximity, her perfume, and his libido operated in sync with Linda's plan.

Seizing the moment, Linda pushed closer until her whole body touched Phil's. She pulled Phil's head down so that she could whisper in his ear, "Gin, do you remember the times that we'd go to up to the Gap in my dad's Caddy? You weren't so shy then. Do you remember how I could make you feel?"

Phil pulled back a little and looked at Linda's face. He remembered how much it meant to him to see the smoky, far-away look in her eyes during intimate moments when they would fall over the edge together.

"Yes, I remember," Phil said. "But we were a couple then. You weren't married."

"I was pretty good for you, wasn't I? I always put a smile on your face, didn't I?" Linda asked, ignoring Phil's comment.

"Every time. Yes, you did," Phil recalled.

"I'll bet you've missed me and the way I made you feel, right?" Linda pressed.

Linda chose that moment to kiss Phil. It began as a small peck, then she pressed her lips to his. When he began to kiss her back, she multiplied the passion.

Phil—setting aside his better judgment and letting the alcohol mute his inhibitions—responded to Linda's advances. He hadn't expected Linda to be so aggressive. In high school she'd always wanted him to take the lead.

Phil felt caught up in the moment. Thinking about it later, he admitted that it was a near thing.

If Linda hadn't chosen that particular moment to entice Phil by flashing the suite's room key, he might have succumbed. Once Linda produced the key, Phil went from white-hot to blue-cold in record time. The room key caused him to flash back to the hotel in Boston in the winter of 1937. He was still hurt by seeing Linda having sex with that other guy. In less than 20 seconds, he sobered up, lost his ardor, and stepped back from his embrace with Linda.

"What's the matter, lover?" Linda asked teasingly, as she tried to pull him back.

"Linda, this is not going to happen," Phil said, with menace creeping into his voice. "You're a married woman. I'm an Army officer. Get a hold of yourself!"

"Oh, so the baker's son is too good for the trashy rich girl, right? What are you saying? Fucking someone else's wife violates your precious military code of honor? What a bunch of hypocrites you Generos are!" Linda said, demonstrating the same hair-trigger temper as her father.

"What in the hell are you talking about? Are you crazy? What hypocrisy? I've avoided you for years, precisely because I didn't want to be in this situation," Phil shot back.

"It's OK to stand here in the hallway, groping my tits and ass, but its fucking adultery if we go to my room? That's hypocrisy, mister!" Linda shouted at Phil, drawing the attention of the desk clerk, who'd come to investigate.

"You came on to me, Linda. I was minding my own business, trying to take a leak. You grabbed me first."

"What a bunch of shit! All of you Generos are liars and hypocrites. You're no better than that slut of a mother of yours."

Without thinking, Phil reached over and grabbed Linda by the front of her dress. With all of his considerable strength, he pushed her hard against the opposite wall of the hallway. The desk clerk and a half dozen customers and guests—who'd gathered in response to the yelling—watched helplessly. No one had the courage to confront the outraged paratrooper.

"That got to you!" Linda taunted. "Didn't you know that your sainted mother has been sleeping with my bastard father?"

"My mother wouldn't give your fucking father the time of day. Junior is a pig," Genero screamed back as he held Linda against the wall.

"Ask your precious mother why she shacked up with my dad when they were in D.C. last month. Ask her why my dad fired her ass. Well, don't bother! Dad got tired of her after fucking her for over ten years. He's a rich, powerful man. He can get any woman he wants in this town. He doesn't need your stupid mom anymore."

For an instant Genero contemplated killing Linda. *It would be so easy,* Genero thought. *I could snap her neck and this vile, evil bitch will be dead. How could I have been so wrong about her? How could I not have realized the extent of her manipulations? How could this piece of trash inhabit the same planet as my mom?*

Just then, Phil felt a gentle hand on his shoulder. Holding Linda against the wall with just his right hand, he spun 90 degrees to his left to confront the interloper. It was Uncle Angelo, who'd heard the yelling and screaming and had gone back to the rest rooms to investigate.

"Gin, let go of Linda. She's not worth it," Uncle Angelo whispered.

Phil nodded. He took several deep breaths. After a moment, he released his grip on Linda and she slid to the floor of the hall.

Leaving her shaken but unhurt, Phil pushed past the patrons in the hall, including one confused junior executive. He jogged through the restaurant and exited through the small west door of the grill. Uncle Angelo followed him and caught up with Phil on the side street. He grabbed Phil's shoulder, turned him around, and said, "Gin, Linda's drunk or crazy. She's become the biggest tramp in Carlisle. Half the men in town have been with her. She's just bitter that you won't play her game. I've never liked her, even when you guys dated in high school. You can't believe anything she says."

"Don't worry about me, Uncle Angelo. I'm OK. I know Linda's a bitch. Kari always warned me about her, too. I should have listened," Phil admitted. He felt lost in time, as if the Linda of his past had never existed and the reality of her true nature hit him like a wave, washing away the evening's joy.

"Uncle Angelo, I don't feel like going over to the bakery just now. I'll walk back to get dad's car and go home. I've had enough for one night."

"OK, son. I'll walk with you."

"No, thanks. I want to be alone for a while. I'll be all right."

Angelo agreed. He wanted some time alone, too. After getting Phil's promise that Angelo and his Uncle John could go with him to the train station the following afternoon, he turned to go to the bakery, where he could use the business phone. *As much as I hate to admit it, I've been suspicious of Marta. I knew something was up,* Angelo thought. *Linda's angry tale has the unfortunate ring of truth. Damn! Something scandalous has happened between Marta and Junior.*

Linda's primal scream gave the whole town a plausible explanation for Marta's recent behavior. It was a tawdry story that many of the gossiping wags in town would love to spread.

*I've got to call my brother right away and tell him what happened. I don't want strangers to get to him first. I'm worried about how Phillip will react.*

Angelo watched his nephew as he walked east on High Street toward the square. After a few moments, convinced that young Phil would be OK, Angelo turned and headed west toward the bakery. Had he continued to watch, he would have seen Phil stop dead in his tracks, contemplate a life-altering decision, and abruptly turn north. Phil hurried off in the direction of the main office building of Monarch Industries.

Junior Monarch pushed back from his desk, leaned back in his chair, and took one last, long look around his office. He loved the dark, old-world wood, his gleaming baroque desk, the shelves holding secret mementoes of his conquests. Sitting here, he felt powerful.

*I've caused a lot of people an enormous amount of grief from this desk. Every one of the sons-of-bitches had it coming,* Junior gloated.

He'd pulled off the biggest embezzlement in the history of the Commonwealth. *It's surreal. I've been careful. I've been creative. I've been bold. I never thought I could actually pull it off with this much cash. But I've done it! As of this morning, all of Monarch's cash reserves, liquid equity, contract prepayments, and loan proceeds are sitting in my secret accounts all through the Caribbean, Central America, and Brazil,* Junior thought. *Naturally, I'd have preferred numbered Swiss accounts, but that was not realistic, not with a war on.*

Sneaking vast sums of money to Switzerland during the war would be problematic. When the war was over, he'd want his embezzled money in a country with a stable government and a strong financial sector—hopefully Switzerland would come out of the war with both intact.

In the next few days, when his embezzlement came to light, the board would learn that it had no capital to make payroll or to continue any vestige of the operation. *How sweet that will be. If only I could be a fly on the wall at the next board meeting,* Junior fantasized.

Junior laughed out loud, as he thought how much fun it would be to read about the directors' desperate and futile efforts to save the business. *These little turds will be lost without Monarch Industries. Fuck them all! It's ironic that my son-in-law will be among those left holding the bag. The investigation will eventually lead to him. He might do a lot of time in prison. That's too good.*

Junior had carefully salted the books and records of the company with false, forged, and misleading receipts, deposit items, checks, contracts, and bills. Monarch was a realist. *I know that the feds and the state investigators will realize that I stole the money. That's obvious. Even with the false identities and blind trails—the feds may find me in Brazil,* Junior conceded. *But if the feds and state investigators have a few high-level scapegoats, like Phillip Genero, to prosecute and incarcerate, they might not be as rabid about tracking me down.*

Junior laughed again when he thought of Marta wailing as agents of the FBI escorted her husband off to federal prison. That would be the ultimate revenge. *The stupid bitch could have had it all with me. It will serve her right,* Junior thought.

All Junior had to do is grab his briefcase, go down the back steps to the car—parked in the alley—and head out to the train station. He needed to get the last train down to Chambersburg, where he had a small plane waiting.

Using the specially chartered private plane was a stroke of genius. It would fly him to Miami. Even with a war on, he'd booked passage to Rio. With his false documents and passport, he would be in his first-class stateroom on the boat to Rio by early Sunday afternoon.

Junior reached into his vest's watch pocket and pulled out his dad's gold pocket watch. *Jesus! It's 11:30. Tempus Fugit,* Junior thought. *I'd better get moving.*

Suddenly, the phone began to ring. *Who in the fuck would have the balls to call me at this hour?* He wondered.

Junior toyed with not answering the phone. It would be better if he left. When he heard the sixth irritating ring, he picked up the receiver and held it to his ear without saying a word.

After a long silence, Junior heard the caller identify himself. "Mr. Monarch, are you there? Is that you? It's Anderson from the Hessian Hotel. Are you there?"

"What in the fuck are you doing calling me here at this hour, you little weasel? Are you looking to be unemployed? I've half a mind to call the hotel's manager," Junior exploded at the desk clerk.

"Sir, I'm sorry to interrupt, but this is important."

"It fucking better be or it'll be your ass!"

"Sir, there was an incident here at the hotel a few moments ago involving your daughter and the Genero boy."

"I heard that bastard was back in town. What happened?"

"Mr. Monarch, your daughter and the Genero boy got into a fight. I don't know what started it, but they were screaming at each other."

"So, the fuck what? They've had arguments over the years, especially when they were kids. Is that why you called me, you old fool?"

"No, sir. I thought that you needed to know what your daughter said to the Genero boy about you and his mother."

That bit of news stopped Junior cold. He asked Anderson to explain what in the hell he was talking about. Anderson complied, giving a full account of what he saw and heard. He noted that there were ten other witnesses to the public argument.

"Sir, knowing Carlisle, your daughter's accusations are spreading all over Cumberland County, even at this hour."

The blood ran from Junior's face. *I might be in a real jam,* Junior thought as he slammed the telephone back into the cradle. *The maggots in Carlisle and Cumberland County live on gossip. A juicy rumor will spread faster than the speed of light. Damn! Anderson's right. People are calling their friends, waking them up, and telling them all of the details.*

*Somebody will talk to Phillip Genero tonight about the fight and the accusations,* Junior worried. *This could get dangerous. Both Phillip and Gin are war heroes. I've heard the stories of Gin killing several men with his bare hands.*

*My bitch of a daughter has made my exit more complicated with that big mouth of hers. It might be too risky to use the train. Somebody might see me and remember. Maybe I should drive myself to Chambersburg. But then I'll have difficulty disposing of the car. Thanks to Linda's bullshit, I have to leave now. I would like to pay that little bitch back. Maybe a small dose of poverty will do the trick.*

Just then, Junior heard someone stomping up the front stairs. No one was supposed to be in the building. The sound of the steps seemed ominous. The skin on his arms began to crawl with fear.

Hearing the footsteps come closer, Junior opened the desk drawer and pulled out his short-barreled Smith and Wesson .38 caliber pistol. After the beating that he had taken those years ago from the steel worker, he always kept a gun handy. He also had a .25 caliber pistol in his briefcase as additional insurance. Junior checked the cylinder. The .38 was loaded. He stood up, held the revolver waist high, and pointed it at his office's outer door.

As the footsteps reached the top of the landing, Junior pulled back the hammer of the .38 and extended his arm, locking his right elbow.

Finally, the footsteps approached Junior's office door. Then, there was silence.

"Who's out there?" Junior yelled, his voice quavering. "What in the fuck do you want?"

Phillip finished the last of his coffee and placed the cup on the table. He closed his eyes and said a prayer.

When Phillip opened his eyes, Marta stood before him. She was dressed for the ride into town to see Phil off.

"You and Gin were out very late. Neither of you got home until after four this morning. Where did you go, Phillip?"

"Angelo called. Gin and Linda Monarch got into a big fight. My brother was worried about Gin. I went out to look for our boy," Phillip lied.

"Honey, I know all about the fight. After you left, I got a few calls, too. I know what people are saying about me and Junior," Marta admitted sadly.

"People love gossip," Phillip said. "They'll be vicious with this one. But I don't care what they say. I love you. I always have, and I always will."

"Phillip, I swear that I never had sex with Junior Monarch. I would never do that to you, or to myself. I want to tell you what happened in Washington."

Phillip nodded, as Marta took the chair next to him at the table. She related the events at the Willard Hotel in May. When she finished, she was holding Phillip's hand.

"Why didn't you tell me when I first got back from Hawaii?" Phillip asked.

"I was afraid that if I did, you'd get so angry that you'd try to kill Junior. He's a pathetic excuse for a human being. He's not worth you getting in trouble."

"You're probably right. When Angelo told me about Linda's accusations, I got so mad that I couldn't see straight. I hadn't been so angry since the Argonne."

"Honey, did you go to confront Junior last night? Be honest with me," Marta pleaded.

"No, I just went looking for Gin," Phillip lied again.

"Why did you stay out so late, then?"

"I couldn't find Gin anywhere in town. I went up to the Gap, to see if he was there. I didn't see him until we both got back here, early this morning," Phillip responded, more honestly.

"What happened when you two spoke? He doesn't want to talk to me," Marta said. "I'm his mom. I love him! He's the only baby I have left."

"Marta, it'll be OK. He loves you very much. He needed a little sleep and a little time to calm down. Gin knows what a worthless slug Junior is. Just watch. He'll be down for lunch. We'll all talk and things will be fine. We'll resolve everything before he leaves today. I promise. Honey, I've thought it over. I can't work near Junior anymore. I'll resign from Monarch later this afternoon. Junior won't hurt anyone in this family ever again."

Marta reached over and hugged her husband passionately. "I love you with all my heart, Phillip!"

"I love you too, Marta," Phillip said, trying to mask his foreboding.

# Chapter 42

THE CARLISLE EVENING SENTINEL
SUNDAY, JUNE 20, 1943
MONARCH EXECUTIVE MISSING
Federal and Commonwealth Investigators Puzzled

By Thomas McVicker

**HARRISBURG, Pennsylvania** (June 19, 1943)—The United States Attorney in Harrisburg, Frederick V. Follmer, revealed late Friday that Federal and State investigators have obtained warrants for the arrest of Mr. Randal J. Monarch, Jr., the Chief Executive Officer of Carlisle-based Monarch Industries. The affidavits supporting the warrants claim that state investigators and FBI agents have discovered evidence of fraud in several contracts that Monarch Industries has executed with the United States Army and Navy.

Monarch Industries is a major manufacturer of apparel and one of the largest employers in the Cumberland Valley. Since 1940, Monarch Industries has entered into several lucrative contracts with the buying commands of the Armed Services to provide uniforms for the military. "Until recently, the quality of the Monarch uniforms has been first-rate," a War Department spokesman told the Sentinel upon the condition that he would remain anonymous. The same source revealed that certain questions arose when unexplainable deficiencies began to surface in numbered lots of uniforms that were earmarked for the Marines in the Central and South Pacific. The arrest affidavits reveal that the Federal investigators have been working for several months and have obtained evidence from confidential sources that support their claim that probable cause exists to arrest Mr. Monarch.

Though arrest warrants have been issued for Mr. Monarch, the Federal agents have been unable to locate him. The U.S. Attorney admitted that a thorough search of Junior Monarch's main office and home on Friday and Saturday revealed that he might have been tipped off. Authorities believe that Junior Monarch has fled the jurisdiction. The U.S. Attorney considers Junior Monarch to be a fugitive in interstate flight to avoid prosecution. Sources suggest that Mr. Monarch may have planned his flight in advance and may be in route to a country that does not have an extradition treaty with the United States.

Other sources have revealed that Junior Monarch embezzled $24,000,000.00 in Monarch company funds. The allegations cannot be confirmed until the banks and financial institutions open for business on Monday. These sources fear that an embezzlement of so vast an amount will result in the corporation's bankruptcy.

On Saturday, the Monarch Industries board of directors met in an emergency session to address these issues. By unanimous vote, Phillip E. Genero, formerly the Vice-President of Marketing, was elevated to acting-Chief Executive Officer. In a brief statement, Mr. Genero asked all Monarch employees to be patient and to remain at their jobs until the allegations against Junior Monarch can be resolved. Mr. Genero revealed that Federal agents are in the clothing plants and administrative offices conducting their investigation. All Monarch employees are asked to provide whatever assistance that the Federal authorities request.

The FBI regional office in Harrisburg has issued an all-points bulletin for Junior Monarch's apprehension. Anyone with any knowledge of his whereabouts is asked to contact Special Agent Carroll T. Roberts at the Harrisburg office immediately. Monarch Industries has agreed to pay an award of $25,000.00 for information leading to the arrest and conviction of anyone associated with the alleged embezzlement.

# Chapter 43

1030 Hours
July 6, 1943
Office of the Flight Surgeon
Naval Medical Center
Wisconsin Avenue
Bethesda, Maryland

As he read the results of the various tests and the summary of the final report in the pilot's folder, Commander Lee Coulter looked up from the paperwork and stared across his large wooden desk at the unimpressive-looking young man. The flight surgeon shook his head.

*It's hard to believe that a man who's absorbed such tremendous physical trauma would volunteer to go back to such a dangerous circumstance,* Coulter thought. *Mister Sullivan is lucky to be alive. It's a miracle that he's not blind in one eye. If the plastic surgeon in Hawaii hadn't been so skilled, this young man would have an ugly scar on his face for the rest of his life.*

*Sullivan's been seriously wounded in both major engagements in which he's fought. This guy ought to go to Pensacola and be an instructor. With his two confirmed kills and his citations, he'd be a natural. He ought to leave the combat to guys with a little more luck. He might make it home that way.*

"Well, Mister Sullivan, it looks like everything checks out. All of your medical tests are satisfactory. You're cleared to remain on flight status. We won't interpose a medical objection or limit your duty with the air wing in the Pacific fleet," Cdr. Coulter stated.

"Thanks, Doc! I've been back flying for a few months and I didn't expect any problems," Sullivan responded.

"Then I'll note that you didn't encounter any difficulties due to your wounds and injuries in flying the dive-bomber," Coulter stated, as he scribbled a notation in Sullivan's medical jacket.

"Actually, Doctor, I'm not flying the SBDs anymore. I'm now qualified and checked out on the F6F-3."

"You're flying the new Hellcat? I've heard that it's a real hot fighter, right?"

"Oh, yeah! It's hot, all right. Compared to the Dauntless, and even the Wildcat, this crate sizzles, Doc," Sullivan said, leaning forward in his chair, excited about his plane.

Commander Coulter was not a pilot. As a flight surgeon, he had an ambiguous relationship with pilots. *These boys are brave, but they can be irresponsible,* Coulter thought. *Sometimes I think that pilots don't have a thimble-weight of common sense among them. But it's their courage that enables these boys to fly the new hot planes into combat.*

"Hmmm, your medical file reflects that you're rated as a dive-bomber pilot," Coulter said, as he thumbed through the thick file, trying to verify his information.

"I used to fly the Slow But Deadly but I'm a bona fide Hellcat jockey now. That shouldn't make a difference. I'm still good to go, right Doc?"

"I suppose so," Coulter conceded. "I should re-confirm the data. Now that you're a fighter pilot, you'll be flying a whole different way. Am I correct?"

"Yeah. Hopefully, I won't get shot so often," Sullivan joked. "The F6 is the hottest thing we've got in the air right now, Doc. I suppose the Corsair jocks might dispute that. Most of them are jarheads. Can't expect them to know shit about aircraft design.

"The Hellcat is a huge improvement over the Wildcat. It's got a bigger, more powerful engine. It flies faster. It's more maneuverable. It climbs like a scalded angel and has a bunch more range. You know, it's even bigger than the old Dauntless, but it's a whole different bird. I love it! The Japs are in for a very nasty surprise. We're going to take the skies back from the fucking Zekes," Sullivan finished, his eyes bright and his face glowing with excitement.

"Oh, yes. Here it is!" Doc Coulter said as he found Sullivan's new designation and orders in the file. "You're to be assigned to VF-9 on the Essex. That's one of those new, fast carriers, isn't it?"

"Haven't seen the Essex yet, Doc. She deployed in the late spring. She's somewhere in the Pacific. I'll catch up with her out there. I'll be the exec. Commander Phil Torrey is the skipper of VF-9."

"Well, Mister Sullivan, there's nothing in your file that will keep you on the deck."

"That's good, Doc. Real good. If there's nothing more, I've got to get moving. I'm leaving for the west coast tonight. Got to be in San Francisco by the end of the week. Wish me luck!"

"I do indeed, Lieutenant Commander Sullivan. I'll say a prayer for you."

"Save your prayers for the Japs, Doc. They'll need them more than me. We're about to turn this war around."

Sullivan shook the flight surgeon's hand and grabbed his file. He slipped his medical file into the large manila envelope with his pay and personnel records, turned, and left the office.

Doc Coulter watched Sullivan depart and thought, *I have no doubt that with boys like this one, the Japanese will be defeated. I just hope that this cocky Irishman is alive to see the final victory.*

# Chapter 44

1645 Hours
August 9, 1943
Mountain View Hotel
Gordonvale, Queensland
Northeastern Australia

C aptain Tom Gilbert strode out of the cool winter evening and stepped into the warmth of the Mountain View Hotel in Gordonvale. He could feel sparks fly off his chest as small shock waves shot up and down his short, but powerful, arms. Though knots twisted and untwisted in his stomach, his chest puffed out a mile.

Late in the afternoon, Gilbert had attended a special briefing from Phil Genero, his old friend and basic infantry course classmate. After more than eight months of hard training, forced marches, practice jumps, and unrelenting chicken-shit details in tropical Queensland, the 503d Parachute Infantry Regiment would jump into combat in New Guinea.

*Man, this will be quite a show,* Gilbert thought. *We'll have to take extra precautions to insure secrecy. We can't afford any mistakes.*

Gilbert walked through the hotel lobby, looking around for his friends. Just outside the doorway to the public house, he recognized a number of older men, who were leaders among the local Australian farmers and merchants. They were having a heated discussion about the latest war news.

Two of the friendly Aussies saw Gilbert and bid him hello in the Australian manner: "G'day, Mite!"

"Good day to you, Mates," Gilbert shot back, waving at the Australians, as he continued to look for Major Genero and First Lieutenant Escheverria.

"Gil, you bloody Yank bastard! C'mon over here and we'll shout you up a pot of Four X!" Michael Kirk, the largest of the Aussies exclaimed.

Kirk then turned to his mates and changed the subject to his favorite topic. He said, "Ya know, if we could just teach the bloke to play rugby union, Gil'd make a bloody great forward—a strong side prop, I think."

All the Aussies within earshot nodded at Kirk's observation.

"You're right, Michael," one of the farmers observed. "He'd have no trouble supporting a hooker. With his huge upper body and trunk-like legs, he'd make a superb prop, given a few years to learn the game. No question, Gil was bred for the scrum."

"Michael, I'll be there in a minute." Gilbert said from across the lobby. "I'm waiting for one of my mates, just in from America. Soon as he gets here, I'll bring him in and introduce him. Don't get so drunk that you won't remember him. Save us some Four X."

Gilbert saw the two American officers, Genero and Escheverria, coming out of the latrine at the rear of the small lobby. When they spotted Gil, he waived them over to his spot in the lobby near the pub. As they got within reach, Gilbert shook their hands and pulled them aside to insure a little privacy. Genero smiled as he returned Gilbert's powerful grip.

Phil's thin smile hid the fact that he was exhausted. The last seven weeks had been a wild, crazy ride, and it looked like the madness wasn't over yet. The afternoon briefing that he'd presented to select regimental officers completed his mission's first phase.

In the next month, there would be little time for celebrations, reunions, or beer drinking. Tonight, at this small Australian hotel in a tiny sugar-milling town, deep in the shadow of Walsh's Pyramid—the highest natural freestanding peak in the world—Phil could make a small exception.

Gilbert's excitement bubbled through his speech. "Gin, Tommy, let's go into the pub before we eat. We could use a few beers. I want you to meet my Aussie mates. After we have some Four X, we can get some tucker. Maybe later we can scare up three sheilas. What do you say, Tommy?"

"Sure thing Gil." Escheverria responded.

"Tell me. What does *tucker* mean? Genero asked, not having had the opportunity to absorb any of Australia's culture.

"Major, *tucker* means food. For a man who speaks so many foreign languages, you must think you're in Oz. I guess you didn't have time to study *Strine* at Penn State. Tommy and I will translate for you tonight. Basically, we all speak English but the Aussies use a lot of words that we don't. They use a lot of words that we use in a different way. At times, it's almost a different language. You'll get used to it. It can be embarrassing, but it's fun. These blokes are some of the finest, most genuine—what they call *fair dinkum*—people on earth. They are totally unpretentious. Just be yourself," Gilbert explained.

"There were places in Britain like that. The cockney dialect in London can be downright incomprehensible. But I get what you mean. Translate for me and make sure I don't screw up."

Phil looked around the lobby to make sure none of the locals were in earshot. "I don't think that I'll have the opportunity to soak up much of the culture down under. We've got an important job to do in the next few weeks. We screw this one up and we might all be legs next year. That's assuming that any of us are still alive," Genero explained.

Phil's last statement threw cold water on Gilbert's exuberance. He hadn't seen Genero since Fort Benning—almost three years earlier. Phil had been more fun loving in those days.

Phil had seen serious combat, illustrated by the ribbons and the three stars over Genero's wings. *If I live through the next few months, I wonder how the combat will change me,* Gilbert thought.

Gilbert motioned toward the pub. "OK, mate; let's waltz into the pub. I'll get you a pot of Four X and we'll bring each other up to speed. I guess you knew Tommy before he went to OCS, right? Just be careful. Don't try to impress us with all the stories of your female conquests in jolly old England."

With that, the three men walked from the lobby, stepped inside the pub, and Gilbert began the introductions.

After Phil bid his mom a tearful farewell at the Carlisle train station, it took him five days to get to San Francisco. Four days later, Phil left the United States for the Southwest Pacific Theater and General MacArthur's Headquarters. Until he found himself in the belly of a B-17, Genero thought that he'd be relegated to another arduous seaborne transit. The indecipherable administrative codes on his travel orders provided for high-priority transit to Brisbane, Australia.

Over the next week and a half, Genero flew from San Francisco to Honolulu and eventually to Brisbane, after spending two full days in Hawaii and about 36 hours in Noumea, New Caledonia, for crew rest and refueling. In early July 1943, Phil reported to the American Headquarters in Brisbane.

Within two days, Phil was back in the air. He flew on a C-47 north across the Coral Sea to MacArthur's forward command center in Port Moresby. There were big plans in the offing and one of MacArthur's senior staff officers thought Genero could make an unusual contribution.

As soon as Phil reached Port Moresby, he learned that he had a meeting scheduled with Major General Moses, his old boss from War Plans. Moses now served on MacArthur's staff as a special advisor. Phil reported at once.

After arriving at headquarters, he received a correct—but cool—reception. For the next 90 minutes, Moses gave Genero a personal briefing of the situation in this theater of war.

Gesturing at the large map affixed to his office wall, Maj. Gen. Moses illustrated the status quo. Since the fall of the Philippines to the Japanese Empire, the Americans and their British, Australian, and New Zealand allies had fought a series of bitter land and naval battles to thwart the Japs' strategic plan for imperial expansion.

By the late spring of 1943, the allies could finally claim that they had stopped the southward expansion of the Japanese Empire. To accomplish this impressive feat, the allies had achieved costly victories on Guadalcanal in the Solomons, as well as less public—but equally important— tactical successes in the Owen Stanley Mountains just north of Port Moresby.

"Major Genero, in the next several weeks General MacArthur will go over to offensive operations in this theater. Since we have limited resources, we will use a two-pronged strategic approach that we will coordinate with Admiral Nimitz and his Pacific Fleet," Maj. Gen. Moses explained.

Moses walked closer to the map, and pointed to New Guinea. "While Nimitz attacks the chain of islands in the central Pacific, our forces will strike at pre-selected sites along the northern coast of New Guinea. We're looking for isolated vulnerabilities, so that we can hop over Jap strong points. In this way, we will use our forces most efficiently, avoid direct assaults on enemy strong points, and limit our casualties.

"Once we bypass a strong point, we'll allow it to whither on the vine and starve them out. The port city of Lae, almost directly north of our encampment, will be our first target," Moses elaborated, as he pointed at the town on the northeastern coast of the Earth's third-largest island.

"The attack on Lae will require an amphibious landing near the port. We'll use an Australian infantry division for this exercise. Of more interest to you, we are planning an airborne assault to the west of Lae. We want the 503rd to capture a small airport in the Markham Valley, near a village called Nadzab," Moses said, as he moved his finger to a spot on the map, directly west of Lae.

"After paratroopers seize the airport, we'll air land another Australian infantry division, which will pass through your lines and attack Lae from the west. We think that once the

Japanese find themselves in this tactical vise, they'll have to stand and fight or withdraw to the north.

Turning away from the map, Moses faced Genero, and continued, "Major, we've established complete air superiority in this part of the theater. If your airborne forces do their job, the Japs won't know whether to shit or go blind. We're not concerned about the seaborne landings. The Aussies have had lots of experience with amphibious operations. Unfortunately, Major, we do not have the same confidence in the airborne phase of the upcoming assault."

Surprised by the general's comment, Phil squirmed in his chair and looked back at Moses. "Why is that, sir?"

Moving away from the map, Moses leaned against the corner of his desk. "Genero, as far as we can tell out here in the Pacific, none of the American airborne commanders has managed a truly successful operation in North Africa or the ETO. I've personally reviewed the top-secret reports of the three jumps in Africa and the two that Gavin and Tucker recently executed in Sicily. I've also studied the new intelligence that the Pentagon has developed on the German air assault on Crete. None of this information inspires any confidence.

"Frankly, Major, the senior Army leadership in Europe and the United States has begun to question the whole concept of vertical envelopment. In fact, there's a real issue about fielding airborne units above the battalion level."

Shifting his weight in the chair, Phil pondered the meaning of this news. "General, I knew we'd had difficulties. I had no idea that the brass in Washington questioned the concept of large-scale airborne assaults."

"You probably haven't heard this detail because it's very close hold. Let's just say that virtually nothing went as planned in the airborne drops in support of Operation Husky," Moses said as he turned, picked up a file marked *Top Secret,* and thumbed through its contents.

"During the assaults, the inexperienced transport pilots had trouble finding the drop zones near Gela, Sicily. The Air Corps wound up dropping the 505$^{th}$ and 504$^{th}$ all over the island," Moses continued, as he scanned the classified report.

"American paratroopers landed just about everywhere on the southern third of Sicily except the designated drop zones. Worse, units were widely scattered, making cohesive operations, even against targets of opportunity, extremely difficult," Moses said.

"Major Genero, it turns out that the coordination between the naval and air forces was so bad that Anglo-American naval gunfire caused significant casualties—dead and wounded—to the airborne soldiers. On the night of the second jump, Colonel Tucker's 504th suffered badly from trigger-happy sailors on station in the Gulf of Gela.

"Worst of all, the British glider-borne force lost nearly ninety gliders in their initial assault in southeastern Sicily. Over five hundred gallant British soldiers died without firing a single shot at the enemy. It was appalling.

"Although the individual American paratrooper fought as expected, demonstrating great courage and tenacity, none of the pre-invasion missions got accomplished in time to be effective. Once the airborne units managed to coalesce, they performed magnificently. Unfortunately, it took far too long for this to happen," Moses concluded, as he turned away and tossed the report on his desk.

"Sir, this is very bad. I don't know what to say," Phil responded, as he stood up and walked over to the map for a closer look.

"Well, Major, according to the top secret reports General Eisenhower has communicated to the commander of all Army ground forces, General McNair, that based on the disappointing performance in Sicily, he no longer favors the concept of the airborne division. Eisenhower is prepared to put this opinion in writing."

Gen. Moses was not airborne. He never intended to be, not with his trick back. He was not enamored with the concept.

Getting large airborne formations to the heart of the enemy meant that staff officers had to supply food, medicine, arms, and ammunition to the airhead. Logistics operations would tie up a large proportion of any available air transport until friendly forces could link up with the paratroopers.

The reports from North Africa and Sicily suggested that the lightly armed airborne forces could not sustain intense combat operations against a determined enemy for more than a few days. Moses believed that dropping paratroopers too far out would be like forcing them out on a limb, then sawing it off at the trunk. Phil's experiences in Algeria and Tunisia only reinforced the general's pessimism.

Major Genero requested permission to ask a question. Satisfied that Phil now had all the facts, Moses told him to go ahead.

Turning away from the map to face the general, Phil said, "Sir, it's obvious that you have serious reservations about the use of airborne forces in this theater. Just how do see me assisting you in the planning for future operations against the Japanese?"

"Genero, were it my decision, I wouldn't deploy Colonel Kincaid's paratroopers in anything larger than a company-sized operation. I would rarely use airborne troops and then only against special targets. I'd adopt the model that the Germans used early in the war on Holland's western front. There were no mass tactical jumps in Holland, Belgium, Denmark, or Norway. Yet the operations were successful and made the difference in more than one important offensive operation.

"I agree with Eisenhower. The airborne division is too large, too cumbersome, and too hard to sustain at the airhead. Division-sized airborne operations are too complex, too costly, and too difficult to plan or execute.

"General MacArthur does not agree with me—and he's the boss. He wants the entire 503$^{rd}$ to secure the western flank in Markham Valley, when we go after the Port of Lae. Neither your opinion nor mine count. We'll make a regimental-sized combat jump in early September. End of debate," Moses observed.

"What's my role, sir?" Genero asked.

"Your role?" Moses asked. "Absurdly simple, Major Genero. You'll spend the next few weeks explaining to the staff every aspect and minute detail of the combat jumps that you've made. We'll evaluate your experiences. We'll cull from them the things that we think will work and reject your mistakes. In other words, Major, we'll look at what you did in North Africa and try something else. Your contribution will be to relate those tactics that failed. Sorry, that may not seem glamorous, but it may save hundreds of lives."

Overwhelmed by the realization that he'd spent two-and-a-half years on a very dangerous mission, only to be told that he was useful simply to relate the details of his failures, Phil pulled his handkerchief from the inside pocket of his blouse. He partially unfolded it and used the larger surface to mop the sweat from his forehead.

Phil took a deep breath. He fought to control his growing frustration, anger, and sense of total uselessness.

Then it struck Phil like a bolt. He was that rare man who had a second chance. Phil Genero resolved to take full advantage of his opportunity.

*Maybe assisting in the planning for a successful airborne operation out here will make up for all of my mistakes, misjudgments, and misdeeds,* Phil thought. *God help me! Maybe I'll earn some absolution for all my grievous sins.*

Capt. Gilbert stood next to Phil at the pub's bar, watching him carefully. He could see his friend's shoulders slumped in exhaustion. *Maybe we should have an early night and give Gin a break,* he thought. *He looks like he could use a drink. That should help him get some sleep.*

"Gin, you want a beer?" Gilbert asked.

"Gil, I've been working my ass off and traveling so much that I haven't had anything to drink in weeks. I've got to be careful. Whatever I get will go directly to my head."

*After Oujda and Carlisle, I have to be very careful. I can't trust my temper if I drink too much. This assignment might be my last chance. I don't want to blow it,* Genero thought.

Gilbert tried to get the barmaid's attention, but she was busy pouring several pints for the regulars. Before she could respond to Gil, Phil spotted a pump handle with the Guinness Brewery logo in an untended spot. During his time in England, he'd acquired a taste for the dark, creamy—but light—Irish stout. *A tall glass of Guinness would be perfect.*

"Can I have a pint of Guinness, please?" Major Genero asked the barmaid, whose lush contours seemed to belong on a steamy, sensuous beach and not in a crowded pub.

Annette O'Dowd stopped dead in her tracks. She looked hard at the new Yank officer who'd bellied up to her bar. "Are you serious, Mite?" she asked.

When Tom Gilbert heard the order, he winced. He looked over at 1Lt. Escheverria. The younger officer shook his head in mild embarrassment. Every Australian at the bar had heard the request. Their silence was deafening.

As Gilbert scanned the crowd, he could see the barmaid and most of the men staring at Genero in disbelief. He'd only ordered a Guinness. Phil hadn't cast an aspersion on someone's wife. In Gordonvale, it might have been better if he had.

"Annette, I'm sorry. My friend doesn't realize that British beer is unpopular here," Gilbert said. "He's new and has never had a Four X."

"Sorry, miss." Phil added, flashing a smile, while devouring Annette with his eyes.

"I expect you would be, Yank." Annette shot back, noticing Genero's leer.

Annette was popular with the customers, who were all men. They respected her beauty, her moxie, and her willingness to work hard. The hotel in this rural part of Queensland did not have a ladies' lounge, so there were no other females in the pub. A smart, tough young woman, Annette tolerated sass from no man.

At 22, Annette had already lived an entire lifetime. Her dad died when she was eight years old. Her mom had worked in the sugar mill to support her and her younger brother. Since the war began, the Army had posted her brother to New Guinea and her mom had become disabled from an accident at the mill.

At 17, Annette had married her sweetheart. She thought they were happy newlyweds until her husband disappeared two years later. She had no idea what had happened to him—or if she were the cause of his departure—and now she trusted no one.

To help support her mother and to make ends meet, Annette worked two jobs. She tended bar at night and packed parachutes for the airborne regiment during the day.

In addition to the threat of invasion, the war had been tough on Queenslanders, like Annette. Men her age were in the military and posted far away. Though she was lonely, she rejected the constant barrage of offers from the older Australian men. The influx of Americans, especially the perpetually randy paratroopers, only made the situation more difficult. Gordonvale was a small town and she was not about to become its most notorious harlot.

Annette had known for months that Captain Gilbert was interested in her, though he'd never asked her out. For a big man, he was actually quite shy. She liked him, but he was not her type.

Her type had just walked in the door and had embarrassed himself in front of half the remaining men in the town. Though he didn't know shit about Australia, this Yank major had a twinkle in his eye and dimple in his grin that gave her goose bumps. The basic chemistry was compelling—not that she'd let him know.

"Excuse me, Mite," Michael Kirk, who'd also noticed Phil's interest in Annette, interjected. "You're a mug here. Better mind your manners with sweet Annette. Days, she packs parachutes for you Yanks. Watch out. Next time you jump, it could be her silk. As for the stout, we don't mind shouting ya a pot a beer, but we ain't going ta invest in no Pommy piss, if ya gets me drift. We ain't like those fancy wowsers down south in Sydney. We're Four X men here."

"OK, mates and Miss Annette; I'm new here. I don't want to offend. I appreciate your hospitality. I'd love to try a Four X. When in Rome!" Genero responded.

"Just right, Mite," Kirk agreed. "In Rome you'd have some dago wine. Here in Queensland, we drink Four X."

Gilbert watched as Annette served Phil his XXXX-labeled beer in a cold, frosty bottle. Genero took a sip, smiled, and drained half of the beer.

"Like it?" Gilbert asked.

"Oh, yeah," Phil responded. "This beer is first rate. It's a lot better than Rolling Rock and on a par with Schaeffer's."

"It's too bad that my time in Australia is short. I could grow to like this place. I already like the people," Phil said to Gil as he made eye contact with Annette, who met his gaze and gave him an alluring half-smile.

Tom Gilbert noticed Phil's interest in Annette. He also saw her smile at his friend. A positive reaction from Annette was a rare event. A pang of jealousy sliced through Gilbert's massive chest like a hot knife.

*Jesus,* Gil thought. *I've been coming to this pub every chance I get for the last five months and not a fuckin' flicker from Annette. Gin waltzes in here and smiles at her and she wets her pants.*

Shaking his head, Gilbert turned to the locals who wanted to know more about the war news. *Beats watching Gin get lucky,* he thought.

As Genero sipped his beer and listened to Gilbert and Escheverria talk with the extroverted Aussies, he tried to engage Annette in a conversation, so he could use his considerable intelligence-gathering skills.

Annette was very busy taking orders and pouring drinks. Though the hour before closing was always hectic, Annette also wanted to find time to learn about the good-looking Yank major. She made it a point to bring him a fresh XXXX when he'd finished his first one, aware that he watched her while she worked.

"What are you so busy looking at?" she asked as she set down his pot.

"I'm not sure yet. I haven't gotten past your eyes."

Annette blushed—something she hadn't done in months. "You know, Mite, you can be very charming for a Yank."

"It's easy to be charming when you're in the company of a beautiful woman."

"Look, I hear a lot of yabber from these dills, mostly when they're rotten with the grog. I can't be had by some slick Yank artist with a fancy tongue," Annette said defensively before she regretted her strong response.

"I wouldn't think of it, Annette. Just making conversation. I'd like to get to know you."

"Sure, Yank, sure," Annette said, rolling her eyes but experiencing a small flutter in her chest.

"When do you close this pub?" Genero asked.

"Six."

"Would you like to get some tucker after you close?" Phil asked.

Annette smiled at Phil's use of the Australian term. "What about your mites?"

"Annette, I'm sure they'll understand. I'm permanently assigned to the regiment. We'll have plenty of opportunities to have chow. How about it? Want some dinner?"

"Maybe," she said, "but only tucker."

"Sure, Annette, sure," Phil responded, smiling like a Cheshire cat.

Tom Gilbert had managed to extricate himself from the Aussies and had moved back toward Genero just in time to hear Annette agree to have dinner. He felt the hot knife again, this time in the pit of his stomach. Disappointed and dejected, he moved down the bar toward Tommy Escheverria.

"What's up, Gil?" Tommy asked, as Gilbert motioned him to lean closer so that they could talk over the din of the bar.

"Let's grab something to eat and then head back to camp," Gilbert suggested.

"What about Gin?" Tommy asked.

"He's busy. He's got a date with Annette."

"No shit? Gin's melted the Gordonvale ice princess? God, what an operator! Gil, you should have seen him at Benning and Bragg..." Tommy said before Gilbert cut him off.

"You can tell me over chow, Tommy. Let's move out," Gilbert said, as he waved at Genero, signaling that they were leaving.

Phil gave both his friends a broad wink, a smile, and a nod.

*So much for Gin's early night,* Gilbert thought.

# Chapter 45

August 16, 1943
2030 Hours
Quarters No. 21
Debden Airdrome
Essex County, England

Major Jim Corbin—tired, haggard, and in need of a shower—paused in the approaching dusk on the rain-swept curb outside Paul Reilly's quarters. Corbin, a veteran of the Eagle Squadron and a plank member of the 334th Fighter Squadron, needed to recover from a long and dangerous day—a day that still had one delicate mission left.

Corbin and Paul Reilly had served together for more than three years. Their friendship had grown close during their time in two different air forces, and included the Reilly clan. Colonel Anderson, the 334th's commanding officer, knew of their friendship when he assigned him the mission to the Reilly home.

*I'd rather be down at the Officer's Club*, Corbin thought. *Maybe if I wait a minute or two, I could get some reinforcements.*

With any luck, Col. Anderson, LtCol. Peterson, LtCol. Blakeslee, and the group chaplain would arrive soon. In the presence of so many senior officers, he might not have to be the first to explain to Katherine.

Although Corbin had just turned 24, his combat experiences had hardened him beyond his years. Paul Reilly was not Jim's first good friend to be shot down in combat.

While he waited on the curb, Corbin reached into the inner pocket of his dark brown leather flight jacket and fished out the crinkled, largely crushed, almost-empty pack of Pall

Malls. Corbin peered into the pack and poked around with his right index finger until he found a cigarette that was still intact.

He shook the pack, removed the cigarette with a practiced flair, placed it between his cracked lips, and lit it with his silver Zippo. Corbin drew the smoke deep into his lungs, longing for the nicotine-induced rush to begin. As he stood alone on the edge of the curb, Corbin pondered the fortunes of war.

*The battle today was an overwhelming victory,* Corbin thought. *The spooks confirmed that the group shot down eighteen Kraut aircraft, mostly one-oh-nines. Jesus, we kicked their asses!*

*We lost two good pilots, Major Reilly and Captain Matthews. Shit! Even with our great success, I can't feel good about it. It's not going to be the same at Debden without Paul around to fuck with.*

*The rest of the guys will miss Paul too. He's a great leader, a patient teacher, and true friend. He's been a real ball of fire for the squadron. It's funny. It may be that Paul's leadership and aggressive style did him in. He always had to be in the front, where it was most dangerous.*

*Well, up to this afternoon Paul's aggression had worked for him. Early in the battle today, Paul got a piece of a Jerry plane,* Corbin recalled. *I guess that's the way to go out.*

Maj. Corbin also had a confirmed kill. He and his wingman had jumped a Kraut who was on the tail of Don Gentile. When Corbin got to within 300 yards of the Jerry, he gave the pilot three long squirts. The second and third shattered the 109's control surfaces on the tail assembly and starboard wing. Some of the rounds must have hit the engine, since it began smoking badly and streaming oil all over Corbin's windscreen as he closed the gap.

Corbin initially engaged the German at 19,000 feet. Their brief encounter ended at 12,000 feet, but Jim and his wingman followed the Nazi down to the deck. They watched as he spun out and crashed inverted in a neighborhood of apartments east of the Seine in Paris. Jim wondered how many civilians died as a result.

Maj. Corbin had no sad feelings for the German pilot. *The motherfucker had it coming. The Krauts had been attacking a large box formation of B-17s on a mission near Paris when we bounced the Jerries to help the bomber crews.*

Corbin didn't see what happened to Reilly during the large air battle. The Americans were trying out a new tactic. LtCol. Blakeslee orbited high over the air battle, orchestrating the effort and directing the American fighter pilots. Blakeslee had sent Reilly and Corbin off in different directions.

Blakeslee's tactic had paid handsome dividends. Yet the cost of losing two valuable pilots was significant, especially to Paul's pretty wife and their new baby boy, Timmy.

Just then, a staff car with the group's senior officers and the chaplain drove up. Corbin took one long, last puff of his Pall Mall, closed his eyes, and prepared himself.

As the men exited the vehicle, Chaplain Brohm walked over to Corbin. "Jim, did you give Katherine the news?" the chaplain asked.

"No, Padre. I just got here."

"Good. I'm glad we caught you, Jim," Chaplain Brohm began, handing the young pilot an official document. "Here is the formal notice that Major Paul Reilly is listed as Missing in Action."

"What do you mean missing?" Corbin snapped. "I thought he was confirmed killed," Corbin stated, now glad that he'd waited.

Col. Anderson said, "Thompson was the last guy to see Paul after the three Jerries shot up his plane. He remembers seeing hits at the wing root, fuselage, and canopy. By his account, the Krauts badly damaged Paul's kite. Though he lost him for a moment in the midst of the air-to-air combat, Thompson swears that he saw Paul's Bolt crash in central Paris. He remembers seeing a parachute floating about a thousand feet above the crash. He can't be sure it was Paul, but he knows it was a fully deployed parachute." Anderson tightened the knot in his four-in-hand tie and tucked it back inside his green blouse.

"Gentlemen," Anderson continued. "The Nazi propagandists will be all over this. Paul was one of our top aces. The Krauts have a dossier on him. If Paul died in the crash we'll learn of it. If he survives and is captured, we'll know within the month. I've decided that despite the damage to Paul's plane, we'll list him as missing for now. Katherine is a tough cookie. She'll understand. Play this straight. Don't give her any false hopes, but there is a slight chance that Paul survived. We owe it him to keep the faith. Got it?"

All of the officers agreed. Together, they moved toward Katherine's front door. The chaplain stepped forward and knocked politely on the old maple doorframe.

A few moments later, Katherine Reilly—holding her new baby, Timothy Sullivan Reilly, on her hip—answered the door. Katherine looked beautiful with her clean, fresh face and simple dark dress. She'd not been forewarned but when she saw the entourage, she understood the nature of their mission.

"Come in, gentlemen," Katherine said in a steady voice— though her eyes filled with sadness. "I knew you'd come one day. I've been expecting you. I'll fix us all a spot of tea."

# Chapter 46

0430 Hours
August 20, 1943
Los Baños Internment Camp
University of the Philippines,
School of Agriculture
Laguna de Bay
63 Kilometers South of Manila

In the late 16$^{th}$ century, wealthy Spanish colonists began making the short trip from Manila to the southern shore of Laguna de Bay, the largest freshwater lake in the Philippines. Suffering from arthritis or gout, they sought the soothing waters of the hot springs that flowed from the base of Mount Makiling. Sandwiched between the dormant volcano and the lake, the town of Los Baños sprung up to cater to the stricken pilgrims.

By the early 1900s, the Philippine Commonwealth had established a university with an agricultural school in Los Baños. For the next 40 years, two generations of Filipino landowners, animal breeders, and agricultural scientists learned their trade at the school.

Everything changed with the Japanese invasion of the Philippines in December 1941, which began ten hours after their attack on Pearl Harbor. After their victory over the American and Filipino forces, the Japanese became the islands' new masters. They had special plans for the Los Baños agricultural school.

By May of 1942, the Japanese had become the custodians of tens of thousands of enemy prisoners and a large number of enemy civilians. Since the code of Bushido despised surrender, the Japanese treated the prisoners with contempt and barbarity.

Initially, the Japanese command housed all of the captured military nurses, both Navy and Army, on the grounds of the University of Santo Tomas in Manila. The Japanese withheld food, medical treatment, medicine, and supplies of all kinds. As the population of the prison camp increased, survival became difficult for the internees.

In May 1943, to deal with the grossly overcrowded conditions at Santo Tomas, the Japanese moved 800 men to a 55-acre compound on the campus of the agricultural school at Los Baños. The transferees represented a cross-section of the pre-war expatriate community in Manila. They included several different ethnic groups, occupations, and professions. The Japanese allowed a few male doctors to accompany the transferees and see to their care.

The doctors asked for volunteers among the nurses at Santo Tomas to join them at Los Baños, and all 13 Navy nurses stepped forward. The Navy contingent included nurses who'd been captured in northern Luzon, Manila, Bataan, and after the fall of Corregidor. Lieutenant Commander Betty Landry became their executive officer. All of the Army nurses stayed behind.

After the transfer to Los Baños, the conditions for the prisoners improved a bit. The Navy nurses established a 25-bed hospital for the men. The doctors and the nurses provided the best medical care that they could, given the fact that they were short of every necessity.

Since life at Los Baños during the summer of 1943 was better than Santo Tomas, the nurses sarcastically referred to their camp as the country club, though it was anything but. The nurses settled into a routine of providing care to their patients and ministering to each other's morale—a serious issue.

Not only were the Japanese cruel administrators, they also held the prisoners incommunicado. In the year and a half that they'd been held captive, the Swiss representative from Geneva had made only one visit to Santo Tomas. No Swiss emissary had ever been to Los Baños. These neutral-country inspectors verified conditions in the camps. They needed the occupying country's permission to enter the camps, and Japan gave it with grave reluctance. Until mid-August it was unclear if the Swiss knew that a camp for prisoners existed at Los Baños. Many of the internees had received no word from their families during their entire incarceration.

On August 19, the Japanese commander, Warrant Officer Sadaaki Konishi, had informed the senior American prisoners that a Swiss emissary would visit Los Baños during the following week. Konishi wanted the Americans to clean the place up and put on a good show to make the best possible impression.

The news about the visit electrified the prisoners. A visit from Geneva could mean mail from home, boxes of supplies for the prisoners, and insurance against anonymity. As long as the prisoners were anonymous, the Japanese would not have to account for them—creating death sentences for many allied captives.

The chief Navy nurse, Laura Cobb, tasked Commander Landry to get the facility up to snuff. Unfortunately, during the night Landry had fallen ill. She spiked a high fever. After midnight, the chief nurse admitted Landry as a patient in the little hospital.

Landry had chills, a headache, and was mildly delirious—like a bad case of the flu. Her skin took on a slight yellow tone, indicating that her liver was involved.

Dr. Richards, a civilian contract surgeon for the Navy, had been due to return to the United States in January 1942, until the Empire of Japan spoiled his plans. Since the move to Los Baños, he'd proved to be a valuable asset for the prisoners. Around 0300 that night, Richards examined Landry and diagnosed her condition as a relapse of the malaria that she'd contracted during the siege of Bataan. Although it was not the worst relapse the doctor had ever seen, the lack of adequate anti-malarial medicines could complicate her recovery.

At 0400, Doctor Richards sat at Landry's bedside mulling over a serious moral dilemma. *I've managed to hoard a small amount of Atabrine,* Richards thought. *If I use some of it now, I might alleviate Landry's symptoms, but I could also seriously deplete the stock of the drug. If I don't use the medicine, Betty's condition could deteriorate. Commander Landry could suffer kidney failure, irreversible liver damage, and even death. I've seen far worse relapses where the patient recovered without Atabrine. But I hate playing God. With malaria rampant in the camp, it's only a question of time until I get a more severe case.*

As he was considering the problem, Doctor Richards sensed the presence of another person in the small room. He looked up and saw her, his heart racing. She always had the same effect on him.

Ensign Kari Hansen had come to the ward to see about her best friend. For the three months that Doctor Richards had been at Los Baños, the two women had been inseparable.

Kari was a very good nurse and a loyal friend. Like all of the prisoners, she was wafer thin from the lack of adequate food. She was still one of the most beautiful women Richards had ever seen.

She was also cool and distant. During the internment, she'd given no signal that she'd welcome an advance from any of the men in the camp.

*She's supposed to be married to a Navy doctor,* Richards recalled. *The rumor is that he was killed in the Pacific. The Japs claim that they've destroyed our entire Navy—but I'm not ready to believe the Nips just yet. That fucking MacArthur claimed that he'll return. If he doesn't, then that will mean the Japs were right.*

Dr. Richards watched as Kari fussed over her friend. *God, she's so beautiful. She has the nicest hands I've ever seen. She wears no wedding ring. That's odd, since she's so committed to her vows. Maybe the Japs took it from her. Or more likely she had to trade it for something.*

While she tended to her friend, Kari said nothing to the doctor. This silence was not unusual. She was persistently taciturn. Kari had the thousand-yard stare. When she was off duty, she would look off in the distance, as if she were expecting something vague and undefined to come racing over the horizon.

Although Hansen had worked with Richards for more than three months, they had seldom exchanged anything but professional conversation. Even so, Doc Richards had overheard Kari fretting to Betty about her family.

"How is she doing, Doc?" Kari finally asked, although she could see for herself that her friend was not faring well.

"I'm trying to decide on a course of medication," Richards replied.

"Do we have any anti-malarial left?" Kari asked.

"I've hoarded some in my trunk," Richards replied, wondering why he was admitting his great secret to Kari.

Kari turned to Richards and looked him directly in the eye. "Get the meds for Betty. I'll get us more and I'll make it up to you. Doc, don't let anything happen to her."

Kari's statement was far more an order than a request. Richards knew he would comply. "You don't have to worry about making anything up to me. It's my job to treat her. I've already decided that she should get what's left. Besides, how would you get us more?"

"The Swiss emissary is coming. We can make a plea for more drugs. Or I can always find something to barter with the camp guards," Kari explained. "One of the men who used to teach here thinks that he can make contact with the Filipino resistance. Maybe they can help."

"Well, let's wait to see what the Swiss emissary can do for us. The Red Cross packages may have some anti-malarial drugs in them," Richards responded, not getting his hopes up about the resistance and not wanting to know what commodity Kari Hansen might be willing to barter for the life of her friend.

Just then, Commander Landry began to waken. Despite the clammy weather, she had the chills. Kari pulled the white bed sheet up over her friend's shivering body, tucking it in just under her chin.

"Kari, is it your watch already? Have I been asleep that long?" Landry asked through chattering teeth, as she looked up at the younger woman.

"No, Betty. I couldn't sleep. I came in to check on you. I've been talking to the good doctor here. He says that you are going to be fine in a few days. Right, Doc?"

"That's right, Commander Landry." Richards responded. "You'll be right as rain in a few days."

"I want to be well for the Geneva man's visit. I've got a few things to say about the commander here. I'm the only one who'll have the balls to tell the truth," Landry observed, using the inaccurate anatomical reference to emphasize her point.

"You just rest now. Doc's got some meds he'll give you. You'll probably sleep the rest of the day. You may even start feeling better by tomorrow," Kari predicted.

"Thanks Kari. You're a pal. Just think—maybe next week you'll finally get a letter from your family. I'll bet there's a whole stack of them. I know Mark and your mom and dad miss you very much. If these Japs weren't such assholes, you'd have had your mail months ago, "Landry said.

"A stack of letters, now that would be something," Kari admitted. "I won't get my hopes up."

# Chapter 47

October 21, 1943
Jackson Strip Encampment
In Route to the Papua Hotel,
Wharf District, Port Moresby, New Guinea

A steady afternoon rain soaked the long dirt road that led from the camp of the 503d PIR. Intent on getting to Port Moresby, Major Genero drove far too fast toward the front gate of Jackson Strip, causing his Jeep to slip and skid in the mud. At a treacherous turn, he narrowly missed an Army truck that was bringing supplies from Port Moresby to the Strip.

As Phil approached the front gate, he slowed down. An Army Air Corps private first class stepped out of the shack and waived the Jeep to a halt.

The guard walked toward the Jeep with his M-1 carbine slung over his left shoulder. As he watched the young soldier, Phil flashed back to the Italian sentry he had stabbed to death in the rain in the Tunisian foothills 11 months earlier.

Genero remembered the gruesome struggle, the sickening sound of his knife's blade as it entered the Italian boy's throat, the intense pain in his hand as his victim's teeth severed tendon and bone, and the pathetic gurgle when the boy died. Phil glanced down at his left hand and looked at the stubs of his two fingers, a permanent reminder of his own vulnerability.

*That was a lifetime ago*, he thought to himself. *Poor hapless son-of-a-bitch!*

As the enlisted guard approached the Jeep, he noted that Phil was brass. He snapped to attention and gave a sharp hand salute.

"Can I help you, Private?" Phil asked, impressed that at least one Air Corps soldier knew how to salute.

"Not sure, sir," the guard responded. "I can see that you're a major. I know you don't need a pass, sir. I was confused. I never saw an officer drive a Jeep before. Sorry to delay you. You can pass, sir."

"No problem, private. Way to keep on your toes. Would you like a little advice?"

The private did a slight double take. In the 15 months that he'd served in the Air Corps, no officer had ever been so polite to him. *The major is wearing one of those paratrooper jump suits,* PFC Renton thought. *He has to be one of the hot shots from the 503d.*

"Sure, sir," the private said, wishing that the major would get the hell out the front gate and simplify his life.

"Private, if you carry your weapon slung like that over your shoulder while you're on guard duty, one of these nights a Jap is going to slip up behind you and cut your throat from ear to ear. It would ruin your whole evening and make your momma a very sad woman. Private, be ready to use that weapon. Stay alert—it just might save your life."

As Phil shifted into first, gunned the Jeep's motor, and sped out the front gate toward Port Moresby, the guard shivered. Watching the Jeep fade into the afternoon rain, the PFC thought, *Jesus, this major must be the kind of madman who could actually sneak up on a guy and slit his throat without a shred of remorse.*

Phil had stolen the S-2's Jeep. Taking the vehicle was unauthorized and contrary to established policy. The regimental commander didn't want the majors and light colonels driving themselves around New Guinea.

Earlier in the day, Phil had received a *most urgent* directive to report to General Moses at his quarters in the Papua Hotel in Port Moresby. Despite his best efforts—spanning three whole minutes—Phil could not locate the commander, the executive officer, the motor officer, or the S-2 to get permission. Since it was his duty to obey all orders from general officers, Phil decided that valor would be the better part of discretion and he would err on the side of throwing caution to the wind.

*Besides,* Phil thought, *Colonel Kincaid is in no position to give me any shit. Kincaid can't be his normal self, not with General Krueger's Inspector General conducting an investigation into his persistent flamboyant and abusive misconduct and dereliction.*

As Phil entered Port Moresby, he drove toward the wharves of the small harbor. The Papua Hotel was situated just up from the Wharf section in a seedy part of town.

Though the hotel's exterior was unimpressive, it was well appointed inside. Compared to the accommodations in the field, those at the Papua Hotel were beyond luxurious.

The hotel rooms had real beds with clean white sheets, soft pillows, and spreads. Each set of quarters had a room where just one person could take an actual bath or shower with hot water. These rooms also had toilets, where a man could actually urinate and defecate without having a general conference with all of his comrades.

During his time in New Guinea, Phil had never gotten to stay at the hotel, though he had been to the bar—now an allied officer's club—on two previous occasions. While the bar had ice-cold beer, it also attracted too many colonels, generals, politicians, and power brokers for Phil to be comfortable there for long.

Today, his trip was official. He was on his way to see Gen. Moses, who occasionally took his meetings in the bar after a long and grueling day.

Genero had been expecting this summons for some time. He was tardy in providing the general with his version of events on the airborne assault on the Nadzab Airport in Markham Valley.

Maj. Genero was proud of what the 503d had accomplished. Yet with all of the complaints about the regimental commander, with the IG interviewing witnesses under Col.

Kincaid's nose, with the low morale of the unit, Phil hadn't wanted to give his report—which was actually very good—and provide a totally misleading impression about the condition of the unit.

*Despite its great success in Markham Valley, despite its total vindication of the concept of vertical envelopment, despite the extremely high quality of the vast majority of the officers and men in the unit, the 503d—as a regiment—is in a serious mess,* Genero had lamented as he thought about what he would say to Maj. Gen. Moses.

An hour after his arrival, Maj. Genero sat fidgeting at a small table in the rear of the officer's club bar, near a tiny window that provided a view of the dreary Port Moresby wharves. Phil was still in his jump suit. Though it had been washed, starched, and pressed by the local natives, it stood out in stark contrast to the more appropriate attire sported by the staff officers who frequented the bar.

Normally, Phil would not have been permitted in the bar at this hour, not in his battle dress. However, this evening he was a guest of the Special Advisor to the Theater Commander-in-Chief. He had a special dispensation.

While he waited, Genero mentally reviewed his report. *Five weeks ago in the steamy Markham Valley, almost due north of this very bar, the 503d executed the first successful regimental-sized combat jump in the short history of the American airborne. Some of the credit for the successful result rests with my contribution in the planning stages.*

*On the other hand, after all the work that the regiment had done since its arrival in Australia—after all of the sweat, pain, tears, and blood—the success in battle had not boosted the low morale in the regiment,* Phil concluded. *Although I've only been with the 503d since late July, I've had enough experience with these men to understand why things are so bad.*

*There is no doubt about it. The problem is Col. Kincaid.*

*For a regiment that has just set the mark in a difficult feat of arms and should be basking in the glow of very dangerous mission accomplished, the 503d is facing a serious crisis. The trouble has been brewing for a very long time.*

Phil had heard that during the months of training in the tablelands of northern Queensland, Col. Kincaid had been an unforgiving, uninspiring martinet. He'd heard talk of training accidents, serious injury, and unjustified deaths.

It is unimportant that the soldiers like their leaders. It is only necessary that they respect them. In the 503d, the enlisted men and non-commissioned officers neither liked nor respected their colonel.

*It's not that Colonel Kincaid makes things too tough,* Phil thought. *These paratroopers are hard as nails. They can deal with anything. I've served under Edson Raff. I've seen Colonel Gavin train the men of the 505th. Kincaid could never be more demanding than Raff and Gavin.*

In addition to the enlisted men, many of the regiment's officers had lost confidence in the commander. Several had put their lack of confidence in the regiment's commander in writing to the Sixth Army Commander.

As he sat sipping his cold XXXX, Phil remembered how thankful he'd been when he received his summons to the Papua Hotel. *I'd been scheduled for my interview with the IG. I'd rather be flogged than attend that interview,* Genero thought as he drained the beer in his glass and signaled the waiter for another.

*This whole situation with Kincaid is detrimental to the good order and discipline of the regiment. The word around Jackson Strip is that Krueger will relieve Kincaid. As long as they delay that decision, the unit's morale will suffer. On the other hand, Krueger will probably replace Kincaid with Lieutenant Colonel Jones. That would be a very good thing. Jones is a great officer.*

Just then, Gen. Moses entered the club. As he walked through the bar, the room fell into a respectful silence. All of the allied officers understood that Moses wielded great power, subject only to the imprimatur of MacArthur himself.

Phil stood up from his chair as the general approached. Moses waived him back down. Moses knew he had power. He understood respect. He was impatient with the trappings.

After he settled in the small chair opposite Genero, Moses ordered a cold beer from the waiter "Thank you for meeting me here, Major Genero," Moses began, knowing full well that Phil had an obligation to obey his summons.

'My pleasure, sir!"

"Genero, this evening I have three agendas. I have yet to hear your version of the jump on Nadzab airport. I would like you to tell me how the operation went. I've read Kincaid's after-action report. It seems a trifle too glowing. Secondly, I'd like your assessment of the morale in your regiment, along with your recommendation about how to fix it. Finally, I have a little chore for you to perform in the next few months. At the end of this meeting, we'll take a little stroll and I'll tell you all I know about it."

Phil gave Major General Moses a direct and simple account of how the 503d had implemented Gen. MacArthur's assault plan on the Markham Valley airport. "Glowing reports or not, sir, the regiment executed the plan flawlessly," Genero began. "If I may, I would like to review the process."

"By all means, Major. I want your unvarnished perspective."

"Lieutenant Colonel Jones, as the Exec, organized the Oplan with the S-3. They identified three different battalion-sized drop zones at or near the airport. The first battalion got the airport, itself. I ended up jumping with them," Genero began.

"The second bat jumped on the DZ just to the north of the airstrip. I've got an old Infantry Basic Course classmate, Tom Gilbert, who commands Dog Company. He gave me a full, first-hand report after the action."

"I've heard of Captain Gilbert," Maj. Gen. Moses said. "He has a good reputation."

"He's first rate, sir," Phil continued. "Let's see, the third battalion got the drop zone on the east side of the valley, closest to the Japanese positions on the outskirts of Lae."

"That's right, Major. I recall approving the plan as you've described it."

"Sir, the planning was almost perfect. For a bona fide combat jump, it was a good as it was ever going to get. As you intended, the regimental planners learned from the mistakes of the 509th in North Africa and the 504th and 5th in Sicily."

"Genero, I don't want to seem impatient, but I'm well aware of the excellence of the plan. I am most interested in how well Colonel Kincaid and your regiment implemented it."

"Sorry, sir. Well, in executing the operation, General MacArthur spared no expense. The transport pilots trained hard for the jump. They practiced a lot, which was one of the keys to the mission's success. Two days before the assault, the transport pilots did a dummy drop on a similar airstrip in friendly territory."

"I was aware of that. So you feel that practice drop made a difference?"

"Absolutely, sir. It gave the fly boys a lot of confidence and did wonders for the coordination."

"OK. Please continue."

"We did not use pathfinders to guide us into the drop zones because it was daylight when we jumped and the Air Corps thoroughly prepped the DZs with 20 specially config-ured B-25 gun ships. You know the ones, sir. They're armed with eight .50 caliber machine guns in the nose, where the bombardier normally sits. The gun ships carried small fragmentation bombs in their bomb bays. The B-25s strafed and bombed the airstrip and other DZs before the jump."

"As I understand it, Major, the Japs did not have substan-tial forces on any of these target zones. Do you think we overdid it with the preparation?"

"No, sir. You're right. We found less than twenty Japanese bodies around the airport. However, had they been there in force, the preparation would have saved hundreds of air-borne casualties. Besides, sir, it was good experience for the next combat jump."

Maj. Gen. Moses paused and looked critically at Genero. He knew that he'd made his skepticism about large airborne operations clear when Phil first reported for duty. *These paratroopers are stubborn,* the general thought. *They don't want to give up on their glamorous concept. It's a pity that it may get many of them killed.*

"The jury is still out on future airborne operations, Major. Continue."

"OK, sir. On September 5th, the entire regiment assembled and loaded onto 82 C-47s near Port Moresby. We flew north over the Owen Stanley Range and began the final runs on the three DZs in Markham Valley by late morning. Sir, from the time the first man jumped, until the entire regiment had gotten on the ground, less than five minutes elapsed. That's a record for a three battalion mass drop, especially in combat."

"General MacArthur was in a B-17 orbiting near the operation. He watched the whole exercise. He told me that he was very impressed with the 503$^{rd}$'s efficiency."

"Thanks, General. But even more importantly, all three battalions landed exactly on target. There was no dispersal. The Air Corps hit the center ring in the bull's eye."

"Major, that's the fact that impresses me the most. Since your units landed in a cohesive manner, you could begin effective operations immediately. From my perspective, that's the whole purpose of parachuting behind enemy lines."

"Yes, sir. In addition to the flawless execution of a good, well-practiced plan, the casualties were very light on the day of the assault. Over the next few days, there was little contact with the enemy. Apparently, no Japanese considered the airstrip worth defending. It was a stupid mistake on their part."

"How did it go after the regiment got organized?

"After the paratroopers and Army engineers cleared the debris and tall Kunai grass off the runways and taxi paths, the Air Corps—using the same transport planes—air-landed an entire Australian division in record time. As planned, the

Aussies immediately moved east, passed through the third battalion, and began the assault on Lae from the east. Eventually, they linked up with their countrymen who'd been attacking from the sea.

"After suffering serious losses, the Japs withdrew northwest, up the narrow and difficult jungle trails. Even without the Americans or Australians chasing them, not many are expected to survive the trek.

"Sir, the only sad note in the entire operation was the loss of several paratroopers in a sharp firefight between elements of the third battalion and a Japanese flanking force, which stumbled into our patrol, as the Japs tried to cover their commander's retreat to the north.

"The third battalion patrol acquitted itself with honor. Among the dead, sir, was First Lieutenant Tomas Escheverria, a handsome, bright, dedicated airborne soldier from San Marcos, Texas." *Since I'd known him longer than anyone on the regimental staff, I had to write his mother on behalf of Colonel Kincaid*, Genero thought, as Maj. Gen. Moses reflected on the briefing.

Satisfied that he knew all he had to know about Phil's version of the Markham Valley operation, Moses asked for Genero's views concerning the morale of the 503d, and Col. Kincaid's exposure in the IG investigation.

"Sir, I'm new to the regiment. I'm not in a position to make a judgment. I'm certainly not qualified to criticize anyone in this matter. Besides, I've avoided the IG investigation precisely because I did not want to give testimony against Colonel Kincaid. Sir, I've been out of line myself on more than one occasion. I'm a lot of things, but I'm no hypocrite."

Gen. Moses looked at Genero for a long time. Moses had a habit of thinking over what he was going to say before he said it.

"Genero, I've known you quite a while. I know far more about you than you realize. Since you left War Plans, I know the reputation that you've earned. I've read your record carefully."

"Yes, sir," Genero said, as he cautiously examined the general.

"Do you think for a moment that I didn't know it was you who beat up those SS officers in Marseilles?"

"What? Major Jardine told you about that?"

"Don't be absurd. He considers you his most talented protégé. We never discussed it. Brigadier General Jardine— he's now the commander of division artillery in the 25th— would never have ratted you out. He and I simply engaged in a little willful blindness. If no one accused you, then I wouldn't have to have you court-martialed. I thought the way he got you out of Washington and into the paratroops was very creative. From the looks of your record, you've more than earned your reprieve. I'll never admit this to another human being, but I only wish that I could have been with you and helped to send those vile specimens of the master race to the hospital."

"I don't know what to say, sir."

"Well, that's actually a good start, since your mouth is part of your problem."

"How so, sir?"

"I also know all about what happened at Camp Kunkle. You're going to have to do something about that temper, if you want a career in the Army," the general began. "On the other hand, you're an honest man. Even people who don't like you—who think you're too emotional, perhaps a bit immature—believe that you are truthful, responsible, loyal, very brave, gallant, and decent. I share that belief.

"I suppose that a man who would defend his former commander's honor at the expense of his career, as you did in Morocco, cannot be expected to respond enthusiastically to my inquiry about your current commander. By the way— speaking of Colonel Raff and the events in Morocco—we just received a notice that General Ridgway's G-1 has declined to approve Colonel Raff's recommendation for the award of the Distinguished Service Cross for your gallant actions at Fariana. He downgraded the award to a Silver Star. So you can attach an Oak Leaf Cluster to the one you have, if you can find one in New Guinea," Moses continued.

"That's fine, sir. I never thought I deserved a DSC in the first place. I don't need another medal, cluster, or ribbon. As for Colonel Kincaid, I'd just as soon take a pass, sir."

"I expected nothing less from you regarding the DSC. However, your loyalty cannot be permitted to interfere with my job. Answer my question about Kincaid."

"I'll answer your question, sir, but only to this extent," Genero said. "I cannot give testimony to any of the allegations against my regimental C.O., because I did not witness any of the behavior that led to them. I can honestly tell you that the morale of the unit is very low, despite the brilliant execution of the mission in Markham Valley. The IG investigation is a serious distraction. It will generate negative dividends unless it is closed quickly. One other thing: I'm very worried about Colonel Kincaid. I've only known him for a few months, but I think he's very depressed. He knows he's about to be relieved and I'm concerned that he won't handle it well."

"All right, Gin," Moses said, using Phil's nickname in a show of rare informality. "I'll let you off the hook on this one. I hope you're wrong about Colonel Kincaid's mental state, but I've heard similar concerns from others."

Getting up from the table, Maj. Gen. Moses motioned for Genero to follow him outside. "Let's finish our talk on the veranda."

Once they were outside, the general pulled Genero off into a corner. Moses looked around to be sure that they were alone.

"Major Genero, normally I'd have you report to our secure room in the forward headquarters to have this discussion, but time is of the essence tonight. I'm leaving for Brisbane at 0345 and I don't have time to fully brief you on your mission, so let me summarize your predicament," Moses explained.

"I don't understand, sir," Phil responded to this unusual cloak and dagger behavior.

"I know you don't. So, just stand easy and listen to me for a moment," Moses offered. "The Anglo-American high command has appointed Lord Louis Mountbatten to be the new Commander-in-Chief of the Southeast Asian Command in India. He'll be arriving in the theater soon. Mountbatten has transmitted a personal, by-name request to General MacArthur. He is asking that you be sent ahead to his command for six months detached duty. Until Mountbatten arrives, you will report to Joe Stillwell."

"What?" Phil said incredulously.

"I know you're being ambushed with this, but I have no choice. Neither do you, by the way. We're not asking for you to volunteer," the general pointed out. "MacArthur has already approved Mountbatten's request. Your orders are drawn up. You'll leave in forty-eight hours for Ceylon, then Mountbatten's new headquarters in India. I believe you have about ninety-six hours to report."

"Sir, do you have any idea what this is all about? You say this is a by-name, personal request?" Phil asked, still very surprised and confused.

"I think I do know, actually. But I'm not authorized to speculate. I can tell you that you'll be working with a Free French Colonel by the name of Anton," Moses responded.

"Anton!" Phil exclaimed. "Sir, is that a Louis Anton?"

"Why, yes. As a matter of fact it is. Colonel Louis Anton," Moses replied. "Obviously, you know of the man. He claims to know you too. There must be a fascinating story there. Too bad I don't have time to hear it."

"Sir, are you sure that Louis Anton is a colonel? The last time I saw him in Morocco, about six months ago, he was a captain."

"No, Gin, I'm absolutely sure. Anton is a Free French colonel. By the way, along with the orders, I'm to give you a message from him," General Moses remembered.

"What message was that, sir?" Phil asked intrigued by the assignment, which had come like a bolt out of the blue.

"Colonel Anton presents his compliments and is pleased to inform you that you are invited to accompany him home to meet his family. I suppose that's some kind of code between you two," Moses speculated.

"Oh, my God!" Phil exclaimed, fully understanding the implications, as a chill of fear and raw excitement coursed through his body. *I'm going to Indochina!*

"Major Genero, I think I know what you are about to face. It will be very dangerous. However, I'm convinced that you are qualified by experience, talent, and training to take on this mission. Regardless of whether I'm right or wrong, I want to wish you *Bon Chance!*" Gen. Moses offered, extending his hand.

"*Merci, mon* General! *Merci beaucoup!*"

*Well,* Phil thought, *at least that gets me out of the interview with the Inspector General.*

# Chapter 48

11:45 AM
November 26, 1943
Office of the Acting CEO
Monarch Industries
Carlisle Pennsylvania

Tired, haggard, and showing his age, Phillip Genero sat at the ornate desk in the bare and cavernous office space. Shorn of its fancy trappings and expensive artwork, the room mustered all the charm of an empty basketball court.

Given the choice, Phillip would have worked in the one of the smaller offices down the hall or on the floor below. Whenever he sat at the oversized desk, he could sense the malign presence of Junior in the very texture of the place. The office generated so much bad karma that on several occasions Phillip had to remember what was at stake in Carlisle. He had to reach down and tap his personal discipline to refrain from storming out of the room and throwing in the economic towel.

The court-appointed receiver had taken over two of the other executive offices on the top floor. The Federal investigators and War Department contract officials used two other prime spaces in the building, leaving this museum of corruption for Phillip to do Monarch Industries' real work.

There was so much judicial and military oversight working at the corporation that Genero struggled to make progress. In the factories, you couldn't operate a sewing machine without stitching up a Federal agent.

Though these were still dark days and Phillip was operating on fumes, the crisis had challenged him to his core. Phillip arrived at the same decision sitting at Junior's desk at

Monarch Industries that he'd made lying wounded in the glade in the Argonne forest. He might not survive, but he would die trying to safeguard the business.

He and Marta had begun to fashion an industrial and economic miracle at Monarch. Starting with over $20 million in debt, Monarch's executive staff had spent the last six months struggling back from the brink of financial disaster. They were not out of the woods. In fact, no one could see the edge of the woods. Yet the business promised to be viable, after a fashion.

Phillip, the acting CEO, had reached out for help—and found the community rallying behind the company. Local banks and businesses provided loans and with additional help from the government, Phillip could make payroll. Even the military showed flexibility in finding solutions—allowing Monarch to change lot sizes, delivery dates, and some final specifications.

The company—and by extension a large portion of Cumberland County—would survive.

As lunchtime approached, Phillip glared at the three pages of unintelligible gibberish before him. These interrogatories, which had been served on Monarch's lawyers by their creditors, were written in impossible legalese. *Why couldn't these damn lawyers just use plain English?*

As he was trying to fashion an answer to the tenth unfathomable and illogical question, Marta slipped into Phillip's office through the private door in the back. She walked over to her husband, leaned over, and kissed the top of his salt-and-pepper colored hair.

Marta looked over Phillip's shoulder and read one of the interrogatories. She crinkled her pretty nose at the language. Even Marta, a woman with the soul of patience, had a hard time with these Harrisburg lawyers.

Sighing with frustration, Phillip looked away from his work, and up at Marta. He smiled. She looked ravishing—and ten years younger.

Marta had thrived under the crisis. Two years ago, the chaos and fear would have overwhelmed her and pushed her towards a bottle and away from Phillip. Now the two of them worked as a team. They could handle the chaos, especially with Junior out of the way—both personally and professionally. Marta's eyes shone with optimism and pride.

Even the letter that he and his wife had just received from their son, informing them that he was now in India, had not troubled Marta.

The assignment sounded routine. *Hopefully, this transfer will keep Gin out of combat for a while*, Phillip thought. *Tomorrow is Thanksgiving. We'll go to Mass at St. Francis and say a prayer for him.*

The buzzer on Phillip's intercom chirped. Phillip reached over and hit the button, ending the noise.

"What is it, Ann?" Phillip asked, as he gazed into his wife's lovely brown eyes, smiling his secret invitation for later. Marta smiled back, signaling her interest.

"Phillip, there are three Navy officers here to see you. It's your one o'clock appointment; they're a little early."

"Which uniform contract are they interested in?" Phillip asked, as he reached out to touch Marta's hand.

"I'll ask them," Anne responded, closing down the intercom.

A few seconds later, the intercom chirped again. "Phillip, they say they're not here to talk about a contract. It's personal and very important."

Phillip remembered the last time the Navy came to see him about something personal in the spring of 1942, tearing his heart from his chest with the news that Kari had been killed.

"Ann, ask them if it's about Mark?"

"Phillip, they won't discuss it with me. They want to see you."

Phillip looked up at his wife. The passion in her face evaporated in that awful instant, replaced by utter desolation. Her shoulders slumped and her breathing became ragged and shallow. She reached out to Phillip to steady herself. *Dear God! Please don't let this be about Mark. We've suffered so much,* Marta thought.

"Ann, tell the Navy officers that we'll be out in a moment. Go ahead and get your lunch."

Phillip needed to gather himself. *Damn the luck!* He thought, as he turned toward Marta.

"Baby..." Phillip began before Marta cut him off.

"Phillip, please don't worry, honey. We lost our way for a while, but now that you and I have found each other again, we can overcome this. We'll deal with the news from the Navy, whatever it is."

As Phillip straightened up, Marta remembered Mark's visit to Carlisle in August. Earlier in the summer, the Navy had recalled the *Enterprise* to Washington State to have a complete facelift and refitting. Like the rest of the *Enterprise* crew, Doctor Hansen had received a 30-day furlough. He spent five of those days with Phillip and Marta.

Mark's brief visit in Carlisle was bittersweet. While both Marta and Phillip had been glad to see that Mark was safe, his presence reminded them of the loss of their daughter. They were relieved when Mark started back for the West Coast to meet up with the Enterprise for redeployment in the Pacific Theater. Now he had gone back to the war—and back into danger.

Phillip stood up from his chair, adjusted his shirt, tie, and vest, and started for the door. Marta reached out for her husband, pulled him close, and held him very tight.

"OK, honey. Let's go out there and face the Navy. We owe it to Mark," Phillip said.

Arm in arm, Phillip and Marta walked to the door and entered the small secretarial office where Marta had spent many miserable days fending off Junior's advances. *One more bad memory,* Marta thought. *This room must be cursed.*

Five people stretched the capacity of the small space. "Good morning, gentlemen," Phillip said, extending his hand to the ranking officer. "I'm Phillip Genero. This is my wife Marta. Do you have news of Lieutenant Mark Hansen?"

"Good morning, sir. I'm Captain Grettle, from Admiral King's staff. I have news for you and your wife. But it's not about Lieutenant Hansen," Capt. Grettle explained.

"What is it then, Captain?" Phillip asked, as he turned from the naval officer and looked at his wife in confusion.

"Is there somewhere else that we can go, sir? You need to sit down first."

*Oh, God no, no, no! Please, God, don't let it be Gin!* Phillip thought.

"It's not about our boy, is it?" Marta asked, her voice barren of emotion.

"No, Ma'am!" The captain said, realizing that the Generos thought he was there to give them bad news.

"Mister Genero, Ma'am, I'm very sorry. I've made a serious mistake. I'm not here to give you bad tidings. I have fabulously good news for you."

"What news is that? For God's sake, man! Just tell us!"

"Sir, your daughter, Ensign Kari Genero-Hansen, was not killed in action. Her death was mistakenly reported during the confusion after the fall of Corregidor."

"What!" Phillip spat. How can this be? Why did you tell us she'd been killed?"

"Phillip, what are these men saying?" Marta croaked as she grabbed her husband's arm.

"Ma'am," Captain Grettle continued. "We're not sure about the details. We may never sort it all out. But the Swiss Red Cross has confirmed that your daughter is still alive. She's a prisoner of war of the Japanese Empire with twelve other Navy nurses in a prison camp about thirty miles south of Manila. It's a place called Los Baños."

Phillip stepped forward and grabbed the captain by the lapels on his Class A Blue uniform and squeezed the material until his fingers turned white. "How can you be sure of this, Captain? A year and half ago, you people told us that our daughter was dead! You told us that she had been blown up and decapitated in an explosion outside the tunnel in Malinta Hill! Are you now telling me that you people made a mistake? For God's sake man, we have Kari's wedding ring and a St. Michael's medal that I personally gave her!"

"Sir," the captain began. "We've had to read some of the letters that your daughter has written to you from the internment camp. Apparently, the Japanese withheld them for many months and never forwarded them. We had military intelligence reasons for doing so," the captain tried to clarify, as he nodded at the young Lieutenant who held up a large box that contained scores of letters.

"In the letters, Miss Hansen explains that she'd asked an Army nurse to hold her personal items while she assisted in surgery. A few days before the Rock fell, the Army nurse was listed as missing. Your daughter didn't know what happened to her. In the chaos of the battle, these mistakes can happen. I'm here, in part, to express Admiral King's sincere apology for the unnecessary heartbreak that our confusion has caused during these very difficult months."

"Phillip, Phillip! This means that Kari is still alive. That's right isn't it? These men are telling us that my baby girl is not dead!" Marta yelled at her husband, as if he couldn't hear. "Kari's alive! My God! Kari is alive! Oh, thank God!" Marta wailed, as she hugged her husband with an inhuman strength, her tears finally starting to fall.

"Yes, ma'am. Miss Hansen is alive! The Swiss emissary obtained letters for you and for other families who didn't know the fate of their loved ones. I'm told that you can write to her and the Swiss Red Cross will try to deliver a few letters before Christmas," the young lieutenant confirmed, as he handed the box of letters over to Marta.

Marta set the box of letters down on her old desk. She lovingly fondled the envelopes and opened one with great care. It would take her a long, long time to get through Kari's letters. Phillip stood behind his wife, his own back now turned on the Navy men. He touched his wife on her shoulder, and whispered, "We have two children whose fate is in God's hands. We'll say a special prayer for them both at tomorrow's Thanksgiving Mass. We have so much to be thankful for. Our girl is alive. And our boy is safe in India."

# Epilogue

On Thanksgiving Day of 1943, a weak cold front stalled over Lake Michigan, north of Cook County and Chicago. The weather east of the front, all the way to the Atlantic Ocean, was stable and very mild. In the Mid-Atlantic States, it was the most pleasant Thanksgiving Day that anyone could remember in many years.

Though the temperature was unseasonably warm in the hills and ridges above Carlisle, the fall transformation had passed its peak. Most of the brilliant, multi-hued tapestry that had covered the Gap now lay in soggy, rotting piles, carpeting the forest floor all the way from the lakes in upstate New York to the hills in Tennessee.

As with the changing leaves, the hawks, eagles, and falcons had flown south, down the Atlantic flyway in their yearly exodus. Cold weather threatened and the wise, experienced, and healthy predators had departed Waggoners Gap, migrating toward their winter aeries in South America.

That afternoon, local farmers could see a lone male golden eagle high in the powder-blue sky, gracefully riding the thermals that flowed east over the ridgeline at Waggoners Gap. Some of the farmers saw this event as a powerful omen, foretelling good fortune. More than one called out to his family urging them to abandon their preparations for Thanksgiving in order to witness the unexpected exhibition.

The eagle's mate was very ill. She could not negotiate her way south along the flyway. Though she was young and in her prime, she would not live to see another season. Since golden eagles bond for life, her mate would not abandon her in her final days.

A few weeks earlier, the female had taken a fish that a New York farmer had baited with poison. The young eagle was dying.

Her mate could not fathom what evil force had caused his beloved to act so strangely. He decided that they must stop their migration and rest for a while.

This afternoon, the male eagle circled over Waggoners Gap in search of heavy tree branches to build a temporary nest. Perhaps with rest, his mate might regain her strength. He would hunt for a rabbit or maybe a small bird for her.

At the time that the Genero clan sat down to dinner gathering to celebrate the first truly happy Thanksgiving in years, the eagle spotted a small mound of dead branches, twigs, and leaves in the hidden saddle—the spot so favored by the Genero family.

Swooping down to the mound, the eagle snatched branches in its talons. He flew off toward the dead oak, two miles to the north, where his mate rested. On his fourth trip to the saddle, the eagle began pulling on a small branch, when he uncovered a bright yellow object that reflected the late afternoon sun in a dazzling display.

Curious, the eagle pulled at the round, glittering gold object. He persisted until he'd uncovered the yellow disk from the branches, twigs, leaves, and loose earth in which it had been buried for over five months.

Grasping the golden object in its talon, the eagle tried to dislodge it from the pile of branches. No matter what the eagle did, it could not release the antique solid-gold pocket watch with the Monarch family crest from the strong gold chain. Though the eagle fussed with the object for several more moments, the chain remained firmly attached to the watch pocket of Junior Monarch's vest, which rested in the shallow man-made depression under a few inches of the loosely packed earth.

Tiring of the frustrating exercise, and repelled by the spoor of rotting human flesh, the eagle abandoned the shiny gold watch. As darkness approached, the predator resumed his task and worked during the balance of the day to complete the nest for his dying mate.

# About the Author

Tony Peluso currently practices law in Tampa, Florida, representing law enforcement in federal and state courts.

Born in Pennsylvania, Tony grew up in Phoenix, Arizona, where he graduated from a Jesuit prep school. Dropping out of Arizona State University after his second year, Tony volunteered for the Airborne and served in Vietnam from 1968-1969 as an enlisted paratrooper with the 173rd Airborne Brigade (Separate).

Intensely motivated by his war time experiences, Tony returned to college, graduated with distinction with a degree in history, graduated from law school, passed the Texas bar, and obtained a commission as a Captain in the United States Army, Judge Advocate General's Corps in 1975.

Tony served 17 more years on active duty as a JAGC officer in different assignments, including tours with the 82nd Airborne and later another with 18th Airborne Corps. In 1992, Tony retired as a Lieutenant Colonel to take an appointment as an Assistant United States Attorney in the Tampa Division of the Middle District of Florida. Tony served more than 14 years as a federal prosecutor in the U.S. Attorney's Office until 2006, when he retired from the Department of Justice to assume his current responsibilities.

Made in the USA
San Bernardino, CA
05 December 2019

60915909R00324